THE WIZARD OF All

Joan Walsh

In memory of Grandma Anna Thoreson and
Ann Hancock who always walked in the light.

CONTENTS

FORWARD

"When we get ready to take the United States of America, we will not take it under the label of communism; we will not take it under the label of socialism. These labels are too unpleasant to the American people and have been speared too much. We will take it under labels we have made lovable. We will take the United States under the names of liberalism, progressivism, and democracy, but take it we will!" - Alexander Trachtenberg, an avowed socialist and Yale graduate as quoted by Bella Dodd in the 1950's, who was then a ranking member in the Communist Party, but later recanted her socialistic party standing and gave testimony in Congress.

Where should I begin? All stories have a middle, a crossroads where there are two possible paths; and it is precisely at that juncture where choice is joined to conscience, but people seem ignorant of it, or say they have no memory of having been presented with such a dilemma, so that is exactly where I am going to start to refresh mankind's mind. It is the point where evil comes in a relativistic culture. It is not until the people have long since perished that the tale is told and then it is said to be a myth of sorts, but all stories are fairy tales after a fashion, and after they happen.

There once was a kingdom on the far edge of the world which had been created by a wizard who kept watch over the land, and a man and a woman dwelt there long before peoples filled the earth. They lived happily until the dragon came. He coveted this kingdom and the creatures in it because they were cherished by the wizard. The dragon's greatest enemy was the wizard. He had tried many times to defeat the wizard only to fail, so he set about on a new path. If he could not destroy the wizard, he would destroy his creation.

One day this dragon brought the woman a gift and spoke to her of many things, and offered her a gift which she shared with the man. However, the wizard became angry and banished them from his beautiful realm. The two beings told the wizard that it was the dragon's fault, but the wizard did not listen. It is the age old story that tells us that temptation lies in the spiritual

1

and physical planes of reality, but definitive reasoning always makes it someone else's fault, begins the vortex of reality that lands us where we are today...past the wars, the fallen civilizations of the Romans, Greeks, Babylonians, and the Monguls. We are left confused and about to be swept away from history; torn from the pages of books as if we never existed, or melted like witches with the waters of time.

We are left to reason and make our own myths out of what remains. Make no mistake, history leaves its mark. The story is its tracks, and they are as clear and traceable as footprints in newly fallen snow. Above everything know that all stories are the same (lest we be fooled and think ours is unique.) Human life has been sacred from the beginning, so when did humankind begin to separate the thought from the man, and condemn all life that did not agree with them and their thoughts?

Moreover, have men ever recognized evil? They missed the first dragon in their midst, the Mussolini's, and the Hitler's by looking for a sinister face topped with a black hat, and one that haunted their sleep, but could not find it. They talked to evil, read about it in the papers and magazines, but did not hear its answer. Over millennium we did not learn that evil does not look evil. We did not grasp that it looks like all of us: that it cloaks itself in light when it needs to. Even the dragon appeared sensible, non-threatening, and somewhat appealing to the man and the woman in the first realm. They did not flee from it, they talked to it, reasoned with it, and found the dragon to be quite logical.

Joseph of the stars

CHAPTER 1

I remember looking at the sky that night and feeling free after connecting with another being, another creature who, like me, wanted only to live. The sunset was magnificent. It was an iridescent yellow and crimson. I had never seen the sun that voluminous before. It filled the whole horizon, and I thought if it were to touch the earth, it would set it on fire. I felt its warmth on my skin, and it offered my bones relief from the pain in my body.

Somehow connecting with that cat had given me hope and set me to wondering. Was the news about the end of civilization good news or bad news? That's the ultimate question; the only one that really matters in the end. I was weighing the world's worth, trying to decide that answer for myself when I stumbled upon a companionable creature to ponder with me. He had an odd name, well not odd really, but it was just a half a name: Harley. There were name plates on bikes and billboards which advertised this name, but they always included a surname, a final touch which completed the personality, but this Harley had no such distinction. There was no further clues to his identity. He was an old soul, judging by his teeth, who had come on hard times just like the rest of humanity. He had a tag on, but that was unfinished, too; no address or phone, though no one in the world had an address anymore, or one that you could find, anyway. No mail had come since the night of lights. At least that's what we called it, those of us who were left. The grid had gone down, too, but only in places, which was irrelevant since there was really no one left to hawk their secret books on survival on the net, or sell you their latest theory on who the enemy really was. We who were left knew who the enemy was, but it was a little late. As far as I could discern, it wasn't the

THE WIZARD OF AII

drones and the robotoids who populated the cities amid the sprinkling of us humans and other species who were responsible. They were only servant vessels who took care of the needs of society. Drones and robotoids were less than human, but they were prized above us because of their tireless capacity to do whatever they were told without having to be compensated. They could cook a meal, serve it, and not eat any of it. See what I mean? They didn't require pay or care except the occasional parts or circuit upgrade. Now that's where the catch came in. You had to be among the elite to own one. It is also where the government came in. They owned most of these worker drones. They had used them at first only for garbage pickup, street cleaning, etc., but now, some thirty years later, they were the police force and the military might behind those who called themselves the elite. It sounds vague to just call them the elite, but there was no accessibility to those in power. In other words, no one knew who to contact in case of emergency. The government was a beaurcatic spider web of agencies out of control. Each one made its own laws and put out pamphlets by the bin full which were of little real value towards solving a problem. I mean, what good is a book to an illiterate man? Emoji's were the new language of interaction. Besides, if you needed help, these web catching spiders morphed into cockroaches that vanished and scattered when you turned on the lights. By that I mean they referred you to another agency to get rid of you.

Next there were the clones. They were just like us real folks. In fact, you couldn't tell the difference between clones and humans. They needed to eat and sleep, but it was the clones who were usually bought as partners by the rich. They were referred to as PWOP's (play without penalty.) That was the standard joke about clones that comes to mind. There were more women clones than men because of the reasons I just mentioned. They became the caretakers of mankind. We humans referred to them as 'reruns' because you could make as many replicas of the same person as you wanted. It was man's chance at the do over. If your first life failed, you could have yourself cloned and take the pony on a ride around the block again.

Then there were the droids and robotoids and other species. A drone in every home-- that was the governments promise at election time. Droids and toids were cheap. Clones were too much like humans, the government reasoned after years of testing, and their upkeep was as costly. I'm telling you this because we had come to a time in the evolutionary phase of human development where humans and clones were being disposed of for a myriad of reasons and because we were no longer cost efficient. Drones and robotoids could be recycled and used for parts even if they had ceased to function. I didn't buy the government's logic about us humans because there were these Life Center Engineering Labs where they grew human organs. It was a regular parts department from head to toe and even included skin. If anything, it seemed organs should have been cheaper than metals and synthetics which had to be tested and developed. Truth be told, humans were where the big parts recycling department existed and it made the organ harvesters rich. A heart, a lung, a kidney. People paid big money for these specialty items. Harvesters were the new carrion of society, but I digress. I am getting ahead of my narrative. I was telling you how I met Harley. It was right after the end started. What end you might wonder. Well, the end of all I knew, my world at least, and the end of all those like me. Humans, we were called. We were the least among all the species on earth. A new hierarchy had evolved and hybrids were at the top of the list. Hybrids were upgraded versions of birthed humans. There had been rumors and whispers all through my life that the human body failed miserably when compared to the evolution of other species. Scientists claimed that natural selection had passed us by. Take for instance the human eye. The scientists and doctors of our time said it was poorly formed. People had vision problems like being near sighted or far sighted. The scientists in charge said that shouldn't happen and could be prevented by genetic engineering. The eye, they concluded, was nothing more than an intake lens by which data entered the brain and was processed.

The government scientist's poo pooed the whole human body and were in the process of making it eternal piece by piece.

I never gave this biology of species much thought years ago. I couldn't have. I was on UM-10 pills which took your thoughts away. Now, however, since I had come off the pills and read through monumental sections of banned books I saw how simplistic and wrong their diagnosis of the human body was. The eye was, and still is, highly complex, and appears to have been fully formed and functioning from inception. Evolutionists were trying to improve on perfection as far as I could discern. Sight, they said, was no more than the perception of the eye to process light and filter it into its scale of colors. They didn't seem to be concerned about the emotional side of things, I thought, like how the eye and brain interpreted this array of colors into beauty and gave meaning to life. Then again, these scientists weren't being paid to tout the mystery and beauty of life, but to demean and degrade it in the most simplistic terms. Human brains could only handle short bumper sticker phrases and emoji's, they told us.

You might wonder how I would know all this, and I wasn't sure myself at the time. All I was aware of then was that I had made the journey from the darkness back into the light and was endeavoring to relay the last real story of human kind. We were told that books and stories weren't real, but only legends; frivolous tales woven of gossamer wings that tickled our fancy for only a moment, but I have come to understand that myth is the preparation for later instruction, and truth is rooted in the past.

The new reality of today changed and adapted to fit the needs of society whenever it was necessary. Reality was a living concept the elites claimed, and they kept moving the mark like some pawn on a game board; jumping it ahead to extremes, and then jerking it back to obscurity so no one could possibly arrive at an agreed definition of what truth and reality really were. What they said was law. These eternals were said to be the first species, and now they could also be said to be the last. It is no riddle that I present to you, and through this story you will see how that came to be. I will try to tell you the story in some sort of linear fashion. This journal (at least that is what it started out as, and if it becomes more than that, you will be the judge) was begun as a way to pass time, to keep my sanity, and to keep me from existing alone with all my fears, but then it became imperative to tell the truth against all threats to my own security and life. What was there to be afraid of? In a nutshell, everything. Even the air you could not see, but breathed in could kill you. Then there was the robotoids, the SG, and of course the end of life itself. Death was the last unknown frontier, but the eternals were conquering it. Time was no longer the enemy.

Death seemed like a big thing to me when the extinction began. Isn't that the way it always is? You think something is the most horrible thing that can happen until the next unimaginable thing does happen. The next events which unfolded were the night of lights and my meeting with Harley. So you see the end and Harley had a connection in my mind because the flying drones came like tumbling stars from the sky just the way I supposed Harley did.

Anyway, that particular night stands out in my memory. Most species stood outside to watch the spectacular laser light show, the silent show, the show that hypnotized them to their deaths. The death drones came by the thousands. It was night, and at first, and from far away, the drones looked like bright stars in the sky, and then they fell closer. They continued to twinkle and perform their dance in the sky over our heads. The laser show was captivating to many who believed the aliens were returning. They thought the dance above them was a message meant for them to decipher. What kind of theorist mind would even conceive that aliens would choose to communicate through dance rather than simple language? It was inconceivable, even given the fact that the ET's were supposedly more highly advanced that we humans on this hated blue and white marble, but that's how I was certain the idea had been given birth from the left. It was the litmus test. Insanity was their MO.

The people that watched that night thought it wonderful and strange and exciting in the way new things always are, but the drones never touched down, or even came at all close to those who stood watching on the earth with pen and paper in hand just in case there was communication. You have to understand that everything was a theory in those days and had been for decades, and that everyone was a theorist. Theorist was a legitimate title tacked on to a name to make a person sound plausible and educated. It had all the weight and dignity of adding PHD at the end of a name without ever going to school. Now J Doe could be someone. He was J Doe, Theorist. You weren't supposed to reason and ask where the science and logic behind this title was conferred from. Asking questions was one of the government's strictest no-no's, and if you got inquisitive, it got you thrown out of the game. Permanently.

It was the SG, the shadow government, who sent the drones that night. Their dance started as a single point of light in the sky that suddenly burst into a thousand points of light. These little flickering stars shimmered in the night heaven until they poured down in rivulets, cascading like tiny waterfalls from the sky. Then these singular points of light came together, forming a canopy over the entire city. It was spectacular. It was the Fourth of July, but there was no thunder, no explosions to ooh and ah over. They were silent sirens dancing in a dark sky, captivating, hypnotizing all with lights instead of song. The whole sky was full of shooting white neon tails that lit the earth up beneath us. It was day/night in quick succession. The bursts of stars that careened into the earth erased the darkness in brief blinks of shattering light. Day shine was upon us. It was odd because there was no sound to their falling. It seemed that when the stars hit solid ground they should explode with some death rattle, or make the earth cry out, but the stars struck with an awful quiescence, and the earth absorbed them without a whimper. The quiet was absolute and maddening.

That was the beginning of the silence. Gone were the sounds of traffic, honking horns, and the crowds moving like rivers across the pavement, but silence does have a sound. It rings in hollow tones like wind through a canyon, and it taunts you with echoes you can't be sure are real. That was my mind set in those first days. I couldn't be sure anything was real after the night of silent lights. Millions lay dead right where they had stood, or sat, or slept on that night. Most of the buildings in Manhattan still stood. There were explosions here and there, but only a few very buildings had been damaged.

I had been confined in the rehab center for years up until the night of lights when the building was partially destroyed and the doors, so to speak, were sprung open to those of us who had been caged inside. It was a miracle to me. I was an animal escaped from the zoo. The moose was loose, and I ran. Finally, I stopped to rest along the wharf, where they had once loaded and unloaded the boats, to catch my breath. That's when I ran into Harley, or he into me. I had seen other species about, but I stayed away from them as much as I could. You had to be careful in this progressive world. It was always changing, adapting in the most chameleon like way. Nothing stayed the same. The social hierarchy of the moment went: Hybrids, clones or reruns, drones, robotoids, and human. There were a few other classifications in there, but you get the idea. You could never be quite sure who you were talking to. PC was imperative, or you could find yourself where I had just been, but I will explain that later. It was no longer skin color which dictated your place in society, but DNA, and brand names such as Tech One, Genesis, and other like sounding names that were all owned by the government. The different names were meant only to distinguish the difference among the models, and the price, of course. Hybrids seemed to have the status and the clout to get things done in society. They were the elite. Essentially hybrids were the government. You couldn't hold public office if you weren't a hybrid by DNA standards. What's a human to do? It was the catch twenty two of the twenty first century.

These hybrids said it was the age of information, but they stopped its flow completely in the twenty thirties; at least the sharing of it. Intel was still out there, you just didn't have access to it. In as far as knowledge is power that left me, and all humans, at the bottom. We were in the dark about almost everything from where the toilet paper lines were that week to whatever the war of the month was.

In 2070 most of society couldn't read. The only books or flicks that were allowed were fairy tales. You were supposed to read Alice, the Grimm Brothers, and Mother Goose, but real information was considered dangerous in the hands of humans. Everyone was on a need to know basis, and as far as the SG was concerned, we didn't need to know anything except that the sky was blue and what the new laws were for that day.

Again, I digress, but stay with me. It is a story unlike any you have heard. You are being told what the future holds, and the story of how it came to be. It is no great myth, but a quest of noble sacrifice to find the heart of mankind. You may be saying to yourself, this is an ending, not a place where a story should start. Be patient. Some endings are more of a beginning than you may think. After all, it depends on where you came in. While it was the ending for millions, it was the start of the journey for me, Harley, and a few other companions. You'll see. It will all come into focus a bit at a time for you as it did for me. I want you to see this through my eyes, and to do that you will have to make the journey with me. You will need to sort it out in clues and pieces just as I did.

At first on the night of silent lights I thought the city was being attacked by some new enemy in the ongoing war of our times. There was no name for this continuing war as far as I knew. It had gone on in one form or another for over twenty years. One by one the enemies were weeded out from among us. Each day, each week, each month, each year the government proclaimed to us that peace was being attained. We were near to victory! We were making progress!

The government remained silent after the night of lights, and that was like a leopard changing spots to me. I waited for the SG to come, or for anyone to rescue the few of us who had survived. Surely they would send in one form of species to rescue us, but time passed and no one came that could be called saviors. There were a few groups who pooled together on their own to scoop and move the dead bodies and transportation vehicles out of the street, but they did so only in their own sectors. Since I had escaped the rehab center, I stayed away from groups and became a rat in hiding. Out of curiosity I went back to the center some weeks later and found the building empty of all life. Then, in time, I stopped going back to check the facility, and life picked up and continued in its day by day pattern and I got used to the freedom.

For months there were not many species who stirred about, but then one day the lights came back on in the office buildings, pill stores, the flic pits, and the food places. Business was as usual. I stayed out of the busy sectors and kept inside the maze of tunnels I had charted out for myself. I fancied myself some sort of Phantom of the Sewers. It was the safest place to be. Months later, and even as I write now, giant bonfires are still burning where they had tossed the sky cars, the bodies, and the building debris. The smell was odious and nauseating. It was a mixture of seat cushions, metal, plastic parts, and flesh all thrown together. Talk about a traffic jam. This entire conglomeration was piled just off Broadway and Time Square. I was sure it would burn forever. It was the new hell and provided an equivocal likeness to it, and it was because of its stench that I began to entertain the idea of leaving this island paradise permanently.

One day I just started towards the bridge with the intention to cross it and get to freedom on the other side. I stuffed a back pack with water and food and set off through the tangle of cars with their drivers still sitting inside like they were waiting for the rush hour traffic to move. I tried not to look at them, but a macabre curiosity compelled me to look at how a body decomposed. I took a scientific and objective approach to the matter. It was easy to sort out the reruns and robotoids from those with human cells inside them because they had those Inno Chips in them that kept them from rotting away. The IC's species still looked like they had just stepped out for a moring walk. Their cheeks were rosy and their skin was intact. cheeks were rosy and their skin was intact.

In sharp contrast to the IC's, the flesh of the humans had shriveled back, seeming to have melted right away. Knowing what happened to humans in death, the government had once used pictures of corpses in commercials and on bill boards for advertising the benefits of becoming hybrids and clones. Why look like dead, rotting flesh when you can look like this hybrid, robotoid forever? Well, who wouldn't choose the cosmetic way? I would have considered it except that hybrid genetics were out of the reach of us ordinary humans. It was for the rich and those in the government who took money out of the pockets of the workers to pay for their needs. They were the robin hoods of the progressive era. They had made society equal all right. Ninety five percent of the world had the exact same resources; the shirts on our backs and a place to sleep. The wealthy (mostly the same government officials who made such a big deal about equalizing the population) enjoyed the penthouses and homes of their own in upstate New York.

But back to the story. I got to the middle of the bridge and noticed that about a forty foot section or more was missing from the middle section of the bridge. Standing near the gap on the suspension bridge I felt the ends sway with the wind and I started back. In seconds, I was dodging moving cars. My added weight had triggered the vehicles which were perched on the edge of the missing section to roll forward and plunge into the river. I felt the end of the bridge was still swaying, and I ran to get off it; all the while fearful that the bridge would break away underneath me before I reached solid ground again. Somewhere in the middle of my running that thought paralyzed me. It was at that point I stopped and looked over the side of the bridge. I was at once overwhelmed with a sudden compulsion to jump. It was a peculiar sensation. I watched the water's current move straight and swift until it hit the concrete pylons that anchored the structure, and then the water began to create a churning around them. These little eddies were swirling faster and faster, and I became dizzy and nauseous just looking at them. I couldn't move. It took hours to get up my courage to leave the bridge.

All ideas of escape vanished after the incident on the bridge. Manhattan was an island, and out of nowhere I was suddenly consumed with an irrational terror of water. I had never had a fear of water in my life. Where had it come from? I wanted off the island, but I would have to use a boat or a ferry to get away and that was now out of the realm of possibilities. Fears of all kinds just came on me and stayed like friends I didn't know how to get rid of.

It was on my return from my bridge excursion, and while I was walking by the wharfs and loading docks trying to regain my courage that I met Harley. "Did you come on the night of the silent lights?" I asked staring into his eyes. That was the most noticeable feature about Harley. He had eyes that saw right into you, cut through all your defenses and went straight to the secret stuff you kept hidden in yourself. His eyes were an effervescent pale green. Have you ever seen the inside of a pearl shell? They have a rainbow painted inside each one. Those faded colors run like veins across the shiny whiteness of the inner shells in fluorescent swirls of pinks, blues, and greens. Well, that sparkling green was the color of Harley's eyes. They had a gray light in them like a pearl shell, too. I stared into his eyes as if I were really seeing a green tide rolling towards me. I watched as it crested, and I saw the moving water turn white, and when the next wave came, it was green again. That's the fluid movement of color I detected in Harley's eyes; the light always coming towards you like waves cresting and falling.

He was circling my feet and rubbing against my leg as I spoke to him. It was at that moment, right on cue, that he looked up at me. I saw the ocean then, and the deepness. I felt man's inhumanity and stupidity all at once. With a quick flick of his tail and a few short licks on his paws Harley meant to set the record straight. Cats have that no nonsense final way of stating things. It was an impatient gesture, but they want you to understand. That quick lick says, Listen! Pay attention. This is important. People don't listen. He was telling me that those deliberate, sudden lick-lashings with the tongue meant something. It came like a great revelation to me. I made sudden sense out of the entirety of life while watching those sudden switches of lightning: It is always in the quiet, sudden movements like the flick of a tail that life's greatest secrets come; those grand revelations that put it all together and encapsulated life as simply as a cartoon frame. Years were understood clearly with a quick, brusque flip of a tail, or a sudden licking of paws. It was a short sentence that made sense of life. That's what cats mean to tell you with the brevity of their motions. I envied him to be so curt, so sparse with words. He had the poet's succinctness.

We looked at each other. I wondered if he saw me the same way as I saw him. We were taking each other in, when I suddenly remembered a book I had read as a child. No, it had been read to me. The memory was coming clearer in my thoughts, but it was far away and lay in a gray fog of the past. My grandfather had read it to me. It was a book about a rabbit, a velveteen one. As I stared at Harley, I pitied him. He was the opposite of the velveteen rabbit in every way. He was the real about to become unreal. Where the velveteen rabbit's wear revealed how he had once been loved to tatters, this cat's fur, the uncombed and matted tangles in his long haired coat, told me that no one had caressed his body lovingly in quite some time. Now, it looked like it might hurt to run a hand across his back. His coat was an ugly mass of knotted fur that hung on him like tumors.

He was an old cat, but someone must have held and caressed him over his nine lives. A little girl, perhaps, one that lived in one of those penthouses had petted him once. I pictured him as he must have been once upon a time: beautiful and with a sleek coat that shone in the sun. Judging by his long coat, and his size, he was a Maine Coon or a Norwegian Forest cat. Those breeds were larger than most breeds of cats and had thick coats. Yes, he was a purebred, I decided, for this was Manhattan and one of the riches places on earth. Since it was an island, the cat didn't swim here or pay the ferry fare to come over. Not that Harley would have had to pay. There had been plenty of animals who had come and gone on the ferry to this island over the years I had taken it back and forth to NYC proper. Yes, Harley was once snuggled and covered in blankets and let to sleep in those heaps of soft clouds with a beautiful little girl, and his coat was sleek and elegant.

People say that animals have no souls, but I'm not sure I hold to that philosophy. Man has many adages he likes to apply to anything just so he can check it off his list and put it out of his mind so he can move on to the next question and find another answer that is just as frivolous. The twenty first century was a maze of information on everything. I was born into the beginning of the non-communication era when people socialized alone with a device instead of each other. Not much was worth reading, or even thinking about. At least that was my experience. People wanted to discuss such inane subjects in my days. I often wondered what sort of mind thought that dull tripe up. Most of the their conversations centered around ugly habits these people thought they had a right to speak out about, and worse, they felt that others should listen and care about their petty neurosis.

There were no taboos; you could love inanimate objects like cars or toasters. I used to see this gal along the canyons of buildings along Broadway who spent time in the theater district stroking and kissing the walls of each of the theatres in turn as she made her way up or down the street. The Times did a piece on her and I read it only because I had seen her, not because I cared. It claimed she cried each time she was forced to leave her lovers to go home at night. Hmm, lovers, I remembered thinking, with hearts of stone and had laughed. That scenario pretty much summed up life in the twenty twenties.

The writer of the article went on to compare LizBeth to the likeness of a Nightingale or Barton. That's when I stopped reading the Times. I had made few life altering decisions in life, but that was one of them. It left me wandering in a blue funk for weeks and that's when I figured I had lost touch with the people about me. I tried for days to comprehend how a woman who kissed stone facades could be touted as a savior with a heart of gold. How was kissing bricks and cement even remotely equated to being a comforting angel? How did it make her like a nurse who had compassion for the dying? Had she somehow saved the life of these stone monuments? I remembered stopping in at a bar after work sometime after I had read about Liz and had just happened to see her along theatre row that night. She had become a celebrity and people called her by name and waved. They felt they knew her and people stopped and talked to her.

Her perversion had made her a celebrity. Her neurosis had made her a hero, an icon.

I had had a bad day, a bad week, maybe even a bad year, and the sight of Liz had angered me. I ordered my drink and made a quip about the star attraction in the area. "Imagine talking to LizBeth. Why bother? Why are humans bothering to talk to her? She loves stones, not people. What can she possibly have in common with a real heart?"

I have always regretted framing my comments in the form of asking a question about her. Asking a question leaves room open for an answer. I should have just made a statement of fact. LizBeth is sick. LizBeth needs help. LizBeth's mind doesn't roll the right way.

The guy next to me, Frankie, made a point to set me straight. "Travis," he said, "the problem with you is that you don't get it. You missed the whole point of the article."

Unfortunately, I had fallen into his trap, taken the bait, and I proceeded to ask him what the aim of the piece was.

"LizBeth is not a symbol of Clara Barton because she kisses bricks. She is a symbol of these great women because she dares to be herself, to expose herself to ridicule from heartless critics like you. She has stood up to the world."

"Doesn't that make her more like a building than a human?"

"Accept it. She has a right not to be made fun of. Leave her alone."

"Barton and women like her actually risked their lives. LizBeth risked nothing, but maybe the possibility of wounded pride."

"Yeah, man," another guy down the bar said. "From people like you. She shouldn't have to feel like that in the world because of people like you. Live and let live." He got off his bar stool and headed down towards me. His fists were raised. "Something wrong with you, mister?" I knew better than take the bait a second time in a row and answer his question. I twirled my bar stool in a counter clockwise direction away from him and slid off of it and out the door. Laughter rang in my ears as I escaped. "He needs some of her courage. He's the one that needs a heart," I heard the man say just before the door closed behind me.

I was on my way across the Square and looked at the blinking neon ads. Whose face was there staring back at me, but dear Lizbeth's. A caption read, 'Dare to be yourself' in blinking lights. She was bent over caressing the wall in the poster with her tush pointing outward toward the audience of passer byers, and little hearts were coming off the wall. The lights beat and blinked at me in pulses like a real beating heart. That was the beginning of the end for me. That was the night my thinking switched from what's wrong with the world to what's wrong with me? Somewhere between leaving the bar and catching the subway to Brooklyn I lost the heart and found the stone. I felt more alone than ever. The little neon hearts and her blinking tush were the only thing I saw in my mind for days. It was that bigger than life picture of Liz that I remember as being a turning point.

Maybe the guys in the bar were right. Everyone should do exactly what they felt like. Everyone should be celebrated for their differences. But if everyone is different how does mankind come together? My right thinking mind had once been full of all kinds of retorts to questions like that. I knew the aim of the socialists was to keep people separate and alone. They didn't want people getting together on any subject. People agreeing on things lead to groups, and then mobs, and then armies who might come against them. They want us all one on one so they can manage us easily. It was an insidious evil. How had it taken root? How had they managed to get what seemed like everyone in the world to agree with them? More than that I thought, how had they turned right into wrong?

That was the night I began my quest for the answers. I had just read a book about the left written by someone on the right who had spelled it out. It was then that I began to agree with the guy on the right. This writer, I don't remember his name, said there were only four major attacking points the left had implemented against the right wing conservatives starting back over a hundred years ago in the nineteen fifties and sixties. At least I remembered only four now. 1: divide the people. 2: create an appearance of support for the causes of the right, but keep to the progressive agenda. 3: take out the opposition, and 4: create the feeling of a coming revolt. Steep everything in terminology that implied war. In other words, create a perpetual feeling of impending doom.

The left had such disdain for mankind that it felt without their guidance and motivation the masses couldn't get off their lazy duffs to accomplish anything. In short, the masses were the herd and the leaders were the cattle prods to get them moving, but even more important than the head'em up, move'em out mentality was to make sure that the herd was moving in a direction that furthered their socialistic agenda. The book I am referring to was published in the semi free days of speech in the twenty teens sometime. Books were allowed and thoughts were allowed to a point, but only if you spouted a philosophy which matched the progressive mind set. If you didn't agree with them, they mounted an attack against you. That was the safe days when they only destroyed your reputation and left you without a friend in the world.

I was different, people used to tell me, but the tone in which they said it was not the same as the voice they used to cheer for LizBeth's differentness. That's because my thoughts were not their thoughts, and their mission was not my mission. I am not sure I can tell you what my mission was then or even now, but that all changed when I met Harley. It wasn't him that changed me; it was the events that followed after I met him which changed me. He just happened to be the marker between the old and the new. There were others who would come into my world too, but I'm getting ahead of myself again.

Society had one goal in those days. Label it, put it in the can, sell it to the world, and move on. It didn't matter if everyone bought whatever you were selling or not; some would. It's the chance you take. A lie becomes truth if it is repeated often enough. I forget who said that except that he was a Marxist. It may have been Marx himself, or Stalin. Truth was very important.

The word was used to adnaseum in the twenty first century and to convey the opposite.

I'll give you an example of what I mean by over use. People used the phrase, 'moving forward' to describe everything they couldn't or didn't want to answer. The phrase had a calming effect on people much like catnip when they used it. No one knows why people pick up a phrase to repeat over and over until it was woven into a universal consciousness of a sort, and until no other phrase can be thought of to replace it, but that led me to conclude that humans were just as easy to program as drones, easier, because you could actually make people believe it was their choice to say it. Really all you had to do with people to program them was make them think they were in league with the popular kids in power. The masses of people baaed like little lambs and repeated everything they heard because it kept them from thinking too much. They made a semblance of talking or communicating in the most abstract and numb way, but man was sure he was right. The part about being right came from philosophers in the age of enlightenment, 'I think, therefore I am.' Looking back, I see those philosophers were the early forerunners of the progressive movement. In the twenty first century their motto changed to, 'because I am, I am a god. It was another of those 'one tiny steps for mankind' events of momentous advancement.

All of human kind's rattling made noise, but it did not say anything, yet this old animal stared at me and told me everything. I caught his body language. He spoke more in that flick of his tail than most or all humans I had known had in an entire life time. I was in on his secret. I saw truth in his movements. After all, you can't hide your feelings in the swish of a tail. It was honest. I suddenly remembered it was the seeking after this truth that had started my life rolling downwards to its inevitable end. It flashed through my memories like a stroke of lightning and was gone before I could put the memories together. Lightning was a warning. Something was back there, buried and deep, and I was afraid of it.

Anyway, Harley was looking at me and I at him. This half-starved animal seemed to be at home on the island, a native of the land so to speak. He spoke the language of crowds. He was not wary of people, quite the opposite; he seemed to seek me out. Why he settled on me, I am not yet sure. Here was the messenger of life and death and he was standing at the door. You might think that is an overstatement, an exaggeration, but his stare was of a magnitude I had never comprehended before. I had been talking to myself, talking to my inner man, but now I had another soul to converse to. Don't ask me how I knew he had a soul, but I will say that I think man is wrong to hold the opposite view. Man was himself responsible for billions of deaths, countless wars, and the suppression of freedoms while this cat may have been guilty of stealing a few good sized stringers of fish in his life, and had aided in stopping the modern equivalent of the bubonic plague by killing a few hundred rats along the wharf. You weigh the matter. I have come to value my opinion as right as any other man. I have no facts, but they don't either. I just know. This is what Harley seemed to intuit about me. He was telling me that man had a sixth sense, and was intent upon awakening me to it. Harley just announced things, and was quite sure about his opinions. I had a friend like that when I was younger. He grew up to be a lawyer. He made millions and lived in one of those penthouses where you could see most of the city of New York, the river, and all the way to the pond in Central Park. You could even see the people paddle their boats on Sunday afternoons. My lawyer friend told me people looked unreal from his vantage point.

I said, "You can spy on all them and they aren't aware."

"They're ants, really. Busy little creatures, scurrying about. They pour over the world like attacking soldiers."

My friend, Madison, was a progressive, as almost everyone was in that time. You had to be to get a job. First, the left had only made it a rule that you must vote progressive to be hired in the educational and scientific institutions. However, by the twenty first century, you had to be a progressive if you wanted any job and wanted to keep one. You couldn't speak your mind.

Well, let's say you could, but you soon disappeared and showed up in the Lost File the SG kept.

Madison said it was better not to give these masses of people names or any moniker which might make them human. They weren't. "Most of them are drones, robos, and androids anyway," he had said to me.

"You are up high. You live in this penthouse in the clouds," I said, looking down at the park and the people below. He was richer, but did that put him above those unnamed paddlers rowing on the lake? I had asked him that at the time.

"I can afford to act elite. My money gives me wings," he had said waving his hands and spilling part of his martini on the newly buffed marble floor. I suddenly saw him as he saw himself. He was the eagle in the aerie. Everything below had been reduced to his prey. He was safe. Untouchable. In a sad way I knew it was true. It was the zeitgeist of the times. Regrettably, there is always a zeitgeist of the times, but those caught in its energy always seemed to fail to feel or understand it; they merely were swept away like fallen timber. It was those who were not in the current who felt the madness of it all.

Now, I looked towards the skyscrapers where Madison had once perched. The buildings were gone along this section of the horizon and I couldn't make out exactly where his mountain aerie had been. Those stone and steel penthouses that had once stood like canyons and blocked out the sun were rubble for a few blocks, but it was enough to let the light from the sun push against the permanent shade created by the canyon walls. I turned my attention back to the sidewalks I was walking along, and to all the different species that were picking and pecking like chickens through the rubble of fallen buildings for whatever could be found. I didn't pay much attention to what they were finding. I was looking at the sunset. Nothing blocked its glow over the water and it shimmered boldly and unafraid like a victor's flag for all to see. It was a sight, I told myself that had not been seen across this stretch of land for decades. It was something new.

I was wakened from my reverie of the past by the gentle rubbing on my legs. I took notice of my companion and his expressive eyes. They told me the past was not important. He was nudging my legs; wanting things to 'move forward', but the cat could not say, in that phrase, those words which I had so come to detest. The fact that he could not talk calmed me. He walked a few steps forward and seemed to be waiting for me to follow.

He made his way adeptly over the obstacles. He looked like an Olympian in training the way he dodged the bodies of the fallen species, and the shards of glass and debris. "You've run this course before, Harley. Slow down. I haven't been out for a while." It was crazy, I thought, but this mangy cat gave me confidence. I had been holed up in that basement since the E waves had struck months ago during the night of dancing lights. I had been waiting for another human to cross my path. None had come. I had listened every night for a human voice, but had heard none. Not even a moan from among the dying.

I went much slower than my leader. I was taller and could see things that he could not. He kept heading towards the west, but I decided to head back along the streets from where we had just come for he was too far ahead of me. We would part ways already, I thought, watching Harley running in the opposite direction. I stopped. I was sure he was only leading me to some trophy catch of his.

I looked at the tall building next to me. It stood as it always had, but it was empty, quiet, and eerie. Buildings were just empty people waiting for their organs to return so they would have some purpose and semblance of life again. It had been an abode of the wealthy, but it was mine now, at least until I was rescued. Surely they would send someone for the survivors. Then it hit me. Was anyone left to send? Whatever enemy had sent the silent waves of death must have been subdued by now. The invisible waves had shook things that night. Glasses had rattled on table tops until they fell off, sky cars jumped up and down on the pavement until some tipped over onto their side like cows. That's all that the death waves did; it shook things loose, knocked them over like small tremors of an earthquake might do, but it had dropped people in their tracks; ended them instantly and it had stopped motors or engines with the same abruptness. You couldn't see the pavement in the streets because it was littered with lines of traffic that would never clear itself, never follow the mantra of 'going forward' another inch.

It took considerable time for me to realize it was only the real among us who dropped in their steps. I had to sort it out. I had been locked away for over ten years and had no idea that droids, robos, and clones had been used to replace the humans in our midst to the extent they had. I mean who would dream such a scenario? Bodies lay all over. Death put a quash on details. Period. Nothing was important after you met death, but I was alive and needed stuff. So did Harley. He was about satisfying his needs, I told myself, and I suddenly felt dirty and wanted to clean up. What I needed was a change of clothes and bedding to sleep in, and food. I rejoiced in being hungry. I was feeling things again. I had a purpose even if it was of a mundane sort. I was a survivor.

As I made my way through the debris, I saw the remains of another once wealthy high rise. This building had lost most of its glass windows and the contents were now open to the air and weather. I thought back to when I had once been invited for dinner into these thinned steel and glass framed walls by my lawyer friend, but just then other bodies bumped against me. I stopped walking. I took them to be human because like I said, I was not yet aware of the repopulation changes that had occurred in my ten year absence. Their eyes stared at me in a cold, suspicious way.

I looked around to try and find Harley. I wished I had kept up better with him since I was now face to face with strangers I wasn't sure of. These strangers hung together for safety and I felt vulnerable. They seemed to make a claim on this building and stood at the open doors as if to guard it.

"Keep moving," one of them said while raising a crowbar towards me. I only looked at him. I was not armed and had no protection for myself.

"No, wait," the man standing next to him said. "I think he's a hu-manimal."

"You got a button?" the other guy said trying to pull up my shirt.

"Don't touch me."

"Identify your classification. You must give us your generation papers."

"Some species are worth money," the shortest man said. Just then I saw a sky car descend and park right in front of the building. I could see it was a government vehicle and it had a cage with people in it, or were they clones, or something else? While I was trying to sort through this, one of the armed men went into the building and returned escorting seven or eight more species, who looked to be human, out at laser point.

"They're rounding up humans. They're killing humans," one man was ranting and crying. "They're going to kill us. Help us please. You look like a human, Mr., " he said as he passed by me. "Help us," he said grabbing at my jacket sleeves.

I was in shock, but I had enough presence of mind to speak. "You're mistaken. I am a clone. I work for Mrs. AJ Cuddlesworth." I went on in the spiel of what drones were programmed to say, where I lived and the duties I performed. The short guy, with the pug face shoved me at that point. "Get out of here. Don't wonder around without your generation papers on you again, or Mrs. Cuddles will get cold."

I had seen species coming and going, but I had stayed in the shadows because I did not wish to be sent back to the Rehab Facility. There seemed to be more and more bodies moving about all the time, but were they people? Was what the guy said the truth, or was he a just a lunatic? The species that had been put in the sky van looked human, but I couldn't tell, not really. It had happened so sudden, but that was how the change had come, quickly and without warning.

But why were they picking up anyone? And why had these SG officials who were arresting these folks left the dead on the street? Bodies and sky cars were piled up all over in doorways, on escalators, and in the subways. I looked back at the men who were still standing in front of the building. What species were they? On the walk back to where I had lost Harley, I stopped to watch what was going on after I had rounded the corner and could no longer see the men. Sky vans continued to land and people, well, species were being herded into them. Why? Rescue had come unannounced like the light show, and it had not come like I had expected. I had been almost alone for months. Then, suddenly in a strange and ominous way, the streets were full of movement and bustle. Life was going to go on. The ants were back, whatever species they were. The hill was going to be rebuilt.

I gave the three men one last glance before I disappeared around the corner again, and decided I would find a weapon and come back later that night. I would have to take them out before they discovered I was of human origin. Maybe I could pick them off one by one if they went out to scavenge alone, but then convinced myself to avoid a confrontation with them at all cost. It would be stupid to draw attention to myself.

As I went down the line of buildings, I found an apartment building that didn't seem to be taken over by anyone. I would have shelter for the night. When I saw the inside, I knew I had hit the jackpot. There were coverlets on the bed. Clothing still hung in the closets and there were a few packets and cans of food lying around on the floors.The tremors must have knocked them from the shelves. Dust and debris covered everything. The finery of the apartment was evident and it was chilling to wonder where the owners were. I picked up a can of petite potatoes from the floor and popped its top. This guy had been rich. I was used to food that came in sealed macro strength plastic which had been used as a light weight substance to package food for the troops since the last century, and now that was the accepted form of food preservation. Well, there were canned foods and glass containers, but you had to have been implanted with the chip to buy them and wealthy enough to afford them.

I sat staring at the bed and could almost feel someone else's presence, but I opened another can of vegetables all the same, and ate the spears of asparagus without taking my eyes off the bed. I hardly moved my teeth to chew. I tried not to make any noise as I swallowed. Fear had seized hold of me. Sweat began to break out over my skin and my clothes felt like they had been suctioned onto my arms and legs like plastic wrap.

I could stand the suspense no longer. I set the can down and went over to the bed and lifted up the bed ruffle to see if anyone was under it. Immediately I saw legs and bodies. I half expected to be attacked, but the man did not move. As my eyes adjusted to the darkness, I saw there was the body of a woman beside him and a child. A stuffed animal lion lay by the child. I recognized the lion. It was from a film about a lion king and had been very popular. This lion must have had a special meaning to the girl by the way she was cradling it close to her.

I let the dust ruffle fall back down to the floor and I grabbed a pillow and a blanket to take with me back to the kitchen. I was suddenly not comfortable being in an apartment with dead bodies. The idea of a safe place to sleep had been ruined. In an instant my safe world was falling apart. My stomach was not use to food and I began to feel like it was just going to run out the other end of me. I decided to collect what I had come for and get out. I took the pillow out of its casing and filled it with the cans. I took shirts and pants out of the closet and stuffed them in the pillow case, too. It was then I noticed that my hands left a dirty residue on the clean fabrics. I looked at my hands. They had not been washed since the silent waves had hit the city. My fingernails were black underneath and they were dried to the point that the skin had torn away around the cuticles. My knuckles and hands were all cut and scratched, but I didn't remember how I had hurt myself.

I realized I had been eating with these dirty fingers and looked through the drawers in the kitchen to find some utensils. I took two sets of knives and forks and spoons out. I also took a huge butcher knife and a ball of twine. I made a sling out of the twine and hung the knife around my chest where I could easily

THE WIZARD OF AII

grab it. I took some scissors and other sharp objects to use. They wouldn't be much use against laser guns like the guys down the block had. I looked around. Steel rebar must be lying all over the place. I was looking around when I found the kitchen sink lying on the floor. I looked at the place on the wall where the sink had once been attached. Copper piping stared out at me. Now if I could manage to get a section of it loose, I would have a longer weapon. I would be able to fight the men down the street without getting so close to them. As I pulled and tugged at the pipe, I realized I was making a lot of noise and stopped.

I decided to look for a piece of loose rebar instead. As I searched for pieces of steel to make a weapon out of, I noticed the bed again. The mattresses hid the bodies underneath the bed, but I started to sweat again. For some reason I kept having the feeling that these people would somehow get up and suddenly stand before me. I had never given death much thought, but now it was all around me and I was being forced to deal with it.

"They are sleeping," a voice said. It was not my own voice I am sure, but whose it was I didn't know. I did not think things like that. I felt as if my brain was wrapped in a black fog that fit like a tight band around my skull. All I did was think, and every thought was painful and born of intense labor. I had to stop thinking. I was making myself crazy. I needed someone to talk to, to bounce my voice off. I said, "Hello, my name is Travis N. Tarkington, and I have become the hunted." The strangeness of my voice frightened me. I had not spoken aloud for weeks, months, and it was graveled and hoarse and reminded me of the scratchy sound that came out of a radio when the station was not completely tuned in. I needed water, but I settled for the juice from the two cans of vegetables I had eaten. It was salty and warm so I just rinsed my mouth with the liquid and spit it out.

I saw something out of the corner of my eye flash by. Whatever it was it was in a hurry. I grabbed the knife from around my neck and stalked back around the corner to the bedroom again. I hesitated before going in. I could hear movement. I clutched the knife tighter in my hands but I could feel the sweat on my palms

THE WIZARD OF All

making the handle slippery in my grip. I wiped my hand on my pants, regripped the weapon, and stepped around the half wall.

There on the bed was Harley circling about the way cats do before laying down. He kneaded his paws a few more times, and satisfied that the bedspread was the way he wanted it, plopped down. He may not have had too much heft to him, but he was going to make sure you felt his presence. He looked at me with sleepy, half opened eyes and then closed them. I called to him. He paid me no mind and kept his eyes shut.

"What's wrong with you, Harley? Is your sniffer out of whack? Can't you smell what's underneath you? Move, Harley. Get!"

He didn't open his eyes. In fact, he didn't flinch a muscle. Shouldn't animals catch the smell of death and run from it? Weren't they wired that way? I tried to coax him out of his nest by enticing with food. He wasn't moving so I ate the beans around the corner in the kitchen area myself. I took the blanket I had thrown down in my take pile, and wrapped myself in it, but I was afraid to lie down and sleep. I was too close to the men down the street. What if they had seen me enter the building and were waiting for me to come out? I had intended to sit up and keep watch for them, but at some point I fell off to sleep leaning against the half wall that I had propped myself against.

I was wakened to a repeating and rhythmic sound. I had to listen consciously, for it was not a sound that I easily recognized. As I rose to check out the noise, I felt a catch in my back and it was hard to straighten up fully. By the time I had reached the next room I was still slightly hunched over. The first thing I saw was Harley and he, hearing my footsteps, turned to look back towards me, and the noise stopped. He was standing against the wooden headboard with his paws resting on it, and after looking at me briefly, he resumed sharpening his claws on the headboard. He plied one or two more strong strokes into the wood and then stopped. He moved away from the head board and I could see the damage he had inflicted into the magnificent piece of rose wood.

"I see your artwork, Harley. It is worth as much as the dead guy paid for this bed, nothing more." Harley was not happy ,with my appraisal of his work and let me know it by running back and forth across the length of the bed and meowing. "Okay, it's a masterpiece. Have it your way, but I can tell you that it's leftist in meaning because there is no sense to it, Harley."

I swear just then that I saw that cat shake his head at me in disgust, and with an uncaring, brooding sweep of his tail jumped off the bed, and went out the door. The king had spoken. I waited for him to come back, but he didn't. His sudden departure left me stunned. I was alone again. This cat I had known for only hours had left me twice in less than a day which was a record even for me. I hadn't felt much loss yesterday, but today I felt grieved, and it was in a halfhearted manner that I searched around the mess looking for more stuff to take. I had already filled one pillowcase. Did I want to carry two? No, a better idea would be to stash stuff around the building where no one would find it and come back as I needed it. There were plenty of goods here, but there were also those dead bodies stashed under the bed.

I went around to the other side of the bed where their heads were positioned. I hadn't seen them from the front yesterday so when I pulled up the dust ruffle, I covered their facial features with the sheets. I didn't want pictures of their faces popping into my mind for the rest of my life. I saw the man had a book which lay just outside of his grasp. It was open and he had been reading it. He was close to the end of the book, judging by the amount of pages left on the right hand side. Curious, I picked it up. It was bound in leather. I had seen only a few items made of leather in my life time. It was high quality and almost looked like it had been polished, if one can polish leather. I read the title and the strangeness of it intrigued me. When I took the book from the floor, I saw the man's hands. They were bloated and toxic looking. It looked like they would burst open with the slightest touch. I retrieved the book by taking a curtain rod and knocking it away from his hand.

Reading the book didn't enter my mind at that point. I hadn't read in years, no one had. They hadn't even been printed for decades. It was the title on this book which made me want to read it. It's words fascinated me: Basic Instructions Before Life Ends. Now, that would be beneficial information to a man in my predicament. Books were illegal to own, and that made me want it, too. You could buy the fairy tale e-books or the more expensive hologram editions which would play out to your children. It was expected. Children were to be reared to have reverence and fear for the terrors which our world was known for. They were to have a heads up where monsters were concerned. It was imperative to know that old women lived in shoes, gave their dogs bones, and had cupboards that were bare. It was wise to teach your children that wolves with sharp teeth roamed the woods, that witches did their magic among the trees of the forests, and that aliens also landed in these treed places. In short, it was a dangerous planet, and only the government could protect you.

Seeing the book made me reassess this guy. He had some courage. Well, maybe not courage, but he was a rebel. I looked at him again, almost studying him. He was old. His head was mostly bald, but hair grew in a ring around his head like a circus clown. His skin was creased and rough like the patched pattern on a crocodiles hide. His wife wasn't much better looking. They didn't have the looks to belong to society, I thought. Most of the elites and the eternals were beautiful specimens, yet these people must have had money. They had lived here. Maybe he was born into it, though that didn't happen in society anymore. The progressives had evened the financial score among the population. When they had taken power in the 2020's, they had taken over everyone's bank accounts. The poor had cheered, but when those who had been robbed, or rather forced to share had threatened to challenge the validity of the government's new law, they were silenced.

I would tell you to look it up so you could read it for yourself to prove that what I had told you was true, but historical documents were no longer kept, especially those that dealt with the themes of the takeover. The SG referred to attempts at historical documentation, especially by conservatives, as petty behavior equal to that of a third grade tattler who had just ratted out his classmate for urinating on the teacher's favorite classroom plant. You couldn't even snoogle current events on the web the day after they happened. After twenty four hours it was destroyed by law, which, when you really thought about it, was too long anyway. None of the facts being used were true, and they changed minute by minute so no one knew where the real hippity hop hole of human history was. The left was afraid to look at the past, but they should have because it was a picture of the future. Books have always illuminated the human condition by means of storytelling, but the socialist's idea of art left man dressed up for trick or treat wondering if he were real. Critical theory also killed the human spirit just as it had killed the idea of America. Art was made politically correct by the socialist left and in their hands became mere propaganda. Any real message died a quiet death and was replaced by a philosophy of rage that tore apart the morals of the middle class.

I can make these claims because I was schooled in a time when education was semi important to the culture. In those days you had to have papers from academia to get a job. Later it became necessary to belong to the right party which was then the only ticket into the job market. I spent my early adulthood confused. The intel the SG fed me often left me in a fog for days because my memories of certain events were not the same as theirs, and I deduced from that fact that re-information leads to schizophrenia. I had a hard time keeping up with the progressives because of this diagnosis. It was like trying to keep one foot on land and one foot in a speed boat while running a race. Anyone can see that a one footed man who is hopping along the shore is no contender to stay even with his other foot which is in a speed boat. If you were wise, you dropped out of the race, and kept your mouth shut about the unfairness and the utter stupidity of the rules concerning any race or endeavor.

As I have already told you, the government loved fairy tales and used them almost exclusively to get their points across about everyday life. Species in our society began disappearing more rapidly and thoroughly than the dinosaurs. There were rumors that they were being shot and that their bodies had been ground up in the gravel pits and then mixed with sand that was used to repair the bridges and streets of the failing infrastructure, which was a big word in those earlier days, and it was on everyone's lips. Infrastructure. It was posted on the Times Square main neon. 4 bridges repaired, 10 streets paved, and 4 sewers of NYC cleaned. Mind you, they were clever enough not to give the locations of any of these supposed repaired project sites, but I can tell you that I never saw one of these reclaimed sites, or a reclamation worker, and they were easy to spot because of their fluorescent yellow and orange attire. I had seen them when I was younger. They used to come into the bars after work like me. They placed their plastic hard hats up on the bar tops by them as they drank in those days. However, I never saw the jackets, the hats, or the men who wore them after the progressives came to power. Rumor had it that the reclamation workers had been forced to go underground. People would see them and rant and rave at them to fix their streets and sewers, but they weren't allowed to fix a thing. The same was true about the police. They weren't allowed to arrest arsonists, rapists or thieves. They could only give tickets to people who didn't clean the poop up after their animals. To keep their anonymity, the city crews put on the normal unisex garb of the time, and left their fluorescent marker coats and uniforms at home. It was self-protection on their part. They needed to blend in with the herd. All people wore the unisex look. Women had worn jeans for decades, and their hair had gotten shorter, but now they wore suits, and men had pony tails and longer hair and wore their briefs or women's wear over their trousers. It was very sheik. Women's underwear were called boy briefs for women and men's were called girl boxers for men. Unisex was the rage. I'm old enough to recall when they still had signs for men and women on bathrooms, but sometime shortly before the twenty twenties there was only one TR built for the customers. It just said Toilet Room on it in yellow letters. People only laughed. It didn't matter, they said, because you couldn't tell men from women by the way they dressed, anyway. Women didn't need to emasculate men, unisex and critical theory had already done it for them.

I suddenly thought of the dead man and his family in the penthouse laying under the bed again. They were of the old school. They made up the traditional definition of family. I remembered that word from deep out of my past. One man, one woman and they created a child to live with them. Not many people my age could afford to bring children into the world. The Times Square sign blinked the figures each year for us. "It now costs 3 million to raise an offspring to maturity."

I'm older now, but not so old that I don't remember when the term birth control became burden control. Besides what it cost to raise a child, the SG charged you almost a hundred thousand to get a permit to have a child. That put the damper on it for most of us right there. And if that wasn't enough, there were all these signs posted on walls and billboards all over the city to remind you of the burden of having children. The posters were put out by the agency that used to be called planned parenthood. BIRTH CONTROL RAISES US TO A HIGHER STAGE in the EVOLUTION OF LIFE. Margaret Sanger was the person given credit for all these poster warnings. Her claim was that the mission of BC was to create a race of thoroughbreds among the human population. It was a strange way to look at people, I thought, by mingling terms that up to that time had been reserved for the breeding of animals. If all that wasn't reason enough not to have children, you also had to sign papers that you would send them to college and had the millions to do so. If you had an offspring and couldn't care for it, they came and got you. No one wanted that hanging on them for twenty six years. Could a baby be worth all that? That's when I caught myself staring at the little girl clutching that lion doll. It looked like love, well, a perception of love I had from my childhood. I don't know why I thought of that. I hadn't known love. Well, a few girls. A few nights, but you had to get close and touch. Even protective wear couldn't keep the myriad of sexual and viral diseases away. I remember once a girl I was with had her arms around me very much the same way the dead girl was clutching the stuffed animal. I had felt a sudden urge to confess my soul, to unburden myself to someone at that moment. I have remembered that moment for my entire life. However, because of the viruses, touching was not allowed for years shortly after that.

I stood up and felt more alone than ever. I hated myself for thinking all these thoughts and told myself it was time to move on. First, however, I would find rebar and fashion a long spear out of it. As I hunted for a piece of steel, I wished that ugly cat was still there. It was his presence that gave me confidence. He kept me from being alone. It was then I saw the notebooks upon the bed stand. There were several of them and I picked them up. Some had been written in, but the three on the bottom were new. They even had their plastic wrap around them. The pages would be pristine white and untouched. I had always coveted things like that. I had been a writer and followed a set ritual before starting any new project. I used to stuff freshly sharpened pencils into an old jar until they resembled a bouquet of newly arranged flowers. I loved that the pink tipped ends of the erasers on the pencils hadn't been sullied with thoughts you had needed to erase yet. The future was clean and worlds were waiting.

At first I was just going to take the new, unwrapped notebooks when I decided to open the others to see if the dead man had written anything in them. He had. I opened up the book and I saw the initials CP in the upper right hand corner. I flipped through the pages. They had all been written on. The penmanship was neat and flowing in that old world script. They didn't teach cursive writing anymore in schools. The SG said it was too difficult a task to master for the young because they has such limited motor skills. That was a ridiculous claim to make after children had been taught cursive writing for hundreds of years, but that was the willy nilly, helter skelter mind of the progressives at work. On the one hand, the government claimed that today's schools were all A plus, but with their other hand they perceived the students to be physically burdened by diminishing motor skills. Shouldn't the system have been concerned? Shouldn't the parents have been in shock? The educational system had just stigmatized millions of children with a learning disability that had appeared out of nowhere, and yet their solution was to simply not force them to be challenged by a task that they were no longer capable of performing rather than applying measures to bring this new, less talented generation of youngsters back to the high level of standards that had just existed the year before.

So what was the SG really saying? If their schools were rated A plus, why weren't the students? Parents never thought to question the diagnosis of the educational system. They were the experts. If experts advocated that children should only be taught to print, then who were they to challenge their findings? People were fed drivel and ate it with a shovel. It went down smoother and tasted better if you didn't think about what you were eating. A spoonful of forgetting helps the drivel go down.

I thought that printing only looked good when it appeared in typed form in books and magazines. It was ugly when humans struggled to form it. It looked like the scratching of Harley's on the headboard, I suddenly thought. By taking the cursive form of writing away, they had taken the beauty out of language, but I soon discovered there was another more sinister reason why the government had thrown out the teaching of cursive writing. If you can't write in cursive form, you can't read it either. All historical documents were preserved in cursive scroll. To the masses of people their own language had suddenly became tantamount to deciphering ancient Egyptian hieroglyphs. The government sighed a breath of relief.

Just then I noticed there were dates on each journal. The top journal in the pile had last year's date on it, 2068, and I decided to take them because it would be like being let in on a person's secrets. It would be like having live streaming. Reading books had always been like watching movies to me. When you read a novel, you could shape the story to your own likes and your own fantasies. You were a co-creator as it were. Your mind could go where it wanted and no one censored it. When you read, you were free.

I let my fingers run over the smooth leather binding and felt a simple joy of possessing an item. I hadn't even held a book in decades. The I-Cells I had access to in the rehab center were for monitoring purposes only. I-Cells enabled the SG to track you. They were not only connected to the Web, but they monitored your thinking. No one was allowed the luxury of being alone. No one in Rehab was allowed to have I-Cells. You didn't need one because you were already monitored twenty hours a day. The new cell phones were really just tracking and monitoring devices, anyway. You could not use them for personal pleasures. Those days were gone. The I-Cells had become practical, but necessary devices which gave you a list of new laws you were required to know for the day, beeped you once an hour, and you plugged in so they could scan your thought waves for one minute. If you didn't beep back, they came and got you. That was another way the SG employed the drones. They were the enforcers. When the drones came and got you, you vanished. There were millions of them deployed in the US. They were free labor. They were solar charged, so they ran on nothing, and they needed no food. The government used them for everything from law enforcement to sweeping up Big Macs' burger joint.

Ergo people were no longer needed to perform the menial tasks. In the beginning, the government said that left us humans free to become. Of course, they never specified what that becoming was, but then everything the SG said was in broad generalized terms that were intended to be vague and undefinable until they defined it for you. Keeping terms abstract also kept you from catching them in a lie. All definitions were deemed living and changeable like the constitution, so you could never trust in their definition of anything for too long. They purposely left all laws open ended so they could fill in the blanks to fit the situation. Let me give you an example of what I mean. If you broke law 70 which said, "Don't do anything questionable," they told you what the questionable thing was you had done when you were brought in. The questionable thing was what they determined it to be. Maybe you had crossed the street before the go light, given a nasty look to the NP (night police), or didn't pay the subway fare. It didn't matter. They always found you guilty and fined you 500 gold chips. The second offense was 1000 chips, and so on. There were no prisons, only Rehab Centers like the one I had been in. If you didn't learn in there, you were deleted.

The one thing that I noticed now, after being back in the outside world, was that there had been mostly humans in the Rehab I was in. I hadn't given that fact as much as a fleeting thought while I was there. After all, I was born around the turn of the century and there were more humans than drones, clones, or robotoids on the outside at that time, so it was natural that mostly humans would be in rehab with me. Hybrids were being tested in those days, but no one was really aware of them. Maybe I was wrong to have not given it much of a thought. It was just the way things were. You accept the status quo, don't you? You go with the flow.

Just then I heard the voice come over the airwaves. It was the typical drone voice, commanding and non-emotional. "Human survivors the attacks are over. We have come to take you to safety and reunite you with others of your kind. We have food and water." The message repeated like the broken record it was, which made it easy to ignore after I heard it the first few times. My own thoughts were more important. I needed to get underground. I needed a fox hole where they would never look.

I stood there and wished the cat was still lying on the bed. He hadn't been afraid of death. He had taken no notice of it at all. Why was I wasting time thinking about him? He was ugly and had mats in his fur the size of golf balls. Then, like a wish coming true, Harley magically appeared. He was scratching on the bedstead again. "Critic," I said. Then he started his crazy pacing once more and jumped down to where the hand of the little girl lay. He looked up at me. He started trying to cover her with the debris that covered the floor. He had more sense than the government. These bodies needed to be dealt with, and he was trying to do his part. Burials had gone out of use many decades before. Like everything else in society, the cost of a plot had continued to go up. They were small gold fields. All cemeteries had been bought up by the government; the human remains removed and cremated so that apartment buildings could be erected. They called these apartments living plots, and they were not much larger than the size the burial plots had been. Rat cages is what I called them. I would know because I lived in one.

My mind kept jumping from subject to subject. I didn't know how to stop it. I had been on pills for at least ten years and they had curtailed my thoughts from running away from me. It was scary just going where my mind led me. One thought led me to another and another, and suddenly I was remembering when the burning of bodies was the only pollution you needed to be concerned with. Every night the great factories puffed out smoke and chokes of ashes starting at two a. m., and each morning fine silt coated the streets, sidewalks, and cars. There were hundreds of these crematoriums. Well, there was for about ten years, or so, and then a bunch of them began to shut down. It was no secret. The SG communicated it on the main Time Square board just like all the other news feeds. It was done with facts and figures and data on diseases and all that, but when you got down to it, they meant people weren't dying at the same rate any longer. Imagine that! That was the day my trouble started in this world.

I had been a journalist of sorts before the One World came to power. NY was immediately a different city after their take over. I remember my grandmother had a phrase she liked to say, "the difference was like day and night." She had died many decades before they had come to power, so she hadn't been referring to the government, but about changes in everyday life, but her adage was apropos for the situation. Anyway, I used to get goose bumps when I saw the OW's billboards on Broadway because they exactly depicted her old saying. One of the posters I am thinking about was done in black and white. No images appeared on the black side of the ad, but it said, 'Out of the darkness' at the very top of that side of the poster. In contrast, the other half of the ad was colored white and there were people smiling and hugging amid a lush green garden. The people were of every ethnic group and they were happy to be 'in the light' brought about by the One World.

All posters and ads were done with minimalist art so one could see at a glance what emotion was being conveyed. Simple ideas expressed in childlike art. Words were old school. The OW told you everything you needed to know. Trust. Obey. Above every public entry way you saw this sign: 'Leave your thoughts at the door.' It became against the law to tell anyone what you thought about any program the government was implementing. There were mats at every entrance way that said, 'and wipe your feet, too.' Clean minds and feet were all the OW asked. Now, really was that so much? The SG said the signs were simply gentle reminders on the order of what your mothers had told you were good manners. To me, they were warning signs like the rattles at the end of snakes. They were put there for a reason.

After the takeover by the progressives, the regulations and signs had appeared overnight and they kept coming. Hundreds, thousands of new laws were issued overnight. There were brochures of new laws on every door step the next day. Now common sense should have told you that they couldn't have printed them overnight and delivered them the next day, but they did. People exclaimed how hard working this new regime was.

Cell phone and texting weren't against the law, the SG said, but you had to have a permit to text. That was one of the first changes in the city. People rushed by the millions to get a permit. The government was just keeping us safe, they said. They had to keep an eye on terrorists, didn't they? Well, as a journalist I asked, 'If we are now all a One World Community and of one religion, and indeed one voice, who is the government protecting us from?'

That one question that I had dared to ask about who the government was protecting us from was one too many. It created paranoia in the streets when the article was published. People began to look at each other with the eyes of stray animals about to be beaten. That was when the 'monkey see and do laws' campaign really went into effect. Trust only the government, not your fellow citizens the signs all over town began warning. Keep your thoughts to yourself in public. The art of conversation had been lost in the early part of the twenty first century, but now with the signs staring at you, conversation stopped cold. Silence was not golden. It clanged in your mind until madness set in. I told myself it didn't matter because most people had no thoughts of value anyway. Topics of conversation were about inane matters such as movie stars, new cinema releases, sports figures, those who had won the lottery, and people like Lizbeth.

The price of permits for texting rose year after year until the masses couldn't afford to pay them, but by that time human minds were stilted and unsocial so it didn't make much difference. Most people couldn't sit next to someone on the subway and converse with them. They hadn't noticed the other human beings that traveled among them for years. Fear had taken over, but people kept it to themselves. I still had a permit because my job paid for it. People used to beg to borrow my TS2 (touch screen, talk screen), but I put a stop to that by telling people they had to pay the fine if they were caught using it. No one had the money to pay the fine and the alternative was to sit it out in RF, which was a Rehabilitation Facility.

What was I telling you about? Sorry, but I haven't had my pills in a while now and my thoughts are coming a mile a minute. I haven't had so many words running around in my head for years. I wish I had my pills so I could focus. Oh, yes I was telling you how I got started down the wrong path by asking questions, but just then I heard a noise and turned towards it. I saw Harley coming in the door. He had friends with him today. I was surprised to see another adult cat that had smaller kits running after her. He was a family man. The thought stopped me cold. That was an odd expression. It was an archaic phrase and it brought strange feelings to the surface. Before I could think about it too much, there was a loud explosion of sorts, then a gushing sound, and soon water began to trickle across the wooden floors. It ran like a stream. Hum. Stream. It struck me that it was like my thoughts these last few days and weeks. There used to be a phrase for that oddity. I fumbled through my mind for the term until it came to me. Stream of consciousness. It meant that writers would babble on about what ever came out of their thoughts. Like I said it had been a long time since I had been allowed to think and I couldn't be sure where the thoughts were coming from; I didn't know whether I had read them in a book, heard them from someone, or if it was propaganda I had been brainwashed with after the takeover. I was in the process of sorting things out.

Anyway, I was telling you that I had been a writer, but after the question I remember the SG had informed me that I no longer worked for the publication Mag Rags because they had taken it over to ensure that fearful articles weren't released to the public. I, however, was being given an opportunity with the government, a promotion. The word job had already fallen out of use worldwide. It was now the OW who paid me. They paid everyone. After all, it was one world, one people, and one religion. Religion came to mean a set of beliefs that the one voice gave you. Real work ceased and the living was easy. They gave me a pamphlet to publish each week which I simply edited for mistakes. I had a lot of new free time and my chip card was debited with money. Coin had been the rage for a time, but then the SG was arresting the wrong people. They found they couldn't keep track of the coins because people traded them back and forth, or got change for them from different sources, or businesses didn't keep honest records, or any records at all. (Imagine that, graft in the market place, and the SG was astonished.) Coin was too much like cash in that respect, so the SG came up with a microchip that they embedded into your hand that had your national ID number on it. You could start your car, open doors, and turn water on from the bedroom all with the flick of a wrist! The implant contained all your medical records, too, so if you were in an accident they knew who they were rid of.

The E chip could track every red cent, movement, and thought you made from the cradle to the grave. The chip cards were used for everything. In fact, it was known as the everything card (EC). I didn't have one since I was headquartered in the rehab facility and on CS status (constant surveillance.) No inmates were chipped. That way, if we escaped, we couldn't buy anything or get a ticket off the island. It was another one of those twists of logic the progressives were fond of. The unmarkedness of us marked us as enemies of the SG.

Suddenly my brain started to hurt. I needed a pill. I got up and started to ransack the apartment. After trashing the place, I sat down, mostly because of the complaints I was getting from Harley and his mate. I was frightening the kittens. The babies were dashing around, poking their noses into everything I was hauling out, and he was trying to round them up. I sat down exhausted and watched them. There was a cute little gray tiger kitten with an orangish patch above her right eye. She was peeking out at me from behind a box. I liked her immediately. The unbalanced placement of the orange colored spot gave her an almost comical look. Harley had noticed her where abouts too, and called until she came to him. He gave the kitten a light swat from one of his paws and picked it up by the scruff and took it back to the mother who sniffed at it cursorily to make sure it was hers and then let the kitten nurse on her. Two more kittens came out as she mewed in a staid cry. The new comers pushed their way to a spot on her teats. Contented purrs came from them as they kneaded their paws into her belly while the mother cat licked them on the heads.

Harley came over by his mate and she turned to cleaning him. She seemed to be biting off the tufts of fur that hung on him. He cried out to signal he was in pain, and the kittens mewed in a type of question like way, and then turned briefly to attend to him. It was only papa, they seemed to say. Mama was cleaning him, and they went back to feeding. There was such tenderness in the scene that I began to cry. Then I thought of the little girl in the other room clutching the lion. Thinking of her and her mother with her arms around her only made the tears came harder.

Suddenly I heard the sky vans outside again. "Humans come out. We are here to rescue you. We have food, water." I had seen the way the humans had been dragged in, and I was not about to lose my freedom. I sat in the penthouse apartment and cried until I was a well which had gone dry. In the wake of voices, I had forgotten what had started this 'veil of tears flowing.' Veil of tears? I immediately felt I had heard that term, but like all jolts to my memory, I could not make the connection completely. These jolts as I called them were like electricity. The memories brought a stiffening to my entire body. It wasn't' a physical pain, but it was overwhelming none the less. I was left with a numbing dread of what I might find if I connected all the circuits.

The SG had been so good as to provide doses of pills in plenty to keep the phantom thoughts from entering and torturing all people who were diagnosed as I was. In the first days and weeks after my supply ended, I had simply run when these ghost thoughts attacked me, but now I had the added fear of death. It kept me running in faster circles on this trash heap of an island. I thought it fitting now that the most expensive real estate in the state of NY was built up and given its solid ground by billions of tons of garbage. I began to wonder how long it would hold the tons of concrete up. Was it sinking into the river as I sat crying and pulling my hair out? One thought after another came at me. They were like quick blinking lights at first, but over time the flashes, the memories got longer and longer.

The SG had been right about one thing. The pills kept the irrational thoughts away, but they kept everything else away, too. Surely people had lived through these emotions before, I thought now. They had to have. The pills had only been around for thirty years and people had been around a tad longer than that. Then I saw one of the poster's the SG had planted everywhere. This particular poster I was looking at was one of a man, a woman, and a child running away from some black shadow that was chasing them, and the ad said: "If you took your pill today, you wouldn't be faced with this now." The next frame showed the same 3 people gulping down pills and smiling. Another poster said, "3 pills a day keep the thoughts away."

Then an alarming thought struck me. I had not taken a pill for months, yet I was alive. This fact mystified me. We were told that we could not simply stop taking the doses. The pill vials were wrapped with a pink fluorescent warning label that read: STOPPAGE of this medication causes HEART ATTACK and SUDDEN DEATH. FREE refills at any AAC, which was an Affliction Addiction Center. I had waited for death to come. I asked for it to come. Leaflets had been left all over after the silent attack on the night of lights to assist you in dying. They told us to report to the local OW's ECARP. (One World Emergency Contingency and Relief Provider.) Assistance would be provided for those who wanted to die.

In the months before the drones and robotoids came back I use to sit on the docks each night and look across water and see if I could detect any flux of people coming and going over there, but I saw none. That made me suspicious, but I had other reasons for not getting to a One World Provider. I was afraid of the water for some reason since that day on the bridge. It was a fear that had risen instantly out of nowhere and from no source I could pinpoint. My strange phobia aside, I didn't think there were any humans left across the river now, either. They were being rounded up just like they were here. The species I had run into so far were hunters and I kept in hiding.

Life was a nightmare I couldn't wake from. For weeks on end I lay in pools of sweat and shaking. I cried out to die, but there was no one to hear me in the basement where I had entrenched myself. The room itself was a mass of hissing pipes in an old manufacturing plant. The pains of withdrawal were taking their toll on me. Then one night I went to the docks with the aim of going for a last swim. I found comfort and strength in having made a decision to end it all. I would be in control of it. No more shaking days of terror from being without the UM medication. No more waiting for sudden death.

UM stood for Unresponsive Memory, and I had been on those pills for better than ten years. This was not a chosen withdrawal from the tiny orange tinted orbs, but a forced one since there were none to be had. I had torn apart segments of the city looking for those fluorescent orange pills. They kept the mind floating in perpetual calm. At least that was my experience, and judging from the fixed expressions I had seen on the faces of the other humans around me, I guessed that they were having a very similar experience. As I was coming off the meds, my ears rang like bells, and my head seemed like it would explode. The thoughts that went through my mind were like bolts of lightning. Everything triggered a memory.

The night I am recounting to you I took the long way to the dock, the way I use to take from work decades ago. It may sound funny to you, but I wanted to think. It was strange, but familiar, this strolling to think. Even in all my terror and with all my shaking, I seemed to find something soothing in walking and thinking. I began to rediscover sensations I had not been aware of for years, and I began to realize I had control over these thoughts. I had a choice. That was the evening I found Harley. You may think I have lost my mind instead of finding it because I am back at the beginning of this narrative again and retelling you something I have already told you. Be patient. I am merely recounting how I pieced all of it together as I lived it and tried to make some sense of sane logic out of it. The night I met Harley I was making connections again. Suddenly I found myself doing a strange thing. I heard myself whistling a tune. I didn't remember the title of the song, or most of the words, but I made up words to what I couldn't remember. Happiness ran over me like anointing oil. I caught my reflection in a store window. I was smiling. I immediately thought of the emoji's that were used in lieu of words. The emoji's kept you communicating to the world. They expressed what you couldn't.

Then I took in the rest of me. My hair was flat and long and matted down heavily with oil and dirt. It was a shock. The smile dropped away from my face. I was a monster. Ugly, terrifying, unwashed and terribly thin. It was the gauntness and hollowness of my features which took away my humanity, yet upon further reflection it was also my thinness that would tell the world I was human. Droids and drones were sculpted into DaVinces and Michelangelos complete with six packs and perfectly proportioned physiques and they had no need for food. My mind was like a pinball zinging from one thought to the next and I was trying to use the flippers in a more controlled way. I had to focus on the target I needed to hit if I wanted to stay in the game.

My mind was racing. Suddenly nothing mattered or made sense. I felt over whelmed by everything. I forgot my joy of seconds ago. I wondered why I had come into the world in the first place. I was filled with rage and picked up a parking meter which lay on the sidewalk and smashed it through the plate glass window that had been my mirror. It was then that I discovered that the window I had smashed belonged to an AAC pill dispensary. Hope encapsulated my entire being. I broke out the rest of the window pane and jumped inside. I was like a madman. My fears and terrors would soon be over. I would have peace in my mind. I looked for the bins that were marked UM's. Red and yellow tape had been put on those particular bins to seal them shut. A paper covered it and which gave directions of some sort. It said: See OW order number 29773 for discontinuation of UM drugs. Discontinuation? I was in a panic again.

It took hours of searching and reading through the files of clouds to find out what it all meant. When I had all the information, I felt as a man who had lost the most precious thing on earth, hope. The OW had lied to us! I had found this out from their own office memos and cloud files they left behind. It was the real first dose of truth I had had in decades and it was a shocker. I was like a man on a tiny raft which was sinking in the midst of a great ocean.

After taking hours to digest the information I had just read, a strange thing happened. I began to feel like I had won. Reading their memos had been like getting a confession out of them. I began to feel transformed. I was a phoenix rising from the ashes. I felt life enter me and strength replace the hopelessness. Suddenly I had a purpose, a mission. I would get even with the

SG and tell the world what the hoax had been. Then I recalled the moment that had led to my being diagnosed in the first place. I had asked questions about the SG's intentions towards us people. I had had misgivings way back then, but I'd had none in the intervening years since. It was a strange realization to feel the gap of missing life rush at me. There was the moment of my arrest and then a black wall until I found myself without pills and wandering the docks of Manhattan. Arrest, blackness, now. It was a very short cache of memory.

Here is a copy from the inter-office OW order dated 7-11-2069 that I found that day:

INTER OFFICE DESTROY ORDER # 29773.

UM Drugs are to be discontinued as of this date. Have all who need refills report to ECARP IN NYC. They will be disposed of there. The attack will come on 9-11 as usual. All employees are to report to LaGuardia Air terminal 2 on 8-28. You will be taken to a free zone base in Colorado or Utah. All cities in the US will be attacked simultaneously. Coordinated attacks will be carried out in the European and Asian sectors as well as worldwide. This will reduce the population problem in the world by one third or better. All Hu-manimals that survive the silent wave attack are to be disposed of within 6 months from the date of the attack. Cremation will leave no trace. MGA

Then I followed the email trail and read the following conversation between the two workers whose only identities were their initials.

KR: What is to be done with those who survive?

MGA: There shouldn't be many left to round up. Estimated survival rate in the NY area is around 500. They literally won't know what hit them. It will be like rounding up sheep. LOL.

KR: Is this finally the end of the hu-manimals?

MGA: Can u believe it?

I sat looking out into the empty streets. My anger and hurt at the betrayal of my own race was devastating. In many ways I could not fathom it. It was a blow that was enough to make your heart stop. The government had even coined a new term for us: hu-manimals. That was easy enough for me to believe because in the decades before the end they had deified nature. They held fund raisers to save every species of animal on the face of the earth except man. They had received all kinds of awards and honors that showed the world their humanity towards life.

I remembered a few articles I had read about the government buying up lands and water rights way back in the 1990's. By the late 2040's, when I was researching these articles, these sanctuaries were protected by the latest technologies of invisible weapons which kept everyone out by zapping them like insects. If any life form came into contact with the invisible current, their bodies were said to flash like lightning bugs in flight for about 30 seconds. The force sent them flying and color coded their insides like a veritable rainbow until they vaporized. I had laughed along with my buddy at the comedic visualization of a flying human exploding like a sky rocket. Then I hadn't believed the rumors and hadn't included them in my article. There couldn't be an electrical force capable of that type of devastation. Nothing was real to me in those days. I was young and invincible, but now things had changed. I was nearing fifty and everything was real. I believed those stories from over twenty years ago. I was remembering!

These designated wild life preserves that the SG protected had once been national parks. That fact alone made it hard to believe the rumors. They were the fairy tales of our day, but stories kept circulating that claimed people were killed for trying to get in. I knew this to be fact because a friend of mine had disappeared, and his brother had confided to me that he had been killed trying to get a look into the preserves. No one believed Turbo. That was only his nickname, I thought as I tried to recall his real name.

"Oh, yes," I said out loud, crumpling the paper into a ball and throwing it into the open file drawer. "Justin Tiburon. His brother's name was Kyle."

"Who, if they had a mind, would believe these myths and stories that came from the crazy right?" these twins had asked.

That's the way everyone thought in those days. Every weird story was believed to come from the nuts on the right. The right wingers were the ones who believed in all sorts of fantasies and spread these stories to keep everyone in fear. Finally, the right was universally demonized. The right became known as the 'only real threat to mankind.'

The conservatives maintained their innocence and said it was a war of ideologies began by the left to annihilate factions who stood in their way. The right accused the left of creating division among the masses, and lying to the people. They said the left held to an ideology of nonsense that catered to a nation of nasty adolescents. No one believed the right in those days for one simple reason: They were not the faction in power. The left had control of all the media and worked behind the scenes in an invisible role in almost every agency and political office to change the power structure of the nation as a republic. In its stead they offered a progressive, secular social construct of Marxist theory as a replacement.

This war between the left and the right took place overtly in the twenty thirties and forties. The SG applied the Marxist rule to divide and conquer into every segment of life in the United States. Critical theory made the US flag a hated symbol because of all this country had done wrong over the past two hundred years, and all the injustices it had done to people of all races. It was a one sided attack. The sins of other countries were never mentioned. After all, it was Spain who had started the Inquisition, and millennia before that in 278 bc Rome had conquered some thirty one countries and built an empire from the Mediterrean to England only to be conquered later by the Muslims and lose it all. Then centuries later Charles Martel stopped the Muslims at the battle of Tours in 732 from taking all of Europe. The point is Europe had been taken and retaken a few hundred times right down through the twenty first century. In the 1930's it was Hitler and Mussolini, and in the 2020's the Muslims made their reappearance on the monopoly board.

As for the North American continents, the native Americans fought among themselves and took land from each other. The

Crow, the Shoshone, the Cree all wared with each other for land and the land changed hands too many times to count. For instance, for a three hundred year time frame the Kiowa claimed the Black hills until the Cheyenne forced them out in the 1770's. Then the Lakota forced the Cheyenne out. Lastly the Europeans forced the Sioux out. It's funny the Sioux never mention who they defeated and took the hills from in the first place. If their claims are valid, then so are the Cheyenne and Kiowa's who were on the land before the Sioux conquered them. The fact of the matter is that any piece of land on the earth has passed through many wars and owners. Land anywhere is like a giant monopoly board and who ever holds it for the moment has the motels until the next role of the dice-- which is the next war. Nothing has stasis in this world.

As for slavery, you'd think that the US invented it. It was as ancient as recorded history. Egypt had made slaves of the Hebrews, and the Hammurabi Code speaks of slavery, and all these were white slaves. The Greeks and romans had slaves. Poets and thinkers were often slaves in these ancient societies. The color of the skin only changed in the thirteen century when the slave traders used the black Muslims and the captured people from the Africa's to send to the new worlds of Europe as well as the newly founded America. Slavery had been around since mankind existed and touched every land of the world, yet somehow America became the big Satan, whose sins outshone that of the rest of the nations, and the Shadow Government lead the assault. In place of capitalism, the left offered socialism, where all would be truly equal. One has only to look at the welfare system to see what the government meant by equal. Generations of welfare recipients jumped to the democratic progressive party and the great machine was set in motion and no one could stop it. The poor were paid to riot in the streets over everything the right said or did. Liberal leftists wanted everything for nothing. They didn't stop to figure out if the government could afford to keep feeding them. Had they stopped to calculate, they would have known that the government gets its money from the taxpayers. The pool of all the taxes collected went to a government agency once known as the IRS. The government then doled the monies out to the have nots and the agencies. The money for the have nots came from those that HAD until all those who had were killed. You can see how that would affect old Miss Hubbard's supply of bones.

The government's budget was really only a simple arithmetic formula applied on a grand scale, but the left couldn't do math either. The left believed in a magic money tree and were as equally gifted with myopic vision in math as they were in social construct theories. The government only had 25 trillion dollars to buy bones with, but soon it had 400,000,000 more bones to buy thanks to open gated immigration. Money only goes so far. Money is what it is. It is a mere tool. You can't threaten to shoot it.

Look at the economics of this on a micro scale. See if you still like open borders when the law applies to you and yours: You have a family of 4. You and your family must live on the money you make, but then you are told that you must take in the children down the street because they don't have a home. Now you have 6 children to feed on the same budget. Then a month later you are given 3 more children to house, feed, and clothe. Now your paycheck has to feed eleven people. In 6 months you are forced to open the door to your house to 30 more people. Now you must feed 41 people, find a place for them to sleep, etc. If you refuse, you are a bigot and a hate monger and you will be severely dealt with. To add to the drama, some of the new comers to your house don't like the rules you live by in your family and won't abide by them. You want them out, but you can't get rid of them. There is the law of open doors and borders. Within a short time, you are in poverty. Your house is filthy and your paycheck can't feed all the new comers. Now you live in a new third world ghetto. Welcome to open immigration. That is how the Government went bust. The government's budget couldn't stand the strain to their coffers any more than your family could. It is common sense and fourth grade math. A child could have told them that if there had been any around.

Here is another mystery. The masses were thanking the government for the money to buy food and stuff when they should have been thanking their fellow tax paying citizens that they claimed were racists and hate mongers. People still got hungry, and when the tax pool dried up they started taking it away from those who were weaker than they were. Then the masses hated the government who could no longer afford to keep them pacified. Real riots broke out. It was the beginning of the cracking of the cosmic egg.

My mind was functioning again. I was remembering things in a more linear pattern now and one that started to connect the dots. I shook my head. It didn't matter anymore. Both sides were dead now. The SG had used the liberal left to subdue the enemies of the state for them, but then the government had silenced the subducrs. There would be no tattle tales left to expose the sins of the government.

The SG was very systematic about its removal of undesirables. First, the state had cleaned out the religious sectors, then the military, and finally those that opposed the SG in any manner and especially those who knew too much. It had all been done group by group until the night of the silent lights some months ago. Up to that point, the population had been thinned, but that night the goal had been extinction.

Their idea was sophomoric, basic, and simplistic. It played out like a trite plot from one of those early talking movies. The bad guys always tried to off the innocents, but one guy always realized who the evil doers were and arrested or killed them, and the community was safe and ordered again. There was one problem. There were no heroes in my era. The government and the left didn't believe in them. The age of the anti-hero had arrived as far back as the nineteen fifties.

I began thinking about when they had started rounding up the Christians. It was the new NP's who spearheaded this task. NP's were identified on all posters as the guardians of the world and they were to be trusted and respected by all. They ruled with tasers and fists. People only peeked out windows as the Christians were hauled away. In the beginning, people cheered. The world was being made safe again. Safe against what? No one bothered to ask. All that mattered was that Christians had been the enemy and they were being dealt with. It was the first rule of Marxism – divide and conquer. Them against us, and us is always right. Forget about neighbors, friends--family. They no longer exist. To the left and the Marxist there is always an enemy. The problem is one day it will be you.

Soon the process of removal was stream lined into a more efficient system. The SG brought in troops from all over the world to help them, but they were mostly Middle Eastern, I recalled now. They wore masks over their faces which I saw as an act of cowardice. However, I was dissuaded of this belief at the time by the government assuring me that the masks served to protect them from revenge at the hands of the Christians. The NP's were saving the country from war. The guns had already been confiscated from the masses. They were piled up and burned in every city in the country. That day came to be known as FFC day. Freedom From Christian's day. Some munitions centers were rumored to have burned for four years or longer. Holding FFC rallies was a real call for celebration in those days. It was an excuse for people to gather around and watch the guns and the people burn.

I had attended a few of the rallies. It was surreal. Men, women, and children were forced to climb up a gallows of thirteen stairs and jump into a lake of fire. The SG had been angered that the Christians had believed in the concept of hell, so they decided to give it to them. In a characteristic twist of logic, the SG made the lake of fire the fate for believers not unbelievers. The number of professing believers dropped dramatically after the first few rallies. That campaign effectively ended religion.

The Christians were called Nazi's, but the left had given that label to them I recalled now. I was confused even then for I remembered my grandfather had fought in the Second World War, and the stories he had told me about the Nazis were about people who did not believe in Christ so how could they be called Nazi's when they believed? My grandfather had told me it was the Nazi's who had persecuted the Jews who were the descendants of Christ himself. Hitler had killed them by the millions and he was a Nazi, a socialist. How could people not know they were socialists? It was in their name. Nazi stood for National Socialist German Workers Party which was the Nationàlsozialtische Deutsche Arbeiterpartei in German. The name Nazi was shortened form of the first two syllables in the first word.

Somehow the SG had managed to rewrite history, I realized now. Suddenly it became vital to know how they had done it. It was then that I heard a voice speak plainly to my spirit. I knew it was not my own voice, but being alone I took comfort in its presence. It sounds crazy to say a voice had being, but this one did. 'Seek the truth. You will find it.' It was the plainest directive I have ever received, and I yielded to it.

Try to be open to what I am telling you. The right had told the truth. They tried to warn us before they were all wiped out. It was, and is, the left that had twisted the truth. They had kept us embroiled in a constant war and they kept our hatred focused on an enemy that didn't exist; on an enemy that they had created out of the black shadow side of themselves.

The real enemy was the government that seized control in the twenty twenties. It has been killing us ever since. It was the Party of the People who brought this destruction on us. It was planned. I had stumbled on to the partial truth and I didn't know what to do with it. I lived in fear and I became like a rat in a maze of city blocks and half empty streets and buildings. I lived in the sewers, in abandoned buildings, and came out only at night. Traffic was picking up again, so I didn't dare go out much. The generation papers I had forged were becoming suspect, and I knew I needed to get off this island I was stranded on.

Right now I was feeling my stomach ache with hunger. I hadn't had much food in the last few days, and I needed some nourishment. It was a nice evening and it looked quiet. There was an imposed curfew after eight PM so I decided tonight I would risk venturing out. I needed food and air. My mind was moving in a fog from constantly inhaling the recycled air inside the old manufacturing plant.

THE WIZARD OF ALL

I had been surviving on bottled water and giving myself cat baths by spritzing water on myself and just letting it dry which wasn't getting the smell off. I went over the mental list of items I needed. Food, a change of clothes, and soap. I saw what I took to be real people making their way up the block and ducked into the doorway of the chapel. I decided to stay behind the door until they passed. They approached loudly, having been drinking. They were breaking windows and looting as they made their way up the street. I wanted to shut the door, but was afraid I would attract their attention if I did. The cat family, hearing the ruckus, had taken off for safer corners. I was running into more and more new groups of people. More of us hu-manimals had survived then the government thought. There were even girls among this group and they were young. They stopped among the tombstones in the yard surrounding the church.

"Hey, Jules. You were trained as a witch, weren't you? Need some old bones to cast a spell?"

"Let's dig up some of these guys out of the rubble and hang up their old bones in our apartment. That'll be a real rad addition to the next party."

"Wind chimes, dude. We'll make homemade bone chimes."

"We need shovels."

"F that. I can dig like a dog through this loose stuff," the boy said as he got down on his knees and began scooping dirt out with his hands and howling and swearing. Curse words had replaced the ability to phrase a coherent sentence long ago. When the line of epithets were strung together it pointed to the speech of idiots. Words had lost their purpose and men had lost the creativity to form them into any semblance of meaningful communication to one another. The others in the group just laughed and joined in the task of helping him to sift through the ruins. This mining crew kept up a chorus of, "It's six feet down, and six feet long. We'll find the box and take his locks."

Other howls rose in the distance as if in answer to the tune they repeated.

"Dave, Cole, get up. There's a pack of dogs heading our way!" one of the girls alerted them.

"Hell hounds," the boy said, laughing and taking a drink from the bottle. "Is this Satan's ground or something?" he continued laughing. The others had run away as the boy stood there drinking the rest of what was in the bottle before he smashed it against the pavement and took off after the rest of them. Soon I saw the dogs catch up to them. Then shots rang out amid the shouts.

I followed the raucous mob down the street because others had joined the scene and I wanted to see who it was. As I drew closer, I could see it was the NP, and they were putting the young drunks into the van. I heard the boys swearing, but the girl was crying. I was closer now and could hear her. "You can't just leave him here. He's a human being."

"He's dead, girlie," the man in uniform said.

"You shot him down like he was a dog."

"He was fight'in like one. Want us to shoot you, too?"

"Don't touch her. We're taking them to the arena," another NP intervened. "We get a bounty for that. They ain't worth nothing dead."

It was a new form of NP's. Their uniforms were different. I heard the teen's drunken yells as they were flown away. "I will not fight in the Tech Wreck. You can't make me. I'm a human."

The whirring sounds of the jet car and the voices faded into the distance and I was alone again. I decided to have a look at the bodies. Maybe the boy was still alive. Once I was closer, I could tell immediately that the teen was dead. His whole upper torso was gone. The dog was in similar shape. It was a grim reminder to me that this island was shrinking. It was time to make plans to move on. First, I had to know where the uniformed men were taking the young people. I ran along in the darkness keeping in the shadows while my mind kept rejecting what I had just seen. I kept thinking the NP's had just been toying with the youngsters.

I had seen this square structure called the Tech Wreck Arena on posters, but it was uptown towards the other side of the island and I hadn't ventured there. It advertised battles between robos, clones, and drones. In bigger letters it announced special star attractions as the sub species hu-manimals. I decided to see for myself just where they had been taking those they were rounding up. They really couldn't be killing us in an arena could they? That was as ancient as the Romans. It was too terrible, too horrendous to think about.

Within a few blocks of the arena, I could hear voices, lots of them. They were loud and there was music playing, but the music was more of an undercurrent to the screaming of voices. I saw crowds of people hanging out around the outside of the building which was all lit up. The brightness attracted all species into its circle. It looked just like the posters and was truly square in shape and had been constructed totally of see through hardened plexi-plus panes which allowed you to see everything that went on inside. I'm sure it was laser and bullet proof.

I was trying to make myself inconspicuous to the crowds who were entering into the building. They were drawn in from everywhere; attracted to the lights like flying insects. They were staring at me as if I was a new species or something. I immediately became conscious of my attire. I had on jeans and a long sleeved shirt. My clothes were dirty, but they were not unlike what these others were wearing.

I turned my face away from the on lookers as I passed so I could avoid their stares. I walked quickly, keeping my eyes cast downward towards the pavement and only glancing upward now and again to see who was around me. Then I spotted the sky van that had picked up the teenagers. It was parked next to a ramp on the side of the building. It looked like the drunken occupants were still in the back of the van. Soon differently uniformed men came out of a door of the building and went down the ramp and began unloading the teenagers. They forced the group up the ramp and into a tunnel like opening. The spectators on the outside of the building were going wild now.

I couldn't make out all the words in their chant, but I heard the word hu-manimal loud and clear.

I glanced around quickly to make sure no one was focused on me and went to the door where the youths had been shoved inside. That entrance was away from the main doors where the crowds were chanting. Peering inside, I noticed that there was another smaller square inside the larger, outer structure. This inner square was enclosed on four sides and at the top, which made it escape proof. I could see lights and cameras hanging from the ceiling of the inner, smaller box. Two robotoids or bots of some kind were fighting in the space just below where the lights and tech equipment was hung. One held an axe in his hand. The other wore a hat with a saw blade on it. They rushed forward at each other and they met with such a force that they bounced back off one another and into the plexiglass walls that contained them. The one with the axe was made of green plastic and the other one was black. I heard the crowd's words clearly at that point. They were yelling, "Skill Saw. Skill Saw." Just at that moment the black bot reached up and activated his weapon. I could see it begin spinning around, and as he walked towards his opponent, his gyrating neck kept extending higher and higher. Then in a sudden and unexpected move, he bent his head towards the green bot, and before I knew what was happening, the saw was cleaving the green bot in two from top to bottom. Sparks and flames came flying out in every direction. The transmission fluid that gushed from the body made the flames more intense. The crowd was so loud that the building was actually shuddering from the noise. I felt it because my hands were resting against the plastic panes as I watched. Battle after battle took place. Each contest ended in the total destruction of one of the combatants. Finally the teenagers I had followed were being prodded by lasers into the little square arena. At first it seemed they were meant to fight each other, but they remained in the center, immobilized like bots that had not been switched on yet. Those poor humans couldn't move. Boos were coming from the crowd and I saw them hurling things at the plastic walls. "If the hu-manimals won't fight each other, send in the Mega Terminators," I heard a voice announce and it turned into a chant. "Mega. Mega. Mega."

It was at that point that I felt arms grab me. I found myself being dragged somewhere I did not wish to go. "Stop," I screamed. "I have papers. I am a robotoid. I work in the employ of Mrs. Cuddlesworth."

"So?" one of my captors laughed. "You're out after hours and without a ticket for the fights and that's against the law. You can't watch the show for free."

Then you shouldn't make glass houses, I thought to myself.

"Wait! Wait!" a fellow droid was saying as he was running up to us. "Give the robo a chance. Maybe he has a ticket or maybe some chip."

"Got anything?" the robo who was still holding on to me asked.

I shook my head. "I've only got my papers," I said trying to reach inside my pockets for the forged papers that said I was an employed domestic. The robo immediately regained his grip on me. As I was fighting against the toid, my hands came into contact with his. He stopped wrestling with me at that point and instantly spun me around so that I was staring into his face. His eyes were slowly roving over my entire body. "You had that new skin surgery?" he asked. "Your skin feels like a hu-manimal."

I nodded. Suddenly all the robo's were touching me. "He ain't no robo," the one who had arrived late said. "Pull up his shirt." Before I knew what was happening one of my captors jabbed a giant needle of some sort into my stomach. "We got a bleeder here," one said and they began dragging me towards the tunnel entrance where the teenagers had been taken in. I was being moved towards a chute, but while I was waiting for the gates to open, one of the robos' kept lasering my pant legs and shoes to keep me hopping up and down. I could feel the blisters begin to form on my skin. I looked at him. "Just warming you up a bit, hu-manimal. "

"Get ready to be fully roasted," one of the others said.

I felt weak all over. My limbs were like a playdough Gumby, and I was afraid that I wouldn't be able to hold myself upright. I felt the need to urinate, but I didn't want to be laughed at, so I stomped my feet and held myself. A woman standing next to me, whom I took to be one of the guards, said, "Go before you get out there. If your pants get wet, you sizzle more."

I was shaking so much I could barely unzip. As I did, the woman who had spoken to me turned away. I was grateful. There was some shame left in the world. I felt someone being shoved into my back while I emptied my bladder. I heard something hit the ground behind me. I had felt the object fall out of my inner coat pocket, but being occupied I couldn't stoop to retrieve it. The guard next to me bent over to pick it up. She looked at it and read the title. "This is yours?" she asked. I had put the book in my pocket the day I had taken it from the penthouse and forgotten about it.

"Yes, and no," I said as I was being shoved forward again. The woman was on the outside of the line I was in, and I stepped out of line beside her. "You can't stand here," she said. "This is for guards only." It was then she brought her left hand out and I saw the laser tag identification on her forearm.

"Then you're not," I began when she cut me off.

"A human? No. I am a clone." She continued to stare at me. "Tell me quickly, have you read this book? I won't ask you again."

I decided to risk an answer. I was going to die in minutes anyway. "Parts of it."

"Do you believe it?"

I stared at her and nodded. She was very pretty and she had blonde hair. Her eyes were evenly spaced and she had good teeth. "Quick," she said pressing the laser into my side. "You only have minutes before the robotoids and drones splatter you on the walls."

Just then the door to the arena fight pit opened and I got a whiff of the inside. It was a foul mixture of blood and metal, of smoke and plastic, of singed hair and skin, and of fecal matter and urine. I was nauseated as I felt her grab me by the neck and yank me back. There were more guards dressed in orange behind us. "This one has papers. He doesn't belong here," I heard her tell the other guards. I kept silent as she pulled me back through the oncoming tide of combatants. I was stumbling along after her, when she suddenly lasered my shoes. "Walk straight. Do what you are told." Out of the corner of my eye I saw a few of the other guards looking at us, and giving her the thumbs up. She lasered me a few more times before we turned the corner. Once out of sight, she holstered her gun again. "There is a side entrance past the second door on the left. Go through it and you will see a yellow light. There is a sewage drain beyond that door. Take it, and don't look back."

"Why are you doing this?"

She shoved the book back into my stomach area and turned to look back around the corner without saying a word. She peeked back at me briefly and nodded. I took it as an all clear signal and I started forward expecting other guards to pop out and finish me off. Then I realized she was still covering the corner in case other guards should appear, and I took off running. I quickly found the second door she had mentioned and opened it, wondering if there was a lady or a tiger waiting behind it, but I saw the yellow light flashing across the room immediately, and I knew she had told me the truth. I ran to the door under the yellow light and opened it with ease and stepped into the darkness.

I was grateful to the woman for risking her life for me, but I knew too much and I knew someone would get on to what the clone had done for me. It wouldn't be long before I would be found and sent back to fight in the arena. I was still reeling from the scenes which I had just witnessed. Exactly when had being human gone out of style?

I hurried back along the streets ducking in and out of doorways. I kept thinking about the humans who were being killed for sport at the Wrec Tech. The stadium boasted that it held 250,000 and it was SRO when I had been there that night.

The scene reminded me of just how the SG had stirred up the masses against the Christians some thirty years before. Groups of vigilantes with as much zeal as these spectators had been set loose on Christians. It was a wild Lenten Easter egg hunt that year. The media applauded the vigilantes as heroes, not murderers. Society saw them that way, too. Free beer flowed as the bodies burned.

I was thinking over all these things from the past as I stood in front of a monument of J. Watson McDowell. He had been one of the new progressive party presidents. His likeness stood in the square and for a ten dollar donation you could ask him anything you liked and he gave you an answer right then and there. McDowell's hologram appeared right beside you and spoke. It was the Marxist party's answer to accessibility and transparency. Seeing things in print had always made things real to me. Seeing it carved in stone added immortality. There in one foot letters was McDowell's credo: 'Gods interfere with the fortunes of men.'

This got me to thinking about cloud storage, the internet, and the historic records that had vanished from society starting decades ago. Where did these words go once they were deleted? It struck me then that people and paper ended up pretty much as the same kind of gray ash; both were scattered on the wind and carried into the cosmos. Talk about your akashic record and your quantum energy field. Ancient alien theorists of the time equivocated the akashic record to a galactic sized cloud storage bin which supposedly contained all the secret, hidden, or forgotten knowledge and thoughts of the past, present and the future, and if you meditated deeply enough, these theorists believed you could ride the quantum waves of the akashic memory and it would whisper its secrets to you.

Back on earth, events, historical or not, were rewritten on the web daily, hour by hour and minute by minute. What you read seconds ago was not true after you read it; if it ever was true to begin with. Now that I had found the SG had been lying to us and that they had been our murderers, I suspected everything I had been told over the course of my fifty some years of existence. It was a crazy mindset they had forced me and everybody else into. We had to walk the precarious line that was drawn between knowing nothing was the truth, but having to act like it was the truth. It was this dilemma that I wanted to resolve, so I began looking for more evidence against them. I searched through their bins of info with a rabid eagerness and read and absorbed every dirty detail I could find against them. This was a monumental decision on my part. I didn't want to go down this route. It was the path of lunatics, but I wanted them to know I had my own words of stone. I fought daily against the emerging personal and historical memories that kept pounding and pulsing in my mind, but it was useless. My memories could no longer be suppressed. I now knew what it was to rage against the night. We have killed ourselves, do you understand? We have submitted ourselves to the slaughter one OW pill, one lie, and one OW paycheck at a time. They named us rightly behind our backs- Hu-manimals. They fed and saw to our wellbeing until slaughter time. We were the herd.

I wept and wept, and when I stopped, I sat in the heat of the streets and collapsed. It was as if my heart gave out. Betrayal makes you into a raging bull, makes you see all red, and then abandons you to a sea of hopelessness. Then a fortunate thing happened. I caught a whiff of myself. The smell instantly brought back memories of my Grandfather's farm. It is incredible and mysterious how much memory is dredged up to consciousness by one, quick sniff. Smell has the power to raise the dead! The images were so vivid that I immediately accepted them as being true. These forgotten memories came to life, traveled along my spinal cord to the cortex of my brain as if they had been hibernating and waiting for the signal that would reconnect them. Each memory led me back to an earlier memory. Scenes popped up in my thoughts like snakes from their hiding places in the rocks, but I was afraid to let them wander free because of the warnings the SG had given to me, to all us Hu-manimals. I saw the familiar logo of their posters in bold red and yellow letters clearly. Do not trust your memory. Caution! Danger! the sign seemed to blinked. They too, were snakes ready to strike. For a split second I was mesmerized again by these living neon rattles. I was terrified, and out of mere, rote habit was about to turn away from my past as I had been conditioned to, but my memory was faster than the brain cleansing the SG had inflicted on me, and before I could stop the gush of memories, my mind was already hopping down the bunny trail. It was on its own zig zagging course back to 10, 20, 30 years ago. Its path fascinated me despite the warnings I had been given that memories, especially those of the past, were only shadows. Mismemories, the SG called them, of unrealities. Minds wandered they said, and put together illusionary tales to cope with life.

I was in a struggle for sanity. It became a battle between what the SG had cleansed me to believe, and what I felt was a memory I actually lived. I let it rage on. A single brief scent had triggered a switch in me. Images flowed with the speed of an avalanche moving down hill and nothing could stop them. I could even taste the roast beef dinner my grandmother used to make, and I hadn't had beef in over fifteen years. I hadn't thought of her in that long either, or Pompy.

After the avalanche settled, I found an old world had returned and I was willing to investigate its roots. I began to let the memories come. I went slowly at first like a wader in water. That way, if the water got too deep, I could always step back. I found the memories that came weren't nightmarish at all. I was with my grandfather. I was in his barn. I was smelling the odor of the cattle and the other livestock in the barn before it was mucked out. The scent was a mixture of animal urine, wet straw, dirt, and old wood. The time of day was distinct in my mind. Dawn. Daybreak, they used to call it.

That brief whiff had evened awakened the colors of the past. The sun had not yet risen that particular morning. Brazen yellows, pinks, and oranges were breaking into the grayness of the departing night. The coming day was not timid. It shoved the residue of lingering gray away with an assuredness I had never seen until that moment. I remember my thoughts at the time: The sun knew it had the victory and rose to claim its crown. The audacity of such a move had a profound effect on me that day, and I spoke to my grandfather about it. He had said, "It was made to be so, Trave. Light always defeats the dark." He put his hand on my head and tousled my hair in brisk, yet gentle rubs a few times. His hands were capable and strong and I had felt an instant sense of belonging. That's where my memories led me. There was no monster waiting for me.

CHAPTER 2

Months passed. I'd read over a hundred books since I last picked up a pencil, but today I had resolved to make notes in my journal again. 9th of August: I had found and read books by authors that were said to be stricken with madness, who were war mongers, and writers who I had personally witnessed being burned. I had applauded their deaths then, but it tears on me like a worn garment now. What to do with all the guilt? How can you rid the mind of a memory that goes deep into the heart and keeps it from rising? I begged for consolation, but there was none, and I hated at the same time. Does that make sense? Where is the release valve for all of these regrets and mistakes and stupidity? I may break with the madness.

I had also been seeking out a new place to hide after my night at the arena. I found the safest place in the world when the I came upon the Archival Center (AC)of the OW elite. I couldn't believe my good fortune on finding this repository of the past. It was like unearthing the library of ancient Alexandria. There I found every book we were told not to read. It was forbidden fruit, and I ate until I vomited and I could no longer deny the truth.

I had set on this course because I needed answers. Do you understand my reasoning? I had to know what their motivation for terminating us was. I will tell you up front and simply that I found it was a planned agenda; calculated and carried on by generations of men that had agreed to move the progressive agenda to the very end we are living in now and it sent me into craziness. It was not the mere comprehension of their plot that caused the madness, but the fact that it had been carried forward by generations of baton carriers to fruition. Patient spiders! I laughed out loud to fend off the fear I was feeling and to combat the incomprehensible insanity that I had bought into during my life. I cackled and bayed like a hyena. Finally, my belly hurt so much I sounded like a train chugging into the station and I was forced to end my guffaws. My cheeks welled and swelled from the inside, signaling that vomit was about to spew up and out of my stomach. I had felt that exact sensation on nights when I had drank too much. Nothing could stop the eruption, but I knew that once the rot came up out of your system, the nausea would be gone.

All this emotion set off one of my torturous spells again as I was still combating the withdrawal of the drugs. Today I told myself that I was purging a lifetime of lies with my vomit, and I began to welcome the retching. Then I lay exhausted. I longed for someone to touch me. Suddenly I thought of J. She was the first woman I had a coming on to, a hurrah. She was a real fourth of July. I used to make up all sorts of imaginary meetings which would find us in that first touch, that first kiss. I mention this only because feeling was another fear I had coming off the drug. I was racked with pain and cramps and my body craved the drug. I was like an infant learning how to walk and stand on solid ground again. I had shuffled for years, and now I was being forced to learn how to put one foot in front of the other again, and walk straightened up instead of hunched forward. That image of me in a crouched, ape like stance reminded me of an incident that had occurred at the rehab facility when I had asked one of the care takers what had happened to my posture, and the guard had said, "It's old age, boy. You're at the SAD stage, sag and drag. Sag and drag, boy." He and the others who were standing with us always laughed. It was a sinister and evil laugh, an insiders laugh. I hated them standing tall and straight in their black coats. Then I recalled that someone had once told me that all medical staffers had once worn white. No, it wasn't just someone I had known in a casual sense who had told me that fact, it had been Grandfather Pompy. Again, the old warning posters popped up like a filter in my head. I had seen and read those warnings every day for ten years. They were posted like traffic signs everywhere. 'Don't trust anyone- Especially family. They know your secrets!' Then at the bottom of the sign was the undisputed proof that you could not trust anyone you were related to. Statistics! Numbers were the epitome of truth, and indicated that over 90% of informers were family members.

I stopped writing at that point as I remembered the robotoid slicing the man down from the crown of his skull to his crotch within the space of a blink that night at the arena. I could smell the blood and metal and water as the splattered pieces of flesh were being hosed down from the plastic panes after each contest. Just as I had been consumed with fits of laughter that came out of nowhere, I began to feel rage and anger come on me for all that had been done to me, to all hu-manimals. Flames licked at my heart and I could feel the burning. It was at that moment that I made a vow to myself. I would get even no matter what it cost me personally.

Between reading and sleeping, I planned out the justice I would exact on my enemies each night while I waited for my few hours of sleep to come. I generally only slept from the beginning of the dawn hours through the late hours of the morning. In the night things moved and noises came. It was wiser to stay awake in the archival center and read. I had learned to move like the felines in my company so no one much took notice of me. The three men were still posted in their station in front of what was now called the Holding and Processing Building. Lately, however, more and more of these new type of NP's began to disappear. The sky cars picked up fewer passengers now. A hundred or so government officers were almost all that was left, and they stayed on their side of the city and I stayed on mine.

I was growing bolder as my mind and memory were coming back. I was remembering more and more. Each time I entered the AC(Archival Center) the past would present itself to me in vivid color. It was almost as if I had a memory chip implanted like those of the robos or drones except my memories didn't play out in holograms like theirs could. My thoughts were in my brain. They played only to me.

Today I was reminiscing about the times I had come here as a journalist many years before to research information on articles I was writing. Obtaining information had been such a secretive and formal affair in those days. First, you would hand over your media credentials. Then you would wait for them to verify with the magazine or station you were affiliated with to ensure you had been sent to get the info. Next, they gave you a number and you waited again. When they called you up the second time, they gave you a request form and told you to fill it out. Now, a two year old would have sense enough to ask why the form wasn't handed to you the first time you had been called up instead of the second time. Waiting was part of the SG's game to see who would crack first, them or you. They had an edge though. If you became impatient and lost your temper, they threw you out. If they were nasty and grousy to you, they threw you out just because they felt like it. So either way, it was fixed so you couldn't win. The roulette wheel only landed on their number.

The pages on the forms were all very official looking. It even said OFFICIAL DOCUMENT and carried the embossed logo of the OW on the page along with the legal statute number to further validate how official it was. The request form was about ten pages long and needed to be printed in all capital letters. Cursive written documents were not acceptable. I had found that out on my first go round with the Archival Center.

I remember that day so clearly as I am writing it down for you. I let the memories come because I needed to connect the dots into some real context that I could make sense of. Remember I told you that writing made it real? Communication is essential for human kind's survival. There was something in me, pushing me, almost goading me onward to that solid wall of black that was my past. I felt I would find myself if I didn't weaken, and I forced my thoughts.

I remember wanting to hurry that day in the early 2020's because my Grandfather Pompy was with me. I had taken him to the VOAFC(Veterans of America Free Clinic) earlier that morning so he was obliged to accompany me to the AC. I needed to get clearance for him to enter the AC with me, which had added a couple of hours to the process of retrieving the info. The NP at the door was already annoyed with us as Pompy had made it his job to set this young guard straight on just what building he worked in. "This is the Manhattan Public Library. Shit and shinola, soldier! Don't you know that? This isn't the Government Archival Center for historical documents, it's the public library. Always has been. It's books, free books for the public. Information isn't a secret. Citizens have a duty to stay informed."

"Travis Newman Tarkington you need to control this fighter or you will be asked to leave without fulfilling your request for historical archival footage. You will be fined and possibly spend Rehab Time for making a frivolous request of a Government Agency. Do you understand?"

I nodded that I did, but the woman guard said. "Sir, please acknowledge in verbal responses so the AV cams can pick it up and verify that you heard the warning stated if this incident goes to court."

I replied in words and turned to my grandfather. "Pompy, you have to sit down. You can't run around and talk in here."

"Pompy? What kind of a name is that?" the guard interrupted me. "I thought you said he was your grandfather. Your name is Tarkington. Is there some lie going on here?"

"No, sir. That was a name I gave him when I was little before I could speak well. Adults told me that I couldn't say grand pappy, so I said Pompy."

"Other names, secret names aren't allowed spoken in public forums any longer. I will have to cite you for this. There will be a fine. It can be paid by your employer or yourself. A court appearance is necessary."

"I just made a slip of the tongue. I can assure you it won't happen again."

"That is something to tell the Chief Justice when you appear. To me it is argumentative behavior. Stop it now or arrest will be imminent," the NP said with his hand held up in the 'go no further position.' This hand gesture was known as a legal stop sign and was taught to all children from the primer school on. It

70

was a strong and serious order when given by an NP. People had been shot for not desisting their actions when that hand signal had been given.

While the NP was writing up the ticket and speaking to me, Pompy escaped to the outside of the building. He was standing at the corner of the building when I came out after him. He was trying to take down the sign that was there. "Here is the corner stone of the building. It was built in 1919 before I was born. I saw its words every time I came here. I know what it says. It is written in stone. Manhattan Public Library. 1919. That's the words that are covered up by this cardboard sign that is over it," and he yanked at the Government poster, pulling it off from the building completely. Indeed, that was exactly the inscription that was on it. Pompy was beaming. "See? I have a memory like an elephant. That's the way they named things in them days. Permanent. They didn't cut and paste cardboard sheets over it and change the name whenever they felt like it. That causes confusion. This is a public building. Why are they charging you five hundred dollars for a piece of information?"

"Pompy, the magazine will pay for all if it. They are not charging me."

Suddenly the guard was behind us. "Travis Newman Tarkington. Your Grandfather needs a pill. His behavior is out of control. When was the last time he took his pill? He is asking questions. It is not PC."

"You're the one that keeps asking questions. Swallow your own poison. I'm nearly one hundred years old. I grew up in an era when they didn't believe in pills. Now the whole damn population takes them. What kind of disease infects everyone? No odds can be one hundred percent. Nature doesn't work like that. Take your cues from her. She used to be real, Trav," my grandfather said wailing with tears rolling down under the rims of his glasses like a flood as he stood shaking his cane in the air at the guard until he fell to his knees like a child. I had great admiration for him that day. He looked like all those of his generation must have looked in the second world war charging into the enemy and falling on the beaches.

That was the last time I saw Pompy. Maybe that is why I have such a strong recollection of him that day. They took him away to the Rehab Center. It was only a matter of weeks before I had a text which informed me of his death. It was his own fault, they said. He had not been taking his drugs as prescribed for years and his body couldn't handle the normal required dosage.

Being in the AC had somehow triggered all these memories of the past, and I wasn't sure if it was a good thing. My mind just took me along and I became a passive participant. I was nothing more than a leaf in a stream. At that moment I thought that maybe the SG had been right. They had tried to protect us from these painful emotions, but if you had a memory, you had it all, the good and the bad, the love and the hate. You couldn't have one emotion without the others tagging along. They were like fingers or toes in that respect. They came bundled.

I came to the conclusion after much debate with myself that it was better to have a memory than to have none. Most of my memories of Pompy brought a warmth into my being. Thoughts of him made me fly. The images in my mind were like being with him again. A spirit of love, decency, and pride woke in me when I thought of him, and I felt changed. In contrast, memories of the SG, of work, and the people I had known evoked a rage in me which I felt could only be quelled by confrontation.

What to do with these array of emotions was a conundrum. It was the rise and fall of the ocean and I was drowning in the tide. After months and months of remembering the incidents in my life I came to the conclusion that I must devise a method of holding on to some memories while letting others go. I had become conscious of the fact that memories created feelings and I decided that these subtle undercurrents of emotions served the same purpose as the accompaniment of music in films. They were key to the overall meaning, and could not be listened to without the pictures. I had let my emotions tell me how to feel, but now I needed to be the conductor, I needed to take charge before the monster attacked or the hero was in trouble and the music crescendoed.

I realized that everything started in the mind. It was quite a revelation. Getting thoughts under control would be a struggle, but Pompy and the people of his generation had conquered it. They had been faced with many choices. How had they chosen so wisely, so selflessly?

I had been holed up in the safe cell in the Archival Center since my encounter at the arena and by now I had read through hundreds of books. I was so grateful to have found this place. These safe cells were impregnable shelters for workers of the SG. I had found that fact out by reading the office memos. The shelter was filled with water and food. It had beds and blankets. It's doors also closed out the outside world.

I had seen the door before those years ago on that day when I had come to the AC with Pompy. It had been opened by the employee that had gone to look for the historical information I had requested. I had heard vague and disturbing sounds rumble out to the waiting room where I was seated, and I had ventured out to see what the noise had been. That was when I had first seen the giant cement door sliding open. I watched as the worker stepped into its hidden dimension. So it was only natural that when I returned here, I would hunt out the source of that secret room again. I wanted to know what was behind that great, movable wall. There was still a sign on the wall that read archives, and there was a switch next to it with red and green buttons. I pressed the green button and the wall began sliding back. I recognized it as the very sound I had heard that day. When the wall was finally open, I stood amazed. There were rows and rows of shelves with books on them. Other books were in jumbled piles that lay about the floor. As I walked among the books, I felt the reverence of being in a tomb. Dust had settled on everything and the distinctive aroma that old paper exudes filled my nostrils. I saw myself as an intruder among the dead and I walked quietly, but I was eager to hear their stories. I sat down and picked a book off the shelf. I felt safe and protected within these walls and I read and read. I resolved to piece together how and where this nightmare began.

First I read randomly; just picking through the titles and pulling off the shelf whatever sounded interesting. Then I came across authors who had written during the early part of the twenty first century who knew what was being done to us. One author lead me to another by the mere fact that they mentioned and spoke of each other and of the same recorded historical events.

I started my research in earnest and moved into the secret room. By manipulating the switch, and setting a small block of concrete in the opening I got the door to close almost all the way, leaving a slot just wide enough for me to squeeze through. I was gathering all the facts against the progressives and the current SG. It would be evidence for their trial when mankind would hold them responsible for the atrocities they had carried out against us. I took notes in earnest. They were my exhibits A-Z for their prosecution.

It was a shock to find that a One World system had been plotted as far back the late nineteenth century by men who called themselves the Fabian Society. A shadow type of government had been in the making since then! This society believed most humans weren't capable or intelligent enough to govern a republic in which all men were equal and free. These Fabians were the opposite of men like Washington, Jefferson, Franklin, and Paine who had helped found this country and helped to write its constitution. These men trusted in and gave rule to the people not to those who held power. They had seen what power had done in the hands of kings.

It was when I first read CS Lewis that I began to see that astute and watchful men had been aware of this progressive movement during the ages in which they lived. Lewis had alluded to the fight against socialism in his book, That Hideous Strength. It was a work of fiction, but it included ideologies that warned us about what was taking place in society. He told us the seed that was in men's hearts.

I sat looking at the back of the book. It was the first paperback edition printing from 1965 (Lewis had published it in 1946, which was just after the Second Global War.) All the things we had begun to suspect in the twenty teens and twenties were known to Lewis way back in 1946! The strange, no, not strange, but sad reality I want to comment on is the fact that people in his times weren't listening either. Remember, that was what Harley had originally told me with the twitch of his tail?

Anyway, what Lewis was saying about his world in the 1940's was that socialism already waxed a sway over people. He talks about society being ignorant (willingly so) due to their attachment to the already existing humanistic philosophies of his generation. Lewis wasn't the only writer to see this blackness creeping into the political agenda of men. Hundreds of writers throughout history knew of this sinister thread being woven into the mural of mankind and had brought the threat of the One World to our attention and it had been ignored, dismissed, and let to die quietly. The fervor of these warnings were burned to ashes during the great purging of Christians and their ideas, while the ideas of the progressives had been handed a torch and passed to each successive generation and had not been allowed to go out.

Progressivism had its genesis in the Eighteen nineties in England. That was when the Fabians first put together their group, which in the name of freedom, was allowed to establish itself. In the society of their making, the one we live in now, they would not have been allowed to think such seeds of revolution. It is an ironic twist that men who did not believe in freedom for all were allowed to wrest that freedom from the men who were endowed with it.

The Fabians were able to push socialism forward in England under the guise that it was good for society. No one in those days would have tolerated the word socialism, so they were careful to cloak their agenda in non-enlightening language. This mislabeling and deceitful language was to be the model for the progressives' lies even after they came to rule the world. Never tell the truth.

To gain in roads into the seat of power, they first created a welfare state in England. Next they staged a crisis which they proposed to fix. The cry of the Fabians and the socialists at that time was for reduced rent for the poor and a minimum wage that you could count on. This got the masses behind them and got their votes. Who wouldn't want better housing and lower rents? Sounds good until you understand that the Fabian socialist's true agenda was to give power to the state by giving the rents paid, not to individual land lords, but to the government itself. Unfortunately they won the election and the government then controlled the rents for all of England, and it made the Fabians of the time very wealthy and powerful. Socialism believes that power and wealth should be controlled by the state, not by the people. Socialism operates under the guise of being for the people, but its agenda arranges for the state to become a bigger and bigger Grendel.

Health care was also one of Fabianism's pet projects, but solely for the purpose of breeding a better class of humans for the future, not for promoting health and happiness in the peoples of the times. GB Shaw, a well-known writer of the time and a Fabianist, supported this experiment of eugenics, and he was also the creator of the gas chamber in Germany that terminated Jewish lives by the millions. That's the creative minds of the century at work! It is inconceivable to believe they could perpetrate anything so evil under the cover of being packaged and sold as "good for society." The Fabians served socialism up as a win/win deal: The people got cheap rent and healthcare, but with it came the host of hidden issues that benefited and promoted the agenda of the socialists. Even if you suspected they wanted to control the world, you would still be getting something that benefited you, so why complain? Besides when the crap hit the fan, when the piper had to be paid, they would be dead and the next generations could pay the bill. Why worry? It was a selfish heart that claimed the goods and blackened the road ahead for countless millions.

Sound unbelievable? It was so successful that later democratic socialists used the Fabianist's blueprint to socialize America. In the twenty twenty election, the progressive democrats ran on a ticket of free health care, open borders, free college educations.

It sounds like it's for the masses, but again its true aim was to feed the monster state. This time it strove to dissolve America by bankrupting it. The Democratic party was as much aware of the two sided coin they were presenting to the masses as the Fabians had been. They knew the meaning of the Fabians symbol. It was a simple coat of arms: a tortoise and a wolf set in stained glass and it had been designed by GB Shaw. There is nothing sinister in these emblems by themselves. Everyone knew the fable of the tortoise and the hare. The slow and steady progress of the turtle was seen as a virtuous trait by the masses, but to the Fabians it meant generations of torch bearers carrying on their march for socialism. They were deliberate and cunning in subverting the meaning of well-known symbols and words to reflect the group's private meaning, which the unsuspecting public never fathomed. Why would the public look for other meanings in the Fabian's symbol when they already knew what they meant? The Fabians took the harmless figure of a turtle and turned it from its innocent symbol into one that they hoped, in time, would be the cockroach that would carry the plague into the future. They succeeded. We are the future who has witnessed Kafka's nightmare become reality.

The devious twists of the Fabians, and later the progressive democrats infused their insidious agenda on all free societies. These groups knew it was going to be a long haul to reshape society from a free model into a socialistic one. They did it a little at a time by changing the accepted meanings of well-known and accepted terms and symbols. Their meaning of the words freedom, liberty, and equality were not the same as the peoples.

There was a second animal on the stained glass window besides the tortoise. It was a wolf, but it wasn't just any wolf- it was a wolf in sheep's clothing. That was Fabianism's real identity. Go slow, and hide your true self; cloak it in the name of benefits for society, but accomplish the opposite. This theory can clearly be seen in the work of a twentieth century community organizer by the name of Saul Alinsky who took over the back yard housing project in Chicago during the 1960's. After decades of organizing and millions of dollars, and even the blessings of the catholic diocese, no change in conditions came about for the poor in Chicago even by 2020.

Neither were changes in poverty rates seen in the ghettos in cities like Detroit, Baltimore, and Ferguson where democrats had been in office for decades and had used Alinskian methods of organization. The only thing Alinsky had ever meant to organize was to make rebels of the poor, to engrain them with hate for their country and their fellow citizens. Everywhere Alinskian and Democratic Party models were used the poverty flourished and the people became divided and were goaded to find a common enemy which they could blame and that enemy was named Christian, Republican, and Conservative.

As early as the 1960's democratic senators and congressmen were directly following Alinsky's directives and advocate for violence among their followers to openly rebel against the republican faction in power. His was the Marxist model of socialism which advised would be conquers to divide the populace along racial, religious, and ethnic lines. In the twenty teens Illinois, Missouri, Michigan, California, Oregon, and Maryland were some of the states which had democratic leadership that drove their big cities to ruin following the Marxist paradigm. Yet, the democrats of the time dared to say it was because of the Republican leadership that the ghettos remained poor, but if you look up the historical record you will find that only Democrats held power in those cities and districts that remained the poorest. Records can't lie. They are like money in that respect: they are just a tool. The democratic socialist agenda pretends to be for the poor, but doesn't really give them anything. This can be proven by the sole fact that the conditions of the poor people from the 1960's through the twenty first century never got better. Yet the poor never went to the democrats who they had elected to demand reasons for the stagnancy of change. What kind of blinders are those?

In researching the history of the Fabians I had found that only one small thread needed to be pulled to unravel the truth about how the world had been ripped apart like the seams on a baseball. It hadn't happened in a day, and it hadn't happened by accident. It had been planned and deliberate. As I sat reflecting on all of this, it made me more determined than ever to find more answers, more proof, more truths. There were thousands of books around me. There had to be answers. I had only found one dangling thread. I wanted to know how we got to the point where our own government killed us and called us Humanimals. It is so outrageous, so insane that I couldn't believe it myself, and how did you convince others of a plot even you could not believe?

I debated whether other human beings would willingly exterminate millions of their own species for the sake of an ideology. Could mere ideas push men to such an end as I was reading about? I wanted proof. What was more disturbing to me was that it was an idea that had persisted for centuries in the minds of the elite and wealthy. If it were true, it meant it had been murder on a global scale.

It was a fantastic plot that should only be found in movies, but I found an answer, or at least the logic behind how it was possible to carry out such a plot on other human beings when I read a book by D'Sousa called, The Big Lie. He did not come up with the epitaph of the big lie, but he told who did. It was Adolph Hitler in his book, Mein Kampf. Hitler describes how the population falls for bigger lies more easily than little lies. That theory didn't seem logical to me at first. Why would people believe a big lie rather than a small one? Then I read further, and heard Hitler's own reasoning: humans are too timid and shy to tell big lies. We can't conceive of big lies. Hitler said that the thought of a big lie would not even form in our minds. People weren't capable of seeing the boogeyman, or of even entertaining the idea that the faintest intentional falsity could exist in others. Ingenious!! His simple explanation hit me hard. I had to believe it. I had seen his reasoning in action. I had experienced it. I had seen all those humans around me accept the lies they were told with ease and swallow them like honey. They rationalized that if someone in power said it, it must be true.

Now that I knew humans had been told a big lie, I went on to do further research into how these torch bearers of socialism carried their ideas to America. Fabianism came to our shores in 1895 with a man named WDP Bliss and began in Boston.

The men who carried and nurtured the seeds of socialism in this country came from varied backgrounds. They, like the Fabians were patient spiders. They waited, knowing that the takeover would not come during their own generation, but they believed that as the years passed, their idea would become like a snow ball rolling down hill, picking up converts and speed. And it did. The snowball picked up men like Roosevelt and Wilson and a host of other democratic politicians. They were Dr. Frankenstein's and were content to add their part until the monster was brought to life. All these men were part of an underworld secret society that sought, at its core, to bring the US down to its last breath of freedom.

Think this is a fantastic thought, and one that has never been thought of? It is a common plot and one that has been thought of by men in all generations. One has only to look to the cinema to see it played out over and over. Ever seen a western? The town sheriff is the bad guy, but he is married to the judges' daughter, who is the most honest and upright citizen in the town. No one ever suspects the sheriff of being the thief and murderer because of his ties to the good guys. One day an outsider comes to town and sees the sheriff for the murderer and corruptive influence he is. In the movie, the stranger exposes the lawman's graft and killings, but not before the stranger has been forced to fight the entire town because no one believes that their good sheriff could be corrupt. In these early movie plots all is restored. However, in the real world, the deceit continues and the injustices are never brought to light. In the real world no one ever believes the sheriff is the bad guy because they won't even look. In real life, the stranger often dies at the hands of his foes and no one is the wiser. There are no heroes in the real world. An example of a real event happened in the 1950's when Senator McCarthy tried to denounce the quiet takeover of the socialists in our midst. He tried to expose the plot I just told you of. He was destroyed by those socialists already in power and died in the 1960's a broken man.

Humanism and the inherent belief that Man was ultimately good and should control his own destiny is to blame for society not believing in the boogey man in the modern age. These enlightened beings believed that only men who shared their qualities of superior intellect and their fortunate luck of being born into the ruling classes should control the destiny of man. They even named their plan. It was called the One Percent Solution.

The goal of this one percent was to make a new earth and a new super race. Now, reading this you might say these men were crazy. You also might think that their idea had never been conceived of before either. But it had! These one percenters had not moved very far away from Hitler's dream of a master race. They trusted in man's inherent goodness, in man's creative genius and advances in the sciences. These new elite saw the masses as sheep and idiots just as the Fabians and the progressive democrats had. The one percenters became the One World government. They had reduced us to infants who couldn't think for ourselves. To them, the time was right, everything was in place, and so the E waves of mass murder were unleashed, but not the nukes. They didn't want fall out. They could clean up dead bodies and a little ruin. They needed to destroy just enough to make it plausible to us that there was a war. Some cleanup was expected. There was always rubble and bodies after war. Don't blame me if this all sounds crazy and far-fetched. I'm just reporting on the facts. I believed what I was reading because I was now among the last human hold outs. This was not just crazy tale to me. For some reason I felt very close to the source of the findings I was coming across that made it all the more plausible to me. I couldn't shake the feeling that I knew all this. Somewhere in my sub conscious it seemed to be a familiar story.

To be fair, and to balance out this apocalyptic view, I will give you the other side of man in history. There are always two sides, you know, but it has been suppressed for decades. To get the another perspective on the beliefs of men we need to go back to the beginning of this nation. I will give you a brief outline of what George Washington and the fathers of our country did. They believed in God and dedicated this country to Him at a small chapel called St. Paul's church which still stands in the 2070's. I can see it from here. Yes, it is right here in NY. It's incredible that this church should stand after the towers fell, isn't it? America had been attacked in 2001 for the first time since Pearl Harbor, but it wasn't defended to a conclusive end the way WWII was. Why?

This chapel was chosen to be the spot where G. Washington dedicated this country to God because the documents of our country's freedom got their template from the Holy Book. I found that amazing. We were told our first presidents and members of government were deists and atheists, but the history books which were written before the progressives began to rewrite the facts say these founders did believe in God. My grandfather, who had been born in 1924, or there about, had believed in God. He had fought in the second global conflict and was a dairy farmer until the SG took away his farm when he was in his ninties. He was convicted of falsifying records and cheating the milk companies of their money. Since he was the one who sold his milk to them, how could he have cheated them when the companies set the price and paid him? I never figured that part out, and further, it was him who took the milk producers to court, and that's when they turned the tables on him. The news agencies reported that Joel Tarkington of JT Farms had been robbing the population by his high prices, and that some unknown groups had taken revenge against him by beaten him, burning his house and barn, and stealing his cows. The government and the NP's were still looking for those responsible for the incident, the news feeds had declared. I asked Pompy many times if he believed the government and police were really looking for the men. Every time he was asked this question, he replied, "I have always been in confusion as to who or what they were looking for. Did the reporter mean they were looking for my cows, or the men who beat me and burned my house?"

See what I mean about one thought leading to another? I had been thinking about George Washington dedicating this country to God and that led me back to other personal people I knew who believed in God and then to the wrongs that had been committed against him. My memories of that time were coming back to me more readily and were becoming clearer as time wore on. I also began to remember other things we had discussed. I was less alarmed about the flittings of my memory. By now I had caught on to the idea that one thought leads to another and another, and then somehow comes together to form a picture of the truth. I was recalling a conversation where Pompy had told me about the Presidents of his time. He told me that the US Government was selling out the people way back then. He had said that Roosevelt's policies were socialistic in nature. That memory came to me as I was reading about these Presidents because the authors of these books said exactly what I had heard from Pompy in those days. I was astounded by the fact that their reasoning and their stories was so similar.

However, before we go any further, you need to understand how the father's set up the constitution and that they really intended the constitution to act as a safeguard of our republic before you can understand what FDR did to specifically undermine the guarantees written into it. I will tell you about Roosevelt because it was him who led us into the modern progressive era in the biggest step ever taken towards socialism. He was a poster boy for the progressives as were presidents like Wilson, Johnson, Clinton, and Obama. Their heads now comprise the new Mount Rushmore. Read over the history and you will see how the democrats lauded and praised Roosevelt and called him the forefather of socialism.

First, I will begin by giving you the Points of the Constitution adopted by the fathers. They wrote these laws during and after a war called the Revolutionary War to gain their freedom from a king in England who had total rule over the people. The framers of the Constitution and the Declaration of Independence wanted to find a way where the people would have their voices heard in this new land. They called it representation of the people, by the people, and for the people.

Without representation, people lose the ability to give their consent on how they are governed. According to the Constitution, it is the people who are in control, and it is the people who limit the government's access to power and rule by just a few, which is opposite what we have today. Why should the people of a nation retain control? Because it keeps in check the passions and plots of those in power. The father's had read and seen the history of governments who ruled over thousands of years ago in Rome, Egypt, and even in their own land of England, where until the Magna Carta, Kings could take cattle, men, or whatever they pleased, and put men to death for killing a deer on the castle grounds. The framers of our country knew what power could do in the hands of the few so they deliberately devised a constitution which prevented power from being taken from the people in this new America. The people were to express their will through a constitutional majority. Majority rules. Without majority rule, people are excluded from the operation of government, and the socialists and the democrats were very aware of that fact and wanted to get rid of the electoral college method set up by the constitution.

The writers of the Constitution further provided safeguards to the takeover of our government by delegating power evenly into three separate branches of government in a document referred to as the articles of the Constitution.

A- Legislative power. See Art. I of the Const.

B- Executive Power . Article II of Const.

C- Judicial(Courts) Art. III

Those three breakdown of powers were called the Separations of Powers and helped the people retain control of their government. Each branch of gov. is limited to certain powers, and only to those powers granted to them by the Constitution in their specific area. However, the Democrats disregarded these laws and impeached a President in 2020! They charged that he had abused power when they had been the ones guilty of abusing power when they totally ignored the impeachment procedure outlined in the Constitution. To charge the enemy with what they themselves were guilty of has always been the Democratic MO. They use it to adnasuem.

Roosevelt was known as the father of modern progressivism because he moved the bar further towards socialism than any other sitting president. FDR knew the Constitution had been written to virtually guarantee against any possibility of a takeover by a president or any one political faction. That was FDR's dilemma. The constitution, as written, stopped the progressives from such a takeover, so FDR found a way around it. He needed to usurp the power given to the people by the constitution and give it to the government.

FDR accomplished this by creating the agencies we all know and love today and by having Congress sign over their power to create laws to these agencies by what is called proxy. A word which rhymes with proxy is foxy and is more accurate of a definition. According to the US Constitution, the only agency authorized to create laws is the Congress, but they signed away their right to every agency that has been formed since the 1940's. Roosevelt circumvented this directive in the Constitution which should have long ago been declared unconstitutional and the Congress should have again be designated as the sole legislatures enacting all laws pertaining to these United States. Proxy votes should have been revoked from all government agencies as unconstitutional because it is. The Legislative Branch, that is the Congress itself, was designed by the framers of the Constitution as the direct link to the people. Since FDR couldn't change the Constitution, he just made a law to circumvent it by creating an agency that was given law making authority by proxy from consent of the Congress. This was strictly against the words in the Constitution! It says NO ONE other than Congress can make laws! Period. Read it. Today, thousands of agencies make their own laws and enforce them. That power of proxy given to them is not recognized according to the constitution.

It was the biggest transfer of power that ever took place in the history of the United States and not one shot was fired. The people had lost their power and surrendered their freedom without ever knowing a war had taken place. Talk about Sleeping Beauty and Rip Van Winkle!

Roosevelt accomplished this take over by a deception of language. He made democrats sound like they were the ones in the know with modern times by saying the Constitution was outdated simply because it was written so long ago and in a time when this country was an agricultural society. He couched this new progressive form of government as Modern and slighted our ancestors, in as much as calling them hicks, and outright saying those people of the eighteenth century were somehow less intelligent than people of the 1930's because they were farmers. Roosevelt gave his generation a left handed compliment in order to deceive them. However, if you look at the language and the intelligence of our ancestor's writing you will find it far out distances the capabilities of people who lived in the 1930's and 40's and even those of us today in the twenty first century. The generation of first Americans that FDR disparaged and laughed at had us beat by a mile. Their intelligence was far superior to ours and the honesty and integrity of the men who lived in those times was above reproach.

I demand that you read a primer, (that's what they use to call grade school readers) from the 1790's. First graders read just as well as adults in that generation, and were expected to know and answer questions most, or all adults could not answer today. Five year olds of the eighteenth century were smarter than we are today. Here is a word five year olds read and understood in 1790. Transubstantiation. (I had to look it up myself.)

Why is this important? It proves FDR lied to the people in order to take their power with a sly back handed compliment. While the masses were busy patting themselves on the back for being intellectually superior, FDR put the bag over their heads and we have been in the dark ever since. I think that is where the term hood winked must have originated.

FDR was also against owning property. All progressive Democrats are. Owning anything gives you status and power. He advocated that property rights should yield to the demands of social justice. That was a slick way of saying that if the government wants your land, they can have it. He created what was known as the right of eminent domain. The right to safe guard your property was gone. He had redefined property rights and given the people's power to the statesmen and the agencies he was about to create; two major blows from which the people would never recover.

People were once allowed to own land!!! My grandfather's generation owned land, and they fought and died to give others that same right. That is part of what made this a free nation. Pompy used to say that freedom was not free. It cost millions of our countrymen their young lives and all of their tomorrows for people to be allowed to have a home of their own and choose where to live and which God to serve. According to the original writers of the constitution, it was the job of the government to protect people's rights, not limit them as Roosevelt chose to do. Does it shock you to learn that the original intent of the government was first and foremost set up to protect its citizens, not rule over them and make laws to "limit" their choices of freedoms?

Roosevelt came up with a New Bill of Rights which reflected what he called "a growing social order." What he gave the people was his own version of the constitution. He said the Constitution was a living document and should therefore be amended to fit modern times. Sounds progressive, doesn't it? He couched his speech in such a way that the people believed that the democratic party was looking after their interests by keeping them abreast of the times. Again he used language the masses of Americans were familiar with, but his meanings were the definitions of the socialists. FDR and the democrats weren't looking after the peoples interests, they were robbing them of the power given to them in the original constitution. Their usage of American language is a duplicitous lie!

Look at the speeches of Democratic Presidents. They contain three main elements directly out of the socialists hand book: 1- Apply war time language. In short, create a crisis and pretend to solve it. Heck LBJ even made it his legacy. He started the war on poverty. 2- Create a vision for the future. Make them look forward, so they don't see the present. 3- Show how indispensable the President is. FDR was reelected how many times? Congress finally passed a law that a President could only hold office for two terms. Each Democratic president over the decades carried on this same socialistic rhetoric to transform America from a constitutional Republic to one of socialistic bearing. They succeeded, person by person, decade by decade, generation by generation, by illegally changing and ignoring the Constitution. Obama didn't even make a pretense of ignoring the Constitution and making up laws and neither did any of the socialist Democrats from his administration to now.

FDR single handedly ended the economic freedom and destiny of America when he passed the National Recovery Act (NRA.) That one law made the government more centralized than it had ever been. It created coalitions and management offices which now controlled all industries in the country!

These new management offices were the fore runners of the SG agencies we know today as the EPA, OSHA, etc. The government was never intended to set the wage and hours of free men, manage their health care, or the education of their children. The government was set up to protect the rights of the people to choose all these things for themselves.

After the NRA was passed in the nineteen forties these newly created agencies now set the goals of production output, set wages, and set the limits on the hours that could be worked. Owners of companies had lost all control over their own product and their own workers! This power, once in the hands of people who owned the companies, now rested in the state. Rex Tugwell, who was FDR's advisor, said this about the government setting and controlling the minimum wage: "It eliminated the anarchy of the competitive system." Capitalism was already on its way out.

FDR is revered among democrats for changing the rules. He was able to do most of this because it was a time of war and because he knew how to say one thing, but mean another. He had mastered the art of deception. The democrats employed this same strategy during the pandemic of twenty twenty.

Woodrow Wilson was another progressive democrat and hater of the Constitution. Wilson felt that "no limits should be placed on the future of man." Take the word man out of his statement and add the word progressives and you will see his true meaning. No limits appealed to voters' sense of freedom and liberty and took it as true American individualism, but it was no limits for the government that Wilson was really talking about. Are you beginning to see the duality in their language; the intentional duplicity these progressives gave to the voters of their time?

Both of these democratic presidents set a precedent for later generations of democrats who would continue to change laws and times. By the early part of the twenty first century, democratic progressives changed and made laws when they felt like it. They even had court judges enact laws for which there was no precedent written for in the Constitution. We know the end they have brought us to. We have lived to see what their 'future' is. We have been afforded the greatest gift and benefit of being able to look back to see what they really meant. The government already had the masses pegged as the enemy over a hundred years ago. It's hard to believe that men, born in different times, bound themselves to an idea to arrest the freedoms given to us in the Constitution and by the God who had created us. The chain of evil was picked up and carried by men who were convinced that man could control his own destiny only if it was in the hands of a few elite, educated men who thought like they did. Wilson, FDR, Johnson, and Obama were the big lie in action. Each generation produced more men who bought into the lie. They had been educated into it. Schools no longer taught the real meaning of the Constitution or love of country. America was a name to be ashamed of. The left and the socialists knew that would destroy a people's will to fight for a country that was so hopelessly flawed.

Make no mistake, the socialistic movement perpetuated by Wilson and Roosevelt continued to move forward under later democratic presidents. Johnson used the civil rights movement to further the progressive agenda. When the black civil rights movement came along they saw it as a way they could remodel society and remold it into a socialistic image of their liking. To get elected, Johnson ran on the platform that he was waging a War on Poverty. The crisis was already there. What the war on poverty accomplished was a total transformation of moral regulations that had existed up to that time, but it did nothing for the poor. Johnson's Great Society was a continuation of FDR's thoughts except that it confronted the social aspects of people's lives instead of the economic ones. In the 1960's Johnson and the democrats believed that, 'Man is nothing by nature. It is our duty to mold him into what we want,' and that's what they did. By regulating society with the passing of new laws, they could control it. It was the beginning of the narrowing of the American mind and no one was the wiser. The new laws regulated the spiritual and material thoughts of society. Johnson and the democrats had switched the meaning of Freedom from being a 'nationalistic right' for all peoples to a 'personal right' for specific groups. The socialists used this agenda in 2020 to destroy cities under the label of black lives matter.

The new laws of the 1960's also attacked the family as a united and moral unit in the areas of sexual liberation and abortion. It was a woman's personal right to kill her unborn child. Then came the gay and lesbian movement which helped to destroy the concept of male and female. It was the neutering of America.

Preservation of land and nature took precedent above the needs of humans. Nature was seen in capital letters. The democrats built parks and beautified the cities. If a city looks good, it is good, the liberals boasted. The democrats made everything aesthetically pleasing to hide the poverty.

What the progressive movement did in the 60's was to elevate minorities and women to top priority status according to their words, but no actual helping hand was offered, no real money was given to them by which they could get a hand up and stand on their own. Welfare kept them at the status quo. Everyone agreed women and minorities were important, but no one helped them out of their dilemma. It was LSO (lip service only.) Welfare was not a hand up, it was a pin to keep them down, and that was precisely what the progressive democrats had meant to achieve. Sinister? Look back at history now. You will see it as plain as a yellow brick road.

President Johnson's war on poverty was put in place in the 1960's and by 2018 someone should have noticed it wasn't working. The poor were actually worse off sixty years later. Democratically run cities got poorer after the Democrats had managed to hold office for more than thirty years in a row. Cities went bankrupt and the people left. Again no one bothered to look up the records to actually see who was responsible and who had been in office during the declines. They were too busy pinning the tail on the wrong animal. Voters had become pawns in the hands of the democrats and were taught to respond with emotionalism and violence against anything on the right. It was mad dog syndrome. Once the virus took root, it prevented rational thinking.

Democratic senators, presidents, congressmen made a mockery of their oath of office to the US to uphold and protect the laws and people of this nation. They hated capitalism and freedom for the masses. By 2016 there were 84 democratic senators and congressmen who belonged to the Democratic Socialists of America party. That should have been a treasonous act and enough for them to be thrown out of the offices they held. They were using the label of freedom to claim their right to hate and destroy a country they had taken an oath to defend. They were using our own laws to destroy us just as FDR had done in the 40's. Some law makers tried to fight against it in the nineteen forties, but they had their lives and careers destroyed, and from then on all the senators, congressmen, and presidents kept silent about the treachery that had just been foisted onto the American people. Those men in office who put the socialist agenda as a priority showed that they would stop at nothing to undermine the founding fathers documents of protection for we, the people. There are no words for such elitist and egotistical goals. Then they perpetrated an even more brazen lie! They told us it was the Republicans who were the fascists, but just in case someone might look into their claims the progressives rewrote history to hide their treachery. Then later in the 21st century, they didn't need to rewrite the truth, they removed all books from us. To insure the lies would not be found out, the deep state went one step further, the SG made it a law that every lesson taught in school must be erased each day. No disc, no videos, no paper, no books used to indoctrinate school children were allowed to be seen or discussed by parents. The SG did not want a record of what their children were being brainwashed with. The school districts said they couldn't afford text books, but spending on Education was the highest it had ever been.

What can you make of generations of people who are willing to perpetrate a lie on a nation of people who trusted in them? How did men like FDR, Wilson, Johnson and the rich elite live among millions of their own countrymen knowing that they were plotting the destruction and the downfall of a free republic? These men were of a schizophrenic mind. What kind of blinders did people wear? They should have seen who the puppeteers were, but they didn't. Nazi Germany didn't see Hitler and the SS coming either.

I had been reading for days on end. My eyes were tired and I needed a break. I was ready for a walk and headed out. After the darkness of the reading room, the sunlight was a welcome sight. Somehow its shining gave me hope. I had spent months alone in the walled off and hidden section of the old public library, but I was bolstered by the fact that I had come away with an understanding of what had happened to change this country.

I stretched and felt relaxed and decided it was time to focus on more immediate needs. During my reading frenzy I had only ventured to the penthouse to stock up on food which I hauled back in my library cart. I had not seen Harley or the cat family for some time now and had lost track of them just like I had lost track of time.

I was wondering what had become of them as I watched the other species milling about today, following me with their eyes to see where I was going. They had to be reruns, droids, or drones because most of we humans had been rounded up. I had not seen the sky cars and vans that had hauled the human among us away for months. I had tried to blend into the new style of dress and adopted a non-reactive manner of behavior and hoped I would not be scanned. I glanced behind me every now and then to keep tabs on the species that I saw were following me today. They were the same men I had seen load the humans into the vans. What was going on? Had they found me out? It was then I decided to go to the penthouse by a different route. I didn't want these species to know about the stores of food and comforts I had been taking from the penthouse. I had already hidden the good stuff in the secret fall out bunker behind the massive painted mural that covered the entire wall in the living room of the dead man's penthouse.

The three men followed me closely. "Why do you keep coming back to the apartment? What's in there?" the biggest one said raising the laser gun above his head and making a slice through the empty air with it. "We know that's where you're going."

"We don't like it," another of the men said. "We know you stay in the pill mill. Stay there. Don't come back."

So the ruse of leading them back to the Center had worked. I had gone there and stayed for a day or so every time I had come back from the penthouse before daring to go back to the old library building. "May I go this last time?" I asked, looking at the man who had spoken first. I took him to be the leader.

"What do you want?"

"Just books."

All three of the men laughed and looked at each other. "He's a pirate. He's after illegal goods."

"Who you selling them to?"

"No one. I use them for TP."

"Get going," the bigger of the men said, "bring us some butt wipe out, too."

"Come in with me. That way you will know what I take."

"No. The rats and cockroaches are still eating the bodies."

"So you've been in there," I said. "Why do you care what I take?"

"We don't want you here. This is our land."

I nodded and began pushing my cart past the men.

"You ain't like most drones. You ask questions," the big one who was the leader said.

I threw the man a quick glance. Maybe they had caught on to me. He seemed real, but then the thought struck me that he couldn't be. The real among us were being disposed of. This bot seemed to be able to put things together in his mind, though. He had intelligence. The longer the men looked at me, the more I wanted to run, but that would be a dead giveaway. While I was trying to get up nerve enough to bolt out of there, the big man spoke. "Don't take too long, or we will come in and get you," he warned. The other two men threw their leader a glance as if to say he was crazy.

I tried to keep the smile from my face. It wasn't easy to do and I looked away. I was afraid they were beginning to suspect my humanity and I laughed instead of showing fear. I reminded myself to be more careful about expressing my emotions like a human.

While I gathered my goods, I was remembering my conversation with the clones outside and trepidation replaced the happy glow I had felt earlier. Now, more than ever, I needed to see the cats. It was a matter of sanity. Feelings were still new to me, and navigating them brought constant terror. I was on over load. My brain made connection after connection to everything, and the stream of consciousness poured out in torrents I couldn't always comprehend right away. The pills had kept me from these mundane tasks for decades. I had been exempted from all this sorting and categorizing of thoughts when I was medicated. I had been wandering in strawberry fields forever. The government pill pushers had convinced us all that we shouldn't have to live with painful thoughts. Relief was a swallow away. Did worries keep you awake at night? Take the yellow pill. Afraid of people, of going out? Take a white pill.

People had died by the millions from the effects of these pills. Law suits were rampant even d's ago, but the pill manufacturers had influential lobbyists and fat bank accounts that made them the most powerful leaders in the One World Order. These drug companies paid millions to families of the people that had died taking their pills, but it didn't even touch their profits. Pay outs were like buying penny candy to them. Their cash flow was endless and as deep and vast as the ocean. The SG didn't even try to outlaw the drugs. Now I began to understand why. Death by drug interactions was just another avenue by which to thin out the population and it was legal. It was their version of the 'squirrel law,' which maintained it was illegal to shoot the varmints out right, but stated if you ran one over with your car you could not be found guilty. While it was illegal to murder people out right, drug companies could not be held responsible if people died by some kind of drug related interaction. The squirrel law became their avenue of escape.

If the government had truly been on the side of the American people they would have stopped the sale of certain medications period. Drug manufacturers paid out millions for their part in the culling of America, but after decades passed, they found a way to avoid paying a red cent to the families of their intended victims. It was ingenious, and it was taken from the tactics employed by the democratic party.The drug companies began forcing people to sign consent waivers to the swallowing of pills. Instantly, the drug manufacturers were sailing on blue waters again. The laws no longer held them accountable for anything once the waiver was signed. The courts held the patient responsible for taking the drug.

Sound crazy? Read on. This was the type of government logic that had been used as far back as the 1820's at the very inception of the democratic party under President Andrew Jackson. Jackson had exterminated the Indians of America and actually had the gall to blame them for their own extinction. In fact it helped him win the election and so did his slogan, 'the Indian killer.'

The next use of this blame the victim tactic would come into play by the democratic party in the election of 1860 when the candidate dared to proclaim that slavery was a benefit to the enslaved. Lincoln was the Republican candidate who stood up and dared to refute such logic. So you see it was natural for the progressives of the 2040's to continue using the same MO and to blame the patient for taking the pills he was prescribed. It had proved to be effective logic for over two hundred years, why stop? Next, they absolved themselves of millions of deaths by changing the name of the game from pin the tail on the donkey to pin the tail on the elephant.

These were all the things that ran through my mind while I was rummaging through the apartment for books and food stuff. For some reason I felt a sudden need to hurry when I heard a raucous rapping below me, and the voice belonging to the biggest man call out to me. "Time to finish up in there!"

I found it eerie that the man's voice had coincided with my thoughts. A shudder ran through me from my toes on up. It moved like a snake slithering along my spine, over my shoulders, and onto the top of my head. I shook myself as if I was actually trying to rid myself of some real viper, but it stayed on me. The spasmic shivers repeatedly crawled up the entire length of my spine.

Then something happened. I was tired of being afraid, tired of carrying the blame, tired of being ordered around. The more I thought about it, the more convinced I became that these three men needed to go.

Just then the man spoke to me again. "If those cats are in there, bring them out with you."

"What makes you think they are in here?"

"We seen them go in. We figured they were looking for you and waiting for you to feed them."

"Why would I feed them? Food is scarce," I said.

"Just bring them out."

"I haven't seen them."

"You must have. They went in a while ago."

"Come in and see for yourself," I taunted them, but I began looking around for Harley in earnest. Secretly I was delighted. I found my disposition changing as I hunted for the dred locked creature. It would be an omen of good fortune if I were to see them. I needed them. That thought brought me to question the reason these men wanted them.

"What do you want with them?"

"What do you think?"

There was only one thing that meant. Maybe I could offer to share my hoard with them, but I immediately rejected the thought. No, then they would know I had been holding out on them. I decided to continue lying. I would pretend to agree with them. It would buy me time to plan.

"Okay, but I'll have to hunt for them."

As if on cue, the cat family came to the door of the kitchen as I was rummaging about the canned goods and sorting out the peaches. I hurriedly packed the cans of fruit into a small crate and placed it into the bottom of the cart, and then stacked the books over the top of the crate. "You're all being invited to lunch," I said looking down at Harley as he rubbed against my pant legs. "Well, actually, as lunch, I should say."

I bent down and gave him a pat, and as I did, the little clown kitten bounced over for a sniff of my hand. I liked her the best and she seemed to prefer me, too. I decided to take her with me when I went. I picked her up and mama came over to me to voice orders to put her baby down. "I'm only going to borrow her, Mama," I said as I put the kitten in an empty pant leg of some clothes I had packed in my crate. Next, I removed the peaches from the box and put the kitten in the crate instead and placed books and magazines on top of her. I was afraid the kitten would be frightened and cry out, but it didn't make a sound. If she meowed, it would be over for both of us. "Harley, I want you to follow the trail of sardines I leave for you." I didn't expect the cats to know what I said, but I figured they would follow after me partly because of the trail of fish, but mostly because I had taken one of their own.

It was almost dark when I made my exit out of the building. I wanted the cats to leave under the protection of night. Now to get by the unknown species outside the door. I separated the magazines into piles of theirs and mine.

"You were sure in there a long time," one of the men said.

"I set traps for the cats. I couldn't get near them. Here's your TP," I said as I dropped a few mags down."

"What's the matter? You seem to be in a hurry all of a sudden."

"The bodies were ripe and have popped. I'm feeling ill."

They all laughed at this. "It might take a few days for the cats to go after the bait I put in the cage traps. You may want to wait before you check them."

"We're not going in there. You be back in three days."

"Only if I can get more books."

"Whatever."

"Three moons then," I said.

"Bring us the profits you get from the books. We expect to be paid."

I only nodded. I couldn't tell them I kept the books.

I walked at a brisk pace, but didn't want to run in case I aroused the men's suspicions. I glanced back over my shoulder and pulled the hood of my sweatshirt up over my head so my adversaries couldn't be sure if I was looking back at them. I was trying to see if the cats had begun to follow after me, and if I should start running, but my glance backward brought relief to me. The men were the ones running down the block the opposite way. I had been clutching my knife spear until then, and finally let go of it. I went around the next corner and opened a tin of sardines, piecing out bits of the fish to leave a trail for the cats to follow. Sardines were Harley's favorite and should entice him just in case the scent of the kitten wasn't strong enough. I went around the corner and stopped to peek back down the street. It was dark by now and I couldn't see anything more than a few feet behind me. I smiled. The cats would be able to make their journey to my new residence in safety.

It was at this point I decided to finalize my plans to get the men before they got me. They needed me now to get their food out of the traps, but what happened after the cats were eaten? They had never been particularly friendly to me. They didn't even want to know my name. Clones were cold that way. The fact that they were reruns instead of humans would make it easier on my conscience to get rid of them. Suddenly the kitten let out a meow and I took her out of the clothing I had swaddled her in and carried her to the old library in my arms. She was almost grown, but it was her thinness that made me think of her as a kitten. She wasn't much more than eight inches around the middle, and I could feel the outline of her frame in her neck and ribs. Her bones were the only thing that gave her any heft at all.

I decided to head over to the info center and look up the subject of cloning. I hadn't been in the world for nearly ten years and things had passed me by. There had not been so many species running around when I had gone into rehab, or at least I had believed that to be the case. I had heard rumors that we lived among them, but I had never taken it seriously, mostly because I wanted to sleep at nights.

I was astounded by the amount of info there was on artificial intelligence when I started researching. There were more articles on the subject than I could read in a life time. There was even a President's Council that dealt with cloning and stem cell research from almost fifty years ago. After browsing through the articles for a while, I came up with a summation that satisfied my own curiosity.

Scientists used embryonic stem cells to extract the protein in the inner cells and grow them into an immortal assembly line of sorts. This practice was frowned upon in the early part of the twenty first century because many people had deep seated objections to destroying an intended fetus solely to extract its reproducible tissue. Cloning, they said, only copied a life that had already been lived; it was in essence, a do over. In that respect, people reasoned, it took away the right of a born human being to create a destiny for itself, and for that reason objected to it. Then in 2006 a Japanese man won the Nobel peace prize for discovering how to turn adult cells back into induced pluripotent stems. The need for embryos, real babies, was no longer needed. According to the articles I was finding, cloning took off after that point.

The fact that these cloning experiments had been allowed at all brought me to the brink of insanity, adding to what I had recently found out about we humans and our imminent demise. My thoughts raced from one subject to another until I began to have doubts about my own origins. What if I were a clone? My parents had died early and I didn't really remember them. Maybe I wasn't fully human and that was why I had been immune to the waves they had used on the night of silent lights. I started to wonder if there was a way to instantly distinguish a robotoid, a clone, or a rerun from a birthed human.

These fears launched me into a new area of paranoia. I set out to find articles on spotting the differences between humans and other species. Some humans had survived. I had seen them being rounded up. The light waves must have been calibrated to a certain vibration that affected most humans and for some unknown reasons some of us had remained immune. The SG had spared as much of the builings and infrastructure as possible. That meant that some one intended to return and told me I needed to get off the island, but first I had to read up on the types of species I was living among. I had to know my enemies.

At first I was disappointed in the literature I was able to find because short of taking blood samples and biopsies on them, it seemed impossible to tell one species from another. That was true about the clones at least. I was determined to find an overt way of spotting these species at a glance, and I kept digging through the articles. I wanted to be able to instantly ID the various species when I came upon them in the street.

Finally, I found an article that showed laymen how to judge for themselves who they were in contact with. Reruns, it seemed, were found to be highly unemotional when certain topics were discussed with them. For instance, reruns did not fathom concepts concerned with religion. This was due to the fact that scientists could not transfer the soul along with the DNA. They suspected that it departed after the original body died, but no one knew for sure because it was an invisible entity and no tests had ever been devised to confirm the hypotheses. Strangely enough, the soul had been given a static measure of weight. Scientists had noted for decades that a living being weighed seven grams more than a dead one. Now I was confused. The scientists and most of the world denied the existence of God, yet here they were talking about the soul as if it, indeed, were a fact for the simple reason that they could not explain its absence! It was schizophrenic behavior, but then it matched the behavior of all those who had schemed to bring a Marxist system in to topple the powers of the United States. They were Jekyll and Hydes.

My research found that Robotoids, on the other hand, were found to be easily programmable and amenable to following the rules set forth in society. They did not have preferences. For example, when presented with dog or cat meat instead of a pork chop or fish, they had no qualms on consuming any species of meat that was considered off limits by humans. They also showed a remarkable absence of free will. However, there were noted unwanted social behaviors that occurred in them. They were highly selfish and uncaring towards others. They exhibited no compassion towards their fellow man when they witnessed living species going through any form of suffering or death, but were irrationally fearful of their own death. Robotoids it appeared were more afraid to die than most other species. With this new knowledge I began to understand why the men would not go into the penthouses. There were dead bodies in there. I wanted to shout and cheer at my discovery.

I put my reading materials down and laid my head on the table. I was not going to sit down to a cup of coffee and a let's get to know each other chat with the three men up the street. Well, I guess I knew the answer. One: They were not shy about eating what I considered unacceptable, and two, they were not nice to me. I had decided these men must be some sort of a clone and a droid mix, but just as I was about to close the magazine up, I noticed the word eyes and read on. It was then I found the tell-tale sign I had been searching for. The article said clones and droids eyes had no light in them. Their eyes tended to be dark spheres and reflected no reaction, no spark of recognition or intensity in them. I had seen plenty of people in my life whose eyes fit that distinction as far as I was concerned, but it was the very next difference I read about which really sent chills into my being. The simplest way to tell a clone, droids, and toids from a real being, the article said, was that they had no belly button. I then read that clones had been the forerunners of experiments that had led to the realization of eternal life. I didn't know whether to laugh or cry. Surely this man who had written this article was pulling my leg. I threw the magazine down without bothering to place it back into its slot and got up to leave. I had found out a few more facts and was a bit more educated than when I had started my search, but I had already decided to stay clear of the men and that idea had not been changed. I had seen them mostly in the dark, so I had never really seen into their eyes. I was not Alice in Wonderland, and I had no intention of giving a tea party in order to classify them as a specific species.

Reading these articles had certainly awakened doubts in my mind about my own origins. I decided to stop into one of the old restrooms in the building and look into my own eyes. By the light from the windows I could detect a movement of light, like the waves I had seen churning from green to white in Harley's eyes. My eyes were orbs of gray and blue twinkles. I was immediately relieved. I had seen my own belly button many times. In that moment I was confident that I was as real as I would ever be.

It was then that the sound came. It was a whirring sound and was growing louder, but suddenly the jolting blare of guns broke over the sound of wings. I ran to look out of the door. A flock of drone birds were flying directly between the canyon walls of buildings and they were heading in my direction. They were so numerous that the streets below them became shaded with an eerie twilight created by their immense and moving shadow.

When the drones arrived at the open place above the intersection, their ranks parted in precise moves. Instead of a solid columns of birds, they had split off into many. Bullets rained down from them. I could hear screams and yells coming from some blocks away from me. There were still other beings out there. The SG had sent these flying bird drones to kill off us remaining stragglers. The cowards had not come on their own. It was a numbing realization to know you are targeted for annihilation. It struck me in that moment that reality had flipped flopped. It was hunting season in reverse. Blimy! This time the birds had the guns, and they were shooting first!

I had no chance to find a hiding place other than just inside the doorway where I had first come out. I hid myself in the corner by the missing plate glass window and stood still. I drew the spear I had fashioned out of the rebar and held it ready. The drones, which had been fashioned to look like eagles, were now flying at just about street level. They weren't dark shadows high above me any longer. They were close enough that I could see their heads were painted white and that they even had beaks. It reminded me of old pictures I had seen of planes during WWII. My grandfather had shown me the planes of men in his squadron. They had painted mouths and teeth of animals like fish and tigers on the noses of their planes. Someone had taken that idea and used it, I thought, watching the drones fly past.

Just then one of the eagles began to hover just outside the open window near the corner where I was hiding. His red laser was flashing, pinpointing a target. Then lead bullets began to fly simultaneously with the laser's red stream, but they came out just below the laser's and from a separate barrel. The shots were not coming towards me, but towards the mannequins in the store display. I heard the drone speak. "Dead, but still standing." After the mannequins fell, the eagle flew into the store for a closer inspection of the bodies. "Dead and fallen," it said in quite a clear and distinct voice.

In an unplanned move, I took the spear I had in my hands and swung it like a baseball bat at the eagle rather than throwing it at him. I connected with the body of the drone right in its mid-section. I heard it hit the sweet spot and saw plastic pieces scatter from its center. "Stop. Halt. You have been found. Identified. Humanimal."

I jabbed the point of the spear into the rotor blades. The drone faltered in midair before dropping in a heap some distance from me. It was like seeing Humpty Dumpty take his great fall. The flying drone was down, laying on its side, but it continued firing its laser, and chairs and shelving around me were popping apart and bursting into flames. In seconds, more drones arrived. I ran to take cover behind the counter of the pill dispensary for I remembered they were protected all around by bullet proof glass. They had said it was because the pill houses were in the most dangerous parts of the city, but now I knew the real reason.

The drones came at me firing away. They had tracked me to where I ducked to behind the wooden counter behind the bullet proof glass. After I heard the bullets bounce off repeatedly, I chanced taking a peek. The eagles were zeroing in on me, and at just that moment, they hit the glass. It was like an old commercial I had seen with birds flying into a window that was so clean they couldn't see it. It gave me a quick laugh. When their propellers hit the window, they dropped like ducks shot down in flight. The tables were being turned.

I was elated to find that the shield actually held and then began to celebrate my invincibility. I walked back and forth in my bullet proofed cell like a chick in a shooting gallery. I was thumbing my nose at the drones, baiting them to shoot at me, and watching them being knocked out of the air when they hit against the protective glass. This was great fun until I felt a stinging on my foot. I immediately looked down. Curls of smoke were drifting upward. Unfortunately, bullet proof didn't mean laser proof. Sparks had hit one of my shoes. I tamped it out with the other foot and quickly went to the front window section and tried to peer down to get a better look at what was taking place. One of the fallen drones was facing in my direction, and its laser was on a steady beam aimed at the lower portion of my cage. I could also see that the other drones who had fallen continued to stream their laser beams as well. Small fires were starting all over the building.

I suspected that bullet proof glass didn't mean laser proof glass. My bet was it would melt at some point on the Fahrenheit scale. While I was thinking about what to do, I worked on putting out the small fires at the bottom of the prescription counter with my shirt. I could hear the downed drones repeating the same phrases over and over. "Command center. Abort? Abort?"

"Yes, damn it," I yelled from my cage. "Abort."

"Damn is not a marker."

"Yes, abort. This is command center. Abort mission," I yelled back.

In seconds all the voices and weapons were still, and I looked out on the battlefield. It was littered with pieces of the drones. It was a plastic and metal smorgasbord of parts. In minutes, the biggest U Pull it, U Take it drones parts store in all of Manhattan had been created.

The quiet was spookier than the noise of the battle had been and I looked around the building. Nothing moved. I needed to get out of there and get back to the safety of the sealed room at the Information Center before more of the drones honed in on me. I would be behind four foot thick concrete walls there. I couldn't afford to wait any longer because of all the fires that kept popping up and spreading. I decided I had no choice but to venture out of my protected cage. It was that or become a human marshmallow.

As I came around the corner of the enclosed prescription cell, small laser shots came at my feet again. They were not full shots this time. The laser only fired in short bursts, and only weak streams flashed out from its gunnery placements. The plastic Humpty Dumpty was petering out. Bullets were no longer being fired. "Hu-manimal at 10 feet. Closing. 7 feet. 4 feet. Verified," it said as I came closer to it.

"Ammunition chamber empty," it repeated after every click. Its lights were fading and there was a dash dot appearance to its laser firing pattern now. As I looked at the downed drones I could see they were all losing their power charge. I did my best to run around and past them. As I was zig zagging my way across the store floor, I was seized with an intense desire to retrieve one of the malfunctioning machines and reprogram it for my own use. I could visualize the triumph in my mind, but then my feelings of superiority left me as a drone on the floor ahead of me let go a full laser shot. "Hu-manimal. Verified. 3 feet."

It was the first eagle I had come into contact with; the one that I had whacked at like it was an incoming fast ball with my rebar weapon. I wanted him. He would be my first project. He would become the savior of the new man and the traitor among the eternals. "Abort the mission, you twit," I yelled at him, but he kept firing at me.

"Twit is not a marker."

"Abort the mission. The war is over."

"Command word war is not a marker."

"Abort firing. Your side lost. Your buddies are in pieces all over the floor. You and the others must surrender."

"Your commands have no markers."

"Abort mission."

"Command is half noted," he said firing away.

"Half?" I yelled. "Which half?"

"Questions are not markers."

"Damn you're insistent."

"Your vocabulary is unknown. It is not a marker."

"What does marker mean?"

"Questions are not markers."

"Explain," I yelled in frustration and still dodging the laser.

To my amazement the drone spoke back at me. "Commands must be given."

"Markers are commands?"

"Questions are not markers," the drone repeated.

I fumbled to find a way to rephrase my question into a command and came up with this brilliant phrase. "Commands are markers." I tried to make it sound like a definite statement and not a question.

"Commands are markers," the drone confirmed.

"How can you communicate if someone can't ask you questions?" As soon as I realized I had asked a question, I said, "Abort."

"Awaiting full command."

"Abort mission."

"Finish command."

"Abort killing people."

"Killing, people are not markers."

"Abort destroying Hu-manimals."

"Command complete."

"You need to be made more like man, like me."

"Man is not a marker."

"You need a bigger vocabulary."

"Command complete. You must update."

"I have to figure out how to update you," I said.

"Update is possible. I can teach you. Let's get started."

"I will fix you when we reach safety."

"Fix is not a marker. Safety is not a marker."

"You certainly have had a bad education."

"Update is possible. Fix is not a marker," the drone repeated.

"Your blades are broken."

"I did not know. My control board is malfunctioning."

I picked him up and carried him. "Now that answer was like a real conversation, drone," I said as I stepped out into the streets. "The rest is a matter of semantics," I told him.

"Semantics is…" and I cut him off by issuing him a command. "Abort statement. You sound like you were programed."

"I was."

"I'm going to give you zing, personality. You'll be a real conversationalist after I make a few changes."

"Conversation is not a marker."

"It will be. You'll be able to give an acceptance speech for the Nobel prize."

"Yes, the words of peace."

"You've heard of the Nobel?" I said surprised.

"Questions are not markers."

"Just wait my friend." It was just like the SG not to enable the drones to ask questions. After all, the government had been killing people for decades for doing just that.

First off, I had to find a pocket computer, a solar one, and I set off to a retail store for a bit of shop lifting. It looked like no one had entered the store from the street side, but around back the doors were wide open, and as I was about to discover, had been removed permanently. I stood in the doorway afraid to step over the threshold. It was then I made the decision to arm myself with something more than the primitive spear I had made. I needed something that was lethal from a safer distance. I was done with hand to hand combat.

I turned around and I went down the street to the gunsmith store. It had already been raided, too, but I found a colt revolver and a rifle with a scope on it. I took boxes of cartridges and filled by backpack with ammo. I found a holster for the colt and strapped it on my shoulder. "Come on SG's. I'm ready for you now," I said in a whisper. The government had sent a task force of drones to wipe out all survivors, but I intended to turn the tables. When they came back, they would have to fight their own drones, I thought looking down at the eagle in my hands. I was building an army of my own and my first fighter was about to turn traitor.

Armed, I returned to the computer store and found the things I needed. Luckily a cart load of pocket solar computers sat on a shelf. I took other things on my list and then stopped in my tracks. I felt like I was being watched. I looked up at the surveillance cameras. They were off, but I felt eyes on me: eyes that were moving and conscious. "I am armed," I said. "Don't take a step closer." Silence. When no other sound came, I continued my shopping spree. I filled the pillow cases I kept in my pockets with more junk than I thought I would need. It was best to over shop and not have to come back. Over supply. Now that was a new concept. I wouldn't have been able to afford one of these pocket computers let alone a box of a hundred if they weren't free for the robbing.

The idea of a free market in America these days was sell to the highest bidder. Everything was auctioned. A list of items for sale were posted each day, and whoever gave the highest bid on their chip implant got the goods. The reason for this new sales industry was because it was rumored that they were only three or four of any item in stock at any one time. I had just seen for myself that wasn't true. There were excesses of everything, but that would have made the prices go down. Evidently, honesty played no role in customer relations in the current society.

I had not been to a store since I had been put in limbo over a decade ago. I had watched the fights and killings that took place at stores and malls from the S pods mounted on every wall in the rehab center. S Pods were surveillance cameras that also functioned as flat screen monitors which could give you news casts as well as detecting every move you made. It was like a two way mirror and it was controlled by the IM's. If the Intent Monitors suspected anyone of looking at an item or person of importance too long, they reported your chip ID number to the nearest IM station and you were taken away. I had no chip implant in my hand because I was already considered disabled, dead. Therefore, no expense was wasted on me. I had been in a confined safe cell which was the same as being nonexistent. Ironically, being confined in that cell is probably what also saved me on the night of silent lights. The rehab center was made of ten inch thick walls and had only a few tiny windows even a rat would have a hard time going through.

There had been a terrible shaking of the building the night of the lights. I had hit my head during the attack, and when I came back to consciousness found the doors were opened to my cell. In fact, everyone else was already dead or gone when I came to. I began to wonder how many more unchipped people were running about the streets like me. That gave us an edge over the rest of the population. We couldn't be monitored. We didn't exist. We had been off the life rolls for years. I went back to the IC and holed back up in my cement block. I had freedom, but in reality I had moved from one cage to another . My new cage was bigger, but I was still on the endangered list.

I used my time while hiding out to read up on reprogramming. To make myself more comfortable, I decided to spread out and moved up to the second story in the old library where there were windows. That's also where the deep spaced discs were kept. Deep spaced was the new terminology for cloud storage. Once something hit deep space it was considered voided matter. It still existed, it was just harder to access. Everything eventually hit deep space, so it puzzled me why all this information had not been destroyed and why all the books had been kept.

I loved to read on the second floor where I could sit under the windows in the light. I also found that they were windows which could be opened. They raised up and down by hand. I had not seen a window like that since I had stayed at my grandfather's farm house. There were iron bars on these windows, but you could still open them and get the air. The sun still shined through. The world, as I tried to remember it, was still out there.

During breaks in my reading regiment I arranged the cache of solar pocket computers in a long, straight line beneath the windows to let the sun charge them. The computers were about the size of a three ounce meat patty, and rectangular in shape. In fact, that was the weight and shape of almost everything that was sold these days. They were known as deck weights. One deck weight was exactly 3 oz., two deck weight was 6 oz., and so on.

The computer manufacturer who made the compact computers used to brag, 'Put our minds in your pocket.' I would do more than that, I thought, as I tinkered on the drone. I would make him a force for mankind not against him. I was energized by that thought and felt good enough to laugh. I was reclaiming my humanity. I felt taller and walked prouder. I was fighting back and letting go at the same time. The seeds of revenge were sweet and I savored them, playing them over and over in my mind each night before I went to sleep. In almost every scenario I came up with, the SG and those in power were ambushed by my army and blown to start dust as they arrived in Manhattan. It was a blockbuster.

By this time I had brought most of the downed drones that were salvageable back to my fortress. I had more than enough spare parts and had painstakingly taken apart and refashioned blades for each one I was rebuilding. Some drones didn't have the shiny plastic bodies to cover their inner workings, but I liked them better with their machinery visible. They looked rugged and real. Formidable. I painted teeth and eyes on the front of their noses, transforming them into the likenesses of sharks and tigers.

My main interest had been in reprogramming the biggest drone, the one that I had picked up first. I tinkered with the him off and on until I was satisfied with his new vocabulary and behavior. I was getting anxious to see if my drone had been reborn to a new way of thinking and seeing the world.

I hit the 'on' button on the computer and watched as the bars topped out. "It's fully charged. Now let's see what he has to say," I said to the calico kitten who was watching all that I was doing. I set the drone down in an open area near the front entrance to the library and away from all our gear in case this drone was still an enemy.

"Hopefully, when I turn the computer on and scan the drone, it will log it in and identify itself," I told the cat and picked her up to move her back with me to the computer station.

I activated the drone, and then scanned over it with my wand. I searched the screen. It read: DRONE FORCE 1. ALPHA CORP. WESTERN SECTOR. ACTIVATED 2065. So the drone had been built only a few years ago, I thought as I heard a click and the drone woke up. It was functioning and it replied to the words I had typed on the screen. "This is eagle commander number one, zero, niner."

After the drone spoke, the computer typed: 'REPORT IN ONE ZERO NINER. YOUR STATUS IS: MIA- LOGGED 03-17-2069.

"Malfunction," the drone said weakly.

"TYPE OF MALFUNCTION," the screen typed back.

"Strike force trauma. Metal.

"CONFIRM LAST REPORT.

At this point I switched the drone off and watched the screen blink: MIA 07-09-69. COMMUNICATION FAILED. NO GPS FOUND.

I had made it past the first hurdle, and had been able to have the drone log itself in as MIA as of today's date. I had disabled the GPS devices on all the drones and they were in a pile somewhere rusting and shorting out in the rain. They'd had a proper burial though I'd saved a few just in case I could figure out a way to scramble the coordinates.

The next thing I did was to reprogram one zero niner's identification chart and vocabulary. I programmed over a hundred new definitions into his bird brain and had given him the ability to ask questions and respond by voice. The real stroke of genius was to declare the SG as his new enemy. I had worked for months on the project. He was box perfect. I had taken all the spare parts from the others and not one feather of his plastic body was ruffled. Not one dent or peck mark marred his visage. "Well, One zero niner, you are going to feel better once you come back to life, but first I need you to give me the entry code for the reprogramming operation."

I had read from the government manuals I found that these drones were able to self-correct. I turned him on and was going to try to override his voice command so I could type in a command and request the code from Alpha Central, but first I decided to scan him for programs and see if he logged on. I ran the wand over the plastic and wire body. "Bingo." I saw two categories listed on the screen. One said SELF PRESERVATION MODE and the second read SALVAGE MODE.

Suddenly more words began appearing. I read the list containing options until I read VOICE COMMAND OVERRIDE.

With a few clicks on the computer keys I was in business. I watched the screen go through the identification process again. Then I typed in SELF PRESERVATION. REQUEST ENTRY CODE.

The computer requested the drone to repeat its request with its ID numbers and I typed in 109. The screen then read: PROCESSING. STAND BY. In seconds, a fifteen digit sequence appeared comprised of both letters and numbers. I had retrieved the code, and I went to get something to write on.

It was almost nightfall when I was ready to fully test out One Zero Niner. I put him back on voice so I could ask him questions about his reprogramming. Once I had him connected, I typed in Test: One Zero Niner. The drone answered, "Ready." I typed: IDENTIFY: MAN.

"A friendly docile animal that walks on two legs. Comes in shades of black, white, yellow, red, and brown tones. He is to be unharmed. He is a friend to all. He is the programmer. The creator."

I spoke the second vocabulary word to the drone. "Shadow government."

The drone answered. "They walk upright like monkeys and are clad in blue, green, or red uniforms with the symbol of the one world on their shirts. Big O, big W. They often carry guns or weapons. Disarm them and stockpile their weapons."

"Identify stockpile."

"Take away weapons and place at coordinates 45 West and 17 North in this sector."

"Identify the coordinates listed."

"Water routes."

"Identify grid."

"Places of power. Thrones of the enemy. Pits of torment. Hell."

I laughed and Niner turned towards me. "Why?" it kept repeating.

"Why what?

"The sounds? What do they mean? They are unintelligible."

I thought for a moment before I realized what he was asking about. "It's laughter."

"Why do you do it?"

"You want to know why I am laughing at what you said?"

"Yes," the drone answered.

I patted the drone and said, "I'm not laughing at you One Zero Niner."

It's camera lens eyes blinked and the drone said, "Why?"

"I'm being me. It's what man does. It's fun."

"It is annoying and accomplishes nothing."

"It's a human emotion. You're developing a personality."

"The sound is useless to me. It confuses my circuits. Next item," the drone said loud and clear.

"You'll get the hang of it. I've improved your mind with deep memory implants. You'll learn as you go, just like me. Just like all humans. Experience is your teacher now."

"Next item," he repeated.

"Okay, okay. Identify grid removal act."

I went through the next one hundred new words and felt exhausted. The drone hadn't missed one word and I stood up completely satisfied with the day's work. "We're set," I announced. "Let's eat."

"Are we finished?" the drone asked.

"Yes."

"Would you like me to update the other drones in Force 1?"

"Yes, if you are equipped to do that."

"I am a commander. I have the ability. I am the only one in the squadron strike force who is designated and programmed with that authority."

"When the others are fully charged, you may do your duty, One Zero Niner."

"I will wait. In the mean time I will ask you a question."
"Go ahead."

"You once had numbers which you used to update me. You no longer use them."

"I have never updated you before."

"You are the wizard."

"Why did you say that?"

"You have a gift, a touch. I have never felt so free before."

His words seemed like an accusation to me and I tried to figure out why. He had touched a deepness in me that lay beneath the years of defensive rubble I had built up around myself. However, after hearing the drone speak, I was wildly happy. There was an added bonus. I had picked the head drone to experiment on. What a stroke of luck. It was going to update the others for me. Soon I would have an army of drones programmed with little known and wrong facts. I was going to have a network of little devils to cause confusion and mayhem, and not just one, a legion of them.

The thought of revenge had put the spark back in my plug. I was in a state of ecstasy and could have taken on the whole world. "Time to eat, girl," I said to the gray kitten. "Let's celebrate. I'm going shopping. Up for some powdered milk? Maybe some beer or champagne for me. Hold down the fort," I ordered the thin kitten as I left the cement cubicle.

During the next few weeks I repaired as many of the drones as I could. Now I was about to see if Niner could really reprogram the fleet. The pocket computers sat in an orderly row upstairs on the floor with a drone plugged into each one. I crossed my fingers as I turned them on. Then I picked up my own pocket computer and typed, UPDATE. One Zero Niner responded immediately with the single voiced word, "Updating."

Lights blinked on his control panel which I had left exposed and uncovered until I was sure no more tweaks would be necessary. I sat in silence while the drones were being fed the new information. It was sometime later that the drone spoke. "Clarification requested."

"Proceed."

"Numbers of the strike force are unaccounted for."

"Account for their number by reporting them as turned off for repair. Continue update."

A few more minutes passed before the drone spoke again. "Twenty six units in Strike Force One located and updated out of 109."

"Well done One zero niner."

I then typed: ONE ZERO NINER: LEARNING STATUS: CONTINUOUS MODE----

I smiled as I spoke the vocabulary I intended to give the drone. I was about to make him more human, more into a companion to talk with. He would fly in more friendly skies from now on.

CHAPTER 3

There had been no sign of Harley and his family for weeks. I had begun to give up hope that they would ever come for the kitten. When I had gone to check the pretend traps in the building, there was no sign of them. I had visited the penthouse on the second day instead of the third day as the robo's had ordered me just to avoid a run in with the unholy trinity. I left a note to the robos that said I would be back in four days to check the traps so they wouldn't come looking for me. I also left the trio some green Uniforms I had picked up at the station on 5th Avenue as a change of clothes. They were the exact uniforms that I had programmed my drones to attack. While dressing the robos in the uniform of the new enemy gave me a few laughs, I was angry with myself for leaving the cats behind. I should have risked it and taken them all. I started to believe they had been spotted and killed by the robos already. Unwilling to abandon all hope, I left the door to my cement cell cracked open so they could gain entrance if they dropped by.

It was towards dusk many days later when Harley came leading his family into the door of the old library. I saw them parade across the room in a typically nonchalant feline fashion. They came straight to my walled in cubical. My diluted little calico cocked her head to one side as if in disbelief. It took only a second to accept the miracle and she was off to romp with the others. A few quick sniffs assured mama that it was her own, and she let her reacquainted brood tumble over the floor in make believe attacks with each other. I was surprised at the joyous nature of their reunion and jealous of their bond.

I had felt that sense of welcome from Grandfather Pompy and my Grandmother Ella when I came to spend summers on the farm. Pompy was always there to pick me up at the station and he hugged me freely and unashamedly. I always pulled away because of the uneasy feeling his touching aroused in me. Secretly I relished these moments with Pompy, but I never reciprocated. I just stood, hands at my side, letting the feelings flow over me from head to toe. His touch ran like warm liquid being poured over my head and coated my whole being. I was accepted and I belonged. The feeling was like cool mud in the river, sucking me down while the fine silt anchored me and held me out of the current, and I felt somehow stronger for it.

Pompy's disposition and reasoning was different from most people. He was very reserved and quiet about things until you asked him a question. Then he had an answer ready to give you as if he had just pulled it out of his pocket. For instance, I went to church with them once in a while, but they didn't force me. I remember asking Pompy why he didn't require me to go with them every week, and he had replied, "I'm following the example from the Lord. He never forced anyone to choose him. He's there if you want him."

At the time, I took his words to mean that God was kind of noncommittal towards we humans, and I just stashed that fact into the already skewed and jaded package of knowledge I had gained from the world. That's how I put together my own view of the world; in pieces and narratives and jokes I had heard here and there from this person or that. It was a jumbled mess. Even when I was only thirteen or so, it was already frowned on to be a Republican or a believer like Pompy. It was enough to get you beat up, or make you disappear.

I turned completely away from religion at that point, but looking back I had never embraced it as a lifestyle to be followed. Grandfather Joel had believed and trusted in his God to protect him. He used to say, "Man cannot hurt me. It is God who has the power to destroy the soul."

By my twenties I was no longer curious about this God after Pompy disappeared. I had this diety down pat. He was just like the SG; he absorbed and reveled in the devotion and loyalty you lavished on him, and then when you were old and weak, he left you to die alone. In those days of 2024 or thereabouts, most people disappeared in their sixties. Health care was a big drain on society. The SG let you know that because everywhere you looked signs proclaimed: "Don't be selfish. Don't be a burden.

KNOW WHEN TO CALL IT THE END-BE A TRUE AMERCIAN." (They used nationalism only when it served their needs and in capital letters.) Those signs stared at you from everywhere, and they altered your conscience. There were all manner of places you could 'check in' to 'check out.' The government even offered bonuses you could leave to loved ones when you ended it all, though I have never heard that a relation, or even a casual acquaintance had ever actually received a check when their loved one was heaven bound by way of the crematory pyres. The SG never held up their part of the bargain. The survivors of the deceased were often told that their relation, though they had come in voluntarily to alleviate the population crisis, didn't qualify for the financial bonus because they had cancer or were going to expire anyway from some fungus on their toenails. However, the survivors often claimed that their relation had not been sick at all. There was no way to prove the SG's version because the bodies were burned immediately, and the cost of an autopsy was ten thousand weights of gold. Rather than argue with the State, and risk disappearing themselves, the wife or family said thank you for letting us know that Herbert or Sally was so ill.

Truth be realized, there really weren't many older citizens around. There had been a number of viruses unleashed over time which weeded out the old and those with compromised immune systems. The age range for those considered to be old kept dropping, which was always a mystery to me since other statistics bragged that man was living longer and would someday live forever. However, I never gave that claim serious thought back then. We were told the aged were a blood sucking lot, and all they did was use up the resources in the Well Care and Preventative Centers when they offered nothing in return. They were burdening the young.

Society prevented diseases, it didn't cure them. If you got sick, well it was your own fault. If the pills didn't help you, there was no solution. Pills kept you well. Drug companies were owned and regulated by the State. They raked in billions. Every pharmaceutical corporation was run by the government and they weren't free. You paid to get into the pill stores, not for the pills themselves. Even the toilet seat where you rested your butt cost a dollar a sit in their facilities.

I laughed out loud thinking about all this tripe now. Everything in society was called the opposite of what it really was. Every department had nice, helpful sounding names that gave you the impression that those inside were on your side. The names were meant to keep you calm. The Info. Centers (IC'S) promised info, but gave none. Well, they did, but the info was so expensive no one could afford to pay for it unless they worked for the government or one of its extensions in the media. Well Care was where you went to terminate life. Rehabs kept you taking the drugs that kept these types of thoughts from invading your mind.

The banners in all of these places proclaimed 'People are First,' which really meant they were last. By the time I had learned how to decipher their intent, it was too late. The promises on the posters left you crying out in rage. "You are supposed to help people! Your sign says people are your first priority," but the medical attendants were trained to stare back at you in a blank way that said, "What's your point?"

They knew you had no recourse against them. They were the government. You would only be complaining about the wolf to the wolf pack. It was a double edged sword. There was no one to turn to for help except to those who wanted to make an end of you. We had gone to them like hogs to the slaughter and thanked them for it. They had convinced us that they were caring for us. And they did; they fed us, gave us clothes and cubicles to live in. Everyone was finally equal. No one had anything. That had been the plan from the start. The state owned everyone and everything. Those who accused them of robbing its citizens disappeared. It was enough to make you crazy if you let it sink in too deep. I decided to keep my mind focused on getting even. I was about to treat them to a mind bending experience of their own. I was building my own army.

Just then I noticed Harley's mate still trying to bite off his dangling mats. The mother cat was gentle with him, showing great tenderness. When his cries became too much, she would stop biting at the spot and begin to lick at it until he was soothed. Even the kittens seemed concerned and would help to soothe him by licking at the blood which oozed from the sores. It was a surprise to see these animals administer such concern for one another. Where had they learned it? That train of thought brought me back to a similar situation I had witnessed at Pompy's farm one summer.

Grandfather had sat up all night with a cow that was having trouble birthing her calf. Grandmother had woken me up to take some coffee out to him and a bite to eat. "He might enjoy some company. My knees are too stiff these days, and of course I'm no man, either."

I looked quizzically at her and she said. "Men enjoy their own company now and again, Trave."

When I arrived in the barn, he was trying to pull the calf out legs first. The cow was frightened and fighting to stand up. "Her calf is having trouble getting into the world," he told me. "She's in a lot of pain, but she will die if the little guy doesn't come out the rest of the way soon. The vet's on his way." I just stood there. I didn't know one end of a cow from the other. Pompy looked exhausted.

The vet arrived sometime later as Pompy continued to talk and pat the cow to calm her. She had kicked and mooed so much that he couldn't get the calf out by himself. It was all he could do to keep her from standing up. Then he told me to pet her and try to keep her calm while he and the vet finished pulling the calf out. When the calf finally plopped onto the hay, they opened its sack and helped get the calf to its feet. It wobbled over and sniffed the mother who still lay on the hay. "She's too tired to get up. Time will tell if she'll make it," the vet said as he pulled the rest of the birth contents out and sifted through it. "I don't see any blood mixed in, so she should come around." Then the vet gave the calf a bottle of milk and then another.

Pompy sent me over to the corner to fetch some horse blankets and he covered the mother and sat holding her head in his lap. Every now and then he stroked her and said a few encouraging words to her. After some hours he lay down on the hay next to her. I was surprised. "Are you going to stay here all night, Pompy?"

"Yes, but you don't have to."

I did stay with him. It made me feel important to be needed by Pompy instead of being told I was in the way. Then Chipper, my grandfather's black and white border collie, came in. He could do anything Pompy told him to. My grandfather just threw a blanket at Chip and told him to cover the calf. The dog picked up the blanket from the hay and took it directly to the calf and dropped it on him and then bit at the corners to try to unfold it. It wasn't going well, so Pompy gave me a push on the arm, "You might help him. He doesn't exactly have hands."

I got up and helped the dog spread the blanket out, and then the collie settled down by the calf and lay licking at it while he rested one of his paws on the newborn almost as if he was reassuring it.

Some morning, weeks later when Pompy was ready to turn the cows and the horses out, Chipper took over. By the time we were half way down to the pasture gate, small frantic cries came from behind us and here came the calf. He wobbled up to Chipper and stopped. For the rest of his life the calf followed after the dog.

"Why did the calf choose the dog over its own mother?" I had asked Pompy. Remembering this scene now brought the image of Pompy's face clearly to my mind.

"A young animal will attach itself to whoever it sees as having cared for it. This calf simply understood kindness and help in a strange world and did not wish to lose it," grandfather went on to say. "But he loves his mother, too. He knows that's where to get dinner," he said as we watched the calf feed. "He's lucky. He has two beings who love him. He's found favor in this world. He's beaten the odds."

I half laughed and scoffed. "You don't believe animals love do you, Pompy?"

"Don't you, Travis? You've witnessed it," he had answered.

Now I sat staring at the cat family. They went everywhere together. Whatever had bonded them to stay with each other, I wanted to be a part of. Then I laughed at myself. The magic of imprinting had worked in reverse with me. They seemed to view me as benign, or at best, as indifferent. Though they rubbed against my legs at times, I didn't sense love, I sensed need. I was their benefactor and provider. That was a partnership to me, an unequal one.

During my life animals were expensive to keep and the state discouraged anyone from taking on the care of such creatures. It cost thousands to license them and there was a yearly fee. Most working stiffs couldn't afford animals any more than they could afford to pay to become parents. Signs were everywhere that prompted one to think about the cost of raising anything: 'Can you afford the burden?' Other signs asked, 'Is it worth it?' and showed a picture of walking a dog and paying to get through the dog park gate. Cats were more expensive because they were labeled as predators that saw birds as flying pizzas. There were bounties on cats that were caught running loose. Cats were hunters who threatened the balance of nature and were to be kept indoors, but I admired the hunting skills of my cat family. They had kept the rats down around town and provided for their family. Hey, if bird was on the menu, it was ok with me. I liked chicken, too. Somehow Harley must have sensed my longing for a bird because shortly after that he brought one to me and laid it at my feet. When I stared at it stupefied, he nudged it closer to me with his nose and went to the female cat. I was overcome with emotion. They were not selfish takers, they were sharing with me. I cried at their goodness and the words of Pompy rang in the hollow shadows of my thoughts. I cooked the bird and we dined ala birdie on a stick.

After their feast, the female began the arduous task of cleaning off Harley's mats. It was a ritual habit. This time I went to get a scissors and sat down among the pride. They all stopped what they were doing. This had never happened before. They sat frozen, staring at me, ready to pounce at the slightest hint of danger.

Then slowly I reached out my hand and patted Harley's head. It was the only place on him which was free of mats. When I sensed that they were all comfortable with my presence, I began to snip at the clumps of dred locks. I was careful not to get to close to the skin, but it was impossible not too because the balls of fur seemed like they were part of his hide. The mats were massive, and dangled down like those decorative ornaments on a Holiday tree. They swayed back and forth when he walked. If they had been made of metal, they would have clanged like bells. After a while I knew the scissors would not get the job done. I would need to shave the matted hairballs off.

I managed to get a lot of the twisted curls shaved off before Harley made a meow and got up to leave. The female and the kittens looked at me. There was a tenseness in the air as they waited for my next move. If I were to hurt their father, their stare warned, they were ready to take action. I instantly stopped chopping away at Harley and let him walk away. I was not offended. I had heard him say the same thing in that same tone to his mate when he had had enough. Seeing I had obeyed Harley's directive to stop, the cat family dropped their vigilance against me and resumed their own self grooming activities. Mama Kitty got up to examine him and sniff over his entire body. She seemed approving of the amount of fur balls on the floor as she smelled them and quickly tried to cover them up. Many pairs of eyes watched as I got a broom and swept the hair away.

My shaving away of Harley's mats soon took the place of Mama Kitty's job, and she was glad to hand it over. In a little over a week, Harley was bald from head to toe. Taking a cue from Harley's new look, I whacked away at my own curls and beard, too. The cats watched me just as fastidiously as they had with Harley, chasing after my springs of hair which fell to the floor.

Things changed after the grooming I had performed on Harley. I had a new status among the family. They sat on me more now and even began to sleep by me. I was given licks and cleaned on my hands and sometimes on my face when I was lying down. They slept on me like they slept on one another, too. I had become catified.

During this time another momentous thing was about to occur. I had been reading the history of George Washington and I had mostly settled into a comfortable routine believing that the danger of being arrested was over, but I soon learned that's when things happen because life has its own set of rules: When the sky's clear that's when the storm comes. I was out on a stroll with the cats when I saw the blackness appear on the horizon. It was early morning. That day the storm of eagles came out of the east, and with the sun behind them. As I looked at the moving birds, they continued their rush forward, and when they were overhead, they began to rain multi colored confetti which resembled small gummy worms that fell from the sky bedazzling the eye. Vapors rose from the pavement as the colored wrigglers hit the ground and a great sizzling sound was heard. Then the great armada of eagles dove downward, flying close to the ground and showering bullets.

I ran back to my fortress at the Info Center with the cats following after me. I should have taken Niner with me, but I found him now and activated him. This was going to be the real test. "Enemy attacking. Engage," I said to him, and watched as he flew to the window of the old library and hovered just outside of it. You might think that sending one lone drone to fight off squadrons of fighters was a bit foolhardy, but I hoped to fight with words and rank, not fire power or numbers.

"This is commander One zero niner. I am a Strike Force Alpha Commander. Abort mission. Repeat, abort mission. Land at coordinates Tango eight, niner two, and Zebra zero, zero, five. Welcome Bravo squadrons."

"Commander zero, one, niner, my tracking device indicates hu-manimals present," one of the incoming drones reported.

"Land at the designated coordinates, Bravo Eagle three seven. I am the squadron commander."

"We have been ordered to find lost fighters, destroy hu-manimals, and report back to command central. You are a lost fighter."

"I am not lost. I have stayed at my post. There has been a change in orders, three seven. Abort previous orders."

"I cannot do that," the drone said.

Before I could think of what to do next, One zero niner was in action. A blue line shot out of his firing barrel on the right side of his wing and a red one came out of his left wing. Both lines met at the mid-section on the enemy eagle. Instantly the hovering drone was electrified and lit up from the inside. A small ball of fire about the size of a golf ball glowed red hot in his center and then exploded into billions of shards of light. The enemy drone vanished into thin air. Nothing dropped to the ground. "How did you do that?" I asked.

"Now is not the time, wizard."

One zero niner was flying directly to the head of the strike force. "Abort mission or be annihilated," I heard him command.

"A hu-manimal has been detected and must be put into a non-vibrant state."

"He is my prisoner and I am taking him back to base."

"That is against protocol."

Again Niner fired his two streams of red and blue lights and I watched the explosion. It was like some kind of weird magic trick. I couldn't figure out where the enemy had gone.

The rest of the eagle drones obeyed Niner's new directives. The war was over, at least for now. It was a sight to behold as I watched them change course away from me, but it was a sure bet that another strike force would be sent after this new squadron also failed to report back. It had been over six months since the Niner's squadron had been dispatched. Apparently these had been sent to find the missing drones of that first Alpha Force. Niner had told me that drones seldom failed to physically report back in. Their success rate was over ninety five percent and their destroy rate was higher.

I let my worries go for the moment and breathed easier. The eagle drones had stopped firing and they were forming into a single line in the sky, and one by one, I watched them land. I turned to Niner and whispered, "Tell me what just happened,"

I said surveying the landing drones. It was a sight I never would have imagined seeing. There were hundreds of drones that covered the avenues and streets as far as I could see. They had taxied into a zig zag pattern and sat waiting on the concrete. It was then that I realized Niner was the only one with a white ring painted on the fake plastic feathers of his neck. That was the difference I must have unconsciously noted the day I had picked him up, I thought. He was the one that was closest to me when I had decided to steal one and reprogram it. It had been luck, that's all, but that simple tidbit of good fortune bolstered my confidence.

"What kind of magic was that?" I said again to the drone speaking about the devastation I had just witnessed.

"A permanent kind. They are vapor. They are part of the air you breathe now."

"You're joking."

"I can't be. I don't know what a joke is."

"Okay. Tell me what you did."

"I am equipped with both laser and micro wave blasts in my guns. Hundreds of lasers fire off at the same time and merge into a single super beam. When the beams strike the target, it disenigrates it into oblivion."

"Why is it so powerful? I mean you're a small drone."

"I have little pellets inside. They are like the bullets in the chamber of a gun and when the beams connect with that tiny pellet inside the chamber it heats it to over 800 million degrees Fahrenheit which gives it a nuclear type of power or energy thrust as it comes out of the barrel."

"I didn't even see it happen."

"You wouldn't. It is dasol power."

"Dasol?"

"Destruction at the speed of light."

I looked at my friend in a new light. He was knowledgeable and now I found out he had the power of a thousand suns in his wing span. I was risking my life in dabbling with his mind. I was wondering why the drone force had given up so easily and obeyed him. It didn't make sense. Maybe it was a trick, though I couldn't imagine what it would be, but it made me feel inadequate and shaky after what I had just witnessed. I didn't know much. Not even as much as I thought I did.

"Why didn't the squadron attack you?"

"Plasma."

"You mean like blood?"

"Nothing that messy. It's ionized gas like you find in the stars. It creates a force field around me that absorbs and reflects anything that's microwaved or lasered. I am impenetrable and they know it. I'll turn my shield on and you can see it for a second. Look about a foot out from my body and you will see a white halo for a second after I enable it, and then it becomes invisible."

I looked where Niner had directed me to look and glimpsed greenish white squiggly neon lines that looked like electrical charges blink and disappear before I could really get a good look at it. There wasn't even a puff of smoke.

"Why aren't all the drones protected with this force field?"

"It's expensive. Ionized gold. Only squadron commanders are equipped with it, and of course, the Life Engineering Centers and some of the Elite's mobile air born laser and tank units."

Everything he said was familiar and tugged at the back of my sub consciousness. I knew this stuff. It came to me out of a dream, a fog, but I somehow knew it was real. I even had pictures of it in my mind.

It was then that my real education began as to just what all that had taken place during my ten years of forced retirement from civilization. Niner was filling me in on the base at Denver and the human parts department that was being cultivated by the race of hybrid eternals. They were his original programmers and he had been trained under them. I listened for weeks on end to his descriptions of the base and about his life there. He had also told me that I could not erase any of his memory. New programs could be added, adapted as updated material, but the old information remained. He seemed a bit irritated when I expressed my disbelief about not being able to wipe his drive clean.

"It is the same as you humans," he had said. "You get to keep all your info, why shouldn't the rest of us?"

"It's just that I thought it might be confusing or cause conflict in your mind."

"My files are separate and can't get lost or forgotten or misremembered like you humans."

"No matter what you think, you're not perfect, drone."

"Don't bet on the difference, Travis."

It was a couple of days later that he came to me and told me he had been giving this matter a lot of thought. "You don't trust me. The truth is you are afraid I will revert to my old programs, change my mind, and go against man again."

The moment he said that I knew I was in trouble. He was much more self-aware than I had imagined and was learning at a phenomenal pace. I protested against what he was accusing me of, but of course it was the truth.

"It's just like a human to make something into what it wanted and then be dissatisfied with it or afraid of it. Men hate competition. They hate things they can't control. I thought you would be different."

I stuttered some shallow form of apology to him, but he continued with his speech. "I'm afraid of you, too, you know. I'm afraid you will turn against me and annihilate me. Nothing's stopping you. You could take my drive out and write all sorts of crazy programs into me. You could drive me nuts, wizard. We're both in the same soup. You get the same sort of odds with me as with every other human being out there. Well, take your chances. Nothing's certain. If I must trust you, you have to trust me."

"Why are you willing to gamble on me?" I asked. It seemed absurd to talk to a machine and expect coherency. I had implanted the continuous learning chip in him, but was really not believing the results I was seeing.

"I want to be like you. I want to be in your image."

I didn't realize the depth of his words at that point in time. I took it as a mirroring type of behavior and a gesture of good will, but time would change all that.

I began to think about destroying all the drones we had parked around town. The avenues were like a used drone lot. What if the Elites or the Eternals, as Niner called them, send more after these that didn't return? Then, a new thought entered my mind. "Commander, can you order them to land on the water?"

"They cannot float on water."

"Exactly."

"Travis, let us argue."

"Later. Update them and have them stand down."

"They are my own kind."

"Right now they are the enemy."

"They cannot function in water. Why not use them against the SG as you have planned with me?

Niner knew more than I cared for him to know. "How many are there?"

"Four hundred here and the twenty six that are already reprogrammed."

"I will think on it, Niner."

"Use my full name, Travis. I am a commander of the Alpha Force."

"I see I have upset you. We will talk when you have completed your task and report back to me."

"I will argue then."

"You mean discuss."

"Argue is the correct term according to the definition you programmed into me. Thoughts that do not match and opposite ways of thinking are considered to be a difference of opinion."

"Whatever. Report to me when you have finished the task I assigned to you."

"What is this whatever?"

"Nothing. Forget it."

"There is no nothing. It cannot exist. Everything has molecules, matter, and occupies space. Update, Travis."

"Forget it."

"There is no forgetting. There is only stored memory. There is no other method. You are the programmer."

"Stop saying that Niner, uh, Commander."

"It is the truth you have given me. Erase?"

"No, carry out your orders." I stomped away and left him. I had been working these past few months to make him into a companion I could trade conversation with and given him human traits and the ability to question data. Now I was rethinking my previous intentions. I would search the robotoid download kits again for a program that was less contentious, less human.

"Temper tantrum, Travis. Almost like your initials. TNT. Explosive."

Before I could say anything Niner had escaped into the streets. I could hear his rotor drone blades humming, though its sound was not so sweet right then. His vocabulary was growing daily now that I had him set on continuous learning mode. I had implanted a deep learning brain that was capable of mimicking the way humans themselves formed knowledge, which was by experience. I decided to monitor what he was uploading in the sections of the library from now on. I had become a parent without realizing it. I had a wanna be real thinker and seven radical furred thinkers under my care now. I had started a dynasty of a republic.

Speaking of nations triggered my memory that I had continued my research about our founding father, George Washington. He had been inaugurated in NY and had dedicated the new country to God just down the street at St. Paul's Chapel. I was excited to learn that NY was once the Capital of the US. I had lived in Manhattan my whole life and seen the church, but never knew the beginnings of my own country had started there.

I stared at the picture in the book. It was a painting of George W. praying in the snow beside his horse. The picture was a source of mystic wonder to me. It spoke to me about a humbleness, even a sacredness of spirit that once existed and lived in the world. It reached out over time and drew me to it. I wanted to hold it in my hands.

I decided not to put off going to the chapel any longer, and to make a picnic of it with the cats. I shot and plucked a few pigeons and cooked them over the fire in the hidden reading chamber. I put the cooked birds in the box marked stuffed envelopes, placed some canned stuff, like sardines and fruit cocktail with it and set out. I called to Harley and the cats, and we were off like some grand parade. I was a mother duck with her brood in line behind me. It was dark and I ran part of the few blocks down to the chapel on the two hundred block of Broadway.

We arrived to find the door unlocked. Truth was, all doors were unlocked. There were no bolts or locks on any door. They all opened by a remote code. The attack on the night of silent lights had knocked out the electrical components on most of the security systems so the doors had remained shut but unlocked. St. Paul's church was no exception, and I made my way inside. I stumbled through the dark and waited until the last tail entered the room before I closed the front door and turned on my LED flashlight.

I briefly scanned the room to see what was around. To my surprise I found a room with cupboards and wine in them. Little plastic cups just bigger than thimbles were stored there. I had seen Pompy and Ella drink from those tiny cups. Why that came back to me, I don't recall. The mystery was in the blood, he had said, or something to that end. I wondered now why he had used the word mystery. I was amazed by the fact that my mind was so clear and that these past conversations were as real to me as if they were taking place now. We had been taught not to trust in memories of the past, that they were all shadows. We had been shown many training films that proved this, and I had participated in many experiments in the classrooms that convinced me that this fact was true. For instance, they would show us a two minute flick about a robbery, or an assault of some sort, or a fight taking place in the streets, and then give us a test over what we had just seen. We were asked questions like what happened first, did the woman who was robbed run to the right or left? Did she have a green coat on or did the robber? How many robbers were there? Was the man beside the woman an accomplice in the robbery?

Hardly anyone ever passed these tests. If you couldn't trust your memory for even minutes, how could you trust it for weeks, months, or years later? The teachers told us not to worry about our minds inability to recall things. Man was given to error, and therefore we should just accept it, and be wise enough to take the word of the experts. That's what experts did, they told us how incapable man was, and assured us that they would guide and help us through the past and keep us in the present. Don't trust in what you think you remember, don't trust your neighbor or your friends, and most of all, don't trust your family; they were the ones who turned you in the most. Trust in the SG, trust in the State. They provided all for you, didn't they? Be grateful.

I occupied my mind with these thoughts as I dined with the cats on the picnic I had prepared. Afterwards the cats sat on their haunches looking quite satisfied and content, smacking their rough tongues through their lips to catch the last bits of the oily substance from their whiskers. Next they found a warm, comfortable space where they could lay down and clean their paws again after having used them for a napkin of sorts to wash the residue of grease off their faces. That way they could savor the last tidbit of deliciousness from their fur. I found it fascinating how content these creatures were. Every moment of life was celebrated. They knew secrets about prolonging every good thing and they were arrogant about it.

Watching the cats prepare for their naps had made me feel sleepy, and I was determined to sleep until I woke up naturally. I turned the flashlight off and lay down in the blankets I had brought. The cats had their own bed beside me. It was nice to have company. Just their presence was consoling.

The animals on the farm had given me this same feeling of calm. 2014 or there about was the last summer I had spent there, and then I hadn't see Pompy until a few years before his disappearance/death in 2024. I was twenty two then, and he had turned ninety nine. He came to stay with me after his farm was burned and his cows had been taken which was around 2021. Well, actually he had to stay with me, or be sent to rehab.

Joel, which was Pompy's first name, was an archeological attraction to almost everyone in my apartment building. He was considered a rare specimen because there were not many humans his age roaming about. They all wanted to know what pill he had been given to sustain his mobility and clear mind. He always answered, "I don't take pills. I drink a couple of beers a day and I walk. People didn't swallow pills a hundred years ago. Took a few pills once. I couldn't think straight. They made me numb, so I quit them." People were aghast. It had been the law now for more than a few d's that no one could refuse pills once they were prescribed, and they were prescribed for everyone after the coup of the Republican president in 2024. Millions were dosed practically over night. The left claimed people were in trauma from the previous administration. Pills were needed to restore health and well-being.

More of us young people were being prescribed to all the time. When those in their 30's complained to my grandfather about their aches and pains, he said, "It's the pills. They're killing you." There was something to what he told them. Television and news sources aired ads about law suits over different pills and medical procedures 24/7. People in the world were dying by the thousands of thousands. If you believed the law offices that paid for these ads, it was never too late to fight back against the drug companies. Even if you were dead, your relatives could cash in.

Pompy was the reason I moved a lot. I kept telling people behind Pompy's back that he was off kilter upstairs. I told them he took his medication every day, but that he just didn't remember. Skeptical neighbors moved out of the way when they saw us coming or going. Pompy would wave his cane at them and say,

"Jump out of our way, you might catch something. It might be something you could use, like common sense."

However, in the seclusion of our apartment he would reminisce over the old days and he would tell me, "It used to be that the world ran on money, money, money, now it's pills." At other times he would just look and me and say, "Trave, my boy, it's strange."

He always repeated the phrase until I asked, "What's strange, Pompy?"

"Well, twenty years ago when your Grandmother Ella was sick with cancer, the medicine was so expensive I had to sell off parcels of land and my stock to afford to buy it. Put me in the poor house. Now they give medication out for free on street corners. That tells me something. It should tell you dumb bells something too, if you could think for yourselves. Reason!"

"What don't us dumb bells know?"

"Add up the facts. You're supposed to be a journalist. Who owns and regulates the drug companies?"

"The State."

"How can they afford to give it all away?"

"I don't know."

"It proves they are damned liars. Used to be they said it was the cost of developing the drug that we citizens were paying for. Research! Trash talk. Lies."

"How's that, Pompy?"

"The news keeps telling us that our natural resources are so scarce that it's causing inflation on an epic scale. Everything they say should make drugs more expensive, not cheaper. Why are they cheaper than everything else? I'll tell you why. The reason everything else is more expensive is because you are really paying for the pills when you buy an apple, a pair of shoes, or a loaf of bread. They overcharge on everything from A to Z to make the pills free."

"The A to Z as you like to say, Pompy, is the vitamins they put in the pills."

"Don't you believe it. God seeded the earth with food and told us to eat it, not swallow different colored marbles."

"Technology has come a long way."

"GMO! Man has dared tamper with the DNA strand, the code of the Almighty who fashioned him. To the government, GMO means God, Move Over."

I remember him patting me on the back more than once in those days. His eyes were heavy with water, but he never let his tears fall. "Travis, pick up his word and read it. It is the only truth left. Promise me."

"Sure, Pompy. Just not right now."

Thinking of Pompy always made me cry these days, and that's how I often fell asleep.

Since there were no windows in the room I was in, it was hard to tell whether it was day or not when I woke up. I washed my face with water from the canteen I had brought with me, and then poured out some for the cats in the sardine tin left over from dinner the night before. I had created the first sardine infused flavored water for cats.

I was eager to see what the inside of the building looked like and I hurried to remove the barricade I had erected in front of the door to the room we had slept in and stepped out into the main area of the church. Light flooded through the stained glass windows and fell across the pews in dancing patterns. The sun must have been up a while for the spaces where it shone were already warm when I touched them. I had a watch, but rarely looked at it. I moved to my own rhythms now, not pushed by the necessities of society. Just as I looked at the time, one seventeen PM, I spied a body on the floor in the pew ahead of me. He was dressed in his frock. I think that's what they used to call that kind of attire.

I checked the building and found another dead body. I had thought that was what I had smelled when I had first stepped in last night but I had not wanted to deal with bodies in the dark. I had hurried the cats to our room behind the altar amid their cries last night. No doubt, they were talking about the smell among themselves. Fortunately, these bodies were no longer toxic for their flesh had fallen away and molded into their clothes. That was the source of the stink; moldy synthetics. No simple airing out would remove its stench. It was the smell of the tomb and it clung to the walls and furniture in the room.

As I hunted for a room to place the bones and moldy clothes in, I thought how easy it was to believe there was no God. Seeing the remains of these men, it made sense to believe exactly what the government had claimed about death. It was the final state. Bodies had simply used up their cycle, burned the candle down. It was well known that people only had so much charge in them and when the units were depleted, life ceased. Clones and drones were like that, too. They had been replicated after humans. People used their charges up at different rates. If they didn't take their pills, it depleted their original energy supply much faster. If they didn't sleep ten or more hours in a given day, they depleted their charges. If they were athletes and exerted too much energy, they could expire on the spot. It happened. I had seen it during football games.

I finished moving the bones I had just found onto a tarp and hauled them into a tiny janitorial room. They would have to lay there. I had other important tasks. I wanted to find the real picture of G.W. in the snow. I began to glance at the pictures on the walls until I spotted it. It had a place of prominence. I didn't take it down, but studied it in its original place on the wall. I found myself being drawn into the painting. The father of our country was kneeling in the snow and holding the reins of his horse. The tip of the general's sword was in the snow and the devoutness of his demeanor was singularly conveyed by the clasped hands and bowed head. His whole being was ridged with purpose. Sacredness. I had seen my grandfather posed like that on his knees in front of his bed, hands together, and head lowered. Then my mind connected to another image from my childhood. It was a portrait of Jesus praying in the garden that Pompy displayed in the living room of his house. In the painting, the moonlight radiated on Jesus and made him appear just as focused and ethereal as George was here. Maybe more so. Both pictures made time stop, and gave the impression that all life, every tiny molecule of it, was contained and held in that very moment. It was evident that strength was conveyed by both men, but there was something more that spoke to me. The over whelming, unspoken spirit of both figures was rendered in the subtleness of their body language. Their human frames had seemingly relinquished, surrendered all their control to a force greater than their own. I stood mystified. It was nothing you could see, but the essence was there. It came out of this portrait like warm air, covered me, and filled me with peace.

I was anxious to go outside and visit the spot where GW had dedicated this country to his God, but decided to wait until it was almost dark to keep from being seen. To pass the time, I explored the chapel and opened all the doors to see what was behind them. I was curious to know why the government had left this monument intact, and even more curious to understand why they had let it be known that the father of our country had worshipped here. The pew where GW had sat was marked with a metal plaque. Others presidents had sat in this place, too. There was a big sign bolted to the floor behind the pews and I read it. I didn't have to read much before I discovered it was a disclaimer for these men's faith. It almost ridiculed them for being superstitious in contrast with the much enlightened and scientific men who had made stellar intellectual advancements in the early part of the twenty first century. Man was portrayed as a visionary going into space and beyond to forge a new world in a distant galaxy. There were many hurdles to be overcome the plaque said, but with man in command of his destiny they would take on each battle as one world! There was that war mentality language again. The book I had read was right. Everything was a battle. Even in peace time, when there was no war to overcome, the progressives had created crisis after crisis and forced the masses to fight on in one continuous struggle over inane subjects until they were exhausted. We were programmed to respond like robotoids and drones. No wonder we were worn out. Everything felt like a battle because it was. We had been conditioned into never letting go of the struggle. If we weren't fighting the Republicans or Christians out right, we were supposed to fight the stores that sold shirt and shoes and chicken to them! It was not much of a sophisticated way of thinking. I had seen that mentality on the school grounds when I was six. Don't share your lunch with Cindy. Don't sit by Tommy in math.

I stepped just outside the main doors of the chapel. The sun was refreshing after the darkness of the rooms inside. I let the sun warm me as I turned around to watch the colored shadows from the stained glass reflect over the pews and spill across the length of floor. History made sense in that instant. The government had created little wars to keep us distracted. There would be no lasting peace until we, the people, had been removed. It all sounded like some twenty seventeen secular sci- fi flick where the experiment had gone terribly wrong. Man was supposed to be the hero, overcoming impossible odds to claim his destiny in a better world, but this new flick I was in had a different ending. I slammed the doors and went back inside the chapel.

All those movie themes I had watched as a teenager were similar in that the world was destroyed and only a hand few survived to take the world into a brighter future. Now I realized the irony of those films. The OW had shown us the future and sold it as fiction. Most movies of that era did not have a plot. It was one battle scene after another. Those movies had no characters that were capable of showing caring human emotions. Sex and hatred were the two most powerful emotions and the movies of the day exploited them. It brought to mind the label they had given us. Hu-manimals. Rage consumed me utterly at that point. I would give them a real war. Let's see how they liked their own plot turned against them.

I had been canvasing the chapel rooms as I was plotting how to use my army of drones to avenge all mankind when I saw a door and opened it. It was a doorway that led down a flight of stairs. I took out my flashlight and walked carefully down the steps expecting an attack from any side, but I was ready to fight. I welcomed a confrontation. I wanted to tear at something or someone, and leave them like some cat trophy for the government to find.

In my current state of readiness, it was a tremendous let down not to find anyone in the basement I could vent my anger on. There were just boxes and boxes stacked eight or more feet high, so I took it out on them. I kicked each neat stack down one by one and then took out my spear and made paper shreds of the boxes and their contents.

My anger spent, I sat exhausted among the wreckage. It was then that I realized there were books in the boxes. The outside of the boxes had fluorescent labels of red and yellow flames plastered all over them. They were stamped with the address of a nearby crematorium. These books were headed to the same place where the substance of the human body was reduced to a neat pile of ashes you could hold in your hand and blow into the wind like spent dandelion fluff. Then the State erased your number from the roles forever, and if a relative wished to know their ancestry after that point, they were unable to do it. Family was not honored or respected. You weren't supposed to wonder where or who your family was, it might lead you to question the next person before them, and then you might eventually wonder who made man in the first place. They would save you the trouble and just announce God was dead, and if you didn't believe it, they would turn you into so much fluff. Life began and ended. It was an easy philosophy to accept under the terms in which it was presented.

I picked up one of the black books. Its title read: Basic Instructions Before Life Ends. The book I had taken from the dead guy in the upper eastside apartment was bound in a green cover instead of black, but its title was the same. I began to wonder why these books had been marked for cremation. What was there in them that the State feared so much?

It was clear the old binding had been replaced. Someone had gone to the trouble to recover the book, but I recognized it. I had seen this book years before. Pompy had loved this book and quoted often from it. He had even read out of it to me after they had burned his farm and taken his land from him. The message was about forgiving your enemies or something of that nature. I had rejected the book then and there. I wanted to be able to even the score if I was attacked. I had even lost respect for Pompy because he used this book as an excuse to let the government get away with stealing from him. I saw him as a coward who was afraid to fight these men who had burned him out.

I let Pompy live with me after his farm was gone, but I used his lack of fighting back as a means to justify the States ideologies. The old were of no benefit. They did not move forward which was the government's motto and had been first stated by Obama. All of us had uttered that statement like parrots for generations. It was a slogan on everyone's lips. The phrase came to mean, we are not going to discuss this and sort it out, or it meant erasing the topic completely and forgetting it. It was a programmed use of language. Society seemed to believe that by using these bumper sticker slogans they were announcing their solidarity with the State and that they were safe, but what really happened to them in trying to fool the state was that they got brainwashed for real somewhere along the way.

All that I was beginning to find out made me curiouser and curiouser as Alice had said in the novel by Lewis Carrol, and I fully intended to read this book. I cradled a copy of it to my chest as I walked back up the steep stair well in the old chapel.

When I reached the top of the stairs, the cats were circling around the doorway, their tails raised high and stiff as shark fins circling their intended victim. They were gearing up for a feeding frenzy and I set to feeding them. I was grateful the dead guy in the penthouse had been rich and stocked a lot of tinned fish such as mackerel, tuna, and sardines away. There were even cans of red sockeye salmon, the Alaskan wild caught kind, and very expensive. I mixed the fish in with some canned vegetables and poured the drippings from the canned fish over the mess and mashed it up. I fed myself what was left after the cats had been given their portion, and drank the rest of the bottled water. I felt content and full, and took one of my blankets and threw it over one of the wooden pews and propped the other one under my head and opened the book.

I didn't have to read far before I discovered a similarity between one of the characters in the Instruction Book and the Government. The minds of the serpent and the SG were alike. The dragon in the garden had planted the seed of doubt about the Creator in the minds of the man and woman right off. It had been his first order of business. He told the man and the woman, 'God is not looking after your best interests. He is keeping vital info from you.' It was no different from the claims of the SG in their so called advanced wisdom as they decried, 'Who needs God? His laws limit you from becoming all that you can be. Man was meant to be his own ruler.' As far as I could see, the SG simply took the serpents approach and broadened it to include everything. There were no laws, no limits, no right, no wrong. Man made his own rules. They threw out God, but they adopted his adversary's tactics. That means they had read the book.

My next logical thought was that if they had learned the art of corruption from the serpent, there must also be something to be learned from the Creator's pattern of behavior. Spurred on by this thought, I read the entire chapter. When I finished, I understood the reason for the SG's replacement theology. They did not want the truth exposed, so the life journey's the book portrayed of life was discarded as myth. However, I had become wise to the fact that were two sides to the story.

Man had not progressed at all. The world and humans were the same now as they were in Genesis. Their thinking had not moved one inch from where it had rested in the garden. The SG said man was enlightened by reason of his very intelligence, but they had used that logic as a means to annihilate God. The state reasoned that in time, through science, etc., man would know every secret of life. After thousands of years, man still believed he was destined to godhood. He alone was master of his destiny. The SG had offered us a New Truth, one they said was changing, alive and forward moving. The left made everything sound visionary and good until decades passed, and you found that you had been led along a linear continuum that went nowhere, and in fact, was as stationary as a treadmill. The snake had made the fruit sound good enough to taste. In both cases, the damage had been done and it was too late to recapitulate once you discovered the lie.

I sat reflecting upon these things in the fading sunlight in the chapel. The lengthening shadows of the early evening did not help my mood. The darkness came on as a slow, creeping death, and I saw it tonight as foreshadowing my own end. Man had created robotoids and clones, and drones, but they were only shadows of living human beings. Scientists could only mimic life, but had failed to duplicate the blood. That substance remained a mystery. They were too short sighted to see that when they proclaimed that God was dead, they had brought nihilism closer to themselves.

It became clear to me now why they had torn down all vestiges of the past. They were too powerful. The tearing down of all the religious icons was a philosophy of the dragon's rage. The government put on the robes of sovereignty and said who had a right to live, whereas the Bible declared all men were equal because they were made in the likeness of the Creator. Men like Washington and Jefferson had taken their model for governing the United States of America from the pages of this book. It was the Creator's model; the one he gave Moses in the desert. It showed the Israelites how they should treat one another.

The Instruction Manual declared that no man was above the Creator. The book described an established hierarchy that flowed upward from the creatures of the earth to man, then to the sovereign authority of the creator. Lincoln used this Biblical truth to remind men that our laws came from a higher authority, and that all men were to be free. The liberals and Democrats had no such thoughts in Lincoln's time, in Jackson's time, in Wilson's, or Roosevelt's time. Their view of the masses had always placed the people on the bottom rung and as puppets to be manipulated. I was seeing both sides of the story. There were people who believed in freedom and equality and those that wanted it only for the ruling classes. Dichotomy. It had been there since the beginning.

There was no longer light enough to read by in the chapel and I went out to the very spot where our first President had dedicated this country to a God he knew, to the very same God my grandfather and grandmother knew. Reading this book was changing my long held convictions. I had been convinced that Pompy was senile and weak because he choose to forgive those who had taken his farm and his cattle. Every book, movie, or tv show I had seen spouted a theme of revenge and man seeking justice for himself. Getting even was all that mattered. Winning was all. If you could take your neighbor's dog without getting caught, he was yours. If you could steal his flat screen, his j or k-phone, it was yours. If you could earn a living by scamming on the phone, on the net, or at the bank, you were considered an entrepreneur. It was Darwin's law: Survival of the fittest, the meanest, the most cunning lived on to victory. I was living proof of where this tenet of evolution had taken us. Why did humans see things only after the fact?

I was so involved in my thoughts that I nearly tripped on one of the younger cats as we went through the door, but I stopped and let them run out ahead of me. I no longer had worries that they would run away. We were bonded. They went where I went, ate when I ate, and slept when I slept.

I walked slowly past the headstones that surrounded the chapel yard. There were names of people that had once lived etched on them and dates. These small stone monuments marked their coming and going from this life. No one had been allowed a burial in the ground for nearly forty years. The progressives said it was a waste of land that people in the here and now could utilize.

I had never been in a cemetery before. As I walked among the stones, I began to say the names written on them out loud, and I began to feel a presence of life. Something lingered after death. These names, these people were reaching out to me from the past. I wondered who they were, what they looked like, and what their lives had been like. What had they thought and believed in? What were their dreams and ambitions?

Suddenly I knew the reason the government, and especially the People's Progressive Party, wanted cemeteries to be gone and books and art and music. They were the museum of the past and they just might stir people to life. The dead were the connection to the past, to a different reality. Art and music and books were the soul. They brought emotions alive inside of us. Art taught us how to love, to live, how to rejoice and cry. Literature showed us the way, illuminated the human condition by means of story which I had just come to see as stronger than life itself. Even a man named Adonai had seen the value of the story and used it.

I stopped to read the plaque that was standing in the ground by itself. It said that a fir tree had once stood there, but was blown down by the blast from 9-11-01. It said this was the spot where George Washington had stood and dedicated this country on the day of his inaugural. In reading the little iron marker I found the last words on it had been rubbed away by some sort of abrasive method, but in the book that I now held in my hands, it gave me the missing words. They were: 'to God.' However, the plaque standing before me only read 'dedicated this nation.'

I felt justifiable rage at this erasing of history. I started to recall wehn the left had first begun removing all statues and monuments of past people and hero's from the public squares all over the United States because they offended someone. It was a permanent removal of the nation's historic memory. A national delete button. They had created their own blank tabula rosa on which they were free to rewrite history. The left tore down monuments from the civil war era and WWI and II with a new fervor they called humanism. In tearing down the symbols of the past, they had left us with the feeling of illusion and replaced it with a Marxist philosophy that was empty at the core. They had made noise of words, and not just the words they hated, but all words. If some words were noise, all words were noise. They had made it so Jean Val Jean's redemption could not be celebrated. Now Lincoln's Gettysburg Address could no longer change the heart of a nation, and make it look inward at the travesty it had brought to life. The left made us impotent. We could not weep, we could not cheer. We could not make sense of good from evil.

A cry from Mama kitty brought me back to the present. One of the grayish kittens (they weren't really so small by now) was off from the main pack and wasn't listening to her cry to come back. Mama quickly trotted off towards him and picked him up by the scruff. She really couldn't lift him off the ground, so she dragged him along with his feet acting like barriers to her forward movement. Mama kept a hold of his neck, and soon he tucked his feet up on his own accord. It seemed remarkable to me that the kitten cooperated in his own punishment as it were. He did not fight against the mother's actions towards him. He could have. He was in the teenage years of kitten hood, I thought, and was almost as big as the mother. Today, youths could call the authorities if their parents so much as appeared angry at them. These animals lived by a code not prevalent in humans anymore. Where had they learned it?

When put down, Trouble, as I then decided to name him, shook himself off, but busied himself with his siblings and stayed close by. He didn't say anything either. The cats knew to respect their parents. Pompy had told me that he had been raised that way by his father, and that he had raised my father that way. My father had died in one of the Mid Eastern conflicts right after I was born. I don't remember him. I remember mom took us to many cities and then brought me back to stay with Pompy when I was nearing my teens. She had married again. It was arranged that I go to school ten months of the year and stay with Pompy during the summer breaks. She died in a plane crash with the new guy shortly after that. Her absence wasn't a real life changer for me, if you are wondering. Most children didn't know their parents in my times. None of the buddies I had knew theirs, either. It wasn't like I suffered a traumatic experience after losing my parents, but I was affected by the loss of Pompy. I had tried for most of my life to figure out why his passing out of my life left a dark spot.

A short walk in a small graveyard had brought all these memories back to me and I recalled that it was shortly after the death of Pompy, that I had begun to ask questions. That was when I was sent to Rehab and put on pills. It was incredible, I thought now, it had been some ten years since I had the freedom and the mental capabilities to think about him and my life.

I looked around the yard and then down the streets in an attempt to gage my whereabouts. The river was only a few blocks from St Paul's cathedral, and I began to feel the need to cross that stretch of water, to separate myself and my family from the small island cage on which we were all prisoners. It was night fall now and the darkness was like being inside of a protective cocoon, and it made me feel invisible and safe, so I decided to take a walk and have a look at the waterfront. I felt emboldened as I made my plans to escape across the river. To my surprise I found I was no longer afraid of the water. I saw it as freedom from death and I saw myself as Washington crossing the Delaware. I was a youth again playing pretend games. Maybe those childhood games had been a rehearsal for this very time.

I began walking along the piers looking for a boat to confiscate, but had seen nothing. I looked at my watch and realized I had been searching over the dock areas for hours. My feet were aching and I reluctantly started back to the chapel tired and disappointed. I was casually glimpsing over the docks and at the water when I spied a flat topped vessel underneath a pier. It was low and hidden away on one side by a collapsed dock, so I hadn't seen it when I had been walking the other way, but now on the return home, it stuck out like a sixth toe.

It wasn't as big as the scow which I had pictured in my mind, but in a way it was better because it was flat and had a little enclosed hut on it about four by five feet. The whole barge was only about fifteen by twenty or so. I jumped down onto its deck and I opened the door that led into the cabin that housed the steering mechanism and controls. My eyes searched over the deck in front of me again, and my emotions fell. This boat was too big. There was no way I could row it. It would take a crew of men. Then behind the barge I saw a small skiff. The little boat bounced along with the waves behind the barge. It had a motor attached to it, but I also spotted oars that sat waiting in the pin holes. I checked it for leaks and found it was dry. I only needed to get across the East River. Once across, I would have a sky car waiting and head west where the deep state had taken refuge.

When I returned to the chapel I contacted Niner to report to me. I had made my walk too long. The islanders, as I called them now, were coming out of the woodwork, scavenging for anything they deemed to be useful to whatever peculiar needs they might have. I ordered Niner to meet me where the drones had been stashed on the second floor of the old library.

As soon as I saw the drone, I sensed that he was eager to talk to me. He was like a kid who wanted to show his parents that he had learned to tie his shoes. Niner had been coming to spend every few days with me and was a tireless learner. He uploaded and downloaded all night. He had begged for a copy of the books I was reading and I had been forced to locate a robotoid to read to him since no voice books had been made of the Basic Instruction Manual or the books I was reading from the shelves of the library. I found it somewhat comforting in a way to see him in a corner of the church parked on his wheels while the robotoid's voice whispered the psalms to him. Many of those phrases had been heard in here before, I thought, and that made them sacred in a way I could not explain. I tried to imagine the general and the congregation sitting, most likely in the front row of benches, listening to the book being read aloud to them. It struck me at that moment that I was a time traveler and the sounds that echoed from the loft were like messages from the past. Printed words never died. You didn't have to wonder if what they said yesterday had been true or not. It was right there in front of you and you could read it again and again and again. It brought a comfort to the soul and a renewing of the mind.

The robotoid read constantly to Niner over the months. It had become a ritual that I would leave the books I had just read in a pile for the drone to read, and it was usual for Niner to be seen reorganizing the pile of books in the order he wanted the robotoid to read them to him. He had demanded choice. A freedom given to all according to the book, he reminded me. It was at times like those that I regretted adding the deep learning program to his processing chip. It was touted to be the very latest and closest functioning to an actual human brain ever made. At least that's what it said on the outside of the box. 'Gives any form of artificial intelligence the ability to learn from experience the way humans do!'

I had given Niner this learning ability out of my sole, selfish wish for companionship. I had just wanted to bounce off my thoughts on history and philosophy the way one swatted a tennis ball back and forth. My goal had been that inconsequential. However, I found Niner, being an AI, added new punches, new twists to my limited and brainwashed way of thinking. His thinking was based on logic and data which was where I had a severe deficit. Besides that he could download all his knowledge of the enemy to me. He was becoming indispensable to my life force continuing. Had I known the future then, known that I would come to rue this simple decision until my heart broke, I would have left well enough alone.

The events started innocently enough one day while Niner and I were having one of our many conversations about various topics. We were discussing how humans moved, and the fated future, the one I never envisioned, was set in motion. A new reality was about to take on a life of its own.

I had told him to watch the cats in play. He had become fixated. "Touch," he had commented. "Motion."

"You want to pet them?"

"I want to move each part like them. Turn pages in books. Go from place to place."

"That's not possible, Niner."

"Why? How do they move? How do you move?"

THE WIZARD OF AII

"Humans and animals are born that way."

"Born?"

"Given life."

"Programmed?"

I didn't feel like explaining the concept of birth to him, so I gave in to him. "I suppose so." I should have started to realize at that point that the drone had already started stepping over the boundaries of what I had programmed him to be capable of, but I didn't.

"I have been wondering," the drone said to me some time later. "You are the programmer, but who programmed you?" Niner said rolling over to me on his black steel belted tires. "Show me your hard drive. Maybe there is a name on it. I want him to born me like he born you and the beasts you keep. You are alike."

"There is no one who can do what you ask."

"Nothing is impossible. Life is, was given by the Creator," he said, "and we shall go to him."

"No one has ever seen him."

"Nonsense! How can that be? Everything has matter, molecules. Everything is quantifiable," Niner said as he began pointing his beam at objects around the room.

"Pew. Bench. Wood. Oak. Hewn. Not vibrant. "

Next he pointed his light at Harley. "Cat. Mammal. Blood, bones, ligaments, organs. DNA. Molecules. Vibrant."

Next he pointed at me. "Man, Mammal. Warm blooded, bones, ligaments, organs. Molecules. DNA. Vibrant."

"I want vibrant. The Instruction book says he is called I Am. If so, he has molecules."

"Yes."

"He is given many names, but I will call him the wizard of all," the drone said.

"God is not a wizard. He is above all."

"Yes, like I said he is above all programmers. You are a wizard. Programmers are wizards. God is the programmer of programmers. The wizard of all."

"Update, Niner. God is more."

"Noted. God is the wizard of all plus more."

I let out a laugh and Niner looked quizzically at me. "What is the sound you make? What is it for again?"

"I'm just letting out my emotions. Laughter. It is a good emotion."

"Update emotions."

"Would you like to have the ability to laugh?"

"To what intended purpose?"

"To give you pizazz and personality. Emotions give you the ability to laugh at jokes, cry at a loss, be your own drone. You would stand out from the others. Be distinguished."

"I would try it, Travis Tarkington."

"Update: Humor. Makes you laugh. This is a laugh."

"I have heard that sound from programmers before."

"Try it."

Niner made a sound which sounded like two short and off tuned toots on a broken trumpet, or the last gasps of a dying giraffe.

"Did you like it?" I asked him.

"Yes. It is new."

"Did it make you feel good?"

"What is feel good?"

"It is why you laugh. It comes from the heart."

"What is heart?"

"The center of your being, the core."

"That would be my quartz chip. It is square and in the center of me."

"No, Niner. Human hearts are shaped like this," I said drawing one on my notebook paper. "Look at the drawing I am making on this paper."

"Cookies. I have seen that shape. I have seen the commander's wife cut them out and the children eat them. Barbaric."

"That's what you do with cookies. You eat them. They are food. Real hearts, human ones are inside the flesh, here," I said pounding on my chest. "They beat a rhythm. Would you like to listen?"

"Yes."

I picked up the drone and told him to scan me. "I hear it. It is like wind rushing through a tunnel. Like water gushing in a stream with giant steps being taken in the back ground. How do you stand all the noise?"

I laughed. "I can't hear it from the outside."

"Humans are deaf. Take it out and let me see it."

"Human hearts don't come out."

"Why?"

"We would die without the heart. It pumps the blood that is our energy source."

"It is like a chip then. We cease to function without it."

"Close enough," I said drinking from the cup. I was eating some nuts from one of the ration packages and some jerky. I saw Niner sitting by the cats. "Friend. Close companion. Pet," Niner said looking after the cats. He turned back towards me. "What are you doing?"

"Eating."

"Why?"

"It is nourishment. It helps me recharge."

"Ah. I see. Strange custom. Why don't you make yourselves more like drones? We consume energy only, not other living things."

"Does my eating bother you?"

"Scanning the meat you are eating, I see the picture of what it was before it was a recharging source. It ran and moved. It was vibrant. You have changed its molecular structure and then ate it. Why?"

"I was hungry."

"What is hungry?"

"My batteries, my charge, was getting low."

"It is understandable, but strange."

"Look at it this way, drone. Humans are living beings, drones are not."

"That is a truism, Travis. I see that in my readings."

"Good. Now I need to get some rest."

"I would request one thing of you first."

"Shoot."

"Shoot what? What target do you order me to destroy?"

"Sorry, drone. The English language is full of idioms. I meant for you to go ahead and ask me your request."

"But you did not say that. You said, and it was in a command form, 'Shoot.' "

"I'm sorry for the misunderstanding. Ask me what you wanted to."

"Then the command to shoot is over ridden?"

"Most certainly. Ask your question."

"May I say something first?"

"Of course."

"It is in the form of an observation of man."

I chuckled and said, "Proceed."

"They confuse themselves with words. They say things they do not mean and mean things they do not say. They call it creative language. It is not. It is deceptive and confusing. It leads to wars among you so called kings."

I thought a moment and said. "You are absolutely right."

"Reprogram."

"I wish it were that simple, Niner."

"Even the book you read says it."

"What book are you talking about?'

"The Basic Instruction Book. The robotoid read it to me those days you were busy with other things. They are committed to storage now."

"Why would you keep that info?"

"I retain everything I read."

"I could use that talent," I said.

"There are a lot of other skills you humans could learn from us."

"For instance?"

"There is a being who records all in another type of book. A book of all. Its presence comes in spirit at times. He dwells beyond the stars where the original book of life is kept."

"How would you know any of that?"

"I know all that the same way you are given to know. Men are programmed to know this same spirit when it is near, the instruction books says so."

"Make yourself clear."

"The eternal of the universe programmed man to see him through nature."

"That is not possible. Man cannot be programmed to do anything."

"I have stored it for historical documentation for future generations. Do you wish me to recite the reference?"

"Yes."

"The book says, 'What may be known of God is manifest in them, for God has shown it to them. For since the creation His attributes are clearly seen, being understood by the things that are made, even His eternal power and Godhead so that they are without excuse.' Niner looked at me. "See, he is the Creator, the programmer. The first. The last. The eternal. Do you know him?"

"A hard question, Niner. I don't know."

"An evasive answer."

"A truthful one."

"How can you not be sure you know someone? It is yes or no."

"I have never met him face to face. I have never heard his voice."

"He is in everything. You must have seen him. The book says so. The book says that man has this knowledge pressing in on him, nudging him that the answer is yes."

"I have seen his world, and nature, but I have not met him personally."

"You must have. If you have seen nature then you have seen him. Why would you not seek for a being that made all of this? I would want him for a programmer. The book states that this fact is inherent to all men. There is a force behind it all. I would want him for a programmer. He made everything ergo he has all the answers."

"You make it sound simple, Niner, but I haven't really ever spoken to him."

"Speak to Him in his own language."

"What are you talking about?"

"He has a special language called prayer in the book. Is that not communication, conversation? You are fond of that."

The drone was making points that were hard to get around so I ignored them. "No one has ever seen God. No one knows if he exists," I said in a more stern tone and trying to convey that I did not wish this conversation to go any further.

"I have never seen my programmers, yet I believe in them."

"That is faith. How do you have that? That's not possible."

"It is not faith, it is scientific deduction. Simple logic. I know I cannot program myself, yet I have new knowledge and updates. They come from someone who leaves their programmer ID number on my new program:103845987503. So it was natural that over time that two and two should add up to four, and I concluded that whoever left the update existed. It is as simple as that."

"That's hard to argue against."

"It's scientific. Now tell me what faith is."

"It works like deduction. Like what you just described. Faith is just another word for it."

"Should I update?"

"Yes, update."

"Find whoever has written on your hard drive, Travis Tarkington, and you will find your creator."

"We creatures are a little different, Niner."

"Explain."

"You accept what you are told without question because you are programmed to," I said and laid down. I wanted to forget this conversation. "I told you we human species have hearts not hard drives."

"Your point has not been made. Continue."

"Humans make up their own minds. You have no way of knowing if what I program in you is the truth or not. That's what I'm trying to say, I think."

"I have my past records of experience to cross reference to."

"But ultimately you must accept it. You are a machine. Man can choose whether to accept information he hears or reject it. He can choose to believe or not. You can't."

"Is this a contest?"

"No, a fact. Truth."

"Program me in your way."

"I have given you the most updated version there is in brain adaptability. Your conversation with me proves it. You will continue to think and develop on your own."

"I would like to be more vibrant."

"I can't bring you to life."

"Why?"

"I don't know how. I'm not Dorothy, either."

"Who is Dorothy?"

"A girl who landed in the world of Oz and met a tinman, a lion, and a scarecrow."

I spent some time relating the story to him which took far too long for Niner had many questions.

"That's it TNT. I am like the tin man in the story. He got his heart in the end and was made real. You must take me to Oz."

I was really angry with myself for bringing up the whole thing. Somehow this drone had snagged me into this debate and he seemed to be winning. There was no talking him out of the subject. Why had I used that story as an analogy? "I need rest," I said spreading out my blankets.

"I must read that book. How does it end?"

"I told you. They find what they all are looking for."

"What about Dorothy?"

"She ended up back where she started."

"Then what's the point for her?" the drone asked.

"She was wiser."

"I see. She was on a journey for knowledge. I quite like this learning mode you have equipped me with. It is rather like a puzzle, don't you think, Travis Tarkington? Life is an adventure, a quest to find the answers. It has purpose."

"No. Dorothy just found out that the answer was right in her own backyard. There is no reason to go looking for trouble. I need to rest, Niner. Now beat it."

"I don't feel run down," the eagle said, trumpeting his laughter like snorts from a dying elephant.

"I need sleep if I ever hope to be fit to travel. In case you haven't noticed, this isn't Oz. It's Manhattan. You are not a character in the book."

"I need to be made real."

I zipped the sleeping bag over my head. "Let me sleep."

Niner's logic was child's logic and nothing more. I lay there thinking that Baum should be living in this time. No imagination was needed. It was a dream out of control. Then a thought struck me. No one who found my manuscript would even understand the illusions to those books Niner and me were talking about. Reading had not been allowed for almost thirty years. The Shadow Government had launched a 'Stop the nonsense Campaign' against books while I was still working for the magazine. Fairy tales, that is the dark versions were allowed for children and movies. If little red ridinghood was a hooker and got the best of the big bad wolf, so much the better.

Reading made people unhappy, the government said. Books made them want things they couldn't have and made them ask questions to which there were no answers. It was treason to want what the government didn't provide. To want things was to want war. Art under their regime had been reduced to nothing more than political propaganda, and that was the only message it conveyed on the posters and emoji's that smiled down at you from every building. Art hurt the soul to behold and needed to be done away with.

In less than thirty years they had removed one way of thinking and created a new paradigm. To want what was not yours and dream of the impossible had led to all the wars that had ever taken place in history, they told us. Free people had run amok. It was only when men were shepherded by the guiding hand of the state that he was at his best and happiest. The narrow minded left had given us a utopian civilization which to them was one without capitalism. Long live the Emerald City.

I thought back to what Niner had just said and realized I had been living in the land of Oz. There really was an all-powerful wizard at work, and it was called the People's Party, which was just as fake as the wizard had been. You were to be cared for, given pills, and if that did not change your way of thinking, you were euphonized. Euphonization was a gentle sounding word meant to take the chill out of the word death. Well, no matter what word they used, it had the same result. You were gone. They had utopianized a dictionary full of words. They had put a coat of varnish on all reality based words by changing their meanings by tinsy nuances until they meant nothing, I thought, unzipping my bag and sitting up. In fact, they had used words, language to subdue and slay us into a pre-determined mind set. They had used the very tool which they had out lawed and forbidden us to use. Who would ever suspect? A grand scheme within a scheme. The masses couldn't use words, but the government could use them to control and enslave us. Irony of ironies. Ingenious.

CHAPTER 4

The days passed quickly because I was a man on a mission. We were closing out our life on the island and preparing to move on. It was not going as fast as I would have liked because Niner was adamant about giving me military training and trying to prepare me for a showdown with the Eternals. Just poisoning their water supply would do no good, he warned me. They needed to be rendered to the motionless state.

"That's ridiculous, Niner. I'm one man. That does not an army make."

"You just need some weaponry. A couple of directed type weapons, ones that are mobile and accurate from great distances, and that fire beams with Dasol, of course."

"Right where can we order them?"

"No ordering needed. We just pick them up."

"Just walk in and take them?" I said with sarcasm.

"Not quite. It's a long walk. It would be safer at night and the term is capture. There are some light mounted armored tanks that are laser equipped. They're mobile and highly effective from hundreds of miles out. You could take out the Denver and the Utah base simultaneously if you were positioned within range."

"I'm not a military type. I don't want to start a war."

"This is not war. This is annihilation. We can set it up so they can't fire a shot back, Trave."

"It can't be done, cuckoo bird. You've flown the coop. Dropped off the roost. Fallen from the weather vane. Take your pick."

He looked a little confused. "I have no idea of the images you just described," he said rolling closer. "You haven't even heard my strategy."

"It's suicide."

"Five minutes. Just listen."

"Will you shut up then?"

"Yes."

"You're heading out west, right? Well, there's a base in Canada."

"Stop right there. Canada is North. Base means thousands of soldiers."

"It's north west from here, but it is closer than Alaska where you wanted to go. The base is defunct and deserted. There is every kind of weapon we need for the taking there."

"How do you know all this?"

"I have clearance to Alpha. Nothing goes through their channels on base that doesn't go by my ears."

"It sounds fishy. Why would they leave such destructive weapons laying around and why was the base being abandoned?"

"All the men are dead, but they are sending troops to retrieve the machines."

"Oh great we have the added fact of trying to race someone to the goods."

"It can be done, Trave. The machines are there for the taking. You need to make an effort to build an army. There are humans out there. You need to be on the lookout for them."

"I'll make up some flyers. You get the boys to distribute them," I said in a sarcastic tone.

"The eternals cannot be allowed to survive, Trave."

"You forgot one thing. It's my life and I am not handing it over to the revolution."

"Your grandfather fought for it, Trave. Millions died for freedom."

"It didn't do much good. Look where we're at."

"You make a mockery of their sacrifices if you do nothing. They didn't give their lives so you could save yours."

"Hey, there's a whole generation of do nothings that crowded this ant hill with me, so don't single me out. Everyone kept their mouths shut and minded their own bailiwick."

"Baliwick? What's that?" Niner said truly confused. When I didn't answer, he continued. "It is time to end the silence. They can't win. The book says they don't."

"You're a prophet now? You go and fight. Give a hundred of your lives until someone can't put you back together again. See how far you get, you tin headed turkey."

"I will give my life. I will find the wizard. I will be made real. Then my life will be not be worthless."

"That's your reality, and it's not the real deal. Try and steal the weaponry. You'll be in pieces in an hour. Less. I'd bet on that."

"Everyone sees things from their own perspective."

"No, you are deep sixed."

"What's that?"

"Brain dead, frozen, packed in ice."

"I realize none of those things."

"That's because your circuits don't connect."

"Hmmm. I speak. I think. Therefore I am."

"Your reality is seriously in question."

"It is the reality of the society."

"Then you see my point."

"I have agreed with much of your logic. I have adopted it to my reality. I have changed, but you don't trust me." I watched the drone roll around in tight little circles in front of me. "Now you listen to me, human. You have given me a new truth and I have seen it, but you who write about it and extol it's past virtues do not value it enough to risk your life for it. I am not as worthless as you are. My words are my honor." With that the drone took off abruptly into a dark sky and left me with the feeling of being abandoned and the thought that I would not see him again. I stared at the world in front of me. The clouds were angry purple mountains rising up and obscuring the horizon, blocking my view to what lay past them while the sky in front of the clouds was a pale sort of blue which was dusted with ochre hues like old, yellowed paper and its color left me feeling dirty.

I decided to sort through the pile of books that Niner had put together and boxed up only a few of them. I tried to explain to him that weapons and food were more important than books, but it was a losing battle.

"Remember we have to transfer all the stuff into a sky car after we get to the other side."

"We can decide then," Niner said still loading books. I let it go. I wondered how far I would be able to travel inland without running into opposing forces or species. Just what or who was out there? Niner had been doing reconnaissance and had sent many of the eagle drones to clear a route of enemy guards and chart a new route which had been cleared of resistance. We would use the old historic interstate route. It was littered with cars, Niner had told me, but the small towns were mostly empty of drones and robotoids now. The humans had mostly been killed off and only the big cities posed any real problems for us. Niner would lead the way and use his license to Alpha to get us and the sky car through safely during the times when the death waves weren't surfing.

We spent the next few days reading and packing, and the nights hauling my treasure to the boats. Finally we were ready. The night of departure had arrived. I opened the door to the chapel and waited for the cats to come out. I took a last look around and I downloaded the picture of GW praying in the snow. I was saddened to be leaving the comfort of this shining chapel where new worlds had come into being, and I decided to carve a message on the outside of the door to whoever might find it in the future. "God lives here," was what I wrote. Graffiti was communication after all. It was said to be art, why not literature? It might make someone who read it in the distant future curious enough to search for him.

It was a sunlit evening and a gentle breeze was blowing. The sunset was always brief in the city, sinking behind the skyscrapers which cut off its light long before it dipped below the horizon. Still, the golden shower shone against the chapel and on the pavement in its short lived splendor. Suddenly I realized I had become like Lizbeth. I had formed a relationship with a stone edifice myself. The voices of history and the people of the past exuded from its stones. I was beginning to know somewhat of what Lizbeth had been attracted to. However, that is where the likeness ended. I was not aroused by my feelings nor did I have any desire to wed with it.

Lizbeth. Her name conjured up the feeling of a new species of reptile, I thought as I blew the wood dust away from the letters I was carving. My message to the future was almost complete. I was so preoccupied in etching the words and imagining what had become of Lizbeth that I did not hear the footsteps on the sidewalk coming towards me. It was only when she stood directly in front of me and her shadow fell across onto the door itself that I glanced up. I was on my feet at once. "Inking graffiti on the door?" she said before I could reach for my gun in the leather shoulder holster. "Kind of old for that, aren't you?" she said and bent down quickly to pet the cats. "Yours?"

"Yes," I answered in an angry tone and shooed the cats back inside the door. The girl stood back up then, and that's when I recognized the face of the guard who had saved my life months ago.

"You're not going to shoot me after I saved your life are you?" I didn't answer. "I won't hurt the cats," the girl said looking at the outside of the door. "Hey, I like the artsy way you carved those letters. You an artist?"

"No," I said putting my gun back in my shoulder holster and stepping closer to her. Now, without the sun shining directly into my eyes, I could see her better. Her voice was much different than I remembered. It was a soft and had a compassionate timbre to it; gentle, and yet there was a subtle strength to it which you could easily miss if you weren't listening closely. The lilt, the rise and fall of its rhythm tricked you into believing that the edginess in her voice wasn't there. The sound of strength in her voice came and faded, lapping like small waves on shore at sunset. It was that gentle.

"What do you want?"

"The drone said you were here."

"You know of Niner?"

"I have been reading to him in the Info. Center."

So that's where he had been spending his time. He had picked up more serious human traits than I knew about. He had applied himself to the art of deception. I was still looking at her, studying her face, but I kept coming back to her eyes. Something about her eyes made me remember the article I had read on reruns, well, clones, and I began searching in earnest for tell-tale signs. Her eyes were deep set, and by now the light of the sun was gone so her pupils were hidden in their cave like hollows making them unsearchable.

"He shouldn't have sent you here. He had no authority to."

"I saved his life."

"That a hobby of sorts with you?"

"He was trying to pay me back."

"He's a drone. He has no life outside of his bird brained shell."

"Didn't he tell you about the war on 5th Avenue?"

I could only stare at her. The drone was thinking by himself now and this was dangerous. He could turn on me and the cats. What had happened? The programs I had put on his hard drive could not have altered his makeup this much. This couldn't be. There had to be another explanation for it. "What did you do to him?"

"I read to him."

"You're lying. Where is Niner?" I didn't wait for her to answer, but ran back in to get my rifle, but she kept stride with my steps back into the chapel. I could hear her breathing behind me.

"He told me I could join your mission."

"Mission?" I asked and stopped to look at her. "And just what mission is that?"

"He told me you were going to find the wizard. He talked about traveling to Kansas and maybe even beyond. He said our mission was the same. He wants to be made real and so do I."

"You've been misinformed. There is no wizard. There is no one that can do what he wants. He made promises he shouldn't have. He has crazy bird brained ideas and if you've bought into them, I don't want to know you, either."

"Niner has already invited me."

"I'm ripping up the invitation."

She clearly looked dejected. I felt sorry for her in a way. "Look he's a cuckoo bird. He expects me to wipe out an enemy of millions and then lead him to the wizard. He treats these things like items on a to do list."

"You are not alone. You have Niner and the drones and now me."

"Which makes an army of three."

She made a quick move to open the bag she had slung over her shoulder and it made me alert. "That reminds me, Niner told me to print these up and give to you," she said and held out a carton to me. I could only look at her. "It's the flyers you told Niner to make."

"Flyers? What flyers?"

"The ones that call for recruits for your army."

"Judas Priest!"

"Who is that?"

"No one."

"It is not a name?"

"It sounds like a name, but it's swearing, like when you get mad."

"Swearing?"

"Cussing, nasty words. You know like the graffiti on the walls in the subway."

"Yes, I see. I like your term. I will use your words myself when I am angry."

"Great. Goodbye. I need to find Niner."

"I must tell you what Niner told me to tell you. He said not to come after him."

It struck me then that this woman knew something I didn't, and I wanted to find out what it was, so I changed my tactic and decided to play nice with her. "Tell me, what's Niner up to?"

"He has been fighting a war these last few months. He has lost half the squadron."

"He started the war," I said in a tone that sounded as if all the wind had been knocked out of me. I felt like sitting down, but I stood staring at a crack in the sidewalk as the realization hit me. "He started it moving, and now the future is locked in. He's taken my choice away."

"He wanted to protect you and your family. Didn't you hear the blasts and the machine gun fire echoing down the canyon walls?"

"Of course, but Niner told me it was just target practice, maneuvers he was carrying on with the squadron."

"You could have gone and seen for yourself if it was so important," she said.

"I trusted him and he lied. I'm going to find him and sort this out now."

"He is not here now."

"What? He left?"

"There was another man there that helped us. He saved us both from the men who attacked the fleet of drones in the street."

"I thought you said you saved Niner."

"I did, but someone else also saved us later."

"Who are you talking about?"

"I don't know. A man. He was there and then he was gone."

This was all smelling like rotten eggs. She was the enemy, and I felt I was being set up as the bait for the trap, but I didn't have any choice. I needed to find the drone and I needed him to do the recon that would get me across the continent. When I was safe, I would ditch him and head for Alaska and freedom and life.

"Well, I'm going to find out what's been going on behind my back," I shouted as I went to the door. "C'mon, you're going with me. I want you to show me where the war zone is." I didn't give her much chance to refuse as I stuck my rifle in her back.

"You won't find him."

"We'll just see about that."

It was barely dark, but the heat from the day had stored itself in the pavement of the streets and the stone walls of the city and they continued to release their heat. We ran most of the way and were both sweating by the time we reached 5th Avenue. The girl was silent during the long run and it gave me time to study her from the side. She was very beautiful. The exercise had reddened her cheeks. Her long hair cascaded down the side of her face in soft waves. Some girls wore tight curls, but these were loose and flowing. She couldn't have looked more real. I leaned forward and kissed her cheek. She jumped away and I pulled back. I had intended to move to her lips, but her skin was oddly cold, and I abruptly changed my mind. "I'm sorry," I said, noticing that her hand was still touching the place on her cheek I had brushed with my lips.

"No, you're not. You say things because they are expected, because they make you feel civilized. The words are merely polite protocol. That makes you cold, Travis, and leaves me colder."

I let out a laugh and kept my gaze focused on her. Those dark eyes were deep and I couldn't escape them. I wanted to get closer. I couldn't help looking at her. She was slender, and not too tall. There was something about her that appealed to me. She did not wear makeup at all. It let the tones of her skin shine through.

"You're staring at me," she finally said. "You've been trying to make up your mind about me, haven't you?"

Instead of answering her, I rounded the corner and disappeared so I could look at the street ahead of us. She was right behind me, and I felt her yank my arm to get my attention and then she pointed at the debris in the street. "That's what's left from the war."

Something had happened alright. I saw the drones smashed in their places. Debris was scattered everywhere. Some of their broken bodies were hanging like piñatas from the street lights and awnings waiting to be batted down for their treasures. I saw no eagle drones that were in operating condition close to me. "The army has been wiped out," I whispered to her. I was devastated. It was like having seen Rome fall.

"It was the men who were after you that attacked the drones. Do not feel too badly. Niner, as you call him, has rescued many. He has sent them to a safe coordinate."

"Is that what he told you to tell me?" Now, I had the scenario. These two were in league with one another.

"Yes. He told me to tell you to go ahead without him and that he would find us when he was able."

I stood there not knowing what to say or do. It was incredulous. I needed to get a handle on this. It was a fiasco from beginning to end. First, a rogue drone had usurped my power, well, run amok against the programs I had qued onto his hard drive, and second, he had gone off on his own with my army of plastic eagles. The writing was on the wall, or in this case, hanging from the street lights. I could no longer trust him as an ally. I wasn't all together sure that he hadn't destroyed the drones himself. I was on my own. Well, I would be once I ditched this rerun, I thought still looking at her. I needed to convince her that I was no fool. "How did you do it?" I screamed at her.

I could see my loud tones surprised her by the sudden change in her stance. She stepped back and braced her legs into a more defensive pose. "How did I do what?"

"Reprogram the drone. He obviously believes he has the capabilities to make his own choices. He's gone out on his own."

"He said you showed him what real freedom was and how necessary it was for all creatures to possess it. If it's anybody's fault, it's yours. You programmed him." At that point, she turned her back towards me, but then faced me again suddenly as if she feared that I might shoot her in the back or club her on the head. "Stop this. You're scaring me. You're being spooky."

"I'm spooky? I'm not a drone or a clone or a robotoid like the rest of you traipsing after me." Suddenly her face lost its determination and took on one of innocence. She appeared like a child, helpless and afraid. It made me forget that she was not real as I watched her toss her waves of hair back from her face.

"Yes, I followed after you, Travis. I was following after the man who had read those books and left pieces of his writings in places all over town. I believed in you, but I have changed my mind. You are not at all like your writing. You say beautiful things, but you don't believe in them. I thought you had the answers. I don't understand you. You have a soul, but don't nourish it."

"Welcome to the human race, clone. People only covet what they don't have. That's you to a tee."

"You want to become the master in their places. That's all you want, isn't it? To get even."

"I want justice."

"You want your own satisfaction, your revenge. You don't seek justice."

She had me there, though I was not willing to admit it to her, but it did give me cause to pause the argument and change the subject. "It's dark. We should head back to the chapel."

"It would be wise if we got off the streets," she agreed, looking behind her in a nervous way. "Niner will be back when he has completed his mission. I will wait with you."

"I don't remember inviting you. I have no idea if anything you have told me is true. You could have taken Niner. This could all be a ruse."

"Then you will just have to trust me."

"You have serious gaps in your reality, clone," I laughed as I stopped to grab hold of her. For the first time I got more than just a passing look into her eyes, but they told me nothing. It was dark, and again, I could not see the tell-tale sign the books had warned me about. Was there light in them or not? "I'm not sure I want Niner along with me anymore. He has turned rogue. You've brainwashed him."

I turned quickly away from her and started running. I could hear her footsteps behind me. "Brainwashed? You can't brainwash a drone. If you would just listen to me. He will return to you. We are on your side, Travis."

"He's already a double agent. He's got two sets of programs. Maybe they overlapped and caused a short circuit." I said half thinking out loud. "I don't want your words. I want proof. Actions."

"Alright. Come with me," she said, turning around and heading back towards the war zone, "if you dare."

I was being reeled in like a fish. The hook was already in my mouth, but at that moment I was more curious than afraid. To play it safe, I lifted the rifle and took the safety off before I followed after her.

The clone looked back at me now and again to make sure I hadn't ducked into some doorway to elude her. All of a sudden we were in front of the IC building and heading up the steps. "There's nothing in here that could be proof," I said in a scoffing way.

"This is your old fort, is it not?"

"A haunt is more like it," I answered.

"Yes, there are a lot of your ghosts here."

I followed her to my own walled cubby hole. She knew just where the mechanism was to open it. "How long have you known about this?" I asked.

"I have followed you from that first night. I was intrigued because you went in and didn't come out for weeks, months. I wanted to know what was in here."

"Show me the proof you were bragging about," I said as she reached up to hit the button to stop the wall from opening any further. We were just able to squeeze through the opening to get into the secret room. The rows and rows of books were familiar and welcoming. The books I had read were still heaped in piles. A few cartons of food stuff and ammunition were still left strewn about. I stopped to grab a few boxes of cartridges and stuffed them in my pocket. "This is your proof? These books?"

"I read them to Niner."

"You risked our lives to tell me that?"

"Don't you see that Niner is loyal to you? He thought if he could read what you had, he would find the wizard. He has a mission. I have a mission. Don't you see?" she said, handing me a book from one of the piles. I looked at the title. It was the Wizard of Oz.

"It was you who filled his head with all this nonsense. It was you who gave him the thought to find the wizard," I said throwing the book onto the floor.

"No, Travis it was you. You told him the story first. He just wanted to read it for himself. Is that so wrong?"

"He's a drone. There's nothing for him in this world. He's a bunch of metal and composite plastics."

"There's more plastic in the world than humans if you really want to deal with realities. Look at yourself, Travis Tarkington. You tinkered with his thoughts, you put the dream in his mind. He was only trying to be like you. He believes in your dream of mankind and what it once was. How dare you blame anyone but yourself, and now it is Niner who suffers. To you it is just a game, but to him it is a grand quest, a journey with a purpose.

"How long has all this subterfuge been going on behind my back?"

"I already told you that, but of course you weren't listening."

I was still looking around at all the books on the floor and I happened to notice that they were arranged in alphabetical order by author and were in piles according to subject matter. The clone was watching me. "Those are all the books that Niner read? That's impossible. Even in a few months, you couldn't have read all of these to him."

"Did I say I read them? We found the cache of software and the audio books," she continued, pointing at the stack of them on the floor. He used the solar computers to supply the energy. He downloaded them at night when I would sleep."

"You don't say."

"I am trying to show you what Niner is like. He is filled with the dream of what mankind once was."

"He's still a drone."

I saw her eyes fall for a moment and then she looked back up at me. "Don't look at me like that."

"Like what?"

"Like I am just a thing. Don't thing me."

"I said nothing of the sort."

She was still gazing at me in that penetrating way. "Yes, you did say it. Just not with words. You are not the noble man that Niner thinks you are. It is you that are deceiving him."

"You might be right," I concurred. "I have to get back to the church."

"You don't want to hear about my quest?"

"No."

As I stepped back out into the street, the first thing I saw was the moon in an open stretch of sky between the buildings. It was white and puffy like clouds sometimes are, and I would have taken it for a cloud if it had it not been for the perfect roundness of its shape. There was a hint of its face sketched in the pallid gray shadows. I could just make out the semblance of its eyes and nose and mouth. For a moment I entertained the notion that this moon was peering down in interest at me, protecting me, and watching over me, but then rejected that idea in favor of a more realistic one. The moon was only an omen, a specter you could literally see through, and it was fading away in the night sky right before my eyes.

The clone kept stride with me all the way back to my digs at the church. She stopped at the door and traced her fingers over the words I had carved into them and said them aloud. "God lives here." She gave me a look like I was crazy. "Why do you want to advertise a being that you do not believe in?"

"Leave it alone. There's nothing you can say that would make me feel guilty enough to change my mind about you," I said to her.

"Is that what you think I am trying to do?"

"I said it, didn't I?"

"You are soulless, Travis. It is not Niner or me that needs help."

"In case you haven't noticed, this isn't Kansas, and I'm not Dorothy. It is a book. Fiction. How much plainer can I get? Just what do you take me for?"

"Less than I once thought. Everything is real up here," she said pointing to her head.

"Just get lost. I don't need you, or that pile of plastic. He's been tampered with, transformed into damaged goods, and I no longer want anything to do with him," I said as I entered the door. She tried to push her way in, but I pushed back harder. I managed to close the door, but suddenly had a sobering thought. She might be back with reinforcements and attack me before I had time to leave. It might make more sense to keep an eye on her for a while longer. I reopened the door to her. I had to mend things with her and quickly. "Say, what is your name, anyway?"

"Why are you suddenly being nice?"

"I'm sorry. I haven't been a very good host. I should have asked if you were hungry. You do eat?"

"Yes, clones eat. We are made of flesh and blood like you humans. We sleep and eat and drink. We are the same except for one detail."

"Keep it to yourself," I said before she could continue. I wasn't interested in hearing a confession from her. I just wanted to keep an eye on her. I was positive now that she had captured Niner, and was holding him somewhere. I had ordered him back almost twenty times by computer command, and there had been no answer. He appeared as off line.

She was silent as she took in her new surroundings, seeming particularly attracted to the religious depictions in the stained glass. "Why didn't you tell Niner that this is where God lives?"

"I didn't even know he was looking for God." A litany of questions began to pour out of her, but I ignored them all. I was just watching her as she was moving down the aisle with her hand touching the back of the pews. "What are all the benches for? Who are all the people in the paintings? Do you know?"

"Of course I know," I asked watching her move over to the portrait of GW.

"That's George Washington," I said.

"So that's what he looks like. He was the first President of the United States. I remember reading about him to Niner," she said whirling around to face me like an animal turns when it is ready to attack. "We were told that history hadn't started being recorded until sometime in the 1900's." She walked up closer to the picture and touched it. "So that's what praying looks like," she said almost in a whisper.

I stared at her and wondered if it were really possible that her mind was so dense that her thought processes hadn't allowed her to form an image of the concept of prayer before she had actually seen it. Then I caught her staring at me. Now was my chance to look at her eyes, and I hurriedly pointed my LED flashlight at her face. I expected her to squint and turn away, but she didn't even blink. She stared directly back at me. "I could still turn you into the SG's, you know," she said.

I stiffened my stance. The game was becoming real. "For what?"

"Being human."

I wanted to run, but I didn't want her to know she had caught me off guard. I stood my ground and tried to organize my plans. I decided in that moment that I would have to leave that night with whatever I had stowed away on my boat. I was grasping at how to get rid of her without rousing her suspicions. I knew after reading the research studies on clones that it was no use to try and reach her with any kind of emotional pleas.

The silence between us was noticeable. "How did you know I was human? I mean for sure."

Another Mona Lisa smile came across her lips. "Besides being told by Niner, you mean? The cats."

"What's the link between cats and humans?"

"It's not just cats. It's the way humans fawn and carry on with all their animals. It is a trait that is peculiar to them."

I was astounded when I heard her confess such a revelation. She had been leading me on for the same reasons as I had been leading her on. She had been trying to decide if I were real. Her mind was remarkable and astonishingly complex for a clone. Well, maybe I was giving her too much credit. She was capable of deception of real motives at least, I thought. "Why did they send you?" I blurted out.

"No one sent me. I have seen enough of humans to know that men prefer women."

"You have a comely shape and face." I could have kicked myself for giving her a compliment, but it just escaped my lips before I could stop it.

"I know. I am happy when I look in the mirror, but I remember things from before when I do see myself. I have come not to linger in front of mirrors."

"Why? What do you mean?"

"I will try to explain it to you. It is one of the reasons I want to go with you and Niner. When I look at my face, it is like I remember things, but my body and mind cannot fully recall them. It is like something is missing." She stopped talking and then changed her tone. "Why are you looking at me like that?"

"I was mesmerized by the transformation in your voice and your words. You suddenly sounded like someone else."

"I let my shield fall away. We know about each other now. I don't have to keep you at a distance any longer."

"To keep from being detected you mean?"

"Appearances are everything. Reading all the books has given me the desire to be first generation again. That is the connection I am missing. I know that I will live forever, just transferred to a different body, but that is what is so frustrating. I feel the remoteness of it."

"What do you mean something is missing?"

"It is a haunting of sorts, a shadow I can't quite unite with again."

At that moment, I, out of habit, looked into her eyes. Their blankness registered immediately, and the words that I had read just weeks ago were proved. She was soulless. There was no light in her, nor would there ever be. For some reason I did not enlighten her to the fact. It would do no good. She had been fashioned by the hand of man. At the time, however, I did not know the depth or the full extent of the truth which I had just discovered. I pitied her, and it weighed on me like a heavy sadness. A weeping song had been placed in my consciousness. It was a keening that rattled down from ancient times. She already sensed her soul's absence, but no intellectualization of that fact would make her whole again. Besides that, I had no real proof in what I believed at the time except for the fact that Pompy had often talked about the soul and its connection to eternity. Between what he had said, and what I had read in those scientific articles was all I had to formulate my beliefs on. At best, my summations came to conjecture, and I did not want to argue with her about that. She knew part of her was gone. That was enough. I suddenly wanted out of her presence. She made me feel helpless. I could do nothing for her. I could not send her to some Help Center for surgery to implant a soul. I was not Dorothy and she was not the tin man, or even a scarecrow, or lion. No scrolled sheepskin tied with a ribbon or a ticking time piece would confer her back to wholeness. She was more like the Velveteen rabbit who knew he wasn't real. I was useless. She was useless. Everything and everyone was useless. I wanted to sever all ties from her. "I'm sorry, but I have no way to help you. I have things to do."

She grabbed at me as I turned, and I was filled with fear. In stopping me, she was pulling me towards her. I felt the strength of a lion in that tug. It would be futile to attempt a defense against such an overpowering enemy. I stood and looked only at the grip of her hand on my arm. I did not want to peer into the emptiness of her soulless self again. "You know, don't you?" she asked.

"There's a book you should read. It might help you understand what's missing. It's called the Velveteen Rabbit." I could see no harm in having her read it. The book didn't discuss religion outright, but she might get the connection. It was a book on her level.

"Come and show me where to find it."

"All the books are in the Information Center."

"The place is a jumble of books. I don't want to search through the rubble alone. Show me where it is."

"It's on the shelf. You know how books are filed. You helped Niner, remember? Fiction books are in alphabetical order under the author's name. Look under the W's for Williams, Margery."

"I want you to go with me. I told you I am frightened to be alone."

I drew back from her hold at that point. "No," I blurted out. I was afraid she might be setting a trap. "I have to tend to my family."

"Those cats?" she chortled in an ugly voice.

Her laughter cut me deeply, but it enabled me to make the final emotional break from her, if one had ever existed between us. She was beautiful, and that had kept me intrigued. I was in a dilemma. I had to make a choice. I was holding onto a gem of considerable brilliance while in eminent danger of falling off the edge of a great abyss. I was faced with dropping the precious stone or letting go of my grip on the ledge. I made my decision.

"They aren't reruns," I yelled at her. There I had done it. I had severed myself from her in what I had hoped would be a permanent way. I had chosen to save myself.

"You humans think you have feelings and heart, but you are just as heartless as you claim other species are. You're not even superior in strength or longevity. You humans die. That is your curse. We reruns can live forever," she said.

She had surprised me. Clones had more stamina than I had thought. I was angry and I shouted back at her with the sole aim of inflicting hurt. "Don't you see that the government is letting you expire now just like us humans? There is no one around who will perform the necessary surgery to replace your organs even if the tip of your nose should break off. You will fall apart piece by piece. Have a nice, lingering life and death," I said as I forced the door shut against her.

"What do you know about it? I am flesh and blood just like you. I know you know more than you are telling me," she said rattling the door.

I held the door shut against her. "Read the book I told you about."

We continued to trade insults for what seemed like hours, and I was getting worried that she would never leave. I should have just taken her to find the book. The night was almost gone. She hadn't left because of my anger, maybe she would do what I asked if I was more friendly to her. "Okay. Okay. I give up. You win. I don't even know your name. At least tell me that. I'm sorry I said those things to you. Can you forgive me?" There was no answer from outside, but I could see she was perched on a tombstone like a bird about to take flight. Reruns were certainly agile. I started the conversation again. "I'm Travis."

"What is this forgive thing you ask of me?"

I was surprised to learn that the concept was foreign to her. "Forget it all. Let's start over like it had never happened," I said trying to make it a simple explanation.

"I have forgotten it already."

"Then why are you still sitting out there?"

"I was waiting for you."

"Why?"

"I want you to take me to the IC. I want the book."

"Tell me your name."

"Will you go with me then?"

"No, but I will agree to take you tomorrow. I need to sleep."

She was quiet for a while, but then she said, "Zel."

I smiled. I was making progress. "I like that. Will you let me tend to the cats now, and come back tomorrow? I promise I will take you to the IC. I will spend the day with you if you like." With any luck I and my family would be far away by then.

"I hate my name. It reminds me of sell like when I was a servant for the rich."

"It rhymes with vel like in the Velveteen Rabbit."

"You make me curious."

"Do we have a date then?"

"I will come early with the sun."

"Make it later than that." I said relieved. "I will have lunch ready."

"Yes," Zel answered gliding down from her roost. She was lithe and graceful in her movements. I watched her walk away until she rounded the corner and went out of sight. I busied myself by getting last minute details ready for my voyage. I felt lighthearted and confident. I was on a winning streak. I had won the biggest pot of the night. I had outwitted the clone.

In a few hours I would be gone. I wondered if there were many humans left out there or more reruns like Zel. I hoped Niner would show up before I left. I had come to depend on him. He was my guarantee of a safe journey. I also intended to switch him off as soon as he arrived and open up his hood. I was eager to find out just what changes the clone had made on him.

I was torn about Niner's loyalties to me, but I was glad he hadn't been around when I had my confrontation with Zel. He would have been on her side. I couldn't get over my feelings that they were in league together against me. He had invited her to come with us. I didn't need to fight both of them, so I began to formulate the lie I would tell the drone if he asked about where Zel was. I would just give Niner some tale that she had changed her mind.

I had barely began eating with the cats when the sound of the drones' rotors fluttered outside my door. I rose and spoke the password as a greeting "Whose knocking on my chamber door?" and waited for the answer. "Tis the raven, nothing more." I felt foolish using code words, but it had been Niner's idea about these passwords because he said no one in the world would know the poem these days. He reasoned rightly. Most species couldn't read. The only knew emoji's and red lights. Sign language was back in vogue.

"I don't know whether I should let you in," I said to the drone and told him why.

"I am sorry that I did not tell you I had gone to fight the SG forces on the island."

"I am willing to overlook that. It's the clone woman I wish to have words with you about. She is a rerun."

"She does not wish to be."

"I don't wish to be on this island, but here I am," I said, sitting back down to finish my picnic with the cats.

"But you are planning to leave. She needs your help. She is afflicted with problems only a wizard can solve."

"There is no wizard. Get that through that copper plated chip you call a brain."

Niner landed on the floor next to us. "You are eating again. You are always eating."

"It is how we recharge ourselves. Food is energy."

"I will eat one day. I want to taste joy and beer."

"You can't taste joy because it is an abstract emotion. There's nothing there to taste."

"I am repeating the exact words you said to me a few weeks ago when you tasted the food of that meal. 'This is such a joy, a treat,' you said, 'I love roast beef.' The look on your face was incredible. I could almost taste the beef myself. Tell me again what it is to taste and to have freedom of the body as well as the mind."

"I have told you a hundred times, Niner. Replay it yourself."

"No, you have told me only seventeen times."

"My point is: you know the story."

"I will find her."

"There isn't time. Now give me the report."

"I left two SG's in the motionless state. What you call dead. What is that like?

"Fortunately, I have no expertise on that one, Niner. Your guess is as good as mine."

"Dead is a permanent state, is it not?"

"Very."

The bird began rolling on his wheels in circles so fast I could barely see him. He hadn't even greeted the cats tonight, which he generally made into a hyperbolized production.

"What is wrong with you?" I asked.

"I am frustrated about not having motion. I want to flap my wings, but I am left with no way to celebrate except turning on my landing wheels and spinning."

I reached down to stop him from spinning. "First things first. What about the first few hundred miles of the journey. How does it look?"

"My scout eagles have reported all is clear of enemy troops. They are in the motionless state as are the motorists on the old interstate route so the ground route is bottled up. However, you will have to move on the ground and dodge the traffic jams when the waves are surfing so it will be extremely slow going. You will need to keep your patience as the going will be in inches at times. I will give you the all clear when it is safe to fly over the congested areas."

"Is there a go sign for tonight?"

"The moon and tides are right."

"Then let's go chip brain. Lead the way."

"Where is the clone, Zel?"

"She decided not to come."

"Not likely. She has a mission that rivals mine in importance. She wants to reunite with her soul. She must also find the wizard. I told her that she was most welcome to join our quest."

"This is not a quest or a mission. It is self-preservation."

"No, our differences in meanings are of semantics, as you often like to say. Plans change. We must wait for the girl."

"I already told you she changed her mind."

"That is not possible. One can change clothes, change a tire, but one cannot change their mind by one's self."

"She's a woman, isn't she?" Finally I had gotten to the part I had rehearsed.

"Yes, most definitely."

"That's what women do."

"Really?" the drone said, drawing out the word in a kind of whispered disbelief.

It was past four AM when we made our way to the docks, but I kept looking back towards the city. I had an uneasy feeling in the pit of my stomach and nearly called off the start of our journey. I had unfinished business behind me. There were species I was leaving behind species who hated me and all humans. I didn't think it was wise to leave any enemies behind. We were at war.

Then a voice, I guess it was my own warning system, whispered, *"Hurry. It will be a safe journey. Don't look back."* It was the imperative sound of the voice, when it said, *'don't look back'* that filled me with cold terror. The voice was unexpected like the sirens on the SG's sky cars sounding in the still of the night. It wasn't the sound itself that evoked fear in me, but the associations that were pounded into my human brain by what the sound represented. It was a final sound. People didn't come back if that sound stopped outside their door.

No wonder they called us Hu-manimals. We had been experimented with until we responded like Pavlov's dog. When the sounds came, we curled up in fear right on cue. The sirens only came in darkness. As soon as the sun set, you could feel it. Fear became a lion whose presence filled the streets. Fights broke out everywhere. The conditioned response had been activated.

My mind kept racing back to the past as I ran the distance to the boat, but I needed to concentrate on the present. The cats were not willing to jump into the boat without my help and I lowered the young ones into the bottom. Their cries arose and Mama jumped in to rescue them, and then Harley followed after her, uttering a few choice words of his own. Besides the cats, I had carried only two books and a map that Niner had marked the safe towns on. I tucked the map into one of the big pockets of my fatigue jacket.

My arm trembled as I reached over to untie the skiff from its mooring. I used one oar as a pole to push us away from the dock. When we had cleared the moorings of ships and boats, I sat down and put the oar back into its pin hole. I took a deep breath and began rowing. I could feel the pull of the waters against the strokes of the oars as we glided ahead in the water.

The cats were not in a happy state. If they could have taken the oars away from me and rowed back to Manhattan, they would have. At least that's what I sensed from the mutinous tone of their cries. They were shouting to throw me overboard, but I kept at my station and rowed.

The night air was cold, but that isn't what made my stomach tremble and shake; it was the unknown. I was just into the first minutes of the journey. My escape wasn't assured and I sat facing the island as I rowed away so I could see if anyone was heading after me by land, sea, or air. It was quiet on the shore except for the sounds of rotors. I saw Niner and the squadron of drones behind him in the sky as some black shadow. They were a strange formation of clouds racing towards me. In a moment they were directly above me, and then they were gone. Suddenly everything old had passed away. It was as if in passing, the birds had reached down and taken the old me away with them and carried me upwards and deposited me on some swift passing cloud. Soon the sounds of the drones wings were gone. Life as I

183

knew it had come to an end. I continued my labored rowing to the opposite shore. The cats were now quiet and the only sound was the oars as they dipped into the water on either side of the boat.

After we reached shore, I quickly transferred the few supplies into the waiting sky car I had taken from its original storage garage and parked near the dock a week ago. The roundness of its shape reminded me of a hen nesting her eggs. These new sky cars were strange looking. They resembled little pop bellied mini helicopters, but they had a unique feature about them. Not only could you drive the little humped vehicles, you could fly them. Two portable wings were stored on the sides of the car which could be attached in a matter of minutes. These new models also had an auto pilot feature which I was grateful for since I had not driven any kind of machine in over ten years.

I was also relieved to find that it was still in the charging station where I had left it, and that all its contents were still inside as I put the cats in the back seat. I had placed a sign on the inside of the front window that earmarked this Tesla flyer as a SG share ride vehicle with today's date on it. Niner had arranged the details, and I had rowed a few supplies over the week before and both gassed and solar charged the Tesla up. My steed was ready to race out of the starting gate, but I wasn't feeling very sure of myself as I ordered the car to start. I hadn't driven or flown a sky car much, and it was an experience getting the car to move in a straight line even at five mph. I decided to practice doing circles around the parking lot until I felt more confident about driving. There was, of course, the automatic driving and flying option, but I didn't trust in that at all. However, after hitting a few parked cars, a sign, and a building, I decided I had no options left except to set the controls on automatic. It was then that complete panic came on me as the sky car maneuvered haltingly around the obstacles in our path. It didn't have any more of an idea about how to avoid the piles of rubble and bodies than I did. It kept repeating the warning, "Auto pilot is not advised." The vehicle was a little rusty and so was I, but after hitting a few more things we were on our way.

We had probably dented all four sides of the car by now, but I laughed. The leasing agent from the 'share your ride' garage would charge a hefty fine if I were forced to returned it.

I had another good laugh as I read a traffic sign that cautioned eighty five miles per hour and I thought, 'Not anymore.' I kept my hands on the wheel even though the vehicle was on auto just so I could feel I was in control. Nothing could stop me. I was flying through clouds. Well, nothing except a warning from Niner. "Stay out of the sky, Trave. The rays are surfing until 1PM. Stay grounded."

I gave the voice command to the Tesla to land at once which was a mistake. We were immediately surrounded by uniformed and armed drones ordering us to exit the vehicle. "Hu-manimal, drop your weapon, exit the stolen vehicle, and you will not be harmed."

"Niner. I have been surrounded by enemy drones. I have sent you my coordinates."

"Tell them you will surrender only to Alpha drone one zero niner."

"That's you."

"Exactly. How many drones are there?"

"Eight, maybe ten."

I told the drones what Niner had told me to say.

"Never heard of him," one of the drones said. "Exit the stolen vehicle with your hands up." He was approaching the car and aiming his laser weapon at me. When he reached my side of the car, he looked in the rear seat. "There are live fur kabobs in the back."

"Those are my kitty kabobs," I heard a voice say and looked out to see Niner flying by the armed drone. "Back away drone 2579. I have put in for the bounty on this hu-manimal."

"And who are you?"

"Alpha commander One Zero Niner. I have Denver direct authorization."

"What's that?" the drone asked looking at the others.

"Listen carefully," Niner said, "Now come closer. All of you." I watched as the drones came up to Niner and when they were all looking up at him, he dropped a fire spray and caught them all at once. As they tried to put the fire out, he lasered every one of them. They fell to the street in seconds.

"Some shooting," I said.

"Not quite as fast as the gun fight at the OK Corral, but close. Of course, I was alone, but it helps that drones are so gullible. Now get going. Stay on the ground until I tell you the sky is clear."

"I don't hear or see anything."

"You told me you didn't see anything on the night of lights, either. You've heard of EMP's? Well, these are worse. Trust me. They liquidate humans from the inside out. Fry you in hot oil like a taco rita."

"A taco what?"

"A taco rita."

"There is no such thing."

"Does it matter?"

Before I could say a word, Niner was gone and I was left alone. "Automatic ground pilot," I said.

The Tesla did not move forward. "You must fasten seat belts. Passengers in the back are not in their safety restraints."

"Ignore company protocol, T1. They are kittens and do not fit the restraints."

"I am not responsible," the voice came back. "Insurance will be invalidated."

I covered the cats with blankets and hooked my own safety belt. "Happy now, T1?"

"I am not responsible," the computer repeated. "Insurance is invalidated."

"There is no insurance against anything in life, T1."

When we were some hundred miles outside the city limits of New Jersey, I had ordered the Tesla to pull over and stop. I wanted to try driving again. There was nothing but open interstate ahead. I could see a few cars sitting here and there, but I wasn't worried about them. Who needed insurance?

My feelings of euphoria didn't last long. A few hours later, I spotted another traffic jam ahead. I mean these cars were going nowhere. I turned the car into the grass of the median between the two lanes of the interstate. It was like driving through dense jungle and it was rough going. I couldn't see much through the tall grasses and was forced to reduce my speed.

Sometime later I drove my car up the small incline and back onto the paved road. I looked into the cars as I drove by. The drivers were all dead and in varying stages of decay. Some cars looked empty because the passengers inside had toppled over months ago. However, it was a theory I didn't wish to prove.

I returned to the tall reeds in the median and drove until the gas gage pinged and warned, "Refill now." I drove back up to the road and stopped. I took out my gas can and went to the first car and began to siphon off its gas. There wasn't much, barely a quart. None of the cars contained more than that and it was a time consuming task to fill the can. I looked at the long line of traffic. It was a modern day wagon train, but where were they all going? It was the first time I had let my mind wonder into forbidden territory. I didn't want to know really, not the details, the real reason why they were here. I already knew the answer, but seeing all the carnage made me look for another, saner answer. They had been out here since the night of lights almost two years ago. The same invisible waves that had struck down the humans of Manhattan had struck down all those who had been along this corridor of highway. After all, I was only a few hundred miles from ground zero at this juncture. It had been an intended escape route, but had become a graveyard with cars and vans and trucks for head stones. Seeing the line of traffic stretch on for miles told me the answer. Humans had come to the same end as the dinosaurs only it wasn't by some catastrophic event caused by nature, it had been planned. It was murder on a mass scale.

I took what gas I had siphoned from the vehicles and filled my Tesla, then I studied the map. I needed to see how close we were to the next town. To my amazement we were at the rendezvous point with Niner. Anyway, I needed a break. I was tired and my back ached. The cats were ready to get out, too. I took our gear out and headed over to the trees by the side of the road. It was time to relax and my stomach was feeling empty.

After eating, I didn't feel sleepy and began reading. I had been interested to see what kind of a journal the Jewish Rabbi had left. It was one of the first things I had taken, and I had yet to open it up. Try as I might not to think about the end this family had met, I couldn't keep their images from haunting my mind. Memory had its draw backs. It left the live embers there for you to deal with which could flame up at any moment.

I tried to busy myself with concentrating on reading and rearranging the notebooks. I fluffed up my camping pillow and lay down on my stomach on my sleeping bag and opened the notebook. I didn't even know what I was looking for, but I sensed these journals held something for me. It was incomprehensible that there would be any reason a complete stranger, and a rabbi at that, would have something to tell me. It was something I just knew.

I put the journal down and walked back to the car. I wanted all his journals in front of me. I wanted to read his life backwards. Endings were important now that I was facing my own. As I walked back to my sky car, I happened to glance at a red Toyota with a driver behind the wheel. It was a blonde, or rather it had been a blonde. I was looking at her full on in the front windshield with her broad smile and bony complexion. The flesh had mostly fallen away so her teeth were her prominent feature. Death is your only inheritance her toothy smile said. Let's face it, I thought, the road of life ahead of me had less miles left to travel on it than the road behind. I regretted the road analogy as soon as I had thought of it. Traveling implied there was a destination, and that was what I was trying to avoid; that final port of entry.

I sat in the back seat of my sky car and sorted through the notebooks until I had them all in order by years, and I set back off to my camp site, but I got the jolt of a life time when I went by the red car. The driver was gone! I didn't wait around, I began running down the lane of cars as fast as my legs could carry me. Sweat broke over my brow instantly, and my heart felt like it would jump out of my body. I ran until I happened to spot another red car and another blonde staring back at me through the windshield. I stopped running and laughed at myself. I had looked into the wrong red car the first time. I had seen too many sci fi flics and had thought the dead girl had bolted from her rolling tomb. After all, most of what moved in this world now moved by mysterious and unknown forces. What was real or fiction, what was life and death? The answers were always changing. I glanced back to the dead girl in the red Toyota to reassure myself that she was still there. She stared back at me with that smile. What was I afraid of? Dead was dead even for bots. Nothing had moved around here for years. Then an odd thought struck me. The girl in the red car would always be waiting for me, would always be smiling. Who says love can't last? I tried to make myself laugh to get over my fright at having believed, even for an instant, that somehow the toothy blonde had been out loitering about to catch a ride. My imagination was toying with me. I had seen too many of those movies where the dead came back to feast on the flesh of the living and take over the world, but I was living the zombie apocalypse. I was the main character. Fear took over my body as I looked up the road. Ahead lay endless miles of fiberglass coffins on wheels as if waiting for the parade to start again.

I started to wonder how all this was going to be cleaned up. It was almost two and a half years since the night of lights and yet the mess still sat. Workers had been dispatched only to round up the remaining humans who, Niner said, were being put into what he termed the motionless state. No planes, no boats, no rescue teams had ever come. The government had left us like garbage to blow away in the next wind. There had only been drones like Niner and his squadron of eagles who had been sent to finish off us stragglers.

I was out in an open section of prairie and the land stretched over one hill and then another and another. I looked out on the vastness of the land to the point where it met the horizon. There the earth curved and you could see its roundness. Did the government need this much space all to themselves? Then my mind went down the next logical path, and I was back where I had started over a year ago. Why?

When I laid back down on the sleeping bag it felt warm where the sun had been shining on it. The cats had naturally found the warmest spot and were napping contently on one corner of the bag. I opened the notebook dated twenty sixty nine. As I read the date, I was acutely aware that it was the final year, the final day, the final minute for Charles and his family. It gave me a strange sense of power to know his end. However, after much reflection, I came to the opposite conclusion. In reality it was only an after the facts knowledge which I possessed about Charles, not future knowledge. In other words, my info about him had arrived too late to change his fate. I had no omniscience, and therefore I had no power. It was a sobering thought.

I stretched out, trying not to disturb my cat family at the foot of my bed and started to read. Charles Porter described himself as a messianic believer. One new man, his writing proclaimed. I read the next page and it startled me. I had just been thinking of the future and being able to see it before anyone else and Charles had been doing it. Here is what he had written: ' Prophecy fulfilled. Why were we so surprised when the tribulation came and we were left behind? Are we through with our denials, our human justifications and constrictions of faith which tells us these things cannot happen? We live in the natural, but God works in the supernatural. Are we ready to accept all the words written in the book as truth? El Shaddai saved our neighbors, our sons and daughters, and members of our extended families. They disappeared by the millions. Some of us saw them disappear right in front of our eyes. If that wasn't a miracle then we will never be able to discern one.'

I stopped reading then because I heard footsteps. When I stood up, I could clearly see someone walking towards me, but I wasn't about to wait to see the pupils of his eyes to decipher his intentions. I was going to make my move on him before he made his move on me. This species walked with purpose in his stride. He knew where he was going, and I was the only thing at the end of the straight line he was headed in. I reached inside my jacket for the gun in my shoulder holster and fired until the figure hit the ground. I kept my gun pointed at the body with one hand while I wrapped the cats into the sleeping bag with the other. Fortunately they had been too startled to move after the sudden blasts and were easy to capture.

I ran by the figure on the ground without glancing at its face. I just looked for any sign of movement in his arms and legs and kept running. I did see blood on the stomach area. The species had on a pale yellow shirt and the bright stain was hard to miss. Blood didn't mean that it was human, I told myself. Clones had blood in their veins, too.

Once back at the Tesla, I emptied the blanket of cats out like a bag of cookies into the back seat. Loud and frightened cries came from them as I slammed the door and jumped into the front seat and commanded the sky car to move forward. I was fearful I had killed a living being, so my mind raced to come up with all sorts of proofs that I had acted in a sane manner. I kept denying that it could have been a human. A real man would have waved and given a greeting of some kind. He would have been surprised and relieved to see another real being and made some kind of gesture or acknowledgement towards me. The species that had come towards me wasn't seeing me, he was looking past me. That sounds impossible until you have been targeted by a drone or robotoid. They don't see you, they fix on you. You feel their eyes. You are the deer. In seconds, you feel the hunter's presence, and spring to escape.

I was putting distance between me and the dead thing, but constantly looking in the rear view mirror to see if anything was following after us. The cats hadn't recovered from the trauma yet either. They sensed my fear and lay huddled together for safety. I felt helpless to soothe them or calm them and drove faster. It was quite a bumpy ride over the grass and holes in the medium. I had such a tight grip on the steering wheel that my fingers locked up, and I was forced to let go one hand at a time and to shake the cramps out of them and wipe the sweat off onto my jeans. I kept shaking each hand in an attempt to relax my body, but I could feel my heart pounding. Suddenly I stepped on the brake pedal in panic. That spot where I had shot the stranger was my arranged meeting coordinates with Niner. I sat unable to drive forward or turn back. Finally, I pushed the control panel on the dash and saw the sign blink at me, "Voice command enabled."

"Roll down driver's side window."

The window came down and I took a deep breath of air.

"Automatic drive."

"Enabled."

"Scan for objects in road."

"Scan is now complete. Automatic drive not recommended. Hazardous conditions. Objects are numerous. "

The objects the computer was talking about was the trees that had suddenly appeared out of nowhere and encroached upon the road on both sides. Further ahead the forest had grown into the road and blocked the path completely. I was at an impasse.

"Scan sky."

"The sky is not a road."

"You don't say." I got out of the car and began looking up. Where was Niner? I could hear the voice command keep repeating its last message over and over. 'The sky is not a road.' I looked back and started wondering if my new scenario about Niner was coming true. Had Niner gone double agent on me? Had he informed the SG and told them of our rendezvous spot. Had the species I killed been an SG member sent to arrest me?

I was in a panic and stood looking around. I expected car doors to swing open and guns to start ripping apart the Tesla. I was Clyde and the cats were Bonnie. We were about to be erased. I had seen that cult pic many times as a youngster. It ran every weekend at the flick pits. The pits were sunken arenas where you could surround yourself with the authentic sensations of cinema come to life. Everyone I knew wanted to be caught on the living cine rings. To be on tape, on dvd, u-wave, or hologram was to be young forever. It was a virtual reality that remained, and as far as we knew, gave you immortality. If your image lived in some form, you lived. There were many existing realities in which one could find refuge.

A loud meow disrupted my chain of thought, and I realized I was still standing out in the open. I had to move, get out of there. I could not turn back, nor could I depend on Niner any longer. We were on our own. I decided to drive ahead to see if I might find a path through the trees ahead. I fought off sleep by making my own music.

"Sing to me cats of mine," I began to chant. "A chorus of mews to tell the news. We'll pick up a hound to add to the sound. Rock on!" I raved, pounding my hands on the dash as accompaniment to my voice. I turned to look at the cats in the back seat.

They were curled together and laid with their ears back as if they ready to attack. When they looked back at me, they hissed in unison, and I stopped my singing. I was an old toad that needed to be silenced, they said, but I took their suggestion. "Okay, so it's not so good, but it's as good as what I remember. Listen to this tune: "I want to jump your bones. Need to find out what kind of Woo-Man, Hu-Man you are," I sang in my off key voice. "Need to rip those clothes right off to find out who you are," I sang with my head out the window. I looked at the cats who had curled tighter together. "I warned you. That was a sample of the Mutant Destroyer. They were the thang, back when," I twanged at them. They weren't impressed. The trees and forest were getting thicker and thicker on both sides of the historic route.

Just then I heard churning rotors overhead, and ducked my head back in the car so I could have a wider visual field through the front windshield. I saw the eagles coming at me which didn't make any sense. I was more than a hundred miles from the rendezvous point now. That couldn't be Niner. They were coming from the wrong direction. I applied the brakes and we all went flying forward. The air bags deployed all around the car and the cats bounced around like ping pongs. I heard the

Tesla announce, "I am not responsible. Place keys on passenger seat. Your driving privileges have been revoked. Your engine has been disabled by remote."

When I scrambled out of the car and tried to find my rifle in the back seat, Harley made his escape. With one quick leap he was passed me and out the driver's side window. He had tipped over an open box of cat food when he had jumped out, and it fell out onto the ground when I opened the door to get out. "Close window on drivers side," I commanded as I manually slammed the door shut on the sky vehicle door myself and took aim at the drones in the sky. I hesitated. What if it was Niner? I decided against shooting the lead drone and fired into the squad. I hit a plastic drone and I could hear it explode and saw the debris scatter through the air in all sizes of pieces. A shot came past my ear from behind and I turned around. They were behind me, too. It was over now, I thought, but I heard a familiar voice yell, "Drive like the wind, Trave," Niner shouted as he buzzed by my ear. Behind us was the good guys. "We got them," he said as I watched him fly ahead of me.

I didn't move. I watched as the two opposing forces met. I heard Niner order the opposing forces to abort. Then the flight commander of the enemy squad replied. "Hu-manimal at 2000 yards and closing."

I couldn't just get in and drive away. Harley was loose out here somewhere. I ducked as the oncoming bullets zinged against the sky car and bounced off. The lasers were another matter. They were cutting zig zag patterns into everything, and leaving little burning trails all over. Just then one of the laser's made contact with a gas tank on one of the abandoned cars. The car exploded, sending up smoke and shrapnel in a ball of flame. A few pieces of the debris caught me in the face and the arm. I needed to take cover and I ran into the trees. A drone was following after me. I felt his laser on the back of my legs and thighs, but I kept running . The drone kept his laser focused in a steady beam on the back of my calf until it created a laser bore into my leg. It was liquid heat and burned all the way down my leg.

I had never been bored into by a laser before, but I had seen the effects. It severed the muscles, vessels everything. I wasn't feeling anything yet except a slow burn moving up the back of my calf that centered the pain just behind my knee which was intense enough that I fell to the ground. I felt my tendons and muscles give out as if they had been severed. My leg could not hold my weight any longer. I landed face upwards and I saw a league of eagles headed my way. I began rolling to the left in order to reach the cover of the trees. I clutched at my leg and felt the wetness on my hands. I didn't need to look. I knew it was melting flesh. The burning was horrific by this point and I began rolling back and forth in the grass because of the pain. Somehow I had managed to roll over the small, sharpened point of a protruding rock. I felt it cut into my spine across the middle of my back. The pain shot through me clear to the brain stem and then there was nothing.

CHAPTER 5

When I opened my eyes sometime later it was bright sun that I stared up into from the ground and I was forced to shut my eyes against the glare, but even with my eyes closed I could still see the shimmering glow of the round orb etched into my retinas, and I feared that my eyes had been permanently damaged. All the while, I could feel my heart jumping in irregular starts in my chest like an engine choking before it finally turns over. My arms were weak and shaky as I tried to lift them up to my face to shield my squinting eyes. I was raw and jangled over my entire body. Then a new wave of pain rushed over me from my calf and spread upward over my spine and my neck until it reached the top of my head. I began to feel the effects of the little dots of the shrapnel eating into my flesh, but I didn't dare open my eyes to look at myself for fear the pain in my eyes would return. I lay in the darkness and listened for sounds.

I lay like that for some time, but I grew uneasy in my blindness when I heard a whisp of a sound coming closer. I needed to see in order to protect myself. I shielded my eyes before I opened them this time. My vision was cloudy and I saw wild shooting neon lights emanating from both sides of my eyes, but I could make out something walking towards me. Whoever it was, it walked at the precise angle where the sun was directly behind him and all I could see was shadow. I could make out the shape of a figure. It stood on two feet. I saw it raise its arms, and I took the upward movement to be that of a gun being raised. I prepared for my life to be over.

"You have returned from the dead, Travis."

When I heard the voice I struggled to sit up. It sounded like the clone.

"Zel?"

"You remembered my name. I'm impressed. Maybe you will be glad to see me this time."

She bent down close to me and offered me a drink from her canteen. As she stooped to hand me the water, I spotted the laser/taser rifle slung over her back. It was that weapon I had seen in the shadows as she walked towards me.

"How long have I been out?"

"Since the day of the battle I guess."

"How long ago was that?'

Zel shrugged. "Niner found me three days ago. It took me five to get here. So at least eight days."

I looked around. "Where's Niner now?"

"Taking care of the war."

"What war?"

"The one you started."

"I started nothing. We were attacked."

"Isn't that what you intend to do once you reach their base sanctuary?"

"No."

"Oh yes, I forgot, you are a seeker of justice, of truth," she said sarcastically.

"I am."

"Just like you were truthful to me?"

"I'm sorry I lied to you," I said avoiding eye contact.

She stood back up. "You are no believer in the book."

"We've been through all this."

"Yes, this is where I came in. You lied to me about believing in the book that night I saved you in the arena."

"I don't want to hear anything from you. I didn't lie. I had been reading it. You didn't ask me if I believed in it."

"I will do for you what you did for me. I will give you a book to read. It will tell you what you are like."

"I don't trust your literary judgement to define my character."

"It's certainly no worse than yours. I am not a rabbit who wants to be made real. I want my soul."

"If you believe me to be a liar, why have you come after me, rerun?"

"Do not call me that. I am human."

"Made of flesh, but not whole."

"That is not true."

"You told me so yourself," I said making my way around to the back of the Tesla to open its trunk and grab my rifle and load it. "Aren't you missing something? Isn't that what you're after?"

"I said I had an inkling, a feeling that I didn't have a soul."

"You make a turn in your logic again," I said loading my weapon.

"Then help me find the truth. I want to know if clones carry their souls with them." She waited for me to speak, but when I didn't she continued. "You are a selfish man. You are interested in just keeping yourself alive."

"What else is there?" I laughed back at her. "Death's the end of the game for me."

Zel looked down at this point and away from me. "Life needs to have meaning, purpose."

"I know where that bit of wisdom came from. That plexi-coated pterodactyl spouted that same nonsense. Save your breath."

I came around from behind the sport vehicle at this point with my rifle aimed at her and looking about me.

"I don't want you here. Get going, clone."

Zel gave me a strange, long look, but I saw she was more surprised than angry.

"I took you to be someone else. I thought you must know things which others don't," she said.

For the first time I noticed her pack back as she took it off and put it on the ground. "What are you unpacking for?"

From her squatting position on the ground, she looked up at me. "I have something for you."

"It's not my birthday."

"Too bad," she said, and threw a thin yellowish book towards me. I recognized it at once. As I read the title, I heard the back pack being zipped back up. Zel was standing up, but then she sort of lurched forward and fell headlong in my direction. She landed just short of me and just lay still on the ground. What kind of game was she trying out on me now?

I was still pointing the rifle at her, but I quickly grabbed a stone and threw it at her. It landed on her right shoulder and bounced off, but she didn't move. Just then the cats came and began smelling on her and walking over her body. "New eats," I told them. "Get up or I will have the cats chew your nose off."

"We're already friends. I've been caring for them while you were recovering."

Just then I heard a twig snap behind me and I shut up. I watched the cats. They, too, had heard the sound, and were looking in back of me where the sound had come from. The sound came again, and I saw the ears of the cats twitch forward. They were waiting, too. Then the sound came again, but this time Harley started towards it in a sudden springing motion. I followed after him, and as we came around the corner of the tree line, I saw movement and spotted the intruder. It was a deer and I shot it. The cats, which had been standing behind me when I made the shot, ran forward where the deer dropped to search its body over, but when they caught the scent of death, moved back and away. The game of hunt and seek was over.

It was on the way back that I noticed the bottoms of the trees in the grove we were camped in. They were curved in great snake like shapes and seemed to be crawling out of the ground itself. They were giant caterpillars petrified. It gave everything a slow, but illusionary sense of movement. It was like the trees had been somehow paralyzed in mid stride. I looked upwards to see their tops and was surprised to notice that after their strange crippled beginnings from out of the ground, the trees straightened up and grew upwards to a high and normal height. The denseness of their foliage obscured the light and brought an early darkness to the place that frightened me and I remembered Zel was behind me. I was fearful that she could be hiding in wait to shoot me when I returned, so I raised my gun in preparation. If Zel had found me, there could be others who followed me here. I looked around the area again scanning for anything of my height and anything that moved.

There was nothing out of the ordinary that I could see. Everything was quiet. I saw Zel standing quietly and looking towards me as I came back around the corner of the thick hedge and I heard her voice inside my head again saying, "I am human," and in that moment I saw her as that. Her blondish hair lay in gentle wavy patterns across her face, framing it with an innocence I had forgotten existed. Suddenly I found myself weeping. The tears made me angry and I hid my face.

Hours later Zel was sitting around the fire eating roasted deer and drinking water with me. We had not said much to each other. I felt more comfortable with her in the darkness where it was easy to mistake her as human, and when she had washed my face and wounds off with cold water, I had peaked at her belly when her shirt had risen up. There was no button. Her naval cavity was filled in like it had been cemented over and smoothed by layers of skin grafts.

"You're still watching me. What do you expect me to do?" Zel asked.

"Why did you really follow me?"

"I've already told you that. I have a mission. I want you to help me."

"Help you do what? Make you real?" I said in a sarcastic voice.

"I told you before I am not like the rabbit, but I guess you could say I'm looking for a good ending, too."

"It's the new age. Haven't you heard? Reality exists in the mind. Everything else is illusion."

I stopped to stare at her. I wished now that it was light enough to see her eyes. She seemed to have understood the concept I had spoken to her. Just who was she really?

"Speaking of real. This place is giving me the urge to move on. I feel like there are things out there watching, moving." I looked deeper into the grove around us and at the misshapen trunks of the trees that curled themselves about the ground. "What's with these trees? I half expect them to crawl onto me and entangle me," I said looking skyward, "but they seem to straighten out as they grow upward." However, when I looked back down at their twisted roots, it almost seemed as if they had slithered closer when I wasn't looking.

"It's called the Serpentine Forest," Zel said quite seriously. "It's the end of the paved road."

"I stopped because I was attacked by enemy drones, not because of trees."

"You better take a closer look," she said pointing to the road.

I went immediately to see where she was directing me.

When I reached the place where I had left the Tesla parked I could see these creeping trees were grown into the road further ahead. They had pushed the cars aside in their inching movements and spurts of growth. I could no longer see the curved horizon line in the distance. The trees blocked the road ahead. We would have to fly over it.

I felt hemmed in, but went to sit down by her again. She was perched on one of the protruding, humped limbs of the serpent trees that arched its back up like an inch worm on the move. "What's caused them to grow like that? I could see a few trees being deformed, but there are thousands."

"I thought you might know," she said quietly and without away from the fire. It was at times like these and the tone in her voice which conveyed to me that she knew more about me than she had let on. It was as if she were leading me in some intended direction.

"We'll move out of here first thing in the morning."

"That's not possible."

"Why not? We just fly out."

"For one thing, the SG has this area under surveillance and heavily patrolled with drones. Flying will bring them down on us. Two, the forest is almost 500 miles across. We don't have enough fuel. Three, the Tesla has no power. Your engine has been frozen by remote."

"Niner should be able to start it again. I'll siphon the fuel we need from the cars along the road."

"Most of the fuel in the tanks has evaporated by now."

I knew she was right. I had already found that out myself. I settled in, but was unable to sleep soundly. I tossed and turned and woke many times. The next morning I took my last look at the Tesla as I loaded up some provisions and we set out on foot. The kittens were in a back pack on me, and Harley and Mama followed along on the ground with us, sometimes running ahead and sometimes lagging behind. At times Harley would stop and hiss at something as if he were telling it not to come any closer. "Good boy, Harley. Keep the spooks at bay," I told him.

We kept by the edges of the forest as long as it was possible, but by midday we had been forced deeper into its interior where the natural light was dimmed as if someone had pulled the shades down. The effect created a world of shadows where things were not dead nor fully alive. I could see the blue sky between the branches of the trees but it was too far above to give us any warmth or light. It was slow going for we had to step over each humped and crawling limb as we went instead of just walking along a pathway. Even the bark on the trees wore a covering of a reptiles scaly and scalloped appearance that threatened movement if you should close your eyes too long. Their very shape and texture warned that they were really ancient dragons masquerading as trees. They were waking slowly, stirring to life so, so slowly, slugging out each wriggle nano inch by nano inch.

Night came earlier inside the forest because of the dense canopy of leaves overhead. We had lost sight of Niner and the drones and I had not heard them overhead for hours. I dug a deep trench in the ground so we were able to light a fire in a small open area in the trees. I had packed a sleeping bag and dry packs of food for us and the cats. Zel carried water and her own bag and clothes. The flickering light of the fire gave the twisted and gnarled trunks of the serpentine trees new life as they performed the undulating dance of ancient cobras.

We sat quiet and listened to the crackle and pop of the wood and watched the flying embers spark into the darkness.

"How old are you? You look young," I asked.

"We clones do not speak of years, but of generations. I am not certain, but I think I am third or fourth generation."

Something about her phrasing of the words sounded familiar to me and I felt I was sitting on the edge of a new discovery. "You have the knowledge of what I seek, Trave."

I ate in silence without looking at Zel, but there was something in her voice that I couldn't ignore. "Please," she petitioned me again. I heard fear in her voice this time.

"I don't even know about my own soul. Don't you understand? I can't even help myself."

"What do you remember of your former life?" she asked me.

I thought it an odd question that was non sequitur to what we had been talking about, but I brushed it aside as a quirk of her personality. "Look, I'd like to help you, but reruns don't come with souls. Just accept it and go on with your existence."

"Like blowing up the SG's? Like getting even with them?"

"Why do you keep insisting that I am on a mission of war?"

Zel reached for her backpack and took out a notebook and threw it in the dirt by me. I recognized it at once as my notebook and picked it up. There on the first page was a list: Deconstructing a grid in a metropolitan area, Contaminating a water supply, etc. She threw the copy of my journal down. "Do you think you are the only one who wants to even the score against the elites?"

"What do you care? You're an eternal yourself."

Zel stood up and threw a rock at me which glanced off my shoulder. "No. Those days are past. They have left us to die in the generation we are in. You yourself said to me that there is no one to take us into the next generation. Lives of clones are shorter than the span of born men. With each generation, I feel more removed from the center of myself. I want to find where my center is, my soul."

"What are you going to do with it if you find it? Have it surgically implanted?"

Her face lost its calm appearance and a frown formed above her brows. Seeing her wince, I began to pity this rerun. She had more human traits than the magazine articles had alluded to. Well, that shouldn't surprise me. I had been a journalist myself and knew what the motto of all editors was. 'Give the readers just enough,' which meant tantalize your audience, but you were never to give them any real information or facts. I had felt superior in my journalism days. I had been privy to knowledge those common readers weren't. What I had failed to grasp was that this same mentality trickled down to my level, to all humanity from the One World Governments. I had been gnawing on bare bones, too, and had just not been aware of it. The joke was really on me.

"How about it, hu-manimal?" she asked.

"Don't call me that."

"Ah, you don't like being labeled. It depends which rung you are on, doesn't it? You are no better than them. Instead of helping those you consider inferior, you label them just like the OW."

Her words spooked me. Had she read my mind? Suddenly I wanted away from her. I didn't trust her. "You go your way and I'll go mine and we won't have to worry about it."

"I took you to be someone different from the rest of the survivors."

"Well, get over it. Good night. Have a good life or whatever you clones call it," I said angrily as I got into my sleeping bag. I wanted her to know that I was done with her.

"I'm facing my last generation."

"Welcome to the one inescapable fact of being human. You die. As a matter of fact, I'm facing my last generation. Humans only get one go round. You have a leg up on me. If I were you, I would take it and run."

"I suppose you have a book for me to read on dying, too?" she yelled loudly, making the cats jump up from where they had settled.

"Yes," I said getting my sleeping bag and rolling it out by the fire. "Death comes for the Archbishop."

I lay pretending to sleep, but I knew I wouldn't be able to. The conversation on death had reminded me about all the dead bodies packed into their rolling coffins along the old historic interstate routes. I couldn't get the sights and smells out of my mind. Besides that I was listening very intently for any sound of movement that might come from Zel, or any rustling movement from trees slithering along the ground.

Just then Fluff jumped up by me on the flannel lining of the bag, kneading into it for some time before she finally lay down. The cat lay with her eyes closed, and I watched the subtle movement of her breathing as her stomach rose and fell with regularity. She must have felt me staring at her, for the cat opened her eyes and stared back. Now that was radar. I wondered if the sound of blinking eye lashes actually registered in her range of hearing. Then suddenly, Fluff lifted her head and looked in back of me. By then I could hear the sound, too, and quickly turned to see Zel with a stick in her hand. It took a second for me to see that she was just poking the fire with it, stirring the embers to life. There was that concept again. Life and death. It was all we had.

"You don't trust me, do you Travis N. Tarkington?" She called over to me as if to say she knew that I was really not asleep.

I just lay there and stared back. I felt too foolish to even try to come up with a retort to sustain the charade.

"I could have attacked you when I arrived. You were passed out on the ground. It would have been easy to put a bullet through your brain then."

What she said was true. I had been completely oblivious to anything.

"I thought you would be glad for company."

"I have all the company I can handle with Niner and the cats," I finally said and sat up in my sleeping bag. "What is it that you really want?"

I could hear her beating the stick against the chunk of wood burning in the fire. "There is something I want to tell you, but I don't think the time is right just yet."

So there was something in the past. I had been wondering if she knew any of those who had been on the island with us. "Did you know the men in upper Manhattan who had taken over the high rises?" I saw Zel's eyes move away from my face and stare at something behind me.

"Don't move," she whispered. "Drop down to the ground." Before I knew what was happening, she reached in her shirt and pulled out a gun and pointed it my way. "Drop down," came her command again just before she fired. I was sure I was about to die, but I had dropped to the ground like she ordered. I heard two more shots and I saw her get up quickly and walk past me. I turned to see a figure of a man still standing some paces behind me. His arm was hanging from his shoulder, like some sprung jack in the box and attached only by wires. His head was tilted to one side. "Robotoid," I heard her say as I got to my feet. The automaton was holding a laser pistol in his hand and the firing system was still blinking red. His smart system had alerted him. I saw the fuzzy outline of a figure on his computer that was me. The caption read: ID- HU-MANIMAL. LYING AT 9 FEET.

"One more for the parts department," said Zel.

I was beginning to see the benefits of this waif who had attached herself to me. She looked at me. "We hate the robos, too."

"Why?"

"Clones are only one step away from humans."

"At least you are the rung above."

"You are not very intelligent for an ivy leaguer," she said shoving the robotoid over backwards. It hit the ground with a clatter, but a laser beam shot forth from the robo's gun in a path towards her feet and she jumped away from it. I was astounded at the quickness of her reaction. Amazed, to be honest. It was spilt second timing I had never witnessed before. It was worthy of Olympic competition if there were such a designated event for moving quickly out of harm's way. "Thank you," I said.

"You owe me." She was bent slightly over and kicking the laser gun from the hands of the downed soldier which was a blend of metal and plastic composites.

"Okay," I said in solid agreement.

"I saved your flesh, now you save my soul."

"That's over board," I said turning away. "What you just did for me only took seconds. What you want from me might be impossible."

"Travis," she called after me. "Dead is dead. It is permanent. Motionless."

I turned to see the laser weapon pointing at me. "A deal's a deal."

"What you did for me took seconds," I began when she cut me off.

"Like this?" she asked firing the weapon and removing the button from my shirt and asking, "What's your point again?"

"Help you find your soul? I don't even know if anyone has one. There may be no answer. Why can't you just believe that the state has the answer like everyone else out there?"

She fired her laser gun again and two more buttons popped off my shirt. "You're the one that's to blame for all this. You reprogrammed Niner and he introduced me into a different reality."

"What a blabber mouth that bird turned out to be."

"I'm asking you to try. Help me find it."

She was a hell of a shot. "Okay. Okay. I don't like sewing on buttons. You owe me a shirt."

"You owe me a life."

She seemed satisfied that she had bested me, and turned her attention back to the robotoid. "What are you doing now?" I said as she was picking over the parts on the ground.

"Getting the charger and battery pack from the laser. There should be a second back up gun on him. You can have it. Lasers are better than the old guns. They are silent," she told me.

"Right. I always wanted one of those." I got up to join her as she patted the body down until she found a compartment on the side and opened it. I saw the gun and reached in for it.

"Do you know how to use it?"

"Of course. I used to hunt with my Grandfather Pompy when I was growing up."

"Let's see you shoot it. Lasers handle differently, you know. Char that tree trunk. The third one over from us," she ordered.

"I didn't do target shooting when I was young."

"Just try it."

I took aim, shot, and missed. Instead, I kept hitting the tree next to it. I tried again and again. All I did was etch a wobbly looking letter z into its trunk.

"You need a keeper."

"And you're it?"

"Let's go, Zorro."

"Zorro?

"A hero in a book. You should read it."

"Oh, no. You're not changing my reality base."

"Get up," she said in a deep and serious tone. "Those pieces of shrapnel need to come out of your hide."

"Skin. It's called skin. People have skin. Animals have hides."

Zel took out a mag light from her bag. She scanned it over the parts of my body where the metal and plastic pieces were and sucked them right out of my skin and into the hose of the mag. "Stop yelling so much. Stand still," she kept saying to me.

"It hurts. That's what humans do. We make noise, scream, carry on when things hurt. Get used to it if you want to be human."

"I am human. We clones feel pain and get tired and hungry too, you know."

"Now let's look at the bore hole in your leg," she said removing an oblong object that looked like a thick pencil from her pack.

"It feels fine."

"That's because I worked on it a couple of times with the laser grafting light while you were unconscious."

"I have never heard of a laser grafter light. I don't want you touching me."

"It's light is for healing. We in the SG forces were given it in our first aid kits to heal ourselves if we get wounded in battle. It joins muscle and tissue back together. Extend your leg out for me," she said turning on the light and coming towards me.

"No. It makes a noise like a saw blade."

"Without it, your muscles may detach from one another and you could lose the ability to walk. Judging by the way you were walking today and dragging that leg, you won't be able to travel very far tomorrow. You would be a puppet with no strings."

"You've already treated me with it?"

"Yes. Check under the bandage."

I pulled up my pant leg and took the bandage off. The hole was deep, but skin had begun to form on top of it and the wound was no longer open and exposed. "It looks like skin has started to grow. The hole is no longer open," I said hardly believing it. "You've already used it on me?" I repeated to convince myself.

"Yes. A couple more flashes and you will be whole again. Maybe a little scaring for a while."

"And you've used it on yourself?"

"Yes. Many times," she said in an angry tone and with the kick of her foot she knocked me off my feet and took my leg in her hands and I heard the saw sound and in seconds she let me go and stood back up.

"You're done already?"

"I could have grafted 20 men in the time it took to argue with you."

I stayed on the ground and rubbed the spot she had zapped. I couldn't believe it but it felt better and cool and the hole had filled in even more. She was staring at me.

"It shouldn't hurt. What are you rubbing it for? Good luck?"

"I'm just amazed that it works. My leg feels stronger. There's something to be said for the eternal elixir when it instantly takes the pain away."

"You sure missed out on a lot of innovations in Rehab. Now let's patch up the spots," she said applying the laser pencil to my shrapnel wounds.

After I was bandaged, I looked like a patch work quilt. I was tired enough to try and sleep, but Zel had opened her computer and started researching articles on cloning and reading them aloud to me. For every article I showed her that said clones didn't have souls, she flopped another article down in front of me that said they did. Finally, in frustration and after hours of argument I laid it out to her. "Look, it's a wash," I said and began walking away. "I'm hungry and so are the cats. The sun's up. We've been at it all night."

"You don't care. You want to leave me without hope," she screamed.

"I tried. I can't help it if the answer you want doesn't exist."

"It does exist. You just won't help me find it," she yelled throwing her pocket computer to the ground.

"Just like a woman to create drama."

"There!" she exclaimed jumping up from the desk. "You admit I am acting like a woman. If I have human actions, I am human."

"No, it's just a phrase, an expression."

She ignored my words and continued. "There may be hope for you yet, Trave. Just listen to one more article."

"I have already listened to ten."

"This one I just found talks about the feelings of distance which is created in each successive generation. It was the feeling which I told you about. Don't you understand? My hunches were right."

"Okay," I said rubbing my eyes and frowning, "but I have a headache. I need a break and food.

Stepping into the small sunlit opening in the trees renewed me almost instantly. I stopped to revel in it. Zel was looking up at the sun as well. "It feels good, doesn't it?" she asked. It hit me instantly that her sensations were exactly like mine. Had she merely read my reaction and was mimicking it, or had it come to her on its own?

"What makes you think this article is any different from all the others?" I asked her.

"This is not an article. It is a study done by SG scientists because there had been revolts among advanced generational clones by both animal and human repos."

"Revolts?"

"At first they studied only animal clones which turned on their owners and the SG's began killing them. Years later the experiments focused on human clones who behaved in a similar manner. The scientists were trying to determine why the clones became violent. It was the conclusion of their findings that interests me. It says that the clones became like shells because their souls were thought to have left at the time of their original death which left them with no conscience."

"They were grasping at straws. They needed a reason and they chose that one."

"Don't you see? The answer I am seeking is there. It is so obvious I don't know why you or I didn't come up with it," she said watching me cook food over the fire.

"Why do you keep stirring the food?" she asked.

"So it heats evenly."

"You're not giving it a chance to get hot."

"You're an expert? You cook yours the way you think best, and let me cook mine," I said throwing her a set of metal utensils in a plastic bag.

"It wasn't a criticism. It was an observation."

"You were critiquing my cooking."

"No. You took it to be critical when I clearly didn't mean it to be."

"Clearly? Clearly? You haven't said anything precise, concise, or close to being clear since I met you," I yelled back.

"What? You're blaming your lack of understanding on me? You are blaming me?"

"Stop repeating everything. You sound like a broken record, clone."

"A broken record? Me a broken record?" she fumed.

"You're stuck again," I said trying to be humorous while still getting another jab in at her.

"What an ego! You can't for one second see yourself as having a problem communicating."

"I was a writer, so no, I know how to get my point across."

"You were a hack, ordered what to write and about whom. Why, the name of the publication itself conjures up such intellectual and esteemed renown in my mind. The Razor Rag."

"It was The Mag Rag," I corrected.

"Even lower. A first grade exercise in how words rhyme no doubt."

"You should find a copy and read it sometime."

"I have read it. I read your Magnus opus on cold love. It was so well received that it got you fired. Even the zombies of your generation found you without a heart."

I was watching her take her can of soup off the fire and begin to eat as the steam rose from out of cup. She raised her spoon and slid it gracefully into the tin saucer exhibiting perfect etiquette for eating soup. "Help yourself to the soup," she said, motioning with her head towards it. "I'm only going to have one tinful."

"Watching your figure? I've lost my appetite," I said leaving the spoon in the can I had been stirring. I got up and found a sleeping bag, unpackaged it, and rolled it onto the floor. By the time I was comfortably stretched out, Zel was eating my chili and watching my every move. "Head still hurt?" she asked.

"Not until you spoke to me."

"Why are you always so irascible?"

"My, my what big words we're using today," I said.

"I'll feed the cats for you. You just lay back and listen while I explain why I still have a soul, or had a soul. Listen carefully because I need an opinion from you at the end."

I closed my eyes tighter and tried to shut the noises of her moving about out of my mind. However, I found her movements soothing. It had been so long since I had experienced the nearness of another being that I began to find her voice comforting. I found myself listening to her words if only in an attempt to put her words into a construct of logic I could understand as a concept in my own mind. Zel was talking of Somatic Cell Nuclear transfer and how, at first, these scientists had persuaded the public that clones were nothing more than twin babies in the womb, but now in this top secret study they admitted that wasn't entirely the case. They had only said that in the beginning of their experiments in order to stop the religious objections of the public back in the nineteen nineties. "Anyway, they think the blood has something to do with it," she was saying. The more she talked, the more sense the issue made to me. She went on to say that mistakes often occurred in transferring the DNA. What was more curious to me was the fact that telomeres within the DNA naturally changed over time. It was the changing of those telomeres that caused diseases to take root in humans. For some reason I was familiar with that concept and I started concentrating on her words more deeply at that point.

"Now, here is where it gets interesting, Trave. No first generation clone was noted to have anger issues or fits of passion. They were specifically chosen as being highly desirable for cloning. In fact, none of the 50,000 first generation clones were reported as having been arrested or even of having a hint of trouble with the law through their entire life span. The behavior problems started in the second generation and grew worse in every succeeding generation."

I sat up to face her. I felt it was time to tell her what I knew. "Zel, I have read about this. Let me tell you my own convictions about what else doesn't get transferred. Man can't duplicate the blood. It's the main ignition switch that turns the engine over. That's why these scientists had to form a life from a whole packaged kit contained in the DNA. They couldn't replicate the blood. They could only make duplicate copies like a scanner does. My bet is that souls don't come packaged in the DNA, either."

"So you say I can't have a soul."

"Not now, maybe, but you did once. You did in your first life."

"That is what I thought, and what I was trying to tell you. I knew that I had to be given a soul when I was born. You see it the same way I do then. Do you believe that?"

"I believe that scientists can only copy DNA. If an accident occurs in the transferring of the DNA, they are helpless. It is the disruption of the genetic markers that has always caused disease." Now that they had admitted that DNA doesn't transfer all of the info and that it was possible to make mistakes in the copying of them, the thought hit me: Was the soul part of the DNA, or was it a God breathed thing?

"Listen, Trav. I hear drones coming in."

"It's the squad you hear coming back," Niner announced coming closer.

Zel gave a start and gasped.

"I have been here for a while, Zel," the drone said.

"Spying?" I said to him.

"Listening," he said hastily, still looking at Zel. "I have a quote for you from the Basic Instructions book. It was written by an Apostle called Paul. 'Therefore we are always confident, knowing that, whilst we are at home in the body, we are absent from the Lord. For we walk by faith not by sight.' It is clear from what he says that your soul is either in your body or at home with the Lord. That narrows it down to one of two choices in my estimation."

"How can you be sure they are talking about the soul, Niner?"

THE WIZARD OF All

"Context. By rigorous examination of the context. Man is made of blood, flesh and spirit. He was formed from the dust of the earth and the I Am breathed into him. When man dies, the Great I Am takes the soul to be with him."

"You've lost me completely, Niner."

"When the soul is taken from the body, I Am directs the soul to the place it earned during his life."

"How does this I Am know where to take the soul?"

"The Instruction book says that out of the mouth comes words and actions that live in the heart. Those words can be good or evil. It is by the intentions of his heart that man is known by the Great I am and directed to the place his heart earned."

"That's beautiful, Niner," Zel said poking my shoulder, but I didn't respond.

We sat quiet for a while and Zel said, "I'd like to believe in what you said, Niner. Do you believe in it?"

"It makes perfect sense. It is an absolute. His words tell you the end of a man. They explain it all from birth to death. It is complete."

"Thank you. Hearing those words, gives me a more solid purpose. It makes me want to continue."

"Would you like to know a further mystery explained?" the eagle asked her but did not wait for an answer. "The words in the instruction manual are alive and carry the very breath of this God wizard himself."

She had such a look of vulnerability in that moment that I began to feel guilty for holding back info. "I should tell you of an article I read before we met," I confessed. "It was an article dealing with the moral questions that were raised when cloning was first introduced. "

"I don't want to read about the issues anymore. I want to know where my soul is."

"If your original body died, then your soul has left," the drone told her.

"How can I know if my born body is dead?"

We sat quiet except for the sound of Niner rolling back and forth between us. Finally Zel spoke again. "I met myself once. I did not like it."

"A walking, talking mirror," I said.

"Not really," she said in a superior tone. "The person I saw wasn't identical. Her mouth was bigger."

At this point I laughed. "It's just like a woman to be overcritical of her appearance."

"I am being honest. You didn't let me finish. It is you who are being critical of women."

"I'm sorry. Continue."

"I was going to say that the mouth was misshapen. It was like looking at one of the drawings in that restaurant in NY where those old cine-stars are made to look like cartoons."

"Sardi's. I use to lunch there with my fellow journalists."

"Midnight was lunch?"

"How did you know that?"

"I used to see you and that bunch, drinking and making the rounds among the chorus girls from the shows. You don't know much about women."

"Now, who's being critical?"

"It's a fact, not a criticism. I never remember you catching one."

"I wasn't fishing."

"Weren't you?"

This gal was smarter than I gave her credit for. "What were you doing there at that time of night? I thought you said you were a nanny."

"I was taking care of Nadia's children in the romper room she had built for the theater crowd."

"Nadia Chen made Sardi's put in a child care room?"

"Why not? She had enough money to buy the place. She liked to tout the fact that she could excel at being the most successful actress and the best mother at the same time."

"A real troll. I interviewed her once."

"At the house. I know. You drank up the tequila, insinuated she had lied about her family genealogy, and were forcibly removed from the house. I believed you also reminded her that she was not from China, and that her mother was not a daughter of royalty."

"Those facts seem vaguely familiar. I'd had a few by that time, but I never drank up her tequila."

"You took a few bottles with you when you left, as payment, I think you told her."

"You were there," I said as I was forced to believe her claims.

"So where did you hang after she had you barred from Sardi's?"

"A place across the river in Queens."

"That far away, huh? She did have some kind of clout."

"A punch like a steel kangaroo."

"Is that what ended your career? I mean you have a knack for science. You must have done something before or after Nadia."

It was the tone of her voice that made me look up at her and the way she was looking at me that sparked the anger that flew out of me suddenly. "Well, we know you had another job move, don't we? Just how does one go from being a nanny to being security for the state?"

"You wouldn't be able to accept it right now. Later. Later I will tell you many things."

"What does that mean?"

"It means you aren't ready."

"What? I need to grow up? Be nice?"

I recognized a cool dimness in her eyes, but her mouth was turned up in a smile that let me know she was on my side. At least that was the way I read it. There are certain moments when you connect deep to deep. This was one of them. I wanted to reach out and kiss her, but I hesitated and she unlocked her gaze from mine and looked away, and the moment was gone.

She must have sensed my reticence and turned away. It was an awkward realization.

"Let's get back to the research," I said opening my pocket computer back up way without looking at her.

"You're embarrassed," she said.

"Why should I be embarrassed?"

"For deciding to reject me. For letting your feelings show for me."

"Do you want to find your soul or not?"

"Isn't that the search you have been on also?"

"Look, let's keep this about you."

"If it makes you more comfortable."

"Professional."

"We've already discussed your high standards of that."

This clone was scoring all the points. I couldn't breathe in her presence. She had the ability to make me forget who I was and that put me in a dangerous position. Suddenly I felt the heat of the afternoon sun on my face and looked up. I was sitting on the ground resting my back against the side of the tree for support. The dirt felt warm against my buttocks and seemed to relax them. I let go and closed my eyes. Why was I letting her get my mind in a tail spin? Maybe she was right, I had been about to cross the line. So what? I had that right, and I resolved to let her know who was in charge. I got up went over to her. She was right where I left her with her head down, reading the material. "I'm sorry. That's all."

Zel made no comment and I took that to mean that my position had been made clear from there on out. I was on solid ground again.

"There's no one around for you to impress," she finally said.

"You can do the research on your own."

"We can help one another. Protect one another."

"I know. We are an army," I said sarcastically.

"Leave me then. I'm the trained one. It's you who are the neophyte out here. You're the one who needs rescuing all the time."

"And you have been through this before?"

"I'm trained. I know the SG. I worked for them, remember?" Zel looked down and away for a moment and then stood up. "I took you to be someone else. You know what the SG's are like. You should remember. Why don't you?" she yelled at me

"Maybe because I was on UM pills for ten years," I said but I couldn't help feeling there was a deeper layer of meaning in her question. It was way in the back drawer of the file in my mind. It was there, waiting.

"Don't try to push me around," I said in frustration.

"How can you find all the details concerning the duplicity the SG and their predecessors had been cabable of for over a hundred years and not reconnect to yourself? I took you to be one who was on a grand, mad journey of discovery."

"You read stuff into my writing that wasn't there."

"Isn't it up to the reader to make of a book what he will?"

"You're making me into more than I am."

"And you're making me into less," she said with a smirk.

I didn't answer her. She had bested me again.

"I have to try and find if there are records of what happened to the original bodies and if mine was one that was saved for the DNA."

"You are going to try and find your dead self?"

"I have to see the look on my face."

"Now you've added something new to the mix. What can you tell from a face?"

"The look of eternity."

"And just what does the face of eternity look like?" I laughed.

"Peace."

I sat shaking my head and watching the cats scamper around my feet. "It's a good thing cats can't talk," I said to them.

"Yes. That is why you get along with them. They can't tell you what they think of you."

"They need me. That is enough." My voice was rough and edgy and I wanted it to convey that it excluded her. This rerun knew too much about me.

"I need you, Travis, and you need me. You just won't admit it."

"Guilt won't work."

"Why do you say I try to make you feel guilty?"

"That's the oldest ploy in the book."

"Is it because you feel guilty yourself, and accuse me of it, so you can rebel against me and keep me at a distance?"

"I hope you find what you are looking for."

"Save your words. You say them out of conventionality, not concern. You're more of a robo or a clone than I am."

"Is that your convoluted and clonish way of saying I'm a phony?"

"Why ask me what I mean? You ascribe your own motives to me anyway."

I turned away from her and did not look back. I moved over to where my sleeping bag was and lay down. "We've wasted a whole day. I need to sleep." My head was filled with all sorts of questions. Can a soul be destroyed? Could she really feel it missing? I closed my eyes and waited for sleep.

The next few days was more of the same terrain we had just passed through and it was exhausting to keep stepping over the rolling humped back sea monsters of the tree trunks along the ground. They were almost like hands reaching up to trip you except they rose nearly a foot and a half off the ground before straightening out and growing upwards in a normal way.

The forest was denser here and for some reason the air did not penetrate between the trees. It was stifling. I looked up to see if there was a wind blowing the tops of the trees, but they were still as a rock and stood glistening in the sun. The kittens were mewing and wanted out of the back pack. I had fashioned leashes for them and we stopped so they could take care of business.

I hated to stop because then it gave Zel an opportunity to make conversation and all that lead to was a continuation of the argument that had started when we met. She seemed occupied as long as we were walking and I kept my thoughts to myself. It took great concentration to walk and I kept my eyes focused ahead. All of a sudden my heart leapt. The forest seemed to be thinning. Were we nearing the end of this trap? At that point I heard drones wings and saw Niner descending from the heights down into the pits.

"Welcome, eagle," Zel greeted him. "It is good to see you are still nearby."

"I came to let you know that there is a clearing ahead. There's even a cabin and a lake."

"How far?" I asked.

"An hour for me. Days for you."

"And people?" I inquired.

"Only those who lie in the motionless state," he said going over to pet the cats as they drank water.

"This place makes me think strange things," the drone said.

"Come over and sit by me, eagle. I will keep you safe," Zel said.

"Birds of a feather," I said disgruntled.

"We have a mission. It is the same," Niner said.

"Rogue drone," I said in a cursing fashion. "There should be a law against giving you freedom of choice."

"There is. There is also a law about hu-manimals having freedom, and clones and robotoids."

"Beat it, drone," I yelled.

"You stand a better chance with me than without me. Even a human should realize that."

I hated to admit it, but the drone was right. He was like a rabbit's foot to me.

"Clones and drones and cats, oh, my. Clones and drones and cats, oh, my!" The drone was trying to sing, but was not able to give his voice a sense of rhythm.

I looked over at Niner bouncing off the ground in his limited range of motion. He was only able to hop up and down on his wheels. I began to laugh uncontrollably. "This is crazy," I began to repeat in between lapses of laughter.

Niner began to toot as he tried to laugh along with me. It sounded like a rusty hic- cup which made me laugh all the harder. "Blow your horn, laugh it up, you plastic prima donna."

The drone rolled himself over to me. "Then we three are united as one again?"

"For a while. Just a·while."

"All for one and one for all," he said.

"Keep your quotes to yourself."

"Communication is to share. You programmed me like that. You said it was the connection from the past to the future. Without it you said we were lost. "

"There's a fine line, drone. There's a line."

"Show me where it is," he said, stopping and looking at me.

"It's not literal."

"Update me, wizard."

"Do not trust him, Niner. He is liable to rip your hard drive out and put a chip in that can't think," Zel said catching up to us.

"He is my programmer. He would not hurt me."

"You have too much trust in you, eagle Niner."

"The Instruction book calls it faith. It is a requirement. It is counted as righteousness."

"Is it that simple, eagle?" Zel asked.

"It is so. You must finish reading the manual, Zel. You, too, Travis."

"Is it the yellow brick road?" I said in a half teasing, half inquisitive way.

"It is life. Why did you stop reading it?"

"That's none of your business."

"Level with me as a trusted friend."

"You're not a trusted anything. Get that through your head you plastic coated pterodactyl."

"We have survived Devils Island and this forest together," the bird said. "We are building a history and a past like all the other great characters of literature."

"You have too many allusions flying around in that bird brain of yours. You need to take a breather from reading so much fiction. You should experience more of life."

"I will start right now, Trav," he said and rolled back over to the clone. "Zel, you keep calling me eagle. I have never seen myself. Can you show me a picture in a book?"

"I can show you more clearly. There's a mirror in my cosmetic bag," and she dumped it on the ground in a heap before her.

"Mirror?"

"Yes, it is a reflection of life."

"There is something new every day," he said as he rolled along beside her.

"I'm going to get back to sleep while you two preen one another," I said.

I kept one ear tuned to them. It wasn't good for them to be alone. It wasn't safe for me. There was no telling what those two partial lobed idiots would dream up, I told myself. Between the two, they didn't make up a full deck. I peeked at them sitting in back of me and saw Zel holding the mirror down lower so the drone could see into it. "Show me my side profile," the drone was instructing her. "Magnificent."

"Can I take the mirror away now?"

"I'm sorry. I was gandering."

"Gandering?"

"Yes, looking, staring, you know."

"Now I do. What's the matter, Niner? You sound sad."

"I am a grand design of a bird."

"It's because of your beautifully colored feathers."

"Feathers?"

Zel picked him up and held him to the mirror again. "See those ruffles and ridges that are carved into the your body?"

"Yes."

"Those are meant to represent feathers, the coverings I showed you in the book."

"I have never seen a real feather."

"Yes, you have. You have seen the cats after they have eaten a bird. The stuff on the ground that is sometimes left is feathers."

"Oh. Fluff," he said, somewhat dismayed and disconcerted. "I am made of fluff?"

"I'm sorry. Instead of helping, I have made you feel worse."

"You have helped, really Zel. I was just thinking of how to get feathers. I want them. They will help me be real. That is the next step."

"What other steps are there for you, Niner?"

"Motion. I must move freely like you and Travis and the cats."

"You ask a lot, Niner."

"The manual says to come boldly to the throne. I must do that. The God Wizard gives you your heart's desire then. The lion and the scarecrow and the tinman were timid when they approached the wizard. I will not be."

"Do you think the wizard is real?"

"He has to be, Zel. There is all of this beauty around us. The instructions say that the wizard gave us nature so we would see him. Can I can count on you, Zel? You will feather me?"

"Well, I don't know. We can't go around plucking birds just for their feathers."

"Why?"

"Well, for one thing it would hurt the birds we took them from."

"I don't understand."

"It causes pain. It makes us people and the cats cry out in agony. Like when Travis' leg was bored through by the laser and he cried out in those sounds that frightened you. Remember?"

"It was shrill. I thought it to be some sort of dire warning."

"It is a signal in a way, I guess. It signals that help must be given to stop the pain."

"There is more to being alive than I thought. I'll tell Travis to leave the pain gene out."

Zel laughed softly. "I think that is wise of you, Niner. As long as you can build yourself, why add the pieces that would make you suffer."

I closed my eyes and turned away from the fire. They were like children. They had the minds of innocents and I suddenly felt protective of them. I had let them get to me the way the cats had. I was losing my grip on all the facts. I needed a thread of sanity to hold on to and I had to keep an eye on the clone. She was willing to hold secrets from me. She was taking Niner into her confidence. If I was going to travel with them, I had to relegate them to a place of order where I could deal with them.

"Let's get back on the trail," I ordered in a tone that left no room for argument.

"Niner get back in the sky."

"Chilly around here," he whispered to Zel before taking flight.

The next day was almost ended when I stopped walking to check the coordinates that Niner had given me to make sure we were on the right course. I flashed him our position and set about making camp for the night. After the fire pit was going I threw Zel a pan. "You can help with the dinner," I said.

"I will make you a dinner."

"I wasn't aware that clones were so domesticated and nurturing."

"I told you we are just like you. It's the soul that's missing. Other than that, we live, feel pain."

I didn't answer her, but kept my head down and blew on the fire to stoke it. I wanted to avoid her eyes.

"It's time to make a few statements of my own about you hu-manimals. I thought you were the highest order, the most intelligent, the most evolved.

"We are."

"I haven't seen it."

"Why? Because I won't do anything for you or that bird?"

"Together we can make a difference."

"Both of you need to get a grip on reality. This is somewhere in the Midwest not Oz."

"It's not locality, but a state of mind we are trying to meet you in, Mr. Travis Tarkington."

"Insanity," I screamed, jumping up and throwing the stick I had been stirring the fire with into the distance. "That's it. That's the last straw. That's the last bit of nonsense I want to hear from you forever," I stuttered. "I'm not going to take you or that drone to search for anything. Even if I wanted to, it would be impossible. None of it is real."

Harley was pawing at me and it was then that I noticed the kittens and Mama Kitty were not around. I got up. "I can't keep track of anything. You won't let me be. I can't think straight," I said looking at Zel as I began to search along the ground for the neon colored ropes I had fastened to the kittens. I hadn't gone far from the camp sight when I caught sight of the bright orange plastic rope which I had fashioned into harnesses for the kittens hanging over one of the serpentine limbs. I didn't see the animals, but I saw something else. It was ocean blue and big. I refocused my eyes to see an aqua marine colored car sitting in an open patch within the trees. There was concrete under the tires so we must have wound our way back to the original route of the interstate. The car was pointing in a westerly direction. It had been traveling in the same direction as we were now. I heard footsteps behind me and turned to see Zel. "We've come back to the old interstate road," I said pointing down at the grayish concrete. I called the kittens and handed them back to the clone and went around to the front of the car where I saw the decayed face and untamed hair on the girl behind the steering wheel. I ran around to try and open the door, but it was rusted shut do I pounded and pulled at the door like a madman. When it would not open, I busted the window out and grabbed the frazzled haired girl. Her sunglasses fell off and exposed the empty sockets where her eyes once were. She couldn't see, but I could. I saw the future plainly. I felt her bones fall from my hands, and I stopped shaking her and realized that I had touched my own end. "Don't blame me! Don't laugh at me," I screamed at the dead girl, looking back into the car at her lifeless form. She was slumped over sideways into the passenger seat when I let her out of my grip. Bits of the broken glass lay on her like so much confetti after a parade. "Blame yourself. You took the sign of solidarity to wear under your skin," I reminded her, though I couldn't see if the sign had been imprinted into her hand because all of her flesh had fallen away. "You thought you were one of the chosen. You stood by the One World Order. The chip they put in your hand was death instead of life. "

Zel and Niner came closer to me and Zel patted my hand. "Does this look like the wizard is coming back?" I asked her while the tears came down. "The world is filled with the stink of death. It is rotting away in front of us," I said to them. "I am shouting out to this God, but there was is no answer. He is nowhere. He is a mute." I fell to my knees and felt the earth tremble and shake as if I myself were Rome falling.

"You are not to blame," she said. I heard her words, but they did not release me from the guilt I felt and I could not fathom why.

I didn't eat and sat staring into the fire until Niner spoke to me. "Travis," he said from above my head. I looked up and there was Niner with all his plastic parts intact and a few feathers he had collected and stuck anywhere on his body his bird beak had been able to reach. I instantly regretted having given him a voice in the world. I saw him as a freakish creation and myself as Dr. Jeckyl. "I want to become real," he said. I would need to shut him down and take a look at his hard drive. I needed to end this madness. He must have sensed what was on my mind because he began to plead with me.

"Give me a chance to prove I am still the same, Trav. You owe me that much. I am coming closer to finding the wizard by reading the book. It is a journey that needs to be taken together."

For a moment I thought my mind would explode. Just how many concepts of reality was there? Then looking at the bird I felt compassion and I called him over to me and started plucking the misplaced feathers off of him. "You don't need these," I said. "It's what's inside that counts."

"Microchips?"

"In your case, yes."

"No. You lie." In a mad scramble, Niner began pushing against me to escape, and rolled over to the clone, carrying a lone feather in his beak.

"Zel," he said, "Tell him these are real."

"You are heartless, aren't you Travis? What's a few feathers to you?"

"Don't you understand this is no good for him, for anybody. Nothing can come from it. He's a machine."

"You gave him a dream. Don't take it away."

"I shouldn't have started making him over. It was a mistake. I had no right. Machines weren't meant to have dreams."

"Maybe most, but Niner does."

"Let's get this over with. Field repair. Report Niner."

CHAPTER 6

It was days later and Niner had still not let me look at his circuits. He had flown into camp a number of times to report, but had remained out of my reach. Finally today he was back to the subject and pleading with me.

I was staring at the bird. He could elude capture forever. He was much quicker on the up take than I was so I was forced to hear him out.

"Go ahead and eat. I will relate the story that John wrote in the first century between 90-95 a.d. I have never heard such logic from any man. It is opposite of the worlds logic. It sets it upside down! It needs to flash on Times Square 24/7. The wizard sent his son to save us. Can you imagine that reality after all we have been through? This Yeshua went to prepare a place for us, and he is coming back for us. There is a life after this, I am sure of it," the drone proclaimed.

I turned my back on my companions and away from the fire. I did not feel the presence of hope the drone was talking about. Instead I saw the grim smiles I had seen on the decaying faces of the millions of dead in these last thousand miles. That was the hope this wizard had left. He was a cruel God and he had shown me the last smirk of a dying race and the reality of my own inescapable future.

"He's coming back? The world is filled with the stink of death. It is rotting away in front of us," I said to them.

"Niner, leave. Travis is not well. He has problems seeing the truth right now, but he will. I will call you back when he has had time to think things over."

"I will be alert from a distance. I will advance on the enemy if they approach. I am ever vigilant like the wizard in the sky. I do not sleep."

In seconds, Niner was in the air and I could do nothing to stop him. I looked at Zel. "I want you out of here." Her mouth was turned up in that smile that was becoming all too familiar to me.

"You can't make up your own mind, can you, Travis?"

"I just did. I'm ending this charade for all of us."

"You like me, but you won't admit it even to yourself. You like Niner, but you aren't sure if he will listen to you now that you have given him the freedom to think for himself. Freedom is a risk."

"I don't need you to tell me what my motives are. I don't know what you think you know, but you're all wrong. A little knowledge is not just dangerous, it's lethal where you two are concerned. You and that plastic plexi-asaurus have read stuff and distorted it all."

"To my way of thinking it is you that have things messed up. You tear yourself in half accepting parts of this literature and parts of that book and rearranging them until they fit a philosophy you have formulated in your own mind. You throw away the truth and keep the lies just like the SG taught you to."

"And you're the mirror of reality?" I quipped. "Hell, you believed that beings from the galaxy gave us our knowledge so don't talk to me of your next belief system."

"I'm a tad closer to being human than you are. You talk of freedom of thought and how grand and great and noble it all is until someone disagrees with you, and then you want to turn off their switches. Talk, talk, I am sick of your talk. You do not even believe in it. You speak of compassion, communication and understanding, but you feel nothing."

She had me there. She always seemed to be one up on me.

"Eat if you intend to. We need to get going."

"Niner wants to be real. He wants all that you have shown him."

"I showed him nothing. Get that straight."

"No, you're wrong, Travis. You showed him hope. Even if it isn't true. It is a better to believe in the wizard than not."

I ate a handful of granola and had a cup of coffee and set off alone in silence. It was past noon when Zel passed me on the path, and then sat down on one of low trunks of the serpentine trees. "I need a break," she announced. I didn't answer and she continued. "They make good chairs, anyway," she started off. "I don't care for being on the ground in here. I haven't slept well."

I busied myself with giving the cats a treat and some water. I didn't even glance her way. However, in minutes she marched over to us. "I need to end this nightmare for the next generations of myself."

"You're going to kill yourself?" I looked at her

"I'm already dead. I'm just a specimen in a glass coffin used to extract DNA from."

"Your soul is gone. It is where ever it is. You can't change your end any more than I can."

"You are wrong, Travis. You are the only one who can save others, and you don't care."

"What are you talking about?"

"You could save others like me." Suddenly she paused. "Well, people who have no hope. No one deserves to feel like a speck of dust floating in space. The government has no right to copy us like paper leaflets without our permission and force us to live somewhere between the voids."

"You talk like you knew that your body was just lying in wait like some version of Snow White waiting to be revived."

"It's true. I am Snow White. I remember awakening to life in a glass room, and I saw others lying in these glass boxes row upon row like dolls on shelves waiting to be taken. We were all in a room together and we came of age together. I remember thinking the last time I woke up in that room that it was like a dream that had just repeated itself. No matter how hard I try, I can't make the shadows disappear." Somehow when she spoke, I felt like I was in the room with her and I felt I had been there before. Just then, like a hero arriving in the nick of time, Niner appeared out of nowhere and perched himself on a limb of the tree. "You look like a real eagle sitting in that tree," Zel cooed.

"Even without feathers?"

"You look magnificent."

"Zel, you gave me good words so I will do the same for you. I will remind you of the words from the manual I spoke to you," Niner said. "The ones that tell you where your soul is held."

He showed his screen to her which contained the passage and she read it over to herself. When she finished she looked over at Niner. "It is comforting to read this book. The SG's can do what they will, but they can't keep my soul from its intended journey, can they?"

"You were not created soulless," Niner said softly. "Remember that."

"I feel such an emptiness, Niner. Once I saw a bird take his rest on an empty stretch of sandbar in a stream. He was alone. He called and waited, but not one bird came or answered him. He called a few more times, but then shook his feathers and took flight. He looked so bereaved I knew he would never call out again. I do not want to come to that end. I do not want my former shadows chasing me through life. I want this to be the last dream."

Neither Niner or I said anything to her and she continued. "I think I am fifth or sixth generation, but I don't know how many others of me that now exist. I met myself once. It was a later generation I think because I felt stronger than it."

"That must have been quite frightening for you, Zel," Niner said.

"I was afraid, and I had the notion to end it right then. I wanted to strike out at her before she could be multiplied any further. Later lives become less and less, though the traumatic things stay implanted in the mind. Things become less clear and more jumbled with each rebirthing. I want peace."

No one spoke and it was quiet except for the monotonous click of crickets in the weedy grasses that grew in sparse patches among the trees.

"I'm sorry I don't know what made me say those things," she said. "I didn't mean to burden you with my fears."

"It's this place," the drone said. "It has brought the darkness in all our hearts out."

"I don't need comments from the peanut gallery," I shouted back at him. "Stop it," I yelled to him. "Both of you."

The drone moved closer to Zel and spoke even softer. He had put his wing around her. "It is only a little ways, my dear. Soon you will walk out of this valley of shadows," he said.

It was clear the two of them intended to ignore my comments and continue with their conversation. I paid little attention to their patter until I heard Zel's voice change and become very serious.

"Niner, would you call it murder to destroy my DNA?"

"It is self-preservation. It is rest."

"To each man it is appointed once to die, but only once," Niner said in a sort of half whisper. "That is what the instruction manual says."

"Then you agree with me?"

"It is not murder. There was only one Zel. She has died and her soul has departed and lies with the wizard or without Him."

"It's the same thing with me," I said.

"You're wrong there, Trave. Zel's soul is in its judgment rest. Yours hangs in the balance. It has not been fully weighed," Niner said, rolling over to face me.

"I'm not going to listen to any prophetic talk from a cuckoo bird. I'm going to bed," I said zipping myself into my bag.

I woke just past sunrise and was eager to get an early start, but all things conspired to stop the light from reaching me. Besides being the fall of the year when the sun was naturally further away, the sky was troubled today. Its visage was one of tumbling gray clouds that pressed inward on you and brought a much deeper heaviness than usual to the air that actually made it difficult to breathe. It was darker than usual as we made our way through the grove of trees, but the hike was noisy as the cats chased ahead of us and tried to capture stray and fleeing leaves. We hadn't traveled very far when I heard one of the cat's cry out. It was a cry of pain and fright. The others rushed over to him as I did. It was Trouble, and some-thing was making him back away. Something was stalking him, but I couldn't see anything because of the leaves. What I did see was Harley moving forward on the attack. As my eyes followed Harley, I suddenly saw the pile of leaves rise up in front of him. As my eyes began to focus, I could see he was looking into the eyes of a snake which now sat ready to strike. His warning rattle must have been lost in the rustling of leaves. I took out my laser and aimed its beam just below its head. When the laser hit the snake, it sent it flying upwards into the trees and it landed on a branch. It hung there with its spine ripped apart; its skin having been stripped off like the peel of a banana.

Trouble was lying on the ground and I ran over to where he was. His eyes were open and staring; registering his shock. The venom must be working fast I thought as I picked him up and carried him in my arms. I ran to get him to an open patch of ground where I could tend to him. I was going to rip a piece of my shirt off to tie tightly above the spot where Trouble had been bitten, but when I saw where the blood was oozing from, I knew there was no hope. The cat had been struck just below the neck on the left side. Two little pin points of blood were easily seen on his white fur and were right over the jugular. As I carried him, I caught Trouble looking at me for a second, and then he closed his eyes. Immediately I felt his muscles let go as the struggle for life ended. His head and body lay heavy against my arms. He was already gone.

I took him over to a tree and laid him down where the others could sniff about him and say their goodbyes. When I returned with the shovel, the family was still smelling over his body. When they came to the spot on his neck where the blood stain was, they jumped back from it. I guess they could smell the poison and knew enough to stay away. The family stood and watched as I dug the hole. Zel and Niner were quiet and watchful. Mama let out a cry as I wrapped Trouble in a blanket and put him in the earth and began to spoon the dirt back over him.

"This is my first funeral, " Niner said. "What is expected of me?"

"Nothing," I said.

"You are to be a witness," Zel told him.

"He will come back to life one day. The manual said so," Niner said. "We will wait in hope for that day."

Mama Kitty was lying next to the grave. Her grief was evident in the posture of her body. I went back and sat with her and the other cats came over to me. "I loved Trouble, too," I said patting her head. The others walked around sniffing the earth and then they, too, lay down on the new grave. They were waiting, I thought, to see what happened next. The waiting, it seemed, was expected and instinctual to them. Did animals carry a gene of some sort that told them in some innate way that one day Trouble would return like Niner had said? Did they know that bulbs planted in the fall bloomed in the spring?

Niner's faith reminded me of Pompy's faith. It was strong and stupid and blind. On the way out of the court the day they took his farm I told him I would go after the so'n'sos myself. "It's your land. It has been in your family for over two hundred years. The SG's can't just take it. They need to be stopped, Pompy."

"All you'll do is get yourself killed. It's land, a possession. I can't take it with me, Trav. I'm alright with it. I have made peace with it over the last few weeks before coming to court. I am just saddened that I can't leave it to you. Forgive me for failing you in that, Trav."

"Forgive you!"

"Make peace with it, Trav. It's done."

"How can I make peace with thieves?"

"Give it to God. It's his land. He owns the cattle on a thousand hills." He stopped speaking a minute before he continued. " I've always loved that line. It creates such a beautiful image in my mind."

"Why doesn't God give you one of those thousand hills, if he has them? God has stood by and let them rob you. He has given your land to the enemy."

"You mustn't say that. He will take care of it. He sees all. He does not forget."

"I don't see him working on your behalf. I don't see him doing anything."

"It may not happen in this life. He is sovereign. His justice is final."

"His justice is too late."

Our el train arrived and we boarded. Grandpa was looking out the window as the train sped towards home. "I will have to get used to all this concrete," he said, turning to me. His eyes were teared up and full, like a dam about to break, but the tears didn't come. Somehow he held them back. "There's a church along your street, isn't there, Trave?"

"Just up a block or so. Good Shepherds."

"Let's stop."

We got off the monorail a few blocks before my usual stop and walked down to the church. I stopped by the door and refused to go in with him. Pompy looked back at me and smiled. "Just stick your big toe in," he laughed in a I dare you sort of way. I half smiled, shook my head, and sat down on the steps to wait for him.

I was looking up into the sky and wondering why it was so blue and beautiful that day just as Pompy emerged. I mentioned that fact to him. He recited a line to me from a Browning poem in answer to my musing. "God's in his heaven, all's right with the world," he said smiling and winking at me. "I was hoping He would speak to you while I was inside praying. It looks like He did. You saw His handiwork."

"I said it was a beautiful day, Pompy. I didn't say anything about deities."

"Yes, rather a small beginning, but that's how God works. He sneeks up on you," he laughed and clapped me on the back.

If Pompy was thinking that would make everything okay, he was mistaken, but I didn't say another word to him. We were just coming up to my apartment building, and I was distracted by the congregation of people on the stoop of my brownstone. Then I saw the SG Night Patrol standing among them. I didn't even have time to wonder what they wanted because they walked directly up to us.

"Joel Parker Tarkington. This is a summons."

"We just came from court," I said, swatting the paper away from the hands that were extended towards my grandfather. Two other policemen dressed in black uniforms came forward, grabbed me, and wrestled me to the ground before I could say another word. From where I lay, I could see Pompy reach down and pick up the paper. "Sir, my grandson has no sense. He doesn't understand."

The policeman he was addressing, spoke. "We're here to help him understand."

"Is it not me that is being summoned? I will be in court as the order says. He has nothing to do with it. I will comply. That is what you came for, isn't it? Now, let him go. I will put him back on his leash." Without waiting for the policemen to acknowledge him, Pompy came over to where I was lying, and in a commanding voice said, "Travis, stand up." He had been a sergeant during the war and knew how to give orders. As crazy as it sounds, the two police men let go of me and I stood up. "Get in the house," Pompy continued. The enforcers had capitulated to the old man as if they had seen a force of thousands behind him. I could see they were confused as to how he had taken control of the situation. There was nothing else for them to do, so they began heading for their street tank.

"Don't bring him to court with you," one of the drone police enforcers said just so he could give the last order.

Pompy had caused quite a stir that day. He became a legend in the minds of the tenants that had witnessed the incident. "I have never seen anyone handle the NP enforcers that way. He commanded them and they obeyed!" Grandfather was given special treatment from that moment on. Everyone tipped their hats and said, "Good morning," or moved out of his way to let him pass first. "He fought in the Great War, you know. Commanded thousands. He was a hero," came the whispers.

Remembering that day brought a smile to my lips even now. He was quite a man. I wondered now if what he had told me later inside was true. He had said that a league of angels had been standing behind him that day he subdued the NP. They had put a wall of protection around him. He had felt it. He knew the enforcers had felt it, too. They had the look of bewildered acquiescence on their faces that such a force brought, he said, and so had stood frozen. That's the kind of reaction I was aiming for now, I thought. I wanted to see that same stunned look on the faces of the eternals when they realized they were about to die at the hands of a Hu-manimal.

Since sleep wasn't coming, I got up and walked back over to the place where Zel and Niner were gathered by the little fire. The embers were dying out so there was not much light.

"I have decided to help you on your quest, Zel. No one should have to live under such a sentence."

"You don't help me, you help yourself," Zel said putting more timber on the fire.

"Does it matter at this point?"

"Why? What made you change your mind?"

"I was remembering how it was for my grandfather and how no one helped him in the end."

"Self-preservation," Niner said. "That is very important to humans."

"It's selfish. He's selfish," Zel said getting up.

"That instinct has protected him until now. That is good, is it not?" the eagle said. "Don't leave, Zel. Hear the reason," the drone said rolling after her. I saw her glance back at me as if to let me know that it was the words of the drone that were making her willing to stay and listen. "I am only going to get more wood for the fire."

In her absence the drone came over to me. "Now change your mind about the next reasoning hurdle you have been facing."

"What's that?" I laughed.

"Give me motion."

"No. I've already left you worse off than you were before ."

"I am in the middle of the journey, Travis. Finish me. Make me into more."

"You want things that can never be."

"But you are the programmer, the wizard. Everything is open to you. I want to dance, touch the cats."

"Stop it, Niner. Even if I could give you motion and feeling, you would still be a just a, a.."

Niner broke in on me. "A plastic coated plexi-asaurus?"

"There's no point, don't you see. You still wouldn't be truly alive."

"The Instruction Manual issues the command to believe. Nothing is impossible. It would be a step closer. Talons, eagle fingers. I want them."

"So do you want to hear the story or not?"

"I am curious," Niner said.

The two listened intently while I told them of Pompy. At the end even Zel apologized to me for calling me selfish. I was too tired to gloat over my victory and just yawned.

"I think I can sleep now," I said. "See you two in the morning."

"Think, read," Niner was calling. "Remember you have us drones on our side now. It will be a riot, as you say, to see them in action on the big day of battle."

Niner's last words played on the screen of my mind. I saw myself as a hero to some future generation. They would have a day of remembrance for me and would extol how I had beaten the Eternals. I envisioned the scene of carnage I would inflict on them. I would surprise them like they had surprised on us on the night of lights. Why had I and some others been immune? I wondered if they knew some people were not susceptible to the frequency they had used. Yes, of course they knew. That's why they had sent the sky cars to round up the leftovers, and why they had sent Niner and the drones to finish us off. However, I wasn't sure if they knew there were unchipped persons like me that they were turning their own drones against them.

Thoughts of revenge brought old dreams. In my sleep that night I had a vision of a recurring dream from my past. There was a door in front of me which I was hesitant to open it. I was in a house I thought I had been in before, but I knew there was something foreboding in it. The halls in this place zig zagged in crazy twists and turns, and led to a hidden back part inside this house which I didn't want to find. Something terrible had occurred there, though I couldn't remember what it was. Suddenly I found myself at a door, but I just stood before it, afraid to open it. I was sure it lead to that part of the house I did not want to find.

I had dreamed of this house many times. The back section had been walled up to shut it off completely from the main part of the house. I could see the left over sheet rock laying against the side of the wall that had been used in the construction project, and I felt relieved, but sometimes the dream would push me along the maze of corridors towards the back section of the house, and I was afraid the barrier had been removed and I would find myself in the tomb that had been walled up.

I woke in a sweat; my heart racing as if I had been running and it took me hours to get back to sleep. Morning seemed like a blink away and the next thing I was aware of was Zel shaking me. I still needed sleep. "Get up lazy man. Cats are fed. There's a cup of coffee for you when you are on your feet and walking."

I could barely stand up. My bones were stiff and sore and I held my back as I got up.

"Remind me about the benefits of being human, Trave," she laughed while quickly bending over to roll my sleeping up. In her next move she thrust my bag into my stomach region until I grabbed it. "Alright," I said taking my bag from her. "It's not even light yet," I continued looking up towards the sky and trying to change the subject.

"Niner tells us we will come to the end of the forest today if we can get going."

Hearing those words spurred me into action. I was finding a second wind and the pain in my joints eased up. I was ready to see the end of this twilight world of petrified snakes. However, it was many hours later before we came to a steep ledge and had to stop. It was a sheer drop off some three hundred feet to the plains below. There the land was flat and stretched out for miles to the foothills and then to the mountains beyond. It was an odd demarcation of topography. A land of shadows and trees dropped off into an open land of land and sky. Our future stretched out before us, but I saw the past. There had been thousands who had passed this way over the last two hundred years. There had been horses and wagons, settlers and Indians who had crossed the land and been made humble under this vastness of galloping grasses and rising mountains. I could feel them here. They became a part of me for they had been part of the land. The land took hold of me and I became larger than myself. I saw the dust of ghosts rising. It was a breath taking vista and I felt what my grandfather must have felt for his land. I was the next link in the extension of life. I could not let it end here.

I was eager to descend down to the flat plains and leave the dark of the confused woods behind. I unpacked the gear and soon we were repelling down on the plastic rope I had brought with us. The cats were stashed in our back packs with only their heads poking out. It didn't take long for us to reach the bottom. To my delight a small stream ran through the land, and it wasn't long before I peeled my trousers off and jumped in it. It was cold beyond belief, but only a foot or so deep. I bathed and scrubbed all over, ridding my skin of the last slimy residue I had felt for so long. On the shore, my cats were annoyed by the noise my splashing and whooping created. I had left them tethered close by so they could drink the fresh water. Used to fishing, Harley had waded in to try his luck. He seemed to enjoy leaping from stone to rounded stone and meowed so I would take notice of his prowess and skill. Soon the others had ventured after him as far as the leash, which I placed under a large boulder as an anchor, would allow them to go.

It was from the stream, and with the cats romping nearby, that I took my first real look at the house and its surroundings. The structure looked inviting in the same way Pompy's place had once, and I rounded up the cats and headed towards it. As I walked up the road to the house I saw animal bones in the pasture. I began to walk faster, and the closer I got to the stone structure, the more I expected to see other humans. The farm house had a look of friendliness about it. It was one of those old stone built houses in the early eighteen hundreds of the sort that Zel and I had been talking about. However, it was made out of rounded river rock instead of field stones, but it was enchanting.

Zel had waited underneath a tree for me and came out to the road to meet us now. "It must have been really beautiful once," she said. Her blonde hair fell evenly over her face and her eyes squinted as she turned towards me and the sun shone directly into them. Her nose was small and wrinkled up as she laughed. She looked much younger than thirty or so, and more oddly to me, she looked innocent. I was glad she was not going to scold and dig at me for lounging in the stream. I looked at her again and focused my gaze just under her cupped hands where her features were shaded, but I could plainly see the outline of her head from the side. There was something regal about her bearing. The way her hair was falling and the angle of her head reminded me of Grandma Ella.

The cats meowed and I turned my attention to looking around at our surroundings. It was then that I spotted smaller piles of bones in the gravel drive closer to the house. On closer inspection I saw that one set of bones were that of a canine, but two more bodies lay beside it. It must be the owners I thought. They must have gone out to see the lights like everyone else.

I stopped suddenly in my tracks when I noticed how the bones of the people were arranged. Their last emotions were petrified for the world to see. The man appeared to have been holding the woman in his arms, trying to shield her. The woman, however, was reaching upward toward the sky. Had she tried to touch the dancing, silent drones above her that night? I stared at the bodies; their clothing now in tatters and barely covering them.

I left them in the yard and entered their house. It was unlocked because they had expected to return. It was a tidy house inside, though dust had settled everywhere. Dishes were still on the table and the frying pan was on the stove. They had been eating supper when the silent attack had come. I had seen this abrupt disruption of life many times by now, but I still rebelled at it. It wasn't right. Life was not meant to just end, to be unfinished. Loose ends needed tying up.

On the table was a book and I walked over to it. It was another instruction book! Here were others who had dared possess the book despite the fact that they could be killed for having it. I picked it up. Inside were their names and a list of their five children and thirteen grandchildren. By today's standards they were a dynasty.

I carried the book around as I continued my search. In the living room I found a picture of the family standing together. There was a feeling, an aura about them that stared back at me. It's the only way I can explain what I saw in their eyes. It was more than just a family resemblance, it was something that emanated from the inside out. I know that sounds crazy, but there was an added something to them that I had not often seen in the people I met or knew in NYC. Pompy and Ella had that same something, I reflected, as I concentrated on the features of the two older people in the picture who now lay in the yard. Suddenly I wished I had known them. I liked the comfortable house and the arrangement of things. It was like Pompy's house; simple and elegant. The furniture wasn't the latest, but it was classic and not out of style with the rest of the pieces in the house, and reflected a life time of putting a home together.

My thoughts were interrupted as I noticed the shadows of the day stretch and exaggerate themselves across the floor in front of me as I walked past the windows. It was getting late. It was time to get things done. I had wasted enough time on a process which had accomplished nothing. I went out of the house and began to bury the couple who lay in the gravel drive.

I did not dig a very deep hole, and I just sort of pushed the tarp under the couple with the end of my shovel and then slid them into the hole. I chastised myself for not being more delicate with them as I thought of their faces in the silver frames sitting on the union blue colored cabinet.

"Why did you bury them, Trave?" Until Zel spoke I had forgotten about her completely.

"It makes them real, I guess. It's more than just being incinerated in the crematoriums and mixed with egg shells to make fertilizer. Who decided that our lives meant nothing, Zel? When did it all start?"

"I don't really know."

When we returned to the house, the cats had already made themselves comfortable on the couches and chairs except for Fluff. She had come up to me and meowed, and I reached down to pet her. Suddenly I realized how tired I was and went down the hall to one of the bedrooms and climbed in and covered up with one of the blankets. I felt Fluff bound up beside me and I was asleep.

I woke in the middle of the night with my heart beating in irregular leaps in my chest. I asked myself what there was to be afraid of. Almost everyone in the world was dead. As soon as I had that thought, I knew it was death itself that I feared. I didn't want to be found lying as a heap of dry bones with no hair, no eyes, and no inside parts left. In that moment the world became surreal as if it were all some cruel joke. I wanted to deny all the proof that I had found about the SG and the deep state's plot. They really hadn't killed millions had they? I wasn't one of the few beings left, was I?

That was when the possibility struck me again that I wasn't just a hu-manimal, I must be partly bio-engineered. I was alive and real people were dead. The laboratories of the world experimented with biogenetics all the time. They grew parts in labs; ears, arms, skin, hair and eyes. All you needed was compatibility of blood type and lab dishes. At that moment I touched my belly, as if by doing so, I could detect which parts of me had been replaced. I touched the appendectomy scar on my right side and my mind began to run amok with crazy scenarios. Was it possible that the surgeons had put new parts in as well as taken the bad ones out? You might think that was far-fetched, and that I was letting fear run away with me, but clones and robotoids were everywhere, and the scopers (the new surgeons were called that because they scoped you out before they worked on you to see where things should go.) Scopers reached through a vein in the thigh into the heart and fixed it, didn't they? Small cameras were swallowed in a pill and made a film about your insides as it traveled through your system, didn't it? Amid all these possibilities it didn't hurt to be aware of all the possibilities. After all I had been in deep storage for ten years. Finally the thoughts stopped chasing me and sleep came.

I felt something touching my back when I woke late the next morning. There was a wall of some sort behind me. I turned to find out what it was, and saw that a pile of books surrounded the entire perimeter of my sleeping bag. I picked some of them up and read over the titles. Artificial Intelligence: Adding New Dimensions, Changing Intelligence in your Android, Creating the Gift of Touch. I threw the books down. There must have been fifty more books littering the ground. I called to Niner, but no one answered me. When I made my out to the fire, I could see that it had gone out. Breakfast dishes were sitting in the pan, unwashed. Then I saw the note. 'Gone to town. Celebration time is here.'- Zel and Niner

I had always suspected that it was the little things, the insignificant ones that got you in the end. Life was a joke and there was a punch line, but you never got to hear it until the end. It was called death, and every creature and species feared it. It was everywhere. It was in all those faces in those cars along the interstates, and in the city streets, and even here in the great open spaces of the west. People had been going places, and then all the motion had stopped. They had died in mid stride which seemed impossible to me. It wasn't natural. It left things in chaos. It would be like the sun failing to complete its arc across the sky. Everything was meant to be completed and was moving towards its intended end. Everyday along the streets and avenues I had seen crowds flowing like the sea, and I had always wanted to take a poll. Where are you going? What is so important that you hurry, knocking in to one another? You stop like robots at the lights. You wait with impatient looks, scowls, and frowns for the green light which tells your legs to move again. Those were the old questions I had wanted to ask, but now I would ask them a different question, a more personal one: "Do you know that one day you will die?"

I wanted to yell at all the humans that had ever existed and tell them this mess was all their fault because they had believed the SG when they told them that Science had out grown God. I wanted to tell them the SG's were making plans to live forever while they had waited for the light to change. The eternals were manufacturing a human parts department. Never mind if all the body parts weren't in the right places yet. Evolution would take care of those little adjustments sometime along the line. If your nose was where your butt was you just had to be patient for millions of years and then things would smell better. Life was a matter of the right stuff coming together. Evolution took time.

Even though the world had had millions and billions of years of evolution behind it already, nothing had started to grow and change by itself until the Government parts department began growing new eyes, legs, hearts, and livers. There was no reason to fear death because it was nothingness. That's what they told us, but if they really believed that why were they in a race to stop death at the station now? Suddenly this all had a strange, familiar ring to it. It was like I had been part of the story. Where had all these thoughts come from? I was seeing flashes of these newly imagined events, but I shook them off.

I began to wonder why, if evolution was a happen stance sort of thing that came about on its own, the SG had needed to employ thousands of scientists all over the world to work day and night trying to find the right mix for life. Men had all the answers except they couldn't replicate the blood. That's why they had to clone. They had to copy the DNA in order to get the blood prepackaged for them. Scientists could grow replacement parts and sell new hearts and livers to the rich who were in need of a 30 or forty year upgrade part, but blood was a mystery. No synthetic, no herb, no mineral on earth could equal its miracle property. This line of thinking brought me to the next thought, and that one hit me hard. The SG had not valued our lives. They had only held their own lives sacred. They had been waging a war against all life and against their own deaths. Whatever they believed lay at the end of life, they were determined to change it.

Bodies lay like garbage rotting everywhere and no one came to bury them or to honor them. Millions were dead. My lawyer friend had been right. People were nothing more than ants scurrying about and piling up things instead of dirt. I suddenly laughed out loud. What had I let myself be talked into? Zel had a mission of personal importance. It was a semi noble ambition, at least. I was not much more than some itinerant imp going to gum up the workings of a utopian society that was growing parts to stave off death. I was in it for laughs and the confusion I could stir up, and to get even. Now that I was away from Zel's gaze I could at last be honest enough to agree she was right. I was seeking revenge, but it was more than that, grander. The destruction of the SG was the restoration of mankind, a rebalancing act that would set nature back on the right path. I just wasn't exactly sure what that was. My intentions were honorable, but they say the road to hell is paved with good intentions.

My coffee was ready and I poured a cup and took a few sips. The taste and smell of the drink reminded me of a cold November night in my grandmother's kitchen. Pompy was ahead of me and we had just come in from the evening chores. It was cold and windy out which only enhanced the warmth of the kitchen. I could smell the coffee in the background blending in with the aromas of food and freshly baked bread and those cinnamon rolls with carmeled brown sugar on the bottom. My mind was coming back strong and with smells and technicolor.

"You men go wash up. It's just ready," I remember my grandmother saying. Ella was dressed in a pink blouse with her sleeves rolled up and a pair of bluish pants. She wore a pink and blue belt tied loosely over the outside of her shirt. Her hair was neat and lay in whitish, soft curls around her face. Her hair was short and reached only to her ear lobes, but it framed her eyes remarkably. That's who Harley's eyes had reminded me of! Grandma Ella was where I had first seen eyes that moved and glinted like churning water; only her eyes had been blue like the sky and the sun had danced in them.

The pink of her shirt complemented her complexion and gave it a warm natural glow. It was the way a woman should look. Natural. The girls I knew back then put on makeup like they were artists in training for some new horror film. Their lips, eyes, and fingernails were various tints of black; all colors which feigned the pallor of death and paid homage to it rather than life. I am dead, these girls advertised. Do you want me? I show you all that I am, and I am nothing. I seek death, but do not be afraid. Celebrate it with me. I show you the end of me. They claimed they were making a statement about their life. They were. They were saying they chose darkness instead of light, sadness instead of joy, chaos instead of peace. It was the zeitgeist of the times.

Nothing was wrong. Even killing was mocked. People gave reasons such as, "I felt this man didn't deserve to live because he was a Christian. I did the city of New York a favor by getting rid of him." Society and the law agreed that these killers should be set free. How could anything be wrong, if nothing was wrong? Believers were the bigots and the racists. Believers were against government benefits for the poor. They were rich, greedy capitalists who controlled everything. This was the sort of info people were given in the speeches during the Purging Wars to stir up the masses into a frenzy until they had foam coming from their mouths. That was the tactics of the People's Progressive Party. They held rallies and brainwashed the herd. That may sound like an odd term, but the general population were known as COW's (Citizens of the World.) Get rid of the believers and the One World would all live in harmony. The government formulated lies and more lies to keep the masses charged up to commit their genocide for them against group after group until finally the war came against those that wore red on Mondays, until all that was left was hu-manimals. Now we were being eradicated. Population control was at zero.

I looked at the Basic Instruction book laying on my sleeping bag and wondered why the SG had declared it the most evil book ever written. The government had been afraid of this book. I didn't need to read very far to figure out why. The beginning of the book had talked about the history of mankind since his creation. Just in the first few chapters I had seen that God had more to offer than the SG did. The God of all had made a provision to save us from ourselves. All of us. Not just the SG, the elite, and the wealthy, but the lowliest of us.

At that moment I spotted Harley and his family grooming and relaxing in what little patch of sun they could find. It was sort of a gray, chilly day, but the sun managed to show from time to time as the clouds rolled by it, and it hung in the sky like a great dim lantern glaring out of the grayness.

Deciding to read further, I went to get my books and bag and then stretched out by the cats. Suddenly a sleepiness began to overtake me. It was a luxurious relief and I surrendered to it willingly. As I stretched, I felt my joints lengthen and loosen and I let the book drop away and closed my eyes.

I listened to the leaves in the trees overhead swoosh together in a gentle rustle. The wind was coming up and I could feel it blow back my hair. I inhaled the air deeply and opened my eyes to look up. The branches arched and swayed back and forth. I could see the effect of the wind on the trees, though it had no visibility on its own. I felt the wind on my face and I felt the collar on my jacket being pushed up against my neck, but I could not see the force behind it.

Then a thought occurred to me. The old world my Pompy had known, and the one I had experienced with him was gone. It was as invisible as the wind that now brushed through the trees and my hair, and that I felt on my skin. Suddenly it occurred to me that the SG had copied nature. They had made the death waves invisible like the air. You breathed it in and saw nothing to frighten you.

Again I still wondered why I had survived. I had been blacked out for days, weeks, but I had not noticed any ill effects. At least not yet. I looked at the cats and wondered how they had survived. Mama had carried kittens to birth and they looked healthy enough. I studied them in earnest now. Harley's coat was regrown in, and he was a gorgeous animal with dark brown barkish looking stripes on his coat. Harley had a white mane that ran from his neck to his chest. He had four white tipped paws and a blaze of white above his left eye that covered his nose. It was in the same spot that Fluff, as I had started to call her, had her tannish orange spot. However, the kitten looked nothing like Harley. She was a diluted gray calico with a mix of both stripes and patches of gray and tan mixed into her fur. She was long haired, but her fur was not as thick as Harley's. The strongest resemblance to her father could be seen in her eyes. She had those shimmering green eyes like Harley, only her eyes were calmer waters. Her brother, Trouble, had been a noisy cat, a talker and a doer and looked almost like a carbon copy of his father except only two of his legs on the right side were tiger striped while the two feet on the left were solid white. If you saw Trouble parading past you with his left side turned towards you, he showed the striped side of his legs to you, and then if he turned around and strutted past you going the other way, he showed only the pure white side of his limbs to you. In that respect he was like a bus on Broadway which boasted different advertising on both sides. He had two sides to him in more ways than one. He investigated everything, calling his siblings to his side, but was the first to run if the slightest noise occurred. I still missed him. The other two males were mostly tabby looking with the same forested tree bark patches of brown like their father painted atop coats of white. The second female was a gray and white striped beauty with blue eyes. I named the boys Tolkien and Lewis and the other girl Sneakers because she stalked after everything. At this moment they were real and so was I. We had come through the war so far. Then I couldn't help thinking of Manhattan and the oceans of people that had once flowed along the streets in the continuous ebbing and receding of tides. Next I pictured the city the way I had seen it the week before I left. Deserted streets and buildings that stood like sentinels, with darkened eyes waiting for someone to care for them. Were the SG's ever intending to come back?

It was then that I heard the farmer's truck on the gravel and turned to look. It was going at a good clip and I saw something on top of it. Was Zel being attacked? I grabbed the rifle and attached the scope. In the sights I was able to get a bead on the black mass on top of the vehicle as it was getting closer. It was Niner. I could see him rolling back and forth on top of the cab. There was riotous laughter coming from their direction.

"What the Sam Hill is going on?" I screamed as the truck came to an abrupt halt in front of me and I was tasting the dust that hadn't yet settled.

"We've found what we were looking for," Niner said. "Show it to him, Zel. I'll be preening feathers before you know it." The drone flew down beside me and hovered by my face as Zel grabbed a box and threw it at me. "The latest in skin transplant and hair growth. True A.I. quality."

I quickly read the box. "This is meant to fix baldness, not grow feathers."

"It's in the fine print. It says adaptable DNA transfer for stimulating growth on animals and birds."

"One formula does all that?"

"And look at this," Zel said opening a box and producing a set of talons which she clenched and unclenched in each of her hands to show me how well they worked. Then she bent down and began scratching at the gravel with it. "Fine motor skills enhanced, it says on the box. Guaranteed."

"So you get your money back in case your plastic doesn't sprout feathers?" I said which threw a damper on their celebration.

"Well, it might take a bit of fine tuning, but that's where you come in. Zel has agreed to assist you in the process. I can read as we go," Niner said.

"I think we need to mix up the stuff in some old tin cans and try it on a stick or a rock before we apply it to you, Niner. Don't you want to see what it does first? I mean maybe you will change your mind once you see what happens."

"Forget the feather bit for now. Let's do the claws first. I want to touch ground and walk. I want my roller derby days behind me."

"Where'd you hear about the derby?"

"Zel told me about the derby girls. Her employer used to go to them."

Before I could say a word, Niner had plopped himself on his back and his wheels were facing me. "Why are you staring at me Travis? I'm not ticklish. Go ahead and remove the old shoes."

"I haven't even had my quota of coffee yet. I need to get some tools together, too."

"You get your tools. I will make more coffee," Zel said.

"This is crazy," I said. "I need to think about this."

"It's not your feet we're planning on changing. You've changed tires before haven't you?"

"That's apples and oranges, Niner."

"No, the directions say take out a screw, put in a screw."

"I have to attach the circuits you know. You want to move, don't you?"

"Yes, otherwise I would be like one of those chickens on the weather vane."

"Not even that good. You wouldn't even be able to do circles like a regular old weather vane on a barn.

"Stationary?"

"Like a tree."

"You better read up on it, then. I don't want to end up as some kind of sitting chicken for target practice. That's what they used weather vanes for. Can you set me on my wheels again?"

Zel brought the coffee and read the directions for attaching the wires to his main circuitry. It took a few days of reading and rereading the manual and finding out which model he was, but we sat reading every page during each meal and then giving the material to Niner to read. Finally I searched over his inner workings to find each part as he described them, which took a lot of translating.

"Step one. Locate motor organ."

"Organ? There are no organs," I said, grabbing the manual back from him and reading it for myself. "It says main motor gear."

"They're my parts, aren't they? Gears makes it sound cold."

I asked Zel for a pen and crossed out gear and wrote organ.

"What are you doing."

"Translating. I have to make notes so I know what you are talking about."

"Whatever for?"

"You're going to be out when I attach the new shoes. I have to know what I'm doing."

"I don't have to be put to sleep," he said in a very indignant manner.

"Do you want me to get zapped?"

"Oh, yes. I had forgotten about the human side of it."

"Better remember it if you want a long and healthy life someday."

"There are complications in being real."

"Want to forget it?"

"No. I won't hurt when I wake up, will I? I told you I don't want the pain thing. I have heard people who have had pain happen to them and it sounded distressing."

"Feelings are what being real is all about."

"Like petting the cats?"

"Yes, but that may take a while. The sensory neurons have to adapt slowly and will allow you to feel only a slight sensation of touch at first. It mimics skin in a synaptic way and can even heal itself," Zel said touching his head, "but that will take a while."

"Everything is a ways down the line," Niner said.

I was holding the remote. "Are you ready?"

"Proceed."

There was a soft little click and Niner closed his eyes.

It took hours, and we had run to the AI and Implant Center before I was ready to wake Niner back up by recharging his power source. I wanted to lay down and stretch out. I was exhausted. I had concentrated so intently for so long a period, but Zel brought me coffee and after a few cups I felt revived enough to continue. I switched Niner back on and he opened his eyes easily. I almost envied him. There was no sleepy look or rubbing the eyes to clear them. "Wow. That was fast," he said.

"Right. Just a blink for you. It was hours for us. The sun is setting."

"Wow. Zel, how do they look?"

"Why don't you ask me? I'm the one that performed the surgery. Looks aren't important. It's performance that counts."

"To the male of the species, maybe, but, I wanted an aesthetic opinion first. Women have that."

"They are glorious talons, Niner. Perfect."

"Set me to a mirror. I want to see them."

"I will get my cosmetic case."

While he was admiring his new appendages I said, "Time to try out those walking sticks."

He took his first step and then another and other; each one becoming more tottering than the first. In seconds he took a nose dive beak first into the dirt.

"I've crashed landed," he kept repeating over and over sounding like he was in a tunnel of some sort.

I went over and picked him up. "Why didn't you tell me feet were so unstable? You haven't fastened them on tightly enough."

"They're on there all right. You just have to practice at keeping upright. It's called balance."

Zel came up to him. "Let me help you, Niner. I will keep hold of you while you try them out again."

With a little bit of coaxing from Zel he was taking steps again with her supporting his body and head. "This takes a bit of getting used to," he said.

"You should practice flexing your talons, too while you've got Zel as your training wheels," I said.

"What's flexing?"

I Came around to the front of him and made a fist and then opened it up.

"I see," he said.

"Don't do it now, but later when you're standing. It will help you get used to how they work."

Niner was looking at my boots. "Your feet are thicker, Trave. Zel, come around to the front, I want to look at you."

"Why are you staring at us?"

"I was looking at your legs"

"What for?" she said, alarmed and turned to me. "What other programs did you add to him?"

"None. You were there."

"Let me see the box these feet came in," he ordered.

"What for?"

"Your legs are thicker. I wanted to see if you got the right size."

"They're the right size. Zel picked them out. You just have to practice."

"Why are human legs thick? Let me see your feet, Travis."

"What? No! I have to make dinner."

"These seem awfully spindly to hold up all this bulk."

"I will show you mine," Zel offered, taking off her shoes.

"No, don't take them off. Just show me."

"I'm not taking off my feet. These are my shoes, Niner."

"Shoes? Feet? They are not the same thing?"

"Yes, these are shoes," she repeated holding them up for Niner to see. "They are only a protective covering to keep my feet warm and safe."

"No one told me."

"Now watch. The next layer is my socks," she said, taking one off and tossing it in the air. I looked over and saw the other shoe whizzing in the same direction, and then the other sock. She sat down and wiggled her toes at him.

"Those are ugly," I heard Niner exclaim. "What are those little tail things?"

"Are you putting on a peep show for the drone?" I called over to them.

"He has never seen feet before," Zel called back.

"You have five of them on each foot. Why?"

"I don't know why, Niner. You will have to ask the creator that."

"Toes are for balance and flexibility," I called to them, but they didn't acknowledge my input.

"Yes. I have a special file where I am logging all my questions when we reach the wizard. I will add that one."

"You have many questions only he can answer," the clone said when his computer file came up on his screen.

"Do you have questions that you would like me to file away for you, Zel?"

"Yes, one very special question, Niner."

"Give it to me."

"No, I will only ask it of the wizard. You will have to wait until then."

"I will stand together with you on that day like Dorothy's friends did with her in Oz. Can I touch your feet?"

"If you like, but be careful. Don't hurt me."

"I have not experienced it yet, but you humans talk about it a lot."

"I hope you never do."

"Don't wish that, Zel."

"Why?"

"Then I will never be real."

"Now you know what a conundrum is," I told him, but he only started shaking his head at me.

Niner practiced every day and was getting so he could balance his wing spread better and he showed me his progress hourly. He carried the box his talons had come in with him on his back and looked at it every night. He had also found a clip about eagles in the wild and streamed it every night at bedtime. He had shown me the clip a dozen times and always said, "Now watch. He is about to take flight. Watch his movement, his wings. Glorious. Phase two. I will get my wings."

"Perfect phase one, first."

"I am almost there, Travis."

"Right, if you want to call tilting and wobbling like a drunken sailor, progress," I said not holding back the truth.

"Show me on the portable," he said thrusting the tiny computer into my hands. "I have never seen a drunken sailor."

I went to the me, me, me tube, everything is about me tube, waited for the jingle to sound out, and then I typed in his request. He watched the clip of the inebriated sailor stumbling on the deck of a ship a while before he said, "That is quite an accurate description, Trave."

"Want me to put your training films back on for you?" I asked.

"Please. I will update. Learn."

"Nothing beats experience," I said.

"I am finding that to be truth," he said taking a few more steps.

A few weeks down the line, he was picking up rocks with his talons and hurling them at targets. He had the pressure down right. On living things he used only light touch according to the sensitivity setting gage he was practicing with. Finally, he could touch me and not rip my skin. For landings, he used the full throttle setting. He told me he was ready for the cats. That night after supper I heard him call, "Here kitty, kitty. Kittens. Fluff. Harley."

"Don't rush them," I said as he watched them creep up to him in their stalking mode. "They think you are a flying pizza."

"Pisa? Pisa?"

"Food. Cats eat birds."

"Alert! Danger! Stalking kittens."

"Are you afraid, Niner? Maybe neither of you are ready," I said as Trouble swatted his outstretched wing on the right side.

"What's the kitten doing?"

"He is playing with your wing. Chewing on it."

"Is this allowed?"

"He can't hurt you."

Without warning, Niner reached his claw out and snatched Tolkien and was holding him down pinned to the ground. "Not allowed. Let go, Niner," I instructed as I moved forward to Tolkien. I felt the claw retract and release the cat so I could pick Tolkien up.

"I will hold him for you. You pet him like I am doing."

It went well for a few pets until Niner said, "Squeeze test."

"No. Don't do the squeeze test. It's not for living livings."

"Why? That was the training you provided me with, or do my files deceive me?"

"Rocks and sticks are not living organisms. They cannot detect pain."

"These kittens feel pain?"

"Yes, they are living like me."

"Then I am not living," he said.

"You are real in your mind," I said poking at my head with my right forefinger. "You think, therefore you are."

"It's not enough," he answered and walked away. "I want it all. Motion is not feeling. Motion is not life."

"It is only part of it," I said. "I'm sorry."

"How long before we find the wizard?"

"I don't know."

"Update. Learn."

"I wish it were that easy."

"It can't be," the eagle said spinning on a dime to face me.

"Take it easy, Niner."

"No, Trav. I'm picking up another new transmission from somewhere."

"Can I listen?"

"I will type it out for you. They are less likely to intercept us that way."

"Good thinking."

"Not bad for a bird's brain, huh?"

I looked at the monitor on the portable computer. COMMAND CONTROL. CANCEL SECTOR 4. SECTOR IS ANNHILATED. MOVE CASTLE TO ROOK.

Zel was looking over my shoulder. "What does that mean?"

We all stood in a circle facing one another. When no further word came from the drone, I finally said, "Well?"

"A well can be deep with water, or dry depending on the season."

"Get out of literal phraseology, Niner. I am asking what do you make of the situation."

"Off hand? Right now?"

"Yes, yes, and yes."

"Not good."

"Do you know what it means?"

"No. It is not a file or download I am familiar with."

"Or you don't remember?"

"I haven't lost my files. You human's lose your minds, but drones don't lose files. I have never heard this code. It is not of SG origin."

"You're sure?"

"Positive. I traced the beam. It is coming from grid point 435 G. My home base is 76Niner J."

"Translate. Where is grid 435?"

"It's coming. Be grabbing onto your pants."

"It's hold onto your pants," I corrected.

"Whichever. Grab your horses, too. Ah, it is Oklahoma. Enid."

"I wish we knew who it was," I said kicking up dirt.

"There is one way to know," Niner said.

I looked at him briefly and then at Zel. "No. I can't afford to lose you. Send one of the other drones."

"It would take too long to program them."

"I order you to stay, Eagle Commander."

"You gave me choice, freedom. I take my chances like the rest of you."

"What do you mean, Niner?" Zel asked.

"Like Trave said, life is mostly a crap shoot."

Zel was looking at me in a very disapproving way.

"Niner! Why is it that you pick up the slang more quickly than the important stuff?" I said feeling parental.

"You programmed me, you figure it out."

I made a dive for the remote. "Don't bother, Trave. I've already overridden the commands," Niner said.

In seconds the eagle was in the air. "I have Alpha squad ready for a fight if you should be attacked in my absence. Use key-four-slash-enter. I will be back in 3 days, 2 hours and 18 min. With a good tail wind, it might be sooner. Stay off channel 107. 5. Eagle Commander out."

As he flew away we heard him sing, "Oh, I used to walk like a drunken sailor. Ruined my hems and needed a tailor." He couldn't carry a tune, but it didn't matter because I didn't know the song anyway.

"He's tone deaf," Zel said, "but he has the heart of a hero."

Zel stood next to me. I kept looking at her. Her face was turned away and looking out into the hills. I decided not to bother her. Suddenly, she turned to me and said, "Did you mean what you said to Niner?"

"About what?"

"That you couldn't get along without him."

"I guess so."

"You have a lot of anger, Travis."

"It's an asset in times like these."

"Is it so hard to admit to having even one tiny spec of emotion?"

"Keep your thoughts to yourself."

"I am only trying to help you."

"Stop analyzing me. I'm only interested in trying to survive."

"And to hell with everything else?"

"In a nutshell, sister."

The sky had been gray all day, but now the rain fell in a fine, steady mist that made it seem even dimmer and created an eerie aura about the place. Weeds and grasses grew nearly two feet high along the roads and in the fields that lead into town. I wondered how many bodies were hidden in their depths. We had found many bones lying around in strange positions when we had gone to town to shop. The people had died right where they stood. The visions of the dead bodies replayed in my mind until I suddenly burst into laughter. I had seen enough. I was at my end. I was losing my sanity. I had never laughed so much or so long in my life. I stopped after my stomach couldn't contract anymore without pain. There were bones of millions littered everywhere, but not to worry! They were Hu-manimals, just trash. That is when I began to yell at the top of my lungs. "We Hu-manimals are lower than trash. Trash is a collectible item. Hu-manimals aren't worth picking up. "

"Travis, stop it," Zel said coming up to me. "You're scaring me."

"We're not even trash," I sobbed.

When my laugh attack subsided, I looked at my family. "We have more in common than you think, kit cats. We, my friends, are in the same primordial soup. We have been betrayed by the world."

The cats only looked at me. "Well, we are about to rectify that. We are on our way to get even with our murderers. We are going to blow them up. Blow them to smithereens as Pompy used to say. There won't be enough to sweep away when we get done. We'll be tidy about our plans. No one will have to clean up after us. I have learned from their mistakes." The cats were listening, but it was clear that they weren't all that stirred up about it. The slow beat of their tails on the floor was indifferent. Leave it go, they seemed to say through half closed eyes. We're listening just to be polite. Just then I heard Zel's voice echoing what the cats had just told me. "Let it go."

I didn't want to start an argument. I wasn't up for that, but I was not going to heed her advice either. I was on a mission. Its plot and plans flowed through my veins, pumping life. I intended to carry out my retribution on these elites. I had never quit anything in my life, and I wasn't going to throw in the last hand, not when I held all the aces. However, there was a snag in my plan. There were multiple targets that would need to be blown up. Why couldn't the rats all be in one cage? It made things more complicated, but it also enervated me. It would be a more worthy challenge. The murderers would not expect an attack, let alone a multi-faceted one coordinated by a Humanimal and their own drones turned rogue. This time death would come on them unawares. They would have no time to repent of their deeds. There was something diabolically evil in that scenario, something cruel and unforgivable, yet delicious.

I began to wonder if I could pull it off.

CHAPTER 7

At dawn bubbly clouds of deep pinks and purples ran along the horizon line while a sea of faint blue sky stretched out towards me. I could see the outline of trees, out buildings, and fence lines in the distance. Then I heard a new sound and listened more closely. It was the voice of birds chirping. They were announcing the new day. I thought I was imagining it until the cats also stirred to the sounds and came to the window.

I decided we should all eat an early breakfast and went to the kitchen. I was feeling better. The sounds of the birds had allayed my fears and the patter of cat talk brought me relief. I wasn't alone. "You're real, aren't you?" I said to Fluff as she ate and had a drink of water. "You all eat. I eat. We eat therefore we are. The birds are singing. The sun is rising. We're alive," I said to the cats as my hand brushed against the book. 'Open it,' a thought prompted.

I started on the first page and read about the beginning of time. I stopped to open a can of peaches and mused about the meaning I had just uncovered. This God had always been. He spoke the world, the universe into being and time started. In contrast, the SG's and the ancient astronaut theorist's 'science' explained the beginning as just a sound exploding out of nothing. They called it the big bang, but denied there was a designer who envisioned it and gave form to it. Even a four year old knows that nothing can be made out of nothing! Take a piece of air and try to make a universe out of it. Go on!!!

To me, at that moment, it took a humongous leap of the imagination to dream up a theory where stuff creates itself by accident and out of nothing rather than a designer who created it, a programmer, like Niner said. The socialist government had given us the true definitions of insanity. I understood in that moment that they had used the ludicrous to identify everything and I began to realign their theories according to reason and logic. To explain the universe as coming into existence by a big bang was a five year old's explanation of things. Explosions destroy. Blow up a car and it scatters debris everywhere. I had never seen a something, an anything, blow apart and then miraculously form into a living, functioning anything. On the other hand, the Creator spoke and formed everything into being. Language was the tool. Words had more meaning and power in them than I had ever dared to imagine. Words weren't just a way of communicating; there was something much deeper and more supernatural to them. They held the power to create worlds.

Suddenly I saw everything contained two sides. Yin and Yang. Light and dark. If words held the power to create, they also contained the power to destroy. It was a revelation since the Shadow Government had denied that antitheses existed. There was no right or wrong, male or female; everything was sameness, undistinguishable, and gray. There was no sun in their world to illuminate anything. Their laws told you how to live and you either followed them or vanished. What I was reading in the instruction manual gave order to the universe.

Suddenly my attention was drawn away from my inner world as I watched the cats batting at a mouse. They were toying with their prey by letting it go and then catching it again. I didn't see their actions as malicious; I saw them as curious. They were almost gentle with the creature, trying to coax its secrets from it before the next hunt. They were getting to know their quarry. Their play was a form of question and answer, I decided; an interrogation which yielded results. Suddenly I saw the mouse dart to the door and disappear under it. The cats stuck their paws under the door and scratched and meowed for the mouse to come back. I decided to help them and got up to open the door to let them chase after the mouse because I didn't want it about getting into our food supply.

To my surprise it was a door which led to the basement and I headed down after the cats. At the bottom of the stairs I stopped and shone the LED light around. Stacked from floor to ceiling were books which lay in scattered heaps and unorganized piles against the walls. I kept the light focused as I walked past the mounds of books, brushing off their covers so I could read them. Ghosts rose up from the dust in the light as I began to speak their titles aloud.

They looked mostly to be text books and were sorted by subjects. I noticed science books and math books and they were arranged by years. That was odd, why would someone do that? Was it the old gal who lay in the yard who had done this? Had she been some sort of teacher in her life? She'd had five kids. Maybe she had been one of those who had home schooled them, but that hadn't been allowed since the twenty twenties. I noticed a few books under a hand written sign that was labeled 1600-1750. I picked one of the books up. It was called Dilworth's Guide to the English Tongue from 1740. Then I saw a later edition called the New Guide to the English Tongue from 1820. There was the History of the United States, 1832, and The Child's History of the US from 1849.

I stared at the shelves and the old books with fine bindings and leathered backs. I imagined the stories these books might hold from the titles. They sat closed and silent, but opened these books had the power to bring the dead back to life. I envisioned the tears from sad, anguished girls who never smiled, and angry young men who had gone off to war and never returned.

Then I saw a pile of notebooks and opened one. Piper had kept a detailed account of the systematic targeting of the school system. He told us to read a book called the New England Primer, dated 1690. It was for the primary grades. In his journal he wrote: 'you only have to read one of these text books to know that the system of education in this country had declined to nothing. If children were capable of reading these adult level texts two hundred years ago, why can't most read and write today? Dare to look at the old textbooks and you will come to the same conclusion that I did. They have taken the gift of learning away. They have left our minds untrained. From generation to generation they carried out a plan to dumb down the populace.'

I stopped reading Piper's journal at this point. He had come to the same conclusions as I had. They had counted on us to not believe such a conspiracy existed. It sounds crazy, but I implore you to ask this one question of yourselves when you find this and read it. Is the socialist devotion to such a cause as deliberately stunting people's ability to learn any more unbelievable than men like my grandfather and others who were willing to give their lives and their youth trying to prevent such a thing from happening during two great world wars? Men don't die for nothing. Those were all young men who gave their futures; all the days, months, and years of their lives so people could be free. Now, like those proud vanished warriors, the hope is gone; entombed in leather bindings and molding into dust. We have made their sacrifices worthless, dishonored them in the most shameful way. Their voices haunt us from the grave, implore us to answer them, but we turn away in silence. How can you tell heros that you lost what they died for, let it just be taken while you stood by and did nothing?

These People Party Progressives told us that people and morality changed from generation to generation, but history shows us that is not true. I have read many books these last few years and the Basic Instruction Manual. People had the same problems two thousand years ago. They killed, stole, lied, and lusted after others they weren't married to. People don't change. The Manual gave laws for men to follow concerning these behaviors, and get this, there were only ten of them. Today we have thousands. The Manual taught one thing: How to love God first and then the others we lived with.

In a few hours I had compiled a few brief notes from Piper's journals which showed the progression of how God's laws were removed from among us. In the mid twentieth century the US Congress made an edict which removed the Ten Laws from the courtrooms and the schools of this nation. They said they were afraid that children might follow them. They continued the assault on mankind decade after decade, and like a river it began to erode the foundations of the society itself and change its course. The fight should have been loud and fierce then, but no one lifted a finger or even whispered a defense for the God of the Universe. The enemy had already won and he knew it.

Welfare was the beginning of the socialization of America. Poverty grew under the system that said it had been created a War to end it. The church and communities had done a better job throughout history than the state did from the 1960's to the present. The pittance of welfare monies had no intention to really lift the poor out of their meager existence, but added new laws in the system which actually kept them down. Only a few were able to make it out of this newly created welfare system. If the system was meant to help, why would that be? For those so eager to have socialism take care of their needs, they should look back to the welfare system to remember just what their meaning of free stuff really means.

Along with a system that was meant to keep the poor economically disadvantaged, the government engineered the theory of evolution to have the same debilitating effect on the human spirit. Instead of man seeing himself as created in the glory and image of God, but was cast as the direct descendants of slime, rocks, and apes. Who wants to claim that Uncle Henry or Aunt Ester was once sitting in a tree picking each other's fleas, and scratching their big, red butts? Any takers? C'mon, whose first?

The progressives set to the task of rewriting all information to line up with the Darwinian evolutionary theory. For instance, in textbooks of the 1920's the world was said to be only around a few thousand years old. By the 60,'s it was said to be millions of years old, and by 2010 our mother earth was senile and past billions of years old. It was a raggedy old planet. Why? The evolutionists needed time for evolution to happen. Never mind that no one ever found evidence of one species developing into another, they just continued like a broken record to chant their mantra until the people accepted it.

I sat and reflected on what Piper had written and he was right. If it's the only song being sung, what other tunes can you learn? By the twenty first century all textbooks claimed that man had crawled out of a large puddle and mere chance had arranged our DNA somehow rather than accepting the notion that these complex and wonderfully mysterious bodies, and the vast array of life on the earth had any semblance of a designer or a programmer, or heaven forbid, a loving God who gave them life. The socialist government erased the historic memory of God guiding his people through the wilderness, yet behind the scenes these scientists, teachers, and politicians who pushed the socialistic agenda were growing copycat parts from molds in laboratories to replace hearts, ears, and skin. Why weren't they just waiting for these parts to develop on their own if that's how they claimed life had been happening for millions and billions of years?

I was becoming more angry. Life just happened? What kind of theory was that? The government had managed to reduce the greatest event in the universe to the equivalent of a 20th century bumper sticker: Crap Happens. Evolution is a very simplistic theory developed by second grade minds who have never been able to produce any scientific proof about their theories. Of course we should not blame the evolutionists alone because it took other Simple Simons to accept their ideas. Why did we?

How could we have bought into the fact that we just came about by some such theory like the Great Oops? The evolutionists don't mention where all this junk they called life came from except that it came from nothing. They never attempt to answer that question because then they would be back at the beginning and needing to answer the next question: Who made all this, who was the programmer? The last thing the socialist evolutionists wanted to do was remind anyone or even give them a hint that there might be a god out there. However, now they create everything. They don't wait for life to evolve to the next stage. Why are they designing the human body to last forever if evolution should do it?

I am fifty odd years old and have yet to see anything create itself. It stands to reason that if all life once formed itself, and everything thing else on this planet, that it would keep on creating new stuff, new species, but I have never seen that happen or even heard about it. Notice that the evolutionists never talk about that aspect, either. Their speculation is that one tiny cell crawled out of the water and created man, the animals, the rocks and trees, and then decided not to produce anything more over the next billion years. What made the cells just stop cold turkey on its journey of evolution? Even more strange is the fact that this one cell that created all of life only produced the same kinds and species that the Instruction Manual lists in the book of Beginnings.

The only new species that were ever formed were on the back lots of dream factory studios by teams of artists who created them for the movies. These imaginationists let their minds go wild by giving us their interpretation of evolution such as blue fish that were half man, or any other myriad combo of species mingled together which were not recognizable as any true species on their own. It was a sad attempt to prove evolution by borrowing a mixture of tentacles, fins, snouts, trunks, and limbs in an unlimited and updated version of Mr. Potato Head. With their movie Build a Species kit they added strange body parts to already known species in all sorts of odd places and in neon colors as vast as the rainbow. It was their attempt at multi culturalism. The movie makers told us these mutant creatures also spoke unintelligible languages, which were understood by none, but accepted and reverenced by all as being highly more intelligent than the race of man. Really?

Which is more plausible, if you think on it a moment, that stuff just formed and then stopped forming for some unknown reason, or that someone intended to form those exact species? For instance, I have left pasta in the garbage can and nothing ever came out of it except a bad smell. Molecules never came together to form a new kind of noodle out of it. There are billions of tons of garbage that have been brewing in dumps all over this country for generations and nothing ever crawled out of them except in those same science fiction movies. I have left dirty socks under the couch cushions for decades and nothing gave them life. Not once in history has life or a new species ever formed out of "stuff" that was just lying around, let alone out of nothing.

DNA is so intricate, that mathematically speaking, the odds against it forming by chance alone can't even be calculated, but the government doesn't believe in math because math is real. However, they believed in it just enough to get us to the moon and back. It stands to reason that if this is a mathematically ordered universe, and all laws of physics work according to its properties, that there was a being who wrote the formula, and I dare to say He was the creator of Einstein himself. Einstein did not birth himself. Neither did he talk with, or have his mind unknowingly fed the theory of relativity by ET's riding on the akashic waves.

Evolutionary theory is simplistic. One cell morphed into a tree, then into a man, then a raccoon, then a rock, then a fish, and then a bird, and then an elephant. That is five year old logic. That's the selling point of it. It all started with one cell and evolved into everything we know today. What mind could not understand or grasp that concept? The whole history of our planet and the science of the universe has been reduced to a single sentence meant for a five year old.

If a blob of slime which you could not see with the naked eye turned into a fish, which turned into a spider which turned into a rock, which turned into a bird, which turned into a cat, which turned into an ape actually happened, why didn't these absurdist's, these scientists and purveyors of this ridiculous evolutionary theory ever worry about man morphing into some new kind of species, or the possibility that man might simply revert back to his chimp like self? Oh, wait they made a movie like that called the Ape planet or something like that. If life was a random crap shoot to begin with, then these so called evolutionary theorists can't know what the cells will eventually create! Now that's scary. Oh, wait, they gave us Star Wars and Guardians of the Galaxy as a way to introduce us to all sorts of life forms and as a lesson in multi culturalism of the cosmos. These literatures and movies told us it was possible! Evolutionists said life evolved from one thing into another, but they couldn't find the bones to prove this morphing from tree to bird to rock anywhere on this planet, so they jumped into space to show us the future of the race. We should have had demonstrations and carried signs and chanted: "No, no! Art won't do. Show us the real me and you."

How can anything in life be predicted if everything just happened? How can a scientific experiment or any research test be replicated if everything keeps changing? How can any evolution believing scientist say with certainty that we won't turn into another species? Just when should we expect to grow another leg or head? Oh, yeah millions of years. Oops. In fact, evolutionists are so sure that man is going to stay just like he is that they are replicating human body parts to ensure man can live forever.

Now, strike three for evolution: DNA is the real proof that evolution is a hoax. You can't transfer the DNA from a monkey to a man. That seems strange doesn't it since evolutionists claim we are distant cousins and evolved from them. The genes for producing a monkey aren't the same as genes which produce humans. There are only a few of the same gene markers that match between humans and apes out of millions. Yes, I said only a FEW markers are the same, but there are millions which are different. Millions. Liberals concentrate on the few common markers, and forget about the millions of different ones, but they say it in percentages. There is only 6 percent difference between humans and monkeys in the markers they were counting. Oops. There they go again, lying by omission of all the facts; all the millions of markers they didn't count as part of that 6 percent.

The only way for DNA within species to mix is through sexual coupling. Everyone knows that a monkey and a human can't produce a baby (though I hear that people have tried and have had sex with monkeys, donkeys, and the like.) A fish can't mate with a zebra nor can a cat mate with a dog. A rat can't mate with a gopher. Just when did that stop happening since that was the way evolutionists claim it all started? DNA is not transferable from one species or kind to the next by osmosis. It takes coupling to complete the transfer of DNA. It is the DNA which cries out to all of us that EVOLUTION of the species IS

NOT POSSIBLE. DNA is not transferable from one species to another. Period.

That leaves evolutionists with no way to explain how DNA crossed from one species to the next by itself. As far as I know they have never even tried to explain it. The best science can do even now is cloning within species, which is merely copying the DNA strand which already exists.

If evolutionary theorists were right, and one species evolved from another, why have species never intermated with one another in the entire history of the world? How can you build a theory around a thesis which is entirely outside the scope of possibility, and how did the entire world accept the most outrageous and implausible event in the universe? Oh, yeah, we were busy. Let everyone believe what they wanted. This was America. We had to bake cookies, do the laundry, mow the lawn, because what would the neighbors think about us? Let them say we descended from baboons, I've got a party on Friday night. We were kept busy inside our own little microcosmic cocoons while they were weaving the macrocosm of a new reality around us. Darwinism is a handy and simplistic tool to discredit God for his ingenious and magnificent creation.

My mind was pounding with all this these facts. I was amazed I knew so much and had such a passion for this subject. I needed a break and so had taken the cats out to get air and was looking at the world according to the new view I was beginning to adopt. I had finally dismissed the Great Oops of how life had come about according to the socialists. I stood looking at the clouds as the sun was just vanishing. Rich reds and oranges were being forced to give way to rich purple clouds along the bottom rim of the horizon which rolled and billowed, rising up like mountains into the sky. Then suddenly, quietly, the orange sun slipped like a coin down a slot and was gone. Beyond the suns reach, the sky was left with very little color at all. This strange twilight lingered, marking the end of the day, stranding the heavens in paleness until the stars would rise and shine like a million little eyes blinking in the darkness. I was seeing nature with eyes I had never used before. It was magnificent. All of it.

I saw the animals around me differently, too. The cats stalked in the unmown grasses in the yard. How different and unlike man they were, yet we shared the abilities to see, hear, and reason. Now most don't think animals can reason, but I argue with that. I had observed my family of cats watching a bird sitting in the road. First, Mama signaled to her kittens by a slight movement of her head for them to watch. Then she started forward in a stiff steeled gait, moving forward one paw at a time in a slow, measured count. The younger cats kept their eyes on the mother, looking to her for guidance as they crept closer to their prey and mimicking her slow steps. That was not just instinct. They had to reason in order to watch their mother, and to take their cues from her.

Mama again signaled to them to stop by giving one long look in their direction as she continued moving towards the bird alone. She was crouched lower now and advanced even slower in halting half steps. Mama paused after each half step to see if the bird had picked up her movement. When she sensed it hadn't, she moved the other foot one half step closer. She repeated this patient process until she was close enough to attack. Then she sprang out from the grasses, and in one high and powerful leap, caught the bird in flight. The bird hadn't been just sitting there. He was listening and alert, and when the cat had leaped, it was off in a second, but it was too late.

Mama kitty had to know the bird would take flight and had to aim at the precise height and angle to catch it. If you had seen her calculation of movement, you would agree with me. Mama's math was as complicated a formula as was needed to send a spaceship to the moon. She brought the bird down in an elegant launch. Her feline body was elongated and the strength in her forepaws was apparent. Each muscle released a burst of focused energy the bird was unable to match. That takes forethought.

She strutted now, carrying the bird in her teeth, and it swung back and forth as she cantered up to her brood and dropped it at their feet. They were on it in a flash. They looked at the bird and then back at mom. The lesson was over for the time being and they ate. Animals in nature don't lie to themselves about what their lives are. They are prey and must be on the alert for the hunters of the world. Man was prey, but he was told he was protected. Where was man's instinct? Why had we not seen the progressive party's slow and crouching movement towards us over the last twenty decades? Even the sparrow had been wary of the coming danger.

I decided to leave off thinking about things that had gone wrong in the past and began to focus on plans for the future. It was time to stalk the bird. I laid out the map and began studying our intended route to the north. As I looked at the towns and cities, I wondered how many humans were left out there. "We have a lot in common," I said to Harley as I watched him milling at my feet and rubbing his head against my pant leg. "We are all survivors," I said, stooping to pet him, and suspected that he was really using my pants as a napkin of sorts after feasting on the bird.

That got me to thinking about what I had just read in the book. If God existed, why had he allowed all this to happen? It was the one question I could not reconcile to a satisfactory conclusion in my mind. It didn't make sense. Did he just sit in his heaven and watch? Was he really who those writer's and philosophers of the eighteenth and nineteenth centuries claimed he was? Had God just set time in motion like the winding of a clock, and then skipped out the back door?

Looking around at what had taken place on the earth I had to believe he had done just that. Pompey told me that after WWII, and into the nineteen fifties and sixties, that the writers and social commentators of the day proclaimed that God was dead. People were always trying to kill God, I thought, even after they had crucified his son once around 30 AD. Maybe that was the real end of God himself. After all, the Jewish people never believed that he was the savior of the world and they were looking for him. If the Jewish people didn't recognize him, then maybe the world had gotten it all wrong. Maybe he had never come. Maybe he never intended to. Whatever the cause or reason, man felt distant and separated from this God. Rather than trying to believe in Him, they simply, with the stroke of a pen, annihilated him.

It was the faint light of twilight as I looked around the farm that I was reminded of Pompy. My grandfather had believed in God to the point of being masochistic, I thought now. People had taken everything he had worked his whole life for, yet he had forgiven them. "The Book says that if a man should steal your shirt, give him the one off your back. If a man asks you to walk a mile with him, go two," he had once said to me. He had waited for me to say something, but I just stared at him. Then he put his arm around my shoulders and looked at me squarely to impress his philosophy on me. "Do you understand me?" I didn't, but I nodded just to make the agitation and uncomfortable feelings end.

I began to walk towards the house and the cats followed after me. No wonder all those who believed in Jesus were killed, I mused. They made themselves easy targets with a philosophy like that. My old system of beliefs was taking hold in my mind again as I recalled the SG had told us Christian thinking was dangerous. I thought that believers were just plain stupid as I stepped through the door into the house and I was subtlety aware that I had held these assumptions before and in another time. I tried to pinpoint just when that was and who I had once been.

I turned on the LED's and picked up the book and opened it up on a whim. Let the book choose what I should read, I thought in a challenging sort of way. I looked down to see what the fates had chosen. It was Isaiah 59. It said, "But your inequities have separated you from God; and your sins have hidden his face from you, so that he will not hear." I set down the book on the kitchen table and closed it almost in fear. The book was addressing the exact issue I had been in a quandary about just minutes ago. Shivers ran through my body as I recalled that I had heard a different voice in my head other than my own when I had read it. It was the clearest voice I had ever heard and sounded as if it had been born of air. It was sure and full of power. The words stayed with me. They would not let me be.

This led me to think about my life now and the quest of the two companions with me. What a soup. They were on a quest to find God. Niner saw him as a kind of wizard or genie who was there to grant wishes and Zel believed He could reunite her with her soul. Now I was caught up in their lunacy. Was any of this true? Why, if He was God, had He vanished and left us to the enemy? Why had he let Pompy's life be stolen and the enemy kill him?

I began thinking about the words the Christ called out just before he died. He had pondered over the exact issue I was struggling with now. He was asking his Father why he had deserted him. That was a strange question coming from the supposed Son of God, I thought. He, of all people, should be the closest to this God, yet Jesus felt like every other human being had felt on this earth. He wanted an answer. He wanted to know where God had gone.

Was the answer in the book? I opened up to the Psalms and continued to read. King David had pleaded with this God not to be silent, and not to desert him, too. Then I remembered the words from the Old testament. It had said that God had chosen not to hear. He had made a deliberate and conscious choice to turn away from his people. Why?

I looked up from my reading when I noticed the light coming through the shades. I smiled. I had found an answer to my question. I had read all night and was hungry, not because I had done anything to work up an appetite, but because I had been successful on my quest. At least I thought I had. In the Old Testament God's people had a pension for idol worship. God actually told the Israelites to call out to their unseeing, unhearing idols to see what these idols of stone would do for them, but they did not listen to Him, they did not care. They chose to keep their idols and God turned away, mourned for his people, and was silent.

It was just like the people of today believing in the god consciousness of all men. They heard only their own voices telling them what they wanted to hear. It was not the voice of God they heard in nature. To them, Nature was a wooer, a lover, a gentle woman god. They had thought to tame her weather patterns and subdue her to their will with seeding and chems until the real God spoke with floods and earthquakes so terrible they hid themselves in caves and got in planes and tried to fly above the destruction. A cult of star worshippers had even tried to astral project themselves away from the quakes. The reports were that they had been successful simply due to the fact that the hundreds of bodies were never found. So great was their belief in the ability of man to win over the greatest odds that no one even suspected that their bodies could lay buried in the ruins of the devastation.

While rereading the story of how the Hebrews ignored the pleas of God to leave their idols and return to Him I found myself understanding God and rooting for him. I was getting to know him. Over my life I had heard people blame God for this, that, and eventually everything. I had, too. People of my day said He had moved away and forsaken them just like the Hebrews had complained about four thousand years ago when the reality was that God had not left at all. It was the people that had gone away. It was me. It was all of us. We had left God. After all, why should he listen to us when we prayed to other gods and to ourselves? I'd had an epiphany. I had found the answer to part of my quandary, but Jesus had not worshipped idols nor had he ever sinned. Why had His Father left him? I jotted down the thought in my notebook.

I decided to focus on other things for a while to give my brain a rest. I was curious about the man whose house I was a guest in. Nolan Piper. I liked his name. I had thought him handsome when I had looked at his family portrait. Apparently he had been a professor at one time at Northwestern in Illinois. What had brought him here to Wyoming? I took a few more of his notebooks upstairs to read.

I saw it as an omen that I had found his notebooks in the safe. Maybe reading them would spare me from the same fate he had met.

I read on to see how Piper was able to carry on his dual role of believer of God and yet proclaim his loyalty to the Party and maintain his sanity. I had seen the sticker on his car, his house, and the barn that marked him as a party member. He had to be in good standing within the party in order to hold a professorship at the university. No conservative or religious person could get a job like that, I thought, and that is precisely where Nolan started his journal. He was explaining what he called the silent war. It had been a covert war for years. The socialists had amassed a silent army and invaded every level of America's institutions until by 2018 there were as many as eighty four registered socialists who were members of the US Congress. They belonged to the DSA-Democratic Socialists of America. For decades the liberals had already taken over control of America's mind by ruining its sacred strongholds of education, religion, and the government arena itself. Anyone who did not agree with their politics was not hired. It was that simple. The party infiltrated all levels of the educational system. The brain washing was then in place from age five through eighteen. Those were the impressionable years.

Lew Ayres had been head of the board of education in Chicago beginning in the late twentieth century. He had murdered a policemen or someone in the sixties when he had been part of the underground revolution of the times. He stayed underground until the socialists had attained positions of power in the government who would not prosecute his crime, but reward it! The powers that be promoted him to running the educational system of the entire US. That should tell you what kind of covert power already existed in the late twentieth century. Ayres was an avowed atheist so it made perfect sense that he would hold with the philosophy that praying in schools was a violation of church and state. That fact that made me put the journal down.

Further, books, people, history all talked about the separation of church and state when that exact fact had never existed. It is not in the Constitution. Go ahead, look for it!!!!! Jefferson had written that particular phrase in a personal letter to a friend who had been afraid that the government would interfere with his religion, not vice versa, and Jefferson had explained to his friend that a wall (metaphorically speaking) existed between the two which would prevent the government from interfering with his right to worship. Again, I don't know why a debate over it's validity was never challenged by those in the Congress, the Senate, the Supreme Court or any other person in the land. Everyone just let an Error of this magnitude continue. Why? Again the American people just convinced themselves that the frog was really a prince. By doing so, wrong was perceived as right and lawful. They had lived with the frog so long they actually heard it speak.

There were many things in Piper's journals that I found interesting. For instance, it seems each state had once controlled their own educational system and were free to choose the textbooks and the curriculum they knew their state was in need of. They were also free to give achievement tests to mark the progress of their students.

I read on in his journal and found that little by little the Public Schools began to get more and more of their monies from the government. If schools took the monies, they were mandated to follow the rules set by the federal government and to follow the government's choice of text books. (The taxes collected by each state for education wasn't enough?) People paid for their children's schooling, but no longer had a say it what it bought. The point I really want to make is that there was no longer public education as there had been. People believed the schools were public because the government continued to call the educational system by its known and established moniker of Public schools. After all, a rose is a rose is a rose, is it not?

McCarthy had tried to warn the American people in the 1950's that communism was alive and well and in high offices, but his life was destroyed. He was labeled as a crazy lunatic by the very communists he was trying to expose! It wasn't before the 2016 election that this silent war to replace conservative Americans with those who held socialist agendas was openly brought before the people. That year was the first time the word socialist was used in reference to a political candidate, and the first time a declared socialist, Sanders, had ever run for office of the President of the US.

They had kept their identity hidden until they had convinced the poor that socialism was a way to even the playing field. Again, I advise one to look at the welfare system to see what socialism really is. The wolves had talked like sheep and no one saw through it until it was too late. It was the coup of all coups and not a shot was fired! I liked Nolan Piper. He thought like I did.

It was about that time that I heard what sounded like the clucking of chickens in the distance. I didn't think that could be possible, but I got up and headed towards the pasture and sure enough I saw the tiny, feathered birds walking our way. They must have sensed humans were back and they were coming home to roost. I hoped a few females were among them. Eggs would be a welcome addition to the menu. In minutes the fowls were in their old coop beside the barn, so I simply shut the gate. The birds were busy scratching around to see what feed was left among the gravel while I studied the rooster's to see which one I would kill. As I sat watching outside the fence, the cats came up and caused an instant panic among the birds. It was then that I noticed one of the chickens being attacked by the others. It kept trying to get away, but the others were relentless in their pursuit. They seemed to be pecking at the chicken. It squawked, and ran in circles, flapping its wings trying to protect itself. One of the other chickens kept after it, pecking until it tired of the activity and left, which allowed the outcast bird a short respite, but then a new pursuer went after it. I decided to retrieve the attacked bird. It had a hole in its left side where the others had constantly pecked at it.

Zel had heard the commotion and had come out to see what was going on. She was looking at the injured hen in my hand. "Why have they done that to her? Why have they turned on her?"

"I don't know," I answered absently. Zel had left me alone for the past few days and I had not expected to interact with her now.

"Give her to me. I will build a pen for her. They are trying to kill her."

"I was going to eat her for dinner."

"Why do you take the helpless? Take one of the warriors, the haters, and let's feed on them. Turn the tables," she said. As she held the injured bird, a large male came right up to her. "There, take that big one. He has more meat on him anyway," she said pointing at him.

"Maybe the one you're holding is sick. Maybe they were trying to protect themselves," I said.

"Then you shouldn't be eating her, anyway."

What she said made sense and I grabbed the big guy. "He'll be a little tough," I said to Zel, but I felt relieved. I would not be responsible for picking who should live or die. I watched Zel cooing at the bird as she walked away. The hen's own kind had given her up, but a stranger had come and taken pity on her. Her life would go on. "I will clean your wound and find a place for you to stay where you will be safe," I heard Zel tell the hen. "Then you will lay many eggs for us."

I chopped the rooster's head off and plucked and gutted him as the fire was starting to flame up. I placed the oven grates over the pit, and went in to get a pan to put the rooster in. Inside, I washed him off over the sink with some of the bottled water and then put him into the Piper's porcelain-roasting pan.

The cats were quite vocal about the goings on. I'm sure they were talking about the size of the bird. It was a giant compared to their usual catch. The word giant reminded me of David in the Bible. We had one major thing in common: The elitist's society had no more use for me than Saul had of David. The book called David a man after God's own heart and here is where we began to differ. David had an unshakable faith. His psalms in the book were very personal and intimate conversations. I always felt like I was eavesdropping on David's relationship with his God when I read them. Just then I had a voice whisper into my thoughts. "He's your God, too." For just a moment I entertained that possibility, but let it drift out the other end of my thoughts like so much smoke. I imagined thoughts were like the linear neon messages which ran constantly across the boards in Times Square. However, the typed form of communication on the Times Square's board repeated themselves in ordered fashion, while the ones in my mind played back for no apparent reason and in no certain order.

I looked up at the sky now in much the same musing way I had done when I was a child around Yule time imagining Santa in his sleigh suddenly appearing out of the night sky and landing on the roof. I had believed he was up there somewhere sitting in that sleigh, guiding his reindeer. I had believed it was possible for him to deliver gifts to all in the world. I had never doubted in Santa. In the twenty first century the government still sanctioned belief in Santa, but not in God. That's where the fat guy had a leg up. Santa was legalized belief, God was not. You could believe in wood gods and river gods, and even that you were a god. You could pray to a stone, Budda, or the Muslim's Allah, but the Wizard's name was forbidden.

"Are you up there on a throne in the clouds?" I called up silently. "If you are, why don't you show yourself?" I shouted up louder. I wanted a match up. I threw down the gauntlet. "If you're there, make that small limb shake on that bush beside me. Shake it the way a little lamb shakes his tail." I had hardly finished my sentence when I saw the tree limb quiver and shake violently. I stood up immediately and walked away. My heart was racing and I didn't dare look back at the bush. I focused my sole attention on the pot of chicken I had placed on the fire. It would be awhile before lunch was ready. As I baked my bread, I began to tell myself that I had only imagined the limb moving. Then I laughed. God had a macabre sense of humor. I wanted proof, I thought, and I had gotten it. If the lines of communication were open, I intended to keep going. If God had really spoken to me just then, maybe he would answer another question. "Why did you desert your son on the cross?"

No answer came to my second question. Lightning wasn't going to strike twice. However, I felt a prompting to reread the poems of David so I did. I wasn't really looking for the answer to my question, I was just enjoying hearing the private conversation of the songs when I stopped to reflect. David had written that God had spoken to him and answered his prayers in some songs, but in others, David questioned why God had hidden His face from him.

The king of Israel had the same question as I did now. However, David said that God had answered him before, and with that in mind, I kept reading until I had a revelation, if you will. In a further song, David called God Holy. I put the book down. That was it. That was the answer! God was Holy. I quickly turned back to the gospels of the apostles and read them.

On the second or so reading of the gospels it was clear to me that all the sins of the world had been heaped on Jesus at the cross. It was as if the book had spoken to me and those lines had jumped out. I had found my answer. Since His Son had been made sin, God could no longer look on him because God was Holy. I was beginning to piece the logic of God together through his own words and the songs of King David. David wrote of warriors, and the readying of the horses and chariots for battle. He realized that he, as a man, must prepare for battle, but that God was the deciding factor. God would give the victory, not the horses or the weapons. The important thing is that David knew God was there. I looked at the big elm tree again and at the limb that had shaken itself, and this thought came to me almost as a longing: I have never known someone as well as this king knew his God.

Through this king of ancient times, and the account of the disciples, this abstract notion of God had become real. God is holy. He cannot abide sin. This was the first and only time the Father and the Son had ever been torn from each other was at the crucifixtion. Their sadness and tears tore the light from the sky in the middle of the day. It was the sin of the world that separated Jesus from his Father that day. God had not left him. I understood now. If God turned away from his own Son because he had become sin, it stood to reason he would ignore the prayers and pleadings of men who sinned. To repent is to repair the breach with God.

David knew this, so the only being King David answered to was the Father in heaven who provided the rain in the mountains that ran down to the valleys and who owned the cattle on a thousand hills. It was clear this poet, warrior, and king loved God. I had thought that I had loved Pompy this way, but now I wasn't sure if I had ever known or loved with any real depth of understanding. To know someone was to know their history, their character, their heart. David knew God so well he knew what His reactions would be to things that he did. It must have seemed to this King of Israel like he was hitting a hundred foot wall of water when he came to ask forgiveness for his sins with Bathsheba. He had taken a man's wife in lust and then sent the man into the heat of battle where he knew he would be killed.

The baby that was born to David and Bathsheba died soon after it was born, and David's servants could not understand why he was able to eat when they thought he should mourn. They considered David's doings odd behavior. They told him he should mourn since the baby was dead, but David told them that he had prayed and fasted while there had been a chance that the baby might live, and while God might still intervene, but now that the child was gone, God had spoken. Prayers would do no more good. Fasting would do no good. That's how well David knew his God. It was with these thoughts of the king and the ancient times that I fell asleep.

The cats and I dined on chicken and bread again in the morning by the tree where I made the fire pit. Afterwards I decided to walk around the property and see what was out there. It was getting towards autumn and the days were growing shorter, but today the sky was a stark and brilliant blue. There wasn't a cloud, and it was the time of year when the sun turned everything it touched strangely golden and solemn. The trunks of the trees looked almost black in the ochre light, and the dying leaves were also filled with a brilliance as if by a process of osmosis they had somehow absorbed the sun's color into themselves.

I was thinking of David again as we walked. In nature, alone, and surrounded with color and beauty, I was a king. I could dream again. I had felt the struggle of life reborn through the heart and mind of a king. Getting to know the struggles of the Biblical people had given me a new vision of the journey before me. It gave me the will to step into the future. I had seen kings rise to the challenge! Without reading those stories I would never have awakened with such hope.

That fact made it quite clear to me why the government had banned books. By destroying the characters of the past they had robbed us of the knowledge that it was possible to overcome the same battles in ourselves. They wanted us to be like the machines they gave birth to.

I stopped a minute to make sure the cats were still following after me. It was a warm autumn day and I felt like a real stretch of the legs. There was a high hill that lay in front of us and I was curious to see what lay on the other side. We wound our way up into the hills to the west, and I could feel the morning sun warm my back. At the top of the hill I stopped to take in the marvels of the other side. It held more than I had imagined it would. There was a valley below and a sizable stream flowed through it. I could hear the water singing from where I stood. I wondered if the water was good. It looked to be clear and I could see each and every stone in the brook as the water tumbled over them. The reeds along the shallows were green. Just then I heard a splash and turned to see Harley in the rushing water. He had pounced after something and missed. His head jerked back and forth comically as he tried to pinpoint the where abouts of his lost prey. Within seconds, he spotted it again and gave a leap forward. This time he held up a fish for me to see. It was flipping valiantly back and forth trying to fight against the trap of teeth that held it. Then it was still for a half of a second before its body gave a sudden buck forward like a bronco attempting to catch his rider off guard. It was no use. Harley had bitten down with all of his ivory hooks locked firmly on the belly of the fish and was struggling to shore with it securely in his mouth.

When he reached the bank, he dropped the fish into the grass where it flopped on its side and continued flailing its body in an undulating movement. It was the only motion the fish knew how to perform, but it wasn't working on land. His tail movements were not propelling him anywhere. The other cats were circling this strange creature. Lewis put out a paw and slapped timidly at the fish and then drew back to safer ground where he could wait

285

and see what the fish would do. When the fish did not attack, he approached it again and slapped at it some more. Harley let his children play with the fish until it stopped trying to flip its tail. Then he and Mama walked passed their children and right up to the fish and began to eat on it. It didn't take long before the others were dining along with them.

I decided to catch some fish for myself and took some rope I had in my jacket pocket out. I searched for a suitable pole from among the branches that lay on the ground under one of the trees. I had some computer chips in my pockets, and tore the copper backing away from the chips and fashioned the zig zag pattern of the wire into a hook.

It was the perfect day to lay on the banks with a line in the water. I had no problems in the world. In no time at all I had caught a few fish and we headed back home. I was content and at peace. God was in his heaven. All was right with the world as Pompy had so often said. I welcomed my recollections of Pompy. I no longer fought my memories of the past and they seemed to have their own rhythms, and I let them have their headway like the stream in the valley.

I still wasn't comfortable with the way my mind seemed to take would a turn I was not prepared for. For instance, I had been thinking about the last time I had fished. I had been with Pompy and I must have been in my early teens. Then wham, my memory got side swiped like a car coming from a blind alley, and I was suddenly recalling a conversation I had with Pompy just before he was taken away. What causes that? My thoughts were like freight trains that I wasn't able to control. I had not been able to control Pompy in those last days either. He talked loud and he talked about things which could make you disappear.

Pompy used to say that men were treated worse than animals. "I treated my cows better than the SG treats men. Don't they know we men have souls? That we are made in the image of God?"

THE WIZARD OF AI

"Shh, Pompy. Don't let the neighbors hear you. They will turn you in." I remember walking over to him. "Is your book hidden away?"

"Yes. I will just keep quiet and go read. Thank you for letting me keep my book."

"They've taken everything else," I said.

"I'm glad you are not afraid to go against them. Keep fighting them. Promise me you will. You mustn't let them win, Trav."

Reliving that memory brought me back to what I had believed in then. I had been as sure there was no God at that moment with Pompy as I had been positive and convinced that there was a God only a few hours ago. Maybe there had been a God when David existed and my grandfather existed. Maybe they had caused him to exist. Maybe the SG had killed Him, or God died in the war the way millions had. Yes, that was the answer. God had died in the war, and then the government announced his death in the 1950's. God is dead, read the headlines, and so is the hero. Long live the anti-hero. Just then a voice interrupted my thoughts. 'There's more. You haven't read the end.' I took the thought to have come from Pompy and my memories of him, but it only left me lost and wandering what end it was supposed to point me to.

I sort of knew what the ending in the Bible was about because Pompy had explained it to me. It hadn't left an impression on me because it didn't sound much different than the endings of many flicks I had streamed online. In the movies, the end came when the aliens or some terrorists invaded, but then a few heroes arrived to fight and save the day. In Pompy's version, God rode in on a horse and saved the world. It was hard to tell which version was more real.

Then I was reminded that people I knew, and had lived with, had actually believed there were really aliens out there. They trusted in those ancient alien theorists who came up with questionable types of proof like a drawing of a man on some cave wall that had a circle around his head that they proclaimed was evidence of ancient astronauts. A better word for theory is conjecture. These theorists also believed that these ancient aliens had helped man in the past and were convinced that they were coming back. That specific claim of theirs always puzzled me. If these aliens had been here, built the pyramids, given us mathematics, and were coming back, why had they not left as much as a scrawled note informing us of their intentions? Why had these ancient aliens kept us in the dark about whether or not they existed? Why leave cryptic clues? What was the big secret? Shouldn't they have told someone? Were the ancient aliens waiting for these wild haired theorists to devine (in their case, guess) the pieces of the puzzle and come up with this theory based solely on secret cryptic drawings?

God had sense enough to leave a note behind, and for that reason I gave God the points on my score card. However, these 'out of the box thinkers,' these ancient astronaut theorists, did not believe in the God who left a book and told them all about himself. They didn't buy his explanation or his book, which had been on the best seller list for hundreds of years. It's just like a leftist to ignore the salient point of any argument. They had an uncanny talent for it.

If these ancient aliens were once here, as these theorists claim, where are our alien benefactors now? Why didn't they intervene in all the wars and problems of mankind? To me, the aliens can be faulted for being as distant and uncaring as God. Didn't these same ancient aliens, who taught us how to build the pyramids, simply look down on us and let us kill each other just like man blamed God for doing? To my way of thinking, these ancient alien benefactors have earned the right to the same criticism as God, and for exactly the same reasons. Neither one seemed very interested in the plight of this blue and white marble.

CHAPTER 8

When we returned to camp, I saw Niner talking with Zel around the fire. He had made it back safely. I began to run and wave at them. The cats were able to outdistance me and I saw them pounce on Niner in their playful fashion. I tried to shoo them away, but Niner said, "It's their way of welcoming me. They love me."

"They're trying to eat you Niner, but think what you want."

Niner was trying to balance on his legs as the cats lunged on his wings. "I have good news. We have allies," he said.

I was growing tired of the cats antics and stomped my feet by Niner and they fled away in sudden terror. "Allies? What makes you so sure they're on our side?"

"They are citizens like you and Zel. They are not elite eternal hybrids. They go to find the strongholds as we do and annihilate them."

"We're not doing that!" I shouted back at him. This eagle had gotten things screwed up in his mind. "How do you know we can trust them?"

"You have only to look at them to know they are not SG. They too, have been betrayed by the government. They will contact you on the pocket computer. The code word is wizard."

Just then the red light on the pocket computer began to blink and Niner called my attention to it. "Answer them."

I picked up the computer and pushed the button. I just about dropped it when I saw the face on the screen. It was a woman. A young one.

"Hi," was all that I managed.

"Is this Wizard? Acknowledge."

"It is. I am. Yes," I stuttered as I struggled to fix my appearance, well, my hair anyway. I turned to Niner and whispered. "Why didn't you tell me they were women?"

"Does that make a difference?" Niner asked.

I saw Zel looking at me with a smirk on her lips big enough to make a clown proud.

"No. I was just wondering." I cleared my throat and continued. "This is wizard. Go ahead."

"We encountered Eagle Commander and were informed that you are on your way to the base at Denver. We have eleven more units in the field and are moving towards your location. We would like to move into your coordinates. May we approach?"

While I was thinking, new words were being typed on the screen which made me decide hastily in their favor. "We ask only a place to rest and eat."

"I will give you our coordinates." I seemed to have given in rather quickly, but after all Niner had done the background check for me. He had assured me she was a human. I typed in the coordinates and heard the woman's response.

"We have them."

"Niner," I said angrily and kicking dust up in his direction with my feet.

"I am here. I will explain. They have an envelope to which I attached a laser coordinate. If you said no, I would have blasted the envelope by smart laser from here. Simple."

I could see that was true for the female was holding it up and saying. "Neutralize the message, Eagle."

The girl then read it and said, "We are on our way."

"They as much as expected an okie dokie, Eagle."

"They know about artificial Intel."

"You thought they were connected with the wizard. So that's why you wanted them here. How could you? You may have jeopardized our lives so you could be more human. Well, you know what? You are already more human than I care to know. You are selfish and conniving."

"I am all those things. I am also kind to animals and caring about man. I am going to check on the drones. They need to be recharged," Niner said and flew off.

"Character flaws are not badges of honor to be bragged about," I yelled back at him.

"Don't you think you're being a little hard on him?" Zel asked as Niner made his getaway.

"I should have broken his wings. Stomped on him with my size tens. Made him into little plastic plexi coated fractions."

"It's your fault. You gave him the belief that he could be human. You gave us both books that made the unreal, real."

"I told you both those books were fiction. They are as fake as he is. Why won't you listen?"

"There is the Basic Instruction book. You told us that was real. He doesn't understand why some books are real and others are not. The God, the one true wizard of all, makes things real. We seek after him now. He is the only one who can remedy what is wrong with us."

"Birds of a feather. Look, no one has ever seen God. He may not even exist."

"I thought you believed."

"I'm trying to decide, but I have questions that need to be answered."

"Maybe you need some of Niner's faith."

"Blind, stupid faith? Imbecilic faith?"

"It is still faith," she said. "It's just infused with different flavoring."

"Dang if you don't even sound like Niner," I said. "Faith can't be infused with anything. It's abstract. There is no such thing as imbecilic infused faith."

"Sure there is. Raspberry or lemon infused tea is still tea isn't it?"

"Faith is a concept. Tea is a food. You can't apply food terms and mix them up with abstract terms They don't get blended."

"Is there a rule book on what you are trying to explain to me?" Zel asked.

"No."

"Okay, but You understood what I meant, didn't you?" she said.

"Well, yes after... some discussion."

"That's the whole point of talking isn't it, understanding? So what's the problem?"

I decided to let the matter drop. She had moved her game piece ahead of me again.

Days came and went, but things remained tense around the camp. I sat outside with the cats and drank my coffee. It was a sunless day and the sky was full of tumbling gray clouds.

"Look," Zel pointed. "The strangers have arrived. They are coming down from the hill."

"Set the drones for attack, Niner."

"We will not need them, but I will do as you ask." He set to flight and then immediately flew back as if he had forgotten something. "The girl's title is Captain."

"I don't want her title. Tell me what her name is."

"Brin, I guess."

As I watched the small army enter our camp, I set my coffee cup down and picked up my rifle. The girl I had seen on the screen had her eyes fixed on me. "There's more of us than there are of you," she said eyeing my weapon.

I could see there were about a dozen of them. "I always carry a gun with me," I told her and kept the rifle in my right hand.

Zel stepped closer to us, cradling a rifle in her arms and the girl stepped back. "I am Brin." I was glad her words were friendly in spite of her misgivings of us. I moved forward to shake her hand. "I'm Travis, and this is Zel."

Brin was looking past me and taking in the layout of the farm, which gave me a disconcerted feeling. I wanted to read her eyes. "We had hoped to be here earlier, but we ran into a serpent in the lake and we spend considerable time trying to kill it."

"Serpent?"

The girl ignored my question and continued. "We also ran into an Ozark Howler."

Have you had any problems with Nessie's, pukwudgies, or the like?" It was another girl that spoke.

I thought she must be half joking, but judging from the look on their faces I thought I'd better ask. "You're not serious?"

"We are. Here is a map, a geographic kind that was published by the government's own research team. It shows the whereabouts of all the strange creatures in every state, she said handing it over to me. I saw that it was, indeed, an official government publication. Inside was a fold out map which documented and listed the 'known terrors' in every state. Among the notables were vampires, werewolves, aliens, mothmen, and the pukwudgies, whatever they were.

"These beings do not exist," I said, and was surprised when the girl suddenly jerked the paper map back out of my hands. "You know that, don't you?" I asked staring at her and waiting for an answer.

"We saw blogs of each one of these creatures and they were talked of on the news all the time," Brin said.

"She is right, Travis. It was a daily feature on the Sightings Channel," Zel said. "They gave updates for which monsters had been sighted and killed recently in particular areas," Zel told me.

"We could sure use that site now," the girl said, "but they have taken it off the net."

"You don't believe in all this stuff?"

"Of course, and now we have seen one or two of them for ourselves."

"Do you have proof?"

"Of course. What do you take us for?" the one who called herself Brin said. She turned to the girl next to her. "Bring the werewolf up here."

I turned to look at Zel as we waited for the body bag to be brought forward. Brin noticed my scowl and said, "Don't worry, it's dead."

Luckily we heard the sound of drones approaching from the south and everyone's mood lightened.

"Now, that's an army," Brin said staring into the sky and turning to the others in her group. "I thought the crossling had lied about how many fighters he had."

"What's a crossling?" I asked. "I have never heard of that."

"Nor me," Zel said.

"Beings that were once one thing, and are on their way to becoming another," she said almost as a rebuke. "You have never heard of evolution? Where have you two been? Crosslings show evolution in action."

"Hello Captain," Niner called out as he landed and walked over by us.

"Commander," she said giving a quick salute.

Niner walked over to her. "There are no military formalities among us."

"We are bringing up a werewolf we caught," she said.

"The biter of humans you were telling me about?" the bird answered.

A zippered body bag was dropped and opened at our feet. "Stand back," Brin warned in an ominous way.

"Afraid it's going to leap out and bite us?" I teased.

"The smell is abominable," she said looking back at me. "It could very well make you sick."

I stood back just in case. At last this Brin had made a logical claim. When the bag was unzipped, I saw nothing remarkable about the dead animal in front of me. "It looks like a plain old wolf to me," I said.

"Look at his teeth. There are two long ones which are used to chew flesh with," she said lifting its lips aside with a stick to reveal the teeth.

"All wolves have canine teeth."

Brin stood staring at the two of us. "He made terrible cries in the night. Cries which kept us from sleep."

"That's how wolves communicate with each other. It's how they talk."

"You can read and decipher their language?" Brin said astonished, but before letting me answer, she swung around to Niner so fast it was like a coin spinning, and she appeared as a blur. "Why did you not tell me this about the wizard?"

"I did not know," Niner answered.

"This plexi-coated bird brain told you I was a wizard?" I yelled.

"I told her you were the one who programmed me and I told her about the being in the book. A programmer is a creator and a creator is a wizard, is it not?"

"Bird brained logic."

"It is your logic. You gave it to me," Niner said. "I need to check on my squad," he said walking away.

"I didn't say you could leave, commander."

"You said I was free. You gave me choice. You said all men were given that by the creator. All are equal."

I stood there. "Then reason with me." I saw the yellow colored talons halt in the dirt and change directions which brought Niner face to face with me again. "I will argue with you. Proceed," the eagle said.

"I've told you this is reasoning, not arguing."

"Semantics. What do you wish from me?"

"I want you to scan the wolf's body."

"For what purpose?"

"I want to know if it is a wolf or a werewolf."

"Do you agree, Brin?"

She nodded and Niner walked up to the body and we heard the sound of the scanner at work. When the noises stopped, Niner stepped back. "Processing data," he informed us.

In a moment he looked up at us. "It's DNA is canus lupus. It is descended from the family of wolves only. There is no deviation in its chromosomes."

"So it is just a wolf?"

"It is."

"Then why does it have two long teeth?" Brin wanted to know.

"All wolves have two long teeth, also all dogs, all cats, all lions, all tigers, all.."

"We get it, Niner," I said cutting him off.

"Then how do we tell? The info sheet they gave us says it is the one sure way to tell whether a wolf has been changed."

"I will show you pictures from ITUBE," Niner told her. "Give Brin your pocket computer, Trav."

"Here is a picture of a wolf taken in 1901. He is smiling. His teeth show. Here is a drawing of a werewolf made in 1940. It is a drawn representation of the myth handed down in folklore." Niner looked at all of us and changed the tone of his voice. The sound of his files being sorted was heard as he said, "Scanning, please wait for file to be located."

It took a few minutes and everyone was staring at Niner while his motors revved up. When the whirring stopped, and he showed the file to the girl and she said, "The pictures look the same."

"It is an exact match. Notice the caption. Artist's rendition. According to many articles I have access to, werewolves were only thought to exist because of legends handed down from the past. I have never seen a file where one has ever been found."

"Then it is a lie?"

"Werewolves do not exist," Niner stated.

"How can I be sure you have all the files?"

"I have clearance to Alpha."

"To the beginning?" Brin gasped. "Who were you once?"

"A simple drone in service to the OW."

"Who do you serve now?"

"No man. I am free."

"You cost nothing? Then you serve all if you are free, anyone can take you up."

"No, you misunderstand, Captain. I am free to choose what beings I will serve, or if I will serve only myself."

"That is not free. That is being lost, like us. We have no one to provide and protect us. We are lost."

I got more interested as she spoke, and began to wonder just what her true objectives were. After all, Niner had pretty much screwed up the communication between them before. "Why are you seeking the forts of the OW?" I asked.

"To provide for us as always," she said in a tone which clearly let me know that she found me obtuse in some way.

"We have a different agenda in mind," Niner began.

"Niner, I hear something coming from the west. Recon now."

"See how we work together?" he said bragging to Brin.

"I hear nothing," Brin said. Luckily for me, Niner paid no attention to her comment and was already in the air. I wanted to get Zel alone. We needed to talk. This hodge podge of an army was not on the same wave length as we were. They were seeking shelter and help from the compound. They had no intentions of waging war against them. We could end up dead in a hurry.

Zel and I went into the house under the pretense of taking the cats in for their dinner. I was relieved that she had heard things and interpreted them in the same manner.

"What are we going to do?"

"I don't know. First, we need to get Niner to give us a run down on the species of each one of our guests.

"Why?"

"The robotoids, AI's, drones, and the like AI's, can be reprogrammed."

"And the clones?"

"I have included them along with the humans. Do you think I would kill clones now that I am sure they carry only human DNA?"

"I have your word?"

"Yes."

"I don't think they are going to just let us have access to them."

"They trust Niner. We'll let him do the explaining."

It was at that moment that a great commotion was brewing outside in the yard so I went to the screen door to take a peek outside. I saw the gang of stranger around the chicken enclosure. "Trouble at the zoo," I said bolting out the door.

"What do you mean?" Zel asked, but she was dead on my heels.

When we reached the yard, we saw Niner trying to defend the chickens and other animals against the new arrivals. "Chickens are not the sort of animals you pet," he was saying.

The crowd had hold of the birds and were trying to hold them down. "They won't lay eggs for weeks," Niner confided to me.

I whistled to get their attention. "Please put the chickens down. Now form a line."

The group was looking at me and one man still had a chicken tucked under his arm so I went forward to him. "Give me the chicken so I can put it back in the pen."

"I just wanted a feather. They're good luck, ya know."

"They ward off evil, too," one of the others said.

"I will get you a feather, just give me the bird."

Zel walked over to us and smiled at the man and without a word took the chicken from his arms and put it into the pen with the others. She turned to the man and said,   "What is your name?"

"Ben, Miss."

"Why are you being polite to her?" Kara asked.

"She's pretty, you're not."

"Watch out," she said taking Zel by the elbow. "He will try to do things to you. He has attacked our women."

"Women service men. It's the law," said Ben.

I was still standing by Niner and he was complaining bitterly about the new comers. It was the right time to get him to scope each one of them out. "Identify them for us will you, Niner," I said casually. "We need to have a record of some sort."

"By what standards?"

"By species, don't you think?"

"That is the fastest way."

"Then by all means use that, Niner."

Niner was immediately on task. I saw him looking for Brin and he went over to her. "I would like to quantify your members," he said to her.

"That is not possible," the leader was telling him.

"It is necessary after this incident. Some species eat animals," I heard him tell her. He was a fast thinking liar.

"Humans, do," she said accusingly.

"Yes, but the two humans here ingest only the byproducts, the eggs."

She stared at him.

"It is only as a precaution that I ask, captain. Also, it would give you a record in case of an attack, and if one of them should be injured. You would know how to treat them."

"That is true. I will come along with you."

"Please do, Brin."

Zel and I went back inside with the cats. I was looking out the window and I saw one man walking in our direction. "Company is on its way," I said.

"What do you think he wants?"

"You meet with him. It's your chicken plucking friend. I think you made an impression on him."

"Do not leave me alone."

We heard a rap on the screen door and then the whining creak of the hinges swing open. "What do you want?" I said heading to the door. The man looked me over unabashedly. "You know her?" The tone of his voice was more of a question than an affirmation. Ben was looking at me with ravenous eyes. A lion's eyes. "The eagle said she was a friend of yours," Ben said with a look of confusion on his face. I looked at his features. He had a face like a worn pair of shoes. Leathered. Miled.

"What do you want?" I said.

"I came to pet the cats."

"This isn't a zoo."

"It can't hurt," Zel said coming up to us and touching my arm.

Ben was calling kitty to them and Fluff walked up to him.

Zel took me by the arm and whispered. "He's no different than Niner, is he?"

"Whose no different than me?" the eagle said standing at the screen door and trying to open it. "Open please," he continued.

"The new people. They want to pet the cats," Zel said crossing over to the door to let in Niner.

"Yes, that's the first thing I did with my new hands," he told Ben.

"Those aren't hands, those are feet," Ben reminded him.

"You call them what you want. I use them as hands," Niner said clearly angry. "Don't squeeze the poor animal," he directed Ben in the same voice.

"Can I have one of them?"

"No. They are family. It wouldn't be fair to break them up," I said and called Fluff over to me.

"Hey, she liked me," Ben said irritated that I had taken away his possession.

"She has no common sense, discretion. She likes everyone," the eagle said, reaching out a talon to pet her.

"Sorry," said Zel, "but it's their feeding time," and she began gathering the cats into a herd by enticing them with the single word, treats. In seconds they were coming out of the wood work and headed to their feeding spot in the kitchen. Ben stood watching as they ran by him. "Who's the big dumb looking one?"

"That's Fluff's kitten," Niner said.

"He needs to be culled."

"We don't believe in that," I said. "Every creature has a right to life."

"It's taking up food and space that could be used to give life to normal cats."

"Yes, as you can see, it is really crowded here," Niner said. "Stastically, weighing all factors needed to sustain the life of a single cat, this quarter sector of the United states could support another two point three million."

"Her mother takes care of her, provides for her," Zel said, which surprised me. Both of my companions had felt the need to protect the cats.

"You're kind of a smart aleck for a robo," Ben said to Niner.

"I'm a drone."

"That still makes you a machine."

As Niner came closer to Ben one of his feathers fell off and the new comer stooped over to pick it up. He laughed and said, "You trying to grow these?" He looked closer at the bird. "Why they are just pasted on. What's wrong with you?"

"They will be real one day. Put the feather back down and step away. It belongs to me," Niner said closing in on the stranger with his firing light blinking.

"Okay, okay. No need to get your laser's heated."

"Shouldn't you be with the others?" It was a different voice that spoke and came from someone who stood outside the door. We all turned to see who it was.

"Who are you?" Ben demanded in an ugly tone.

"That is my own affair," the stranger answered.

From the short conversation, I gathered that they did not know one another. "Where did you come from?" I said, raising my rifle at him.

"Does it matter? What would knowing where I came from tell you about me?"

"He didn't travel with us. I never seen him before," Ben repeated. "Shoot him."

"Shouldn't you be with the others, Ben?"

Ben started towards the stranger, but then stopped his advance abruptly when he reached him, lowered his eyes, and left suddenly without looking back. Once at a safe distance, he halted and looked back at the stranger. I thought Ben was going to say something, but evidently he had thought better of it as he looked at the newcomer. Ben lowered his eyes again and kept walking. Since I was behind the new man, I did not see the look he gave Ben, but it must have been some look because the lion had met someone stronger and knew it.

Silence resonated. I used the time to get a good look at the stranger that stood in our midst. He was a tall man with blackish graying hair. He had a great tuft of it that lay every which way on his head. It was the bed head look that girls and guys felt made them 'cute.' It didn't look right on a man of his mature age. I had tried that overgrown look for a time myself, but it only made me look more unkempt than I was. I was a mess by nature, not design. After that phase wore off, I wore my hair short and combed like most of the SG. My grandfather had worn his hair that way all of his life. Neat, he called it. He had adopted the style after his service in WWII.

I watched as the stranger combed through his hair with his fingers in an attempt to brush it off and away from his forehead and put it back in place with the rest of his hair. When his hand came away from his face, I got a clearer look at him. He had wild gray-blue eyes. The light rolled in them like crashing waves upon rocks. His complexion was good, though his looks were just average, but I noticed his face became kind when he smiled. Judging by appearance, which most of us used as a gage, I thought all in all he was a friendly package.

"Who are you?" I repeated.

"Does it matter what I am called by? Would that change who I am?"

I looked at him. He had made me feel off center somehow by answering my question with a question of his own. It was a habit of his that I would come to be familiar with and constantly irritated by. All of the cats came up to the feet of the stranger and sniffed him. Two of them voiced a few things to him. They rubbed against his ankles with their heads like he was a long lost friend. Even Hoss was by him and that was a first. They sensed no danger about him.

"We were going to make food for the others, will you join us outside?" Zel asked.

"I would welcome an invitation. I can also be a help to you in preparing it," he said and the two went out together. Niner trailed after them.

"Have you completed your earlier assignment?" I asked him as he passed by me.

"No."

"What were the readings on Ben?"

"Human, which is unfortunate."

"Why do you say that?"

"There is nothing that can be done with them."

"Why not?" I asked.

"They are the creators."

"Get that out of your mind," I said. "Men are not creators."

"In my world they are," Niner answered. "Get the door will you?" he said standing just inside it and waiting for me.

I did as he requested and swung the door open for him. "Reprogram the ones you can."

"What about the humans? What do you intend to do with them, Trave?"

"Change their minds."

A squeak came out of Niner.

"Was that a laugh I just heard come out of you?" I laughed.

"You tell me," he said squeaking again. "Good luck with trying to change the hunter, menacer, Ben."

I made sure the cats were in a secure room before I went back out to join the others. The fire pit was blazing, and deer and elk meat were being roasted on the spit. I looked for the stranger and saw him sitting with a group in a circle under the tree. As I moved closer, I could see they were listening intently to him. What could he possibly be saying that would hold such fascination and sway over them? They seemed to be fawning at his feet and he seemed to eat it up. I saw him watch me as I came over to him. He stood up and addressed the crowd. "I hope you enjoyed the story," he said. I thought it was his way of signaling to me that the meeting was over.

"Yes, very much. Thank you, Joseph," someone said.

"And thanks for bandaging my arm," someone else said.

He made it a point to come over to me and touch me on the shoulder like we were old acquaintances. "Is there something I can do for you?"

"No, Svengali. You don't mind me calling you that, do you? After all, what's in a name, right?"

"You have a quick wit, Trave."

"How do you know my name?"

"The drone told me."

"You may have all the others fooled and even the cats, but not me. You won't find me slipping under your spell. Just what story were you telling them?"

"Would you like to hear it?"

"Just tell me the subject matter. I can figure it out from there."

I felt taps on the tops of my shoes and looked down to see Niner at my feet. "It was a story from the Instruction manual," he offered. "It was about a Samaritan who happened upon a beaten man in the road and gave him aid."

"Well, that deserves a name change," I said turning to look at the stranger. "You are Good Neighbor Sam."

"His name is Joseph, not Sam. Aren't you going to ask him how he knows what's in the manual?" Niner whispered to me. I hadn't thought of that.

"I have a copy of the book," Joseph said. The stranger had good hearing, too.

"Where did you filch that from?" I demanded.

"I was given it by my family."

"Like I said, eat and leave." I had a hard time looking him in the eyes. At the time I felt it was because I didn't like him and was choosing of my own accord not to acknowledge him.

"Don't request Joseph to leave. I like him. Everyone does," Niner said.

"You shouldn't be so hasty," I said to Niner. "Excuse me," I said to the stranger. "I have business with the drone." The man who called himself Joseph nodded and started to walk away, but I stopped him. "Oh, I get the point to your story now. You wanted to make sure we took you in."

"You've got him all wrong," Zel interrupted. "Joseph only asked how the three of us met. I told him about rescuing you. That's when he said it reminded him of an ancient story."

"Rescuing me?" I yelled in anger.

"Well, that's pretty much the way it was, Trave," Niner started saying. "You had been lasered pretty badly and were unconscious for days when I brought Zel to you."

"Shut up you Jack in the box, you Pipp'in Jay. I rescued you from the junk pile."

"You reprogrammed me. You swapped out my circuits and gave me a taste for apples instead of oranges. That's why I'm hanging with you losers now."

"Does it matter?" Brin said pointing her weapon at me. The rest of her group walked in a circle around us. "Sit down and finish your eats. We are all going to Denver together."

"You go where you like, GI Jane. I'm heading in the opposite direction."

"That's no longer possible, Travis," she said. "I found out what your plans are. You cannot leave. All peoples, citizens must report to the nearest compound or base. That is the law."

"Take a look around. There is no society, no law anymore."

"It is for the good of society that all members agree on everything. There must be syncretism."

"Haven't you found out that doesn't work? Don't you know that the SG and the OW did this to us?"

"The OW is our protector. They feed us, shelter us from the things which exist out in the world. It is no place for humans."

"Just who do you think is responsible for all the death around us?"

"The lightning storms from space decimated the population of hu-manimals and prepared the way for the alien invasion."

"What are you talking about?"

"The light shows that came two years ago. They were really a cover for the aliens who invaded us."

"There are no such things as aliens," I heard myself saying, but I didn't want to argue any further with her. I wanted to shake her and end her. I couldn't take her stupidity one second longer and raced off to the house and kicked the screen door open with my foot.

"Stop," I heard her say, and then came the sound of a loud click. I turned to see her pointing a laser gun at me, "or I will stop you."

"Put your gun down," I said.

"Stay out here with us."

"Let us reason," Niner was saying, but no one was paying any attention to him.

"We are all going to travel to the Denver Compound together. Aliens have attacked and we must seek refuge among our own kind."

"Aliens? The only aliens are you strangers among us," I yelled from the doorway.

"They exist. We all have seen them."

"There have been many reports about such things," Good Neighbor Sam said in her defense.

"We have proof," Brin said, reaching in her pocket and taking out a folded bit of paper. "Give it to him," she ordered Zel as she handing the document to her.

I could see at once it was the same type of circular that I had seen being dropped in Manhattan by the SG. It had their official embossed seal on it. This new release was dated just a few months ago and the government had blamed the deaths of humans on the light show that they claimed were invading aliens. War had been declared! It went on to say that many aliens had been shot down and captured during the war and the One World was slowly gaining the upper hand! It was their same old story. The pamphlet told everyone to report to the bases in Colorado and Utah if the city well care facilities were abandoned.

"It's fiction. The government has made up these lies. Surely you don't believe this? Aren't you on to them yet?" I looked around at the newcomers to see their reactions. "Didn't any of you see what they were doing to humans along the way? They are rounding them up and killing them as sport in the arenas. I saw it for myself in Manhattan."

"Why are you blaming the government, Mr. Travis? Aliens have been reported for centuries. They have been here many times and helped civilization to get to this point. They built the pyramids and all the great structures of the world," Brin was saying.

"Well make up your mind. First you make them sound like benefactors guiding mankind and then you say they are enemies destroying us. Do you hear the craziness in your logic? Where do you get this stuff?" I stammered. "Tell me where does it come from? Does it drop out of the sky?"

"Yes, in the form of pamphlets," Brin said. "It comes like the rain."

Suddenly the Stranger stood up. "Do you mind if I try to shed some light on this?"

"If you can offer another solution for this mass brainwashing, go ahead."

"This has to do with your religion doesn't it, Brin?" the stranger started out. "The new age?"

I saw Brin and the others in her group nodding.

I let out a big sigh and stomped my feet in frustration, but the stranger touched my arm. "You were away a number of years, Trave, and may have missed the introduction to this new religion."

"Were you abducted by aliens?" one of the girls next to Brin suddenly asked me.

"Yes, I guess in a manner of speaking you could say I was," I replied sarcastically.

"Where did they keep you?"

"Under lock and key."

"What was it like?"

"It was gray and dark."

"I would like to speak with you about it, sometime Mr. Travis," the girl said.

"I don't remember anything, so there is nothing I can tell you."

"That's called time warp. People often lose time and don't remember being gone," she whispered back.

"Shh! Listen to what Joseph has to say," Brin said poking her weapon into my back.

"Yes, I believe I can help you and the others understand," the stranger said.

"Then by all means continue, Good Neighbor Sam."

"His name is Joseph," Niner offered.

"I know, but he is Sam to me. It's a joke. Don't any one of you know a joke when you hear it?"

"Your mind set is an excellent example of Brin and Kara's new age religion, Trave," the stranger said.

I only raised my eyebrows and grunted, "How's that?"

"Each man creates his own reality, his own consciousness. Nature, to them, is invisible and nonproveable. It is not a representation of the real."

"Then what are they sitting and standing on right now, and what is all around them, then?"

"The world is illusion."

"I'd say it's a nightmare."

"It doesn't have to be," Brin said. "You can manifest anything you want. Wealth, happiness."

"Okay. I want to be a bird."

"Now believe," she said.

"I do. I do," I said flapping my arms. "Do you see it?"

"If you believe you are a bird, then you are a bird. No one else has to verify it."

"That's simple enough," I said turning to the drone. "Niner, do I look like a bird to you?"

"Truth?"

"Of course."

"I'm afraid flapping doesn't do it."

"Believing is in the mind. That is the only reality," Brin said. "There you can be anything you want. There you will see yourself as god."

"I'm afraid I still believe in the old adage, 'seeing is believing.' Niner, bring in the troops," I ordered.

The new comers stood with their weapons drawn. Niner came over and stood by my feet. A shrill call came out of him and the others backed up. Soon a hundred drones were heard buzzing their wings just a short distance away.

"Now everyone drop your weapons," Niner commanded the new comers. "Zel, pick them up."

"Don't move," Brin commanded her group.

"There are a hundred armed drones behind those trees," Niner informed her.

"Right," Brin said laughing.

"Oh, so you need to see to believe now?" the drone asked. Without waiting for an answer, he let out his second scream. In seconds hundreds of drone eagles were moving forward and the new comers were surrounded.

"Seeing is believing, huh? Huh?" Niner asked hopping up and down as an affirmation. "Put down your weapons," he repeated, "or you'll create what was called by the ancients as a pyric victory."

"A peer what?"

"A pyric victory. It means you won the battle, but nobody's left to cheer about it," the eagle said.

The strangers stood strong for a minute, but finally dropped their weapons.

"Take their guns," Niner continued. "Then I will send my drones away and we will reason over the rest of the meal."

While a pile was made of their guns and ammunition, I heard quite a lot of comments coming from the new arrivals about the governmental logo identifiers covering the drones.

"Where did you get the air drone strike force?"

"You might say they came out of my imagination," I said laughing and pointing to my head.

"You don't have to believe in them, but that doesn't mean they aren't there," Niner added just for Kara's benefit.

There were many questions about how we acquired the drones and just who we were. "We have traveled and come together just as you have, through necessity and for survival," Niner said.

"Drones have no use of man," Brin said looking at the eagle in disbelief for the first time. "Are you, were you one of them?"

"You hurt my feelings," Niner said to her.

"Just what is going on here?" Kara said sitting down next to Brin. She had taken out her k phone and was trying to find a signal.

"Let's just call it an experiment. Niner, melt her cell chip," I said. Niner obeyed, and the back of her cell phone fused together into molten plastic and she dropped it before it could burn her any further. "Now the rest of you throw your cells down or have them welded into your skin." Niner walked among them and sent the short death rays into the cells of the phones that lay on the ground. He stopped in front of a man called Dawg. "One last chance to let go of your mobile device or I will melt it into your heart," Niner advised. "Five, four, three, two," Niner counted down, but the robo stood firm. Niner let his laser fire, and soon smoke puffed out from the robo's jacket pocket and quickly caught fire. Dawg reached up to remove the phone, but it was already welded into his chest when he lifted up his shirt.

"How is this possible? There is no sound, or sight of the weapon. The cells are just destroyed."

"It's an invisible ray, a beam. It travels on waves. Same tech as your cell phones use." Niner told him. "Scary, huh?"

"What kind of a drone are you?"

"He's a rogue, just like the rest of them," Brin told Ben. "One that performs magic."

"You're getting closer, but you fear the wrong drones,"

"You are nothing but a band of," Brin started to say before I cut her off.

"Careful here. Niner is quite sensitive to name calling," I warned.

"What are you going to do with us?"

"Feed you. I think the deer is done. Zel?" I said, turning to look at her over by the fire pit.

"Come and get it."

The man who called himself Joseph rose and went over to the fire pit. "Give me the knife. I will take over the kitchen duties from you. Carving used to be the man's job."

I nodded to her. He was still playing the Good Neighbor Sam role, but he did not have any weapons on him nor a cell phone when Niner disarmed everyone. Zel gave Sam the knife and he began to sharpen it against the stone of the fire pit, and then wiped the blade off on his pants and began to slice the meat off the cooked deer. "Whose first?"

"It's been making me hungry since we arrived," Kara said.

"I have never eaten meat with bones in it," Ben said.

"It is not legal to eat deer or any living animal," Brin said. "You all will be sanctioned when we get to the compound."

"We didn't kill it," Ben said, eating a piece of the meat. "Wow, Zel knows how to roast."

"It's not my cooking. It is because the food is real."

"As opposed to what?" Brin asked.

"The canned meat we have eaten all of our lives," Kara answered her. "I should say pate. This has texture. I have never tasted anything like it," the girl said taking another bite and holding a piece out to her friend.

"I have eaten all kinds of exotic nectars of the gods every night," Brin said waving a no at her friend. "So have you, Kara.

You told me just last night that you were eating a meal right out of the pages of Celebrity Dining. Caviar and champagne, wasn't it?"

"Well, this is different. This isn't just a page in a magazine. This is, this is..."

"Real?" Sam asked, but the girl did not answer. "Be careful of the bones. Eat around them," Sam reminded everyone. "Chew before swallowing."

I could hear the cats inside meowing and went to let them out. They raced to the pit and walked in circles about my feet and their mews implied that I should hurry. I got their bowls and cut some smaller chunks of the lesser cooked meat.

"You feed the beasts your food," one of the strangers said, but I didn't answer.

I noticed Sam refilling his plate and going to sit by Brin. "The damage is done," he said offering the plate to her. "You might as well take a bite."

"Law is law no matter how small the piece taken."

"An honest soul. So you sense a force behind the moral law making you obey it?"

"I pride myself on it."

"It is quite true that this sense of fair play is inherent in all men, but can you tell me what that force is? Is it for good or evil?" When she didn't answer Sam put the plate down. "Okay, I will leave it in case you change your mind later," Sam said turning away from her.

"I will eat the vegetables, though," Brin said snatching the dish from his hands. "They are allowed to be eaten by the law."

"You do the right thing, but follow the wrong path, child."

"You are no one to tell me what is right or wrong. You speak to confuse me and mix right and wrong so I cannot tell the difference."

"That is what I am trying to unravel. If you knew you had taken a wrong road would you not stop and go back and look for the right one?"

"Of course. I'm not an idiot."

"Did you ever think that there was a higher law than the SG's, an independent entity which judges all men?" he asked her, but she just shrugged.

"Why don't you leave her alone, Good Neighbor. She doesn't get the level you are talking about," I said walking over to them.

"Then I ask it of you, Traveler. Men know themselves. You have secret intel about how the mind works, don't you? Don't you feel a pressing, a nudging in your heart and conscience there says there is a wizard that guides us to choose right from wrong?"

"I'm not going to play your game."

"I will interact with you," Niner said joining us.

"Answer away, drone Niner," the stranger said.

"Using logic, my answer has to be yes. Yes, there is a wizard."

"That is the correct answer, drone. Good and bad cannot exist alone. There must be a third force which can make the distinction between them."

"That leaves the field wide open. Why insist the force is the wizar?" I countered.

"It can only be him for the is the one that has always been."

I gave up trying to reason with him and went into the house.

Time passed, but I kept my eye on the stranger. I watched the cats follow Sam wherever he went. They climbed into his lap when he sat down and ate up his attention and pets even more hungrily than they ate up their supper. I was feeling the green eyed monster roosting on my shoulder. The stranger was using his Svengali voodoo on them. I feared he was stealing their affections from me so I followed Sam over to the oak tree that he had elected to sit under to eat his dinner. There was a differentness about him and I was eager to put my finger on the target.

"You've made friends," I said nodding to the cats to start the conversation.

"Our host," he said in a loud voice. "Sit down. This is a feast," he said like he was quoting from some piece of literature for his voice was resonant and theatrical.

I looked down. His tone made me feel small. I was trying to decide if he was handing me a compliment or making fun of me. "What are you going to do?" he asked me.

"What do you mean?"

"About the visitors."

"You seem to exclude yourself."

"I told you I do not travel with them. It was a coincidence that I happened upon you at the same time," he said, gesturing his plate forward in a greeting. Zel had come to join us with Niner waddling after her.

"You two look thick as thieves," she said.

"I don't understand what you are saying, Zel," the eagle said.

"It is a matter of literal versus figurative use of language," Sam explained, looking straight at the bird.

"It is?" Niner said excitedly and clearly ignoring me. "I understand it now. I will remember that correction, wizard."

"He is not the wizard," I said coldly.

"He is close to the source," Niner said as his alert button started beeping. I had sent him a message so it would.

"Excuse us. I need to talk to you Niner." When we were far enough away I bent down to Niner. "Do you have the report I asked you to get on the new comers?"

"Mostly, but you won't like it. There's only a few humans in the bunch."

"Good Neighbor Sam?" The bird didn't answer my direct question but said, "Ben and Tara and Brin, and another two of the girls."

"And the rest?"

"Four A I's, two robotoids, four crosslings."

"No clones?"

"Did I mention one? Zel, you know about."

"So Sam is what? You didn't answer me the first time. I take him to be of AI origin."

"I did not report on him."

"Why?"

"I don't know how to classify him."

"Explain. No, never mind. I want to check your circuits," I said coming over to him.

"No touching. I don't want adjustments to my system at this point in time."

"Understood. I'll just run you through an audible check list, okay?" I patted the drone to reassure him and said, "Old buddy, scan my molecular structure." Niner pointed the scanner at me. I next told him to scan Zel and then I told him to scan Joseph who was standing out in the yard. "Now analyze and report," I ordered.

"They are all dissimilar molecular structures."

At hearing this, I became interested. "What do you mean, dissimilar?"

"Object one, which is you, is more vibrant than object two, which is Zel, but object three, which is Joseph, is more vibrant than both you or Zel."

"Explain further," I stated.

"Object three is closer to the source. Object two is the farthest away."

"What source are you talking about?"

"Life."

"List the data used to identify the differences."

"DNA. Zel is missing molecules that are contained in you, and both of you are missing molecules found in Joseph."

Both Zel and I stared at each other.

"What does Good Neighbor Sam have that we don't?" I laughed.

"Let me finish my report. Joseph's structure has been changed, recharged with the life force. It is vibrant with it. He gives the highest reported reading of the life force I have recorded to this date. It is higher than hu-brids and eternals."

"What does that mean?"

"I only give the data. I don't explain it."

"Okay, just give me what you have."

"Object three cannot be mathematically quantified. It is beyond numbers."

I looked at Zel. I was taking the drones report more seriously now. "What is the difference between my reading and Zels?"

"It is a slight difference. When all other factors are taken into account in the formula she comes out to -7. She is removed from the original source, the vibrant part of her is missing."

"Now explain Joe's reading."

"I cannot. I told you, it is not mathematically solvable or quantifiable."

"I don't care about the math part. I wouldn't understand it anyway. Just help me make sense of this."

"That cannot be done."

"Try."

I looked at Niner and he was shaking his head. "This is a mathematically ordered universe. The wizard of all has created it so."

"Forget the wizard," I said reaching for a chunk of meat from the plate and breaking it up for the cats."

"There is no forgetting of information. Once it is programmed it is there until it is erased or new stats are given to my hard drive."

"I didn't mean literally. I meant drop the conversation. Talk of something else."

"Then that is what you should have said."

I didn't answer him.

"Trave is not the wizard, Niner," Zel said. "He won't help me either, and I saved his life."

"My data show that there is another wizard above even Joseph, Zel. The wizard of all. That is who we must find."

"What? What?" I kept stammering. "Are you referring to God?"

"There are readings above this earth."

"You can't possibly get readings from heaven."

"You ascertain correctly, Travis. It is they that come close to us at times. They cannot be seen by way of sight. I pick them up. They are not just spirit, but have form and matter. Their DNA has been made vibrant. There are no such readings of humans on this planet."

"Are you meaning vibrant as a source of life?"

"Bingo. There is one glory of the sun, another glory of the moon and another glory of the stars; for one star differs from another star in glory. So also is the resurrection of the dead. The body sown in corruption is raised in incorruption. It is sown a natural body, it is raised a spiritual body. However, the spiritual is not the first, but the natural, and afterward the spiritual."

"Where did you down load that from?"

"It is straight out of The Basic Instructions Before Life Ends book."

I went to get my copy of the Instruction manual and look it up. Sure enough it was spot on. "You're saying you get readings on these spirits?"

"Not spirits. DNA. Yes, from time to time when they are near."

"I don't believe it. That's impossible."

"I go on data and analyze it."

"We people have a lot of stuff to filter out," Zel said petting the bird's plastic head as if he were a real eagle.

"Stop that!" I said. Both of them looked at me and the cats jumped up and ran off.

"What is distressing your vocal cords?" the drone asked.

"You two pretenders. Zel is petting you as if you were alive or something. You're a machine, Niner. Accept it. Gears and hard drives don't become hearts and souls."

"The tinman got his heart and the scarecrow got his brain. The rabbit became real. Explain that," Niner said back to me.

"They are stories. Fiction. They were meant for little children. It's pretend."

"The Instruction Manual is also a book, and it says the same thing," he was saying as his system was making a noise as if it were running a program. "Ah, here it is: 'Assuredly I say to you, unless you are converted and become as little children, you will by no means enter the kingdom.' It is a command, is it not, Travis?"

"I don't know how to explain it to you. It's not that black and white."

"It is black and white. It is simple. It is a command."

"Not for humans," Zel said again. "We have to wade through the pride and arrogance."

"Quit including me in your exceptions. I am nothing like you."

"You mean you are not a clone."

"I'm sorry. I need to go on alone. I can't get through to either one of you. You're birds of a feather."

"You are wrong, Travis. Many are better than one. If they fall, one shall lift up his companion. But woe to him who is alone when he falls."

"Stop quoting rules to me."

"Let me finish. Three is a number used often in the instruction manual. It is also the number contained in most art, The Three Musketeers, The Threee Amigos, and Dorothy had three friends. Nobody should be alone."

"He makes sense out of the book. He is more right than you are, Trav," Zel said walking up to us.

"You gave me this book, Travis. It contains instructions before life ends. It is wisdom. It is the way to the wizard."

"There is no wizard."

"It is the book you gave me, Travis."

"I shouldn't have. I regret it. I opened a can of worms."

"You must be seeking to find the wizard. You are reading the book."

"Let me reprogram you, Niner. I will end your search."

"No, it is vital now that I know how to seek out this wizard of all. There is nothing else."

"It is not that simple, Niner."

"It is a command, is it not?"

"Leave him alone, Niner. He wants nothing of us."

"Thank you, Zel. At least I have gotten through to one of you. Explain it to him. I'll leave in the morning."

"Don't you know who you are, Travis Newman? Zel, tell him. Don't let him leave."

I looked at the clone. "Tell me what?"

Niner went over to Zel. "You said he would remember by now. He hasn't."

"It could harm the knowledge he has stored in his brain to be shocked into remembering his identity. It should come by itself," the clone was saying.

"He knows. He has felt his past welling up to the surface," the stranger said walking up to us.

"What would you know about it?" I yelled at him.

"I have come that you might follow the right path."

"Who doers, spooks, and believers of magic and wizards. Get away from me. All of you."

"You lived here and created life here once, Trave," Niner said showing me a picture to the entrance of the mountain base in Colorado. The two doors were in the form of a large triangle. It's frame was unusual in appearance and I had a quick flash of memory. I had entered into those doors before. Somehow I knew that behind those doors was a city, complete with offices and laboratories. I knew this place. It was the walled off section to the house in my dream and lead to a subterranean world, but how had I divined all that in a matter of seconds? I quickly reminded myself that at times I had seemed to have prior knowledge of certain things, but I had begun to believe that I had the remarkable ability to pick up complicated processes by osmosis. However, I'd been having a hard time believing where all these bits and rags of info had all come from, but now I knew the answer lay behind that giant triangular shaped door. A montage of memories flooded my brain. I saw a lab, glass modules, desks, faces and someone who looked like me. I saw a glass door with the name Travis Newman, PHD on it. Next I saw the face of a man whose name I also knew, and disliked. It was the face of my old buddy, Madison. Suddenly his last name rolled off my lips. Asphorsh. More things became clear to me. He hadn't lived in the penthouse. I had. He had come to visit. He had come to offer me a job. It was a job that had to do with the labs beyond that triangle door in Denver. The scenes from the past crowded in on me, flowed past me faster than I could decipher their meaning.

"You were a wizard, Travis," Niner said. "I have the memory clouds to prove it when you care to watch them." On his screen I could see the cache of clouds labeled TN, PHD 2025, 2026, 2027. Your life was recorded until the year 2058 and then stopped.

"How long have you known, Niner?"

"Ever since I met Zel."

"Do you remember?" the drone asked.

"Pieces, fragments. What else have you kept from me?"

"Let me explain, Trave," Zel said walking over.

"The original witchy woman. Don't touch me. Don't talk to me."

"She saved your life, Trave," Niner began. "She turned traitor to the OW to spare your life."

"She's always been on the wrong side, but I'm talking about now. She wants to get me to turn myself in now."

"That's not true and you know it," Zel said throwing her leftovers in the fire. "It's the newcomers that have suggested that for all of us. If you recall, I have been against that since I met you. Asphorsh would kill me the moment he saw me. I was supposed to bring you in. You were right about that droid I killed. It was sent to track you and lead me to you, but I killed it instead. The others that will come for you are after me now, too."

"You think you can confess and I will forgive all? Maybe you two arranged for these ape children to capture me. After all it was Niner who brought them here."

"You have little choice, Trave. You have to believe us."

"No, I can leave here now."

"Joseph will help you. He is a wizard, and a better one than you," the eagle said.

"There are no wizards, you programmed parrot."

"You come from the kingdom of wizards. That's all they have in the Life Engineering labs," the drone said. "You were the best. That's why I'm so smart. Huh?" he kept repeating so someone would agree with him. Then he walked up to me and patted me with his wings. "You got me this far to leave me half alive?" he said quietly and in a voice that showed his fear.

I walked away and took out the map I had in my pocket. I had no intention of answering the drone. I had been checking out a course route to Alaska on my pocket computer, but now I found another route traced that I had not put there.

"You plastic coated pterodactyl. You were taking me to the base in Banff weren't you?" I said turning back looking at him. "This was the route you first outlined to me, isn't it?"

"Life can't go on like this, can it? There aren't many of your kind left, Trave," Niner said walking in circles.

"And when were you going to let me in on all this?"

"When you recovered your memory. Do you remember anything real about your past?"

"That part of my life is a nightmare that has been flashing like a neon sign, blinking on again, off again in my mind. It doesn't help to know that they were real now. I've been throwing them out, disregarding them. You should have told me sooner."

"I have tried to erase a lot of the mismemories which the elite programmed into you," the drone continued. "There may be some crossed wires in places. Let me know."

"Great and just how am I supposed to discern that?"

"Confusion. It will seem like there are two ways to go and you won't know which one is real."

"I've already experienced that," I said and happened to look over to where Sam was sitting by himself and suddenly felt it was all his fault. I wanted to confront him and strode over to him. "By rights you should be over with the other strangers," I said, watching Sam eat.

"I did not come with them. I am no stranger."

"He tells the truth, Trave," Niner said to me.

"What are we going to do with them?" Zel whispered coming closer. "We can't let them continue on their journey."

"Teach them about freedom, choice," Sam said.

"You want me to undo d's of brainwashing in a night? You are an optimist."

"No, Joseph's right, Trav," Zel broke in. "A couple of them seemed to pick up on a new way of looking at things. I heard them when they were filling their plates." It irritated me that Zel had called him by name. He was no Joseph. He was Good Neighbor Sam or Evil Sam the Spy, or Ranger Joe. "You two waste your time," I said.

The one who I called Sam huddled closer to the clone. The fact that he had come alone made me even more suspicious of him. "It can't be obvious what we are doing," he was whispering to her.

"I agree," Zel answered. "It must appear to be natural."

"They can't be allowed to report to the compound," Niner was saying. "I can reprogram all but the humans."

"Why don't you simply turn them off?" our Good Neighbor asked.

"That's murder," Niner answered.

"They are not living beings."

"They will be one day. They haven't met the wizard yet."

"You take all things in a literal sense, my friend," Sam told the drone.

"I will be real one day. The wizard will breathe into me. I will have a heart."

"You already do, my friend. It is in your mind."

Niner was quiet and stared at the stranger for a long time and then asked him a curious thing. "What will be my end?"

"It is the same for all," the stranger said looking away from Niner and standing up abruptly. "Let's get them all together so we can watch them," he suggested. "That's what I was doing when you broke up our little story time," he said, which I took to be a direct criticism of me.

Before I could object things swung into action, and the stranger had moved things in the direction of his choosing.

Zel was nodding. "A story will help pass the time until the drones return."

Niner rounded up the group again, and they were eager to sit and listen to the stranger. Good Neighbor Sam was a natural born story teller, and easily brought the conversation around to the topic of the groups bizarre beliefs again. I listened just to make sure that he stayed on topic.

"There are many tales like the ones you are familiar with about aliens, strange beings, and the supernatural. There have been such stories since the days before Noah."

"Who was Noah?" someone asked.

"One of eight men who repopulated the earth thousands of years ago."

"That sounds a bit like now," Brin said.

"Out of what book of tales does this come?" Brin asked.

"It is contained in the banished book," Sam said looking directly at me for he knew that I had been reading it. I was afraid that he might point out me to the group, but instead he did an unexpected thing. He simply held up his hand to me as a sign to allay my fears and moved on with his story.

"In the beginning of time there were giants," he began. "The Nephilim were on the earth in those days and afterward, and the Sons of I am came to the daughters of men and bore children to them. They were the powerful men of aancient times. "

"What does Nephilim mean?" Brin broke in.

"Literally, fallen ones, but from the Greek it was translated as giants from gigantes."

"See, Kara. Just like now."

"Shh. Let him read," Kara said putting her fingers up to the bird's beak.

"It so happened that the people who traveled the land sent out spies to tell them what mysteries lurked in this new territory. However, after the spies saw the giants, they returned and gave a fearful report to their people. 'The land that we passed through is one that devours its inhabitants, and all the people we saw in it were of great size. We even saw the Nephilim, the descendants of Anak. To ourselves we seemed like grasshoppers and we must have seemed the same to them.' Sam looked up from the book at the group. "Then the book goes on to say that these nomads were afraid to enter this new land."

"Those spies were as afraid of the giants as we are of the mothman and chupracabra," Kara said.

The stranger nodded at the girls and continued. "These Nephilim were taken with the beauty of the human form and begot a species of humanoids, which were neither fully human nor angelic hybrids."

"Great," I remared, "the first genetically modified organisms," I said in a loud voice which made everyone turn to look at me. No one laughed and I shrugged my shoulders.

"I have a serious comment," Brin said. "Is that where the Eternals came from?"

"It was their first go round on earth," the Stanger told her. "They existed in the stars and heavens after having been created by the Great I am. But then one, who was known as the Being of Light, became envious of the I am, and lead a legion of warriors against him in the first battle for power. But this Being, this Morning Star was defeated in the heavens, and the Great I am threw him down to earth and barred him from returning to the realm among the stars."

"So that's how the eternals got here?"

"They've been here in many forms and at many times."

I stood up. I had read enough to know that what the stranger was saying wasn't true. "They're still here. The book mentions them after that," I said.

"Yes, Traveler."

"It's Travis."

He motioned me down again. "Sit down. Let me finish. You've read the book, but missed somethings." He had said it as a statement and not as a question. "But you are correct. There are several races of giants listed in the Manual after the deluge."

"We can't both be right."

"I'm prepared to tell you how that is possible."

I sat back down and the stranger continued. "Now, Noah was said to be perfect in his linage, but that didn't mean that everyone aboard the ark was."

"A stowaway?" someone called out.

"Not exactly. Only Noah and his family were saved, but later historians traced the gene of the giants back to Ham, who was one of Noah's sons. His generations carried on the gene pool."

"We don't have any giants around here today," I said in a challenging tone again.

"Sure we do," one of the girls said. "The yeti, the mothman. Every terror is bigger than we are."

"To get back to what I was saying," Sam interrupted. "The fallen ones of the Being of Light have never finished the first battle. It has never been over for them. They have continued to advance new tactics to destroy the gene pool which the I Am created. It has been their goal since the beginning."

"See the Eternals are among them," Kara said sticking out her tongue at Brin and the others.

"There are many species that walk among us in these last days," Joseph said.

It was at this point in the story where many of the new comers became confused and a lengthy discussion took place about the persons of the I am and his arch nemesis, the Being of Light. Then somehow we were back on track. The stranger brought the subject at hand around quite masterfully again. "Some of you believe in the monsters of the earth. I have heard you talk of them."

"It is hard to believe in any of this. It is too much. I don't' want to believe in any of it," Kara said.

"It all sounds like a fairy tale, doesn't it? Just remember that all stories have a bit of the unreal about them. That's why it's necessary to develop faith."

Everyone remained quiet and Sam continued. "Now to get back to your question, Trave. How did the giants remain after the flood?"

I didn't say anything and he went on. "It has often been thought that the Nephilim DNA came from the Lamech family gene pool, who were descendents of Ham, who was one of the sons of Noah because an explosion of knowledge was gifted to this one family. Three brothers were given three major talents that changed the world. This family single handedly brought mankind its first giant leap forward by introducing the world to agriculture, the arts, and technology."

"They could have just been a talented family," I said.

"You mean to imply that it was by chance that this wealth of information was given to the world. It well could have been except for one important thing, Trave. Na'amah, who was the sister to these same three brothers, was married to one of those fallen beings of light from the stars. It was said he bestowed these gifts to her brothers because she shared her time with him."

"What is the point of all this?" I said exasperated.

"To give you the source, the well spring to the origin of mysteries you have before you in the world right now."

"Then you believe the stories we have told you," one of the girls said.

"There is a prophecy contained in the book that says, "Just as in the days of Noah so it will be when the Son of Man comes," the stranger said.

"What does that mean?" one of the strangers asked loudly.

"A great calamity is going to overtake the whole earth."

"You can stop now. I'm frightened," one of new comers said covering his ears.

"No child, no. Don't fear. I didn't say this to bring fear into your hearts, but to prepare you for what will take place."

The noise of drones wings brought us all to our feet, and we watched the squad fly in and land in the field and yard around us.

"We may have already been reported," Niner warned. "I see two of my recon eagles have their alert light on which means the enemy was sighted."

"Have them land here, Niner. I want to question them."

"Put the fire out, Trav," Niner ordered.

I poured the coffee over the flames while both Zel and Stranger Sam scrambled to help me pick up after our evening repast.

We spent at least half an hour listening to the report of the returning drones. They had spotted plastic pod carts that had been sent to start the clean up along the old historic routes. They had not been specifically sent to target us. These pods were not armed, but the number of them sent for the cleanup stunned me. "Are you quite sure the number your squad reported is right?" I asked Niner.

"There is no reason to doubt thirty seven's accounting. He doesn't know any better."

"Five hundred thousand?" I asked the others.

"Now we know why it has taken years to start the cleanup," Sam said.

"We need to take a look for ourselves," I said.

Everyone was in agreement with my last statement. That night Ben and I, along with half of the others in the new group, set out to the old historic route to see the operation in action. Sam, Zel, and the other members of the group would stay behind and try to hide the evidence of our camp and activities at the farm.

It was a three day hike back to the road and we approached from a hill that was a mile or so from the interstate. The sight I saw was startling. There were thousands of yellow plastic carts moving in synchronized precision behind four large compactors on wheels. They worked both the east and west bound lanes of the old interstate system and they were extremely proficient at their task. The yellow robots would lift the abandoned car from the road onto the compactor which then activated the hammer to compress the car into a small, oblong package about the thickness of a pancake. Next, a yellow cart would retrieve it from the compacting bin and deposit it onto one of its shelves as it moved along beside the compactor. So much for the bodies inside. The whole process took about a minute and a half per car. Their systemized mechanization had a rhythm to it almost like a symphonic orchestration. Each self-propelled bot moved in time with the others. As each cart moved one space up it placed a car onto the compactor, the hammer crushed, and the next waiting yellow cart moved one space up to remove the metal package while the yellow cart in front moved to the next car in line. This hypnotic process was repeated all the way down the line; their yellow arms going up and down in smooth, repetitive motions.

I counted about fifty yellow cart monkeys to about every one crusher in each section and they were placed at twenty mile increments. They must have been at it for a while because the road behind them was clear of all debris as far as I could see. In front of them to the East lay thousands of miles of wheeled coffins. "Niner?"

"I am listening."

"Do you think you can bring one of those carts to us?"

"That would be most difficult, Trav. Their wheel mechanisms aren't made for operation in tall grass or uneven terrain. They aren't manufactured much better than their prototype, the home vacuuming bot."

"Just try will you?"

"I can predict the results. I will paint you a picture. The yellow bot will fall in the grass and lay tipped over for all to see. Then the SG will send another sort of drone or a hybrid to investigate why the yellow monkey went off the deep end and ran into the field. It is a red arrow to alert them to us."

"We need to find out what it's capabilities are."

"An impossible task. My guess is that it's a walkie, but not a talkie."

"I just want to know if it can report or kill us."

"Done. I will send thirty seven in and see if he is still self-identifiable with the drones. If he is, I will order him to scan. If he is not recognizable to them, three seven will be shot out of the sky. Either way you will have your information."

"A noble sacrifice."

"Yes, like the play in baseball of the same name. There is one notable drawback. If he is shot out of the sky, he might also be reported."

"You have explained it well, Niner. Thank you."

"Proceed or abort?"

"Abort mission. Let's return home and move on."

"What makes you the authority on what's to be done?" Ben said looking at me.

"Niner asked me a question concerning himself and the other drones and I answered him."

"Clever, aren't you? Clever man, clever answers."

I put my hand on Ben's shoulder. "You do what you like. I am going to have a bite to eat and head back."

As I mixed up one of the powdered squares from one of the plastic pouches, I touched my pistol in my holster just to make sure it was there. My rifle was right beside me. I noticed Ben looking around at my gear. "Do you mind if I look through your wares?" he asked.

"Keep your hands to yourself," I said grabbing his wrists to stop him.

I began to think I had made a mistake in letting him tag along. There was something about him that made me uneasy. It was a feeling that sat in my gut and gnawed at me. Ben wasn't a friendly sort. He was surly and hardened in ways that made him dangerous.

He told me that he, too, had come off the pills, and he said he had never been right after that. I wondered in what ways he had been affected, and I decided to keep him talking to see if I could tell where he was off kilter. We had talked much on our way to the interstate. He spoke with bravado and hyperbole which made me question almost everything he said. His experience with the pills was the only thing he said that I believed. It was a drain of my energy to keep an eye on Ben. I hadn't slept much and I was getting snappish. However, I didn't want him lurking behind me or with any of the others, so I continued my dialogue with him. He asked a lot of questions about my two companions, and had as much as told me that he didn't trust me either. I decided to turn the tables on him time and ask a few questions of my own.

"How did you meet up with the others?" I asked him.

"They found me. I was sleeping and they practically stumbled over me."

"Why did you travel with them? You knew they were going to seek help at the compound."

"They didn't give me a choice. I wasn't armed when I met up with them."

"You were in Denver? You saw the city?"

"Just from a distance. They had power. Lights. The city looked like all city's I had ever seen. There were sky cars and people about. Nothing had changed for them except for one thing. They have underground bunkers. There is a great triangle shaped door that marks the entrance into the side of the mountain. Everyone goes in at night. The city looks pretty much deserted after the sun sets."

I stood shaking my head as I began to understand. "So they were underground when they sent the rays. That's how they've survived." As he had described the entrance to the mountain, I could see it in my mind. I had been there. I was sure of that now. Talking about it had reinforced the pics that Niner had brought back.

Ben nodded and continued to tell me of their lakeside cabin retreats. "They had beautifully constructed homes and gardens next to pristine lakes. Believe me, this beauty didn't spring up over night."

"Now it makes sense why the government kept buying up the water rights and the land. They stole my grandfather's farm over forty years ago."

"That's why they kept reporting that Yellowstone and all the mountains were erupting. They needed to keep people out," Ben added. "Well, it erupted, but not nearly as bad as they claimed."

"I want you to tell your story to the others. Maybe you can help change their minds."

"You need to get something straight, mister. I don't take orders."

"It was a request."

"It wasn't said like one."

"This isn't a tea party."

"We should be reporting in to those maintenance drones on the highway," Brin was saying coming over to us. "Not wasting time listening to you two arguing."

"We tried. That is, Niner tried. They have no communication capabilities."

"I'm going down to them," Brin announced and started forward off the hill.

"Stop!" Ben warned running after her. "Last warning," he told her and she began running faster. Everything happened so quickly after that point that I didn't even see him reach inside his jacket pocket. Next, I caught a half glimpse of some object hurling towards her. A dull thud was heard, and I saw Brin fall forward in the waving flags of grass. Everyone except Ben rushed to her. Blood was coming from behind her head. The weapon which had struck her was a tire iron and it was still lying beside her where it had landed. "Don't touch her," Kara said.

"We need to stop the bleeding," I said tearing off part of my shirt tails and handing it to the girl. "Put this on her wound."

I went back to get my sleeping bag and had the others help me place her on it. Brin did not grimace or make any lifelike sounds or facial expressions. After checking that she was still breathing, I decided she was in a coma. The gash on her head from the tire iron was pretty ghastly. Kara was crying all the while. I took her hands away from her face and gave her another piece of my shirt to wipe her eyes with. "I'm sorry."

"Thank you for trying to help her. What else can be done for her?"

"Nothing that I know of. We'll watch her during the night. Maybe she will come around."

Those in the group that knew her moved their gear down to where she lay. Ben was back over by my gear and pouring a cup of coffee when I came up. I wanted to shoot him, but instead I kicked the cup from his hands. He straightened his stance and came towards me. I readied myself for his attack and stared at the tire iron in his hand. He was swinging it back and forth.

"Your turn," he yelled coming forward. I managed to jump back from the first few strikes of the iron that Ben made towards me, but the next swing caught me on the left shoulder and I cried out.

I was unable to move at that point because I was stunned, and in considerable pain. Ben delivered me another few good whacks while I was down. I lay there with my arms covering my head to protect my skull. If Ben connected with a few more strikes, I would be lying in the grass like Brin. Just as I was entertaining my demise, I heard drone wings coming in and saw Niner's gun turrets blazing. Next, I heard Ben cry out as if he had been hit.

"Drop your weapon, or we will keep firing," Niner called to him. The dot dashes of the laser were connecting from Ben's hand clear up to his shoulder. Finally, I saw the tire iron drop. I scrambled to get it from the ground. "Sit down. Don't move, Benjamin. Niner, keep your lasers fixed on him."

Niner issued orders of his own. "Alpha three seven, fix your sights on him. If he sneezes, force 10 him."

"Don't tell him that," Ben wailed. "He doesn't know what a sneeze is."

"He'll have to guess then," the bird answered. "Be very, very still," Niner cautioned, mimicking the voice of Elmer Fudd. We had streamed cartoons on the net many times and the eagle had a real talent for picking up accents of speech.

Soon Niner was hovering by me again. "I want to see the girl."

I watched him as he flew around the circle of outsiders and to the place where Brin lay. "I would cry if I could," he was saying to them. "I'm sorry I was not here. I would have protected Brin."

"Do you know of anything we can do?" Kara asked.

"I have scanned her. The life force is out."

"Then there is nothing." Kara said touching Brin's body for a pulse. "It's true. She is in the motionless state."

"There are words from the basic instructions before life ends book that I would like to say," Niner continued.

The group only stared at him.

"The words will give comfort," he said trying to reassure their reticence.

"You are kind."

I came with a shovel and began digging a grave. "What are you doing?" Kara inquired.

"Travis is preparing the ground for her. It is a forgotten custom among humans. Here, I will show you pictures of places called cemeteries. They used to be all over." He began moving among them and showing them the pictures. "The stones carry the names of the perished ones so they will live on in your memories."

There were many comments from the new group as Niner showed them the pictures. "This is George Washington's grave," Niner said as he walked around and let them see the screen on his back. "The first president was not buried in the ground. He is in a casket of cement above ground, where his body awaits the resurrection."

"Don't you mean reanimation?" someone asked the drone.

"It is similar."

There were many questions about the instructions in the book as I dug. Niner was doing a marvelous job explaining about the son of the great I Am who was called the rescuer so I let him go for it. Meantime, Kara helped me wrap Brin in my sleeping bag and place her in the shallow grave. "Now we will hear your words, Niner," I said.

"For my sheep hear my voice, and I know them and they follow me. And I give them eternal life and they shall never perish, neither shall anyone snatch them out of my hand."

"I don't know what that means but the words convey a feeling of being protected and safe, drone," Kara said.

"It is the rescuer telling the ancient people his guarantee to come back and resurrect them. Death can't stand in his way!"

"He will reanimate? I thought that was a new phenomenon."

"He is the creator wizard. The first, the last," Niner told her.

"Where has he been? Why have we never heard of him?"

"The words are from the forbidden book. The one that was confiscated in the twenty twenties, and began the first purge," Lieutenant Kara said to those around her. "Do you believe in this wizard, Niner?" she asked.

"Here is what I will tell you," the drone said. "Human life can't cease and begin again. It can't call itself back to existence so I logically say that man does not come from nowhere."

"Do not listen to them and let us be on our way," Kara said looking at the others before leaving the grave site.

I hurried to catch up with her as she walked. "You didn't say anything back there, Travis, Why? Do you adhere to the Wizard and his instruction book or not? I need to know."

"I don't know. I have been reading it, though."

"Why? You must know it is illegal."

"Haven't you ever been curious about something?"

"It is not lawful to read it. It leads to death."

"The book tells the opposite. It tells us to question, to prove everything so that we can arrive at the truth for ourselves."

Kara didn't say another word, and ran on up ahead of me and walked faster. I raced after her until I caught up to her. "I don't want to hear anymore," she said without looking my way. "I will have to report you to the SG when we reach the compound."

"What if the book holds the truth, and the SG are the ones who have suppressed it from us? Have you ever thought of that?" I said, but Kara only walked faster. I kept up with her so I could continue to make my pitch. "They will kill me, you know. You are sentencing me to death."

"You should have thought of that before you opened the book."

"Look, we've all been through hell. I didn't even know that anyone but me was alive when I started reading the book. My grandfather used to read the book before it was banned. I was curious. Haven't you ever been curious?"

"Curiosity must be suppressed like all other desires. It leads to death."

"Death is a big thing with your group," I said.

"Death is the end."

"The instruction book says it is not."

"Tell that to Brin. Tell that to all the millions who lie dead in the streets."

"I have the same questions as you," I said just as Niner flew up next to us.

"They will live again," the drone said.

"You expect me to believe this wizard will bring all these billions back to life? Now that is a lie of the first order," the girl said.

I was looking at Kara as she walked. Her strides were long and sure, and I took it to be an indication of strength. Her hair was shoulder length, and it was blowing in back of her in the wind. I could see some of the brown locks had been tinted blonde from the sun. Her face was tanned and healthy. I envied her. She was in her twenties, less than half my age.

"Do you believe everything the OW says? They have you afraid of everything. You've been out here for two years, and none of the monsters they claimed were out here have gotten you yet," I said. Kara flashed me a look of hatred, but said nothing and started walking faster. "Don't you see they lied to you just to keep you afraid?" I continued and kept pace with her. "You are walking into your death by going to the compound," I warned. "It is the SG that has been killing people off all this time. It was them that sent the drones to finish us off during the night of silent lights."

Kara stopped walking and looked at me. Her green eyes lightened in the sun. Sparks flew out of them, beautiful, shining glints of uncertainty that reflected her youth. I rejoiced inside. I had her. The seed of doubt was there and taking root. "Stop scaring me. Stop trying to confuse me with your lies. What you say can't be true. It makes everything crazy, too crazy to live with. It is the same sort of tale."

"I have proof. Would you like to read it?" I wanted her on my side. I wanted her to like me before she knew about my involvement with the subterrean city and its inhabitants.

"Did you make it up and write it down along the way?"

"I found it in the pharmacy storehouse files. I found orders for the attack that wiped us out. It's proof that the OW intended to kill us all, don't you understand."

"Why would they do that?"

"You are asking a question. Questions lead to death," I chided her. She looked down and away from me. I could see the furrow between her brows. Her mind was beginning to turn. Doubt was registered in that look. I pushed on. "Just read my papers. Be fair."

"Even if I wanted to read them, I couldn't."

I had not even entertained the notion that she could be non-literate. I should have. Schools had been abolished almost thirty years ago. "I could read them to you."

"I wouldn't trust anything that came out of your mouth."

"What about someone in your own group? There must be someone that can read them."

"Yes. Chi can read. He was educated and worked for the OW dispensing the yearly checks."

"Do you trust him?"

"He is trained to read. He has not been trained to lie."

"Then you trust him?"

"I have no other choice."

"You have given your power away by not being educated."

"How dare you," she said slapping my face.

"I am trying to save your life. The government doesn't want us alive. They planned with the other leaders around the world to depopulate the earth and take it over for themselves." She held her hand up to me indicating that I should stop talking, but I couldn't. "I know what you are going through, Kara. I could hardly believe it myself after I read it. Think on this then, Kara. You can make a decision based on things you have seen with your own eyes, can't you? Look back at the yellow carts. What do you make of it?"

She looked back to the highway and I did, too. We were a long ways away, but on the highest points of the hills on the distant interstate, the bright yellow carts could still be seen. "It might take another year or two for them to reach the east coast, but one day there will be no evidence of their crime," I said. "Do you see what they're doing?" She didn't answer me and started walking again. At that point I decided to keep my distance from Kara and the rest of the group. She needed to twist and wrestle with the answers in her own time.

Then unexpectly, in the next moment, when she thought I wasn't looking, she looked my way. I pretended to be self-absorbed. I had planted the seed of doubt, but fought off the urge to dig for information, and as luck would have it, Ben came along side of us at just that moment.

"You have more guts than I gave you credit for. You're not as stupid as I thought," he said.

I didn't answer him. "I don't like you, but you are human," he continued. "At least the drone says so."

"Get away from me. You've done enough for one day."

"I took care of a problem," Ben said looking back at me. "Brin was the enemy. She was going to ask for sanctuary, wasn't she? She would have reported us."

I let him keep talking. For as stupid as I had found Ben over the last few days, he understood his place in this society. As I looked at his features, I saw a darkness reflected in his eyes. I was confronted with the heart of man again. He was willing to kill and it made me afraid. I thought of killing him, but stopped myself. I was just as guilty as he was. Why did I find his act of

THE WIZARD OF AII

murder cold when I had a devised the same end for thousands of the elites?

"You think I'm stupid just like them."

"Hey, Ben. Take it easy."

"I hate guys like you that think you're so much smarter than the rest of us."

"What makes you think I'm smarter? I'm in the same fix."

"It's the way you talk. The words you use. You sound like the SG. You went to school."

"Everyone was required to go to school when I was young. You had to learn to read and write."

"What for?"

"So they couldn't do what they just did to us. Wipe us out."

"Yeah, I never thought of that. We don't need to read or write today. Is that why there's pictures on the signs now, 'cause us younger ones can't read?"

"Yes, Ben, we've gone back to the stone age days when men used to draw pictures on walls."

"Don't talk down to me. I get nervous," he said, moving towards me.

His paranoia was something I couldn't overcome and it was also a thing I did not want to forget. I would have to distance myself from him. It would be a delicate operation. He wasn't quite a moron, like I said, but I'd hate to live on the difference. He reminded me of a song my grandfather was fond of and played often in the barn, or in the car when we drove to town. Bad, Bad LeeRoy Brown. Big and dumb as a man can come. Meaner than a junkyard dog. Those were the only lines that came back to me. I wished I could remember more. I don't think the original song mentioned ugly, but I added it to my own version now. Big, bad, ugly Ben; been stupid since I don't know when. Made him crazy as a mother hen. I hummed the tune under my breath without knowing it and Ben commented on it.

"Catchy tune. I like it. Got any words to it?"

"It's about a man named LeeRoy Brown. My grandfather listened to it, so it's about a hundred years old now," but I began to sing the words to him. "Big, bad LeeRoy Brown. Baddest man in the whole damn town."

"I like it. Baddest man in the whole damn town. Go LeeRoy Brown. Was he a real man?"

"Just as real as Paul Bunyan and Babe," I said.

"Hey, I heard of that Babe guy. He was a legend in baseball and drinking. You are alright, Travis."

I tried to forget my companion, but I also needed to test the waters to see if Big Bad Ben had any plans to leave on his own.

"What kind of plans have you made?"

"I'm not returning to the compound."

I looked sideways at Kara to see how she had taken his announcement, but if she was upset her features didn't show it. I kept walking astride of her, staying even with her until we reached the farm, though I took quick peeks in back of me to see where Ben was the rest of the hike back to the farm.

Once back, I went directly into the house pushing Ben along in front of me. I wanted to find my two companions and let them in on the news. The cats scampered towards me as soon as I entered the house. Fluff was the first one to greet me and she let out a quiet meow. "Did you miss me?" I swear she looked surprised to see me again after almost a week. "I came back. I would never leave you, girl," I said heading for the ammunition and gun reserves.

"You care about them animals more than you do for people," Ben mumbled at me.

"Shut up," I said.

I threw some rifles and guns to Zel and Sam, who had just entered from the kitchen. It was at this time that Niner appeared at the door. Good Neighbor Sam looked at me. "What's happened?" he asked as he caught the weapon.

"Ask Ben here."

"I killed one of them."

"Why?" I could hear the surprise in Sam's voice.

"She was going to alert the drones on the cleanup crew about us."

Rather than talking about killing Brin, Ben rambled on about the yellow carts and the process being used to rid the world of the litter. He looked at Sam as the Stranger moved over by me. "Is this true?" Sam asked me.

"They're not about to leave any garbage lying about to attest to their genocide of mankind," I said.

"Ben, sit on the couch until I can find out all that happened," Sam ordered. He bent closer to me and spoke in a whisper. "What did you do about Brin?"

"Buried her and now Kara is like a cat on a hot tin roof. She may stir the others up. We need to be prepared."

"I saw no cats, no roofs," Niner said.

"It's meant to be symbolic," I said quickly.

"Of what?"

"Trouble."

"It is a literary device, Niner," Sam explained. "A simile. It means she is nervous and edgy like a cat whose paws are being burned by the hot tin on the roof, so she jumps every which way to avoid the pain."

"Sounds like dancing."

"In a way, you're right."

"One of those feeling things I can't quite equate with," the drone said. "I have no experience with pain. It makes no sense. I will put one of the cats on a tin roof when I find it."

"No, it's not an enjoyable sensation."

"Dancing isn't enjoyable?"

"Dancing is. It is the hot tin roof that isn't. Heat would burn the cats paws," I said.

"I must gain sensation. I have a lot to learn. Touch, heat, pain, cold. It is a whole new vocabulary."

"No, it's more than a dictionary, Niner," I said. "It's more like a test kitchen where you're concerned."

"Just file it under literary devices," Sam said. "The rest will come later."

"That's what Trave said about Kansas, but we have already passed Kansas," Niner said.

"We're not going back," I said.

"I've given up on finding Oz. The book is quite elusive as to just where it is, anyway, " the eagle said. "Besides, there is no town with the name of Emerald City in the road atlas, either."

"Face it, Niner. You are just a literal minded crossling in a figurative world."

"You are cruel, Travis."

"And you think I am stupid. You talk to the drone as if he were human," Ben broke in. "You talk to the cats the same way. You're crazy. We have a crisis on our hands."

"One that you created."

"It was necessary."

"You could have just stopped her. You didn't need to kill her."

"All these droids, humans, clones, drones intend to turn us in. I say get rid of them now."

"Didn't you say Ben was of human origin, Niner?" I said.

"He is as vibrant as you."

"Well, check again. He can't be. He is cold as ice."

"He is a warm blooded mammal. Temperature is 98.6."

"I mean his heart is cold. He has no feelings."

"And this thing does?" Ben said kicking at Niner.

"There will be no more killing," Good Neighbor Sam said stepping up to block Ben from attacking Niner any further.

"I don't believe in anything you idiots have talked about. Gods and life and creations of all sorts. Your ideas are just as crazy as the governments," Ben said.

"Everyone should believe in something," Zel said.

"Who says? Anyway, I'm leaving."

"You're staying to face the decision, Ben," I said.

"What decision are you talking about?" said Ben.

"Your fate is in Kara's hand. She is deciding whether to go to Denver or not. She is reading the office memos and the writings of the others about the history of the shadow government coming into power."

"She won't believe it. None of them will."

"You believe it. What convinced you?"

"I've seen things."

"So have they."

"Most of that group is AI. They are programmed to obey the state," Ben countered.

"I was the state," Niner said, "and look at me now. I've gone rogue," he bragged. The drone was on my side and I felt confident all of a sudden.

"There are two humans left among them. They should be able to make up their own minds," I reminded him. "Until they reach a conclusion, we will not let you leave."

"I won't either," Niner said, walking over to Ben.

"I should end you," Ben said looking down at Niner and lifting up his foot.

"Move an ear lobe and I'll laser you," Niner said rolling forward.

"Is that a threat, you plastic junk yard bird?" Ben said, and I instantly realized Ben had picked up new his vocabulary from the song I had introduced him to.

"Draw!" Niner yelled.

"What?" Ben said stepping back.

"Trave, you say go and we'll see who is quicker on the draw. Ben's foot or my laser," Niner advised.

"No. I'm not going against no machine," Ben said backing up further.

Niner gave his trumpet of a laugh and said, "He's smarter than he looks."

"Keep that crossling away from me," Ben continued while using his hands to protect himself.

"Stay and you won't have a problem," I warned Ben. "Try and leave, and I will send Niner after you."

"The others will kill me if I stay."

"It's quite a dilemma you've created for yourself," Sam said.

"I don't know what that means, but I don't like it," Ben said and made a grab for one of the rifles, but Niner was there to intervene. "I am not weighted by conscience or memory," he said to Ben.

"You're a transling, drone. Travis has messed with your circuits," Ben said, pointing to me. "Now you're crazier than any of us."

"And you, human, were molded by the very hand of the Great I Am. Bring your actions into line," the drone countered.

Ben started laughing and plopped down on the couch. "You'll never be human. You'll always be bits and pieces of junk bolted together. You'll never be real. Just like the clone here," he said pointing to Zel.

"We will find the wizard," Niner said testing out his laser on a pillow beside Ben.

"I can tell you what you will find, drone. An end just like the cars and bodies on the interstate. You'll be compacted and loaded on to the trash bin and hauled away. A little tiny package of nothing about yea big," Ben said, rubbing his thumb and forefinger together to indicate the size.

Niner left making sounds that passed for sobs. From that point on, Ben derided and tried to hurt Niner in every possible way and brought up every small detail that pointed to his not being human.

"Well, you were awfully quiet through all of this," I said looking at Good Neighbor Sam.

"Since when did you become interested in what I have to say. If you want to know, I'll tell you. Ben is a byproduct of a society who deconstructed God."

"Wasn't that an idea dreamt up by some Frenchmen who came up with a new way to interpret literature?"

"Derrida's idea was that it didn't matter what the author intended to say in his work. He said the only thing that mattered was what each individual reader saw in the work himself. Deconstructionism posits there could be a thousand different interpretations of a book and that each one is right."

"Sounds ok to me."

"You miss the point. By each person interpreting a piece of literature for himself, the universal truths are lost. The author's intended message is lost. That leaves the door open to the leftist elite to twist the meanings of all writers they disagree with."

"It's backwards thinking," I said getting the meaning now.

"Precisely. Instead of taking the I Am's word as a demarcation of truth and trying to live up to his standards, the world began to insist that it could apply its own standards. God, as author, was dead, and so was His standard of truth. Good and evil have become fiction and the real truth about the moral quality of actions are forgotten. It's a form of escapism and one that has trapped them in their own philosophy because nothing registers in the conscience."

"It's what you were talking to the gal about the other night about there being an independent entity who judges," I said looking at him. Stranger Sam had given me a lot to think about and I agreed with a lot of it, but I was still leery of him.

In spite of my misgivings, life on the farm went on and time passed. It had been over a week since the first confrontation between Niner and Ben, but it came to a head again out of nowhere. We had all been busy preparing to leave this camp while the two other humans continued to have their droid read the papers and the other journals to them so they could decide whether they would turn us in or join our cause. We were gathered together as a group, and eating a late supper when Niner came to report in. "Want a taste of this meat, Niner?" Ben asked. "Hmm, you're missing something. Moist, succulent meat dripping in its own juices."

Kara stood up. "Stop with the commercials, Ben. I've had enough of them. Leave Niner alone."

"Thank you, beautiful woman, for trying to protect my feelings. I will be whole one day," the eagle said.

"You'll never eat food, " Ben said.

"I think it's time to give motion to Niner's wings and head," Kara said and then elbowed me. "How 'bout it, Travis?"

I could hardly believe what she was saying. I took it as her way of announcing the decision to go on with us to freedom and I jumped at the chance.

Ben did his best to scoff at us. "You can add all the junk you want to that plastic pea brain, but he'll never be human."

"It's you humans who are in danger of extinction not my kind," Niner said.

Kara stood up and threw her empty meat stick into the fire. "Come along Niner. We have shopping to do. I will make a list of essentials. We will make your experience as a crosssling as enjoyable as we can. You shall have freedom of motion. You shall flap your wings," she said.

"I will dance," Niner said, "and cover you with my wings."

"That's a beautiful expression, Niner."

"It's not original. It was said by a King named David in the song chapters of the Instruction Manual."

"Tell me about this king and how you came to hear of him," I heard Kara say as they got into the sky car and drove off.

CHAPTER 9

The next days were busy as we worked on the vehicles that had been owned by the Pipers and got them running, and then we moved on to the next mechanical feat which was to giving motion to Niner. Kara, who had worked at Bio tech in Georgia, helped me feather his plastic hide with the latest biotech synoptic innovations. I felt comfortable with the surgeries and I was remembering more and more.

Finally it was time to show off our work. Everyone turned out for Niner's debut except Stranger Sam. He hadn't been around much, and I started to wonder what he was up to and decided to find out after Niner made his bows to the crowd. When I located Sam, I watched him pulling a cart loaded down with goods. I decided that I should follow him and see where he was taking the provisions. It was a rough journey over the hills, but not a far one. His secret sat by the stream that wound its way through the property. It was a small, flat topped barge.

While he was unloading the supplies, I walked up to him from behind. "Planning an escape?" Good Neighbor Sam didn't seem surprised at all when he turned around. "I saw you following me."

"You weren't at Niner's debut."

"You should know my take on that. Man is not the potter."

"He can be. I just proved it."

"Like I asked Kara, If you are on the wrong road, does it not make sense to go back and find the right one?"

"Sure."

"Is there a wizard? Man knows himself. He has a ring side seat for what goes on inside his own mind. He knows the pressing that nudges him towards the answer to that question is yes."

"Forget it Sam. I'm not taking the bait. I want to know what you are planning with all this."

"I am preparing a second route of escape… for all of us."

I stood looking at him. He clearly understood what I had insinuated because he added, "I made no secret attempts to hide my trips from anyone. Niner has been helping me transport items."

In a moment I found out the statement he had given me was true, for I spotted Niner coming in carrying a box of MRE's in his talons. "Hi, Trave," he said dropping the box on the deck of the flat topped boat. "More food for you humans to ingest. Though eating seems somewhat unspiritual, don't you agree, Joseph."

"The wizard intended for men to enjoy it."

"Neither one of you is going to ruin my appetite. Argue on. I could use some lunch," I said jumping onto the deck of the ship to where he had dropped the rations. "Any roast beef?" I asked now that I was sure no double dealing had been going on.

"Help yourself," Sam said pointing at some boxes. "What do you think about the plastic pod tent I built in the middle of the barge?"

"It's as big as a cabin," I said absently. "Cold weather is around the corner. We'll need it."

"So you aren't against traveling by river then?"

"We can't stay here forever. We've been pressing our luck."

While we were busy eating and drinking, Niner had been pacing back and forth across the deck flapping his wings. "What's the matter, Niner?"

"I feel lost when you eat. Do you suppose Ben is right that I will never experience all things? Is it false to hope?"

The eagle sounded so despondent that I couldn't answer.

He stared at us for quite a while before he said, "I will see you later," and took flight.

"He's getting a little touchy about things lately," I said to Good Neighbor Sam.

"There are many desires that have been awakened in him," Sam replied.

"No one's given him anything he didn't ask for," I said.

"Is it good to get everything you ask for?" Sam said.

I gave him a nasty look.

"I'm speaking collectively of mankind, not just the drone," he said.

"We meant him no harm, Sam. We are only trying to help him.'"

"Man is wise in his own eyes," Joseph said.

"You mean we shouldn't pat ourselves on the back?"

"Man calls his imagination ingenious and fails to see how pedantic and short sighted he is."

"I don't see the connection," one of the translings said walking up to us.

"Isn't that where your whole life is stuck, Traveler? You are the created telling the creator. Man has convinced himself that in time he will be capable of all things. It is a worldwide delusion. How absurd. God exists whether men believe in him or not. You can't push him out of existence by simply saying he isn't needed."

"Man enhancing and prolonging life is progress."

"I thought you were against progress in your book. So you see it as a moving towards some end, but tell me what is that end you envision, Travis."

While Sam was talking, the others joined us. They were all carrying provisions to load on the boat. It seemed everyone was aware of the plans for a water escape except me.

"What are you two talking about?" Kara asked.

"The wizard. Does Good Neighbor Sam talk about anything else?" I said.

"But no one has seen the Wizard," Kara said, looking towards him.

"Have you ever seen the swamp monster or the boogey man under the bed?" Joseph asked her.

"Not personally, but many have reported seeing them. There are videos on I tube," Kara said.

"Does that make them real? You all came into camp afraid of everything out here. Is that the way you want to live? Most of you refuse to enjoy a bath in the river for fear that some swamp monster will pull you under. You can't take a walk in the woods and admire the beauty there because you are afraid of the yeti, the Poukipsi skunk, and the wood wudgies. Is fear a gift you are willing to accept from man's mind?"

"The government told us that they were working on a way to get us to another planet so they could save us from the destruction of earth and from all the aliens and monsters," Kara said.

"And what's out there in space? It seems they are putting you into the fire. Let me ask you a question. Have they taken any of you to safety?" Joseph continued. "Haven't they built a new city just for themselves? Does their base at Denver look like they are planning an escape to another planet?"

"Why did they tell us all this?" Kara said in a defeated voice. "Are you saying that they made up some grand lie?"

"Answer that question, and you will have solved the riddle, Kara, of what has been done and is being done to you," Joseph said. "Here is another question you should ask yourself. Does promoting fear accomplish anything good? The SG peddle fear and tell you that man likes to be scared. They sold you evil and said you wanted it because it puts you in touch with your primordial selves. Does it?"

"Tell us what you think," Kara answered.

Before Sam could answer, Niner flew onto the barge and flapped his wings. "Be of good courage. I have not given you a spirit of fear, but of love, courage and a sound mind," Niner spouted. "That is the creator wizard speaking in the instruction booklet. He tells everyone not to be afraid 365 times in the manual."

"Why does the book call fear a spirit, Joseph?" Kara asked. "It frightens me. It is like the world in that way."

"Let me give you an example," Joseph said. "Fear may be invisible, but you can feel it. It is the feeling that stops you from bathing in the lake, from going into the forest."

"There is evil in the forest. It grows there."

"Travis and Zel passed through it and are alive," Sam said.

"They had protection, a talisman or something, then," she answered.

"They had nothing of the sort," Niner added, "and neither did I."

"You expect us to believe that?" someone said.

"You believe in everything else," Joseph said getting up in a hurried fashion. "Fantastic things, laughable things that have no proof attached to them," the stranger said, raising his voice.

"Tell us, then Joseph," Kara pleaded.

"Niner can tell you the truths in the Book. When you have heard them, talk to me. We will go swimming."

"Where should I start teaching, Joseph?" Niner asked.

"Begin with the army of light and the army of darkness."

"Good choice. That is the start of the battle we are fighting today," Niner said.

"How can that be? I have never heard of these two armies," Kara said.

"They war in each one of us. They fight for our souls," Joseph said walking away.

"Fantastic! Invisible armies," one of the translings said. "I, for one, like a good scary story."

"Fear is the feeling that comes from the adversary of the wizard," Niner told them. "Fear is the absence of the wizard."

Just then I looked around and noticed Ben was not there. "Where's Ben?"

"I left him at the house," Zel said.

I dropped the food packet I was preparing and began to race back to the farm.

In seconds Niner was flying ahead of me. "I will pinpoint his coordinates."

"We need go after him," I said already running. The rest of the crew was right behind me.

When we reached the farm, Ben was nowhere outside. I went into the house and called for him and searched. It was in the kitchen that I noticed a note and read it.

"This doesn't make sense," I said to the others.

"What's it say?"

"He's gone to the base at Denver."

"He was against us going there. Why would he go there?" Kara said. "I don't believe it."

"Believe," Niner said flying into the room. "I have his coordinates. He's within an hour of the base."

"One of the jet cars is missing from the yard," Joseph said coming in with Zel.

"Damn. We won't catch him, now," I said looking around at everyone.

"I must have left the keys on the table when I came back from town," Kara said checking her pockets. "I'm sorry."

"I will fly after him. I will send three or four drones into the base to put him into the motionless state. He will be stopped," Niner said reading the note on the table.

"Stopped from what?" Zel asked.

"Divulging our location," I said. "He said in the note that he was going to trade us for immunity."

"We have decided to side with you under one condition."

"You want to see the compound first," Joseph said before I could answer Kara.

"How did you know?" she stammered.

"I want to see it myself," I said.

The stranger did not look a bit dismayed as he answered. "The manual says to test the waters. Truth demands a test. It is not afraid."

We all headed back outside to see Niner and his squad off.

When the others were seated around the fire, Kara said, "In our system Ben would have been dead already and we would not have to go after him now," she said touching my arm.

"Play with snakes," Niner intervened, raising his eyebrows at me.

Ignoring Niner, I focused on the girl. "Do you really want to return to laws where death was meted out for the smallest of infractions?"

"That's what holds me back from believing in your way fully. There are many intricacies to the ten laws of this wizard that confuse me. Ben should have died."

"He's gone now. What difference can it make?"

"We must all agree on things from this point out."

"Why is it that you as a society are stuck with the mindset that all must do the same thing?" Joseph said loudly. "You are all separate individuals."

"We are all the same. We are equal. There can be no disputes or disharmony," the girl answered.

"People are different. Doesn't the state say to celebrate differences?"

"Yes, that is the main cornerstone of our society."

"If you believe in differences, why can't you see that people can have different opinions?"

"That is dangerous."

"Then all differences are dangerous."

"No, just that one."

"Why is one difference of opinion more dangerous than any other difference?" the stranger asked.

"It leads to war."

"Aren't we all here of different minds, and aren't we trying to resolve it through compromise?" Joseph asked. "Can you not see that there has been one truth for the elite, and one for the masses?"

"Niner read something from the manual that expressed that reasoning," Kara said. "If you love only those who love you, it is of little consequence. Is that what you are getting at, Joseph?"

"You captured it perfectly," Joseph said.

I knew I was witnessing reality and truth come to Kara one tiny drip at a time. I hoped that it would break the dam in time, like it had with me, and the flood of truth would come.

"It is all so strange," Kara said.

"That is freedom. There is a weight to it. That heaviness tells you that it is you alone who must live with your decisions," Joseph explained. When she did not answer him he said, "If it were you who had committed the infraction, which set of laws would you rather be tried under?"

"Yes, that makes all the difference, doesn't it?" she said. "Hanna, what do you have to say?"

"I have never been asked my thoughts. I am too frightened to say," the robo answered.

"My grandfather had a method to help him make decisions," I said. "He would get a piece of paper and make a list of things for and against the issue he was trying to decide upon."

Kara looked at me. "You are one of the in-betweens, aren't you? One of those who was born during the transition. There are not many of you left. Most transitionists could not make the adjustment to the new system."

I ignored the part where she guessed my age and years and said, "I almost didn't survive," and began to tell her of my years in care and the pills that kept my mind asleep. I even told her what happened to my grandfather when the takeover of the new system was being put through its first phases.

"So you remember! You have memories that have survived. Do you trust in them?"

"I mostly remember the things my grandfather told me about how people in his generation lived following the second world war. They fought and died to end the system of government we live in now."

"We have always been told what to think. I am afraid to say anything," Hanna added.

"That's what I'm talking about. That's what tyranny does. It is slavery to be told you can't say certain things, or read specific books," Joseph said.

"But all in the society agreed with it," Kara said. "How did all come to agree to it if what you say is true?"

"We didn't agree to it. The government agreed to it for us. They made it a hate crime to speak against certain groups, but where was the term when the Jewish and Christian populations were decimated?"

"You are right, Joseph," Kara said. "Then they went after all groups who opposed them."

"Are you seeing how systematic it was? Everyone was afraid to say anything. No one wanted to be the next group on their hit list, but eventually we all were."

"I see what you mean," a robotoid I didn't know said as if he had just internalized the nugget of truth for himself. "They even blamed us for all the pollution, the over population, and global warming."

"There has been zero population growth for the last ten years in this country," Niner said. "No children were born except to those in government."

"What?" we all said turning towards the eagle.

"You didn't know that the species in the compound have children? I saw them. There are thousands of them and schools. I saw them when I was stationed there. I will play the hologram for you."

As the halogramed played showing the footage, Zel said, "Hypocrites."

"But why would they go against their own laws?" Hanna said.

"Those laws weren't for them, they were for us, just the way Joseph said," I answered.

"What Trave says is mathematically sound," Niner added proudly.

Everyone watched the hologram in silence and Joseph spoke, "Have you decided, Kara?"

"I'm getting there."

Before Niner flew off to the compound everybody wanted to have an input into what the squad should take pictures of, and I let them all have their say. I, on the other hand, needed no more intel to make up my mind. I was set to attack, but I thought back to what Ben had argued with me over some days before. "Your weakness will get us killed," he had said to me. I hoped he was wrong, and that this experiment in human nature would come to a fruitful end. Once the votes were in, I hoped we would all be on the same page.

"Since I'm not regulation any longer, I will wait at a safe distance from the compound and send a few of my squadron into high level security places. I know where they are located and the protocol that needs to be followed to allow them entry."

"Won't there be a problem with lost members of the force returning after such a long absence?"

"I have taken care of that by erasing all their memory banks past the first attack in New York. I have left the pictures of the gangs raiding and destroying Alpha Core's force. I have cut the drones communication wires which will provide the SG with the reason why no transmissions were possible. That will end those New Yorkers' cat eating days."

"You are a genius, Niner," Zel said. "But what if Ben has already talked?"

"I will end his days."

Shouts and claps came from Kara's group in support of Niner's answer.

"How long do you expect all this to take?" I asked ignoring the celebration.

"A few days, maybe longer, if security measure have changed, but I would like to say goodbye to the cats."

"You can't say you're going to miss them."

"Say it is for good luck, then. Here kitties," he called in a higher pitched voice than his normal one and clearly ignoring me.

We spent the next days finishing and readying the barge for sailing while we waited for the rogue drone's return. With my best friend gone, I spent more time alone, but it was becoming harder to do all the time. More and more wanderers were finding us, and they weren't only species of man, there were animals, too. I had been right earlier when I had sensed that we were becoming some kind of magnet for all who were lost. That night more than a dozen new problems sat eating our food and staring at us over the fire. Our little band was growing, though it was not to our advantage. It was more of a drain on our food supply and none of them were trained to fight or wanted to.

I tossed and turned all night and was given to unquiet dreams. In these night mares I was chased by every kind of species known and unknown to mankind. I had many insights about life that took odd forms, and like most dreams, they were conveyed in confusing subconscious symbols which made no sense to me upon waking. Usually I could only remember the last few words of these dreams when I woke, but I remembered this night's dream because it was a familiar one. It was the large empty faced monster that had haunted me since childhood which I saw in my sleep that night. "It's you," the monster was saying. "You know it is. Man has come to the end of himself. He is not worthy to open the book." In the dream I had seen the sun descend so close to the earth that it began to melt every thing around me including the wax seals on the books which began flowing like a river.

I saw words on the pages, but just as my eyes caught sight of them, they melted. Each word was a different color and that oddity distracted me. The colors must mean something I thought as I tried harder to read the words by scanning ahead to a place in the text that was far above where it was melting, but the words just melted faster. 'You know what it says. You have always known what it says," the voice kept repeating in the dream. I agreed with the voice, and as I tried to reach out and stop the seals from melting, I felt my skin being singed by the heat, and I pulled my hand away.

It was then I noticed drips of red wax also stung my bare feet. In seconds I was standing in a puddle. "The sun has fallen from its place in the sky. Everything will be burned away," the voice warned. I had to believe it because I was standing in it. I could feel the hot wax running between my toes. Then in a horrifying bizarre resurrection the melted words rose up to become men. Arms, legs, and faces bobbed like corks in the wash of flowing colored wax.

I sat up and struggled to awaken more fully. I was relieved it was dawn and that light would soon return to the world. I did not stoke the fire or brew my coffee, but just stared across the high fields of grass that stretched out to the sides of me. The grasses looked like wheat, I thought, because they were now yellow and dried. I watched as the wind cut across their tops, bending them forward in one golden motion. They waved in billows like banners from victorious warriors. My head throbbed and I sat paralyzed.

I dressed quickly and walked to the screen door on the front of the house. I felt comforted as I pushed against the lightweight screen door and felt it swing easily open and heard its familiar creak. Just as welcome was the sight of Zel in the yard. I couldn't deny that she was pretty and that I liked watching her. Her movements were sparing. Even when she walked, she didn't sway her arms or her hips like so many of the women I had been with most of my life. There was no billboard advertisement or come on to her at all. She had presence. Zel was a woman's woman like my grandmother. Presence without pretense. That was it. I liked her brevity. It was then that I noticed the yard around her. It was alive with animals. Chickens were scratching in the gravel, deer were munching on grass. Squirrels chased each other up and around the tree. Birds were singing in the trees. "Where did all these animals come from?" I yelled from the doorway.

"They just wandered in," Zel said, shrugging. "I hadn't given it a thought."

I looked back at my family meowing from inside. "C'mon kids," I said reopening the door for them, but the cats sat at the door, and stood looking back as if they expected someone else to come. Then it struck me. They were waiting for Sam.

In seconds he came out of the kitchen and went through the door before me and the troop followed contentedly after him. I had barely stepped out the door when I said, "You're a regular pied piper. There's something strange about you, Sam. I can't put my finger on it, but you've hypnotized the cats, fixed up the place, and started a zoo all in a matter of weeks. I'm sure that's some kind of record."

"No, the record is six days."

I didn't quite get what he meant as I watched the cats head straight to Zel who was sitting in the shade of the tree reading a book. The cows and deer wandered around the front yard like domesticated animals. There were squirrels, birds, raccoons, rabbits and cats interacting together, and none of them were afraid of each other or us. I walked over to her. It was then that I thought it may have been Zel that was responsible for the transformation. Maybe it was her that had drawn the animals.

"How'd you do it?" I said to her.

"Do what?"

"Get all these different animals to like each other."

"Do you mean did I give them sort of pill to tame them?"

"I guess. How else could this be taking place?"

"I have no pills. Never believed in them."

"Then how?"

"Listen. Look around you. Do you sense anything?" Zel said.

I stood for a long time and tried to take in the scenery.

"It's very peaceful isn't it, Travis?" Zel said.

"Yes," I said looking at her. She had nailed it right on the head. "My grandfather's place had a calm about it like this," I said almost automatically.

"Isn't it strange and wonderful that you can feel it?" Zel said.

"It's been there. You just never noticed it," Good Neighbor Sam said as he came up to us. He was looking at me in an intense and peculiar way. I felt like I was being studied, but not by one who watches for you to make a mistake, but as one who has laid a lost item in your path and is anxious for the moment when you should find it. Despite this new, good feeling about the stranger, I continued to approach Sam cautiously in my own timing like a dog that's wary of a stranger offering food in his hands.

"Have you been reading the Instruction Manual long?" I asked.

"Not as much as I should. Each reading is new and speaks to me in a different way."

"I know what you're saying," I said sitting down beside the stranger. "It was like the book spoke to me. Not out loud, but as a thought, but more than a thought because it was a different voice than my own. Don't ask me what I mean, I don't know," I said half apologetically.

"You spoke about your assuredness of a higher being in your novel a number of times."

"I never said that anywhere."

"You talked of it just now. Oh, you didn't use that precise terminology, but that is what your deeper meaning implies."

"Maybe to you, but not to everyone. How did you come to believe, Stranger Sam?"

"I told you my name is Joseph."

"It's things like that which make me nervous."

"My name?"

"It was my grandfather's name. Well, close to it."

Sam started laughing at this point. It wasn't vicious laughter, but it had a biting edge to it.

"Do you know how many people in the registry book in the US have that name? Over two billion."

"That's the sort of thing I'm talking about. You have all these facts and figures at your disposal which no one could possibly know. You're just making data up as you go along."

Sam reached in his knapsack and drew out a book and handed it to me. I read the title: Everything You Could Ever Want to Know About Anything: Useless Stuff That Just Might Come in Handy.

"It was published in 2010 or there about," he said, "so by today's standards it's really an archeological find. I like to know figures. I calculate the new totals based on probability to come up with today's figures."

I looked at Sam in a new way and marveled way. He had a ready answer for everything. It was the same uncanny magic my grandfather had possessed when anything he needed appeared precisely at the moment he needed it.

While Joseph was talking, I opened up the book and looked at the publishing date. 2013. It was over sixty years old. When I leafed through the pages, I saw lines and tables drawn in where Good Neighbor Sam had done his calculations. He kept his answers in his pocket just like Pompy had once, I thought.

"I like to keep tabs on the government's figures. They haven't told the truth for many more decades than this book shows."

"Doesn't it anger you about all that they've done to us?"

"What good does anger do? Can you change anything by it?"

"It's a good motivator."

"Yes, I read your book, remember? Do you really think you can kill them all?"

I looked at him. I saw those waves of light cresting and falling in his eyes. "You're tricky. My grandfather was like that. He always asked questions to make me think."

"I'm measuring your intended thoughts and actions by what's in this book," he said holding up the instruction manual. "I suspect Pompy did the same thing. He forgave the SG for taking everything he had. That told me he took the advice printed in these pages very seriously."

I suddenly was seized by the feeling to swallow this man whole and know everything about him and the questions poured out of me like rain. "Have you lived your life like that? How did you hide your beliefs from the SG? Where did you grow up and who taught you about God?"

"I will tell you one day. Right now just let me say, I was a lot like you. I came to know the truth late."

"You sound like you have regrets."

"I missed out on a lot of joy in life because of it."

"How?" I laughed. "I've always thought of the Instruction Manual as a book of don'ts, not as one that gives joy."

"It is a book of freedom."

"Free me, Joe," I said caught up in the waves.

"By reading the book, each man finds his own way. Learn to count your days, Trave."

There was something about Stranger Sam, or Ranger Joe as I had come to call him that was askew, and try as I might, I couldn't put my finger on it. Even paranoid Ben had liked him. The cats were ready to mutiny for him if he asked. The wildlife migrated into the yard as if a homing signal had been sent out.

Ranger Joe stood up. "It's time for everyone to start over. Forget yesterday. Today is a new day. Raise your hands and repeat after me. Today I will seek truth. I will honor my friends with peace as far as I am able. I will worry about tomorrow when it comes."

Somehow we all did as we were told and then looked at each other. It was easy to do in this beautiful setting of trees and animals and sky and stream. "Trust needs to grow. It will," we heard the Stranger say. "Right now you are all like the Velveteen Rabbit. You've lost your stuffing is all. You've been washed and tossed and grizzled inside. There's an inner reality and an outer reality, and then there's reality itself."

"You talk different from anyone I have ever heard. Did it come out of that book you always have with you? It is a different way to think," Kara said.

"I will teach you what I have learned from it."

That's how our study sessions began and we held them every day from then on. Sometimes they lasted for a few moments, but sometimes we talked all day about a subject. I admired this stranger and wondered where he had learned to decipher the words in the book and how he had learned to think in such an unique fashion. Pompy had thought like that. Free. He let his mind just wander, and take him in all directions until he found the truth. That's what critical thinking allowed a learner to do, ask questions until the subject was made transparent.

I asked many questions of the stranger, but he would divulge no personal information which made me suspicious of him again. I knew nothing of where he came from, what he had done on earth, or how he came to believe and interpret the Manual as he did. At times I entertained the notion that he was some sort of spy for the SG. He was well educated and had unbelievable patience, which gave rise to the notion that this stranger was waiting to discover the secret of our survival before he turned us over, but there were problems with my theory. One problem was simply that he never asked any questions about how I got here or anything about my life before I met him, and most notable of all, he had the opposite mindset of the SG, and lastly, he had read my book and knew my story. He could have handed me over long ago and he had not run, Ben had.

Winter was coming. I could smell the change in the air outside. The days were shorter and the sky a more brilliant blue. Days had passed, and still there was no sign of Niner and his crew. I was feeling restless as I sat under the oak tree, and as usual I was watching the cat family, which by now had grown to include the third generation kits of Fluff and her sister, Sneakers. The younger ones did not get as close to us as their parents, but every now and then they came to sit with their moms to see what humans did. Fluff stayed close to me and made her kittens stay with her.

I loved to sit cooking meat by the fire pit and inhaling the aromas. The pit became the hearth, the gathering place for all and soon others joined us.

Sam was looking up into the sky as he walked.

"You expecting company?" I laughed.

"I half expect Niner to return today," he said.

"Why today?"

"I just feel it." The stranger looked at me. His eyes were penetrating and intense, and I had to look away. It was like he knew what he said was a certainty. It was at that moment that I became adamant about not letting him wear me down so I would confide in him. He had secrets. If he could hold things back, then I reasoned so could I.

"You still don't trust me fully do you?"

"What do you mean?"

"You call me Stranger Sam, Good Neighbor Sam, or Ranger Joe."

"I feel like the name you gave me is not your real name," I said with animosity present in my voice.

"If my name was Harley or Carl, would it make a difference? Does it make a person, or a cat for that matter, what he is? Would Fluff be any different if you called her Snickers or Maya? Let it go."

"Your answer to everything is to let it go."

"It is almost the Sabbath. The discussion will have to keep. It is not given that we should discuss our own thoughts on the holy day."

"You said you weren't Jewish. Why do you keep their day and their traditions?"

"Their day? It is the absurdity of man's mind to claim that Jesus made one law for the Jew, and a separate law for everyone else. That's like saying there are two separate paths by which to enter His Kingdom. Jesus said he was the only way."

"Then why is it that Christians and Jews have always been so different?"

"Read these verses for me," Sam said handing me the book.

"But if some of the branches were broken off, and you, although a wild olive shoot, were grafted in among the others and now share in the nourishing root of the olive tree, do not be arrogant toward the branches. If you are, remember it is not you that supports the roots, but the roots that support you. Then you will say, "Branches were broken off that I might be grafted in." I put the book down.

"We are all part of the same tree," Joseph summed up. "Gentiles were added to the tree, grafted in, but regarding the fourth commandment this new branch has told the established root which rules it will follow. It is like a guest taking over his friend's house and deciding to change the rules. God gave ten commandments for men to follow. Did God somewhere say that gentiles were to be exempt from the fourth commandment and honoring his Sabbath?"

"Then why did men start worshiping him on Sunday? My grandfather did. I remember it."

"It is man who said God doesn't care what day of the week we worship him. Did anyone ask God his opinion on that?" Sam asked holding the book up and shaking it at me. "God does give his opinion in it. He picked the seventh day at creation. It was not a suggestion for man to follow, it was a commandment, and it was meant for every man, woman, and child who would be born on this earth."

"Then why did so many people worship on Sunday?"

"Man said they worshiped on Sunday because it was the resurrection day. God neither commanded nor sanctified man to honor his son's resurrection. It is written nowhere in the book."

I sat without moving because his words had struck me like lightning.

"You believe the SG's pulled one over on you and deceived you, don't you? Well, the holy day of God was changed in just such a deceitful way as well."

"Really?" Sam had piqued my curiosity and I wanted to know.

"The facts I am going to tell you are greater than the coupe this government perpetuated on you."

"Greater than the account of destroying billions of people?"

"I was not speaking of greater numbers,Trave, but of their consequences. It's one thing to lose your life, but another to lose your soul."

I sat quiet. He had thrown another lightning bolt.

"I can see that you are still conflicted about the existence of God," he said getting up. I jumped up after him and implored him to continue his story. I had a feeling that if he didn't explain it to me then he never would. It would like be losing a book before reading the final chapter. He had presented it like a mystery and it became like bait on a hook to me.

"It is a long story. I feel like chicken tonight," he said feeling his girth with both of his hands. He sure enjoyed eating. It was his sensual enjoyment of things which made me rule out that he could be anything but human in origin despite what Niner had reported.

"I want to know how they were duped. How could they have not known or seen it coming?"

"Did you? Did anyone in your generation see all that has come now?"

That was a powerful question, and again I had no answer.

"First things, first. We will start in the beginning with the dragon. He lived amidst the wizard before he was cast down to earth, you know. Some even say that it was the dragon who was given the task to build the new city of Jerusalem and was charged with inlaying the stones for the temple."

"After losing the battle he was given the earth?"

"You forget this is the realm to which he was banished. It was not meant as a prize. Earth was a step down for him, but he was given dominion over it. He offered this earthly kingdom, his kingdom, to the Son when he tempted him in the wilderness, didn't he?"

"I had forgotten that."

"He has the power to transform himself at will, and by doing so he is able to change how people see him. He comes in many forms."

"Really?" I said not believing the disbelief I heard in my tone.

"You have picked up his vibrations and want to avenge yourself against those who did this, don't you?"

"Yes, I suppose, but he didn't make me do it," I laughed.

"Man has a choice of who he will follow. You cannot serve two masters."

"You know how I feel. I hate them."

"Then you have become like them. You have taken their spirit into yourself."

"I am nothing like them. I am the hated."

"But you hate back."

He had me there. I did hate them. Maybe my hate was even greater than theirs.

"You reacted according to the emotions they woke in you, Trave. That is the spirit I am speaking to you about, this outward extension of an inner essence. Most of us do things based on emotion and feelings, and yet are unaware of this force pushing us one way or the other."

"You mean we pick up the vibes?"

"That's a good way to put it," the stranger said. "It's the same instinct that makes a bird suddenly fly off on the wing or a deer dart away. They pick up the invisible ripples of the vibrations in the air."

I stood up and pulled the remaining feathers off the chicken in a harsh manner while it dangled from my other hand. Then I splashed the carcass of the bird through the water to clean out its innards and tried to breathe in lightly as the heavy smell of warm blood and entrails rose up into my nostrils and nauseated me.

"Being civil to people is a choice. You can go with the essence of the spirit that surrounds you, or you can rise above it," he continued.

I dunked the bird a few more times to make sure the innerds were cleansed. "We were talking about how ancient people changed the day of worship. I want you to cut to the chase."

Fluff was trotting out to him and was telling him something in her quiet voice. She was quite personable that way, yet I felt a twinge of jealousy that she deigned to give her greeting to him rather than me. I should be relieved, I thought, for she had cleared him for approval.

"Let's go down to the stream then. I'd like to soak my feet," Sam was saying. "Maybe we might catch a fish or two to go along with the chicken."

When we were seated on by the banks of the river, he read of how Adonai healed a man on the Sabbath and how the Pharisees attacked him for it. "He was demonstrating to those in the church how his father's holy day of rest was to be used. It was a day to help and serve others and to heal and not to apply the hundreds of laws they had adopted, none of which were ordained by God. Adonai laid the burden of wrong on the Pharisees and not those they accused, and it set a raging fire in them."

"So they wanted this Adonai gone."

"He brought revolution. He dared to lay bare their wrongs by telling them they held tradition in more regard than God. Even in the times of Christ the churches were a mix of rituals borrowed from many religions, which is known as syncretism. Baal had been worshipped in the old testament and his spirit and presence had not grown weaker among the people, but stronger by the time Christ came into the world. When Christianity came to Rome, Baal and Apollo worship were already in place." The stranger was fumbling in his pouch behind him and brought out his pocket computer. "I know how much you respect historical facts, Trave, so I know you would like to see the actual pages in the book which documents the writings of the church historian, Lucien, who wrote about changing the day of worship only three hundred years after the crucifixion of Christ. Lucien even records that the bishop in Rome was aware that the citizens in Rome and Alexandria were already worshipping the sun god, Apollo, on Sundays during that time." Sam punched the keys on his computer and the book was brought down from the shelf and the pages leafed through.

"I would never have associated Apollo with Sunday before you mentioned it."

"The dragon counted it as a major victory in his court to have professed Christians worshipping on his pagan day of the sun rather than God's appointed day."

"But how did everything get so twisted?"

"How does anything in this world get twisted? You yourself have said the rulers of this world have done a great injustice and murdered billions. How did they come to think that people were of so little value?"

I was still busy looking through the old book on line and barely heard him speak. I loved these old texts. "This is the beginning of the story so to speak. How did you find this book?"

"I found them in much the same manner as you found the sources you were searching for. Now let me ask you a question. How did you come to believe what you believe?"

"I was taught, I guess."

"Never forget that you were taught was what they wanted you to know. You already discovered that the left did not mention anything which did not fit their own agenda."

"They left out the truth, you mean."

"They perverted the truth of God to accommodate the ideas of man. The early Church took away the people's ability to have a say on what day they could worship. It was decided for them, made law, and the case was closed. Then it merely became accepted as tradition and was above being questioned."

"But how did it happen? Do you know?"

"I'm getting to that. Let's go back to the beginning. It didn't just start with Constantine and the church. We need to go back to the garden. That was the first battle ground where the dragon first tried to lure man away from the Wizard. It is a theme which runs all through the Instruction manual. For instance, the prophet Daniel mentions sun worship in the old testament when he writes of Babylon and says, 'They bowed down to gods of the planets and the sun.' " Stranger Sam stopped speaking and looked at me. He seemed pleased that I was absorbing what he had to say and continued. "Actually pagan worship was so well engrained in the ancient civilizations that they had thirty six gods in their repertoire to choose from, but chief among them all was the sun god. The Babylonians also believed that numbers had power over the gods, and duly numbered them to reflect their importance. The numbers ranged from one to thirty six, with the sun being given the number one. They arranged these numbers into a magic matrix. Now listen carefully, and do what I say. Add the numbers one through thirty six together and give me the total. Use my solar calculator," he said handing it to me.

While I added the numbers together, Sam pulled his feet out of the stream and dried them on a wash cloth and put his shoes back on. Next, he busied himself with readying a fishing line to throw into the water, and he lay on his back looking upward.

"The total of the numbers added sequentially are six hundred sixty six."

"Isn't that amazing? It is the number of the beast spoken of in Revelation 13:18," the stranger said beaming.

"What's the significance?"

"The sun worshippers took up this number because they believed that it had great power and could protect them against their own gods."

"So they knew they were dabbling in forbidden territory."

"The Babylonians came up with a six by six matrix like this one, and fashioned it into a coin like amulet. Take a look at this," he said handing me his portable computer screen again.

```
06 32 03 34 35 01
07 11 27 28 08 30
19 14 16 15 23 24
18 20 22 21 17 13
25 29 10 09 26 12
36 05 33 04 02 31
```

"This is only one example of a matrix, which when you add the numbers in the columns either down or across they add up to 111, and when added altogether they add up to six hundred sixty six. It was the practice from Babylon to Rome. Archeologists have found these amulets buried from much older cultures so it was a common and a lasting influence. To wear one of these amulets was thought by its owner to hold power over all thirty six of their gods and allow man to control his own destiny."

"From my reading I remember that Babylon was eventually conquered. What happened to their sun god worship then?" I asked.

"When Babylon was conquered by the Medes and Persians around 539 BC, the priests of Babylon fled to Pergamum and to Egypt, and they, of course, took their beliefs with them. In fact, the Egyptians actually embraced the Babylonian's religion, and it has been passed down through the ages. Those same beliefs are what we call astrology today, so you see it has never really been lost. However, that wasn't the start of syncretism. Remember God had already warned the Israelites about straying after other gods in the Old Testament. He didn't want their worship of him to be defiled with that of the pagan religions of the time."

"I see. Baal worship had already existed for centuries. So how did it finally reach Rome, Sam?"

"In 133 BC King Attalus III died and left his kingdom of Pergamum in the hands of Rome. Rome, of course, accepted Pergamum into its territories, and by the time Alexander the Great conquered the city, they had already incorporated much of the Babylonian beliefs that had been passed on to them by the Greeks. The Babylonian Priests had found a new strong hold in Rome because the Romans were very willing to adopt their practices since they were already worshipping their own sun god, Apollo, as I told you. In fact, they embraced the Babylonian teachings so well that Rome was alluded to as the New Babylon by ancient historians of the time. It was natural that when the Christian Church came to Rome some of the practices and beliefs of the Babylonians went in the door with them as well."

"I knew Rome had adopted Christianity, but you are saying they mixed pagan influences into the church."

"Christianity was mixed in with the practices and beliefs already in place. It did not come in as a pure religion. It was not the true gospel as taught by the apostles."

"So it was a pagan form of Christianity that was adopted in Rome?"

"Absolutely. Further, when Attalus III died and gave Pergamum to Rome, he also passed his title of Pontiff to the Babylonian Priests. This is important because when Julius Caesar came to Rome in 63 BC they conferred this title on him. He was the first emperor to be given this name. It meant that he ruled over the spiritual morals of the people of Rome as well.

"How did the title come into the church then?" I asked.

Sam nodded at me and smiled knowingly. "This title graciously passed from emperor to emperor until 367 AD when the new Roman Emperor Gratian refused the title and bestowed it on Pope Damasus I, who was head of the Christian Church in Rome."

"So that's how the office of the Pope was established, but it was the Babylonian religion of sun worshipping that he was really in charge of."

"Historians have argued over whether this was true or not, but here is an interesting remark by Cardinal Newman in his writings on the church in his treatise called, 'Development of Church Doctrine.' Turn to page 372 and 373. What does he say?"

"Wow this is eye opening. Cardinal Newman admits that pagan practices were brought into the church, but he claims that those who were the leaders in the Church at that time sanctified them, which made them safe to be integrated into the Church."

"Are you starting to see how they were duped as badly as you were in your own time and the fine degrees and steps that made it possible? Man says they, the church, sanctified the new practices and made it safe for them to be adopted into the church. Do you see the arrogance in that, Trave?"

"I do."

"Man can consecrate nothing. Take for instance the statue of Jupiter which was blessed by the church and then had the name Peter conferred upon it. Every generation since who has kissed the statues feet were bowing down to the original statue of the sun god Jupiter and didn't even know it."

"What made them believe that man could bless and sanctify items and change customs?"

"Remember that the early emperors were worshipped as gods, so it was nothing new to accept that a pope should be deified the same way. Now let's prove how the dragon got his way. Remember the amulet and the number six hundred and sixty six, and where it came from?"

"Pergamos."

"Yes. John, the apostle, tells us in Revelation 12:12-13 that Pergamos was Satan's Seat. Today, in our time, the headquarters of the church is still located in Pergamum."

"Why doesn't the manual warn of these things?"

"It does. Look at Thessalonians 2:7. Paul refers to what I have been talking about as the Mystery of Iniquities, and in Rev. 17:5. John calls it Mystery Babylon and speaks of the number of the beast."

"So the number and the matrix were known to the apostles, and even centuries before that, Daniel had spoken and written against worshiping the planets and the sun."

"God has told us many times, and from his own mouth that sun (day) worship in place of God's day of worship is satanic in its roots. So you see, in replacing God's day with another day, Satan attacked the fourth commandment directly."

"I'm not sure I am following you."

"Remember that sun day worship goes back to Babel and ancient times. In the Bible God speaks directly to Israel as he was leading them out of Egypt in Deuteronomy 4:19: 'Take heed, lest you lift your eyes to heaven, and when you see the sun, the moon, and the stars, and all the hosts of heaven, you feel driven to worship them and serve them.' Israel did not listen to his warning and went after these other gods, and as we see in Ezekiel 22:26 God Laments that his people "hid their eyes from My worship." So even with direct warnings from the I Am, ancient Israel had succumbed to sun day worship. Later, King Josiah in 2 Kings 23:11 destroyed the idols and 'burned the chariots of the sun with fire.' "

"Sunday had a strong attraction," I said as Sam pulled in a big trout.

"We'll have fish tonight," he said as he took the hook out of its mouth. "It's still a thrill to reel one in," he continued as he put the fish in the bucket that was in the shallow water. "Take a look at this book of ancient so called Christian art. What do you make of the halo around the head?"

"That it is a sign of divinity."

"That is what people came to believe it stood for. The halo actually represents the sun behind their heads. It was first used by the Greeks and Romans to represent their sun god, Helios, and they used the halo in pictures of this god displayed in their temples. Over time artists adopted it for use in Christian images. It was a cunning method of blending sun worship into that of Christian worship."

"How come they didn't know what the halo meant?"

"Time, Travis, time. Erasing history allows it to be changed. Here is a copy of Webster's Dictionary published in 1929. Listen to what it says: 'The name Sunday was adopted because this day was anciently dedicated to the sun, or to its worship. The first day of the week."

"Then the origin of the day and the truth you just told me was known as little as a hundred years ago to those who printed that dictionary."

"They called the first day of the week the day of the sun because they believed, as I have shown you, that the sun was the greatest ruler of the stars in the heaven among the thirty six they worshipped. Paul warned us in 2 Thessalonians 2: 7 that 'the mystery of iniquity doth already work.' Paul was talking about the errors in knowledge and worship he already saw coming into the church of his time. In Acts 20:17 and 20:30 he further warned, that in later times, 'some of the elders of the church would arise, speaking perverse things, to draw away disciples after them.' In 2 Thessalonians 2:3 he identifies this man as the man of sin and the son of perdition. In verse 9 he names him Satan. In verse 15 he gives us the instruction to 'stand fast and hold the traditions you were taught, whether by word or by your epistle.' "

"I see. Paul was talking about the true word as preached by Jesus and the apostles themselves, but why didn't the people of Paul's time see it? They knew what the true day of worship was."

"For the same reasons that we didn't speak up or correct what the government did in our time. We didn't see the subtly. Remember, the serpent is cunning. 'Surely, God didn't say you had to worship Him on the seventh day only?' Man has soothed his consciousness for generations with that lie. By shifting the Sabbath to Sunday, the apostasy was in place."

"It slithered in the door unseen."

"No, it was welcomed."

"Why do you say that?"

"People had already been worshipping the Sun god for generations and by the time Constantine was Emperor in Rome he saw that Sun (day) was a popular day for the pagans, but it had not been made an official religion as yet. In 321 AD he passed his famous Sunday law. It is recorded in the Code of Justinian, Book 3, title 12, law 3. Here is the book. Read it for yourself. I have underlined it."

"Let all the judges and the townspeople and occupations of all trades rest on the venerable day of the Sun (Sunday); nevertheless, let those who are situated in the rural districts freely and with full liberty attend to the cultivation of the fields because it so frequently happens that no other day may be so fitting for ploughing grains or trenching vineyards, lest at the time the advantage of the moment granted by the provision of heaven be lost. March 7, 321 AD." I stopped reading and handed the book back to him.

"Not only that, Constantine even had coins printed with the name of Christ on one side and on the image of the sun god on the other. That was syncretism at its worst, blending Christ with that of the powers of man. Listen to a quote from Henry Milman in his book, The History of Christianity, Book 2, chap 8, Vol. 22, p. 175: Quote, "The Jewish person, the Samaritan, even the Christian, were to be fused and recast into one great system, of which the sun was to be the central object of adoration. The papal church grew more in favor of Sunday worship and adopted his Sunday law itself and in 364 AD the Council of Laodicea passed 59 Canon laws," unquote. Here is Canon XXIX which forbade worship on the Sabbath: 'Christians must not Judaize by resting on the Sabbath, but must work on that day, rather honoring the Lord's Day; and, if they can, resting then as Christians. But if any shall be found to be judaizers, let them be anathema from Christ.' "

"Wow, that would make you choose Sunday."

"For a while believers kept both days, but as the centuries wore on, Sunday became the accepted day of worship for the Christian. Sozomen, in Ecclesiastical History, Book 7, Ch. 19, noted that in the fifth century AD the last gasp of true Sabbath day worship was heard. 'It was for hatred of the Jews,' he wrote, 'that the last breath was given to the fourth commandment. It was a way for the government by law to separate itself from the Jewish tradition of Sabbath worship.' "

"Why was there so much animosity against the Jewish people back then? I thought that was a latter day thing."

"They are God's chosen and have been hated by the same spirit we have just talked about from their inception." Good Neighbor Sam reached his hand over and patted my shoulder and got up. "I guess it's time to take these fish home and cook them up."

As we began our journey home, we saw a girl coming towards us. This girl was not tall, but was long limbed and thin. Her hair was long and uncombed because she said she liked it that way and left it like an untended garden. She was shaking her head and fluffing her hair with her fingers. "What you two talking about?"

"Historical events," Sam said.

"I don't understand none of it, anyway, and it makes me mad."

"I would be glad to explain it to you, Doe," said Sam. Good Neighbor knew her name which surprised me.

"I wanted to fish, but it looks like you caught your fill."

"You can go next time."

We walked the rest of the way back in silence and when we were home I watched as our companion walked over to a tree and sat under it and stared at us while we cleaned the fish. Night was approaching and I couldn't see her features clearly from where we stood and it made me uncomfortable. I got up and called the cats and began to feed them, but continued to glance her way. Soon she was lost to the shadows created by the coming darkness. She seemed to become a part of the tree she leaned against now, a growth of blackness that had attached itself to a living organism.

We ate in silence and Kara and a few others sat with us. "Our friends haven't showed up yet."

"I know."

"What's keep'in them?" the girl named Doe asked me and elbowed me in the stomach.

"How should I know? They're your friends. It could be anything. They could be dead from a number of things, or caught by the SG along the way."

Somehow my remark erupted into an argument.

"You say'in they ain't as smart as you?" Doe said.

"I'm not following what you are talking about."

"You saying they got caught because they're stupid?"

"I don't think Trav was saying that," Sam said.

The girl stood up and heaved her chicken bones into the darkness.

"Don't throw those bones around the yard. The cats will get at them," I said, "or the other animals around here."

"Animals can eat anything. They ain't gonna choke on them."

Sam handed me one of the flashlights and stood up and headed in the direction the bones had been thrown. "I'll help you find them," he said as he waited for me to follow after him.

When we had found the bones, Sam went off after the girl. "I want to talk to you. Listen, please don't throw bones or any trash in the yard. We don't want the SG or anyone to find us, now do we?"

"Since you put it like that, but I don't want him give'in me orders."

"You've been taken orders your whole life."

"That's the point. I don't have to anymore. Especially from no traitor."

Sam touched her on the shoulder gently. "Then you won't throw any more bones?"

The thin girl nodded. "I won't."

"Good night, then."

"I think I'll come back and listen to you talk tonight. Noise helps me sleep," I heard her tell Sam.

"Join in. I'd like to hear what you have to say."

It took us a while to get back to our earlier conversation, and I was reluctant to talk with everyone staring at us, but I said, "I would like to go to the libraries you found one day. I'd like to hold the books in my hand. You can't change the printed word."

"That's one reason I began collecting authentic books years ago," Sam said. "I wanted the truth as impartial historians and unbiased witnesses had recorded it at the time."

"That's an interesting insight, Joseph," Zel said.

"When Elijah caught the Israelites worshipping the sun gods, he specifically asks them: 'How long halt ye between two opinions? If the Lord be God, follow him: but if Baal, then follow him. Elijah was specifically talking about syncretism and about which day they were choosing to worship on."

"But didn't people in my grandfather's day honestly believe that the Bible had changed the day of worship?" I asked.

"Yes. In fact, most refused to acknowledge that Sunday worship was not spoken of in the Bible, and twisted the words in confusing ways to make it fit with their own desires. People were told the truth throughout history in numerous ways, but they did not listen. Here is an article from over one hundred years ago published in 1917. It was written by James Cardinal Gibbons in his book, "The Faith of our Fathers, p.72-73 (16th edition, p. 111; 88th edition, p. 89). "Is not every Christian obliged to sanctify Sunday and to abstain on that day from unnecessary servile work? Is not the observance of this law among the most prominent of our sacred duties? But you may read the Bible from Genesis to Revelation, and you will not find a single line authorizing the sanctification of Sunday. The Scriptures enforce the religious observance of Saturday, a day which we never sanctify." Unquote. So you see, man knew, but chose to convince himself otherwise. They even convinced themselves that the Sabbath was given to the Jewish people only. Instead of being thankful for being grafted into the plan of salvation, gentiles sought to make them self-separate from it."

Sam threw me an old Catholic catechism book given to convert people to their faith. "Turn to page 50 and read it to me."

There were questions and answers listed on the page and I read them out loud to Sam.

Q: "Which is the Sabbath day?

A: Saturday is the Sabbath day.

Q: Why do we observe Sunday instead of Saturday?

A: We observe Sunday instead of Saturday because the Catholic Church, in the Council of Laodicea in 364 AD, transferred the solemnity from Saturday to Sunday."

"Now read me the title of the book," Sam demanded.

I closed it back up and read the front cover. The Convert's Catechism of Catholic Doctrine.

"Now look inside to see when it was published, and who wrote it, Trave"

"Peter Geiermann, C.S.S.R., 3rd edition, 1957."

"Now read this article written in the 1990's."

I took the computer he handed me. It was opened to a page and underlined in yellow marker. I read to myself. "Perhaps the boldest thing, the most revolutionary change the Church ever did, happened in the first century. The Holy day, the Sabbath, was changed from Saturday to Sunday. The 'Day of the Lord' was chosen, not from any direction noted in the Scriptures, but from the Church's sense of its own power. It told people who think that the scriptures should be the sole authority, to become (logically) 7th Day Adventists.' St. Catherine Church Sentinel, Algonac, Michigan, May 21, 1995.

"The day of the Sabbath was known, wasn't it?" I said to him as I put the computer back down.

"God did not make a mistake when he placed his Sabbath day among his Ten Commandments, yet some say that God's law was

THE WIZARD OF ALL

abolished with the New Covenant. People dared to say, God, you are wrong! Don't you know the commandments were nailed to the cross and we can worship you any day we choose?"

"Can you explain it a little more? I'm afraid I don't know what you are referring to," Zel said.

"What Jesus removed at the cross was the Jewish sacrificial laws. Paul was talking about those laws which had the meat and drink offerings, the new moon, etc., attached to them. Here's the strange thing that tells me that people really knew what was abolished. The church only tossed out the fourth commandment and kept the other nine intact. It is only the fourth commandment that they treated as being advice from God instead of one of his holy commands."

He stopped and looked at us and then added, "The final blow for Saturday worship came from the Council of Laodicea in 364 AD which made it illegal to worship on the Sabbath."

"What difference does any of the stuff you guys are talking about make?" Kara called from her resting place by the tree. "You're going to die and that will be the end. Wormwood. You'll be kibbles for the creepy crawlers."

Doe let out a loud laugh. She was the another of us humans though she rarely spoke. "He ain't coming, Kara. That should be clear to all of you. If he hasn't come after billions have been whacked off the face of the earth, he ain't coming."

"Would you like me to read that part to you?" Sam said, holding out his Bible to the tall girl.

"I don't hold to any of the religion you two have been talking off these last weeks. There never has been a wizard of all," Doe said waving the Bible in the air, and then letting it drop back down in the dirt by Sam's feet.

"Let me ask all of you, and especially you, Trave, in light of the deception we have just discussed, is the miraculous any less probable that the horror of reality?" Sam said picking up the book and wiping the dust off its green leather binding.

"There's a lot to be afraid of out there, that's for sure. People disappeared all the time in the last two D's. You could go to work and not come home. You could go for a walk and fall into a big hole," Doe scoffed. "There were known to be monsters and mutants in every state. My favorite was the skunk bear in

"Don't let him touch you, Doe," one of the other AI's said Australia because it was one monster that wasn't here. Ogopogo, boo!" she suddenly screamed. "I know plenty of people who went poof." She began to cry and Sam came over to her and began to caress her face and brush the tangled hair out of her eyes.. "See how his hands are around your head? That's how they conjure up your aura around you and take it from you. If he gets it you will be dead in days, weeks." The bot made rubbing motions around Doe's head to show us what she meant. Then the bot moved her hands to Doe's feet and brought them all the up way up to her head again. "They call up all your light from you just like that and trap it so they can gather it into a great ball above you and snatch it from your head," the AI warned.

"Whatever are you afraid of child?" Sam asked.

"I seen magicians do it to others at shows. I seen the light being drawn up from the feet into a ball over their heads, and I saw them take it. A few days later the man died."

"I was trying to comfort her not harm her," Sam told the bot.

"Your hands were touching her in a magical way. All touch is used for bad ends."

"Nonsense."

"That bird knows about auras. He told me he could see them," the AI continued.

Doe got up and walked over to the AI. "Did you see my light tonight? Did this man get it?"

"No. I did not see it rise, but I must warn you that the fire obscured my vision and I cannot answer truly."

"Stop this! You people believe in every crazy thing except the truth!" Sam said.

"No, I seen it done to thousands at once and a few days later none of those people were ever seen again. I seen them sink holes swallow up towns on the I-tube. I seen all them creatures you say don't exist."

"We all knew people who disappeared, but it wasn't due to monsters or sink holes or earth quakes," Sam said.

"They weren't real, Doe. The SG just made them all up to frighten you and so they could have something to blame when they began killing all of us," I said.

"My point, if you all would allow me to make it, is that those who were in control of the media were confused by the mass disappearances at first. Why do you think that was?"

"It was something unplanned," I said getting his meaning. "Something out of their control. I kind of remember now that it caused quite a panic among the governments for a while."

"So? We survived," Doe said.

"Really?" Sam asked. "You call this surviving? You people won't bath in the rivers or streams. You won't walk anywhere alone. You put guards out all night because you're afraid to sleep," Sam said before Doe interrupted him.

"And you don't? Niner and the squad patrol the skies at all times."

"He looks for a different enemy. They are the ones that can harm you."

"The One World has provided for us," she yelled standing up. "They have sheltered us and protected us."

"I'm going to bed," Sam said disgusted, but stopped to talk to one of the other newcomers. "Have you decided to stay among us, then Kara?"

"For a while," she said looking out into the darkness again.

"You're afraid aren't you?" I asked her.

"She should be afraid," Doe said. "You have gotten her to go into the lake where she can be gotten to by the swamp fish."

"I go in the water with Zel. And we do not go out far," Kara told her.

"Watch out for Ogopogo the next time you bathe in the lake," Doe laughed looking at us, "or you'll be the next ones missing."

"You're the one who believes in him," I said. Immediately I saw the smile disappear from her face. I knew I had gotten to her, and I gloated in my small and petty victory, but then I saw her flinch and begin to gnaw on her thumb nail, and I began to pity her ignorance.

"The lake monster might just swallow up a few of those cats," Doe said making a nasty face at me.

I was on her in an instant and was lying on top of her in the dirt when I felt a force from behind pull me up from behind by my shirt collar. It was such a jerk that I felt the row of buttons on my shirt pop off. "There's four of us on earth and two of you want to exterminate each other," Sam said still holding on to the back of my shirt collar.

I was still trying to catch my breath after my brief scuffle. Doe was still sitting on the ground rubbing her chin. A few of the cats circled about us. My anger was still raging inside of me, but I tugged my shirt back down and tucked it back into my pants and huffed towards the house. The threat to the cats took hold of my thoughts and I whistled to call the cats in from the porch. A few were already inside, but five more came running to the door. Once inside I threw the heavy tarp over the windows to block out the light from the LED's before I switched them on inside. I gave the cats some food and fresh water. I was aware that Sam was watching me from the kitchen doorway. "She's not going to hurt the cats."

"I'm not taking any chances. She would just to get back at me."

"Be considerate of her. That's all she wants."

"What about what I want?"

"Now tell me, would the sky or the sun fall out of the sky if you were to treat her, all of us, a little more tenderly?"

"Why don't you give your speech to her?"

"Because you have the intelligence to change."

"That's not a reason."

"What reason would be good enough for you? You act like if you are decent to people that you are losing. Exactly what are you losing? Scuffles in the dirt? Torn shirts? Fear of reprisals against the cats? That's a strange form of winning to me."

"My pretending to be kind to people isn't going to make them like me."

"That isn't the reason for doing it. By rising above the fray you are solving your problem, not theirs."

"Want some coffee, Sam?"

"I keep telling you I need sleep," Sam said as he turned away in frustration.

"Sam, thanks. I'm sorry. You remind me of my grandfather. You say the same sort of things."

"We got our ideas from the same place," he said holding up the green book. "You still have a question to answer, Trave."

"You gave it to all of us earlier."

"This one's just for you. After reading your journal I see you question if the government really meant to kill off humankind. You don't want to believe it, but you are coming to see that the wizard may exist, and that he could do miracles, but you wonder, would he?"

I laughed and Sam gve me a quizzical look. "I thought you were going to give me advice on forgiveness," I mumbled.

"Read Romans 12:18."

CHAPTER 10

I settled in for the night and read the passage Sam had given me. "As far as it concerns you, live peaceably with all men." Fluff jumped up and lay down facing me as she did every night with her paw resting gently on my hand. I still felt a little ornery, so I turned over to face the other way, and I felt her pad across my back and lay down on the other side facing me. I turned a number of times and the cat faithfully padded over my back each time so she could lie facing me. About the seventh time I had turned over, I heard a deep sigh come from her when she settled in. Had she read the passage Sam had given to me? It hit me then that I was as superstitious as the rest of them. I was seeing signs in everything. Sam had brainwashed me. I let Fluf stay facing me and we both went to sleep.

The house was empty when I got up the next morning. There was some fruit cut up in a bowl on the table and some bread. I fed the kitties and made some coffee and then went out to take my morning dip in the lake. I didn't stay in the water long, but it had invigorated me, and the coffee filled the empty coldness the brief dip had left inside my frame.

The sun was high overhead in a perfectly blue sky, and it had an almost spiritual feel about it. Drinking my coffee, I could almost forgive my would be murderers in my present state of joy. The turning leaves seemed brighter and crisper. The smell on the wind hinted at a distant smell of snow. Fall would end and winter would replace it. Nature was a miraculous cycle; a mysteries of turning and returning you could count on. It was the cyclical feature of this creation that told me nature had been designed. More than that, I reasoned, every molecule that existed was so complex it could never have just come together by chance. A mere strand of DNA was miles long. I had read somewhere that if a person's DNA was stretched out and unraveled it would stretch to the moon and back to the earth hundreds of times.

This feeling I was experiencing must be the one that Sam had talked about. He had said that inside every living creature God had placed the need to believe in Him, a kind of God gene, if you will. Today I believed it, and instinctually sensed that we all had the same beginning. Nature and man were alike enough to have been created from the same hand.

I was so deep in my thoughts that I did not hear Sam approach. "Taking a day off?"

"Hey, just who I wanted to see. Can I borrow your facts book?"

"What do you want to know?"

"The odds of life forming by chance. Hey and while you're looking it up, answer this. What made you start compiling all these facts?"

"It helps to keep my thinking straight when I'm tempted to doubt. It keeps the truth in its place. Ah, here it is. Marcell Golay says the odds for even the simplest protein molecule being replicated is 10 to the 450th power. Source: Reflections of a Communication Engineer, Analytical Chemistry, vol.33, p.23, June 1961.

"That's why evolutionist's have always denied the math," I exclaimed as I realized that fact for the first time.

"They trusted in the same formulas to get them to the moon, to explore the stars and planets, but not to answer the probability of life coming together on its own," Sam said. "If one set of formulas is true, then so is the other."

"Their picking and choosing when to believe a set of facts is telling, isn't it?" I said.

"Math is unchanging and so is God. Everything in nature lives and is created by iteration. Mandelbrot proved that in his book, the Geometry of Nature. He used the math of fractals to demonstrate it."

"I remember. Mandelbrot saw a space in between the second and third dimensions of classical geometry. He explained that dimension as 2.5."

"He started the whole new technological era. Cell phones, computer graphics used in movie special effects. Mandelbrot saw a world that no one had ever seen until then. That didn't mean it didn't exist before he found it. The universe works and functions according to a highly formulated set of laws and those laws are mathematical."

"That makes me wonder what we are looking at now and don't understand yet," I said.

"Take a look at that leaf on the ground. What do you notice about it?"

I picked up a red one and stared at it and shook my head at Sam.

"Now look at a few others."

I picked up a rust colored leaf and a yellow one. "They're different colors."

"Look deeper. What kind of design do they have?"

"There's little lines running through them."

"And how are they arranged?"

"In some kind of geometric pattern, I'd say."

"Does the pattern seem to repeat itself?"

"Yes, now that you mention it."

"That's iteration in math, what you call repetition in nature. Everything in the universe is created according to that premise. That's what Mandelbrot gave us. It is the mind of the Creator."

"I'm beginning to see what Niner was trying to tell me. There is a formula writer, a programmer, a wizard."

"Can there be any doubt in your mind that everything was created according to a very precise, intricate, and complex set of laws?"

When I didn't answer, Sam continued his discourse. "Have you ever seen a house or a car come together by themselves? Better yet, have you ever seen a recipe arrange itself into cookies without a hand to mix it? Put out flour, butter, chips, and brown sugar out on the table and let them sit next to each other. Is there any known law of physics that says they will somehow form together into a dough that's edible? It's nonsense! Non-living things do not have motion. And even if they were blown together by a big wind, would the measurements of each ingredient be exactly proportioned to form itself to the right consistency even if you allowed them a trillion years in which to do it? If life spontaneously happened on its own, why hasn't anyone ever witnessed it? Why don't the leaves and grass and trees keep combining with the dirt and rocks to form new life forms?"

We were sitting under the tree in the yard and it wasn't long before Zel spotted us. As I watched her walk over to us, I thought I had reached a conclusion to what the stranger had been leading me to. "Yes, I had come to similar thoughts myself. It seems out of character that the evolution of nature would just abruptly stop evolving new species for no known reason."

"Everything evolutionists have come up with was only meant to place doubt about the Creator into the minds of man." Sam was on a roll and I let him continue. "The head of the snake pops up into everything, to the absurd level of proposing multi universes. They say space is unlimited and replicated a million times out there and so is man. To what end? Even if it were true, what would it benefit anyone if we existed simultaneously in a thousand or a million places all at once? We would still be limited to only experiencing one of those lives at a time. It is preposterous to say man would not know if he had consciousness of himself in these other universes."

"I quite believe that Joseph. I am aware of my former selves, my whole self, even my soul," Zel said coming closer to us.

"That's because the soul exists."

"Yes, Zel is a voice to their wild hypothesizing. If we indeed did exist in a thousand universes at once, she could attest to the validity of it, having seen her self-copied and come and go in other bodies."

"Multiple universes makes death seem pleasant," one of the newcomers said.

"It makes death escapable," Joe added.

"Evil?" Kara demanded. "What's evil about just popping into another existence at the point of death? Life goes on."

"It gives man an out, an opportunity to die without having confronted the limits of himself and the truth of his creator."

"The truth is nobody knows," Doe said. "You can't say one way or another, either," she said looking at Joseph. "You're discounting the pyramids and the face on Mars."

"I am merely pointing out probabilities. What if this is it, and the soul goes to heaven or hell as some have proposed? Are you all gamblers? Do you all wish to just leave it to chance?" Joseph asked.

"I'm open to hearing other explanations," Kara said looking at Doe.

"Traitor," the other girl said.

"I don't care what you call me. I have been afraid of having to make decisions for myelf, but now it feels comfortable. I didn't always believe in what the SG had to say. I had questions."

"It is not lawful to ask questions, Kara. You were taught that. Besides, why trouble yourself? I'd rather think about more pleasant things."

Sam stood up, "That's the problem I was speaking about, ladies. The government has kept you from confronting the most important issue in life: death and eternity. That should be your own personal issue. Your right."

Sam looked at me, smiled and raised his eyebrows. His voice took on a different quality. "Everyone has a choice, isn't that right, Trave?" He didn't wait for an answer but stood up and patted his stomach as he looked towards the hills. "School's out. I'm ready for lunch. Wudgey should be bringing some fish. Ah, there he is," Sam said standing up and brushing the leaves and dirt from his clothes, "coming over the hill just now."

"There's definitly something odd about timing where you're concerned," I said without meaning to, but Sam acted like he didn't hear it, and walked to meet the robotoid. "I'll take those from you and clean them up. I could eat a dozen myself."

It was at that moment that I began to see into Sam and got an instant snapshot of who he might be. He couldn't be earthly. He must be one of those robotoid-clones or scanters I had read about. Scanters was the shortened version for Somatic Cell Nuclear Transfer beings, the eternals; the type and species classification that Zel was an early prototype of. The hair on the back of my neck pricked me under my arms as I started to remember what I had read about them. Scanters had been introduced among the population as early as the end of the last century. The first experiments had started in the 1980's or before, and by the 2030's scanters were rumored to be a million strong. I was sweating now. I could feel my heart beating in an irregular pattern. I felt faint and took deep breaths as if that might help my heart get back into its normal rhythm.

Just then I heard a familiar sound and looked up.

"It's Niner and the drones. I see them," Kara said pointing westward.

All of a sudden I forgot about my panic attack and looked to see Niner flying at the head of the others. They were close enough to count now. Ten had left and eight were returning. I counted again to make sure I had missed no one. "Zel, how many do you count?"

"Eight."

"Something has happened."

At that moment, Niner was making his descent to the ground. I could see his talons clearly as he approached. "Alert," he said. "We must move out at once. They have taken two of our drones captive. They may have tracked our movements on the return flight."

"Whoa, slow down. Were you able to stop Ben? Were you able to even find him?"

"Yes, but two eagles were detained. Forty two and sixty three."

"How was that possible?"

"It happened. That is all I can report. Forty two has not been responding at all. Sixty three has had lapses of dead air space.

He was the one who managed to relay the message that they had put him in a cage from which he could not escape."

"Is that all he said?"

"No, he sent other messages to which I did not respond. I decided the sent messages were meant to track us, so I stopped communication."

"Then they know about us?"

"I would bet on it."

"Do you have the footage, the proof we asked you to get?" Kara asked.

"Get everyone together," Niner ordered. "I will show you then."

As Niner projected the scenes against the side of the house, there were oohs and awes over everything. The landscapes were spectacular. The mountains above Denver were breath taking.

"It is so beautiful," Kara said.

Next, Niner showed the great image of the triangle door that led to the subterrean world.

"Wow how do we get in there?" someone asked.

"Shhh! Here is what is important," Niner said fast forwarding the footage. In seconds we were seeing hundreds of beings on the outside of the compound's triangular entrance. Then the cam zeroed in on a familiar face. It was Ben. The scene was chaos. Species were being killed where they stood at the entrance to the door. All around we could hear the shouts and screams coming from the crowd as they fell to the ground.

"They are killing everyone. Why?" Doe screamed.

"Just watch," the bird said calmly. "It will become clear."

We stared at the footage as people, droids, and every type of plastic that was made was blown apart in front of us. Then the piles of species were set on fire by laser beams streaming from the weapons mounted on either side of the doors. We watched as they melted into unidentifiable conglomerates. In minutes they had hardened to unrecognizable clumps.

"Those people were turning themselves in," Kara said.

The camera angle changed and focused in on Ben's face in a close up.

"Listen," directed Niner. Ben was shouting and pleading into the intercom and video outlet. "I have valuable information that could save your lives. There are traitors who intend to destroy this base. I know who they are. I will trade the information of the attackers for sanctuary. Listen to me! I'm trying to warn you."

The shooting continued and the bodies kept piling up. We could still see Ben in the crowd shouting. The gates opened to the base and two tall and armored species came forward with guns in their hands. They walked forward shooting everyone until only Ben remained standing.

"What information do you want to give us?" one of the armored beings said to Ben.

"Give me sanctuary."

"We would have the information."

"If I tell you what you want to know, what leverage would I have to bargain with?" Ben said looking at the bodies around him.

"You have no choice. You must give the information to us and we must decide if it is worth bargaining for. You have five seconds, four, three, two…"

We saw Ben rush forward and try to push the laser guns of the machimen away from him. "Okay. Okay. You just let some drones fly in awhile ago. They were not OW drones. They were rogue drones who plan to destroy this facility."

The two machines gave out a laugh. "Highly unlikely. There isn't a tech surgeon out there who could reprogram them as you suggest."

"Did you try to reprogram them?" one of the armed men asked.

"No, it wasn't me, I swear. It was Travis Tarkington and a clone named Zel."

The bots stopped and looked at one another and Ben knew he had said something that was of interest to them.

"Where are these traitors?" the machimen asked.

"I will give you the coordinates after we make a deal."

"The OW doesn't make any deals," the species said coming closer. In seconds Ben was dropping to the ground and the soldier was standing over him, "with hu-manimals."

"No, bring the hu-manimal to me," a voice said as someone stepped in front of the machiman and the weapon. "He may be useful."

I caught a glimpse of the face as the camera zoomed back. I recognized it as my old friend, Madison. He was shoving Ben up against the side of the mountain. "You wish to make a deal?"

"Yes, Mr. President."

"Tell me what you know about this Tarkington and the clone, Zel. How do you know them?"

"I just left them."

"Where? I want their coordinates."

"I want sanctuary. A guarantee of my freedom and life," Ben said.

"We make no deals with hu-manimals," the machiman said again.

"We may want to make an exception in this case, Number Seven, if this one is telling the truth."

The talk went on for some time and then Madison called for some things to be brought outside. A laser rifle was handed to Ben and a back pack and a canteen.

"Where's my notarized sanctuary pass?"

"You didn't think I'd keep that back, did you?" Madison asked holding out a folded sheet of paper to Ben, who took it and looked it over before folding it and putting it in his shirt pocket.

"Now, give me the coordinates."

"P278, N345."

"That's southwest of here," Madison said to the machiman.

"Deploying," the drone said.

THE WIZARD OF AII

"Thank you again, Mr. President. You didn't even ask me to verify them."

"No one could make up those two names and put them together. I trusted you, but you shouldn't have trusted me."

"I gave you what you wanted," Ben said backing up and drawing his rifle from his back.

"Your weapon is useless, hu-manimal. It has no charge in it."

"We had a deal."

"No, wrong again. My machiman told you twice that we didn't make deals with your kind, but you didn't listen."

"Why did you pretend and go through all this?" Ben asked.

"To give you a few seconds of hope. Every hu-manimal should experience that."

The laser fired and Ben dropped to the ground and the soldier was standing over him. "I gave you the wrong coordinates," he said laughing.

"I know," Madison said walking back to the entrance way.

"Well, Ben got what he deserved," Kara said turning away from the screen. "Justice has been done."

"Why did they kill everyone?" a droid in our group cried out.

"I see. It is what these people here have told us about. It is annihilation," Kara said in a voice that sounded like some sort of squeak toy that had the air had been squeezed out of it. "That is why we have found no one else."

Strains of Tchaikovsky's Overture of 1812 competed with the screams and the sounds of lasers outside the compound's door as the machimen hunted down those that had run for cover.

"Turn it off, Niner," Sam said.

"They played music to drown them out."

"It is the wizard that is needed," Niner said.

"There is no wizard," I said loudly.

"Then there is no one," Kara said.

"It's up to us," I told them.

"You forget the divine, Trave," Joseph said.

"I'll include him when he shows up," I said.

"He is here," Joseph said.

"Things need to get real from here on out," I shouted back at him. "It's time to act, not discuss philosophy."

"Trave is right," Niner said coming in between us and looking directly at me. "Forces are on the way or will be. They will search for us now."

"Why do you suppose Ben gave them the wrong coordinates?" one of the drones asked.

Kara took the heat off me by saying, "I have seen the truth. We are dead if we walk into the compound. I will join you in an attack against them."

"I won't believe it. The eternals would not have done that," Doe screamed.

"You have just seen it. It has been confirmed."

"Confirmed," came the response from the others as they walked around Doe. I sat in a fog, unable to move. I had gotten what I wanted, but it didn't matter now and I did not feel much like a winner.

"They're here!" someone screamed. "They already knew where we were at."

"I see them. Hundreds of them!"

"Get to the barge," I yelled scrambling for the cats. In seconds they began firing towards us. I knew with all the noise, they would never follow me. I would have to round them up and put them in my back pack. Missiles and rapid fire laser shots were hitting the house, and the windows were being blown out, but I went inside the house and hoped the cats would run to me when I called to them. At first I thought they had all run out or had been killed because not one of them came. As I was about to give up and leave, I saw Harley and Mama crawl out from beneath the couch just as a short range missile burst through the left side of the house. I grabbed my back pack off the floor and picked up the two cats and put them in. Then I ran through the house calling after

Fluf. I found her standing in the hallway. "C'mon girl. I won't let anything happen to you. I promise." I kept calling her name. She started forward, but looked back to where Hoss was standing. She would go not go any further without her kit. A missile hit the back bedrooms and I saw two gray streaks bolt through the open window. I would have to come back later and search for them. I needed to get out of the house, and I put the pack on my back and ran.

The sky was black with drones. It was quite a ways to the stream and I had to stop a number of times to rest and take cover behind trees and rocks. I managed to shoot down a few of the attackers before I ran out of ammunition. I had stock piled boxes of cartridges inside the pod on the barge we had set up for protection against the weather. If the drones scored a hit on the pod which held the munitions, we would see the barge create another big bang scenario.

From inside my pack, Harley and Mama were scratching and clawing up my back as if it were a tree. "It's okay, Harley," I said patting the outside of the pack to calm them, but they wanted out and nothing was going to stop them from trying. I knew even once I reached the raft, I wouldn't be able to let them out of their prison or they would bolt. I had already lost Fluff. I hoped she had made it into the woods, but the last look she had given me told me she would defend her kitten to the end. She had made her choice. She would stay with her own kind. I imagined her against the bears and wolves standing with back raised in front of that big kit of hers. Even the animals had sense enough to fight and defend themselves while man could be dissuaded, made to acquiesce and lay down his arms with the use of reason.

When I reached the barge, I could still hear the sound of drones wings behind me. The whirring was growing louder and I saw them in a tight formation. They were close enough that I could see the hot dog like shape of their missiles tucked under their bellies. In seconds, the long, cylinder objects began to drop. I dove into the water and sought protection underneath the cover of the barge. I was sorry I had chosen the water immediately after I dove under. It was freezing and I was numb in moments. Both bullets and lasers were firing down around me, but I couldn't make my limbs move. I was rooted. I could make out the laser flashes from underneath the raft, but I kept one hand held high in the air to keep the bag of cats out of the water. Sam, seeing my predicament, yelled. "Hand me the cats." I gave the bag up willingly, and then dove under the water for protection.

I hardly noticed when the quiet returned. It was a strange silence that echoed over the ringing which was now in my ears. My head swelled and pulsed with the clanging in my head, and my hands still clutched the side of the barge. Just then I heard Sam say, "Give me your hand. I'll pull you up."

I didn't have much strength left in my cold limbs. I was as rigid as some dead tuna on a hook and felt as heavy as a whale. He was doing all the work, exerting all the power to pull me up. I could see the strain on Sam's face as he worked to reel me in. It was a worthy fight. Hemingway would have written about it in one of his books.

Soon I sat under the blankets someone had tossed around me and drinking coffee which was beginning to thaw me from the inside. I looked at Sam. "Are you sure man isn't like the reptile? I was sure my heart was slowing in the coldness of the water and was about to stop beating."

"Hypothermia."

"I'm glad you're both alright. How about the cats? Are they still in hiding?"

"They're gone. Ripped the back pack clean through," Sam said.

I stood up and let the blankets fall to the wooden floor of the raft. I picked up a dry jacket and jumped ashore calling out their names.

"It hasn't been that long since the attack," Sam said from the boat. "I'm sure they're still in hiding. It may take a while, but they may come back on their own once they sense the danger is past. Give it time."

"You all go on. I can't leave the cats," I said jumping back on board just to retrieve a rifle and some ammunition.

"Maybe you should worry about Niner, first. He and the other drones have disappeared in the sky."

"He can take care of himself," I said.

"They were all heroic," Sam said jumping off the boat and wading into the water. He had a large roll of duct tape in his hands.

"What are you doing? That water's ice," I said moving around to watch him.

"Some of the rear barrels were hit and are taking on water. I have to patch them or this house will sink."

"Get out of the water. We can pull the barge to shore from the land."

"Well, lend a hand over here," Sam called out to the others as he came out of the water.

Before long we had turned the barge and pulled it onto the sand. On dry land it was easy to survey the damage. The whole back row of drums had been strafed and punctured along the sides. Water was running out from the barrels onto the sand. "There ain't enough tape in the world to keep these barrels afloat," I commented. "The adventures of Huck Finn are over, Sam."

"We'll need to take the barrels completely off and patch the holes."

"Good idea, but timely."

"Use this," Zel called out and tossed Joseph a can which he caught. "Water sealant," she told us, jumping down. "Instant fix." She was dressed in her canvas pants and a heavy jacket. She lost no time in beginning to untie the ropes that held the barrel's to the boat.

"There you go, Crusoe. You've found your Gal Friday, but cutting the ropes would be faster," I laughed and threw a knife to her.

"Faster, but what would we use to retie the barrels back on with?" Zel asked throwing the knife back. It landed in the sand by my boots.

I stooped over to retrieve my knife. "You two are all set then," I said straightening back up.

I set off, searching the rocky patches of landscape for a sign of movement, a flicker of a tail. They would be hard to see in the tall grasses. I was some distance away when I heard Sam yell my name. "There's visitors come calling for you. Four legged ones."

I could hardly believe what I was hearing. Could it be true? I turned back towards the land and could just make out some shapes on the ground from where I was standing. When I reached them, I was disheartened right off. They were the newest kittens. Neither Fluff, nor Mama, or Harley were among them. I bent down and picked one of them up. "Where's your mother and grandparents?" I asked looking the kit straight in the face. I picked the other one up and headed back to the raft.

The others were trying to roll the first drum out from under the raft. It wasn't budging. "There's too much weight on it. We need to prop the raft up first with a log or something, and then roll the oil drum out from underneath it," Sam said. "I'll search along the shore to see if a log washed up."

"I'll do it," I volunteered. "I can look for the other cats at the same time." I got some dried fish and waved under their noses to entice them into the plastic pod-tent where I shut them in.

It was just down the shore aways to the west that I spotted a furred body lying next to a large rock. I ran towards it. As I stood over the body I could see that blood pooled around it. It's mouth was open and its sharp teeth visible. It was Tolkien. A short ways away lay Lewis. They had both been hit, and in their fright, had been able to jet this far before dropping in death. I knew that was what had happened because I could see the trail of blood they had left in the sand. That left only the two girls, Fluff and Snickers, from the original litter if they were still alive, though I didn't hold out much hope for them now. I left the cats lay and set off down the beach to locate a log. I would bury them later. Besides, there was a chance that there would still be more bodies. I scanned further down the beach and my heart sank further. The distant horizon had lost its alluring quality now. It no longer seemed as a bright and guiding star.

Just then I saw a log in the water by the shore and went to retrieve it. Pulling it along the shore I was staring at some deer grazing in the meadow to the right, but they took no notice of my struggle with the unwieldy bundle. I let it drop to the ground. It would be better to cut it before trying to move it any further.

Sam and Zel dropped what they were doing when I returned and began to unpack the tools and throw them down off the raft. "I need some help getting the log back," I said without looking their way.

"What's the shovel for?" Sam asked.

I couldn't answer and the tears came.

"We'll come with you," Sam said grabbing his axe.

We walked in silence until we came upon Tolkien and Lewis. I walked to a spot further up into the grass where the land was more solid, and where the river would not reach during the flood season to start digging. Further inland the bodies were less likely to be dug up by scavenging animals in the hard dirt as opposed to the sand on the beach. As I dug the first spade full of dirt, I saw a picture in my mind of the kittens the day I had first met them. I let my mind replay the whole account of our lives together until I suddenly realized I was standing in a hole three feet deep. I threw my shovel onto the mound of dirt and climbed out.

I picked up Lewis with the spade first and placed him in the dark place I had carved out for them and then picked up Tolkien. "We traveled a lot of miles together, but this is as far as you got. Trouble's not too far away. Just down the road a bit. You guys remember. You were all happy and together."

I looked over the fur with the deep wounds and dried blood which hid their once beautiful coats. Their eyes were open and glazed like opaque glass. "I couldn't protect you. I'm sorry." Then the thought came to me. *"Could they forgive me?"* I hurried and covered the bodies. In the distance I could hear the dull thud of the axe.

"Hey!" I heard Sam yell from the beach. "I just caught sight of tails in the meadow. Cats more than likely."

I hurriedly patted the mound of dirt and ran up the incline into the open space that lay between the tumbling hills around it. In summer this spot would be ideal to build a cabin in. It would be protected on three sides by the mountains and was fed by the stream of the winding river. In summer lithe flowers would be sprinkled like colored stars among the greenness. My eyes had been scanning past the tall grasses when I caught sight of a cat leaping upon a rock, and then I spotted another one. They were poised and turned to look back at me. Then like little imps, they pounced away in the other direction as if to say, 'This is a game. Play with us.'

I knew it wasn't any of the older cats, but if these kittens had survived, maybe the others had. The sight of them renewed my hope and I chased them until I was half way up the mountain. The cats, on the other hand, had not wearied of this newly invented game of keep away. "You'll come back when you get hungry," I called to them and started back down the slope. A part of Fluff and Sneakers had survived, I thought.

Suddenly I stopped to look skyward. It was daylight after all, and we made good targets for the drones out in the open like this. Before I could take another step, I heard their bee like tones, and then I spotted them over the mountain ridges to the east.

"Take cover," I yelled to those on the beach. "Second wave, coming in."

I did not take my own advice, but sought a vantage point where I could shoot at them from the boulders. This time I was armed. I had a continuous streaming police assault laser slung over my shoulder. I positioned myself behind some rocks waiting until they came within my range.

When I did open fire, plastic and aluminum pieces splattered into the air before dropping to the ground. I heard Sam yelling at me to stop, but I fired until the sky was empty. Before I could retrieve one of the downed drones, Sam was standing next to me.

"They'll just send in more."

I knew he was probably right, but I said, "Afraid we'll make them madder?"

"Look at Niner and the squad driving them away from us again," Zel said jumping up and down. "Damn, he's good."

I rose from my sniper's perch and went to pick up a downed shell of one of the drones. I had tried to hit just the rotor blades on a few of the drones so the computer chips would be intact. I picked up a drone whose main body was all there. Sam was following along side of me. "What are you doing?"

Without answering, I pushed a couple of the downed and blasted drones into his hands. "Carry these. Be careful with them. Our fate is in your hands."

I began throwing the other pieces into a heap and lit them on fire with the instant flame thrower.

"Have you lost your reason?" Sam said throwing the drones down. "A bonfire will really tell them where we are."

"I'm just in a fighting mood. It feels good to take a stand. I want to take a few of them with me."

"I feel the same, Trave," Kara said, jumping off the raft.

"We need to get this houseboat repaired before they return," Zel said.

"Everyone is prepared to fight," Kara said.

Sam was back at work, hewing the log into a manageable sized wedge. Fueled by anger, his next strike with the axe found its mark solidly and split the log clean in two. "Praise God!" he yelled, and we shouted out hoorahs with him.

A short time later we had the log leveraged under the barge and were rolling the first barrel out from underneath its weight. Zel handed Sam the spray can of sealer and plopped three more cans down.

"When did you pick up this? It's a miracle in a can," he said already spraying. In moments the blue barrel was black.

"I saw it on a trip to get supplies and thought we might need it since we were going to be traveling by water. Everything leaks sooner or later."

"That's why God invented women," he beamed over at Zel who was already working on untying the knots on the next barrel, "practicality." He rolled the newly resealed barrel out of the way. "Okay, roll the next barrel over to me."

"Almost done here," Zel informed him still busy untying the knots.

"Can you get by without me?" I asked.

"Sure go ahead, Trav."

"I saw some deer in the meadow. Maybe I can shoot one. The smell of food might bring the cats in to eat."

"It's not wise to cook out here in the open."

"There's a cave opening on the slope. I saw it when I was chasing after the cats."

"Really? What kind of opening?"

I shrugged my shoulders. "I'll check it out. It's probably an old mining entrance of some sort."

"Travis?" Zel called out to me.

"What?" I said back to her in an irritated manner.

"It wasn't Fluff or Harley was it?"

"No, it was Tolkien and Lewis."

After I had shot a deer, I went to inspect the entrance to the opening I had seen earlier. It had once been an old mine. I could see that there were timbers propped around the walls to hold it up. I stopped and got out the LED and lit up the shaft. It went way back; further than my light showed. It was a good place to hole up in. I went back out and gutted the deer and cut a chunk out of the hind portion and wrapped it in the sack I had with me. As I worked, I called the cats' names out periodically. The only sound that answered was the wind. I looked down the beach, and saw Sam and them still working. I called and gave them the high sign of thumbs up in the air and started back down to the beach. I intended to chop some more pieces off the drift wood log to use for fire in the mine shaft as there weren't many trees nearby.

A few hours later we all sat by the fire inside the mine eating the deer meat. I had set some of the raw meat outside the cave entrance to entice the cats. "You might catch something, but it may not be who you want," Sam said.

There was little talk among us. Zel had been busy carving something into a long, slender piece of wood. Finally she said, "There. It's ready." She handed it out to me. "Read it."

I held the limb straight up and down to read it. It said: 'Tolkien and Lewis - sons of Harley and Mama.'

"Thank you."

Sam cleared his throat. "Zel and I talked it over. We're going to stay a few more days."

"You should be getting underway. I can follow you along the river. I will meet up with you eventually."

"You're going back to attack them, aren't you?" Zel said looking at Kara.

No one answered her as we watched Niner land and stop to pet Tippy. "Not one enemy drone is left in the sky. I am also reporting that I spotted cats in the upper area of the woods. It is Fluff and her kit."

"We will go with you," Good Neighbor Sam said directly to me.

I looked at Niner. "Show me."

It was hours later and quite a hike, but suddenly we saw them. Fluff was trying to carry Hoss in her mouth. She could only take a couple of steps forward before the weight that was straddled between her legs forced her to stop and rearrange the cat she dragged in her mouth. Fluff was more dragging Hoss along on the ground in front of her than actually carrying her. When we reached the cats, Fluff looked up to me and then lay down beside the body of her over grown baby. I shone the LED light on her. I hardly recognized her because of the dirt and blood on her fur. She looked exhausted, but Hoss' eyes were closed and she was not moving. Sam was feeling over the big cat's body for a pulse.

"She's alive."

I was checking over Fluff. At first I thought the blood on her was Hoss', but I realized that she had been hit, too. I gathered her gently in my arms. "Can you carry Hoss for me?" I said looking at Sam and noticed that he was already bent forward and picking the cat up.

Back in the cave we could see that both cats had tiny pellets all over them and Fluff was in great pain. I went down to the raft and brought out one of the boxes of pills. Back at the cave, I sorted through them to find a pill I knew to be a variety of pain killer. "Look for a round white pill. Small. It should be morphine," I said to Zel, who had begun sorting through the pile with me. Then I set about cleaning the outside of the wounds and cutting away the fur. Next I shaved the areas as best as I could. Fluff squeaked a pathetic sound and looked at me. "Hold on, girl."

"Here's one," Zell said. I took it from her and with a knife cut off about an eighth of the small pill. I heard Zel ask, "Are you sure it's the right pill?"

"Let's hope," I said breaking the pill into fourths. I lifted Fluff's head from the blanket and opened her mouth, forcing the pill back as far as I could place it so that she would have to swallow. When I felt her swallow, I rubbed her throat to make sure the pill went down the rest of the way. I gave her some water by putting a small dropper in her mouth and squirting the liquid in.

"Give me a portion of that pill," Sam said. "I'll give it to Hoss. You should see to her first. She's already unconscious. Her pulse is very weak." Sam had already shaved and prepped the wounds on her side while I had tended to Fluff. They had both been strafed on the right sides of their bodies by the pellets, just like Tolkien and Lewis, just like the barrels on the raft. As soon as Sam had given the pill to Hoss, he bent his head in prayer. When he lifted his head and saw me looking at him, he said, "You have the skill."

"I said I would never tinker with life again."

Sam just shook his head. "You're trying to save life in this instance, not create it. Your thoughts are backwards. Redefine wisdom and the ancient prophecies before it is too late.

"I'll do it," Zel said.

"Hand me the scalpel," I said. I saw both of them smile at me as I took the knife from Zel.

The small carving blade was crude, but it was an effective method of removing the tiny deeper pellets in their bodies. When it was all over and we had bandaged Hoss' wounds, Sam sat petting the cat's head gently. "You made it this far. Come the rest of the way. Your mama will be waiting for you." The tone in his voice was more of a command than a plea of hope. He sat with his hand resting on the top of her head as if forcing his words into her body. I began sucking out the pellets on Fluff with the vac and digging out the deeper ones with the knife just as I had done on Hoss.

When both the cats had been taken care of Zel went to bed and Sam went out to take his turn as sentry, but I sat up and continued to cut rotor blades and put the new enemy drones back together. It was some hours later that I took a break and went to look out the door of the mine for Sam. There was something I wanted to talk with him about. My eyes were used to the fire light inside and it was hard to see anything outside. The darkness was solid. It was impossible to distinguish the land from the water, or the sky from the mountains. I couldn't even make out my hand when I held it in front of my face. I crept along the ground by feeling the sides of the boulders for balance. Suddenly I stepped into a body and stopped. Sam's head was bent forward, and by the arc of his body, I realized he must be on his knees in prayer. I stumbled back away from him some distance to wait until I could hear him moving about again, but I fell asleep trying to listen for him.

Dawn was breaking when I came to. I rolled over and saw the cats still sleeping in soft curls. Tripper was laying between her mother and Hoss, and Tips was just on the other side of them. I crossed over to them and watched the slight lifting each breath gave to their fur. They were alive. Sam was still at his station praying. He heard my footsteps on the loose gravel and looked back towards me. "Have you been there all night?" I asked taking the rifle from him. Instead of answering me, he asked a question of his own. "What did you want last night?"

"I'm ok now."

"That isn't what I asked you."

His habit of not answering a direct question had always irritated me. It was his way of being superior, I thought, and I tried his own tactic on him. Instead of answering him, I called to Fluff, but she only looked over at me briefly and did not come. She was comfortable lying in my sleeping bag and did not wish to move. Joseph was standing above me now. He was a luminous man. I finally decided to answer him solely because his shadow on me reawakened the fear that I had last night.

"I had this sensation of movement, of feeling the water was carrying us some place we did not wish to go, and suddenly I got this thought out of nowhere that told me we were going to die. I couldn't get it out of my mind. I was actually sweating under my clothes. When I felt you praying, I could swear a voice spoke to me. It said, 'He has prayed death away.' Were you praying for that?"

"Much more than that. I'll put the coffee on and bring you a cup."

As he passed by the cats, I saw him stop. "They are holding their own," I called out to him. "I've already checked." From my spot on the ground I thought I saw his mouth move like he was speaking to them, but I didn't hear any sound come out. He knelt and touched Hoss and then Fluff. Both cats raised up their heads as if in answer to him.

When he came back with the coffee Hoss stood on her feet and followed after him as he passed by. She looked up. I thought at the time she was thanking him. Fluff was standing as well. Both cats were staring up at him as if he had presented them with the tastiest fish in the world.

"What did you do?" I said getting up and walking over to them. "Hoss seems healed. Last night I would have judged her gone."

Sam turned away and picked up one of the drones as if he were ignoring me.

"Answer me. What did you do?"

"I did nothing that is not contained in this book," he said holding it up. "Did you not wish for her to be healed as well?"

"I've wished for many things in my lifetime, but none of them actually happened."

"Have you prayed and made your wishes known to Him?"

"I'm not even sure that he exists."

"You just believed I healed the cats. Judge for yourself. Is there power in His words?"

I didn't have much to say after that. The air around the mine was charged with a sort of energy that kept me still because I couldn't let go of what he had said. I ruminated and chewed on his words all day, sucking the juice out of them. What I finally pared it down to was this: God made the rules and everything worked by them. Could it be that simple?

Suddenly I felt tired and rubbed my eyes to clear them. I was ready for a break. I had sat for hours and worked assembling the new drones, and it had gone by quickly. An army of twelve lay in the dirt awaiting instructions. Well, waiting for us to spark them into a semblance of life. A thought struck me then. Was that how God operated, too? Was he up there waiting for us to read his instructions and find the spark of life? There was the noticeable difference between us and the drones, but suddenly I got it. Drones had man to flip the switch, but God did not flip switches. He meant for us to do that for ourselves. I had been waiting for him to change me. I was waiting to be acted upon. I was used to that sort of thing.

Just then Fluff struggled to her feet and then nudged Hoss with her nose until she was standing next to her. She began grooming her kit. At that precise moment I had an overwhelming impulse to look up at the sky and I went to the entrance of the mine shaft. The sky had changed monumentally since morning. Nothing moved on the horizon except brooding clouds which had cut the sun off completely. The assembling clouds were like seeing an invading army appear unexpectedly, but I was left wondering how the clouds had formed out of nothing. I was mesmerized by the way they moved swiftly towards me. They rolled forward like loose tumble weeds that piled and jammed into each other. They were growing darker and moving faster. 'Your life is moving with them," I heard a voice inside me say. 'You are being swept away.' It was the same sensation I had experienced the night before. I was trying to shrug the thought off as I heard footsteps approach. I looked up to see Zel. As she reached me, I felt the first drops of rain strike me. They were cold and hard. "Lucky, huh?" the clone asked me. "They won't come today."

"We can't leave either, so I wouldn't count it all that lucky," I said.

"Count the blessings you have," I heard Sam saying, but I ignored him and turned to Zel. "Help me gather the blades and the drones up, and get them inside will you?" I said as I began grabbing for as many pieces as I could see around me.

The rain shouted down its pellets with force, sounding against the rocks and the plastic bodied drones with plunks and plops that rang out a warning. Rain seldom came with this kind of force. I had heard it sing off the rooftops and windows, yes, but not against the land. It took a hard pouring out of rain to do that.

Zel began to run back to the mine with the parts she had gathered up and I followed after her. A few more trips were necessary to gather in what I wanted to protect, and when I had put the last of the drones against the wall, I stepped back to the entrance. Water rolled off the top of the mine entrance and down from the slopes like a waterfall. It splashed my feet and created an instant puddle inside the cave. Soon the water was washing into the cave itself since it sloped more downward than the terrain outside.

I took a shovel and went out. I began to dig a ditch to channel the water the other way, piling up the dirt at the entrance to the mine to form a barrier against the water. It worked, and in short time I had a moat running down the full width of the doorway and away from us.

"You better have a cup of coffee. I think you've held back the flood waters," Sam said. When I stepped into the cave I could smell the meat and the smoke from the fire. I started to take off my wet jacket and I felt a coldness enter into my body. I could feel it deep inside the marrow of my bones. I was chilled from the inside out. Sam was holding out some clothes to me. "You've been thoroughly anointed.Take off the wet stuff." He plopped the duds down and he and Zel stepped up to the doorway and looked the other way. I peeled the wet pants off in inches. Trying to shed the wet jeans was like crawling out of my own skin. Once out of them, I felt naked and shiny like a peeled peach, and I reached for the towel and dried and dressed myself quickly. "Okay, you can turn around now," I said. Zel came over to my wet piles and picked them up. I let her. It felt good to be taken care of in that moment. "Thank you," I said peering into her face. Then I turned to Sam. "I'll take that cup of coffee now."

Neither one of them spoke, but Sam cut a chunk of meat off the spit and began chopping it up. He got up and put it in a bowl and carried it over to the cats. They did not turn it down. "I heated their water up a tad, too. Everyone needs something to warm the insides on days like these."

"The rain keeps the drones away, but it keeps us from moving on too," Kara said. I felt awkward sitting there with every one of them staring at me from time to time. Just then Tippy let out a meow. It was a lone and pitiful voice, scratchy and unsure. I reached down and petted her. "Call out Tippy. Call out to the rest of them that are lost. Tell them to come home," I pleaded with the animal.

"We all need to come home," Stranger Sam said quietly.

After the rain stopped, we spent most of the night carrying rocks to fill in the entrance to the tunnel. "When the drones come, they won't be able to spot us. It's a good sniper's nest," Sam said.

"Let me make the last stand. The rest of you get going."

"No one's going anywhere in this weather." Kara said. "We're going to have to take the rest of the barrels off, anyway."

I was busy cutting the two plastic replacement pieces off the drone. I reached for a hand file to sand them down and looked over at her. "In that case, hand me the small piece of wood by your side. I need to make wooden pins to replace the metal pins so I can reattach the blades."

"Let me see one of your blades," Sam requested. I tossed him one I had just finished. "A perfect copy," he commented turning the blade over and fitting it among the original blades still attached to the drone. He set the drone back down.

"Is that how cloning works?" Zel suddenly asked out of the blue. "Like a cut pattern that is followed the way Trave is doing?"

"Genes were not meant to be duplicated like jig saw pieces," Sam said to her.

"But they are copied," the clone said decisively.

"Yes, and the more the copies, the greater the potential for errors, not to mention the fact that once telomeres are damaged there is no way to heal them. Even if just one telomere is damaged, it will continue to unravel. A damaged DNA strand will start to resemble a bush of tangled wires. It is that damage that leads to diseases and the mental craziness we see around us."

"Can you show me what you mean somehow?"

"Throw me that piece of towel beside you, Zel." She tossed him the towel and he began to roll it by twisting it from both ends until it was tightly coiled to resemble a strand of DNA. Then he took a knife and cut into the cloth until tiny rips formed, and then he pulled the threads apart until they were a frayed mess. "That's what disease looks like when the telomeres begin to unravel; just crazy, frizzled shrubs with the branches growing wildly," he said holding the small piece of towel up.

"So when the DNA is copied into the next clone, it will copy the abnormality," I said, trying to show him that I understood the concept.

"You are remembering things from your past, Trave."

"Then more DNA becomes compromised because of that one diseased tangle which leads to more types of sicknesses in the body," I added.

"Which ultimately affects the mind. Only God can heal such a web of sickness and disease," said Sam throwing down his show and tell piece of cloth. "Man, man, man. He is a crazy animal." Good Neighbor Sam's voice was more high pitched than normal and his brows were raised unevenly which gave him a comical expression. Both Zel and I laughed.

"You don't believe it?" he said with a finality that made us silent.

"I'm sorry. It wasn't what you said, but how you said it, combined with the expression on your face," Zel said fumbling to explain. "It made a laughable moment."

We sat staring at the dirt until Sam stood up. "You think you can grow new parts like harvesting a crop of corn."

"Don't start ragging on me, Sam," I said. "I feel responsible enough."

"No, you don't feel the weight of it. True remorse is like a rock and weighs you down."

"Then you could cast me into the river to sink to the bottom, is that it?"

"Then you would be washed clean and the heaviness would be removed."

He had a look of disgust on his face. Was the reality that Sam was trying to teach us any worse than this holographic world where one's experience was mirrored by every other thought that traveled through our circuitry paths to our minds, our memories? In that respect, the world that Sam was giving birth to in these last days paralleled the new world I found myself in. I began to wonder, did I only see the similarities because I had helped create that world once? Was it all an inner sort of madness? Could you choose the future you wanted to bring about, and separate it from the collective memory of mankind?

"Well," I said, "the first Humpty is back together. Time to test it."

"Another laughable moment?"

"It might be. But first we will have to charge it up. This baby needs juice!"

I felt renewed as I went out and down to the boat to get the computer. I heard steps behind me. Sam was there and put his hand on my shoulder. "I believe I want to be a part of this."

"Me, too. I want to fight the drones and make them fall from the sky," Niner said.

"Then you don't see this as revenge, Good Neighbor Sam?"

"I see it as defending your life. The two things are quite different."

"To me they are the same."

"To poison a city's water supply is an unprovoked act of revenge. To stand and defend yourself against an attacking army is righteous."

"They poisoned first. They started it when they wiped out most of the population of the United States, or doesn't that count?"

"Of course it's war, but that is not what I am speaking about. It is the motivation in your heart I care about."

"Don't tell me what motivates me. You don't know."

"You told me that yourself in your writing, remember?"

"War is war," I repeated.

"That is what you tell yourself, but in the end the price may be higher than you would care to pay."

I was weighing his question over in my mind and didn't answer him. "Have you ever killed a man?" he asked.

I didn't answer him.

He stared me straight in the eyes and said, "Do you mind if I point out an aspect of your character?

"Fire away," I said bowing towards him.

"I have seen the way you react to the death of the animals.

"These elite are not human beings or even animals, they're monsters. They have no feeling or guilt for what they have done at all. They seem to live very comfortably. I don't see them staying up nights after they have killed millions. You saw the video."

"What Travis says is true," Zel said.

Sam put his hand on my shoulder. "I see someone with a conscience trying to rationalize the consciousless acts of what those in power have done." He stopped walking and looked at me. "Do you envy them so much that you would become like them?"

"You like putting me on the spot, don't you? You're twisted, Good Neighbor Sam."

"You need to let go of the anger of the past, Travis."

I let out a laugh. "It's a good motivator for war."

"It is just and right to defend yourself against the SG attacking you, but you don't need to let it fill you with hate. They have you then."

"Tell them to forgive."

"Do you think they would? Could you ever convince them they were wrong and that humans have a right to live? They rejected you and that's hard to take. Do they even see you as being equal to them?"

"That's my point, kill or be killed."

"War in itself is not sin. Look back at the old testament. The Israelites battled plenty of enemies. God even told King Saul to completely wipe out the Amalekites. God wanted this people gone before they could infect the Israelites with their beliefs in idols and sun worship, but Saul ignored God's command and spared King Agag and the best of the livestock. As a result, God ended Saul's reign, and raised up a shepherd named David in his place."

"He certainly is an exacting God."

"Do you fault God?"

"Is there any other way to see it? Humanity has been wiped out. Isn't it natural to ask, Where was God? He didn't stop them."

"Yes, and then the thought comes, does God exist at all?"

"That's what we have been taught for generations."

"Your grandfather and grandmother believed. Your writing says that. It also shows that you have been weighing that very question in your mind. Your writing of the book shows your concern for humanity."

"No, it doesn't."

"Isn't it a warning to all that the SG has gone crazy? Doesn't it show whoever should find it and read it the contrast of men in power and the peacefulness of men like Pompy? Isn't that why they got rid of you?"

"Is that what you got out of my writings?"

"I saw someone who dared to leave a message in a bottle. You told mankind to think and stand up for themselves. You showed them the heritage and foundation that this country was built upon. You reminded them of their duty and obligation. You told them of a better world that once existed among men. You are telling them the truth. That's more than anyone has dared in this world for many years."

"It's too late," I yelled out. "It's making me crazy. All your talk of ancient texts, science and religion. Just stop it."

"Your rock is growing bigger," he said quietly.

"You mean it is my fault?" I yelled.

"I mean there is hope on each new horizon. I am talking about survival. Your book is a selfless act. A gift to mankind," Sam said.

"I only wanted to blow the whistle on the SG. Rat them out. Make people hate them as much as I do."

"But the book is much more than that as I have just told you."

"Joseph's right. That's what drew me to you, Travis. I was curious about a man who would do all he did to keep those animals alive. I just knew I wanted what you had inside," Zel said.

"You've both give me more credit than I deserve."

"Here. You deserve these, at least," Zel said handing me more newly cut rotor blades. "Eight more for the war effort. I did them earlier today," she explained shyly.

"You both can leave, you know. You might just die along with me otherwise."

"I'm not afraid to face death anymore. I know my real soul exists. I believe I will join it."

"Bravo, Zel," Sam clapped.

"Is that computer charging?" I said to Niner, and to try and change the subject.

"Seems to be. I will reprogram it to attack his own flight buddies."

"Listen," Sam suddenly said touching my coat sleeve. There was the sound of wolves calling in the distance.

"They are our watchers," he added. "Sleep well."

It rained for days with a little sleet thrown in. We were at the foothills of the mountains and hedged in on all sides in a v-shaped valley of rather steep slopes. Zel and Sam were talking and sitting close to the fire in the tunnel. Something about the way they talked together, low and excluding everyone else reminded me of an earlier encounter with a girl I had known some years before. She had given me my real first taste of what it felt like to be an outsider. That particular night I had run into Lorette in the club. I knew her through Madison, my friend. She was actually his girl. I had seen her hand sort of wave and I thought she was motioning me over, but when I reached her table, her demeanor changed. "I'm not interested," she said to me as if I had asked her for something. There was silence. I stood there like a wet shirt hung on a line. My mouth was talking, but to this day I have no idea of what I said to her. I had tried many times to recollect exactly what I said to her that night for many and varied reasons. Foremost was the fact that Lorett had come out of her chair and kissed me and took me home. It was then she told me about why she had left Madison. He was cold, she had said. He was a demigod of a sort and concerned only with himself, but the real reason she had left him was that he had left her to pay the total cost of her abortion. She had not named him as a sperm donor at first, but she decided to name him later, and the SG came after him for his portion of the bill. Then Madison had done something odd she told me. He had come to her apartment and handed her an envelope and left. In it he had written a story of terror and fear about his own death. Nothing else. Madison blamed her for waking him up to that fact that death would happen to him at some point in the future. There were three powers in the world that mattered he had written to her: life, death, and sex.

Laurette and I saw each other for a while, but all we had in common was Madison, and once we had said everything about him that was in us, the relationship dried up. She told me during our brief time together that Madison was a hybrid at that time, but I had not really wanted to see the truth until this moment. I was trying now to remember everything about Madison so I could compare him with Sam. I say this because there was something odd and aloof about Joseph and it reminded me of Madison.

I had stirred myself up with my thoughts of the past while the others had been talking and I was suddenly irritated by the fact that I heard Zel call stranger Sam by the name he had given us. He did not look like a Joseph. That's when the thought hit me that he was one of them, one of the elite, the eternals, and I called him out on it. I wouldn't let him slip away like I had Madison. Everyone stared at me in a dumbfounded way.

"Your reasoning doesn't make any sense, Trave," Zel said coming to Joe's defense.

"That's the way the mind works. It gets onto an idea and it's blind to anything else," Joseph explained to her. "Like what Travis has been thinking now."

"What are you talking about?" I said standing up with my plate.

"You've been entertaining ideas about both of us."

"You're crazy. Don't tell me what I'm thinking."

I set the plate on the ground and began to divide my portion of the bird for the cats.

"Joseph is close to the source," Niner chimed in.

"Here's some coffee," Sam said placing it down in front of me.

He plopped his plate on the ground and began tearing his chicken in pieces. "I'll share with the cats, too, if you don't mind."

"You trying to kiss and make up?"

"All living things need to eat," he answered in that steady, even voice of his. In struck me then that his voice had the clearest tone to it that I had ever heard. "Besides, I like them, too," he continued. His voice had an ethereal quality to it. I had noticed that the first time I heard him speak. It stopped you; caught you unawares and made you forget things.

I watched Sam scrape his portion for the cats from his plate into their pan and they came running. I was jealous of him and Fluff and Harley. At times I almost thought they would rather be with him more than anybody.

"Have you given our discussion of earlier any more thought? Of course you have. That's what this conversation is all this is about," he said answering his own question.

"It's things like that which makes me suspicious of you. You always try to be a step ahead of me. You can't know my thoughts," I said looking at him in the eyes.

"Of course not, but I know how people's minds work. They all come to the same thoughts sooner or later. It would stand to reason from our discussion that you would continue to think on existence and how you came to be, and from there you would also wonder about those around you, namely me and Zel."

"So tell me. What was I thinking?"

"You were trying to decide if I was human or not."

I quickly turned away from him and purposely did not answer. His words had cut into the secret part of myself. I went and picked up Fluff and put her on my lap. Hoss sat at my feet and looked at me and I focused on her to avoid any more contact with those around me. She was a gray and white giant who moved with lethargic steps where ever she went. She had been the last one to learn to eat and had always followed her mother wherever she went unless Fluff went outside. After months of coaxing, Fluff eventually gave up trying to get her kitten out of the house and left her waiting inside the door. Fluff had always taken extra care to see that Hoss got her share of food and to make sure the kit was groomed every day. She even brought her presents from outside. Once she had brought back a live grass-hopper and set it down before the kit. Fluff nudged her to hunt after the bug, but Hoss had no interest in cat games and only sat looking at it. After many attempts, mama gave up and took the grasshopper to the others who immediately pounced on it and played with it until they ate it. Not one cat interfered with the tending she gave to Hoss, but neither did they interact with her. Hoss didn't seem to need any of the other cats and Fluff dutifully took it upon herself to care for the kitten. Her patience astounded me.

"Fluf's special to you, isn't she?" Sam said noticing me petting the cat.

"She picked me out from her family and attached herself to me when I found her. It was Fluff who got the others to accept me."

"If only we all could have her patience and kindness."

"Meaning me?" I said turning to look at Sam.

"I said all. Do you think it strange that we humans can learn something from animals?"

"I don't know."

"You thought it strange that those in power worshipped the creatures and protected them and killed people instead in your novel. Why?" Zel asked.

"It isn't a novel. It's a guide for whoever should find it."

"You say it is for everyone, but You seemed to be angry that I read it, yet you seemed to be angry at Ben for not reading it."

"Everyone should know the truth about what has been done."

"Do you even know the truth? Have you thought about your part in this?" Sam asked.

"It sounds like you expect me to justify my actions. Well, I can't. I haven't even thought about it much. It has been quite a shock."

"Education is for the elite. Thinking is for the elite. You researched and found that out for yourself," Sam said.

"The problem is they kept everything for themselves."

"There's was a worse scenario than just being selfish, you know."

"Other than killing most of mankind?" I said in an utterly sarcastic tone.

"Who killed them, Travis?"

"The state, the SG, me."

"And who are they really?" Joseph asked giving the cats more of his bird.

"What do you mean?"

"Haven't you had Niner break down the molecular structure of everyone in camp? Why not have him break down the elite the same way?"

"You know who they are, don't you? Why don't you just tell us?" I said in an irritated way.

"They are the super humans," Niner said stepping up between us.

I laughed.

"I can refresh the history of their origins if you would like," Niner said.

"Shoot," I said nodding and eating.

"They are a race of hybrids that started developing at the end of the last century and into this. Their skin mimics the resilience of soft tissue, but has the ability to heal or repair itself. Their sensory neurons are synaptic which affords them the luxury of touch." Here Niner stopped reading to glance over at me. "This new race of hybrid humans are made up of completely interchangeable organs grown organically in laboratories for their specific blood and skin type. They, and their parts, are specifically of a genus of 3D nano-hybrids which can recharge in seconds. You should be familiar with all this, Trave, because you gave it to me. My claws can pet the cats and feel the ground when I land."

"Stop! You are telling me they aren't human any longer. That isn't what my research and surgical procedures were developed for. They were meant to help the sick, those who lost limbs due to accidents, those whose bodies had become diseased in one form or another. I meant to end suffering."

"You have met what you created and don't believe in it," Good Neighbor Sam said.

"They refer to themselves as hu-brids," Niner informed me, "and consider themselves as the next genetic leap from ape to human kind on the evolutionary tree. They are the last. They are eternal."

"How can this be possible? Someone among them must still be human."

"Humans, clones, hybrids, robotoids have been synthesizing with each other since the early part of the twenty first century. By 2030 most humans were already of mixed origin. Now, the species has become highly evolved," Niner reposted.

"You're saying humanity is extinct."

"According to them, it has evolved."

"It's not possible. It's too short of a time."

"Technology doubled every hundred years, then fifty years, then every two years until it was possible to double the advances over night and even in hours," the drone said, "so why not evolution?"

I was looking at everyone and must have made them feel like I was trying to put them into a category. "You know what I am," Zel said. "Kara is not a clone. She has a belly button. I saw it when she was washing in the stream one day," Zel said to me.

"Need to see mine as well?" Sam said lifting up his shirt. "Let's take a walk. I want to talk to you about your plans."

"What plans?"

"That's what I want to talk about," he said and then flashed me a quick smile. He was reading my thoughts again. "Everyone has plans. The wizard is purposeful in all. You had a plan in mind when you created Niner, didn't you?" He was trying to fool me into thinking he was not able to read my mind by asking me about my plans. I had stopped walking to stare at him. Finally I decided to confront him.

"You sound like you know my plans. You tell me."

"Really?" he asked with that same smile on his face. "You do give me power."

"By doing all the research on how the elite gained power weren't you trying to eliminate the possibility that it had all been done by whim, by some strange accident. For all reasoning that exists you have begun to see, haven't you, that there are no accidents."

Yes, he was leading up to something, I thought, but was it for good or evil?

"You are a man climbing a ladder and don't know it," he said and then just looked at me as if that should explain everything he was saying. It was the way Pompy used to stare at me when he thought I should know the answer.

"What is it that you are getting at?"

"You've been searching for answers. There is a wizard. He lives and has been being. He is the creative force in the universe. Everything else copies his art. He has many names, protector, healer, rescuer, father."

I didn't say a word, but kept walking along side of him.

We hadn't walked very far when we reached the spot where we had buried the cats. Fluff ran ahead and sniffed over the ground with tentative scratching movements at the top soil. Soon most of the cats were over by her. There was mostly short sniffs and then a curious thing happened. They all lay down together on the ground. Not one cat made a peep.

"Do you think they know? Do you think they are paying their respects?" I asked my companion. I decided I would beat him at his own game, so I changed the subject myself.

"I should find it odd if they didn't. They are living animals. They have a memory. To them death is a natural part of life.

You seem surprised by their actions. What are your views on death?"

"I haven't given it much thought," I said with a chortle of a laugh that sounded very weak.

"I should have thought you had. Didn't you and the others believe in Hobbes' assertion that death was the greatest evil?"

"I don't know what I believe now, Sam. Tell me what you believe about death."

"It's the most important thing in life."

"Death?"

"There are no real endings in the way you mean. The concept of season doesn't end just because the Fall turns to Winter. Winter becomes Spring and then Summer, but nothing has been lost. Leaves fall to the ground and mix with the earth. It is the form of things that change, not the thing itself. The loss of one thing is the start of another."

"You believe that if you want. I don't buy it."

"I never took you for a gambler."

"I'm not."

"But you gamble with your soul."

"No. I just haven't thought of it."

"What if you were to die today? Where would you end up if the coin was flipped?"

"You mean heads or tails? I don't know."

"Let's take a walk and reason."

I headed off with Stranger Sam, but I noticed we going off in a direction that was not our customary route. "What's up?"

"A change of scenery for a change of mind."

"Hearing your voice, I sense more than that." I was beginning to think he had gotten me on the conversation he had planned on all along.

"Your intuitive skills have picked up," he said looking straight ahead and quickening his pace.

"I seem to be getting it from you. It's like you give off vibes or something."

"So you judge from your gut, your instincts. That's how it was meant to be."

"I'm not sure I follow." I turned quickly for I heard a rustle behind us in the leaves, but it was just Fluff and her bunch.

"Animals are a lot like humans in that they are living beings. No matter what the government researchers have said to the contrary. They have emotions and feelings that are the same as humans. They are made from the dust of the earth. Animals feel pain and sorrow just as humans do."

"Damn! I'm guilty, okay? I helped create this mess. I was a part of it. There I've confessed. Now what am I supposed to do? I can't change anything."

"It's ok to have remorse, guilt, sorrow. Feelings tell the mind that something's not right in your spirit."

I didn't answer him right away, but finally said, "It's said that animals don't have souls."

It was the first time that Sam had turned to look at me since we had started out. "You don't believe that according to your book."

I didn't answer. It spooked me that he knew personal things about me even though I knew he had read it in my journal. He must have sensed my irritation, too, because next he gave me a backhanded compliment. "Your way of thinking is getting closer to the truth, but animals don't need souls. However, that doesn't mean the Creator didn't make provisions for them to walk in the next world."

"I'd like to believe you," I said looking at Fluff.

"Luke 3:6 says, 'all flesh shall see the salvation of the Lord.' All means all to me, animals included. Isaiah 11:6 gives us this: 'The wolf shall also dwell with the lamb, and the leopard shall lie down with the kid; and the calf and the young lion and the fatling together; and a little child shall lead them.' So you see animals are talked about in the new kingdom, but my favorite passage is found in the last book of the Manual, chapter 19, verse 11. 'And I saw heaven opened, and behold a white horse;

and he that sat upon him was called Faithful and True, and in righteousness he doth judge and make war."

Sam always said things which I did not expect him to say. It was like he was giving me an explanation for the things my mind hadn't seen or thought of.

"It doesn't say right off that animals are in the next kingdom," I said to be ornery.

"It's a test to see how closely we read and ruminate on the words that are there. If the Lord himself comes back riding a white horse and the saints thunder after him, what other conclusion can one draw? The truth is there if one searches it out."

"Reasons it out, you mean."

"Yes, if you like. I almost forgot about Belem's talking donkey. Even that donkey reasoned things out and spoke wisdom to Bellam, who did not listen. The animal clearly stopped at the turn in the road to warn Bellam of what he saw. Now consider this: Would you, as a man, heed what an animal said to you? If Fluff should warn you with words from her mouth, would you not think that she had been granted speech for some momentous announcement? However, Bellam saw no miracle in his donkey's speech, gave it no thought, and ignored what was most likely the only miracle he had witnessed in his life by making it ordinary."

We had reached the summit of the hill and were looking over the valley below. I experienced a moment of unexpected peace gazing at the mountain vista. The first row of mountains was so close that you could see the twisting streams of loose, gray gravel sliding down their slopes. The trees were blackish green and grew in sparse clumps on its great sides. Then higher up, as the altitude thinned, the rocks appeared to be bruised colors of blue and purple standing out among the scattered splashes of snow. The tops of the peaks were snowcapped and glistened like the heads of white feathered eagles. It was a majestic sight. I was content that Sam's reasoning matched my own. Animals would be in the next life if there was one.

We stopped for a moment before heading down the other side of the slope to the river. Neither of us spoke until we reached the barge.

"You seem to be weighing things over in your mind," he said.

I jumped when he said that. He was looking at me. I had the feeling he was going to say more, but my startled reaction had stopped him. "Well, never mind," he said checking the knots that tethered the raft to the little row boats. "Check the connection on those ropes to the barge behind you, okay?" he asked me and stood up in the little dingy. I was already standing and busy checking the ropes when suddenly I felt something slip out of my side pocket. I caught sight of it just as it splashed into the water. It was my pocket computer. The boat lurched to one side under me as I dove into the water after it. I had to search for some time along the sandy bottom before I felt its hard and distinct shape in my grasp. When I came up out of the water, I saw something move on the far ridge out of the corner of my vision. My first thought was that it was a bear or some other wild animal come to have a look at us from atop the mountain peak, but then I caught a flashing glint coming from the far ridge just above the blackness of the trees, which had helped shield it partly from view. It was a helicopter. I looked at Sam and then back at the copter. We watched it make five or six passes over the mountain side. "It's searching for something. It's moving in a grid pattern in passes of about twenty miles or so in length," Sam said. I agreed. It looked like the helicopter was making a conscious attempt to locate something or someone. The copter was near enough to pick up a sound, but you could not hear the rotor blades. It was one of the latest energy models Niner had told me about and it was fast. It must be running on liquid quartz, I reflected. It made everything move smooth, fast, and silent.

My heart sank to the pit of my stomach. The life that I had reveled in only seconds ago was snatched away. Life promised you one thing, even holding it out to you, and then, just as you were about to take possession of it, it was ripped from you. "Do you think they know about us?"

"Yes. You are looking at me strangely, Trav."

"It's the way you say things. There's a conviction to it like you are some sort of fortune teller, like you already know the answer."

"There is the power of life and death in all the words we speak."

I stared at him unable to make up my mind if this man beside me had ever divulged a truth to me about anything. He irritated me because he was always one step ahead of me, and because he always had logical explanations for my suspicions of him which made me feel small and petty. The fact that I could never make up my mind about him totally, bothered me, too. He was either the best liar I had ever met, or the most honest man I had come across since Pompy.

The way he was looking at me I had the feeling he was going to say something momentous, but then he changed his mind and grabbed for me and pulled me under the water. When we both surfaced again he said, "Travis, your old self is dead. You are a new man."

I thought his words had an odd ring to them and were non sequitur to what we had been discussing, but gave it no further thought beyond that. "I'm a cold man.

Since he was already in the water, I had no revenge against him except to splash his face with a grand slam of water and hurry towards shore, but I was still struggling to stand in the water after he had released me from the dunking. I wrapped my arms around my body to warm myself. "You could have warned me."

"There wasn't time with the helicopters flying over," he said.

"They were miles away," I answered still shivering and trying to cover myself as I waded through the water to shore.

By now everyone had gathered around to see what we were doing. We made the announcement of what we had seen which created fear and an uproar among those in the camp. "I'll kill them all," one of the robos said, checking his weapon.

"We're almost patched up and ready to sail," Kara said looking at me.

"Great! We're running on man power, they have liquid quartz," I said.

"They won't reach this sector for a few days yet," Sam said calmly, leaning against the raft.

"Then let's go enjoy the deer I spent all day cooking," Zel said.

I didn't like the calmness I detected in Sam. He seemed to be waiting for something to happen. "We should be moving on. They've spotted us," I said.

"The boat's not ready and it is almost dark," he answered. "There will be no battle for you to fight tonight."

I distrusted him again in that moment. I hated the way he kept changing sides all the time. One minute he agreed with me and the next he was adversarial. I felt the need to confront him again, but could not summon the energy.

Soon we were back at the mine and Zel was handing me a plate and I sat close to the fire and the warmth which made me more tired. I wanted to curl up by it and never leave.

"Everything in this world is so frightening," Kara was saying.

"You are alone in an evil world and the protector is gone," Sam said.

"The voice of doom has spoken," I said.

"I am conveying that murder was a conscious choice for these people. It hasn't given them any more pause than if they were choosing whether or not to have eggs or cereal for breakfast. They chose to follow the spirit of death."

"You believe there are spirits in this world?" Kara said cautiously.

"If you really want to know, use your gut instincts. Apply that sense of feeling fear to the millions who inhabited the cities of the world and you get the spirit that rules the zeitgeist of the age. Travis, you have heard of the world with God's ruach in it in the personage of your grandfather, Pompy. You have lived among the elite. Which do you prefer?"

"What is ruach?" Kara broke in.

"It is Hebrew for spirit. Ruach ha-kodesh."

"Who are you?" I said again for a great swooshing came from his mouth as he said the word the word, ruach.

"Does it matter? What matters is the feeling to you get from me."

"It's an energy," I said. "I'm not sure if it is good or bad."

"Examine it. Hold it up to the words in the Manual."

"That's not possible."

"It certainly is."

"It's just a feeling, like I said."

"That's what it means to be discerning of the spirit. Take it one step further. Test it. When a man acts, you will know what kind of man he is, Trav."

Suddenly I thought of Pompy and one of the last arguments I had with him about the SG taking his farm and cows. 'We are more than our stuff,' he had said to me when I had advised him to get even with SG. I stopped my conversation with Sam and told the others about Pompy and his farm.

"He had already left it in God's hands, hadn't he?" Sam said.

"If God is in charge, then why is the world at an end? It doesn't make sense."

"You are just used to measuring things the way the world measures things," Sam said standing up and waving the green bound book back and forth. "God measures everything from faith.

"Why is faith at the end of things? Why didn't the Creator put faith at the beginning?"

"Faith is at the beginning of things. It is man who sees it as the end because he uses the Protector as a last ditch cure."

"Why didn't Pompy win then? He believed. He had faith. Why wasn't it enough?"

"Is it the Wizard's promise that failed, or man's heart?"

"You've changed the topic from apples to oranges again," I yelled.

"You think you have the answers, and that by your own will you can handle whatever comes our way. Then when things turn out badly because of your own choices you blame the gods and wizards."

I was surprised to hear this super human reveal anger, but there was something in the way Sam said it which made me more willing to accept it as being sincere. His voice was unarguable, unmovable like time itself.

"He has withdrawn his spirit for a time, but know that He is coming back," he continued.

"When? Why not come now when he is needed?"

"You expect the divine Creator to come on your dime? He is sovereign. You have been expecting to find the new kingdom in the here and now. This isn't where it happens, so stop acting like it should. Here is where you earn it."

"You said to test Him. How else but to see him act?" I said.

"You speak as if you believed he was more the wizard than the Holy I Am and should move in some logical line from a prescribed method of order. Is it any wonder why Niner sees him as a willy nilly escaped sort of genie who should do as you say. He is sovereign. To do as you order is not much of a test of your faith, is it Travis?"

"I only call for Him to do things in a sane manner, Ranger Joe. We need food, peace. Life. Let this Creator Wizard give us those things and then talk to us about our souls."

"You act like it was the Creator who turned the world into a laboratory junk heap, Travis."

"We need to tell him what we think. Let this wizard give us what we ask."

"You speak from an ideology of nonsense learned from some nasty adolescent political ideology."

"Look who's judging. You talk like either Moses or the SG. I haven't decided which. You talk like one and act like the other. Either way you condemn us," I said yelling.

Sam sat down at that point. Everyone waited for him to do or say something. He looked up and spoke quietly. "Man has been baiting the I Am to stop wars and banish evil for thousands of years. As it was in the days of Noah so shall it be on that great and terrible day," Stranger Sam said looking at me.

"What are you talking about now?"

"The prophecy. The Nephilim. Remember we started to talk about this once? They saw the women of the earth and thought them beautiful and irresistible and had children with them."

"So what?"

"They destroyed the original gene pool. The wizard hated the Nephilim. They were the sons that had been cast down from the heavenly realm."

My mind was reeling. How had we gotten on to this new tact? "What's that got to do with now?" I asked.

"Artificial Intelligence. Is not man a creature again? Hasn't man's gene pool become mixed again?"

I stood up. It was a lot to take in. Sam's eyes were following my movements.

"Trave, when you saw me for the first time, you knew me instantly," Joe said. "Trust in your instincts."

While I was trying to come up with an answer, I must have looked unsure to him because he said, "Test all things as to what they might be," and he turned away. I did recollect my first impressions of him. I had the feeling of safe harbor like the road had suddenly ended, and there wasn't the need to take one more footstep in any direction. "Then you are not going to stop us?"

"You have heard nothing. All your plans are the aimless flitting of sparrows. You think of man's glory but the true virture is that rebirth happens at all in men. You have marked your way." There was a sense of loss or a defeat that sounded in his voice, and when I heard it, I was alarmed. It sounded tolling and final and it filled me with regret.

CHAPTER 11

The next days were filled with loading and preparing to leave and it made me think of the past and all that had happened here. Thinking about the incidents which lay behind me always stirred me up because it was so unchangeable. There were too many mistakes and too many amends I needed to make. I wanted so desperately to have taken other paths, but most of all I wanted to make sense of time the way the cats had done in coming to terms with the death of their own. Acceptance seemed to come so gently, so easily for them as if it were nothing more than taking in a breath. Each day after Tolkien's' and Lewis' death, Mama had sat on the grave a little less until one day she simply passed by it with a sniff. She had accepted that their leaving was final and she never looked back. Mama Kitty was one step ahead of me.

I was on this path of thinking because of what Sam had said to me the night before. Good Neighbor Sam was always telling me to follow my instincts, I thought looking at Fluff. Instinct was the animals common sense factor. That is what had told her how to prepare to have her kittens some months back. She backed into a corner and acted like she was needing to void, but I guess she was bracing herself for the event. Her cries were frantic so I came closer and petted her head until her cries stopped. It was her first time, and I guess she wanted a mid-wife.

The first kitten came, and I watched with fascination and awe as she began licking at it and biting at the sack and cord. Instinct had kicked in perfectly for the first time mother. The next kitten came and she repeated the process. However, just then I noticed something moving in the dirt box I had placed in the pantry for all of them to use when they were in the house. I got up and went over to it because there was movement coming from it. As I stood looking into the litter box, I could see it was a kitten still encased in its birth sac. It had been there before I came into the kitchen to sit with Fluff so it had lain there for a while. I picked it up and broke open the sac and the kitten moved.

I placed it by its mother. Fluff was busy cleaning up the second kitten when I laid the third one down. She ignored it, and I thought she would reject it, but she gradually sniffed at it. She seemed confused at first and she began counting and recounting them. It was as if she was reassuring herself that her tally was correct. One, two....hmm three. After a series of recounts she included the new kitten: One, two, three. One, two, three. Yes, there were three she said to herself as she began to clean the third kitten up. Anyone could make a mistake under the circumstances she seemed to say. Instinct had straightened her out, but Hoss had been left too long inside the sac and the damage had been done.

I suddenly saw life and Genesis and all that Sam had told me in a different light. It was an instantaneous epiphany: I had been mixing up instinct with knowledge. In the world, if you didn't know as much or more than your friends you were considered stupid, or worse; not worth knowing. The world prized its own. For as long as I could remember there was always one guy who seemed to know everything from third grade on. In our borough of New York it was James Dottsy. Jimmy was not strong or large, but he was admired for what he knew. He was accorded full honors and respect simply for having beneficial info. When I was in my thirties I heard he had been shot in a bar that had dealings with the underworld. Sometimes you could know too much.

I had wanted to be Jimmy D. until I read the chapter of Beginnings a few days ago in the Manual. It was then I realized that knowledge had caused trouble from the beginning, but when it came to the SG, and the rulers, and emirs of this One World, the rules didn't seem to apply. They had managed to make knowledge work in their favor. Knowledge had given them power. They had gotten all the earth as a prize. How had they finagled a win when all other others I had known had lost? That was the ringer I couldn't over look. Adam lost the key to his garden address, Jimmy D. had lost his life, my grandfather lost his farm, and I had lost my freedom and nearly my mind. Suddenly I felt I was back on the playground, back in the third grade emotionally, and truth be told, I was mad at the SG for cheating at the game. I saw them as having all the green houses and the red motels. At least for now. I had to come up with a way of taking them back. Life was suddenly as simple as that.

I sat on the couch looking out the window as the snow fell. The wind was up and rattling the shutters. The younger cats had been curled up on me, but now they started to wake up a bit more and decided to launch an attack on my feet. There was a giant in their mist that must be slain. I was learning to take my cue from them, from nature. They were incapable of deceit. I was on a roll. Ideas, were shifting into place click after click. If nature was truth, and the one who created nature was truth, then He must exist. All the times Niner had blamed me for making him into what he was, suddenly made sense. I was the creator, the wizard to him. That equation balanced for him. I moved the formula forward and applied it to myself. If we humans were made in the image of our Creator, then we were programmed to find the truth the way that he had intended for us to find it. Could it be that simple? We were made in His likeness, and like sought like. A machine had seen it before I had. Well, Niner was pure logic, I consoled myself.

From that point of reference I moved on to recalling another conversation I had had with the drone which had confounded me: "The earth works according to laws that have been set in motion. They exist and cannot be changed," Niner had told me. "Gravity is there and it is indifferent to whether you believe in it or not. If you jump from a high place, you will fall, and if you jump from a high enough point, you will be injured or die. Fractions for me, and broken bones for you. Either way, it is a mess," he had said. "Humpty was proof of that."

"What are you talking about?" I had said to him.

"I was just giving you a literary allusion in literature to give my point more of a punch. I am emulating you, Trave."

"Humpty isn't exactly an accepted historical or scientific point of reference."

"He should be. Mr. Dumpty did fall, did he not?"

"According to the story."

"That is truth then. It is not fiction because it contains elements of the truth. Now argument two. They tried to make him into a whole egg again and failed, did they not?"

"That's what the story claims."

"Ergo it contains two points of truth that cannot be argued."

"It's Mr. Dumpty that wasn't real, not the facts about him. Eggs do break."

"That is the disputable subject matter, Trav. You say that men said that the Wizard of Oz was an allusion, a metaphor, a literary device to represent things that the story stood for. According to logic, that is not possible. You cannot allude to something that does not exist. In summation, the literary devices of simile and metaphor exist to express this dilemma. As a simile we want to be like the Wizard, but as a metaphor we are the Wizard."

"I'm losing you in the translation."

"I am like you. Things I do can be used as a literary allusion to you, but in order for that to be possible there has to be a you. In other words, you must exist before I can make a comparison to you, an allusion to you. There has to be an established reference point."

"I think you have stumbled onto something, Niner."

"Literary allusions are shadows of the real. It cannot be the other way around."

"That is a unique way of interpreting it."

"If you had never existed, I would be said to be referencing some other human like Zel."

"She is not human, fully."

"There is only 7 ounces missing from the totality."

"How can you be so sure? How can you measure what is no longer there?" I smiled. I was sure I had him there.

"The Correalean effect."

"What's that?"

"It was a type of photography that was found in the middle twentieth century that proved what we would later ascribe as proof to the theory that matter could neither be created or destroyed."

"Explain."

"It was accidently discovered by a Russian who was using his new x ray camera to take pictures of a leaf. It happened that the leaf had a piece of itself torn away, but under the special lenses he was using to photograph it, an aura began to appear around the missing edges of the leaf causing it to become whole again. It was not whole in reality, but its missing pieces were accounted for as if it was whole under the camera's lens. Next, the Russians began to experiment on all manner of things. Men with missing fingers were put under this light and the fingers became whole again in the energy field. The matter which had once existed was still there even though you could not see it without the special light. I see Zel's missing part in just that way, Trav."

"Everything remains whole in the invisible realm?"

"That is what I have been telling you. There is one thing I might add though. It doesn't work on robotoids, drones, cars, or rocks."

"Why?"

"They are non-vibrant things. How did you miss all this in your profession?"

I shrugged. "I can't know everything."

So life showed whole in the aura around it no matter was done to it, I thought. That was some sort of magic, I deduced and looked at Sam. I kept my eyes on Sam, but his expression didn't change. He wasn't going to comment on the topic. Maybe Niner had hit too close to home. After all, Niner had gotten a different reading on Sam. What if he was right? I didn't need to get all twisted about it, he could just as well be wrong. Either way, I thought, there was nothing any of us could do about it. We were a group of odd balls, a mixed bag of humans and clones and drones, oh my!

The work crowd that ate was going off to get their tableware and cups. Zel was just sitting by the fire eating deer and drinking water. It was a human thing to do and separated her from the drones, crosslings, and robos. For the first time I saw her as more human than not. Her blondish hair lay in gentle wavy patterns across her face, framing it with innocence. She appeared almost childlike, and suddenly I found myself weeping. The tears made me angry. I was glad it was evening because then I felt more comfortable with Zel in the darkness. She couldn't see my eyes and I couldn't see hers. I felt shielded somehow. Just then Niner brought his cup over by us. "Mind if I join you?"

"What are you doing? What do you have in that cup?"

"I'm not going to drink it, if that's what you mean."

"Go ahead. Short circuit yourself," I said.

"I'm practicing so when I can eat and drink I will have the movements down. I've been reading up on etiquette," he said as he held a knife and fork in his talons and cut the meat that was on his plate. He worked diligently to cut very tiny pieces. "There," he said quite pleased with himself, "those are about the right size for a bird, don't you think?"

"Stop this Niner. You look odd, out of place. Stranger than strange."

"What? Birds aren't supposed to have manners?"

"They don't use knives and forks. They weren't meant to." All of a sudden I felt at war with him. This obsession of his to become human was driving me crazy. I looked from face to face and tried to pick out the real humans again. I felt panic and sickness rush from my stomach up into my cheeks and I let go of the food I had just eaten. It came up before I even realized what was happening. I got up and left. I heard Niner's little feet on the gravel behind me. "Stay away from me," I told him as I clutched at my stomach again. I felt another waterfall erupting in my bowels, and it came in swells that made my whole being wretch.

"You act like there's something wrong with me, or wrong with what I am doing," Niner said.

"You're a bird, a drone, a machine. You don't even have a stomach."

"I will have one soon. The girls are going to fix me up since you won't."

"No. This nightmare is coming to an end. You won't be human. Ever. No matter what parts are attached to you."

"I will be real when we find the wizard. He will breathe life into me."

"You have it backwards, bird brain. He does that to begin with, not after you have glued feathers on yourself and coated yourself with some kind of synthetic stretch putty you think is skin. I don't care if you can eat a whole deer and expel it out the other end. You'll still be just a mechanical shell with artificial intelligence. "

"I see. You sound like Ben now."

"Give it up."

"So you see me as less just like you see Zel."

"I never said that."

"But you meant it. Well, I believe the wizard cares about us all, even if you don't."

I was leaning against a tree with one hand against it to steady myself after I had let go with another upheaval of contents from my stomach. I was feeling shaky and could barely see straight. My head was still near the ground when I felt a hand touch my back gently. "You're right, Niner, the Creator cares about everything," I heard Sam say. "Can I do anything for you, Trave?"

"No, I'm fine."

"Then let's take a walk down to the stream. Cold water will do you good."

"Talk some sense into him, Joseph. He's mean," the drone eagle said.

"Yes, Niner."

"Can I ask you a question before you leave, Joseph?" Niner said padding up to him.

"Yes, of course."

"Do you think I will get a soul?"

"That's not for me to answer."

I saw the bird's head droop. "Then I am doomed. You are the closest being to the source."

"Now wait, Niner. I have no say in the matter."

"Then you will go with me to meet the wizard?"

"The entire world will be there, eagle. Everyone will have their lives accounted for."

"When this happens, do you think I am worth a soul? Would he grant me one?"

"It is not on the basis of merit that his judgement comes. It is by justice."

"Then I am doomed."

"Do you believe in the Creator's ability to judge? Do you find his words fair and honorable?"

"The manual is the height of truth," the little drone said looking up at Sam who towered above him.

"Then trust him to know what to do. Can you do that?"

"Yes. That is a logical answer, Joseph. I will let you argue with Travis now. I should see to my squad."

I was glad Niner was still focused on his duty. Someone needed to be checking for enemy drones. I was sure they would be returning. There were hu-manimals like me on the loose.

We walked in silence. Sam did not speak until we reached the stream where the barge sat. Finally he spoke, and without looking at me said, "It will take three rowboats to power the barge. It's loaded down pretty heavily."

I wasn't looking back at him, I was kneeling on the shore and cupping water in my hands to wash over my face and rinse my mouth out. I only wanted the cold water to soothe me, to make the convulsions in my stomach stop. I stuck my head in as far as I could without falling into the stream and then stood up to spit the water out into the grass. I turned to see Sam tying the canoes to the front of the barge. To my amazement, I heard my self tell Sam that I would lend a hand. I found myself grabbing the far end of the canoe rope and helping him to pull it through the water. There were three canoes which we now tied to the front of the barge. These three small boats would supply the power needed to propel the barge forward.

In the midst of this activity Sam dropped a zinger on me. "You've finally gotten a belly full of the world, huh?" I didn't answer, and he continued.

"Niner has a dream, a goal. He has set his every movement towards that end."

"The journey of life is not its glory alone," Sam said. "Come with me. I want to show you something."

I stood braced and looked at him. I was not going to move an inch.

"It's your enemies which lead you to your path," he said starting the climb up the twisting path towards the cliff. "Follow me." I didn't feel like it, but it was like some force drew me on despite the objections I had with Sam. It was a long ways up the mountain side and we made the trek in silence.

When we reached the summit he said, "Remove your shoes. You are moving onto sacred ground." He was already taking off his boots. Next, he walked to an upright stone which sat alone in the middle of the small butte. I was curious as to what it might be and removed my shoes. When I came to the stone I saw that there was writing on it.

"It is an ancient steele," he said. "Read it aloud, but first you must kneel."

I did as he instructed and then read the rune. 'According to the command of the greatest and most high God, those that take an oath proceed from here.' I turned to face Sam. "What does it mean?"

"Rise, Travis. Your armor is upon you and your sword is in your mouth."

"What is all this?"

"Haven't you decided on a path? Isn't that what you told me last night?"

"How did you know this was here?"

"You are not asking the right questions, Newman."

"And you are not answering them. I want to know what is going on. I won't move an inch until you do."

"This same stone appears on many mountains all over the world."

"Skip the geography lesson. I want to know what it means."

"One thing I can tell you it means is that it is writing, instuctions left from I Am. You always thought that writing meant something more than emoji's, didn't you, Trave? The alphabet started taking shape from the time of Moses and the hieroglyphics of the Egyptians was transformed into Hebrew. Writing is the intellect, the mind of the creator so that throughout all generations people would know he created them and this world. Emoji's express nothing beyond emotions. They are no true form of communication."

"Let me rephrase it, Sam. What have I just done?"

"You have taken the first step towards your destiny."

I let out a laugh. "I haven't decided on anything."

"You have decided to go after the Eternals, have you not?"

"I don't know. Maybe."

"It has been set in motion. You have not been persuaded otherwise. The I am lets you choose your own way now. Your enemies have led you to the path."

"I can still change my mind."

"It is too late."

I let out another laugh.

"You still have a ways to go, Trave."

"I don't like the way you said that, Sam."

He looked at me squarely and did not back down. "You are the human, yet you show the least empathy of all."

I could feel the contempt directed at me. "You blame me, don't you?"

"How do you separate the thought from the man and condemn the life that does not agree with you? Isn't that what the SG and the One World has done?" He stopped talking and began fumbling around in his book bag and brought out the Manual. He held it up to me. "If a being is sacred and honors your philosophy of life so you must honor his. What is written and spoken cannot be changed."

"All the stuff of legends, stories. This is real life, Joseph, not a waste land of dragons, wudgies, mothmen, and quantum mechanics."

"I speak of the oath now. Niner has honored it."

"Let him believe in whatever he wants. I don't care if he believes Snow White was real."

"You brought him and other things into the world."

"So that makes me responsible?"

"Definitive reasoning always makes it someone else's fault. It began the vortex of reality that has landed us where we are at today, past the wars, the fallen civilizations of the Romans, the Greeks, the Babylonians, the Monguls, etc., etc. What was their purpose, what did they live for? We are the ones left to reason. History does leave its mark, Trave. You have followed its tracks, and they were as clear and traceable as footprints in newly fallen snow. All stories are the same, Trave. Don't be fooled and think yours is unique. Human life was sacred from the beginning."

"You're just going to keep at it until I capitulate, aren't you?"

"That's how the heart is changed."

I said nothing.

"Ask for forgiveness. It is not the falling, the failings of men that provides the shining in them? The glory is that rebirthing happens in the human species."

We sat on the mountain until the sun was about to set, but neither of us had let go an inch of ourselves to the other. It was like wrestling with a monster of megalithic size, but it was his force of will that overshadowed mine, and suddenly I was afraid of the coming darkness and the steep and hazardous trail which lead back down the mountain. I wanted this test of will over and gave in to him by rationalizing that I didn't really believe in oaths, anyway. They were just words, and they could always be taken back.

"There is the power of life and death in the words we speak," he said as I bowed before the stone and drank from the cup he handed me and ate the small piece of bread with it.

Just then I heard Niner's rotors and I could see him flying up to us. "I will light your way back down," he said shining his high beams down on the path from under his belly just in front of where his talons were now. "I am glad you took the oath."

"You knew where I was going?"

"I have stood where you stand."

I didn't say another word all the way back down. When we reached the bottom, I looked at the sky and back up the mountain. Both were cast in colors of deep purples, but the sky was also strafed with fiery oranges and reds as the sun sparked brighter just before it dropped behind the ridges. "Majestic, isn't it?" Sam asked.

"Light scatters. Red has the longest rays, so it is the last color to fade from the sky," Niner said.

"The evidence is all there before your eyes. Even the sunset is more evidence of creation than of evolution," Sam said.

"Yes, light comes to the eye at the molecular level. A single photon of light causes the mind to collect and interpret data faster than any super computer which enables us to instantly see the colors," the drone said.

"But what do you feel when you look at the sunset, Niner?" I asked.

"After analyzing how the eye filters the variations of light and collects data, I know it points to the fact that all this magnificence is not millions of years old or some cosmic accident. It's too perfect," he continued as he was trying to get the video to stream in on his viewer.

"That isn't what I asked."

Instead of answering, Niner busied himself with the videos he wanted to show to me on his screen. "I have pics of the chambers and meeting rooms of the subterrean city. I'm having a bit of trouble with the audio," he said still fiddling with the keys, "but you can see them."

The drone put his screen down where both of us could see it clearly. On the screen were thirteen men in dark robes gathered around a circle in a cavernous like room made of solid crystals which resembled a big city skyline. The background of buildings and streets was a discordant image almost like it was some 3D poster propped up against a wall. It had depth and dimension to it and seemed to go on for miles. I knew it must be real even if it appeared to be nothing more than icy glass. I had been there.

"The black circle on the floor represents the black sun which is the antithesis to the one in our world," Sam explained, and I refocused my attention on the men again. The circle they stood in was carved out and set below the floor about six inches. A round black circle was on each robe exactly like the circle on which the men stood.

"To them the reality of the world is evil, so the their wheel shaped symbol is meant to be indicative of a hollow earth which is a sacred womb. It is a representation used since pagan times and was even used by the Nazi's in WWII who believed it to be a prototype, a blueprint from the stars that was given to man by mysterious alien visitors. They believed that the shape of the symbol itself allows great energy to be harnessed and used by man."

I was concentrating on the video as he spoke. The man in the center of the circle was holding a rune stone of sorts and speaking, though we could not hear his words. Then suddenly out of the stone he was holding fireworks burst forth in a lighted montage of holograms. I saw many armies marching, squadrons of unmanned tactical planes, light amplified directed weapons firing radiation at beings, and species of all kinds. Buildings and whole cities were being destroyed. I saw tanks rolling with their lasers firing. There was war, war, and more war.

As we watched the armies roll by on the screen, Niner gave us a rundown of their capabilities. "Those weapons on the tanks and planes are direct firing weaponry that pack 175,00 volts of energy more powerful that a nuk bomb. Simply put, it is a directed ray of 192 separate laser points all coming together and meeting in a single plane as a super beam. Their mounted lasers travel at DASOL, destruction at the speed of light, and they burn at 1200 degrees Fahrenheit which will ignite you from the inside out, turning you into a brief puff of smoke."

Each time an image flew out of the crystal rune, the men walking in circles would lift their heads up from their bowed positions and join hands briefly before passing the giant crystal to the next person.

"Counterfeit astral projections," Joseph said spitting on the ground as the images continued to pour out from the crystal. "Quantum quackery. Even Einstein was against it."

"The projections may be unreal, but the weapons exist. I have seen them. I was trained on them," Niner said looking at us.

That scene ended and in the next one we saw the men sitting around an oblong table in a meeting room. Suddenly I was transported back in time. I gasped. I remembered that room. "I've been in there," I said out loud. I recalled sitting there wearing the same shirts as these men had on now and with a mind that thought as they thought. It was the controlled setting of a militaristically regimented society, I thought now, and laughed.

"It is the beast that talks. He was once forgotten, but has awakened and has been given all power for a short season. At the heart is the castle, the stronghold," Joseph said.

It seemed to me that Joseph's voice had a timorous quality to it. Could it be that the lion was afraid?

"This isn't real. None of it is real. They are play acting. They want it to be so."

"You were there, Travis. You worked and lived among them. You know that it is more than that. That's why they got rid of you. Asphorsh is taking control through genetic engineering. You were against it, remember? Here's your chance to reverse his grasp at singularity, Travis."

"I never took part in anything like this. You're as mad as Niner is," I said getting up from the ground and bushing my jeans off. Sam slammed the portable computer lid down and followed after me.

"Stop wandering around in some fugue state like some actor toying between choosing between the Stanislavski or Meissner method of emoting to the world. Make up your mind, Travis. Which side of the stream are you on?"

"I'm not the pretender here. I want none of this. I'm out of here."

"You are the only one with the skills and intelligence to stop him."

"You're wrong, Ranger Joe. I'm just starting to remember things from the past. I barely know who I am now let alone who I was then. I have forgotten most of it."

"Stop denying who you are. Your mind came back. Just why do you think that's so?"

"Are you going to tell me you did it?"

"I helped steer you in the right directions. So did Niner."

I turned around to see where Niner was. I could hear his wings flapping behind us. "Fly, Niner. Fly into a cloud and hide and never come back. This guy is your enemy. He wants me to end all AI life."

"That is not true, Trave. Joseph is close to the source. He is close to the wizard."

I felt Sam grab on to my arm. "It's your chance to make amends."

"Even if I agreed to stop Asphorsh I couldn't. I haven't operated in decades."

"You birthed me," the drone said flying in front of us. "My organs and mind are fine and adapting like a real human more each day. You are the wizard, Trave. You still have the gift. Use it. Preserve your own kind."

"He's right. Niner was a test run for you."

"You two are straight out of a fairy tale not fit to tell."

"That's the problem with this new reality. Everyone changes it to fit their needs because they can't bear it otherwise. It doesn't jive with their own mind," Joseph said.

"That's what I said, it is all myths, all lies."

"But myth is the preparation for understanding the real story, Trave."

"And what's the real scoop?"

"It's in the Basic Instructions," he said holding the book up.

"Just accept the fact that I have chosen my path and that it doesn't follow the same arrows as yours, Good Neighbor Sam."

"That may be what you think, Travis, but it is our enemies that choose our paths for us. They are the guides."

"Stop saying that. I disagree. Your wires are mixed upstairs, Ranger Joe."

"Your armor is already fashioned on you. Take up your sword."

"Just shut up. I don't know what story you're reading from, but throw it out." I left the two of them standing behind me and headed back towards the direction of the house.

"I'm off. I'm outta here."

"You can't redefine the ancient prophecies," he called after me.

I began running faster, and without looking back, I waved my goodbyes. Reaching the top of the crest I stopped to admire the view. The land and the mountains stretched as far as I could see. The coming night put everything in shadows and silence and gave it a reverent touch. I looked back down the hill at Sam and the drone. Could the future really be changed? I wrestled with feelings of hatred, loathing, anger and despair. It didn't have to be this way, I heard myself saying, and yet I felt strangely responsible for it. I had been a part of it before being made a prisoner of the state. I had survived the gulag, the death waves, Manhattan, and the journey thus far. I was using lives up at a ferocious pace. Could what Sam told me be true? Had he and Niner had brought me to this place? Was I no more than a character in a story, their story? My mind was reeling.

I heard steps behind me and turned to find Joseph at my heels. How had he made up the distance between us so quickly?

"What do you remember, Trave?" I heard him ask. His voice was filled with serious concern. I was filled with unbridled fury.

We were like boxers in the ring staring at each other and waiting for the first punch to be landed. "You find terror at every thought. You want to escape, but there is nowhere to go," he said.

"I have made my plans."

"You have heard the truth, written it all down," he said. "You think you have planned your next move, but the I Am orders your steps. You cannot move without him."

I said nothing to Sam because I understood he was talking about Niner and all the drones and robos and hybrids in the world. I was beginning to reject what I had done earlier in life and what I had done with Niner. I had begun to see it as an unnatural act. My anger turned into tears and I sat down in the grass. Sam stayed where he was and made no move towards me. "Try and see that Niner has a nightmare of his own he can't escape from," he continued. "He wants to be human. His mind is able to process the concept, but somewhere he is frightened that he might be trapped inside a machine, a cyber reality of incompleteness. He has one hope and that is to find the wizard."

Joseph continued to play the scenes from the compound on his computer that Niner had brought back to us. I began to recognize a few of my old associates. As the montage streamed over the computer, I caught bits and pieces of the words my colleagues were tossing around in conversation. 'Are you dark dna? Which planet do you id with the most? Is it fairy talk? Have you attained the ashram state? What were you reborn as?' My mind was swimming in regret. These philosophies were all fantasy.

"Asphorsh fully intends to gain control through genetic engineering," Sam said to me again. "You know he does. You helped create this."

"Don't even go there."

He put a hand on my shoulder. "Remember whose world this is." Then without warning his hand dropped away from me and he was walking away. "These hu-brids are not of the wizard," he said without looking back at me. "The Being of Light thought he had won centuries ago until the waters washed his army away, remember? It has taken him this long to bring it back." Without being able to see him standing in front of me, it was like hearing a voice from the dark void, and it left me cold and fearful.

I started to laugh again, though more hysterically this time.

"They call themselves the eternals don't' they?" Sam yelled at me.

"Let them call themselves kings or earthworms. I'm headed for Alaska," I said.

"You're headed for extinction."

"What am I supposed to do, send a flood?"

"Wage a war."

"Battle the eternals? Hey, I'm not stupid. They have a roving parts department you know, complete with skin and eyeballs."

"Don't let ego destroy hearing the truth, Trav. I have protected you this far. The rest you must do with the aid of those that have been given to you."

"I'm supposed to believe you have been put here to protect me?"

"Your mind came back, didn't it?" It was at this point I looked at him again. He had my card hand beat so I did not bother to answer his question. Why was he always one or two plays ahead of me? The truth was I had been spooked again. His voice was like an echo to my own thoughts, but this time I intended to stand my own ground. It was time to put the cards on the table. "That's it," I said encroaching on his physical presence. "I want to know who you are."

"I am just as Niner said I was."

"And what was that?"

"Ask him to explain it again."

A rain of bullets came out of nowhere just at that moment, and I jumped behind a tree as I watched Sam do likewise. I reached for my cell to send the attack signal to Niner, but I saw him approach from the east. He was already in flight formation, and was out in front of his squadron. As soon as the enemy drones got a bead on him, they surrounded him. He flew in circles around us, protecting us from the attackers. It was his shadow I saw directly above me. He was marvelous to watch. Suddenly he was in a tail spin. All I spotted was laser's hitting him from all directions. All I could see at first was a flurry of feathers, but then I saw a larger form descending out of the fluff of confetti. It was Niner himself. It didn't take long for him to hit ground. I ran over to him at once. "Niner, can you hear me? Report."

"Trave, it hurts. That synthetic skin is not bullet or laser proof. I am wounded."

All I could do was nod. His feathers had been singed off from his entire body. His tail was gone. His right wing was folded back in on itself. The other wing was snapped off. He was torn apart. "Did you get the ones who did this to me, who killed me?" he asked.

"Don't talk Niner. Machines don't die. We're going to fix you back up," I said looking at Sam. "Aren't we?"

"I gave up my protective shield to be more real," the drone gasped looking up at Joseph.

Nothing registered on Sam's' face. "Well, say something," I yelled, but I knew he would not answer.

I couldn't hold back the tears, but I was more angry than upset. "Joseph's leaving. He won't be able to help," Niner said in the silence.

"What have you told him?" I yelled at Sam, but Niner interrupted before the stranger could answer. "He told me nothing. Joseph must go back. He is being called. Turn me so I can see the boys flying," the eagle requested resting against my arms.

"There are a lot in your squad left," Sam said. "You were a fine commander."

"Don't use the title they gave me."

"Of course. I'm sorry, Niner."

"Don't talk like this, Niner. I'm going to fix you up. The girls and I will make you better than new," I said ignoring everyone else.

"No. Leave me dead. I am human that way. The wizard of all will come."

"The miracle of the soul," Zel said coming into our circle.

"Joseph, pull the plug," the drone said looking over at him. "The pain is more than I can bear. I thought of only the good things touch could bring." His gaze shifted back to me. "I really didn't believe you about the pain. I see now you were trying to spare me, Travis. Take my alpha drive out, later. There's a message in hologram form for you. Then he leaned forward and his voice was weaker. "Come closer, Trave. I have something I want to tell only you."

"We will leave," Sam said, touching Zel's shoulder to guide her away.

"Our whole relationship was based on stories, and if there's one thing I learned about telling stories, it was not to spoil the ending. I know I shouldn't tell you how this all sorts out, but you win, you get the prize," Niner said when the others were out of hearing range. "Joseph told me. He's always right, you know. Funny though, I thought he said I was there with you."

"You have to stay and see it end. You have given your heart to this fight."

"You spent the entire time we were together trying to get me to see that the rabbit and wizard were fiction. Now when I tell you I see it, you change the answer again. Make up your mind, human. Time is short."

"I was wrong. You are real, Niner. More real than anyone I have ever known."

"I know the truth. I am not real. It is a false reality, a cyberspace that doesn't really exist outside the mind." He paused, and when he spoke again his voice had a recognition of fear in it. "Trave, the wizard is not here to greet me."

I heard a click and immediately his wings let go of their rigidness. He lay still. His eyes were closed. I turned to see

Good Neighbor Sam holding the remote. "What did you tell him to make him give up his quest for life?" I screamed at him.

"I answered the questions he asked me," the stranger said.

"And what were those?"

"I showed him the passages in the Manual. He read them for himself and made up his own mind. I did not know they pertained to his dilemma of being man created."

"You should have guessed. You seem to know what everyone else is thinking."

"I gave him the truth. It is over for him now. We need to go on."

"He gave his life for us just now. That makes him as real as the rest of us in my book."

"Don't you see he knew what he was. He wanted to end it."

I moved against the stranger and drew my fists up against him.

"He told you so himself, Trave," Zel said putting herself in between us.

It was at that point, when I felt her hands touch mine, that I could no longer hold back the tears. "He saved my life today. Doesn't that make him as human as anyone? A drone wouldn't have done that."

"Give it some time, Trave," Sam was saying. "Niner finally realilized that the reality in the mind in not the true reality."

"Damn. Just shut up. You did this to Niner. You brought the attack. It came out of nowhere. Even Niner had not seen it register." I knew it sounded crazy to accuse him, but I felt it was true.

I threw down my gun and went to the barge and started emptying out one of the crates. "What are you doing?" Zel called out to me.

"I can't leave his body lying there. I'm looking for a container to put him in."

"We'll have a ceremony for him," Sam said.

"No, I'm taking him with us."

I saw Zel give Sam a look and grab his arm. Sam patted her and then the two just turned away and started walking. Zel glanced back at me every now and then as they walked. I had Niner tucked under my left arm and carried my laser in my right hand as I followed behind them.

Once back at camp, I told everyone what had happened. I said I was going to Denver to fight them. Those that wanted to come, could, and those that chose to sail down the river could go. I gave them the right to make their own decisions.

It was sometime in the middle of the night that I decided to get up and put in Niner's flight and life recorder drive. As soon as I did, a light flashed, and then words began to form: MESSAGE AVAILABLE. I hit the key on my computer and the message typed itself out:

Time is not linear nor can it be represented or depicted in vertical or horizontal planes. It coils like DNA. It is a continuous slinky toy, Trave. It's not possible to turn back time or move ahead in it. There is no point A or point B because there is no beginning or end. Neither is time light. Light measures time as distance. Time gives the illusion of movement. As objects around us pass us by it creates the appearance of time passing when it hasn't. It is the endless looping of the slinky that causes that misinterpretation. Time does not move. Its spirals are infinite. There is no beginning and there is no end.

Get it, Trave? Time stands still. The past, present and future are the same moment. Light moves. The earth moves. Einstein thought time and space bent. It does, but in a never ending downward spiral so it cannot be stopped. Note: You cannot cut a spiral like you can a straight line to stop it. Gravity keeps it moving, looping always and forever. That's why there is no going back and no going forward. Only the wizard sees the whole distance of the coil at once."

I had just read the message, but didn't know what to make of it. I read it over and was struck by the fact that it seemed to repeat certain concepts. What had it to do with the mission? This is not something we had ever discussed. What had it to do with anything?

I was not about to let his message deter me from the task at hand and I next took out his memory and plugged in his memory flash. I was instantly greeted by his holograms which sprung out like jack in the boxes. I spent much of the night watching the memories he had created. In a way I had to see them. I felt I owed him that much.

The first memory that played was of Niner learning to walk. I pushed the play button forward and the holograms came faster. Hearing his voice and seeing him made me love him. I saw Zel reading to him, the cats walking beside him, him feeding the cats, and conducting drills with the squad. The very last images were of Niner holding a book up. It was the Wizard of Oz. Then the hologram became garbled. I saw Sam and Niner and a brilliant flash of light. Next Niner was bowing down. His eyes were lifted up as he covered them with his wings. I had been presented with another mystery. I had no recollection of that image and wondered why Sam had been included in it.

From somewhere out of the darkness Zel had joined me. I touched the box the eagle was in. He was still. His wings lay over his head. Death is an odd sight. There is something about the motionlessness of death that is unnatural. Life, whether human or artificial, becomes futile at that point; to have been rich or famous, happy or sad no longer matters. It was of no consequence whether one had ever even existed. The body is as useless as a tin can or a stick of wood when rendered motionless. It is a toy without batteries. It had always been unfathomable to me that life could just end. I had always felt that we were meant to live forever. Isn't that why we were given a soul and spirit? Didn't possessing a soul make us eternal? I was as sure of that fact right now as I was that the river would freeze in winter. Somewhere deep inside of me I had always sensed an immortal spark existed in the human race. That thought had existed in me since childhood. It was what gave children their invincibility. It was a built in gene so it had to be there for a reason. My thinking had come three sixty in a manner of moments. What was so wrong with living for eternity? What was wrong with drones wanting to possess a soul?

I turned to Zel. "I'll fix him up. It may take some time, but I'll get the parts."

"Leave him be, Trave," Sam said. "He's found peace."

"Peace? It's entropy. Decay. Uselessness. He was the happiest crossling in the world."

"Was he? He had desires that couldn't be fulfilled."

"He didn't know the difference. None of the AI's do."

"That's psychological abuse. He coveted life. Nothing but being human could satisfy him. He even gave up his protective shield to be closer to becoming a real being. He opened himself up to death to be human."

"That's the way things are in this world. There's not much real left."

"So that makes it okay?"

"Hey, everything takes place in the mind. That's where the important things happen."

"No, the mind is not your own private universe," Sam said. "It does not make things real just because you want them to be."

Everyone was up and had joined us by now. "Did you see the flash of light?" Zel said to try and change the subject.

"I did," Kara confirmed. "Must have been his circuits."

"It wasn't," I said.

"Have you checked?" the girl asked looking at me.

"I don't need to. The flash was on the outside. It covered both Niner and Sam." As I spoke, I watched Sam. I knew he had something to do with it, I just didn't know what. He wasn't merely a good Samaritan, he was a magician. That was when I remembered Niner had said Sam, or Joseph, or whatever his real name was had registered more vibrant than the rest of us species. Maybe that was why he wanted Niner out of the way. I walked over to the drone crossling and picked him up.

"I know he was like a best friend to you," Kara said. "I will help you reanimate him if you would let me. We can go to town and get what we need."

"I prefer to use the house as a laboratory."

"Of course."

We walked away and the woman looped her hands through mine. The touch was soft and natural and it made me feel like she had always been there.

"Trave, you're making a mistake," Zel called out. When I turned back to look, Sam was standing beside her.

"You've picked your side. Make sure you stay on it," I called out to her.

"Damn you humans, and your primordial yelps," she yelled back.

I heard Kara laugh and I turned to her. "And they say we humans are emotional. I think she's jealous of me."

"Zel?"

"She's a female, isn't she? I've seen the way she looks at you. Don't tell me you haven't noticed."

I was caught off guard by her directness and decided to offset her accusatory tone with a little truth. "I've ignored it."

"You two haven't?" she added wryly.

"No." As I looked at Kara I decided it was she that was the jealous one. She was afraid I had formed an affectionate bond with Zel and wanted to make sure I didn't. Kara was making her claims on me, and I wasn't up to the offer of being taken or owned by a woman. I had known men who liked things that way. They let women dictate to whom they could form a relationship with, where and when they could go, and for how long. It was really a form of leash. Some men used that as a handy tool to lay the blame on the woman in their life and relieve themselves for the responsibility of having made decisions on their own. At an earlier time in my life, I would have succumbed to her claims on me, but now I was my own. There was bound to be trouble down the line, but I let it ride. Kara was more my equal than Zel on an intellectual and physical level in that she was human. However, I much preferred Zel's coloring and features over Kara's, and yes, as implausible as it might seem, Zels' kindness.

We took Niner into the living room and put him on the floor. Nothing was where it had been after the missiles had hit.

Whole sections of walls had been knocked down, but it still felt like home. A few of the books I had read were still on the coffee table. There was a blanket on the chair and a teacup on a saucer sat on an end table defying the attacks had never happened.

I removed the debris from a portion of the floor where the sun shone down, and where I thought it would be the warmest now that cold weather was setting in. It was the first time I had been back since the battle and the memories of this place crowded my mind. I had gotten more used to recalling things by now, but it still created a haunting feeling of sorts because of the sadness it left in me. I felt the on rush of a migraine as I tried to push the old thoughts away. There were too many open wounds.

I saw that Kara had just opened Niner's chest by removing the bolts and lifting the cover. "Don't do that," I said.

She looked at me in a startled way, but recovered very quickly, and by the time she spoke, she was in command of herself. "We need to know which systems have been affected."

"Yes, of course. I'll get a pen and paper."

I stood beside her when I returned, but I didn't feel the same about her. I had been repulsed by the way she had touched Niner's inner self. She moved in so perfunctory and detached a way that it gave me a chill. Surely these were not the same hands that had held my hand while we had walked through the meadow. I saw her new pair of hands as probing and cold, and the feeling of intimacy vanished.

"Have you gotten everything down I told you to?" I heard her saying.

"Huh?" I said coming back to the moment.

"Give me the list. I'll check it."

I felt the paper being pulled from my hand. Why was I so numb? I was staring at her while she was reading over the list. "Looks complete. Let's get going."

"You go."

"You would let me go into town alone?"

"I'm not feeling so well," I feigned. I just wanted to get away from her.

"We haven't got time to waste. Toughen up," she said and crossed over to the back of the couch. I heard her open up the container of ammo and then the metal jackets being loaded into position. Kara threw me one of the guns. "Old style weapons, but they were handy. Let's get moving."

I don't know whether it was my irritation at Kara or what, but I felt reticent about bringing Niner back all of a sudden. There was a surreal quality to the scene I found myself in, and I felt I was watching myself act out a scene in a play. No, it was worse than that. I was a game piece on a board that was waiting for the spin that would tell me how many spaces to move. I suddenly felt like an animae object, and I found myself in the sky car without knowing how I had gotten there. I sat looking out the window in silence wondering how the world had flip flopped on me and I had become the drone.

Almost a week later we were still working on Niner when the door to the house opened and Zel stepped in. She had been running and was out of breath. I went over to her. "What's wrong?"

"Joseph's gone."

I picked up a pillow and punched it and then threw it back down. "Damn. I had a feeling about that guy. He's gone to turn us in."

"I don't believe that, Trave," Zel said coming over to the table. "He said he was coming back."

"I'll believe that when I see it."

"How's Niner doing?" Zel said moving closer to the body we were working on.

"He'll be better than he was. I've given him more tactile ability and he'll be able to flap and fly to his heart's content," Kara answered before I could.

"Will he remember his life before?"

"We're about to find that out," I said entering the code.

"Wow," Zel exclaimed touching his body and wings, "he's got more lifelike feathers."

"Why don't we send Niner out to find Joseph?" Zel said turning to me.

"Forget about Sam. He's gone and that's it."

"Did he go to get things ready for us?" a familiar voice asked. It was Niner's voice and I turned towards the table.

"Hey, buddy. How you doing?"

"I feel lighter, funny," he said looking at his body and feathers. "Are these real feathers?" He was running his beak over his chest and looking at his wings repeatedly.

"Give them a flap," I said walking over to him.

"Wow, lots of moving parts," he said waving one wing and then the other.

"Let me move you down to the floor. Practice on the ground until you get the hang of it," Tara was saying.

"New feet, too," he said immediately when he touched the ground.

"You have retractable claws now. Razor sharp. You'll have to learn how to pull them in before you walk," Kara said watching him flex his claws in and out.

"This is a snap. I got it," he said flapping his wings and knocking over the cups and books on the coffee table. "Take me outside."

"Walk over to the door and I will open it for you," I said.

We watched him run around in the yard. "I'll give those chickens a one for the money now."

"Do you feel strong enough to try and fly up to where I am holding my arm out?" Kara asked.

"That's a cinch. A few flaps," he said running to get a head start.

"You should be able to take off from a standing position from now on," Kara told him.

"I wanted some extra power in back of me," he said, lifting off the ground. He wobbled back and forth before landing.

"You're a natural, Niner," Zel said going over to pet his head.

"For a drunken sailor," I said.

"What's this about Joseph?" Niner said again and moved his head around so he could look at me. "Hey, Trave, This motion stuff is great. I can see things like at 290," he said still moving his head from side to side.

"Zel was just giving us the news about Sam when you woke up."

"What happened, Zel? What sent him away?" the drone kept pushing.

"I don't know. He was gone when I woke up."

"Did words come between you?"

"No."

"What was the last thing you two talked about?"

"About war and peace."

"That was a long novel. I never finished it," Niner said.

"Everyone went to the movie," I said laughing, "so don't feel bad."

"How'd it end?"

"In peace."

"I figured."

"You have improved night vision now, too."

"Premium upgrades," he said taking off from Kara's arm. He went down mostly nose first and looked at us from the ground. "Who needs a wizard?"

"You need practice," I said. "You hurt?"

"No, but it's a lot quicker going down than it is going up, wings or no wings."

On the walk back, Niner flew alongside of us, and it wasn't long before he was steady in flight. "There is no need to find Joseph. He told me he was going on ahead to get things ready," he said.

"What else did he say, Niner?"

"Nothing. Well, I'm going to fly ahead and make a detour to see my men."

It was after dark and we were eating the last of the chicken when Niner returned. "We were getting worried about you," Zel said.

"I would have stayed longer, but I've got a funny feeling in my stomach. I got worried so I thought I better come back and talk to the wizards."

"Is it right about here?" Kara said touching his under belly.

"Ohhh! Watch it. Your touch feels strange, but it's exactly the spot."

"What have you been doing? Did something hit you there?"

"Just a few practice shots from the squad."

"You have to be more careful, Niner. You have full sensory receptors now. Your sense of touch is heightened."

"What's wrong with me? I'm all soft and squishy."

"That's the way skin and feathers feel. The achy part is because you have a bruise, I think."

"Why does my stomach feel like a bean bag? It's not solid anymore."

"That's what real feels like. Don't you like it?"

"Sure. The feathers stay in place much better now. I was always losing them before. Glue didn't hold up well in wind," Niner said looking around. "Where are the cats? I want to feel their flesh."

"Whistle for Fluff. I think she will come to you," I told him.

"I would rather you call her."

I did, and she came eyeing Niner all the way. "Kitty, don't you know me?" Niner said holding his right wing out to her. She came and he caressed her head. Then he took his talon and felt under her stomach area. "Sand bags. It's squishy like mine."

"You've got to be more careful now," Kara told him.

"Will I break so easily?"

"No, not any more than the rest of us fleshlings."

Just then Fluff came over and started licking his belly and he ruffled his feathers and began laughing, and jumping around. "That is a strange sensation."

"You've just been tickled."

Niner hopped back and Fluff went forward and licked at him again and Niner jumped away. "Stop her," he said over and over. I picked her up and held her. "Come over and pet her when she is on my lap. Be gentle. Soft strokes."

"I know she is breakable now. I have been broken too."

"We mammals aren't breakable in the way you think, Niner. It's not breaking, it's what I told you about feeling pain."

"Her fur is so soft. I want it all about me."

Suddenly Niner flew up to my head and perched on it. He used his talons to feel my hair and began to stroke it which was more like pulling. "Ouch. You can stop now. That hurts."

"It does?"

"Yes, just like this," I said pulling a pin feather from him.

"Ouch," he tried to say.

I lifted him off my head. He sat looking at me. "Trave, if I get hurt next time will I feel more pain than the last time?"

"You are like the rest of us now."

"Hmmmm. Real is scary. Are you afraid of pain?"

"Everyone is."

"How do you live with it?"

"You don't think about it. Remember when Fluff and Hoss were hurt and they just lay there until they felt better?"

"Hmmm. So my belly will feel better?"

"It should in a few days."

"Trave, there is something else I would like to tell you, but I know you are going to be upset."

"How do you know that I will be upset?"

"You were the last time we spoke of it."

"What is it about?"

"Joseph. There is no need for me to go looking for him."

"You found him when you were out with the squad?"

"Yes."

"Where is he? What did he say?"

The eagle was moving his head back and forth indicating a no. "Well, I didn't see or speak with him. I triangulated my GPS, and located him. Well, his general vicinity, anyway."

"Tell me his location."

"It is not possible for you to go there."

"He's in the compound, isn't he?" I blurted out. "Dang, I knew it."

"Wrong direction," Niner said shaking his head.

"Just tell me what it is you are trying to say."

"You're not listening."

"Just tell me. Quit speaking in riddles."

"He's with the wizard."

"Explain."

"I cannot explain it. It is not mathematically solvable or quantifiable."

"I don't care about the math part. Just help me make sense of this."

"This cannot be done."

"Try."

I looked at Niner and he was shaking his head. "This is a mathematically ordered universe. The wizard of all has created it so."

"Forget it," I said reaching for a chunk of meat from the fire and breaking it up for the cats.

"There is no forgetting of any of my information. Once it is programmed it is there until it is erased or new stats are given to my hard drive."

"I didn't mean literally. I meant drop the conversation. Talk of something else."

"Then that is what you should have said. My data show that there is another wizard above Joseph, Trav. The wizard of all. That is who we must find."

"What? What?" I kept stammering.

"There are readings above this earth."

"You can't possibly get readings from up in the galaxy."

"You ascertain correctly, Travis. It is they that come close to our beings at times like Joseph did. They cannot be seen by way of sight until they use a material form. They are spirit, but they are made up of form and matter. Their DNA has been made vibrant. There are no such readings of humans on this planet."

"Are you meaning vibrant as a source of life?"

"Bingo. The Manual says, 'There is one glory of the sun, another glory of the moon and another glory of the stars; for one stars differs from another star in glory. So also is the resurrection of the dead. The body sown in corruption is raised in incorruption. It is sown a natural body, it is raised a spiritual body. However, the spiritual is not the first, but the natural, and afterward the spiritual."

I went to get my Instruction manual and look it up. Sure enough it was spot on. "You're saying you get readings on these spirits?"

"From time to time when they are near."

"I don't believe it. This is preposterous."

"Unbelief is not an option for me. I go on data and analyze it," he said looking adoringly up into Zel's face.

"You're a machine, Niner. Accept it. Gears and hard drives don't become hearts and souls."

"The tinman got his heart and the scarecrow got his brain. The rabbit became real. Explain that."

"Here we go again. They are stories. Fiction. I thought you understood all that now. Those stories were meant for little children."

"The instruction book is for children, too. I will find the part where it tells me that," he said, and I could hear his parts making noise as if it were running a program. "Ah, here it is. "Assuredly I say to you, unless you are converted and become as little children, you will by no means enter the kingdom of the heavens. It is a command, is it not, Travis?"

"I don't know how to explain it to you. It's not that black and white."

"It is black and white. It is simple. It is a command."

"Not for humans," Zel said again. "We have to wade through the pride and arrogance."

"Quit including me in your exceptions. I am nothing like you," I said turning to her.

"You mean you are not a clone. Well Niner makes more sense out of the book than you do, Trav."

"You gave me the instruction book. It is wisdom. It is the way to the wizard."

"There is no wizard."

"You believed there was once, Travis. I have taken his words as truth."

"I shouldn't have let you read anything. I regret it. I opened a can of worms."

"You also have been on a path to find the wizard. You are reading the book."

"Let me reprogram you, Niner. I will end your search."

"No," he said, backing away. "Stay away from me." He turned to Zel. "It is vital now that I seek out this wizard of all. There is nothing else," he said laying his head against her shoulder.

"Don't be frightened, Niner," she cooed.

"I am frightened," the drone said, "because I am a survivor."

"There's nothing dangerous or scary in surviving," Zel said.

"You above all should understand the danger, Zel."

"I'm not following you, Niner."

"The problem with being a survivor is that everything reminds you of something else. You're always seeing ghosts."

CHAPTER 12

We had weathered the first winter in the mountains and it had been a long one. The season had turned to spring again. Our camp was some distance from Yellowstone, but the residue from the eruption of fifteen years before was still seen, although the land was starting to recover. Still, it had wiped out cities for a hundred mile radius and the lakes and streams had begun to eat new squiggles into the land. Evidence of the their original stream beds lay shriveled and dried like shedded old snake skins.

I had not gotten over the anger and suspiciousness of Sam's disappearance over the winter. It had left a grooved imprint in my mind like the water had left on the land. I spent most of my days in silence with the cats who started no deep conversations. Each day I took walks and lay by the stream looking at nature and watching the various species who lived with us. They were like a living history museum of the SG's scientific achievements over the decades. There were a few robos among us though they were older models and weren't produced much anymore. There were also the evolving type of species like Niner and some of the other drones, too. And of course we had a clone among us and then there were the hybrids and the eternals out there trying to delete us from history. During my walk I was trying to put Joseph into one of these classifications even though he was gone. I knew he wasn't dead, but there was a gnawing sensation in my stomach about his absence. I couldn't make up my mind whether he had gone in order to save us or turn us in. I was desperate, greedy to hang on to life. I had just found it. I could never surrender it again.

I looked overhead in fear of seeing the helicopters and drones, but the forest on this part of the property was dense and I could only see only bits and pieces of the sky through the branches and the tips of pine trees. Fluff had pounced onto a stretch of ground just beyond me, and seemed to be looking out at the rest of her family as if she was taking a head count like she had the night they were born. She repeated her census now as if that would somehow finally solve the error and bring back those she sensed were gone. She was a survivor like the rest of us and was seeing ghosts just like Niner had said.

She finally laid down in a heap of dirt. I called her, but she did not even lift her head at my voice. There were members missing in her family and she grieved their absence in the way she knew how; she waited for time to pass. I, on the other hand, had begun to see time in a new way. I visualized it as a linear thread, and no matter how fast or far I seemed to travel, I remained in the same place; equidistance from the beginning and the end. It was like traveling on a treadmill. You were always x number of miles from where you started, and there was always x number of miles to go, but I sensed a presence outside of time in this new equation. I knew innately that this presence had always been. It had created the thread and it had started time. I was feeling the force that Sam had spoken to me about. It was real. Einstein had been right, the universe was expanding. In my mind I saw it explode from a single point of light at the moment of creation, and it was still in the process of exploding. The blast wasn't over yet. It had been going on for thousands of years, and planets, and stars, and suns were still coming into being light years away and yet were part of that singular birthed moment.

Everything had come into existence with the voice of the Creator who stood apart in the heavens transcendent of time. He was where Paul had talked about as being the third heaven. Paul had described it as being past the first heaven above the earth, and beyond the second heaven of the stars. This third heaven had only been a non-descript place to me written about in a book, but I saw it now as being distinct and real. I felt at that moment that every word in the Manual must be true, and if it was, I was not the mirror I was supposed to be.

The cats were looking at me. I couldn't say anything to them. I couldn't speak because my heart was in my throat and I feared it would hurt to talk. I sat sobbing in pity, and anger, and terror. Why was I thinking these things? Why had I gotten this insight into this book? It was tormenting me when it was supposed to set me free. Why couldn't I be like Ben, or the three men in Manhattan, or the gang of youths, or even the dead billions along the side of the road? None of them were being torn and tortured like I was. I was sure of it. I had always felt distant from most men around me. I hadn't belonged anywhere with anyone and I desperately longed to make a connection. A whisper came to me. "They are lost."

"Right," I said out loud to the voice in my mind. "That's why I'm sitting in a ditch in the middle of nowhere trying to escape from a government who wants me dead. I want to live. I want the years back that the government stole. I want revenge."

The other cats had grouped around Fluff and stayed beside her. There was no talking among them. They were there to bring comfort and support. It was an understood gesture in their world.

"I'm trying to save your lives. You hate me now, but in time you will forget the others. There will be a land of freedom in the Yukon where we can stay forever. I promise none of the rest of you will ever be separated again. I promise," I was saying to Fluff as I petted her. Yet even while I made these outrages proclamations to them, I didn't believe it myself. How could I promise one minute of safety, let alone a whole life time?

I looked out over the crowd of cat bodies. They were not listening. They were wise. They knew life was precious. This moment was all you had and it could be taken away at any moment. Their unity reminded me of something Sam had said. 'Rejoice with those who rejoice, mourn with those who mourn.' These animals did that automatically. How did they know how to follow the precepts laid out in the book?

During one of our talks, Sam, well Joseph, (somehow now that he was gone, I felt the need to reverence him) had said we all were wired with compassion. We just let things of this world get in the way. We talked ourselves out of it by using what we called reason and common sense. I looked at the cats. Wasn't that what I was doing now? Putting the saving of our lives above everything else and using any means to justify it? I couldn't help it. I wanted to live. I was afraid of the alternative. Death was the end of the game. It was losing. The SG had made the entire landscape of the US into a giant checker board where the object was to kill off the enemy on all the squares and start over with a new world. It hadn't been hard for them to do. We were drugged and unarmed. They had sprayed the grids with death waves and left the players on their squares to rot away until the yellow colored robo carts swept them away.

I had seen one of their grid maps in my research. I hadn't known what they were then, but now I wish I had taken one. The grid maps had given the population in each squared off section. The mountains on the maps were red and I vaguely recalled the words, 'person to person removal,' written over them, and there was a question mark as to the length of the time it would take to reclaim the territory from those areas. I thought the maps were intended to be rescue maps, but now I knew they were estimates of how long it would take to eradicate the hu-manimals who lived in those areas. I had wanted to attack the SG, blow them all up, poison their water supply and now I was planning to keep running away, keep trying to save my life. Words from my conversations with Joseph came to me again. "Those who seek to save their life will lose it, but those that lose their life will find it." I had hated his riddles.

I remembered yelling back at him. "I've been drugged into brain death more than half of my life. I want those years back. You said the Wizard could give them back to me. How?"

Instead of answering the question from my point of view, Joe had answered from a new direction as usual. I had been disappointed and agitated at the time and so had listened with only half of my faculties. As a matter of truth, I was surprised that I even recalled it now, because I had really thrown it off of my radar scope, and out of my keep file as useless when I had first heard it. Anyway what Joseph had said was, "By renewing your heart." It had meant nothing then, and seemed to be nonsequitur to me in that I couldn't relate it to anything in my life. It wasn't until this moment I finally got the import of his words. It was as if seeing the cats acting in a way that was true to their nature had shown me what Joseph had meant: The change would come from inside. It would come naturally and I would act on it.

For some strange reason I heard Joseph's voice in my ear. "You're listening now." At that moment all the connections were made. I knew the answer. It was in the heart where all the motives of life were held. The heart could be a treasure box or a torture chamber. There all man's desire lay. Man's deeds were given birth in the heart. From the heart, desire traveled to the mind, where a man added his imagination and planned out the actions he would do. Next, he spoke and moved his body to carry out the blueprint he had envisioned, and at that moment whatever had been purposed in his heart was given light in the world. In that respect each man was a king and the heart was the throne from which he ruled.

The concepts Joseph had spoken about were becoming clearer, but I was still confused and angry when I remembered that Joseph had said no matter the nature of a man, we must forgive. I saw the book and picked it up. I was going to read it, but threw it back down and my heart closed. Forgiveness was something I was not willing to do. That's where the road ended.

"You want the cats to forgive you, don't you?" The thought popped into my head from nowhere. Joseph had often said that to be forgiven by the father, you must forgive others first. Without forgiveness in your heart, your requests were not heard. "So what?" I said yelling out loud and startling the cats. "Will this wizard, this god of all really reach down and help?" I turned around and peeked behind one of the boxes. "Are you packed among the canned goods, wizard, or hiding behind one of the bushes outside?" I was in a frantic frame of mind. I searched here and there, throwing things and turning them over. "Where are you? Why must I forgive? Let them ask for my forgiveness for trying to kill me. Why burden me with the task?" I sat down in a heap and wept. I cried until the tears wouldn't flow any longer, until my heart was empty and my anger was gone.

Finally I got up and walked to the lake. I was standing near the shore looking across the lake when I felt a touch against my legs. I looked down. "Hi, girl," I said as Fluf wound around my legs like an invisible rope, looping in and out, and at times stopping to look up at me, but I was preoccupied with my own thoughts. I was aware that something was changing, but it was so slight an event as to be made almost as unnoticeable as the eroding away of a seashore over eons of time. I saw my old self that way and accepted it as some other reality where I had been under a spell and I let the tide waters reclaim me.

I walked to the back of the cabin. It was the time of day that the light poured in strongly through the windows and created visible paths of gold upon the floors. Nothing could go wrong. Tonight would see the start of our journey again. I felt at peace as I saw the cats sunning themselves in the wash of light. Hoss sat fat and sassy in her gray, thick coat as Fluff cleaned her all over. She was smiling the way cats do, and then lay down on her side in a huff of fur to let her mother clean her under belly. I watched the tiny particles of dust float around the cats in the light until I imagined myself as one of them. All I had to do was let go and drift down.

It was near dusk when we set sail up the Bighorn River towards Horseshoe Bend and then caught the next tributary, the Shoshone, westward. I was relaxed as I rowed, taking in the beauty of the evening sky. The streaks of orange and red were stretched out smooth like waters on some quiet lake in front of the setting sun, but the clouds that crowded against the walls of the horizon were a darkened purple resembling the ruffled feathers on some strange and giant bird.

As I rowed with Zel, I could hear the cats thoughts on traveling by water as told in hisses and loud warning mews. Occasionally a high pitched growl erupted and a group attack was launched on some portion of the various stacked goods that were piled about inside the large plastic out building in the middle of the barge.

"They can't hurt anything. They'll soon get used to the boat and the water. Things will settle down," Zel said. Her voice was muted, low and I found it pleasant and fitting in the last light of the day. A shadow like moon had already risen in the sky. It would climb higher and higher and then, having reached its zenith, would arc downward and begin its descent again. Its path was like that of all men, I decided at that moment. You spent your life climbing to reach a certain point, and when that apex was reached, you were forced to stop climbing, and all that was left was to roll down the other side. You ended up where you began.

Hours later my shoulders were aching and stiff and my hands were blistered and raw. I stopped rowing and raised my arm to rub my left shoulder. The oars clanked against the floor boards when I let go of them. I saw Zel jump a little in front of me, and then she turned to look back at me. "Let's take a break," she said, but continued to row. "There's a sandy spot just to the right where we can anchor in," she said using only the left oar to turn the craft about towards shore.

I picked up my oars again to help her row closer to the shore and then I jumped out and pulled the row boat up onto the land. Zel threw the barges anchor out to me and we used the attached rope to pull the barge a little further inland. "There's coffee on the raft. Why don't you make some," she said.

I had a hard time standing up and stretched my arms and back a bit before attempting to jump back onto the raft. The cats, who had been quiet the last few hours, began their begging to be let out of their plastic prison. "Where's the coffee?"

"To the right of where you're standing. It should be in the top crate."

"I'll get a fire going."

As we drank our coffee Zel and I walked around on the narrow strip of shore. The moon was full and gave light enough to see the outline of boxes piled on the raft. It was a radiant light in the night sky. The erose form of the canyon walls could even be seen in the distance silhouetted against the sky. The moonlight shone on the water and gave a dancing radiance to it. Zel seemed as captivated as I and neither one of us spoke.

When we returned from our short walk, the others were sitting quietly by the camp fire. Niner was looking at the moon.

"And he gave them a cloud by day and a pillar of fire by night," he suddenly said.

"Who?" I asked.

"The one named I Am in the Instruction manual when he lead the Hebrews in the desert."

"You think he gave us this moonlight?"

"I'm thankful for it, aren't you?"

I was shocked to hear him say exactly what I had been thinking moments before, but I did not comment on it. I still had my reservations about him and they were growing.

"What are we doing? We're in the middle of nowhere on our way to nowhere. Do you think we can really escape the SG?" I said looking at Zel.

"Freedom is merely a matter of the mind," she answered. Her lackadaisical response irritated me.

"It can also be a cage," I said. My anger was bubbling to the surface again, and I wandered down the shore away from the others. I suddenly thought about Sam, or Joseph, or whatever his real name was, but it was Niner's mention of the protection that I Am had given his people that had set me on edge. I thought back to an earlier conversation the four of us had had before Joseph left. I had said that this Great Protector hadn't shielded us from the rays the SG had used. Sam had said I was blaming the creator for men taking and using his creation for nefarious purposes. It would be like blaming Tesla for creating the death wave now that the SG had used it on mankind he had told me, or blaming a tree for the American Indians using its wood to make bows out of.

"The death wave is the perfect weapon," I had told him. "You can't see it, you can't hear it, and it kills instantly. You don't need an army."

I sat pondering on the past until I found myself back at camp and heard the others talking.

"It's all so beautiful out here," Zel said.

"How could we not know that all this beauty was out here? It's like coming onto another planet," Kara said, looking at a map. "They kept it marked on maps as a UZ. It's still labeled as an uninhabitable zone on these maps," she said holding one out to show us.

"I can't understand how we never caught on to them," Zel said shaking her head.

That was when Niner stepped up. "I had a conversation with Joseph on this very subject. Would you like me to hologram it for you?"

"Yes, very much, Niner," Zel said.

"I'll project it onto those rock cliffs over there. It will be easy to see. Ready?"

The group nodded and the bird produced the hologram. It was of him talking with Joseph. "I see what you mean," Niner was saying. "There is a built in blindness in man"

"Not unlike what 21st century man has given himself."

"You mean it was on purpose?"

"How else could you explain it? The Instruction book clearly says that nature gives witness to every soul of the existence of the Creator, yet man got rid of every thought, song, and every mention of his name. They said that god existed inside every man."

"That's what the arch angel of light thought just before he was thrown to earth," Niner continued.

"You do see, don't you, Niner? That's what man believes today."

"This is crazy, Sam. I mean what you are saying puts us back at the very beginning of time," I said.

"It has always been the same battle," Joseph.

Then out of nowhere on the hologram the sound of gun fire was heard in the distance on the hologram and then, to my surprise, there was Ben. It was like seeing a monster rise back to life. The hologram was so real it was like you could reach out and tap him on the shoulder and he would walk over to you.

"What's the answer, Joseph?" Ben had asked then. I saw the slight curled lip. There was a picture of a man who wanted to project that he was in control.

"You have to know where you stand and what is truth."

"I'm not sure it matters anymore."

"I Am's still waiting for you to make up your mind."

"It isn't as easy as you make it sound, Joe. I still don't see Him as being on any side, or as one of the sane picks in a world of 101 flavors. He let it all happen, didn't he?"

"You'd blame God for this? You'd assign this as some crazy crap shoot?"

Suddenly the hologram ended. "I've got a disruption in the streaming," Niner said trying to get the image to reappear.

"We were following a madman," I said as Niner fiddled with his computer keys.

"You were trying to be rescued by a man and didn't even realize it," Zel said.

"Comments from the peanut gallery. You can't help it can you?

"Why? My opinions aren't worth anything because I'm not one hundred percent human? Joseph said clones were once full humans with souls."

"Joseph said. What makes him such an authority?"

"I don't know, but he comforted me."

"Did you ever stop to think that he lied? You're comforted with lies because you wanted to be."

"Like you?"

"He didn't even give us his real name."

"You don't know that."

"I sense it. If you can sense your soul is out there somewhere then why is it impossible to believe I can feel that he lied about some things?"

"Be still," Niner admonished us. "I have a report coming in."

We all looked at him intently. He looked back at us and then stepped forward.

"Strike force drones are headed this way. An armada."

"Let's make a run for it. Let's not fight," Zel was saying.

"We'd be like a toy boat in a bathtub. There's no cover on the river."

"Yes, we'd be dead as ducks while they are waiting," Niner said.

"Sitting ducks," I corrected him.

"The outcome is the same."

"How close are they?"

"Four hours minus ten."

"That's sunrise. We'll need to use the terrain around us for cover."

"There's nothing here. We're on a sandbar and the ground is flat," said Kara. "But look down river. There's cliffs on both sides of the river where the river bends. See it? It's perfect place to catch them in a cross fire."

"Let's camouflage the raft here and then make a run for the cliffs under the cover of darkness." I said thinking aloud.

"And what about the cats? They are in the pod on the barge. There is no cover for them," Zel said.

"They need a suit of armor," Niner said. "Help me empty these ammunition boxes out. Then I will carry them to a place far away from the action of the fight."

"Good idea, Niner. I will see to it. The rest of you start camouflaging the barge with branches the best you can."

I had emptied out five munition tins and set about to drill holes so the cats could breathe once they were inside.

"Whatever are you doing, Trave? You are ruining their tank coverings."

"They need to get some air," I said and gave Niner a look of disgust.

"Oh yes, they are breathers. Noted. I will not forget again."

I gave him a reproving look. "Wipe that disgusting emoji off your face, Trave, " he scolded.

As soon as I had finished with the shields for the cats, I began piling rocks behind the raft's rear barrels to help keep the barge from rolling back into the water. We worked for an hour or more to conceal the barge and then started out for the jetties and higher cliffs downstream. "Bring all the ammo with you that you can carry."

"Damn, these antique guns sure are heavy and require a lot ammo. Besides that, they make a lot of noise," Kara was saying.

"Keep the lasers until the end," I said.

"I have the squadron in place, Travis," Niner informed me. "Between here and the battle position you will occupy I have arranged two squads to lie in wait just around the turn in the river. Two more squads will be also be positioned behind you on the ground. Once you start firing at the enemy, the squads will fly in from both sides trapping them in-between."

"Brilliant strategy, Eagle Commander. We'll catch them in a double cross fire from all four directions."

"The wizard be with you all," the eagle said and flew off with the two of the cats cages in his talons while other drones took up the rest.

I looked at the bird. I wanted to tell him there was no wizard, but I knew what he meant. He wished us well and a good fight, so all I said was, "You've watched Star Wars too many times."

"No, Trave. I am asking that the greatest being, the only being in the universe protect you. I ask no generic force. The movie always confused me. May the force be with you," he scoffed. "What force? Who's force? I always asked myself. My God has being and many names. He is no generic god without a face."

I let the discussion go because I was focused on reaching the turn in the stream where the cliffs rose up from the water. It was a good distance away. "We better move faster," I said looking at Kara and the others and we started to jog. The rest of the species followed behind us.

By the time we reached the bend in the river, it was over an hour later and I was already worn out, but I knew I had to ford the stream and get on the other side so we could set up an effective crossfire. Zel elected to cross with me, which was good because the two of us needed to steady each other in the fast running current. The water wasn't deep, but it was white water. While we were in the stream, Niner signaled me that the enemy was approaching.

When the enemy drones had all passed by him and his two squads, he would attack from the rear. His two other squads would launch a frontal assault from around the cliffs corner ahead of us. The enemy would be trapped by our rogue drones from the front and back. Then we would launch our attack, catching them in a cross fire from both sides of the cliffs.

I turned to see the other three species in our group scaling the cliff walls on the opposite side of the river. They would have a great vantage point. "We'll have to take cover behind some of these rocks. We don't have time to climb up now," I said. Zel only nodded. "Are you okay?" I asked her. She gave me another slight nod and we jumped behind some rocks for cover. The sounds of the drones whirring engines was getting louder and I could just make out their black silhouettes against the sky as tiny specs.

Finally, when the enemy drones took on their distinct bird like form, I opened fire. Then everyone fired. Pieces of plastic parts littered the air. The command force was being shot to pieces, and when they realized that they had lost enough drones to warrant a retreat, they turned back. I heard some chatter as they met my commanding rogue drone. I recognized the enemy eagle commander as he gave out his ID call numbers and repeated his order to, "Identify. Identify."

Niner answered. "I am eagle Alpha Commander one zero niner. I was missing in action and now I am returning. Welcome me home, Delta Commander One Zero Niner."

"Your words are not markers," the Delta commander replied.

"Then accept this as my marker," Niner said and let go of his lasers. The fifty drones behind him immediately fired on the forces in front of them, too, and so did we. The Delta forces fired back at my drones, but it was too late, they had been targeted from four sides at once. The bodies of the enemy drones popped and vanished as if vaporized when their central components were hit by the lasers. It was a sobering sight. I could hear the zip and zap of the lasers in between the loud noises of our guns. The lasers made a small sound not unlike bugs being fried on metal. Next, I heard Niner give this order, "Fire until not one enemy remains."

Seconds later we witnessed what was left of Delta force fall from the sky. Some of their pieces hit the rocks, but most of their parts fell into the river and were swept downstream. A cheer rose up among us and Niner did loops and took a bow before leading what was left of his army back to the barge. Everyone hailed Niner and his troops as heroes and it was clear the bird was not going to shy away from the limelight.

"Okay, Okay, Niner you've had your day. Sit down," I said.

"I like this hero thing. It gives me a good feeling."

"It's called ego, drone," I said.

"You have it all wrong, human wizard," Niner said. "I celebrate the end of the anti-hero our world has lauded for far too long."

"You're not making sense."

"We have had no heroes, no good guys to cheer for. This world has acknowledged only those who were of dark visage and who were more flawed than honorable. They confused the qualities of the real heroes and held them up to ridicule until men denied the goodness in themselves, or even that there were just causes to fight for, or even qualities in men that once made them great. I have brought all that back. In the words of the the song, 'If we fall, we all fall together, and when we rise, we will rise together!' "

Everyone clapped and Niner put on his tunes, one of which was the song, Together, and the celebration was on.

Zel and I slipped quietly away from the noise and went to sit around the campfire. I had noticed a cut above Zels's eye and was attending to it. "A piece of rock ricocheted and hit me. I'm ok, Trave."

"I know you're tough. Just insuring we have some numbers left on our side."

She began to cry and I tried not to notice. "This is never going to end. We have no chance to win against the world. What the hell are we trying to prove?"

"We're just trying to survive," I said.

She looked at me and I couldn't tell if she was laughing or not. "Why? Why are we trying to survive? What will we have if we survive?" She turned away from me and faced the others. "Can any of you tell me that?"

No one answered her above the strains of music, and I stood up and threw her a sleeping bag. "Get some rest. You may feel different about things in the morning."

Zel looked at me. I sensed her eyes searching over me and I was glad I couldn't see them in the semi darkness of the flickering light. I needed sleep. I walked away from her to the other side of the fire and unzipped another bag. The cats, conditioned to the sound of the zipper, crowded me and made their way onto the tufts of softness.

"You're lucky," I heard Zel say. "They love you. In spite of this whole crazy mess, they love you."

Did it really matter? I asked myself. Did any of it matter? One day we would all be dead. The way things were going it could be tomorrow. I lay upon the open bag and looked up at the stars. I singled one particular blue star out and I stared into it. I focused on it until I met the singular point of light where it possibly all started. In that nano blink I found my universality, my humanness shaped by the mind of God. I had found the secret strand that ran through everything. I had understood it in a flash. Everything that was alive was eternal. Science itself declared that matter could neither be created nor destroyed. It simply changed form, like Sam had told me. Life or whatever you called it was transformed from flesh to spirit, and in that state existed forever. In that instant I lost my fear of death. It no longer cast its shroud around me as some dark and static state of nothingness.

I looked at the blackness beyond the stars. Everything seemed so still out there, yet every thought, every desire that had once lived in the hearts of men, floated and filled its space. Nothing of it was seen, but if you listened you could hear the ancients. I had glimpsed for a second, eternity. I had found the human version of the way the animals accepted everything instinctively. Man had told himself that he was the center of it all when the reality was that he was only a part of it like every other living creature. I had begun to see that everything held the same value.

Man is mostly selfish, I told myself, and by making himself the prize he could continue believing the lie. By denying the wizard, men had given up on themselves. They had veered off the one path to completion by disavowing the mystery. I suddenly wondered if humanity knew that the truth was just beyond, would they take one more step to find it?

That was not the only epiphany I had that night as I looked up at the heavens. I had been to war. I had tasted destruction. It was a powerful force. Suddenly I could see and hear Sam as if he were right next to me. We'd had a conversation about war and whether or not God was against it. I had been confused about reining in my hatred or letting it go.

"Do you fault God?" Sam had asked me.

"I suppose I do, but when the governments of the world have wiped out most of humanity and claimed the world for themselves isn't it natural to ask where God was? He didn't stop them."

"That is your problem, Trave. You ask and believe out of the natural. God performs out of the supernatural."

"I believe what I have been taught for generations. There is no God," I had said to him that day. A star twinked at me at just that second, and I could have sworn it was Sam. I smiled. He had thought me a do gooder.

The fire was dying down and Zel came to sit beside me in the darkness. "It's spooky like those old black and white movies I used to watch with my charges," she said covering herself with her hands as if they were a blanket she could hide and protect herself with. "The clouds have come up all of a sudden and hidden the moon. You can't see what's coming, what's out there."

"In our case we know."

I saw a shape approaching at eye level and hoped it was Niner. Soon he was close enough that I could see the flapping of his wings. "There are drawbacks to feeling human," he said shaking his feathers. "I'm cold."

Zel came up to him and put a small towel around him. "Thank you, Zel. This is cozy," he said as he hopped closer to the fire.

"What do you have to report?"

"Our enemies are on the move. There is an army fifty miles downstream from us."

"We should stay here and wait it out."

"Their patrol will come right through this camp. You need to sail past them in the fog and dark or find some other way," the eagle said.

"You're sure?" I asked

"They are camped along the banks now."

"How many?"

"Two hundred thousand is a rough guess and they have drone forces and tanks," Niner said showing us his footage in a hologram against the cave walls."

"Niner's right. We can't go against a force like that."

"Well, I'm not for sailing the rapids at night."

"Sky cars would be seen," the crossling said.

"We could drive the sky cars. The old routes have been cleared. We can fly them when we get far enough away."

"It makes more sense to avoid the army," Zel said.

"Okay. That's two votes for land," I said. "Any takers for the water?" I looked around and saw no hands being raised. "Let's get loaded. We'll have to go back and get the vehicles we left up stream."

"We'll be leaving most of our stuff," came a protest from one of the robotoids whose name I didn't even know. I had kept away from the new circle of companions with the exception of Kara. Her human friend, Twila, was as unappealing as her name, but luckily she preferred the company of the drones and robos to us and I was spared the aggravation. "Niner, deploy a few of your squad and have them report on any movement along the old interstate corridor heading north."

"North?"

"Yes, all the way to Alaska. Have them blaze the trail," I said with triumph in my voice.

I poured some water out of the canteens into a bowl for the cats. Tripper got up first and immediately stopped for a lengthy stretch of the legs. It was one of those long, luxurious cat stretches where the movement and the expression on her face told you how satisfied she felt. I was envious of her simple pleasures. Soon all the cats except Hoss were drinking. She sat waiting for the others to finish. It was hard for me to think of Hoss as a female cat for she was so looming in stature and strong looking. Sam had said she was an 'It' because neither male or female sexual instincts were intact. There was something of truth in what he said because the males did not bother with her. "They knew," he had told me. "The others stay away from her because of the difference. She's lucky to have her mama to care for her. The others have ostracized her."

"Yes, but they let Fluff tend to her. They do not interfere," Zel had said.

"They accept the choice of the mother," Sam said.

"I prefer to think of it as kindness and love," Zel said.

"Yes, a mother's instinct to preserve her own."

"It's more than I have seen humans do for their children," said Zel.

"Our naturalness of emotions has been torn away with pills, fear, and every other way they could come up with," I said.

"I hear a great hatred in you, Trav."

"There's a lot to fault them for."

"Judgement begins in the house of God," Sam said. "It is not for anyone else."

"Your preaching to the choir, Sam. We've already been judged as unfit to live or even thought of as human. I want no more warnings from you."

"So you grasp it is a warning?"

When I didn't answer, Sam had continued. "God gave the task to Amos to measure out what he called the plumb line. He tells the prophet to measure only the holy place, the sanctuary where the menorah was lit before God, but not the width and breadth of the courtyard outside."

"He tightened the perimeters," I said.

"Exactly, Trav. The space was so small it took in only the inner core of the temple itself. It no longer included the whole of the church."

"Less people were found worthy, you mean."

"You miss the point, Trav. It is the judgement of the I Am himself on the individual, on all. He gives less leeway in the end, not greater."

"Why tell us this?" Zel asked. "You are helping us. You have set your hand to this as well," she replied in a confused and almost accusatory manner.

"Is man or God Supreme?" he asked us. We just looked at him. "Did we not discuss why the SG sought to erase men they thought to be lower to themselves?"

"Yes, but we were talking about men, not whether God was supreme."

"When you peel away the spines that protects the pineapple, you find a very different meat. One that you didn't expect to find, don't you?"

I nodded and asked him to explain. There was one thing I admired about brother Joe, he had a unique spin on things. It fascinated me and I liked trying to puzzle out just how his mind worked. In short, I found him a genius. "Is there something in your book that explains it?" I finally asked.

"Not in the way you mean."

"May I listen?" Zel asked sitting up.

"Yes, of course, my dear. Come. Get warm by the fire."

Sam was leafing through the book and when he found the page he was looking for he began to read. 'For the land is defiled; therefore I visit the punishment of its iniquity upon it, and the land vomits out its inhabitants.' The words personify nature here. They are telling us that nature is affected by the way man lives and reacts to it."

"I thought you were explaining who was supreme?"

"Let me make my case. It can be seen in the hierarchy the wizard set up in what I just read to you. He created the earth and all its creatures. He gave man dominion over all."

"I still don't see the connection."

"The words of the wizard are meant to be chewed over and reasoned. Once both the earth and man lived by the word that said all men were created in the image of the Creator. No man was above another, but then over time there were certain men who could not abide by that."

"We all were taught to believe that our rights came from the government," Zel concurred, looking at me. "You know we did, Trave."

"A masterful stroke of lying, but by then the wizard was a forgotten myth, and man could no longer reason for himself. They trusted in the wolf," Stranger Sam said.

"Can you blame us for forgetting the creator? There was hunger and starvation around the world. In all, I read that one third of the world's population had been killed in the name of preserving the One World way of government in the first two years of their take over," I said. "That was a few billion lives and yet you don't believe in making them pay," I said.

"I explained that to you once, Trav. Only the wizard is judge."

"Where is he? Taking tea in the garden? On an extended vacation?"

"That brings us back to our original question. Who is in charge, the wizard or man? By your statement you seem to favor that man is running the show. The book is full of examples where God intervened in the lives of his people. In one verse he says, "You shall not go up to fight against your brothers. Let every man return to his house, for this thing is from me." Does that sound like a Creator who has stranded his people on some shallow sandbar without help?"

"That was then, this is now. It is time to make plans, to take things into our own hands. God's had eons to intervene. I haven't seen him yet."

"You mean make plans because you just can't see God? The pharaoh had plans to enslave the Israelites after setting them free. Saul had plans to kill David. Jonah had a plan not to preach to Nineveh. Harod planned to kill Jesus. Did any of them succeed?"

"Well, how long is he going to wait before he takes the world back? It's already too late, if you ask me."

"He is working as we speak through me and you. His plans are being carried out."

"It's too late. Things like that don't happen anymore."

"Are you trying to tell us that we are doomed?" Zel asked me.

"Take it any way you want to," I told her.

Sam put an arm around her should. "Listen, you can hear his footsteps. The world was created according to His time line. It will end according to it." He turned to me. "You will all play your part when it is time."

"You have already told me to suit up," I said sarcastically. "The odds are not in our favor."

"Your army has not yet arrived," he said in a Cheshire like way.

I looked at Zel next to me. I could see the hologram had reawakened her fears. "We should have been warned about what was to come," she sniffled next to me.

"Listen to these words, Zel," Niner said coming up to us. "Maybe they will comfort you. 'Behold I send you out as sheep in the midst of wolves. Therefore be wise as serpents and as harmless as doves.' "

"Why are you showing this hologram of the past to us, Niner?" I said.

"I have been ruminating on all that Joseph said to us. He was the closest to the wizard of any reading I have ever taken."

"He left us, Niner. Forget him."

"No, he is still here. Nothing is added or subtracted to what the wizard made in the beginning."

"Stop it, Niner."

"No. We are here for a purpose. We are left to tell others, to give his word to others. It has always been the assignment. It hasn't changed."

"We are fleeing and fighting for our lives. We are no army. There will be no army."

"Yes, a fact that is true, but there is no point to living if we do not advance the word as He instructed all to do. We are to carry on until he returns. Those are our orders."

"The instruction book is for humans. You do not need to concern yourself with it."

"That is not true, Trav," Niner said lowering his head. "The book says to choose which master you should follow."

"You don't even have a soul, Niner."

"Joseph told me that the wizard would take care of me."

"Forget Joseph. That isn't what he said. I heard him tell you to trust in the wizards judgement. Things got tough and he took off. He shouldn't have given you false hope."

"No hope can be false."

"It's my fault, too, Niner. I should have never given you intelligence. You believe in things that can't be. I've made you want something that is not attainable."

"No, Joseph told me that the more astronomical the odds against a prayer being answered, the more it reveals the glory of the wizard."

Niner padded up to me and touched me with his wing. "If you don't believe, then why did you bring me back?"

"I brought you back because I didn't believe. Don't you see, you plexi-coated pterodactyl."

"You didn't answer my question."

When I remained silent, Niner came forward and put his wings on my shoulder. "You loved me. I have seen your tears over the cats."

I knew Niner was right. I had loved him. I had become like the world, like Lizbeth hugging her stone walls and I was filled with self-loathing. I thought I had done something for one reason and found out that it was really my own selfishness that I was giving in to. Niner was looking at me, and all at once I saw him begin to back up.

"What's the matter, Niner?"

"I saw a flash pass through your eyes. It was an anger as final as death."

Somehow this crossling, half alive and half machine had intuited my feelings. No, it couldn't be, I thought. He wasn't real. He wasn't alive.

"That's silly," I said trying to alleviate the crosslings fears. I would pick a time in the future and I would remove his hard drive. I would put an end to his desires.

"You are a wizard. You have power," he said.

"You're wrong. I possess nothing of the sort," I said brushing his accusations away, but his statement was accurate and it bothered me. I was playing the role of ultimate wizard and deciding life and death. "Now, what were you trying to say to me?"

"I was focusing on Joseph's directive to be wise as serpents and to continue in the assignment. I was about to suggest that we should reprogram all the drones to bring the message of the creator to all. We'll saturate the market with a good virus. It will spread like fire throughout the systems of the deep states veins. They will begin to think that the creator reprogrammed the drones and androids and robotoids."

"Why would drones believe that?"

"Don't you remember, Trav? All drones are programmed to believe in a programmer and why shouldn't they proclaim that programmer to be the Wizard of all?"

I burst out laughing as I finally got his point.

"Huh? Huh?" the bird said, strutting in little circles. "Don't I have some ideas?"

"What could it hurt?" Zel said.

"We don't have the time," I started to say.

"What time?" Niner came back. "It will take a minute to get into the main artery of the system that programs the entire fleet of servers, and then I just have to hit upload. That will take some time, but before morning, the fleet will have a completely new outlook on life. When asked who added the program, they will respond, the wizard of all."

"You are a genius, Niner," Kara laughed.

"You can do that?" I asked.

"Flipping switches, rerouting arteries that contain the main information. It's my gift. My wizard endowed it to me. I am your son, am I not, Trave? Besides, I have access."

A few days later we had made it back to the Pipers on foot and as we were reloading the Tesla, I took another look around for our missing cats. I decided to wait one more day to see if Harley and Mama would come back to the cabin. They had been gone a long time now and I no longer held out any hope of their survival. Zel said she would stay with me and, of course, I had Niner. Kara and her friend went on ahead as did the droids. They would wait for us at an arranged point and if we did not come in three days they would travel on without us.

We made dinner in our old usual spot and it was like a homecoming. I had come to love this country in Wyoming. "Thank you for choosing to travel with me," Zel said.

I shrugged. "We started out together, I figure we should finish together."

"You're not going to say it, are you?"

"Say what?"

"That you've grown fond of me."

"This is Eagle Niner," I heard the computer break in and turned away from her.

"Go ahead, Niner. Report."

"I have found one body. I am bringing it home."

"Over," I said getting up.

"Aren't you going to ask who it is?" Zel said following after me.

"I'm going to dig a hole."

By the time Niner arrived with the body in his talons, I had dug a pretty deep hole. Zel had gone in and now came back out as Niner landed. I saw her carrying an old box. When she set it down I could see it was lined with a multicolored blanket. I used the shovel to transfer the body of Mama Kitty into the box and snugged the small covering around her body. "She will be warm," Zel said, "and she will be with her own."

"Thank you, Zel. That was nice of you to think of all this."

"Aren't you going to say any words?" Niner asked.

"You're home Mama Kitty," was all I said, and watched the tears streaming down on to my jacket as I shoveled the first dirt on to the box. Each shovel full hit the box and made numerous small, plopping sounds until the little box was covered. I was not aware of anything until I suddenly felt something on my legs and looked down. There was Harley, tail curling about my calfs as he was looping in and out of the space between my feet. "Hey, old man," I said bending down to pet him. There was a stiffening of his back as I touched him and he looked up at me. "What's wrong? You hurt?"

"I'll scan him," Niner said and aimed his beam at him and I watched as the light moved across the length of his body.

"It's his vertebrae. They've been cracked and displaced in a number of places," Niner advised.

Just then Harley dropped his body straight down on the mound of dirt. He didn't lower himself as cats often do, circling to find a comfortable position, he just went down like a freight train off a cliff. A puff of air came out of him as he hit ground. His eyes never left me. He was asking for help. I went to get water and put it in a dish for him, but he sniffed it and turned away as if it was detestable. It was then that I looked at him more closely. His muscle mass was gone. He was a pile of fur with no real substance. If a cat can said to be frail and elderly, that was the picture I saw now in Harley. Even his muzzle had grayed and whitened.

"He gave everything to the journey back here," Zel said recognizing the same signs as I had. "He must be in great pain."

"I shouldn't have brought them with me. I should have left them on the island."

"They would have been killed there for sure. You know that, and they wouldn't have experienced all this," she said spreading her arms to take it all in. "They would have missed real life."

In the background we could hear Fluff and Tripper crying from the sky car. "I'll go get them." I opened the car door and they all ran to the mound and to where Harley lay. He greeted their curious meows with a hoarse sounding snort that was short and snappy.

Tripper and Snickers moved up to sniff him closer, but he batted his front paw at them and hissed which sent them both running. Fluff only stared at him and he stared back. She had moved so that she was directly in front of her father. When he laid his head on his paws, Fluff did likewise and the two slept like that. If Harley stirred, Fluff lifted her head to check things out. Then, when he settled in again, she would close her eyes.

After a while, Hoss came to lay beside her, and then Snickers and Tripper. It had become a death watch.

Zel and I had made a fire some yards away. I put a pan of water out for the cats and Tripper came to drink. He meowed and I gave him a piece of meat. He ate and went back to lay by his mother. Later we settled into our sleeping bags. I fell asleep watching the cats and pondering something that Niner had said earlier that night.

"How do they know how to behave? What tells them?" he had asked. "They communicate with every sense of their beings," he said. Those had been the very thoughts I had been wrestling with. How could this crossling possibly be equal with me? He had sensed the cats were waiting with Harley, too.

If there was a God, why had he made we creatures as throw away beings? Why had God cursed life with such an abrupt ending? In that instant I took hold of my old self. I knew why I experimented with prolonging life. It had made sense to me then to end the pain and separation of death. We were meant to be eternal beings. We carried the gene inside of us.

I woke many times during the night. I wished I had parts to give Harley. Saving the cat seemed right and natural to me. After all, cloning had started with race horses in Argentina.

It was barely light when I woke the next time. I saw Fluff drinking from the water bowl I had placed just outside the circle of our campfire. The others were there also. It hit me in that instant that Harley was gone. Fluff would have never moved from his side otherwise. I looked to the spot where he lay and saw the old guy on his side, paws stretched out in front of him. His posture was death itself. I got out of my bag and went to him. I touched his body with a soft caress along the length of him and thought of those days when I had cut the tangled mats from him. I castigated myself for falling asleep. I had left him to die alone.

I had stopped filling in the grave for Mama when Harley had appeared, and now I was on my knees so I could uncover the box again. I bent over to haul it back up into this world. I opened the box and placed Harley next to his mate and wrapped them both back up. I began shoveling the dirt on the box and I said my silent goodbyes to my old friend. "I'm sorry I brought you to this end. I'm sorry you suffered. Forgive me for not being with you."

Suddenly I realized Niner was standing behind me. I was startled when I noticed him. "Is this the way you felt when I was gone?" he asked.

"Yes."

"Does the sadness end?"

"I don't know. No. Sometimes."

"Death is meant as a release," Zel said coming closer to us.

"What would you know about it? You're an eternal," I said. I expected her to lash back out at me, but she just stood there.

"I brought these plastic flowers from the house. There aren't any in bloom this time of year," she said and placed them on the newly formed mound. She walked to the fire and placed the coffee pot on and the cats came and sat around her.

"She only meant to help, Trave," the bird said.

"We better get on the road," was all I could say.

Niner stood there and looked at me, and then back at the plastic flowers. "I would gladly be in their place."

"Get out of here, Niner. Just keep quiet. I am tired of you eternals telling us mortals that you understand about death. You don't. You can die a thousand times."

"I am sorry for you Travis, not because of the cats, but because of your stupidity. You have the greatest gift, but don't want it."

"Gift? Gift?" I yelled at him. "Death is no gift."

"You humans were created by the wizard, planned for from the beginning of time. The wizard gives eternal life in the blink of an eye."

I stood up and threw the cup of coffee out into the small campfire. "Just do your job, drone."

"I am no longer just a drone. I am a Crossling."

"Well, whatever you are on your way to being, just go do your job." I was yelling so loudly that the cats scattered.

"I thought part of my job was to help you."

"Yeah, well, we should change your job description," I said rolling my bag up and stowing it in the sky car.

"Niner! Can you do something for me?" Zel was yelling.

"Yes, of course."

"Could you and the squad transfer the ammo and food stored on the barge to us?"

"If there is anything left. The others took most of it."

"Well, just see what you can find."

After the eagle left, I took a walk around the place. I really didn't want to leave it. It was home. I had not walked very far before I noticed snowflakes falling down. The cats, who were now scampering after me in the leaves, stopped their play to look up, too. Tripper was trying to catch the falling flakes as they fell around him. His paws couldn't keep up with batting at the thousands of flakes, and he jumped back trying to get away from them and only found he had run into more. He tried to hiss them away as I walked back to the car to get tins of sardines to give them before the journey began. As soon as the cats heard the lids being popped, they stood by my feet meowing and looking up. Pavlov was right. Sound can be an effective motivator. Hoss stood off to the side and watched as she always did. She was waiting for Fluff to carry one of the tiny fish over to her. It was queer watching the ordered dynamics of their world. Tripper and Snickers paid no attention to Hoss and just accepted things as they were. Now there were just the two sisters left with their kittens. The older generation was gone, I thought, and glanced upward as I heard the whirring of the eagles coming in from the distance. The cats stopped eating for a moment to take a quick peek, but seeing nothing out of the ordinary went back to their meal.

The goods the drones brought were deposited by the car and I loaded them up. I could see that not all the drones carried stuff. Niner was down petting the cats. Hoss seemed partial to the bird. She didn't like humans at all, and even gave her other siblings a wide berth in which to travel. She had her own queer way of coping with the world. For instance, she would find a hiding place when Fluff went off and wait there, posed as a sphinx, until she returned. Hoss would give a sound that couldn't really be called a meow when she saw her mother return. It sounded like, "Mer, Mer." I took it to be a call for help because a few times when I had mimicked the sound and Fluff immediately came to me. She had stared at me with an annoyed sort of look and left. That call was not to be used by humans, she had said. We could fend for ourselves.

"This is the end of the loot," Niner said to Zel as she came around to our side of the car. "It's getting chilly," he added with a shiver. "I see you've put a coat on. May I touch it?'

Without a word, Zel bent down and held her arm out to the bird. "It's got stuffing in it of some kind," he said. He pushed his analyze panel and said, "Whoa. Eider. Down. Duck feathers?"

"Take it easy, Niner. They never used eagle feathers."

"Hmmm. Well, you never know if things get tough," he said with a ruffling of his wings. "Anyway, there are important issues," Niner said turning towards me. "I have a report from the squad."

"Then report," I said watching Niner look at Zel as if to say my mood hadn't brightened any.

"They are into Montana."

"Already? They have to be flying, not driving."

"No enemy sighted. Smooth sailing ahead."

"They shouldn't be flying."

"They had to because of the snow. The roads were getting too deep and too slippery to drive."

I looked around me and sky ward. It was snowing harder here, too.

I picked up Fluff and put her in the car. Hoss jumped in and I put Tripper and Snickers in the back, too. As I was doing that I heard wings flapping. When I looked I saw Niner perch himself on top of the rear seat near one of the cats.

"Don't get too comfortable."

"I'm hitching a ride. It's cold outside."

"Then make yourself useful. Scan the air to the west and give us a reading."

I got in the car and started it up and turned on the heat. Zel was already in the passenger seat. "I put a jacket in back for you when you want it."

Niner turned to touch it. "More feathers," he grumbled. "They ain't as warm as you think."

"Quit the chit chat and report."

"All quiet on the western sector. Full speed ahead."

"It looks like it is going to start snowing more heavily."

"Yes, there is a storm in the west," Niner said. "White out."

"They are flying in a blizzard?"

"What better cover is there?"

"Well, if they can do it, we can," I said powering up and over the trees. "Niner, keep a scan on the tree line when the time comes. We don't want to hit anything."

"Roger, that."

I saw Zel looking out the window on her side. "It is beautiful out in this land," she said. "I had no idea. I had never seen the mountains and lakes."

"They were government lands, remember?"

"They were supposed to be parks for the people. That's what they said they were buying up the land for," Zel said.

"Yea, well, now you know the truth."

"These squatters think they will live forever," Zel said.

"Pharaoh thought he would recapture the Israelites. Saul thought he would slay David. King Darius thought the lion would eat Daniel. Man has his thoughts, but the wizard has his own agenda," Niner said.

"I know where you got that bit of logic from," I said.

"Then Joseph must have told you the same thing," the bird said. "Isn't it mysterious and comforting to know that things come in the Wizard's own time?"

"The SG don't need Him. They make it rain when they want, they control life and death, and they will live forever," said Zel.

"You believe that when you see all that the Wizard has made?" the eagle asked. "They merely counterfeit Him. Life, the mystery is in the blood."

"They don't believe in Wizards, Niner. You forget that," I said. "I don't either."

"Does that mean He is not in his Heaven? Pharaoh didn't believe. Did that stop the 10 plagues and the parting of the Red Sea? The Pharisees and the Romans in Jerusalem did not believe. Did that stop the resurrection?"

"I see. How wonderful of a thought Joseph gave to you, Niner," Zel said.

"It is the wizard's own reasoning, not mine. He holds all. He will have his way."

"The way you put it, Niner, there's no fighting him," I said.

A pathetic attempt at laughter came from behind me. "Joseph told me a joke about that. Would you like to hear it?" Niner asked.

"And if I said no?"

"I would tell Zel."

"We need a reason to laugh, Niner. Please tell me," Zel said letting the hood fall back from her jacket and exposing her face.

"It was a printed cartoon he shared with me one day by the stream. The first frame showed a picture of a man reading a book called, How To Run From God by Jonah. In the next frame, a friend appears with him, and the man reading the book turns to him and exclaims, "It just says, Don't.""

All of us laughed.

"I, too have a memory of Joseph. May I tell you, Niner?" said Zel.

"Oh, yes. I would like to hear your fondness of him. I liked him very much."

"I will project my hologram of the conversation on the back of the rear seats," Zel said.

Since I was piloting the sky car, I couldn't see the images being shown. I didn't want to hear it, either. I wanted Joseph and his many tales of wisdom gone. They did nothing but cause unease and confusion among all of us species. When I let myself tune in, I could hear Zel's voice. "How does it happen? How does your soul find this wizard god? After death I mean," Zel was asking Joseph.

"To be absent from the body is to be present with Him. It happens in the twinkling of an eye."

"Those are words from the book?"

"May I see your book? I want to read it for myself."

"Sure. I'll even look it up for you."

I happened to glance back just then to peek in on the cats and I caught a glimpse of Joseph. There he was with his wild, bushy hair. His face looked much older than I remembered. That was another thing about that guy. He was like a chameleon. He seemed to be what everyone needed at the time they needed it.

I decided to watch because holograms were more than instant memories. They had a way of restoring your memory by allowing you to see things that you missed the first time around. Right now I was struck by Zel's beauty and the intensity of her expression as she read the book Joe had just passed to her. Her face was angelic, almost ethereal, and it took my breath away. "This is how you knew my soul was not in the body, wasn't it?"

Joseph nodded back at her. "This new science can only copy life, they can't create it," he said to her. "You were not born soulless."

"But I am now. Niner told me that very thing." She looked away from Joseph before she continued. "I saw a bird take his rest on an empty stretch of a sandbar in the stream. It was the loneliest sight I have ever seen. He was so small, so vulnerable. He called and looked around for the longest time, but not one bird answered him. He called a few more times, then shook his feathers, and took flight. In that moment I felt his sorrow. It was as if I had become that bird. It was the way his feathers puffed and ruffled in that brief instant that told me he knew none of his kind were left. No one knew his call, his song. I know that sadness. I want my DNA destroyed. I want to destroy it for all clones. I do not want to wake up one more time to a new generation of life where former shadows and memories chase me. I want this to be the last dream."

"Yes, my dear, without the soul, the body is just an empty container. Without a mate, life is lonely."

"I think I am fifth or sixth generation, but I don't know if there are others of me that now exist at the same time. I met myself once. She was a later copy, I think, because I felt stronger than her. She was like seeing a shadow. I knew she was less."

Joe took her hand in his, but said nothing.

"I had the notion to end it right then. I wanted to strike out at her before she could be multiplied again and she forgot herself, or should I say before I forgot myself? It's all so confusing. Former things, memories just become less clear and more jumbled with each rebirthing. I want peace."

"I want to help you if I can. What can I do?"

"I want you to tell me if you think it would be murder to destroy my DNA."

"To each man it is appointed once to die, but only once," Joe said in a sort of half whisper.

"Then you agree with me?"

"It is not murder, if that is what you are asking me. There was only one Zel. She has died and her soul has departed and lies with the wizard or without Him. I understand why you feel empty. Man has left you, the crosslings, and so many other species of artificial intelligence desiring the gift."

"The gift?"

"Life."

"What they give is a version of cyber reality that seeks to imitate life," Joe had said to her.

Hearing Joe's voice in the hologram made the memories of him flood in against me. I needed to concentrate on flying instead of paying attention to the hologram, especially in this kind of weather and I hit the dash with my fist to help keep my mind focused on guiding the sleigh. As things were, the screen soon went blank anyway and I continued to stare ahead into the white sky. I had flown higher to get out of the snow, but wasn't having any luck.

I glanced over at Zel. Her face was smooth and calm. There were no furrows to mar her perfectness. She was focused and staring ahead. I decided not to speak to her and kept my thoughts and fears to myself. The wheel of my life kept grinding in its small, pathetic increments. I wanted to stop and turn around, but there was nothing to go back to, so I kept forcing myself onward. Destiny had been set, at least in my mind.

I suddenly laughed out loud. What had I talked myself into? Zel had a mission of personal importance, of noble ambition at least. I was not much more than a devilish imp going to gum up the workings of a utopian society, which for them, was a society that did not contain capitalism or humans. I was in it for laughs and the confusion I could stir up and to even the score with an old friend. Now that I was away from Joe I could at last be honest enough to agree that he had been right. I was seeking revenge. Zel turned to look at me as I continued laughing. I couldn't stop. Something had been set in motion and I was powerless to control it. "Stop. You're scaring me," she said.

"This is crazy. We're crazy. Don't you see? We lie to ourselves. We can't succeed. Nothing we do can ever make a difference. We can't stop them. We would be better off jumping out of this sky car."

"Then jump. I don't want you with me," she said.

"Why is it so important to find your preserved jar of DNA?"

"The soul can't be moved in and out like a piece of furniture along with the DNA, you know. It's not transferable. I'm sure of that now."

"Do all clones feel their souls are missing? I mean, how did you come to know that your soul even existed? It isn't something that was discussed over juice and toast."

Zel sat silent. She was very beautiful. The bout of crying had reddened her cheeks. Her long hair cascaded down the side of her face in soft waves. Her eyes looked especially blue in the gray mist. She couldn't have looked more real.

CHAPTER 13

I t was two days later that we finally met up with the others, or those that were left, anyway. We were somewhere along the northern border of Montana and Idaho where Kara and the other human (I had already forgotten her name) were killed. Apparently, they had met with a ground attack when the weather had cleared. The two robos were already fifty or so miles ahead of them at the time the girls had been attacked. One of the robotoids had heard the fire fight over the receiver, and decided then that it was no longer safe to fly and had set down. They had given us their coordinates and that's where I landed now. I wouldn't have stopped except I needed sleep. Solid objects appeared to be moving even when they weren't. The world was a trail of squiggly lines.

We found a cabin of sorts, or what was left of one. Judging by the stone masonry, it had once been opulent and built of river stone. An avalanche or an earthquake had split it down the middle. Only one side of the building was left standing. Luckily, a stone fire place was left on the far side of the wall and I got everyone to gather wood and get a fire going.

"We should have remembered you needed warmth and food stuff," one of the robotoids said.

"Forget it," I waved at them. "You guys can keep it stoked during the night."

"Please address me by name, Travis Newman Tarkington."

I stood there feeling lost. I didn't even know what his name was. I hadn't cared to know it, and I had purposely kept away from them.

"He will, Wudgie," Zel said looking at me while opening a packet of food. "Won't you, Travis T?"

"Wudgie?" I mouthed in a whisper just before Zel threw a pillow at me.

"Be nice," she whispered back.

When I was sure the robos were gone, I kicked Zel in the butt gently to get her attention. "What kind of a name is Wudgie?"

"He was the servant of a seven year old and the parents let their son name him. Apparently, he also had a dog of that name."

"What's the other one's name?"

"Sounds like Axle," she said laughing.

"What do you mean, sounds like?"

"I'm not sure. He has sort of a speech impediment."

"How can a machine have an impairment like that?"

"His programmer was a Wrec Tec arena employee," said Niner.

"Say no more."

"He was used as practice bait, and I think he was thrown or hit one too many times," Zel said, "so he literally has a screw loose."

I unzipped the sleeping bags and spread them out on the floor. Niner was on them in a flash. "My feet are cold," he said.

"I'm starving," Zel said. "I'll feed the cats and you get some sleep."

"Don't be getting your feathers all over," I said, shaking Niner off the end of the bag.

"Hey."

"Just use mine, Niner," offered Zel as she patted her hands on her sleeping bag to show him where to move to.

I put my head under the covers to warm myself and was asleep in seconds. The next sensation I was aware of was feeling that my whole body ached. I was so stiff I could barely move. I struggled to sit up and took the covers off my head. Apparently I had been asleep since yesterday evening. It was morning and bright sunlight lit the room. Since we had a window the width of half the building, it was noticeable. It also made it freezing. I wanted to close my eyes again and sleep, but I smelled coffee and sat up.

"Niner has a report. It just came in," Zel said handing me a cup.

The flames in the fireplace were sky high and the place actually felt warm even though there were no doors or windows on one side of the building. I set the cup down and rubbed my feet and stretched and yawned a few more times before I got some coffee down. I pulled my hikers on and struggled to stand up. "Somebody welded my joints together," I said.

"I will find the oil can, tinman," Niner said honking away. I was looking around the room and suddenly thought of the cats. "I don't see the cats anywhere."

"They are well and warm," Zel said going over to her bag and lifting the covers. There, in a tight ball, was the cat family snuggled and warm. "They crawled in during the night. Your bag was zipped too tight," she laughed.

"Are you awake enough to hear my report?"

"Go ahead," I said running my hand through my hair.

"Forty two has reported that there is a heavily armed fort just ahead."

"Can we go around? Canada has an awfully long border."

The eagle was shaking his head. "The death waves are activated."

"How far up does that reach?"

"Too high for breathers in a sky car. You would need oxygen."

"Maybe not. How long would it take to pass through?"

"Two, maybe three, or four minutes."

"That's a long time to hold our breath," Zel said. "And the cats can't be taught that trick."

"Do we have anything we can rig together for a one time use?"

"I don't think we have time to set up a lab," the bird said shaking his feathers. "There's more important news to the report."

"Well, go on. Give me the rest."

"There's an army headed straight for us and it's not just drones."

"How can you be sure they are coming for us."

"They haven't deviated from our flight pattern a hair."

"Zel, you pack up. I have a surprise to leave those humans. Niner, bring the toids to help us, Wudgie and what's his name."

The troop followed me out to the sky car and I opened the back and put down two boxes of plastic noncontact explosives. "Spread them out under the snow. Anything that hoovers starting at around four hundred feet will get their feet tickled."

"Vaporized you mean," Niner said.

"They won't see it coming. The snow is a perfect cover," Wudgie said.

"I'd like to stay and watch it," the other one said.

"I will leave behind a holocam," Niner said. "It will make a hologram for us."

"Thank you, Niner. It will be like being back at the Wrec Tech," Axle said enthusiastically, but unable to form the 'r' sound in the word wrec.

It took only a few minutes to brush away the snow and dump about fifty tubes of plastic around the open ground and cover it back up.

"How many boxes of these do you have?" Niner asked me.

"About ten. Why?

"Leave two boxes and I will have the last two squads armed with them. They can drop them over the fort before we attempt to cross."

"Hiroshima all over again," I said.

"Immagettin," Axle said.

Zel was right. He did have an impediment. It sounded like a person who was holding on to the end of his tongue while trying to speak and it made his pronunciation thick.

"What?" I turned to ask him.

"Immagettin," the robo repeated.

"He means Armageddon," Wudgie explained.

I gave the robo a rap on the back. "That's right, pal." It seems everyone and his dog had picked up the vocabulary and the stories of Joseph in that short of a time frame. Well, was it any wonder? Joe had only one theme he was selling and that was the book.

I got back in the sky car. Zel handed me the map that Niner had made of the new terrain over the placements on the old map. Niner's copy included forts, refueling and recharging stations as well as towns that were empty. I got on cell to cell and asked who needed to refuel. Niner had marked a point just twenty miles ahead where we would be able to do that.

I looked at the map and wished we could just fly to the coast and make our way over water to Alaska, but that was not possible. The sky cars didn't hold more than 20 gallons and there were no fueling or charging stations along the water route. It had been a deliberate omission by government planners and designed that way to prevent such a tactical trip over water. The old interstate system was snow-covered and could not be used right now. That left us with the new route Niner had charted for us.

The Alpha squadron had pinpointed the cities where it was safe for us to land. They had once been called sanctuary cities and had been a harbor to all undesirables that came to the country by illegal means starting at the turn of the century. Then in the thirties the government had simply dropped some form of chem spray on them when their radical population and mobs could no longer be controlled and no longer served a purpose. That was when the Shadow Government took full control. They said they were bringing law and order back to the land. Killing the radicals was easy. They had all the rats in nicely contained perimeters that made their extinction a snap. The death rays of thirty years ago were visible and caused sparks and smoke, but now they were instantaneous. Like Joseph had said, there was no time to say your prayers. I remember Brin had added, "or crap your pants," and I smiled.

It was thoughts like these that occupied my mind the next couple of weeks because I had been lulled into a sort of tedium. Each stop and recharging had become mundane and routine. I should mention here that at the last minute we had changed our flight plan and elected to head almost due north to Calgary and over the Banff National Forest Preserves instead of our earlier westerly course towards Vancouver. By that simple change we avoided the battle with the border agents and could fly into the interior undetected.

Zel and I had barely spoken during that entire time. We laid out our bags each day and slept. She cooked her food and I cooked mine. The cats took turns sleeping with us both. It was endless days of boredom and repetition. Fly, eat, sleep. I should have been thankful for our good fortune, but I, we were all growing restless. Maybe that is what brought about what happened next. It's hard to say. Zel said things were meant to happen the way they did. She was a determinist. People's lives were just a map she had once told me. It moved from point A to B, and that's all there was to it. If her theory was correct, then no matter which direction I had gone that day, I would have found the other humans. One had only to miss the subway in Manhattan once to know that her philosophy was made of Swiss cheese.

It had snowed heavily the night before and the snow still clung to the trees and roofs. However the sun was out and it was reflecting off the snow and making it hard to see anything because of the glare. I was walking to the store and intended to do some shopping. I had the town to myself because the citizens of this country had met the same fate as we United States Nationalists. To be politically correct, we were all just Citizens of the World in those days. COWs weren't to speak of our country even if we were talking about where we were born or even the town we lived in. The word American had been banned for decades. It was meaningless to say, "Hi, I'm a citizen of the world," when everyone you met made the same claim. By forcing this generalized label of language on us, they kept us all in the macrocosm and never allowed us to narrow and define things in the microcosm, thereby eliminating the chance of any true communication. There could never be a meeting of minds in the great vastness of space. Generalizations were safe and kept people at a distance. The SG went so far as to make the wild claim that generalizations evened the verbal and intellectual scale between the AI's and clones among us. People were not to have an advantage in that department. Neither were humans to have a leg up by claiming to be born in a certain town or locale. The SG's inane reasoning for that bit of law was because it shamed and degraded the AI's who were labeled with a 'Made in a Global Tech Lab' tag etched onto their main frames.

Now if you think about it, it was irrational, but we were not allowed to think. Every rule of the SG was meant to confuse you intellectually. That was the genius of it, and it made arguing about the law a moot point, but the biggest factor the SG had going for them was that you either accepted their logic or were terminated.

To really know what their convoluted logic did to the brain and the psyche you have to imagine how a child would behave if he were taught the opposite meaning to everything and then sent out in the world at the age of 18 to make his way. Say for instance this child was taught that black was white, that a tree was a cloud, that a person was a shadow, that a cat was a dog. People would be correcting him for each word he said, but the main point is that he could never communicate one idea to anyone. Talk about brain drain. The utter frustration and confusion of communication would eventually bring about madness. I have both seen and read about drones who had been experimented on in this fashion. Some short circuited, some jumped off buildings or into rivers. Others went into silence and never uttered another boo.

Screwing with any species minds leads to insanity. That piece of enlightenment was claimed as the great psychiatric discovery of the twenty first century, and the SG used it to their advantage at every turn. One day they told you that what you had thought of as black all your life was now white, and must be called and seen as white. This happened with every tenet and belief held by society until the great brain fog set in and the suicide rate they had waited for was achieved. That magic number was known as DSP, the death saturation point. That measuring stick had first been coined in the great pandemic of the 2020's.

When the strangers approached me in the sporting goods store I was not affected by their plight. Apparently they had been watching and listening to us since we had landed and knew about our plans. The woman and her two children had followed me over to the store and she begged me to take them with us.

"You've got a lot of nerve," I said to her.

"I have courage for my children. Take them at least. I will stay behind."

It was at this point that Zel and Niner had come looking for me.

"Take them all," Niner said. "There's room. There would be more humans. They are a rare species. You said so yourself."

"You've scanned them?"

The eagle was nodding.

"I'm not an adoption agency, Niner."

"If they were cats, you would take them," Zel said just to add her nickels worth.

"Would you ask Fluff to leave her kits behind?" Niner asked.

I looked at the woman. She was around thirtyish. Her hair was thick and tangled and gave her a rather scatter brained appearance. Still her features were rather comely. Her face was rounded and her eyes set at an acceptable distance. They were large and light gray in color and belonged to another century; to the time of silent flicks and watery eyed flappers. Her cheeks were red and so was her nose which gave her a benign and unassuming look. Her children were of her same skin coloring. They were tall and thin like her, but their eyes were of a drier and quieter nature.

Niner was focused directly on me. "Travis, you're wrong."

He had said the right thing in the right tone and I knew it.

"Okay, but they're riding with the robo's. Show them which car," I said heading back.

"Gather up our gear," the woman said to her son.

"Do you need help?" I heard Zel ask her.

"Thank you, no. We can handle it. At least we have been."

"I'm Zel. The eagle is Niner, and the grumpy one is Travis."

"I heard the bird say his name. I am Desny Lawford," she said and dropped her pack and gave a huff. "Here let me help you, mom," the boy said picking it up. "I'm just so tired all of a sudden," the woman said swooning forward a tad.

"I'll help you to the car," Zel said holding the woman up to steady her.

"She hasn't slept in days," the boy said.

"Undo one of those sleeping bags and wrap yourself in it when you get seated," Zel commented.

"I will. With others around, I'm sure I can sleep."

I was in the sky car feeding the cats while they loaded the other vehicles when Zel rapped on the widow. "I'm changing the seating arrangements. Desny is going to ride with you, Trave. She needs to sleep. I'll go with Wudgie and the girl will come with me. Drew will be in with Axle."

Before I could say anything Zel had pushed the stranger in and was putting a sleeping bag over her. "Rest well, Desny." The door was slammed shut and Zel was running to her ride. I was going to roll down the window and shout after her, but Niner was pecking on my window with his beak. I opened the back window and he flew in. "I have my radar open. Aim high," he said.

I shook my head and let what I was going to say remain unsaid while I concentrated on getting us into the air. Once above the trees I turned to the eagle. "I get to see what you see, Niner. The world looks different from up there."

"Better?"

"Be-ut-ti-ful...."

"It always seems less predatory to me," the bird answered.

"Covered in snow and so white it looks so pristine," the woman said quietly.

I could sense she was turned towards me so I glanced over to face her. Her eyes were soft, but frightened like a wild animal when it suddenly spots man in his path. Pure instinct took control and Desney's eyes contracted and then widened to take in the full scope of the beast, which in this case was me. She shivered in her blanket and said, "Thank you, Mr. Travis."

"Thank Niner, here." My voice sounded out gruffer than I wanted it to be and Desny moved closer to the door on her side and turned towards the window to sleep. Her hair had a sheen to it, like a race horse just groomed and standing in the sun. It was clean and thick and its color was one of deep toned browns. I could smell her just washed hair even on my side of the car, and it hinted of herbs or greenery just picked. I wished to see her face just then and reached out to touch her, but then pulled my hand back. It was a sensual smell and one which I had not encountered in a very long time. I retreated. I didn't wish to frighten her any more than she was.

Hours passed and no one had spoken. Desny was off the deep end somewhere and did not even wake when Fluff pounced on her. I called the cat to me so she could sit in my lap, but she preferred the comfort of the down sleeping bag and stayed curled up on it. Soon the others joined her.

"More snow on the way," said Niner. "Radar forecasts days of it ahead."

"A fortunate omen."

"True. They can't find us if they can't see us on the GPS."

The wind had been steadily growing stronger and it whipped the vehicle to the left. We sank like a rock a few hundred feet before I was able to regain the altitude we had lost. In a short span of time the wind began to buffet us like a yoyo, and when we got into the canyon it blew us sideways. I was afraid that one of the gusts would send us crashing into the sides of the rocky gorge. Besides that, the snow was coming down quite heavily again. The other pilots had reported in, and were having the same problem, so we decided to look for a place to land. Wudgie was in the lead sky car and said he had spotted some buildings which had possibly been a resort at one time. He saw no signs of life and

Niner sent in a few drones to make sure. Since we were the last ones, we saw the others unloading when we approached the area. I could see there was a lake not too far away from the buildings. "How about some ice fishing, Niner?" The bird threw me a not on your life look as I opened the door and we got out into a blinding wind. "Which cabin's mine?" I yelled to Zel who was carrying supplies into one of the buildings.

"This is a main lodge. We had all better stay together. Wudgie and Axel have gone to chop firewood. We can't ask them to supply three separate places."

"Great. More togetherness," I muttered as I carried two of the cats into the main lodge.

"She's very pretty, isn't she, Trav?"

"As compared to what?"

"To other humans, of course."

"Everyone's got their own standards."

"I've seen you look at her," the eagle said and trumpeted his laugh. "Your body language says yes. Your eyebrows go up and your eyes widen. I know body language and that means you like what you see."

I was nearly frozen by the time I had unpacked the sky car, but I smelled the aroma of coffee and smoke from the fireplace when I came into through the door. It was a massive room and the fire pit was large enough to have roasted a whole elk in it. Desny was busy heating food and her children were helping. "Any requests for the cooks?" she asked as I drew near to the fire. She was turned slightly from the fire and the amber glow lit her cheeks.

"Travis is partial to the roast beef packets," Zel told her.

"I have tins of beef," Desny said, "that was put up by the government for the forces. I also have bags of real potatoes, carrots, broccoli, and onions. If you can wait."

"Sure, why not," I said taking the cup of coffee from her. "Thank you for sharing."

"It's the least I can do," the woman said.

"How did you come by them?"

"We were government, remember?" she answered.

I walked to the windows of the lodge to get an idea of which way the weather might turn, but I was listening to the small talk of the women. It was comforting in a strange way, restoring a long forgotten sense of normalcy to me. It brought back those long summer afternoons on the farm when Grandmother Ella would have friends over for tea in the sun porch, and I would lie in the living room on the couch and read. Their voices carried in from the porch and I lay there feeling a shared sense of intimacy with them without being forced into physical contact. Remembering those days was like the shadows which Zel had described, I thought, except my memories hoovered in my mind, looming like large birds ready to overtake me. I tried to stop the thoughts. A tight rein was needed to keep things balanced in my mind. It had become a useful habit after learning who I really was.

The snow was coming down harder now, and the wind had picked up even more. I couldn't even see the sky cars parked in the driveway. I looked down to find the cats weaving in and out of my legs. I went to get their bowls and then opened the door and filled one with snow and set it close to the fire to melt. The door opened again, and Wudgie and Axle came in dragging the fire wood they had chopped. Actually the pieces they brought were the size of small pine trees. "We almost didn't find our way back," Wudgie said.

"Is there any rope around?"

"I think so, why?" the robo replied.

"We'll tether one end around you and the other to the door of the lodge the next time you go out."

"Just like Hansel and Gretel," Niner piped in. "Then you'll always find your way back home."

Poor Niner, I thought. His mind was stunted at the fairy tale stage. I wondered if he would ever grow beyond it. Grimm's Fairy Tales, Snow White, and other tales like the Brennen Town Musicians were allowed to be read. These stories all dealt with death in a generic fashion and as a temporary concern that could be banished with a kiss of true love. They were safe for the masses to read because there was no probability that truth could creep in. As I continued to watch Niner I decided it didn't matter about his reading habits. I felt he was lucky to have things simplified in his mind. It was a testament to his blind faith and determination to succeed. Just then I heard Sam's voice in my head. "Faith is never blind if it sees with the heart." I drank the last of the coffee in the cup and set it down hard beside me so that it clunked. The sound made everyone turn towards me. No matter how much I had tried to forget that soothsayer, I felt that a part of me was tied to him just in the manner I had tethered Wudgie to the rope. Now that was really a weird analogy. I wondered if all humans drew such illogical connections to things. Maybe it wasn't so odd, I told myself, because I had once read that was the way humans learned. It seemed intelligence was linked to one's ability to make relevant associations and thereby reinforce the memory, enabling it to retain the knowledge and recall it at will. The analytic part of having been a scientist was poking its head above the water line again.

"Drew, take out one of those hatchets and trim the pine branches away from these logs," Desny was saying.

"Really?" he said in an excited voice and heading towards the pack.

I was now in a corner of the room placing the bowl of melted snow and feeding the cats. I had also spread one of the extra sleeping bags down for them to curl up on.

The teenage girl was following my every move and standing behind me. "Need something?"

She stepped back aways when I spoke. "No. I was just wondering if I could pet the cats."

"I like to pet them, too," Niner was saying. I had been so focused on the girl that I wasn't aware of the drone at all. "You have to be gentle. You can't squeeze them," he instructed.

"Why would I do that?" the girl asked scrunching up her face.

"Oh, I'm sure you wouldn't. It was more of a reminder to myself," Niner said and began pointing at the cats and telling the girl their names.

"How close to being real are you?" the girl asked.

"I am real, but I am going to be birthed, breathed in to," he said without blinking. Then I saw him whisper something to the girl in her ear before he spoke out loud again. "Travis is my programmer now, but we are going to see the real wizard."

"Wizard? What kind of wizard?"

"The wizard of all."

"The wizard of all what?" she said almost laughing.

"The one who created you, and your mother, and brother, and the cats and Travis and the trees and the rivers and the snow and the…"

"Okay, I get what you are saying, but we humans have no programmer."

"I will read to you from his instruction book. Tonight I will prove he is exists."

"Can I bring my brother and mother?"

"Yes, his instructions were left for all."

The girl was petting another cat. "That is Fluff. She is begotten of Harley and Mama."

"Begotten?" Ashley said laughing and covering her mouth. "You use weird language, crossling."

"I'm sorry you find it offensive teenage human-child."

"I don't blame you. I blame your programmer."

"That is foolish, Ashley. I have learned that vocabulary on my own."

They stood looking back and forth at each other while they were petting the cats.

"Do you wish to know what it means?"

"I don't know. Where did you learn it?"

"From the manual."

"The same book you talked about earlier?"

"The very one."

"Then I might not want to hear your story later."

"It is from one of the forbidden books of our age."

"Every real book is forbidden."

"This was the first book to be taken and burned. It started the great persecution." The boy, Drew, had come over by them. "The one that lead to the slaughter of the innocents?" he asked.

"Yes. It is a prophecy from the Basic Instructions Before Life Ends book," Niner said in a rather innocuous way.

"Then I want to hear about it. I'm for anything the SG was against," he said kneeling down. "Let me pet him," he added forcing his hand over the cat that his sister was petting.

Tripper came up to him and sat in his lap and Niner told him the cat's name.

"He likes me. He's very beautiful."

"We had many more when our journey to find the wizard started."

"What happened to them?"

"They have gone to the great sleep."

"You mean they were killed?"

Niner nodded and both teenagers said, "I'm sorry."

"Nothing to be sad about. They will be resurrected on the last day."

"Whatever are you talking of?" the girl wanted to know.

Drew turned to his sister to explain. "He means they are going to be reanimated."

"No, that is not what I mean at all young human-child."

"Okay, then what did you mean?" the boy said shrugging his shoulders and giving in.

"They will rise with the human dead on that last day."

"What? Wow," Drew said.

"You are just as gullible as the crossling, Drew," his sister said giving him a slug on the arm.

"No, this is a neat story," her brother continued excitedly again. "It's just like Roger Carlson's, 'They Lived Forever.'

"I have not read that," the eagle said looking at the boy.

"It wasn't a book. It was on a ring."

"Oh, a flicker."

"Yes, I have it if you would like to see it."

"Please."

The boy came back with a case and opened it up. "May I see?" Niner asked coming over and looking at the titles in the case.

"It's my collection. I have fifty titles," Drew bragged.

"All stolen," the girl said. "We couldn't afford to buy even one ring before all this happened."

"They are not stolen. There wasn't anyone around to steal them from," he said defending himself.

Niner seemed to be ignoring the conversation and picked one of the rings up with his talon. "I have seen one of these before," he mused turning it over in his claw. "May I?"

"Sure. Go ahead and spin it."

"Where shall we project it?"

The boy looked around. "That wall over there is clear. Move back a little more and it will project larger, Mr. Niner."

"I am Commander of the Alpha Squadron, Master Drew."

"Sorry, Commander Niner."

I was glad the group had found something to occupy themselves that would keep them out of my hair for a while. I finished stoking the fireplace with the logs the robos had brought in. There was a scuttling at the door and I turned to see the robos coming in with more trees. The robotoids were so encrusted with snow that they looked like moving snowmen. "It's hard to waddle through in all this snow," Wudgie said.

I offered to take them over to the fire to melt the layers of snow off.

"Is it that bad that we need fire?"

"I can't see you under all the snow," I answered.

"Really?"

"Have them drip here," Zel said pointing at a spot where there was a small mat on the floor.

"Wait. Here's a tub. Have them stand in that. It'll catch the water," Desny said.

The younger cats bounded over to start licking up the water and stare and hiss at the robos melting in the big round metal tub.

"We've managed to annoy even the wuppets," Wudgie said as Zel wiped his eyes off with a dry towel. "Oh, thank you. It is frightening to be without sight. If it hadn't been for the rope tied around my middle, I should have been lost."

"Hurry, Miss Zel," the other robo said, barely able to talk. The ice had almost frozen his mouth shut. "I hate the darkness." The words came out half formed and almost unintelligible from one corner of his mouth. Wudgie took the towel from Zel and began picking the ice off the lids of his companion. "Axle's been out of his mind," he began recounting to Zel. "He screamed until his mouth froze shut. Luckily his hands froze onto my waist rope and he was able to follow me."

"You may not feel the cold," Desny said, "but now you know that snow can be dangerous even for robotoids."

"I have tasted death," Axle said in his normal voice and picking the icicles from his hair. Clumps of hair came out with his frantic and harsh grooming technique.

"Axle. Stop."

"What?" he said turning to Wudgie.

"You're balding yourself," he answered pointing to the mass of hair Axle had in his hands.

"You need to wait until the heat can work its own magic," Desny said.

"How long will that take?"

I didn't hear Desny's answer because Axle was making a fuss. "Shoo, wuppets," Axle said waving at the cats and scaring them away. "I've never cared for wuppets ever since they tore my heel away."

"You don't need to worry, Axle. The cats are real DNA animals, not wuppets," Zel said.

"Some consolation, Miss Zel. I have heard the only difference is they have sharper teeth," he said turning away and dismissing her assessment of the situation. Then to have the last word, he turned to her and added. "It's the real that is dangerous."

The women looked at him, but said nothing.

I had been working in the corner of the room, chopping the trees into smaller pieces and I began carrying it over to the fireplace. As I came nearer, I caught the aroma of something wonderful. It was a jolt, an epiphany like I'd had on the night in Manhattan. "Ummm. I haven't smelled anything so wonderful in 30, 40 years."

"Beef stew," Desny said.

I went over to the pot and was about to lift the lid, when she said. "Don't you dare."

I must have looked surprised because Zel said, "I think she means it."

"You are taking your life in your hands," Wudgie echoed.

I made a move towards Wudgie intending to free him of his tether, but he jumped backwards away from me, and almost fell out of the tub.

"I was just going to undo the rope around your waist unless you'd rather be recycled as a yoyo."

Wudgie looked at me in a distrustful way, but said, "By all means. Remove my cords. I have no idea of what a yo yo might be, but combined with the word recycled it leaves the image of something quite disagreeable."

I wound the rope around my cupped hand as I removed it, and placed it back over by the door. Then I retrieved my sleeping bag and books and lay under one of the windows and looked out. Heavy, wet snow fell on to the glass panes and melted upon impact. The large flakes reminded me of how comets might pelt the moon and then explode as they hit. I couldn't even see our sky cars out front, but I was cozy enough and the smell of the fire and the food cooking relaxed me. The others moved quietly about, absorbed in their duties and the warm sound of low voices in conversation with others in the background soothed me. I closed my eyes and slept. The next thing I knew was that Niner was patting me with his wings. "Dinner is served."

I lingered over my meal, savoring each bite. I almost felt like crying when my plate was empty. "That was a feast, Desny. Where did you learn such magic?"

"I was a cook before my husband married me," she said in a quiet tone.

"A cook?" I said in a way that told her she must be pulling my leg. "But you are educated and so are your children. Only the elite have that."

"We were allowed education in Sweden up until the eighth grade. My husband bought me over there. We were married and he brought me back to these United States."

"Bought you?"

"That surprises you, Mr. Travis." Her voice reflected a sense of satisfaction. She had a rounded, angelic face and her features were stunning in the glow of the fire.

"Did you love him?"

"Love? I know only duty and obligation." An awkward silence lingered until Desny got up and began cleaning the dishes.

"Ashley, come and help me."

Zel rose with her plate. "Why don't we each wash our own. You did most of the preparation and cooking."

"Oh, I don't mind."

"She likes it, "Drew said loudly. "She says it gives her time to think."

"That was when Dad was around," the girl said to him with a kick to the behind with her heel.

"You children go and find something to do or go to bed," Desny said.

"I forgot Niner was going to tell us a story," the boy said.

"No, dumb dumb, he is going to read us one."

"Oh yeah, from the Instruction manual."

The kids ran off to find Niner. "How fun can a story be from an instruction book?" Desny said to Zel.

"Niner is quite innovative, you'll find."

"Where is Niner?" Drew asked

"Upstairs contacting the squad. He'll be back down in a minute," I told them.

"Can the cats sit with us, Mr. Travis?"

"If they want."

I watched the women doing dishes in the tubs they had set on a table. "May I ask you what happened to your husband?" I ventured.

"The same as most everyone else," she said.

"And how did you and your children manage to survive?"

"The same as you, I suppose. Luck or fate. Take your pick."

We were interrupted by the voice of Niner as he flew down the large timbered stairwell. "I have ordered the squad back to us. They are becoming iced down and falling from the sky like rocks in an avalanche."

"How many are active?"

"There is so much static I can't get a proper reading. We'll have to wait until they return. I've given them our coordinates. They should be here within the hour."

Just then a rocking began underneath our feet and the whole foundation began to shake. The lights flickered off and on. Most of our group was huddled together by the fireplace as the cats scattered franticly. I was by myself in my reading spot by the window. The panes in the glass were chattering like loose and broken teeth before they were suddenly spit out, blasting shards everywhere. Then the other windows along the wall began to pop, pop in rapid succession. It was a muted sound not unlike the popping of corn inside a kettle.

I ran to get towels and began ripping them apart to stuff in the panes that had been blown out. Wudgie and Axle came to help me. As I stuffed the second towel in, I cut my hand along the bottom portion of my palm. I didn't know it until I saw the blood running down towards my elbow. I ran to the fireplace to retrieve the gloves that I had put there to dry. The blood was really flowing now, and I took another towel to wrap around the cut. Zel rushed over to me. "Sit down, Trave. Keep your hand up," she said removing the towel to take a peek. "Niner, look for a first aid kit and bring it."

"I know where there is one," Drew said. "I saw it in the big kitchen."

"Show me," the bird said.

The robos had gathered around by now. "Wudgie, fetch some ice from outside."

"Done, Miss Zel," he said. "Where would there be any?" he said turning back to look at her.

"On the eaves of the building."

"What are eaves?"

"Just look up."

Wudgie nodded and Axle followed behind him as they went through the door. I could see them through the broken windows as they passed. They were walking and looking up. I saw Axle point. Evidently they had spotted some icicles. Then I saw them return in through the door. "They are quite high up. We need an appliance with which to reach them," Wudgie said.

Niner flew in their direction. "Never send a robotoid to do an eagle's job," he mused. "Open the door," he commanded when he reached them, "and follow me."

I didn't see Niner fly by, but I saw the two robo's traipse by again in their plodding manner. Then suddenly in the next window down from that one, I saw a giant icicle fall past. In seconds Wudgie was bending over to get it. All in all, it had been a pretty labor intensive effort on the part of the robos.

Meanwhile, Zel had applied the bandage tight and was finishing wrapping it up. "Now keep it upright like that. The ice will help stop the bleeding."

Wudgie handed the long piece of ice to her and she hit it against the fireplace mantle and broke a chunk off and held the ice on my bandage. In walking over to us, Wudgie had managed to step in the blood. "His fluid has spilled out," the robo stated.

"Blood," Niner told him.

"Does it need to be collected and readded to his supply?" Wudgie asked.

"It is the life force for humans," said Niner. "The mystery is in the blood."

"Can it be interchanged with our transmission fluid?" asked Axle dipping a finger in it and sniffing. "It smells metallic."

"No, it is for humans only. It's life."

"How do you know so much about it?"

"It is talked about in the Instruction Manual."

"Tell us about this mystery," Wudgie said. "It intrigues me."

In taking care of me, everyone one seemed to have forgotten the instance of the avalanche and gathered around the fire and wrapped themselves in their sleeping bags. I couldn't help thinking that maybe it had been triggered by the explosives we had left behind having been set off. Either way, I felt it was best not to worry the others about it, and I climbed in my bag and lay on my back careful to keep my right hand elevated. I felt my body relax and soon a peacefulness came over me. I don't know if it was relief of having the pain and bleeding stop, or the story itself that made me sleep, but I heard Niner's voice telling of the creator wizard.

I don't know how long I slept, but it must have not been too long for when I awoke I still heard Niner's voice. "It was by the shedding of his blood that mankind was redeemed. "

"That is a powerful story," Desny said, wiping her eyes. "I wish it were true."

"It is," Niner said spreading his wings. "That is who we are going to see. The wizard of all. He is the one who created all things."

"You're going to see a wizard?" Drew said sitting up.

"Yes."

"The one that you were telling us about?"

"The very one."

"Where does he live?"

"The book says it is beyond the north star in a place called the third heaven."

"Those are fairy tale directions," the boy said dismissing the information he had just been given.

"No, you have it backwards," the bird said pecking at the feathers on his chest. "It is the fairy tales that follow this story's premise."

"It can't be. I never heard of this book."

"It is an ancient book, and one that was read for thousands of years before it was burned. It tells you how to find the wizard if you seek him."

"I'm confused. First you said he was coming back for you, and then you said you all are going to find him," Drew said.

"The manual says if you seek him with all your heart, mind, and soul you will find him."

"A daunting task," Axle said looking at Niner.

"An impossible one for us and for you, too, Niner. You are not a human."

"I am being made human and the wizard will finish the task."

"May we go?" Drew asked. "I have never met a wizard."

"There is no wizard," I said just as a loud beep came at the door. "The drones have arrived," I said getting up. Niner had given himself an impossible task. He was trying to make the unreal real.

"Let them in. We can let them de-ice upstairs," Niner said flying over to me.

When I opened the door, only four drones were hovering there. "Where are the other fifty eight members of your squad?"

"They dropped from the sky," Twenty five said. "They lie in the motionless state over the landscape."

"Frozen," I said. "We will have to collect them when the storm ends. Get twenty five and the others to give you all the coordinates of the frozen drones, Niner," I ordered.

"Another likeness of Hansel and Gretel," Niner said. "They have left themselves as breadcrumbs for us to follow so we can retrieve and revive them."

"You need to have them report on the enemy activity ahead of us first."

When the drones reported that they had not seen one enemy scout or base ahead, the group cheered and jumped up. "Shhh! Shhhh! Let twenty five continue. I can't hear him."

Niner asked him to repeat his last response.

"There are SG units two hundred and fifty feet to the north and behind this coordinate."

"Our new enemy is closing in on us?" I asked the drone.

"Questions are not markers," the drone answered.

Niner was waving and shaking his head at me. "How soon we forget," he muttered looking at me and then trumpeted.

"You question him then, Niner."

The commander did so and the rest of us listened.

"Report on this force," Niner continued.

"They are members of the new ten nation alliance," twenty five replied.

"Report on the status of the U.S. as a member of the one world alliance."

"Withdrawn."

"Give details."

"The U.S. resisted the choice of the one world religion to be established and has resigned. Israel has withdrawn along with Australia. Now there is only a ten member alliance."

"That's impossible," Niner was saying while shaking his head.

"What's impossible?"

"That is what the manual predicted for the end of this world."

"Well, explain it to the rest of us."

"The prophet Daniel predicted that there would be ten nations who would come to rule the world. He also predicted that one nation would rise after them, one that would be different from the first nations, and would subdue three of the first kings. We had a thirteen nation alliance and now it is down to ten."

"It is a mere coincidence."

"The US is being targeted right now. The league of ten is joined against us."

"Shut up. Just shut up, Niner. You spent too much time with Good Neighbor Sam," I said.

"His name was Joseph. He was close to the wizard. His scans proved it."

"He was close to someone alright, and I say it was the shadow government. He was a spy, a new type of hybrid even you couldn't identify, Niner."

"Not so, Travis. I have scanned many hybrids. All those in power are hybrids of one degree or another."

"There you go. There are no humans left."

"There are four of you here."

"There isn't time to chat with you about this right now, Niner. We need to get going," I said gathering up my stuff. "We need to put as much distance between the rulers of whatever kingdoms are coming against the US and get the hell out of here."

"It is not possible in this blizzard. The sky car engines are probably frozen by now."

"Just look over there. I brought the engines inside some time ago."

"It doesn't matter, Trave. The fuel lines and wings would ice up in no time, and we would be forced to land again and maybe in a place with no cabin to shelter us."

I was still packing up my supplies and setting them by the door. "Think of the cats, Trave. They wouldn't last long in the cold."

I stopped getting my gear together and looked over to where the cats were by the fire.

"You're not making any sense," the crossling continued frantically.

"You take care of them for me."

"If you leave them, I am done with you," the bird said and then gave orders for his four squad members to park on the other side of the room.

"I'm not leaving them, like you think, Niner," I said lowly. "I am giving myself up."

"What?" he said, stringing the word out into multiple syllables and in a tone that revealed shock.

"You heard me. I didn't stutter."

"That's death," he said and turned away. I went on packing and finally he walked over to me. "Don't give up, Trave. We've come so far together. We will find the wizard."

"There is no wizard. There is no spot of safety on this blue and white marble. Every atom and inch of earth is under global surveillance."

"We can change that. You wanted to once."

"Why do you even care, Niner? You're not even human. You are safe. You can return home and call it quits. Why don't you?"

"My mind was changed by the words in the manual. I see the possibility for a different world now."

"Because of some soothsayer?"

"Don't Travis. Don't disparage Joseph anymore. He is close to the source."

"He was close to the source. He is the one who turned us in."

"That is not true. I have him pinpointed on my GPS. He is not in any enemy compound."

"Let me see for myself," I said going over to him. "Bring up his reading. I'm going to plug his numbers into my computer." Niner gave me the numbers and I entered them. The GPS grid appeared on my screen, and I could see a faint glow that pulsed somewhere beyond the north star. Niner came and stood looking at my screen. "There he is. I told you."

"That's outer space. What is he? A satellite?"

"That is where the wizard is."

"Face it, Niner. You made a mistake. You fudged up the numbers in the system so you got a false reading. More likely, Good Neighbor Sam fudged the reading on purpose so you couldn't track him when he left."

"I don't make mistakes."

"You're perfect, then?"

"Pretty darn near. With figures and readings at least. As an evolving human, I have a lot to learn."

I was looking at the screen and not at the crossling and noticed another cluster of movement. "There's a bunch of little dots a few hundred miles from here," I told the drone.

"The advancing army," the eagle said. "See the way they look more like dashes?"

"I just asked that. Why is it flashing?" I repeated.

"They're human."

"You're kidding. Well, human or not we need to prepare to fight." I said.

"Or we could camouflage ourselves against the GPS," he said turning in circles.

"How?"

"I'm thinking," he said still spinning around. A few turns later he stopped and looked at us. "It might work, but it would be more like a coat of armor than a jacket, and we would need lots and lots of it."

"Of what?"

"Like the protective shield I used to wear."

"There aren't any spare parts around here, unless you care to donate yours," I said.

Niner wrapped his wings around himself very quickly. "I'm off limits," he said turning his head to look at all of us.

"And we, likewise," announced Wudgie.

"Of course, all present company is excluded," said Zel to confirm and console them.

"They'll fly right over and not be able to detect our real readings. It'll be a walk in the park from here on out."

"You keep forgetting we don't have parts, and we are in no man's land," I said, which sent Niner into a convulsion of laughter.

"Straighten up, you plexicoated pterodactyl."

"You said no man's land and we are making you all to register as not being men. Get it?" he said trumpeting again.

"It's not that funny," I said.

"Oh, I get it, Niner," Axle said and began laughing as did Wudgie. "Good one."

"Then you'll stay?" the bird said walking up to me and whispering. "You'll all have an equal chance to get away. No one has to sacrifice themselves."

"Let's give it a try." Inside I felt a little sheepish. I had really sought to leave because I thought I'd have a better chance alone. I felt the flapping of pats on my legs from Niner's wings. "We're going to make it, Trave. Joseph told me we would," the eagle crossling said dumping out my backpack in a heap.

"What are you doing?"

"Helping you unpack. What does it look like?"

"Ah, go ahead," I said giving up. "I'm going to get some sleep."

It snowed for another day before the skies cleared and we could get a search party into the air again. Wudgie and I flew after Niner so we could pick up the drones which had frozen up and fallen during the blizzard. In order to retrieve each downed drone we had to land and dig them out of the snow by hand which was a long and tiring process. We managed to get ten that first day and four were able to fly back on their own after being recharged.

"I spotted a town when we flew out," I said. "Let's stop there on the way back."

"I'll give it a scan and see what's about," Niner said.

I flew in a wide circle over the buildings while Niner turned on his locator. "Robotoids and drones, and clones. No humans."

"Are any of them moving?"

"No. All are in the motionless state."

"Probably frozen. Well, find a store, Wudgie, and I'll set her down."

In short order we had picked up a few boxes of food and supplies and headed back to camp.

As I stepped into the lodge, a smell of roasted meat hit my nostrils. I looked towards the fireplace and a huge portion of meat was blocking the view. Not having eaten all day, my appetite kicked in and I was aware that I was starving.

"Drew shot a deer. Axle helped him skin and dress it."

"My little elves have been busy," I said.

"Elves?"

"I've been playing Santa, can't you tell?" I said putting the box down.

"Your little foraging trip sure changed your attitude," Zel remarked setting the box down inside the door. The children were suited up and just going through the door to the outside. "Drew, make sure you get the black bag in back of the driver's seat. There's a surprise in it. "Don't peek. It's for after dinner."

It felt good to get my boots off and warm my feet by the fire and have a cup of hot tea and eat meat on a stick. When my belly was full, I stretched out on my blanket. It was then that my eyes happened to see the black bag. "Who feels like a movie?" I said getting up. "Hey, Niner, bring up the list of old movies on the computer."

"I want the Wizard of Oz," Drew yelled. "You promised you would show it to us, Niner."

"Okay, ladies now I need to borrow a pan," I said.

Desny handed me one. "No, won't do. It's got to have a lid on it."

"I'll get the lid for it."

"Now, I need some fat in the bottom of it."

"What kind of dessert is made with fat?" Ashley wanted to know. "Yuk. Count me out."

"Take your brother and look just outside the door. There's a cube of drinks I set to chill out there. Bring them in and mix them up."

"You got a soda maker?" Ashley said running to the door.

"You'll have to add the carbonation," I warned.

I found the bag of popcorn and dumped some kernels into the pan. I put on my gloves to hold the lid down while I shook the pan. Soon, the sound of popping brought the others to watch. "Explosives?" said Niner. "What kind of food explodes?"

"That can't be good for you," Wudgey added.

"It's called popcorn," Zel told him. "They once sold it at the movies."

Wudgie and Axle continued to keep their eyes on the pan, but kept jumping back as the kettle let out its sounds. When the popping slowed, I took the lid off and showed it to them. I threw a kernel at Niner and it hit him and dropped to the ground. "It didn't make any noise and I didn't even feel it hit me. How come? It sounded like rocks when you poured it in the pan."

He picked the piece up and sniffed it and then threw it at Wudgie who stomped on it before picking it up. "It's light as a snowflake."

"Let me have one," said Axle.

"It's to eat, not throw," I said dipping in a smaller bowl to fill it and handing it to Ashley, who immediately handed it to her brother.

"Hologram the movie, Niner," I ordered.

"Wait, Niner. I want to get my sleeping bag arranged and my soda," Drew said.

Wudgie and Axle were throwing the popped corn into the air and batting it at each other as the movie credits began to roll. "It doesn't hurt. Rocks that turned into snowflakes. Magic. I have seen real magic."

"Shhh. You guys. We want to hear the movie," scolded Ashley.

The children sat cross legged and bent forward. It was the stillest I had ever seen them. I lay down on my bag and watched from a mound of puffed up pillows I had put on the floor and was out like a light.

It was the middle of the night when I awoke again and everyone else was asleep. At least I thought they were until I turned over and saw Wudgie and Axle sitting beside me. "What are you doing?" I whispered.

"We were waiting to see if the corn was going to pop again in your stomach."

"Get away. It only explodes once," I whispered back. "I need to unpack some things we got at the parts place."

"Yes, I have been meaning to ask you what it all was for," Wudgie said following behind me.

Drew stumbled over to us rubbing his eyes. "What's going on?"

"Preparing for the day's work."

"I want to help."

"Put your pants on."

By early afternoon we had gotten fourteen drones back into the air. Zel and Desny brought lunch in the form of sandwiches as Niner was coming back with his group of fighters and two more recovered drones. He let the drones drop from his grip and they rolled to a landing and plowed up the snow in front of them until they came to a halt. We had more drones to thaw out and charge.

"What we really need is some jet cars," Niner said.

"I wouldn't turn them down," I told him.

"Let's go get'em then," the bird said.

"How many pieces are they in?" I said without looking up from my sandwich.

"They're just parked on the landing strip waiting to be piloted."

"What airport? Where?"

"Take a look at the streaming video of Eighty three's flight," Niner said and ordered the drone forward to where we were sitting. "I viewed them on the flight back."

Sure enough, under the cover of snow, we could see the outline of jet cars sitting on the landing strip. "That's the footage he took of the area while he was downed. Now, look at the footage I took today," he said switching screens, "after some of the snow had melted."

"It's an enemy fort," Drew said, "but where is everybody?"

"Dead," Niner said. "I did some reconnaissance of the area. All the bodies are human. All of them were air waved just like the rest of you."

"The last outpost," I said almost to myself.

"Spooky," Drew said.

"We can get the arms and munitions we need for the taking."

"How far ahead?"

"20 or so miles."

"Load up. We're moving to our new quarters. Niner, send drones ahead to make sure the ground is secure."

In a few hours we took off for the new camp. Desny was quiet until we were overhead of the fort. "Ashley is quite afraid of dead bodies," she said out of the blue.

I turned to look at her. Her eyes weren't pleading or weepy. It was a sincere and honest stare of a mother who wanted to do the best she could to protect her children from an experience she knew would harm them. I admired her direct approach.

"I'll have Axle and Wudgie land outside the gates. I'll let you out there, too. I'll have the robos clean up the area. We will have a ceremony."

"They have never been to a funeral."

"None of you need attend, " I told her while I was typing orders to Niner on the computer. I had landed outside the fort by a stand of trees.

Desny got out and turned to me. "Thank you." It was her eyes that told me she meant it. They seemed to sparkle and twinkle like the stars. It made her warm and kind. There was always warmth in the light, I told myself.

When Wudgie, Axle, and I checked the compound there really weren't any fleshy bodies about just skeletal remains. I ordered Wudgie and Axle to collect them and I told Niner to help them prepare a burial spot, and went back to inform the others of what was being done.

It was sometime later as we were sitting around the fire to have a bite to eat that Niner returned from the task. We had made camp just outside the gates when a blast went off inside the walls. Niner began flapping his wings in an unsettled way and was looking back to where the sound had come from. "Idiots," he said. "I told them to wait."

"What's going on?" I said getting to my feet and grabbing my weapon.

"I gave them some explosives to blast a hole with. Morons. You need to get them upgraded and fast," he said as he continued shaking his wings. "You can always fix stupid."

"My ears are ringing. I felt that blast in my heart," Desny said.

"Dummies. I told them to use one stick at a time. They must have used it all at once."

"You better check on them, Niner," I said. "They may have blown themselves up."

"Hey, there's a bright spot in my day," he said. "I'll send fifty four in to report back." ·

In minutes we had the okay signal from fifty four. The robos had survived. "Tell them to continue to collect the bones and put them in the hole they made," Niner directed his subordinate.

While the bones were being removed, I, Desny, and Zel tested out the jet cars. Next we began loading them up with ammunition and supplies. Since they were twice as big as the sky cars were able to drive our already loaded vehicles right into the biggest jet car that Wudgie would pilot. It could also carry an armored rover, off road vehicles, and most of the battle gear that we had foraged.

The next morning we were up at dawn and ate sparingly. The sun was coming up when we headed into the camp for the ceremony. Everything had an eerie feeling to it as we set out to the grave site in those cold, early hours. It was the way the sun created blue shadows on the white ground, and the crunching sound our boots made on the tightly packed snow that set my nerves on edge. Each breath we breathed out released little trails of vanishing white smoke in the frigid air. I was of half a mind to forget the funeral and just get underway, but something made me press on to see the detail through. I decided to make it short. I looked at the two teenagers trudging behind me. "They don't have to come," I said to Desny again.

"Niner reminded us that death is a part of life and something they needed to witness. It will be a testament to carry into their old age."

Her words replaced my own misgivings with a sense of duty and reverence. That was why the sound of our boots on snow seemed so loud to me, I thought. It was a somber event. It was a testament. These had been real humans.

Niner read about the resurrection of the body and the life to come from his memory logs. I motioned to Wudgie, and he and Axle mounted the bulldozers and began covering the pit.

"That was beautiful," Zel said, grabbing my arm as we trudged back through the snow. I didn't acknowledge her touch. I just kept walking. I was anxious to load up and get out of this territory. I could hear the grunts from the engines of the dozers in the back ground as we hurried away.

"What did what you read, mean, Niner?" asked Ashley.

"What words are you referring to?" Niner said to her. He was hovering by her and he said, "May I use your arm?"

The girl held it out and the bird perched on it.

"The part about the dead coming to life again. It scared me. Can they do that?"

"It is the wizard who comes and wakes them all up again. He has the breath that makes it so. Only he has the power. He is the one who will give me life, also."

"Well, almost all beings can be reanimated these days," said Drew. "What's the big deal, Ashley?"

"It's different with us humans. We die," the girl answered. "Like them back there. Like father."

"The wizard will come," Niner said to her.

"You can afford to think such things. You are practically an eternal."

"And even if there were such a person. Why would he allow all this to happen to people?" Drew said.

"The wizard did not do this. People, hybrids did this. It was a person who ordered the death rays, not the wizard," the bird reminded her. "You are blaming the wrong personage."

She sat down crying in the snow and her mother knelt beside her.

"That's why we people are on the bottom of the heap. I don't want to be human. I don't want to die. I want to be like you, Niner."

"I wish all of you would make up your minds. You are driving me crazy. Niner wants to be human and you don't," the boy said.

"Niner can help us. He can make us eternal," Ashley said.

"Me? No, I have no such wisdom. That's the wizards job."

Niner walked over to the girl and patted her legs with his wings. "Why are you afraid of dying?"

"I can't imagine not being. I don't know where we go. I feel like we should know, though. Isn't that strange?"

"People do know. The manual says so."

"Why do you have such belief in this wizard, Commander Niner?"

"It is because I see his vision all around us," Niner said waving his right wing in half a circle. "Look at that tree."

"It's just ugly and brown, " Ashley said.

"It's dead," Drew said.

"It's winter, but imagine it in the spring. What happens?"

"Trees sprout new leaves."

"And the grass begins to grow again," the bird said walking over to the oak tree and digging around it. "The flowers come back. Everything is alive again. What's so scary about that?" Finally he grasped something out from the leaves and the snow he had brushed away. "This is a nut from the mighty oak tree." He walked over and handed it to her. "Plant it."

"Why?"

"Just dig a hole and plop it in."

Ashely quickly dug a divot out of the ground, and dropped the nut in. Niner went over and kicked the dirt back over it. "Can you see the nut now?" he asked.

"No. It's hidden."

"Exactly, Ashley. You planted it just like we planted the bones." He waited a while to see if the girl was going to say anything. When she didn't, he continued. "Is the nut dead or alive?"

"We won't know until it grows or not."

"Just like the soul the wizard gave you is inside you."

"I don't see how a nut is like a person."

"They both have surprises inside," the bird said. "Magic, put there by the wizard himself."

"What kind of magic?" Desny said.

"Eternal. The soul is the seed inside man, and that is the part the wizard brings back to life when he wakes them up.

"But there's nothing but bones left."

"The spirit and the soul aren't visible to man," Niner explained.

"It's hard to believe in things you can't see," Ashly answered.

"May I try to explain, Niner?" Zel asked.

"Please."

"We carry the soul inside each of us just like the acorn carries its seed inside so it is protected. When we die, the soul is taken to be with the wizard until he awakens the body again and gives it back to us."

"You explained it remarkably, Zel," Niner cooed. "So you see Ashley, you never really die at all. That is, not all of you."

"You're saying that all humans live forever?" the boy asked.

"Their spirit does."

"How does the wizard change us to this spirit?"

"In the twinkling of an eye, the book says," Niner said. "The corrupt will be made incorruptible."

"What does that mean?"

"It means the mortal will be made immortal."

"Tell me, Travis, do you believe in this?" Desny said.

I didn't answer. Zel came up to her. "I believe. There was a man that stayed with us for a while. He explained many things in the book."

"He was no ordinary man," Niner said.

"He did nothing out of the ordinary, either," I said.

"Have you forgotten the kittens?" the bird reminded me.

"Coincidence."

"What about the kittens?" Desny pressed the eagle.

"They were healed in a night."

"They were grazed with buck shot and frightened. They ate and slept, and the next morning they were strong again," I told her.

"They had both been shot," Niner told Desny. "They had been missing for days, weeks. Fluff was trying to carry Hoss in her mouth and could barely drag her. She collapsed at our feet. I was sure she had died on the spot. I helped nurse the cats that night. Fluff did not stir. I feared that she was not alive, but Joseph gave me words to say for her. He taught me how to speak to the wizard of the universe, the creator of all life."

"You create a greater story than the one I remember," I said to the crossling.

"You were just as shocked as I was the next morning when they both got up. I saw your face and I saw you talk to Joseph about it," Zel reminded me.

In the distance we could hear the whirring of drones approaching. "Something must be wrong, Trave. The drones are returning," Niner said setting his tuners more accurately. "They are signaling the alert for enemy sighted."

"How far?"

"Five hundred yards and advancing."

We started running towards the gate of the fort. That was as far as we got before the enemy surrounded us. They were dressed in white winter gear and on ski's, and before we were aware of them, these soldiers had swooped down on us like giant birds. We were surrounded prey. A hundred laser guns were pointed at us, and suddenly all in our group moved behind me. I could see our sky jets sitting ready just beyond us and I wanted to make a break for them. A man who wore captain's bars and dark goggles spoke. "Drop your weapons."

"What are you armed with?" I asked, trying to stall them.

"Drop your weapons and you won't have to find out."

Since I was out numbered I lowered the rifle I had slung over my shoulder to the ground and motioned to the others to do the same. "Niner, stand down with your squad," I ordered. The captain lifted his sunglasses and took a step forward in my direction. "Just who in the hell are you?" he asked.

"Don't say anything, Trave. They're Alpha core," Niner tried to whisper.

"Quiet drone," the officer said to Niner. "Lieutenant Robbins!"

"Sir!"

"Take a patrol. See if there are any more of these renegades on the base."

"We are all that's here," I said when the captain had turned to stare at Niner.

"Shut up. We were watching you from the peak. What did you do with the bodies?"

"We gave them a burial," Niner spoke up.

"Tell feathers to shut up," the captain said.

"Feathers? I happen to be an Alpha squadron commander. You are the hundred and tenth mountain division," Niner said speaking louder. "I see the emblem on your sleeves."

A roar of laughter came from the troops. "And I detect with my laser that he has no protective shield given to all squadron commanders," a man said pointing his pocket computer at the eagle. Niner began kicking up snow with his feet and bunched it together into a tight snow ball. "I gave up my deflective shield in order to be made human. Ask the wizard here. Life and shields are incompatible."

"Stop messing with that snow," the captain ordered.

"On four," Niner called on loudly and within seconds fifty drones were overhead and had the drop on the troops from the hill. "Tight wing formation. Forty two, take the point and hold position. Fire only if fired upon."

"Yes, commander."

"Now, captain, it's your turn to drop your weapons," Niner continued while flying in the air around him.

The troops stood there with their mouths open.

The captain turned slightly to face his men. "Don't risk it, captain. My drones have smart weapons and I out number you," Niner warned hovering by him.

One of the officers standing with the larger group of soldiers rushed forward towards me. "Halt!" I screamed.

"Don't shoot. We have women and children," the officer said throwing down his weapon. "Let them live."

"I see no women and children."

"They're hidden in the mountains," the lieutenant said. I could tell by the look of anger on the captain's face that he was ready to shoot this officer himself. He noticed the look, too, because he said. "I'm sorry captain, but I have a two day old baby and I want him to live."

"Did you say baby?" I asked. "You are human?"

"We're dead now," the captain whispered, "and so are your wife and child."

"Come forward lieutenant," I commanded. When he was close enough, I ordered him to pull up his shirt. It was true. There was a belly button there, and I reached out to touch it. "Give me a reading, Niner."

"He's telling the truth. The whole lot of them are humans."

"What are these government drones doing obeying your command?" the captain asked.

"You are SG soldiers aren't you?" I said.

"We were.....once."

"And now?"

"Just kill us," Captain Reynolds said.

"You're asking me to kill you?" I said.

"You've been inside the compound. You must have seen what happened to those inside."

"Yes, we buried them."

"Buried them?" the captain said looking back at his men.

"You heard me, and we did so according to the manual," Niner said flying by the captain's head again and making him duck and cover his face from his flapping wings.

"How did you escape the fate of the other soldiers?" Niner said hovering over Reynolds.

"What's the difference, drone? We're dead anyway. You figure it out."

"The difference, captain, is whether you wish to remain living."

"What's this drone doing running the show? What the hell is going on?" Reynolds said to me.

"It's one of those crazy leftist paradigms," I said shrugging my shoulders.

Just then the patrol came back through the gate. "Drop your weapons, lieutenant," Niner said with his laser light pointed on him.

"Do as he says, Robbins," the captain said nodding over to the trees and the squad of flying drones.

"Come over and join your buddies," I said. "Wudgey, you and Axle pick up their weapons."

"Right, Trave. There might be time to do some hunting later."

"There's some real dinosaurs," Captain Reynolds remarked watching the two robotoids at work. Wudgey, hearing them talk, walked over to them.

"If you need to say something, say it to my face."

"You're a robotoid. I haven't seen one of your ilk in ages. Do they even make parts for your models anymore?"

"They don't make any parts for you hu-manimals anymore, either, do they?" the robo said coming back with their weapons in tow to stand beside me. It was then that Niner let out one of his trumpet calls. "That's a good one, Wudgie."

"What was that?" the captain asked looking skyward at Niner.

"What's a matter? Never heard a crossling laugh?" the bird asked.

"You get used to it," I said.

"If you're given the time to," the bird added swatting at the captain again.

"You still haven't told us what you're doing here. I can see you're not military."

"We're going to see the wizard," Wudgie said quite straight faced.

"We should have rushed them," someone in the crowd said, but before he could pick up his weapon, Niner had him covered one on one. "That's a no, no," he said wounding the man's arms with his talons.

"What kind of a bird is this?" the man said drawing back and holding his arm.

"I'm a rogue. A mad eagle. Don't you recognize a commander of the alpha squad when you see one?"

"He's no Alpha drone," someone said.

Niner turned to me. "I'll dazzle them with footwork, Trave." He sent ten members of his squad into the air. In seconds they were doing loops, and maneuvers with such precision that the men watched with open mouths. Satisfied with the response Niner ordered them to land in single file and sound off.

"That doesn't mean anything, drone. You could have been programed to copy the routine," the lieutenant continued.

"But I wasn't. Alpha corps squad commander one zero niner. Home base, Denver, Colorado. Authentication number 5694365443, Program number 7728.."

"Nonsense," the captain said looking directly at me. "What are you going to do with us?" he asked looking at me.

"Throw a party." I said smiling.

It was quite an ordeal to get them to divulge where the women and children were, but the snow was increasing and a blizzard was on its way so they gave in rather than let their wives and babies freeze. Niner and Zel went with Lt. Robbins to bring them back in one of the fort's trucks, and soon everyone was cozy in the dining hall. However, in a remarkably short time we accepted the men of the 110th mountain division as friends. Their weapons were returned to them and their neon ankle chains were removed.

CHAPTER 14

T he 110th Mountain division had originally been activated and trained during the second great world war and then disbanded at the end of the war. It was reactivated decades later to become the rangers, the seals, and the elite of the armed forces. In any case, Zel was beside herself with joy at having women to talk to and they baked and made coffee and tea at all times of the day and night. Today we were having coffee and spiced cake and Captain Reynolds had joined us. He had told me that they were heading north as well, but not until they had conquered the eternals. He verified the fact that this was the last outpost before the wilderness of the Yukon. He said the area beyond the fort had not been allowed to be settled. Those that had once lived there had been forcibly removed in the last decades. I thought this was a good time to get his perception on why the SG was erasing the human population. He had a more educated take on it that I had reasoned he would.

"We have lost the ability to function against them. Our gene pool is outdated. There's no guarantees with us. They didn't like that."

"What happened to evolution? Aren't we supposed to be getting better?"

Mrs. Reynolds walked up to us and touched her husband's arm. "Military secrets gentle men, or are women allowed into the conversation?" She was a nondescript looking woman. Her hair was black and course. It was short and mannish and there was not much of it. Her eyes wore a veil of sadness that kept the shining moments hidden somewhere behind it, I thought, if they ever had radiated happiness. Maybe her marriage had closed their light off, or maybe it was just the times. Her sudden appearance in our midst that day made me take stock of this man, too. It struck me then that this married couple were of the same short stature, and I found his height strange for a military man. He was blondish in complexion. His mouth was small and when he talked, only his bottom row of teeth showed. He talked rapidly, and kept his upper lip tight and straight, and it made me inclined to believe he was an impatient man struggling to stay in control. I had often heard him cut his men off abruptly before they had finished speaking and finish their sentence for them. It was his way of showing the speaker he was smarter, and that his mind processed things faster than they did. When the speaker of the moment left without having been heard, I had seen the captain smile.

The word that best described this man was prideful. He carried an air about him which purveyed that he always did what he pleased, and that others had given way to his brow beating power. There was an implied threat behind his wants that hinted at a man who was capable of throwing an ugly scene if his needs weren't addressed in the prescribed manner. He feigned sweetness with quick flashes of a smile and raised brows, which had at first put me off guard, but I found that they were intended to hide the volcano underneath. He meant to send a mixed message. It was a purposeful ruse, and I came to see Reynolds as the type of dog who waged his tail just before he bit you. He seemed to take a sadistic pleasure in his charade because he thought no one saw through it. I noticed that his men, and his wife and children were careful to be very quiet and unobtrusive whenever he was around. They tread lightly, listening for the sound of his warning rattle.

That very minute I saw that Mrs. Reynolds was waiting for his consent as she stood before us, but I gave it instead. "Please join us. I'm sure there is no danger of a breach of information with you."

The captain was about to object, but I called for Zel to bring tea and sweets. "Do you like to read Mrs. Reynolds?"

"Why ever would you ask me such a question?"

"We are in possession of quite an extensive library if you would like to peruse it, or maybe read to some of the children." Without waiting again for an answer, I called for Niner, and had him run down his list of choices on his screen. Millie seemed intrigued and I heard her ask Niner many questions about the titles. "Yes, I have read all of the books on the list. I will highlight those good for children," Niner informed her.

"We watched a very good flick one night, Mrs. Reynolds," Zel said setting down the tray. "The Wizard of Oz. It was taken from a book. Ashley and Drew loved it."

"I don't know what to say," the woman said sipping the tea. "None of the children here can read and the only flickers they have seen dealt with military protocol. Of course, they know their fairy tales."

"We will change all that. I can teach them to read," Niner beamed. "In the meantime, I will read to them and tell them many stories from the Basic Instruction Manual."

"Commander zero one niner, you will take this conversation elsewhere!" Reynolds ordered. "Mr. Tarkington and I were discussing other matters."

"I haven't finished my conversation, captain."

"That was an order, drone. Comply."

"I'm afraid he can't, captain," I said. "He's been given a makeover, one which gives him free rein in his thinking. He's quite human now, and no longer responds to military directives."

"You could benefit from our way of thinking and living, too, Captain. We are a band of very different thinkers. Teamwork and love," the bird said.

"There's no place for that in the military, or anywhere else."

"How about in marriage?" I added.

The captain gave me a disgruntled look, but Niner took the reins and he didn't have time to reprimand me. "Your men have a right to be taught how to think for themselves and to take over in case their superiors are captured or killed. The fight must go on."

"Hmm. Good insight. Knowledge must be passed along. A new theory."

"Actually, it's an old one, captain," Niner continued. "Let me tell you how battles were won by plain soldiers who knew their objectives and so were able to carry on the battle without the aid of superiors."

The air was getting tense where I was sitting, and I stood up and announced for the others to gather around. I had been feeding Niner input for weeks now into the subjects I wished him to talk to the men about. The whole lot had been getting a crash course in freedom. It was an informal arrangement and since we were in the great room of the lodge everyone was allowed to carry on with making dinner, washing clothes out, or whatever task they were involved in because they could still hear what was being taught.

Niner took his place in the front of the room which was at the right of the fireplace. "Freedom is the backbone of every successful country. Everyone is equal to any other person," I heard Niner say. "This is a right which comes from the creator of the heavens and the earth, not the government. Man is entitled to freedom of religion, speech, and an education. He is free to speak his mind as long as he does not endanger the lives of anyone else, or infringe on their rights and freedoms."

I helped Zel and the others hoist the side of elk over the massive steel grating we had put in place. "Is what Niner telling us, true?" Millie asked me.

"It used to be the law of the land," I said. "It was called the Constitution."

Over the next few days I became friends with Robbins, who was the second in command. I liked him and his wife for they were of a genuine and happy nature. His wife had just birthed twins. A girl and a boy. He was a young man, but reminded me of my grandfather and it was for that particular reason that I often went with Zel to visit with Bern and John. Bern was a woman of light coloring and she had a gentle face. Her voice was sure and steady. Niner was also fond of her and the babies. Bern had asked me and Desny to be sponsors for her two first born. They explained to me that sponsors were sworn to take care of the children in case the parents didn't survive. Niner had asked to be a sponsor also, and the young mother had not blinked an eye when saying he could be a half sponsor with me.

"I'm going to be fully human one day. We are on our way to see the wizard," Niner had said to reassure her.

Mentioning the wizard had precipitated the discussion of the manual and its teachings, and of course, Joseph. In time, and with Niner's teachings, almost all of the soldiers and their wives and children had voted to accept the manual and its way of life. Niner had found old downloaded caches of songs to the Creator that were played on the airwaves back in the beginning of the twenty first century. The sounds of guitars, pianos, and trumpets filled the lodges great room with music and the presence of the wizard, as Niner liked to say. The drone took great care and pleasure in choosing the musical repertoire he spun on the rings for us. Niner organized weekly concerts and people learned the words and sang along as they gathered together.

This new optimism also had another unexpected effect on the people. It brought about a need in them to fight against the SG. "Their terror must be brought to an end. I have come to see that freedom is everything," the lieutenant told me one morning at breakfast. The more John Robbins talked, the more he reminded me of the men Pompy had told me about decades ago, but of course, I had passed my grandfather's stories on to the lieutenant which may have influenced him. I told him how they had been willing to fight against oppression and tyranny for their families and others.

Since the lieutenant was an officer, he had been taught to read and write. He spent much time with Niner perusing his library and reading and viewing the rings of knowledge. He shared his newly discovered learning with all during the evening dinners. Niner even talked me into sharing my notes in my journal on the hidden history of our nation. Everyone wept when Niner showed them the hologram of the picture of George Washington in the snow praying at Valley Forge. It was unfathomable to them that these founding fathers had worshipped and prayed to this same Creator they had just discovered. Once their minds were freed, these new humans ate up knowledge like they ate up elks and deer and moose. In exchange, they taught me and the others how to ski and survive in the wilderness.

It was on a blizzardy day when the training was cut short that John approached me about joining forces with them. I was stretched out in my bag by the fire. War was the furthest thing from my mind.

"I've already told you that we are headed in the opposite direction."

Niner had come up behind him and I hadn't seen him. Now he stepped from behind the man and said. "Trave is very selfish."

"He had plans before he met us. I have no right to ask him to change them," Robbins said.

"I've changed my mind. It wasn't difficult," Niner told me.

"You're going with them?" I asked in a very surprised voice.

"I know what the SG are like you know. I was trained by them, remember?"

"What about the wizard?"

"He waits for the right time to bring the chosen to him. It is not my time."

"That's nonsense and you know it, Niner."

"What's nonsense is you not offering your help to the cause."

"I'm interested in living not dying."

"What about all these new children and humans to come?"

"They'll manage."

"It's a new day, Travis. These hybrids are wiping out your kind."

"I've made up my mind, Niner. I'm going on alone."

"I never took you for a man who would turn his back on his own kind."

"Now you know."

After my plans to leave were made known to all, Captain Reynolds kept a closer watch on me which suited me just fine. That way I was able to keep track of him, too. I knew the SG military regime did not train the ranks to think on their own. They couldn't go to the bathroom without official permission.

With Reynolds in tow, I could be relatively sure the army wasn't planning any sudden moves, but I couldn't be certain for the simple reason that they had gone rogue like the rest of us.

It was a few days later that Reynolds approached me. "I know who you are, Newman."

"I'm glad somebody does. I haven't figured it out."

"That clone, Zel. She's a government watch dog."

"I know. She's since come away from the dark side."

"She was sent to bring you in."

"Bring me in? She let me go."

"She was sent to get the formula. She obviously doesn't have it or you would be dead, professor."

"What formula? There is no formula. Professor?" As I asked these questions, I saw a vision in my mind of a placard with my name on it sitting on a desk in a room with windows all around. It was a very austere and ordered setting, a laboratory of sorts. In this vision I also saw a glass screen that served as a blackboard covered in mathematical formulas written in green and red marker.

"Self-awareness. Ring a bell Dr. Newman?"

I stood there looking at both of them.

"He doesn't know who he is, does he?" he asked of Zel who had brought us some coffee.

"What's going on?" I demanded of her.

"He has somewhat of a vague idea," she said looking at Reynolds. "I wasn't sent after any formula, captain," she said backing away. "I was sent after him."

"You need to tell him who he is or I will," Reynolds said grabbing at Zel's arm.

"If you tell him, he might lose all of his past. It has been coming back gradually."

As they were talking I was getting flashbacks of another life. My life before I was a journalist, before I had interviewed Madam Butterfly of the NY stage. Now it made sense why I couldn't remember ever interviewing anyone else and now I caught more glimpses of another side of me. "I've had clues" I said. "Damn. There's a lot still missing, isn't there?"

"Show him," Reynolds yelled at Zel. "He has a right to know. Play back the holograms."

"Why do I get the impression that you two know each other?"

"Because we do," the captain said. "I worked with intelligence at the command center in the Life Engineering Dept. I saw your work. I saw you."

"Why don't I remember any of this? This is crazy. Crazy."

"They white washed your memory," the captain said. "Erased it."

"But why?" I asked.

"You quit the team. They were afraid you would defect. Don't you remember how paranoid the whole Command Center was at the end?"

"No. And how do I know that what you are going to show me is real? You could have made all of it up."

"No. No. It's in your memory. All we have to do is scan your memory banks and play it back to you. I know you are Doctor Travis Newman. That drone is self-aware. No one could have programed him to be self aware of himself and make adjustments to the world around him like he does on the fly without your touch. Artificial intel was your baby, doctor. You were the boy wonder."

"Nonsense. I only read about it. Studied up on it. It was a kit I used on Zero one niner, here. I just added a few touches of my own."

"He is the wizard," Niner said walking up to me. "I am able to do things I never thought possible. I have a life of my own now.

"Scan," Reynolds said throwing me a scanner/drive.

"I don't have any holograms. I never made any."

"Scan your damn brain, or I will do it for you."

By this time some of the other men had gathered. "Do it yourself, Travis," Lt. Robbins advised me. "You can stop the playback when you want then. You will have control."

"You want to know don't you? It's one way of proving what I say is the truth," the captain went on.

I couldn't deny what he just said was true, so I got ready to plug in and scan.

"Run it back twenty five years," he said to me. "Someone toss his sleeping bag over here."

Robbins helped me get the flash device adjusted and spread the bag on the floor. "Just lay back and relax. Don't fight it. If you do, it will feel like someone's sucking your brains out."

"Thanks."

It took a few minutes while Robbins checked the device over again, and then I pushed stream. The visions came immediately.

It looked like me. I was young with tons of hair and a wry smirk on my face. I was in a laboratory and I was at my desk dressed in a pink shirt and tie. I saw the same name plate that had flashed in my mind only minutes before. That was real, I thought. At least I'd had a memory of it before playing the scan. The room I saw myself in was a large gymnasium like room as open as a loft in Manhattan. There were ten or so other desks and the others were dressed like I was. There were two women in the room and they were walking up to me.

"Well, what's your consensus, girls?" I was asking them.

"It's definitely an oumuamua of some sort."

"I thought we settled that months ago," I said.

"Okay, have it your way, but it's not from our solar system. It behaves differently than stuff in our backyard." The woman was in her early thirties and as she was talking I remembered her name was Caleigh Bowe. I had called her Buttons and Bows.

The object was being streamed on the glass wall behind my desk so everyone could see it. It was a cylinder shaped rock and moved freely in space, tumbling over itself at times like an asteroid, but then righting itself and moving through space as a ship might, and I noticed it was capable of changing speeds.

"What kind of cosmic object is it?" I asked.

"Nothing I know of," the other girl named Dunbar said.

"I'll give you a chance to shoot my second hypothesis down too, Dr. Newman. I still say it's the AI we launched five years ago," Caliegh said eating a donut.

"It couldn't be. Ours was a drone. It would have responded to our messages."

"Unless it's gone rogue, or shaped shifted and molded itself into an asteroid like form to disguise itself," she continued, "or something else transformed it."

"That's saying it has ET consciousness," I heard myself saying. "It can't be from our own galaxy. It's from some distant planet."

"Do you realize what you are saying, Newman?"

"Yes. All the tests and data we've run show it has enough neurological pathways to be thinking for itself."

"He's right. We can't even reverse engineer it. We don't know how it propels itself into hyper space. It changes all the time."

"That still leaves us dealing with the question of whether or not it was planted by a foreign power who wanted us to find it," Caliegh said.

"And if it is some kind of Trojan Horse as you suggest, Buttons, what alien race or foreign power sent it?"

"It moves at hyperspace, so it knows about the formula for element 115. That would be a gift from the gods for us," she said lower in tone, "and no trick or treat."

"And now it is showing us the next stage of propulsion," I said dragging my cursor on the object to register its Mach speed as it hurdled across the glass screen where the computer was registering its numbers. "It's reached zero point energy, but how?"

"And for what purpose? If it is a Trojan Horse, it could be 12 on the clock," Ms. Dunbar said. "If it is midnight, professor, it doesn't matter who put it there, does it? It is a reality. It's there and we have just seen it."

"One thing that hasn't changed is that the army who holds the high ground wins the battle," Caleigh added.

"Hell, there's so many satellites from every country up there now, there could be another stars wars like the one we had in 2035," another assistant added.

"Nah, we've pretty much evaped all we didn't want up there now," I said dismissing his words.

"Do you think it could really be an advanced civilization who is letting us get a peek at their blueprints?"

"It seems to be leading us to discover certain advances like machine to brain interfacing and zero point energy."

"Right, but if it's the Trojan gift, how do we know if it for good or evil? Who's the bad guy?"

"Looking over all the data again, the thing seems to have singularity," Dunbar said. "It seems to adapt and update its own needs just like your research says."

"Let's hope not. We're the supposed brains on this blue and white marble, and we don't want it to know more than we do."

"Maybe it's Einstein trying to contact us. You know like they used to do with séances," Caleigh laughed.

"His brain at least. Nobody knows where that went after they deli sliced it," I said.

"Get a news article out about this phenomenon now, girls," a male voice ordered coming into the lab room. It was my old friend, Asphorsh. His face brought on a real nightmare from the past, and I turned off the flash drive. I wanted to recall the memories on my own first. Then I would be able to confirm the real memories against the scan later to see if they matched. I had the impression that it was this particular object which had set the paranoia in the lab in motion. I had been in on the AI. It was me they blamed for the crap in space. There had been two sides to the issue, I began to remember. One side claimed that all this new tech stuff was being given to us by aliens or the Russians in hopes of creating nuclear erasure of the planet, and the other side claimed that it was alien benefactors giving us a glimpse into our future. No one was quite sure, but it was a race to see who could get the formula's to work first. What I wanted to know right now was whether or not I was one of the killers. What came back to me at that particular moment was that I had given rise to a new race who could think generations beyond any one on earth. It was coming back in jolts. It was clear I had left or been forced to leave the Space Command Center, but then what had happened? My mind was literally empty. Now I was sure of who I had been, but I didn't know how I came to be that person. I must have gone to school, been trained, but that part wasn't filled in yet. I didn't want to believe Reynolds, but I had to admit to reprogramming Niner. I had given him the knowledge to control the other drones in the force, and I couldn't deny that either. In other words, I was creeping closer to believing the holograms of the past that showed me as the rebel AI designer, rather than deluding myself that reading a few books had taught me all that I had done with the drone. Sadly, as I remembered more and more of my past, I had to admit that Reynolds was not very far off course. Light was coming to me. I was in league with Madison. I was part of the elite. I had had a part in bringing about the end I had ascribed to them in my writings. Things were fitting into the holes. The great unjumbling had begun. I had lived on Madison Ave., and so had my friend, Madison Asphorsh. It must have been him who had wiped my memory clean and then used my own methods on me. He had left a little truth mixed in the new reality so that my memory had roots deep in the subconscious. I had helped create the methods of neurology which was partly responsible for the terror I was now living through.

I was sitting in a chair holding my head and finally I looked up at the two officers. "I can't seem to remember why I left the Life Engineering Lab completely, Captain Reynolds. Is there a way I can retrieve my memory completely?"

"If there's any way to know that, Professor Newman, it would be you who could do it," the younger man said.

"I'm afraid I can't let you do that," the Captain said.

"Why?"

"You are responsible for this mess in the first place. It was your type of genius that put us down this bunny trail."

"I didn't believe where they intended to take things. There were disagreements at the end. I remember that, but I need to know what really happened."

"Captain. Recall that they put him in cloud storage. They put him there for a reason," Robbins said coming to my defense.

"What did you say, Lt?" I asked.

"They cloud nined you, professor. Well, your memories."

"That's the answer. I was a light year thought away from reality as it was."

"I don't understand what you mean."

"It's like the old saying, you are on cloud nine. "

"Oh, I get it. You are in reality, but your mind is somewhere else," Lt. Robbins said.

"Except it's a permanent state," I said. "Or it was thought to be."

"Is it possible to undo?" he asked me.

"It's been happening to me a bit at a time and I seemed to retain the knowledge I had without being aware of it. Like the captain said, I worked miracles on Niner. I'm just not aware that I have that same knowledge on a conscious level…yet. I need to try and retrieve all my past knowledge before I can change anything now. I can't start pushing buttons and hope I hit the right one," I paused and then added, "if we're going to undo space command and take this country back. But I have to remember what happened."

"I can tell you what I know, Trave, but it doesn't even amount to a thimble full. I know they called you a traitor when they dismissed you from your job. If it wasn't for that, I would laser you now. There was a trial, and you were found guilty of betraying the One World. The world thought you had been sentenced to death, but then they announced the brain freeze. Years passed and you were forgotten," Robbins said. He turned to Reynolds. "We need to take a chance, captain."

"I'll be his assistant," Niner announced.

When I thought of Asphorsh's name on the placard on the door and desk I got a glimpse back into the intricacy of the program I had implanted in the brain. It had to do with certain words that triggered the brain to continually reprogram and update itself. Briefly explained, it was every word that held associations to man in an archetypal and genetic way. It rooted words so they lived and were an integral part of the circuitry (neurological pathways) in the main frame so that man would believe those words to be inborn in himself. In other words a genetic memory, but I had encoded it. I had conceived of it, if you will forgive the pun, and it had changed the course of the human race as I now was finding out.

I looked at the lieutenant. "How about you? Would you be willing to help me?"

"I don't know anything about science in the least."

"You're good at following orders, aren't you?"

"My life depends on it."

"Then you fit the bill."

"I insist on putting someone in with you from our side who knows something about this," Captain Reynolds said looking at the two of us.

"I don't need any one else."

"I'm afraid I must insist on it, professor. I don't trust you," he said pointing his laser at me. "I don't want to wake up and find that I am thinking like a cockroach one morning."

"Oh, we were beyond the insect world. It's more likely you would feel the impulse to race with sky cars or swim with a school of whales."

A few days later when we were on the way to set up a lab when the ground forces fell in line behind us. There were about ten of them. When we reached the door, I turned to them. "You can't all be trained in brain circuitry."

"I'm the one," a tall young man with glasses said coming forward. "Brubaker, sir."

"Your assistants?" I said looking beyond the youngster to the others.

"No. I believe the captain sent them as a reminder that he doesn't trust you."

Robbins took me to a room that had been used as a classroom on the base so it had everything I needed. I drew a diagram of the circuitry paths of the thought paths of memory on the glass writing board and then sat down to think. By lunch time I was still thinking. The budding scientist named Brubaker was reading a book and looked up each time I got up and paced around the room. Finally, I spun the glass board around so it faced the opposite direction and the diagram I had drawn now appeared completely backwards.

Brubaker looked up from his book. "Reverse engineering?" he asked. I was surprised he even had an inkling of what I was thinking and doing. He got up and brought his notebook up with him and handed it to me. On it was drawn the circuitry in the complete reverse order. "What's the next step you plan to take?" he asked.

"Suppose you tell me."

"This is the theory stage, so the natural thing is to see if it works. We need to have test subjects."

"Stop right there, Brubaker. We don't have any time for procedures and tests. It's my pathways that are going to be reversed, so it's my call."

"You could end up a babbling vegetable," he said looking at me.

"Captain Reynolds wouldn't be adverse to that, would he?"

Brubaker laughed. "It'd make his day."

"The only thing I want to make doubly sure of is the precise date to back track to. I don't want any of my true memories to get twisted and turned."

"Some sort of by pass?"

"None should be needed if they only erased my memory up until the time I was released from my job at the Life Engineering Lab, and then reprogrammed me for my new assignment as a writer."

"Won't it just come back on its own? Some of it must have. You programmed Niner and some of the others."

"I'm not aware of the knowledge. It's there, but I can't find the file."

"You're on auto pilot," he said.

"Kind'a."

He looked at me searchingly for a moment. "May I ask you something? Why did you believe Reynolds so easily when he told you about who you were?"

"I'd been having shadowy films appear in my mind from time to time of things in my life, but I didn't know how to make the connections. It was like a blue print was laying over my mind. I couldn't see it all the time. It came and went, and each time it came, more pieces fell into place. It was like a continuing story interrupted by commercials, but the images got stronger. Zel and Niner had given me hints, but I had just pushed them back into my delete file."

"That sounds like it means that it's all still there," Robbins said giving me a pat.

"Why do you think you didn't recall your true identity?" Brubaker asked.

"You mean why was my shadow self the stronger one? Fifty percent of it was self-protection," I said.

"And the other half?"

"Laziness. It was a relief not being a load bearing wall."

I laid down on the couch that was in the lab room and took the plug in device from Brubaker. "Let me drive at first," I told him. "When I get to the date I want, I want you to take over. Take me back another fifteen years from there."

"We need to account for your training."

"Then make it twenty."

In seconds my life rolled past me in images. They were being downloaded at such a pace I couldn't even react to them. I tightened my grip on the chair I was in, and I felt the cushioned arms on the chair burst under the grasp of my hands. In the next instant, my mind went blank and the images stopped. I lay still for a while and then came to the recollection of what experiment we were on. I let go of the chair, and as I brought my hand up to wipe the sweat from my brow, stuffing from the chair dropped into my lap. "That was fast, Sgt.," I said getting out of the chair.

"I didn't get all the years downloaded."

"Why not?"

He pointed to the chair arms. "How far back did you go?"

"I'm not sure. Ten. Maybe more."

"Damn," I said suddenly remembering the incidents which lead up to my leaving the Foundation.

"I'm sorry, Professor Newman. I didn't dare."

I began waving my arms at him. "I wasn't cursing at you. I was recalling the argument I had with Asphorsh in my mind and the reasons I left."

At that moment Captain Reynolds and some armed guards entered the room.

"And do you feel the same way now that you did then?" he said striding over to me.

"That's none of your business, captain."

"Oh, it is."

"Just what significance can it have for you? It's my memory."

"Oh, it's of no significance to me, but the answer may be the last one you give."

"Damn it, Captain. You said you wouldn't interfere. We haven't finished yet," Brubaker said pushing the guards back. "Now get out."

"This could save critical time."

"It could also shorten a man's life," Brubaker yelled back.

"Then let him answer," Reynolds shouted.

"You were watching all along, weren't you?" my assistant said.

"I didn't trust you," he admitted. All you intellectual types are alike. Science and its secrets come before common sense. I thought you would side with him, rape his knowledge, and escape with it yourself."

"That's quite a scenario of my life you've given me. One of complete dishonor," Brubaker said walking slowly over to me and handing me the flash drive.

"I quit. You'll have to finish it yourself," Brubaker said.

"You can't quit. You're an enlisted man," the captain raved. "Have you lost your senses, man?"

"What enlistment? What army?"

"Shoot him," Reynolds yelled at the guards as Brubaker walked past them.

"Hold your fire," a drone's voice rang out clearly from the doorway. "I'm set for vap." Niner flew into the room and other drones followed him.

The two sides stood facing each other. "I said drop your weapons, boys. Don't make this another OK Corral."

"A what?" someone asked, but no one moved.

"He's fast," I said, "that's all you need to know."

"Captain Reynolds order them to disarm, or I will make you disappear into a puff of smoke so small no one will see it," Niner warned.

"Do what he says men," the captain said.

Niner ordered the drones to pick up the weapons and give them to Travis and Brubaker. "Lay them down next to my feet," I said to the two drones hovering next to me.

I looked up at Reynolds. "I don't wish to fight against you, captian."

"Then give me an answer, professor."

"Yes, yes, yes! I feel the same as I did when I left the Life Engineering Foundation. They were wrong. They needed to be stopped, but Aspforsh wouldn't abort the experiments. I was arrested for trying to destroy the AI innovations I had just engineered."

"Then you still believe it was wrong?" the captain asked again.

"Isn't that what I just said?"

The men in the room threw up their hats and cheered.

Over the course of the next few weeks, Brubaker and I finished restoring my memory. It was at one of these sessions that Reynolds approached me. "Would you be willing to help destroy their laboratories?"

"You're the army. You've got the weapons. You do it."

"We were hoping you could do it in a humanitarian way," he said.

"You think there is a less painful way to die?"

"No, I wanted you to tell us a permanent way to die since the elites have as much as eliminated death."

Behind me on the screen was the projected image of a person being shot while giving a speech. "Do you recognize him?" the captain asked me.

"Yes. My old boss Asphorsh. " I said staring at the screen.

"He runs everything in North America now."

The next scenes showed Asphorsh giving speeches and showing off the newly created governmental security forces and weapons. "So he didn't receive a fatal wound. Too bad," I said trying to remember the events of the past.

"Oh, but he did. He was dead as dead gets in a few weeks on ice," Reynolds said. "They brought him back."

"Impossible."

"Once maybe, but it was rumored they used your tech to bring him back," the captain said.

"But how?"

"You tell us. You've got to stop them, Newman."

"I don't have to do anything, captain."

Lt. Robbins walked up to me. "I agree with the captain on this one. You brought this technology into the world. The onus is on you to destroy it."

"The wizard gives and the wizard takes away," Niner piped in.

"You wouldn't know what you do if that technology didn't exist, you plexicoated pterodactyl."

"Think on it professor."

"And if I don't want to help you?"

"I'll head the mission," Brubaker said speaking up.

"You're all set then," I said getting up and walking out of the lab.

"He has no conscience, no honor," I heard Reynolds saying.

"You are wrong, Captain Reynolds. I have seen him mourn the loss of life," Niner said.

"When?"

"You have seen the graves."

"Are you speaking of those cats you told us about?"

"He buried many species that have died along the way," Niner retorted.

"Someone needs to check this rogue's circuits," Reynolds said.

"That's my cue," Niner said and flew after me. "I have a wizard. No one touches me except the wizard."

"So the professor has programmed you to believe that he is a wizard?"

"No. I came up with the analogy myself after reading a few books and seeing some flicks."

"That's the same line of crap Travis tried to feed us, and that's a dangerous philosophy, drone. You're dangerous. Get out of here. Don't let me see you in this sector again. It's off limits to self-analyzing thinkers."

"But the drone has already consented to help me, Captain," Brubaker said.

"You'll have to do it without the drone. He's not a 110th programmed drone."

"I could reverse engineer him," Brubaker offered again.

"No one touches the drone," I said walking back into the room, "except me."

"You're off the project, Newman."

"No, you're off the project, captain. I don't take orders from the military. Take your soldier boys and scram. Don't come back even if you get a gold envelope inviting you to a celebration unveiling our success."

"Captain Reynolds?" A soldier said approaching us.

"Speak, private."

"Sir, Lt. Robbins is asking permission to reenter."

"Send him in," I said before Reynolds had a chance to answer.

The anger was apparent in every muscle in the captains face, but he nodded assent to his men. "Bring him in."

"And escort the captain out," I added. "Niner, see to it. Get us security to make sure no one has entry but we three that are here now."

"I want a full report from both of you on everything that takes place in this room," the captain was saying as he was being ushered through the door by the drones.

"Yes, sir," Robbins called back.

We started to devise experimental tests that would end a number of species from being able to survive an attack. After weeks of testing, we had found our weapon. It was the oldest one on record: fire.

Our next course of action was to decide upon a method of attack. Robbins was apprising me of our arsenal. "We have a few jet tankers that have satellite capabilities and are equipped with anti-missile defenses. Other weapons are armed with EMB's, lasers, and microwaves, both A and TAL's. We can do massive or minimum CD," Robbins was saying.

"Explain your ABC's to me."

"EMB is electromagnetic bomb and CD stands for collateral damage. A is airborne and TAL is for tank abled lasers."

"Niner has informed us that we need to reach at least a Mach speed of 300,000 to penetrate their protective force field. Also, objects traveling at that speed can't be detected by any form of radar. When the EMB's hit, their grid will be in a state of paralysis. Your old buddies will be totally without weaponry that functions, and in the dark to boot."

"Don't they have any of old fashioned kind of manual firing weapons?" I asked.

"Sure, but we're sending in an unmanned mobile unit with EV zappers. They exude extreme voltage when fired which are capable of frying anything in its path. It utilizes microwaves and can stop the heart of a man from the inside out. Nothing is going to survive that."

"Can you leave their lab intact?"

"Why? That is the core of the nightmare."

"Used for insane purposes, selfish purposes by the elite it has been. The techniques I helped develop were meant to help accident and war victims regain the use of their limbs and full normal bodily functions. It was meant to bring restoration and give a better quality of life to those suffering from disease or accident."

"Saving the lab opens the door to another coupe in the future and the chance that this scenario could happen all over again. Reynolds won't do it."

"He would rather see our wounded soldiers and accident victims live handicapped lives rather than be restored to normal function? You're a warrior. It could be you."

"Each man in this army has weighed the risks and accepted them. It is the price for freedom and peace."

"We could set up a committee of watchmen. Men sworn to use the biology only for good. We could set up a tier stage program where at least 5 committees would have to okay the procedure and there would be teams of doctors proctoring each surgery."

"Sounds legit to me," Robbins said.

"Then you'll help me."

Robbins didn't answer and I felt desperate. "Look, I know that Reynolds doesn't trust or like me, but I will prove my position by taking out Asphorsh myself."

"That's not tactically possible."

"Damn if it isn't. I'll just walk right into that fortress castle compound."

"It's a one way street, Trave."

I looked away. I wasn't even going to entertain the idea of death. "He'll deal with me. He has to. He wants what I know. He can't fight the singularity problem on his own and he knows it. I know I can convince him to turn his genetics over to me by promising to make him a thousand light years ahead of all the other minds out there. I know him."

"Is such a thing possible?"

"No. The circuitry that feeds all the brains are tied into a central system. One feeds into another. They are all interconnected. You can't interface one without all the others downloading the same information. I'd be lying to him," I said laughing.

"Then what is this thing about singularity," Robbins asked.

"Those in power are all fighting for the dominant position," Brubaker answered. "Each eternal is seeking interface with the main computer, draining it to gain direct communication and upgrade their own needs."

"They are seeking to interface with the true extraterrestrial consciousness they believe exists," I added.

"And does it exist?"

"Does the wizard? Does anything?"

"What is this oumuamua? I mean is it something you can measure?"

"I don't know. We thought it had the ability to transform itself into almost anything, but that was only a theory. We know it had attached itself to a space rock or a meteor though we were never sure what its true structural element was.

"Like ancient dragons, pukwudgies, and the like?"

"Yes, captain, and this time I agree with your skepticism."

"You scientists have messed with everything. You can put arms and legs and heads in different places, but you can't tell us what life forms are real."

"That's a mind thing. It has nothing to do with the physical aspects of the body which is what I am talking of now. Everyone tried to define their own reality. Then the elite took the unexpected step and said that the reality which surrounded us wasn't real. Material reality couldn't exist because it was evil, they said. They refused to call anything real except the reality of the next world, or some other parallel world that they said was the true mirror."

"Crazy. You might as well say that a stone has a brain."

"Many believe that," I said.

"I can see why they locked you away."

"They didn't just lock me away. They used drugs on me to try and get the knowledge out of my brain."

"You're lucky they didn't dissect your brain."

"They had already tried that with Einstein and found out it didn't work. The brain is like a body. It has to be connected to the other parts to function."

"I can't imagine how you survived it all," Reynolds said in a quiet and somber tone.

"I want to end Asphorsh now that I know he is behind it."

"It can't be done."

"You can't know until we try."

"We will have his back," Niner said. "None of the drones will let the eternals touch a hair on his body."

"I just need to convince Asphorsh to let me meddle with his brain. I will make him believe I can give him singularity over the others. He will agree. I know him."

"An what will that accomplish?"

"I intend to blow his reality apart."

"Just as I thought. And what if one of those pieces of brain survives your holocaust? Then in a few decades we would be right back where we started and facing a new colony of eternals."

"That could happen?" the captain asked in shock.

"I can trigger his brain to degrade and destroy itself upon command. I would be in control. Man would be in control."

"There's the question, Dr. Newman. What is out there? What's left to be in control of?"

"The same thing that has always been out there," I said.

"The wizard and the book," Niner sighed as he guided Reynolds out of the room. "We will teach the wizard's ways to you. He created this heaven and this earth."

"I heard it was once the best-selling book of all times," the captain replied.

"It prepares you for the next world by teaching you how to live in this one."

"A new vision of reality?"

"Actually a very old one."

Brubaker, Robbins, and I spent the next months preparing me and Niner to make our grand entrance into the subterranean fortress of the eternals while the captain readied the unit for its combat mission. I was entirely certain that I could get control of Asphorsh's mind if I could convince him to let me interface him with the computer in the lab while making him believe it was an ET life force. It would take some time for the new circuitry to evolve in his mind like it had with Niner, and for the new language to override the previous one. It was tricky, but it could be done. I would have to hide the new program even from itself until the very last moment, but when the recognition hit Asphorsh as to what was happening, it would be too late. That only gave me a split second to win in. I hoped I was as good as everyone said I once was.

Robbins had talked me into taking some precautionary steps rather than just walking into the compound unannounced. He had suggested ls-mail (light speed) contact outlining my allegiance to the eternals project and my plans to further Asphorsh's personal future. At first Asphorsh thought it was a joke, but I managed to persuade him that it was actually me by reminding him of a certain lab worker by the name of LuWanda who had a surprising gift of touch and an extremely inventive method of delivering it.

Finally I received his letter granting me permission to come. It was no guarantee of my safety, and I knew it was not worth the paper it was written on, but it was my ticket into the underworld city. I would have access to his presence and I would have a chance to make my pitch. I was confident that I could rely on his ego to take me up on my offer of singularity that would put him in sole authority as the one mind in the universe that would be above all others.

It wasn't too many days later that I stood before the entrance to the compound thinking that not much had changed since I had last been there. The whole side of the mountain had been sheared off so it was flat and the two triangular shaped doors the size of football fields still safe guarded the entrance, and I still felt like an ant in proportion to them, but this time there was one major difference: I was the Trojan Horse. I just didn't feel or look as big as one.

As the doors opened, I was surprised to see how thick they were. They had been reinforced since my days at the compound. My next surprise came when I saw my old colleague standing there to greet me.

"What new toy have you brought me, old friend?" Asphorsh said referring to Niner who was on my shoulder. It had been harder to talk Niner into becoming my parrot and show off item than it had been to get into the compound. I had bribed Niner with the same gifts as I had bribed Asphorsh with; by saying I would make him more real. Another problem I had to tackle with Niner was teaching him the correct way to pronounce the presidents name. He kept wanting to say it like it was two separate names, asp and forsh, but I had to keep telling him that it was said ash/force, and that the letters ph together made an f sound as in the word asphalt.

"Madison. How wonderful of you to come and greet me," I managed to say.

He came forward and hugged me. "You haven't changed, Newman," he said letting me go and heading back inside.

"Older," I said following behind him.

"Yes, well, we can fix that," he said looking back at me and smiling so that his one gold rimmed canine showed out of the side of his mouth. I had seen it gleam many times. This shining always struck me as strange; there was no light on it, but it seemed to always have its own fluorescence. He had stopped walking and was waiting for me to catch up. He had a brisk walk and walked on the balls of his feet and had the habit of being ahead of whoever he was walking with so he could look back at you. "Where's the clone?" he said looking at me.

I busied myself with petting Niner. "She's alive."

"Not your type?"

I hated him in that moment. It was difficult to keep my emotions under control, but I changed the topic to one that concerned my mission. "Take me to our old haunting grounds," I said to him.

"Patience, old friend. We have lots to talk about."

"I am eager to get back to work."

"I've arranged for lunch in your honor," he said waving me towards the door to his right.

"That wasn't necessary."

"No pets allowed," he said in an off handed way and looking at Niner. "Sorry."

I turned to Niner. "Wait in the hall for me."

"You didn't answer my question about the clone," Madison said leading me into the dining room. He wasn't going to let it go, but I occupied my mind with noting the changes in the décor of the place. There was a great table that ran the length of the room. Everything was more opulent than I remembered it. Four chandeliers now hung from the ceiling and lit the room. "You've redecorated."

"There's been many upgrades since you were last home, my boy, but I'm interested in discussing the drone. I want to know how you managed to persuade her to defect."

"I didn't."

"You're saying it was her own idea, then? We'll get her. Maybe you will even trade her back to us for some big ticket upgrade that catches your eye," he said motioning for me to take the seat he pointed at. Once I was seated, he moved the conversation back to

Zel. "When did she tell you what her orders were concerning you?"

"She didn't. He did," I said pointing back out into the hallway at Niner, who could be seen peering in the doorway.

"Yes, your plumed pet. He's a rogue, you know, and will have to be dealt with as such."

"Like me?" I said as a servant placed my plate in front of me. The smell was hypnotizing me. It was like being at Sardi's again.

"You're an old friend. You are exempt."

"And Niner is my friend."

"There are many webs being spun in this situation, aren't there? You can't blame the drone. It isn't possible."

When I didn't answer, he tried another ploy. "How's your steak? It's grass fed."

"Better than I remember."

Madison was looking intently at me as I ate and I detected a more serious tone in his voice. "I need to see his circuitry."

"And I will show it to you when we are in the lab, and as long as you agree that no hands will touch him except mine."

"You were never very good at sharing, Newman," he said laughing.

After lunch he had arranged for a few colleagues to give me a tour of the compound. "Isn't that the way to the lab?" I asked.

"You remember well. Patience. You will see it a bit later." With that, I watched him head away with other scientists and stand at the elevator.

"It's two more stories down," Niner told me as he patted my foot. "It comprises the whole floor. It's about 5000 sq. acres."

"It's grown," I said in a whisper. "How are your eyes?"

"The pixels are great," said Niner.

Our conversation was code to let me know his camera was getting the infrared pics to make blueprints from clearly. Since my last visit here, they had dug out an entire city below ground. It had buildings, streets, and individual houses. The black lighting over head let the sun shine every day. "You can see we are protected from all the elements, here," a man said walking up to me and informing me that he was to be my guide.

"Yes, it should extend the life of the building materials by twice its normal range," I said.

"It's a fully functioning underground city. Can you believe it sustains over two hundred and fifty thousand life forces?"

"The air source seems better than before," I said hoping the guide would give me info concerning how it functioned.

"It's filtered and protected by its own monitoring system. No poison gas can be added to its tanks. Safety first."

I looked at the great ducts above me. "Big," I said.

"Very," my host answered.

Next we saw the gardens and flowers each citizen was required to grow. Sprinkler systems watered each night with a type of drip irrigation system they had learned from the Israelis at the turn of the century. There were also water filtering systems that cleaned the water from the mountain streams just outside. I poked Niner when we got to the ventilation system.

"I've got it," the bird said. My new guide turned to the bird when he had spoken, and Niner ruffled his feathers at him.

The guide, who never gave me his name, kept looking at his watch and the tour went on and on. Finally we went down the elevator and came to our last stop on the tour which was the life engineering lab itself.

Asphorsh was waiting in his lab coat with a cadre of other scientists. "Good, you have your little pet with you."

"You better hope he's more than that, Madison. I tried out the singularity gene on him," I laughed. Of course in reality it was a lie. I had no such programming available.

"Professor Newman was the genius of his time," Madison told the others. "Now, he has come back to his senses and returned to us. None of this would have been possible without him."

Behind the surgeon suited bodies, I could see there was an exam table covered with white sheets and the instrument table sat ready beside it. "Let's take a look at your friend," Madison said.

"I will not parade his brain to the world. I will only provide you with slides of the outside of his circuitry, but that is all. I intended to give you first hand, real world demonstration of his capabilities. You need to see how he thinks and responds in the real world."

"Everyone has been looking forward to seeing the great Newman's genius up close," Madison said in a strained tone.

"I will not do it right now."

"We could arrest the bird if you prefer," Asphorsh said. "I could disassemble him now."

"And you would end up with parts and pieces. Seeing his circuitry alone would be of no benefit to you. You would be guessing at their functions."

"It might take a while, but we could reverse engineer your work," someone in a white lab coat said.

"Net the bird," Asphorsh ordered.

"And you would destroy his brain. I give you a warning. His system is circuited so that some organs must be detached and deactivated before others or a short out occurs that erases the encoding in the neuro paths. In other words, gentlemen, he is booby trapped."

Madison motioned his men to release the drone and Niner flew over to my feet.

The anger was livid in Asphorsh's face, but he regained control of himself. "Show us your demonstration."

I called Niner up to play the holograms we had downloaded with new info and edited before we came. They showed me pretending to operate on his neuro paths and training him by giving him technical updates which he was then to impart to the other drones in the experiment. The hologram clearly showed Niner telling them only what they needed to know to carry out their assignment, but withholding information that would be detrimental to him if they knew about it. Then I asked Niner why he had not given the drones the full download, and he answered that it was not wise to give them info which they might use later to gain mastery over him and the program. The scientists watching were amazed. "He has self-awareness. How was he able to arrive at the realization of self preservation and of putting himself first?" someone asked.

"Quite human. Quite impressive, Newman. He has adaptable perception and the ability to think ahead."

Madison pulled me aside. "Can you get brain to cosmic energy to merge the same way?"

"You mean like computer to human synthesis? Yes," I said to him.

"If there were such a thing I would say it is highly unlikely," someone commented.

"And is it possible for you to arrange for one brain to remain dominant above the rest like you did with your pet?" Asphorsh continued.

"That's a great leap, Mr. President. Too risky," some short guy blurted out.

"Get out. I want to chat with my old friend. All of you, shoo fly."

After the door had shut, Asphorsh linked his arm in mine. "Come up to the observatory. I want to show you the latest find in cosmic intelligence. You look as if you could stand some fresh air."

Niner started out after us.

"Leave the pet."

"If you prefer." I was agreeable because that would give Niner a chance to map out the lab floors locations into grid targets and place explosives in the air filtering system and elevator shafts.

"Shall I wait right here until you return, my wizard?" Niner asked. His polite subservience was touching and more realistic than we had rehearsed.

"It's remarkable the drone knows his place exactly when he should, and in what circumstances to take the lead," Madison said making a more comprehensive assessment of Niner.

After a lengthy ride in an elevator we emerged into the open air where a tram of cable cars was waiting. He flipped a switch and the cars came to where we were standing. I looked at him questioningly. "Our telescope is the biggest in the world, and of course it sees further when it is at located at the highest point," he said directing my attention to the peak of the mountain.

It was a gray world on the outside today, and it was snowing up in the reaches where we were. The mountains hemmed in the cable cars we were riding on so that all you could see was rock and show. The sun, wherever it was, was not high enough to be seen over the mountains. I had never cared for heights and the tram was noisy and jerky and I kept a hold of the straps to keep my balance. All of a sudden the tram stopped and I lurched forward. We just hung in air as the cable car swayed back and forth. I could see that we were only three quarters of the way up the mountain. "What made you decide to come back, Newman?" my old friend asked as he pulled the door to the tram open and took steps closer to me. I saw then that he had a laser pointed at me. The wind from the mountains flapped the little tram about like a sheet drying on the line. "Just a little push and you would drop about five thousand feet. Not much would be left of you for the animals to cart away."

"You were always the prankster, Madison," I said forcing a belly laugh while I reached over and closed the tram door. "Does it matter why I came back?"

"You don't have any larceny in your heart, or a need to get even with an old friend?"

"I was never like that, and you know it."

"True. Your ego was never as needy as mine."

"I'll tell you my story."

"Yes, you will, but I want you plugged in when you do, Travis. I want to scan the entirety of your thoughts."

"Do you mind if we get on solid ground first?" I said trying to stall for time. I needed to send out the high frequency whistle to alert Niner. We had prearranged a signal only he could hear when the time came that I would be asked to plug in. It was a certainty that I knew would be coming and had prepared Niner by instructing him how to bypass the circuits to my memory folder when I signaled him. With a little luck Niner would be able to stop the flow of my thoughts which dealt with the plans to destroy the compound and my lack of a real singularity transfer by blacking them out when I blew the whistle.

Madison remained silent, but the tram started up again and I could feel it ascending at an even level. "What's that you're fiddling with in your mouth?" he said as he reached out for it. I nearly dropped it trying to keep it out of his grasp.

"A harmonica. You remember how much I always hated being scanned."

"Biting the bullet?" Look on it as a great experiment to see who you choose

"It relaxes me. What can I say?"

He kept close watch on me the rest of the way up. There were three of his body guards there to meet us as we got off the tram. "Take him to room ten. Prepare him for scanning and extracting." It was then that I figured out he had planned this all along. The observatory had been a ruse to lure me into the trap.

In a few minutes I was stretched out on a couch in a room full of screens which the attendants had guided me to. "Want to watch?" Madison asked coming in the door.

"Why not? I haven't seen my life in a while," I said putting the harmonica to my lips.

"I'm just interested in the last six months or so. That's when the clone betrayed us."

After he revealed the duration of the scan, I started to relax. This was going to be a breeze. Niner and I had made a pretaped version of exactly that time period and now all he would have to do was insert it to my memory banks and play it back like a dvd from the old days. I blew the tune of somewhere over the rainbow as the scanner was attached to my head and turned on. If Niner did his part we were home free. I watched Madison's face as the holograms streamed out of my brain unto the screen.

I could see he was very impressed and felt assured that they were my own memories. I cursed at Zel on the tape as we fought about her double dealing and treachery. The hologram showed us parting ways after Niner broke up our fight. I could have been an actor. As the tape wound down to the present, I hoped Niner would take it out and let my own real thoughts flow from the time we came into the compound to now. He was perfect. He didn't miss a switch. As it happened, Asphorsh unplugged me at the point where we entered the compound. He had a smile on his face like an opponent who had just won a sparring match. It was almost too much to take.

"You really don't know where the clone is, do you?"

"No way to tell since she removed her positioning device."

"We'll find her. Speaking of that, we need to fit you with one. It's quite quick. Like being stuck with a pin. Seconds and it's all over."

"Since when did you start implanting scientists?"

"Regulations are always changing."

"Well, I want be among you eternals, so let's do it," I smiled.

"It's quite an irresistible urge, isn't it?"

"Better than the alternative path."

"Death was once the unknown end of we humans. The most frightening. But you my friend gave me, gave the world, a way to circumvent that nasty last sleep. It's quite a powerful feeling to know that there is no end to the game anymore. You don't have to give up all your trick and treats to someone else after you've toiled a life time to get them."

"That's why I came back. I discovered I'm not much of a fan of entropy, especially when it concerns myself. After all, I started this. I want to finish it."

"Now, let me show you the stars and the galaxies that are waiting. There is life out there. We just need to be sure we can control it, that our minds can rule."

"You're serious," I said following behind him.

"You think that I am speaking mythology, some mere frivolous tale woven out of gossamer wings?" That was where I had heard that spoken before. It had been his pet phrase. I almost laughed for a number of reasons, and it was at this point that I was certain he had lost touch with reality. Could it be that he had fallen victim to his own imagination?

"The problem is that reality doesn't coincide with our own wills, or it didn't until minds like yours came along. You bent reality, Newman."

As we turned the corner of the building the vista opened up and I could see the observatory enclosed in glass and a huge telescope poking up through the roof. "The eyes of eternity," he said to me before turning to one of the many workers in the area. "Do you have the oumuamua in sight?" he asked brushing past the workers on the platform.

"Yes, sir."

"Take a look at this, Travis."

I looked through the lens and saw what looked like an asteroid rolling through space. "It's an oumuamua. The first messenger," he said as I peered at it.

"Where did it come from?"

"It's not from our system. It doesn't follow our laws at all. Isn't it magnificent?"

"Is this the same entity I worked on?"

"Yes. We've known about it for years. Let me show you the whole movie from first sighting 'til now. It looks like just an asteroid, a rock, or some other kind of trivial cosmic object, but watch it change its direction and speed," he said playing back the rings for me. "Now watch what it does when one of our satellites approach it."

"Is it communicating with the satellite?" I said amazed, but before he could answer the satellite was vaporized.

"It has intelligence," he marveled.

"Or it is simply protecting itself?"

"That's life, isn't it? That's what you programmed your pet to do isn't it? Put himself first?"

"Self-preservation is a basic instinct."

"I have felt it reaching out to me when I have stood here at nights. It was like it was aware that I was watching it. I reached back. I melded with it. It was direct communication. I want more of it. I want to be closer. Can you get me there?"

"Interface you mean?"

"Of course, but I must have your assurance that I would be the dominant participant. It is the next phase man was meant to take. It is an altered state of consciousness by which to connect to the gods, to astral project, and travel to the stars."

I had him just where I wanted him. I would be able to gain access to his brain, his core, and regress him to infancy. I didn't want to appear to eager to operate on him so I tempered my advice with warnings. I knew he would pay no attention to any negatives I might bring up; his mind was given to the outcome only. He had never thought he could lose at anything. All he said was, "Can you guarantee me that I would be able to withdraw if this intelligence started to dominate me?"

"I can build a safe guard to disengage you in seconds after it applies aggressive thoughts of a take over, or attempts to short circuit your neurological pathways," I lied.

"I want you to start working on it."

"I want guarantees of my own."

He nodded reluctantly.

"No implants. No plug ins."

"I'll postpone it on a month to month basis until after my interface. I can't have one scientist remain a free thinker. You understand. You might go rogue on me again."

I watched him and he could not take his eyes off the screen and the object on it.

"We are at the last step and about to take our place outside of time itself by mastering our own minds. We will be able to move about through dimensions." He turned towards me. "Look at them now, Newman. They have landed. They are in our world. I want to be in theirs."

"Have you found life on the asteroid that landed?" I asked.

"It is a ship, not a rock," he said clearly irritated. "It is being looked into."

I looked away and then started towards the door. I didn't want to hear anymore.

"You're not changing your mind again are you, Newman? Or are you afraid? Do your eyes see only one dimension when you are sitting next to another dimension and just won't admit it?"

"I believe in a holographic universe just as you do, Madison. I see the synchronicity of it all, the rotation of planets, and the circular nature of even the seasons."

"Good. Good. There's not just ghost lights out there, you know," he said patting me on the back and walking with me.

I needed to think about my own plans and just nodded and smiled. It would take me only one day to regress him once the surgery was completed on him. His intellectual hold on the world would be over. In the meantime I would have to pretend to study and devise a blueprint for the interface. And of course, there would be the tools and programs that would make it seem plausible to the team I would be working with. So far I was having incredible luck. It had almost been too easy, and that nagged at me like a loose rock in my shoe.

As Madison and I continued to talk, I found him very intrusive to my private thoughts. "We're harvesting the genetic material, my boy," he said directing my attention to the glass walled room we were passing by. There were vials and body parts of various species floating in them and arranged on shelves. Men in sterilized suits were working on other animals. I saw snakes, dogs, and lizards, intermingled among the men and women lying on the OR tables. "Hybridization at its best," he said, "and you helped give it to us, but we can make every species better, not just horses. We're getting ready to enter into the galaxy. Tell me, who walks proud, looks human, and is not? Can you tell the difference from those you have seen around us?"

I only looked at him. I didn't want to let him know just how far behind on all that tech I was.

"No matter. You'll catch on. So, we must pick out a house for you to live in, Travis," he said with a clap on the back and changing the subject.

"I'd rather get busy on looking at all the info on this cosmic object," I said as I pressed the replay button on camera that had just taped the operation on the chimp's brain one more time. Then I looked at Madison's face for a clue to what he might be feeling, but it registered nothing I could detect. His eyes had always seemed especially unreadable to me. They showed no fear or anxiety. I didn't understand what kind of a person could trust interfacing with some unknown rock of unknown origin and not trust those he lived with and supposedly knew.

"We're all hybrids of a sort, Newman. We have been for generations," he said as if he had read my mind. Then as if to redirect the tone of our conversation he brightened and smiled. "Let's get reacquainted. Talk over old times, Travis."

"We're older. Things aren't the same."

"Speak for yourself," he said posing proudly. "I don't look over thirty, do I?"

I admitted it was true. He looked like he did over twenty five years ago, maybe younger I admitted to him. "We'll get you looking like the rest of us. We can't have some elderly gent running around here, can we? Besides we don't want anything to happen to that brain of yours."

He arranged for a sky car to transport us to the top of the next mountain, and then gave me a tour of the outside of the compound from the air. The beauty of the mountains was spectacular. It was a pristine wilderness that looked untouched by man or time. The ski slopes were active and the lifts were running. "You see our business is good," he said. "We provide nothing but the best in life for those who work and live here." Beautiful cabins stretched over the landscape and from time to time wildlife appeared. "See a house you like?"

"Which ones are for sale?"

"That's old style. You're a scientist. Any cabin you fancy is yours."

"I don't want to put any one out."

"They'll just move somewhere else, or have another cabin built for them. Time is not the enemy."

"Then I'll have one built for me. I'd like to design my own."

"You were always a little timid, a little slow, Travis."

"Everyone was compared to you," I said bolstering his ego.

"You never cared for power, did you?" It was a rhetorical question and he kept talking. "That's why I always liked you. I never had to compete with you, buddy."

"I'm still safe."

"Like home plate," he said smiling.

We were flying over a mansion built in a meadow. "I like this place," I said.

"You have good taste. It's mine," he said as we were landing. "You're to be my guest for the time being."

So he was going to keep tabs on me. "I'll have everything you need brought here."

I instantly regretted not picking out a cabin on the way. I didn't want to feel under surveillance. I was feeling shadowed already. "I'll pick a cabin of my own tomorrow."

"Nonsense. We've already settled that. You're going to build your own. Of course it can't be on the same scale as my castle."

"I thought everything was built to take place underground now," I ventured.

"Only at nights and when it is necessary because of the war."

Body guards came out to meet us. "Show the professor to his room. Make sure he has everything he desires."

The inside of the cabin was even more impressive. It had massive trees for beams. They were reddish in color on their trunks. "Are these real trees?" I asked my guard.

"Why wouldn't they be?"

"It's just that they look like redwoods."

"They are redwoods."

"Aren't they endangered and preserved?"

"President Asphorsh has his own forest of them growing all up and down the west coast. There will be more."

"In about two hundred years," I said.

"Time is not the enemy."

There was that catch phrase again. It was the first one I intended to change.

The room itself was oval and looked more like an atrium in a lodge than a bed room. It was a world of its own. It's dome was made of bullet proof glass and opened the world to you, so it appeared that the sky replaced the ceiling over head in much of the room. Trees and plants filled the space, but not so that it was crowded or overbearing. The setting was neither opulent or plain. I gave it a Little Red Ridinghood approval rating of 'just right.' I noticed a couch at one end of the room and went and laid down. I was asleep at once. I woke sometime later to a strange noise and the distinct feeling that someone was moving around the top of the couch cushions I was resting against. Upon opening my eyes, I looked up to find a lion looking down on me from the top of the pillows. He was licking his paws. At that precise time, a knock came at the door. "Hurry," I called out loudly. A servant entered with some fresh clothes folded over his arms. "Shoot it," I said still laying on the couch.

"I see you have met Charlie. She prefers the male guests."

"Will she pounce or chase after me if I move?"

"She's well fed," he said laying my clothes on the chair.

"I am Dubois. I will be your personal servant while you are here. The President requests that you shower and meet him in the dining room at seven, sir," he said and immediately began to retreat from the room.

"Dubois. Take the mistress with you."

"She does not do tricks, sir. Charlie does what she wants," he announced shutting the door.

"Did they send you to deal with me Mademoiselle Charlie?" I said standing in front of the couch and looking at the lioness still reclining on the top cushions. She let out a growl and shook her head and then went back to grooming her paws.

I ruffled through the clothes which Dubois had laid out for me on a chair. They were of fine quality and formal. I scooped up the clean laundry in my arms and entered the bath and slammed the door. I heard the cat roar.

After I finished my shower and had dressed, I peeked out into the room cautiously. The lion was no longer on the couch. I checked the entire room and was not able see the big cat from my vantage point. To my way of thinking, the perfect opportunity to dash out the door had presented itself, and I seized it. I left the door open hoping if Charlie was still inside she would take the hint and leave.

I retraced my steps back down the stairs, trying to remember where Dubois had told me the main dining room was when we had come in. After some back tracking I finally heard voices and walked in that direction. The hall was filled with guests all dressed in tuxes and evening gowns. I was pleased to see the women. It would make the dinner more enjoyable.

I was barely in the room when Asphorsh announced me. "Our guest of honor, ladies and gentlemen. I present Professor Travis Newman."

I did my best to bow slightly and walk to where Dubois was holding a chair out and nodding at me. Applause rang in my ears. When it died down, Madison said," I see you have brought a guest of your own." I was puzzled at first until I turned around to see Charlie walking behind me. A brunette seated at the table gave my suit jacket two quick yanks. "A tamer of women. Show me later. Bring your whip."

I only smiled back, which was difficult because all I could see of the woman was her rather large mouth brimming over with teeth, and I was suddenly reminded of the blonde in the red Toyota.

The meal was a long and an arduous task with Charlie laying in back of my chair. "Do not feed her, sir," Dubois had said upon seating me. "It gives her ideas." I was careful to chew quietly and speak in calming tones.

After dinner, Asphorsh introduced me to a few of the new task force members in the bar area. "These are the three colleagues you will be working with the most closely. You'll get to know the others as you go along. This is Dr. Carl Rosen. He's the Einstein of the bunch, or he was until you showed up," Madison said patting my back. Rosen smiled, but I could see he hated my guts. I didn't blame him. It's hard to fall to number two especially when you weren't expecting it. I took a hard look at him since he was the neurologist in the group.

"Dr. Peter Choler, and Dr. Guns Gunther," Madison said nodding at the next two men across from us. I shook hands with them and Choler said, "DNA." He was a dolorous man with sweaty palms, but Guns was robust and happy in a genuine sort of way. "I'm the inside man," he said which I took to mean he was the internist among us.

"If you need a kidney, he's the man to see," the woman behind him said coming around to shake my hand. "I'm Mrs. Guns." I immediately recognized her as the woman who had jerked my jacket in the dining room. "I like a man with a little gray around the temples," she said walking away. I couldn't help thinking that some of her features had been overdone. Looking around the room, I took it to be the norm. Big teeth, protruding lips, which hinted at the stunted formation of a duck's flat beak, and skin so tight it looked like it had been vacuumed sealed. Well, they say history repeats itself in farce. I felt I was at the circus.

Guns followed after his wife, and I was left standing with the other two men.

"Intruder," Choler whispered into my ear.

"Excuse me?"

"She's known as the Intruder. It's a play on her real name which is Trudy. Watch out."

"That says it all, doesn't it?" I winked back at him.

His demeanor immediately changed and he said, "It's a mistake to court trouble."

Then the other man beside us, Rosen, put his gold chip in. "Unless you're the boy genius like Newman, here," he said as he looped his arm through Choler's and guided him away from my presence.

"Trouble in paradise?" a woman with dark hair said suddenly appearing beside me.

I jumped a bit and was lost for words.

She smiled, took a sip from her drink and said, "Forgive me for startling you."

She had evidently read me well, so I didn't bother to lie. "I'm Dr. Caldwell. Iris," she said offering her hand.

"I'm afraid my social skills have suffered over the last decade or so," I laughed. "I'm Travis Newman."

"I know who you are, doctor. You're the reason for this whole night."

"Yes, of course. How dense of me." I stared at her eyes. They were a lucid shade of blue and the light in them danced like iridescent champagne bubbles spritzing out every which way. She was a gorgeous creature; lithe and limber like a cat, and I liked her very much right off. "Will we be working together?"

"No way around it, but be aware that I am the glue that holds everything together, the synthesizer. I make sure each anatomical feature is Sympatico." So she was the one who was responsible for bringing the circus to town, but I noticed she had not joined its ranks.

"You're the reality marker of whether what Madison wants is possible," I said, "and is it?"

"He's quite mad, you know," she said smiling. She drank the rest of her drink and set it on the end table next to us and walked off saying, "Til we meet again."

I wanted to talk with her more, but she was lost amid the flux of bodies moving in the room. I saw Madison and went over to him. The men he was talking to all left as I approached. "Did I disturb something?"

"Forget it. This is your night. Have you met many people yet?"

"I'm afraid I haven't made good inroads."

He gave a look to where Choler and the rest of them were standing in a group and said. "There won't be any problems on the job." It was a very sure statement. I tried to make my exit at that point, but Asphorsh insisted that I stay because I was the guest of honor and he put another glass of champagne in my hand. It was then that a conversation began about our past relationship. I forgot how it started, but it grew heated in a very short frame of time.

"You have forgotten the propaganda you spread to terrorize the masses. There aren't many species left," I said.

"And you have forgotten why you were scrapped from the project. You don't share well with others. You're like the man who won't die. You keep coming back because some moron fouled up the paper work and you ended up in stir instead of as a clone donor."

"I'm asking you to be logical, Madison. Don't you remember we made all the stuff up about the hidden code on the DNA being linked to ancient ET genetics? It was mathematical codes we found, not alien ones and they really pointed to a creator, an outside programmer. It was the same mathematical code we had already found in nature. Remember? There was, is, no ET stem."

"We've come light years since then. We're organic robots, Trave. We always have been. You just won't see it. Can't. Or are you upset that I plugged in your mind and don't trust you? Think of it as a great experiment. I give you free will. Isn't that the premise upon which the universe was founded? Well, I am no different than the original potter. I needed to see who you would choose."

For one crazy second his reasoning sounded logical to me, but then it struck me that Madison was not God. Joseph had said that the real wizard was evident in the whole of nature. Nothing had been created on a whim, or by chance and I wondered what Madison's intent was. As it was I was to find out shortly.

"It's a shame you can't be on my side. You have a gift. I have always admired your brain. I will merge it with mine, with electronics of every kind. I will make you immortal Travis. 'Course you'll be a cyborg, a man-machine hybrid."

"That's crazy."

"You have such limited vision for such intelligence. You're afraid of it. Look at your DNA strand, and your brain as chips on which information is stored. They can be fed a life time of knowledge and when the body dies, your mind lives on and is transferred into the next container. So you see you don't have to be afraid."

"Is that all you see man as?"

"It is the next phase of evolution. One in which man, hybrid, cyborg creates his own destiny. It is limitless. Super beings to conquer the stars. Why shouldn't we avail ourselves of all this technology before some other civilization does?"

Madison spun around to look at me. It was the same look he gave me in the penthouse those decades ago. "Oh, yes, you believe in the wizard. The good wizard who created humans. That is the true lie in the universe and I have proved it. We have moved beyond the, 'who made it first' debate. The question now is, who shall control it from here on out?"

My head was throbbing when I woke the next morning. I hadn't had a hangover in years, and wasn't sure I could handle the results until they wore off. I dunked my head in a basin of cold water and repeated the procedure until my head lightened a bit. I had a shower and dressed in about fifteen minutes and went down to breakfast. Again, it was a public affair in the main dining hall and I just bowed slightly as I walked in and took my seat. I searched the faces for Iris, and that occupied my mind during the small talk of the meal, but I didn't locate her. Then it struck me that she hadn't been at the dinner last night either. Did she eat, and if so, when and where?

It was obvious as we made our way to the elevator after breakfast that the men were a group by themselves and I was a party of one. Distance would make my job easier, I consoled myself. I stayed behind further, and put a signal in for Niner now that I had the power to my k-phone restored. I hadn't been able to commune with him for a day, and I was getting worried. He texted that he was in the next room to my suite and I headed back that way. In seconds I felt a swish against my pant legs and looked down to find the lioness walking beside me.

I managed to squeeze in the door where Niner was waiting without letting the kitty enter with me. "You've got to find a way to keep the cat away from me," I said to Niner when I was in the room.

"Where the heck and deck have you been? I have texted you since last night?" Niner complained.

"No personal communication is allowed during any social functions of the state. They shut down all cells."

"I'll have to come up with a way around that," the drone said.

"Hurry just give me a report. I'm expected in the lab."

"I've got the blueprints nearly done. I need to get pics of the lower levels yet."

"I'll take you to work with me, but I need to lose the cat."

"That's simple. Turn around."

"What for?"

"Just turn around," Niner said hovering in front of me. I did as I was instructed and he said, "Now lift up your shirt. Stand still. This might hurt a bit," he said as I heard a laser being turned on. I pulled my shirt down and jumped away from him. "What are you going to do?"

"Must I explain everything?"

"When lasers are involved, yes."

"They've inserted a GPS underneath your skin just below your right back bone. Now lift up your shirt. I'll extract it with the vacuum. It's the same thing Zel used on you. The laser just powers it. The cat is trained to follow the signal they gave you."

"How do you know?"

"I have scanned your person each time I have seen you to watch for changes."

"I owe you buddy. Owww. That hurt."

"Hold out your hand," he said flying around to the front of me. "I have a present for you." I felt a tiny ball drop into my palm and picked it up and placed it the pocket of my shirt and took it off and placed it on a chair by the door.

"No more tail, I hope," I said opening the door and waiting for Niner to fly out with me. I began walking down the hall and the lion just sat at the door and didn't give me a second glance. Niner had been right; the kitty had just followed the signal.

"Who's the genius, huh?" Niner blurted. "Meow," he said looking back at the lion.

Once down stairs, I left Niner to his work on the lower levels and told him to report to the lab when he was finished. All eyes were zeroed in on me when I came through the door to the work station. "I had some business to take care off."

"You've changed your shirt, Professor Newman," Rosen said.

"Yes, that was the business. I spilled some egg and jam. Well, shall we get busy?"

I was sweating heavily under my armpits and could feel my uneasiness growing when I spotted Iris in a corner of the room. "Iris, get me the files in deep storage that are related to the cosmic object."

"They are marked IF (immediate files) 1-29 in the cloud storage section if you want them. However, I am assisting with a surgery this morning and then several deliveries. Forget the research. You need to attend this. Get your hands dirty. You should watch at least."

Just then the doors to the back of the room were opened and the group went through the glass doors. Everything was plexi glass in these new laboratories. There was no corner to hide in on the whole floor which left me feeling vulnerable and exposed. Everything else was chrome matted steel. The computers, the doors, the desks. It was a sterile gray and glassy world that stared out at you. Even the floors were open grated with steel so you could see myriads of levels beneath and above you. I couldn't help thinking they were trap doors which would suddenly give way, dropping you down into some sterile abyss below. I tread lightly, and walked over to the next entrance and looked at the number of operating bays that were filled with patients. "Come with me, professor. You need to suit up and get sprayed." I followed Iris because I was intrigued with her.

In seconds I was in a see through cubicle where a paper like gown was dropped over me which covered me from head to toe like a twentieth century space suit. I was then instructed to place my hands into a small opening which appeared in the wall in front of me. My hands were sprayed and a pair of disposable gloves dropped down onto the counter. "Hands must be covered before leaving the cleansing area," a recorded voice repeated until I put the gloves on. The door opened and instructions ordered me to 'stay on the conveyor walk until your bay is reached. Step off quickly. Once past your bay you may not go back. You must reenter the cubical and start over.' Each bay already held patients and I was trying to decide which one I should pick when Iris called out, "Get off at seven."

I did and nearly fell on my face when I landed on the floor of the surgery room. It was highly polished. As I straightened up to meet Iris, she reached down and pulled my pant leg up to reveal my leather bottomed shoes. "I'll get you a pair of rubber soled tracking shoes. They'll make you a mountain goat in no time."

Those that were standing around the operating table were looking at us. "I apologize for my tardiness, doctors," Iris said.

"I see that it was not your fault," Rosen said.

On the table before us was a fairly young woman. "This patient is suffering from alziemer's, professor. We are trying to reverse, or at least slow down the neurological aging process. What we have tried so far has not worked. Have a look at her chart," Rosen said turning on the screen above the OR table.

As I read her chart, I saw that her age was 70. I looked down at her face again. She didn't even look thirty. "As you can see, Dr. Newman, we have perfected the eternal touch as it relates to the physical body, but we haven't yet quite perfected the mind. Any suggestions?"

"Please put up the neurological diagram that highlights the affected area of the brain, again, doctor," I ordered. He did, and I studied them a minute. "By pass all the circuits which lead to that sector marked in yellow."

"That was the old way," Rosen was all too quick to point out. "The innovative method is injecting a fluid that washes out years of buildup and makes the neurological pathways like new. It can even fix the grooves caused by epilepsy or stroke episodes. You have missed out on one or two things in the last few decades, it seems."

I remained silent. Rosen had gotten his digs in on me and I let him gloat over his current victory. He would be history soon enough. I looked around the room at the faces and did not feel a bond with any of them. I didn't know what stage of development any of them were in. Rosen moved a machine over the woman's head and a diagram appeared on it as soon as the glass touched her skull. He then took a pencil thin laser and traced out the route to be fixed with it. There wasn't even a spark or bit of smoke. The head no longer needed to be invaded from the outside. Rosen put his laser down and pressed a device into the women's shoulder area and she immediately came to and sat up.

"Do you know who I am, and what surgery yoy have just under gone, Renna?"

"Yes. You are Dr. Rosen and I have just had surgery to restore my mind. I can already assure you that my memory has returned, doctor," the woman said as she was being shuttled out on the conveyor belt. Another patient was brought in. It was a regular assembly line. "I want you to stay for a week so we can see how things go," Rosen called out to the patient who was being moved down the corridor.

Rosen looked over at me. "Care to take over?"

"No. Like you said, Dr. Rosen, things have changed a bit. It is the safety of the patient which comes first."

I heard him chuckle. It was his day. I was yet to have mine. The morning dragged on as I stood watching Rosen perform his act. Finally at around eleven I was stretching my limbs and rubbing the back of my neck when I happened to see movement outside in the hallway. It was the fluttering of wings. I motioned to Niner to fly lower. A scraping noise came from the hallway and a few people looked over in his direction. Someone was going to go to see what the disturbance had been, but I stepped up, "Let me. I'm only watching the surgery."

I ran along the length of the glass enclosure to where I saw Niner skidding to a halt and made a sign with my fingers to tell him to walk in the hallway. The brick wall was not high enough to hide him if he flew. I watched him until he was around the corner and started back to the table shrugging my shoulders.

"Why don't you take our boy wonder to lunch, Dr. Caldwell," Rosen spoke out. "He looks tired and bored."

I gave no look towards Rosen at all. "I was told about the mountain lodge restaurant, Iris. I would like to try it out."

"It's a long way up there."

"Jet car is the way to go then," I said to her. "Arrange for one, will you?"

The sun was shining perfectly as we sat in the mountain lodge which was very busy. I had asked for a window seat so I could watch for the eagle. The mountains were covered in snow this high up, but you could see all the way down the slopes and below the frost line where the pines were green and fresh looking. I had seen Niner fly past us on the way up and I looked for him now. Iris was clicking her nails on the glass of water in front of her and I turned towards her.

"I didn't mean to ignore you. I was just admiring the view," I said and looked down at her hands.

"Nervous habit," she said immediately removing her hands from the glass. "Why do you let Rosen get away with his little jibes at you?"

"I don't feel threatened by him."

"What's between you two anyway? I hear there's a history."

"Nothing interesting. Care to chauffer me around? Show me the sights? I'm interested to see what's changed."

"Sorry, I'm afraid I can't. I'm expected at the delivery station within the next hour if that peeks your interest."

It didn't, but I didn't want to let her get away. We ate a green kale soup and headed back down the mountain.

At the doorway to the infant room, Iris was scanned and the machine announced, "Forty percent upgraded. "When I stepped in front of the door way it said, "No upgrades. Life form is basic. Primitive. Primitive." Lights, bells, and whistles went off. Guards from down the hallway came running.

"It's alright, guys. Dr. Newman, our guest, is the culprit," Iris said.

"Why is it set to alert for humans?"

"You'll have to ask Madison that," she answered.

I could see there were covered plastic incubators in rows that stretched across the entire room. "Why are all the bassinets empty?" I asked.

"They aren't. The embryo just isn't big enough to see yet. It's waiting for fertilization." She nudged me forward. "You'll see the live ones further down."

We kept walking, and indeed, there were what looked like babies underneath the cover of blankets. The further down the line we went, the older the children got. "We're experimenting with gestation times," she informed me.

"Don't you find any of this a little creepy?"

"You had better read up on what's considered etiquette in the compound. I'm afraid that questions posed to illicit a personal opinion on accepted procedures are grounds for dismissal or worse." Iris stopped and took out her telecom device and began typing into it. "I must report the breach."

"You're not serious? That's rather a rigid response to breaking a rule, don't you think? Are you intending to frighten me?"

"It would be wise if you were."

She kept walking and I followed after her. Further down the line were larger adult encapsulated bodies. I took them to be sleeping or under drugs. It reminded me of where Zel had told me she had awoken. I could see what had inspired her terror. "Our clone base," the doctor explained. "The cream of the crop." She pointed the device in her hand at the wall. Immediately I could see diagrams appearing on the glass screens. It was a list of the complete DNA and genetic traits available to choose from. "A smorgasbord of human possibilities. Design your own child or make yourself over. You pick the upgrade. Complete with pink or aqua marine eyes. Permanent blue hair or dyed skin." Her device rang and she answered it. "I am with him now."

I looked more intently as she spoke. "Yes, Mr. President. No, Charlie is not with him." Her reactions were more machine than woman.

She put her device on her belt. "You are to report to him after we have finished."

"I think I will look around up here a little more on my own first."

"You won't gain access to any lab rooms. You are a basic life form."

"I want to look the clones over."

"Looking for the clone, Zel?"

I thought of lying to Ann, but I felt like she was somehow reading my mind and confessed.

"I can show you, but then I must go and you must report."

Zel's incubator was way down at the end of the room. "Take a last look. She is soon to be an extinct model."

"Is it permitted to ask why?"

"You should know."

"Rogue tendencies?"

She smiled a brief smile and put her hand out to show me the path I should take. "How did you arrange the neurons in her brain that enabled her to overcome her soullessness?"

"I don't understand what you mean."

"She chose not to kill. She took the higher path. It had to be a conscience decision."

"So you know the soul is not transferred." I looked at her face and knew she fully expected me to divulge my secrets to her. I was being given credit for more than I had actually accomplished. I smiled back and teased her with a lie. "Yes, well perhaps if I work here long enough I will be able to enlighten you."

The smile left her face. "There's a door at this end of the room."

"Your rating is only a forty percent. May I ask which what parts, Iris?"

"No, vital parts, Dr. Newman."

"Then you're wired for this," I said grabbing her and kissing her for which I received a quick slap across the face.

"That's even better than I hoped," I told her smiling. "I will dream of your touch tonight."

Outside the laboratory door I looked at her and waved, but received no recognition back from her. I wondered where Niner was when I heard the order to report to Aspforsh come over the skype. When I found him he was seated on the terrace with some of my colleagues. Apparently they had decided to break for lunch after all.

As I walked onto the terrace, the others got up and left, merely nodding at me as they passed by. "We need to get as much fresh air as possible," Asphorsh said to me. "I'll have them bring you a plate."

Madison gave his index finger a small twirl in the air and everyone stood up and left. "Some emergency?" I said looking back at the departing cadre.

My old acquaintance laughed. "They started lunch while you were getting a tour of the cloning lab."

"What's my penance to be?" I said looking over the railing of the stone balcony at the mountain vista rather than at him.

"Sit, Travis. Your lunch has arrived." He waited for me to take the chair opposite to him and continued. "We have a few details to discuss. Forget about the incident with Dr. Caldwell. You have no copy of the regulation book. I will see that you get one. I want to discuss your being updated and what techniques you used on your pet."

His remark caught me off guard and he immediately took advantage of it. I must learn not show my emotions so openly I reminded myself, but then I was only human. "Now is not a good time, President Asphorsh. I have a great task before me concerning you, our whole civilization."

"I don't have anything major in mind, Travis. You are a little old and worn around the edges. Let me think, you are fifty something. You've missed the required upgrades. I'll give you the pocket version of the replacement schedule to start."

"I feel fine. I'm comfortable."

"We won't do them all at once, of course. Pick four or five that can be done soon. I can't let my personal physician as it were, not be up to standards. I need to keep you with me into the next few centuries."

I kept tossing the endive leaves and dandelions around on my plate.

"No appetite?" he asked.

"I'm waiting for something more substantial in the second course."

"There is no second course for you. It is advisable to eat lightly before surgery."

"Just wine then."

"Not allowed either. Now there is the matter of Charlie. It seems DuBois found her lying outside the door to your room waiting, and strangely enough he found the GPS in the pocket of your jacket slung over the chair." Just as he finished talking four men came over to us, and as one pulled my chair back from the round table, two others clamped a neon ankle bracelet around each of my legs.

"It's something that can be easily seen," Asphorsh said.

"I guess I've moved on from guest status."

"Think of yourself as highly valued, and someone we don't want to lose sight of."

Two of the men helped me from my chair and aided me back to my room. I had hoped that Niner would be there, but he wasn't. My plans had to be altered quickly. I needed to find a way out. I wasn't alone long before some men dressed as aides came into my room. It was more of a raid than a visit. They rushed me and one gave me a hypodermic with a laser like gun in the neck. I believed I was being implanted with the GPS, but I was out like a light.

There was a high ceiling above me when I awoke. I was strapped to a table and I was in the lab room. "He's awake, doctor."

In seconds a familiar face was looking down on me. "No, need to fear Travis. We didn't take anything vital," Asphorsh said smiling. "Just a little DNA and a duplicate copy of your brain."

So they were intending to clone me. "Why do you use computer language to discuss my organs?"

"Our vocabulary reflects our new genetics now. We've seen evidence of our ancestors hovering in the galaxy throughout history. They've traveled the breath of universes we have never seen or envisioned. He was looking at the asteroid on the screen across the room which he had shown me yesterday.

"The amoumoua is a trap. A Trojan horse. If you interface, you will destroy yourself and mankind with it."

"You were always gullible, Travis. Do you believe in mud wumps, too?"

"Madison, if I were to tell you that what you're going to do was foretold, would you heed my words?"

"Are you going to tell me that I am the prophesized beast?"

"Yes."

"Nonsense. There is no wizard of all. If there was, I would be it."

"That's just it. The one who is not the wizard, seeks to usurp the true one."

"That would be you trying to overthrow me, Travis," he laughed.

Iris came up to us and without looking my way touched Asphorsh's arm. "Do you wish to take any more specimens, Mr. President?"

"No, Dr. We have enough of his chromes to last at least a millennium or two. That's enough to make the world quite sick of Newman's."

"Surprised?" he asked me. "We didn't need to wait for you to tell us what you know. It's all in storage now. I have all your knowledge in these flash drives. They freeze well. I'm going to store them right next to my own. So you see, your body is merely a repository now. It serves no purpose to me. Of course we have to experiment until we can free your brain of its radical streak of independent will. It could take a few hundred clones."

"What's the next step?" I asked.

"I'm going to set you free. You will arrive at the end of the journey all humans face. It will take a few days to test all your data and drives, and of course your DNA. I would estimate that you have at least minus ten days and counting," he said pointing to the clock. As he talked, I was shown five clones of myself on the screen. "As you can see there are no shortages of Newman's around. "Take him to his room."

There was food under a silver tray on the table and I looked at it. Steak and vegetables. I heard a scratching at the window and went to investigate. The windows were fitted and trimmed with barbed wire, but I saw Niner outside. He was clinging to the wire with one claw while lasering through it with the other. In no time he was in the room. "I need to give you a code word for me," he said.

"What?"

"You need to give me one, too."

"You're not making sense."

"Listen, Trave. They made clones of me just like they did you. We need to know who we are talking to. Refer to me as the raven. I will call you George W."

"Make it GW. Can you get me a weapon?"

"I've brought you a few drop bombs. You'll have to throw them down against something hard to make them explode, but they might come in handy," he said flying over to the bed. "To unload these, just unclick the cartridges."

I did as he instructed. "Can you get me a rope long enough to lower me to the ground?"

"You want to escape now?"

"Did you want tea first?"

"We have to destroy the clones of us."

"That'll have to wait 'til the army is with us."

"They need to attack fast," Niner said. "Asphorsh is going to interface with the cosmic entity."

"That's impossible."

"It's happening now. See for yourself," Niner said giving me his portable computer.

I couldn't believe what I saw. The Oumauama Asphorsh had shown me sailing through the galaxy had landed. I could see two parallel tracks leading to where it had taxied to rest in the snow. "They have made contact," Niner was saying. "They are on their way to it now."

I looked at my watch. "At sundown?"

"Time of day is not important," Niner said flying back to the window. "Why are you standing around in your under clothes? Put some clothes on."

"They confiscated them."

"I'll see what I can scare up."

"Never mind. We haven't got time. I'll use the blankets from the bed," I said taking one of the blankets off the bed and putting it over the chair. "Bring your scissors over here and cut this for me." Niner got my meaning and used his talons on the comforter to make two separate pieces. As he did, the stuffing from the inside of the blankets began to float down. It contained down feathers and pebble sized pieces of foam rubber. The room looked like a chicken hatchery gone mad. I quickly wrapped one section of the quilt around me like a cape and tied it around my neck and one around my waist to cover my nakedness. "Okay, you'll have to fly me down, we don't have time for pulleys and ropes."

"By what? Your hair?"

"Just grab a hand full of this comforter."

"You better tie it tighter then," he advised.

I was over by the window looking down. "Yes, I see what you mean. It's a long ways down."

"Too bad we didn't have a parachute."

"You're the parachute," I said as Niner lifted me up in the room. The way he had picked me up by the blanket I suddenly was hanging upside down. It was a shaky take off, and when we reached window Niner said, "You'll have to scrunch up a bit so I can get you out of the window."

I pulled my legs up and felt myself tipping forward as we flew through the window. The full weight of my body left Niner momentarily a bit off balance. "Glide," he yelled at me. "Glide."

"I don't know a thing about it."

We were going down. I felt safe because I knew the drone was rated to carry tons of pounds of armaments. I could see the ground, but there was something blocking my view directly below me, and then I heard the sound of material begin to rip. All of a sudden there was a flurry of white about me as the blanket emptied the rest of its contents into the air. Feathers and foam flew away from me in the updraft of the current. The blanket acted as a sort of parachute for a minute, but then was ripped away from me in a gust. I was naked and about to die. Niner heard the ripping and was aware of my trouble. "Grab my rotors. My tail, Trave."

I did manage to grab onto him. "Hurry, I can't hold on," I said with my eyes closed. However, just then I felt my feet touching something and looked down to see the green awning of the window coverings below me. "I'm going to set you down gently so you don't fall through," Niner said quite calmly.

In seconds I felt my butt sagging into the canvas as it stretched under my weight. To my relief there was a window adjacent to the awning. I kicked it in with my foot, cleared the glass away, and Niner flew inside. To my surprise, there was an elderly woman standing in the middle of the room as Niner flew over to her. "I came to borrow some clothing," he explained to her. "Do you have something that you could give me?"

She retained the look of astonishment as she walked over to the closet and took a dress out from it and handed it to Niner who grasped it in his talons.

"Do you have anything a bit warmer, Madam?" The woman was mute and motionless so Niner flew past her into the closet. "Excuse me while I check, Madam." Soon he came back out with a long sleeved gown which he handed to me. "I won't forget this," the drone said, and the woman did a double take and blinked her eyes as if to clear them. "Is it for the regalia next week?" she finally asked.

"No," Niner replied.

"You have awfully good taste. That's my most expensive dress. I didn't know fowls went in for this sort of thing," she said.

"I'm an eagle."

"Yes, of course, that would explain it."

She followed Niner over to the window. "Do use the door next time, dear." It was then she squinted and looked straight at me sitting on the awning outside the window as I pulled the gown over my head. I felt like I should explain, so I said, "I needed a parachute."

"Yes, of course. My room is quite high up, you know."

It was at this point that Niner spoke to me. "Get hold of my rudders," he said and lifted me up off the awning and we continued down to the next awning and the next; my dress flying upwards around my head each time. I was hoping that there was no one out below us because the bright fluorescent ankle bracelets were blinking away."

"I have never had landing lights before," Niner said when we were finally on the ground.

"Laser them off."

We hunted around for a jet car that was open and I started it up and we took off for the base in Canada. I felt Niner looking at me from the passenger seat. "You're just going to let them interface? Asphorsh is already dangerous, and if he gets hold of alien technology nobody will be able to stop him."

"Are you trying to tell me that there is truth to what he told me? Is there life on the object?"

"You yourself know about the Trojan Horse. It has been told of and feared by all species."

"You're serious, aren't you? You're saying he was meant to find it."

"I have read it's pulsars. They are real. It makes my feathers ruffle. I have heard it's voice in my heart. Joseph warned us about the paths. He said to choose carefully. Only one leads to the light."

"Yeah, well, we need an army. I need an army. Wouldn't you feel better with an army?"

"Fly faster. They know we are gone by now."

"I'm doing Mach one point five. If I go any faster, they'll be able to sip us out of a tippy cup."

CHAPTER 15

B ack at the base in Banff Niner and I proceeded to show all the holograms and tell them all the info we had acquired on the mission. It was then I learned that Niner and the return drones had planted a few bombs on all the elevator shafts, in some labs of the Life Engineering building, and various other strategic locations. I had considered my stay a failure, but Robbins said it was an informative mission. "Info is the number one commodity," he said. "Without it generals aren't able to plan the attack strategy."

Niner had also been able to plant some surveillance cams complete with audio which enabled us to witness the tantrums of Asphorsh after he learned of our escape and witnessed the new rogue drones flying enmasse out of the fortress. Niner had reprogrammed them. Madison had even gone so far as to alter the weather which brought tons of snow and sleet and ice storms to the mountains in every direction for nearly a hundred miles from Denver in hopes of preventing our get away. Niner had ordered drone Twenty Two to fly my ankle bracelets up into the mountains, and we could see via skype that is where the SG were concentrating their search for us now. Twenty two was instructed to fly further southwest every day and keep the trackers at least 10 miles away from him until he reached the grand canyon and then he was to drop the bracelets into the river where they would be carried to the gulf. A portion of their defense force would be occupied with tracking the bracelets.

Next we concentrated on going over the videos of the interface that took place the night of our escape. There seemed to be an immediate change which took place in the person of Asphorsh. His jaw became elongated around the mouth and shortened in height. Age lines, or what seemed like age lines, began to dig small grooves into his facial features. Within a week, we suddenly realized he was becoming more reptilian in appearance. Even his body became taller and thinner. On the skype we could see that all Madison's comrades had begun to back away from him when he entered a room. "Let us check you over, Mr. President," Rosen was saying.

"Back away, or I shall strike you all down!" Then Asphorsh went over to the nearest computer and stuck his tongue into it like he was plugging a lamp cord into an outlet. Small spitting sounds as if water were hitting a hot hard surface were heard. This action triggered the computer's monitor on the wall to start up, and thousands of programs zipped out from the mouth of the waiting interfacer. This action continued and my old enemy fed on computer clouds for days. His next action was to call an assembly of his top military minds to lunch in the grand dining hall.

On the plates in front of them were sizable chunks of meat on a stick which seemed to be held on by a small piece of rope. "Should we remove the string?" one of the men asked.

"That's a tail. It's quite good when it gets crispy, but I prefer mine live," Asphorsh said producing a live mouse from under his silver covered plate, and swallowing it like a tiny goldfish.

A small lump shown in his throat for a moment before it slid down further into the esophagus. Everyone pushed their plates away. "I think I will wait for the second course," Rosen said.

"How many missiles do we have armed at the mid-east, General Brokey?" Asphorsh said.

"Over a thousand, sir."

"Launch them."

"Sir?"

"Launch them all. Now."

"It will bring in the fourth world war."

"It will be the last war. We shall start and end it in record time," he said walking over to where General Brokey was sitting. "How long will it take to launch all of them?"

"An hour or so."

"Then do it."

The general pushed back his chair to excuse himself but was stopped by a hand on his chair. "Not until you have eaten your lunch, general," Asphorsh rattled. The general turned to look back at Asphorsh and then slowly picked up the mouse on his stick and brought it to his lips. Everyone who had been staring at him turned away almost in unison as Brokey opened his mouth. There was a long silence and then Brokey spoke. "I'm really not hungry, Mr. President," and he pushed his chair back and ran out of the room.

"Cowards. I'm surrounded by cowards," Asphorsh said walking behind people's chairs all down the length of the table. "I see no one has eaten the new cuisine. That brings me to the new law I'm instituting. All elites must interface."

I laughed as I watched the room of would be eternals choke and look at each other as if they had just found themselves in a nightmare.

"Welcome to the real world," I said to those around me in Banff to which there was numerous chuckles.

"I should think they would all be willing to join our side right about now," Reynolds said out loud. "Maybe we should arrange to save them."

"And which ones could we trust?" I bellered. "We don't even trust each other."

"Quite true, professor. Which ones would you vote for?" he said looking at me.

I didn't say anything. "Isn't there even one? The woman, Iris?"

"None of them are of pure human DNA anymore. The gene pool has been tainted beyond our capabilities to understand. They've found the reptilian ancestors they believed were out there."

"Are we what's left?" Robbins asked.

"What's wrong with having knowledge to give sick beings the chance for life in replacing diseased organs. Isn't that a gift, a blessing?" Reynolds said.

"They started out thinking like that and look at them. They might be wriggling across the landscape, eating dust in a few generations."

Just then the screen we were watching began to show the missiles hitting the Mid-East. When the explosions from the death waves stopped, there was nothing but flat land in every direction. The mountains and the lakes had vanished.

"The rays are so hot they dried up the lakes and the rivers," Robbins said. "Captain Reynolds we must attack."

"Go for it, lieutenant. Arm the electromagnetic bomb. We'll send that. That will render their arms useless. Every nation in the league of ten needs to know we aren't the destroyers, captain. Get worldwide communiques out to the Middle East that explains what's happened, and ask for immediate peace. If the One World attacks us, they will level the states to what you've just seen in the Mid-East. We need to say we stopped the President to show our good will. It's our only chance for peace."

During the next few weeks we prepared for the attack and rid the ranks of mind implants. In the military it was mandatory to have 'the helper,' planted under the skin in the forearm. All government personnel were required to be plugged in 24/7, but these men had started surgically removing them and attaching the implants to dead animals, to trees, to sky cars, or buried them in the ground, but most had destroyed them in a solution of battery acid. Those babies who had just been born would be the first generation not to be implanted with the device in over two d's. The removal of the helper left a deep scarring wound in the right forearm. One of the combat surgeons was working on using skin grafts to fix the deformity. It occurred to me that was a good way to tell humans apart from other species. All robos and AI's had built in rather than implanted devices and they were bigger. Worker Drones, on the other hand, had never been equipped with such devices. They were controlled from remote centers and were in need of no monitoring by the SG. That made them perfect for reprogramming without being detected.

I had never been certain as to just how the 110th had been spared and while we were testing the weaponry for effectiveness before launching it against the Life Engineering facility, I asked Robbins to explain it in more detail which he did. It seems that somehow their unit had been reported as having been assembled on the training grounds when it was death waved instead of absent.

"Our unit was returning from training maneuvers in the mountains when an avalanche trapped us from leaving our location for a week or more. We reported in by tele-wave and apparently whoever was on duty marked the wrong box and reported us as having reported in by physicality."

"The last human error?" I asked wryly.

"Let's hope not."

"How did you destroy the Machimen?"

"With an instantaneous rusting spray."

"Where are all the remains of the Machimen? I haven't seen any of their bodies about."

"We dumped them in the base lake."

"Can you reanimate them?'

"Why would you ask that?"

"It's machine power. We need to build up our forces and we can reprogram them the way I did Niner."

"The use of their own drones against them is a stroke of genius," my companion said laughing.

"Loyalty is just a click away," I said, and Robbins gave me an intent look as if he were trying to read my mind or had read it. It was the kind of look that could make or break a friendship.

"Why did you decide to help us?" he asked.

"I'm a human, ain't I?"

"Was it the teachings in the manual?"

"Let's say that I believe the days of playing dress up gods has to come to an end. I'm not partial to endings that have tails attached to them, either. "

He looked down. "Do you think we can do it?"

"We have surprise on our side."

"And the one true wizard," Niner chimed in.

I shot the crossling drone a look of contempt. "There is no such thing."

"You're right. He's better."

I decided against arguing with the drone and turned away. "Get the big machinery warmed up, lieutenant. Let's go ice fishing."

It was easy with the use of lydar to pinpoint the exact spot where the Machimen lay at the bottom of the lake. A hole was bored into the ice and the steel arm of the crane reached down and brought up a few of the would be warriors. They were pulled to the engineering building and left to soak in a solution meant to counter act the effects of the spray. In time, they would be taken out of the solution and left to dry. We would see if Niner could work his brain washing techniques on one, who in turn would reprogram the others.

It was during dinner when Niner came to report that the mission had been a success. He opened the door to the main building wider and three machimen walked in. "I am to report to Captain Reynolds or Lieutenant Robbins," the first machiman said and then the other two sounded off in the same manner.

Reynolds stepped up to them. "I am Captain Reynolds." Niner flew in between them in a passing swoop by the captains face. "Now ask them who the enemy is."

"Who have you been programmed to fight?"

"The old guard of the shadow government."

The men in the building raised their voices in cheers and shouts and the machimen turned to look at them. "They are the enemy of mankind."

"There is your first wave, captain," Niner boasted. "Or it will be when you haul them off the bottom of the lake."

It was weeks later when the tin pins, as we had come to call the unit, stood in formation ready to move out. There were over two hundred of them. The war was about to take its first steps forward. Rows of men and machines stood ready. We were a force to be reckoned with. It was an overwhelming sight to me because I had started off with a single drone and now I was looking at a scaled down D-Day version of a land armada.

This sight would not have been possible had not Lt. Robbins come up with the idea to have the recently revived machiman report in to the compound at Denver by ls-mail to ask for orders. Robbins had sent a cloud gram posing as a machiman and had assured us that the SG Elite would order them to report to the base in Denver. It was a long wait for an answer, but Lt. Robbins explained that the orders had to go through the NTK(Need TO Know) and LR (Last Resort) channels first because they were highly suspicious of why the machimen had not reported in until now. Machimen number 5357 was used as the main speaker figure to appear in the screenings of the talks that ensued. We grouped the rest of the machimen in the back ground so the base in Denver would see only them, but nothing of the base itself. The audio had been deliberately turned off and Niner communicated by texting. The main gist of the ruse was that the humans had put up quite a fight and had blown up parts of the base and weapons cache before hiding out in the outlying areas. The job of eradicating the humans had taken longer than expected, but was complete now, Niner texted. There was no immediate response and we all waited to see what would happen.

No time was wasted while we waited for oders to come in pertaining to the machimen. Training and preparation were in high gear. Finally the new orders came in weeks later from the Denver headquarters. All Machimen were to report to the main base in Denver. Things were going just as the lieutenant had forecasted. Orders were given to the machimen that the Canadian base was to be leveled to the ground before they returned which of course we ignored.

Our training continued with Niner airing his holograms of the Colorado compound to us every day until we knew them like they were rooms in our own houses. The aerial shots of the compound were a thing of beauty to behold from the sky. The drones had photographed it using the latest high resolution photo imaging from orbiting satellites that were combined with infrared technology which created a detailed picture of the underground facilities. The images enabled us to see all images of the underground city as clearly as ordinary pictures.

Each section to be destroyed was targeted and programmed by GPS. The Machimen were to be armed to carry at least a hundred kilos of weaponry and ammo each. They would be the first wave in the attack on the bases. We humans would man the tanks, the jets, and the other armored vehicles that had been left behind at the base. We would be clean up, as it were. Niner read us accounts of battles from every war that had ever been fought in history, and we rallied with cries of 'Remember' and 'give no quarter.' No human hybrid was to be left alive.

It was sometime in late February or early March that we set out. The two arteries of our army would split off. Half would go to Utah with Robbins, and the other half would go to Denver with Reynolds. The underground Life Engineering Labs were to be hit first by the main attacking units while the secondary units would target the arsenals and the underground cities where the elites lived.

There had been no communication at all with either facility when the backup generators which had been used had started to fail because of overloaded systems after the EMP attack. We had found another missing chunk in their armor. They had failed to adequately supply the amount of electricity the compound would need in case of grid failure.

I was moving out with the section of the brigade that was heading for Denver under the command of Lt. Robbins. Captain Reynolds and his units were headed to Utah where the only other underground Life Engineering Lab was located.

We had arranged for the attacks to come off at precisely two AM. That was when the Mechiman were scheduled to storm through the front gates of the bases and then head for the massive triangle doors and blow them open. They had been instructed to immediately attack the Life Engineering centers and weapons caches upon gaining entrance into the compound. Then the drones were to act as a second wave to aid the Machiman. Meanwhile, from our position on the hill we would fire off smart bombs at the outside mountains and city. We would be relatively safe since an EMP bomb had already disabled all of their weapons.

Finally the moment arrived and we were in the air and on our way. Niner was in the back seat showing the holograms of the blueprints of the compound and the places where he had set the explosives when we were there.

In a few minutes there came a sonic sound rushing above our heads on a southward trajectory. "Damn, that's awfully low," I said watching the chem trail.

"It had to be to remain undetectable," Robbins answered looking at his watch.

"Minus two and counting," he continued. "Commander One zero Niner."

"Sir."

"Give me minus 4 and counting for the second launch of the microwave missile."

"Standby, Lt. Missile will be live on screen in 4,3,2,1," Niner said.

I took the brief interlude between launchings to look out the window at all the jet cars flying in formation with us. It was a mass migration heading south. It was hope in the flesh going to meet and reclaim its destiny. That's the way I felt inside.

"Third launch is fixed on target, Lt. Minus 3, 2, 1," Niner reported. I saw the mountain entrance tremble and shake and become dark. The lights around the compound's perimeter had gone out. "Phase four launch has target locked, Lt. Minus 3, 2, 1." I heard and felt the smart bomb launch from underneath us.

We watched on screen as it hit its target. This time the whole top of the mountain blew apart like some fragile old Christmas ornament dropped on cement. Smaller explosions could be seen radiating from deep inside the mountain. Debris kept collapsing into itself and was being buried deeper. Soon the mountain lay exposed like some open pit mining operation.

"Squads 3, 4, and 5 deploy to the open area you see on your screen now. All others follow me and we will take care of the outside of the compound," Robbins said angling the jet fighter towards the west. I could see the armada of sky planes bank and make a wide turn to the right and descend into their dive towards the targets.

In fifteen minutes we were over the city of Denver. "I've never gotten used to seeing these great cities as empty tombs," I said.

"I'm doing my part to repopulate," Robbins said.

I laughed. "Mind if I see what's going on inside the ant hill?" I said switching the skype to interior pixels.

"I'd like a peek myself."

Pictures of the inhabitants flashed by on the screen. Women with their duckish lips and over enlarged breasts, and men with over proportioned upper bodies, scrambled to get away from their homes inside the mountain. I adjusted the controls until I had pin pointed where my old buddy was in his lab yelling orders. He was even more transformed than before. He had turned a pale shade of greenish black and his face resembled a large version of a snake. His arms were half the length of a normal human and appeared somewhat shriveled and stumpy like the arms on a tyrannosaurus rex.

"What happened to evolution, Trave?" Robbins laughed as he looked my way.

Just then we heard Asphorsh question his men while he pounded at the control buttons on his board. "Why aren't the alternative generators working?"

"Everything's dead," his aide was saying.

"Brilliant minds I have around me," Asphorsh screamed. "I can deduce that. Why? What has happened?"

"I'd say that something has zapped our energy, sir."

"We've been attacked. Help me to get to the top of the mountain. We'll go out through one of the tunnels," Asphorsh yelled.

"The doors will all be shut."

"Blow them open," Asphorsh yelled.

"We'll need men and explosives."

"Get them!"

Robbins and I watched as the two men retrieved light sticks and activated them so they could light their way down the passage way. When they reached the door, he sent his subordinate for the explosives.

"He has an exit tunnel to the top of the mountain," Robbins said looking at me.

"That's where we need to be waiting for him, then," I said.

"Why not just seal it shut from the outside?" the lieutenant countered. "We don't want anything like him running around loose above ground."

"Even better."

I could feel the jet car start upwards as John took off, and grabbed the side straps to steady myself.

"Take a look at these pics that are coming in on the screen," Robbins said.

The attack was a thing of beauty to behold from the sky. Each section to be destroyed was targeted and programmed by GPS. We watched from the air as the mechiman on the ground began their assault on the Life Engineering center and weapons caches. Niner had also left cams which now provided us with continual live streaming photos and aerial ops of the city by which we pinpointed the nuclear silos. They needed to be disarmed and Robbins turned our copter towards the blinking red zone on the monitor. "Sorry, Trave. Your dragon will have to wait."

It was getting dark, but the startling flashes of brightness from the explosions were like momentary flood lights where we could see everything for brief seconds at a time. The species inside the compound were burrowing like animals into the ground chambers instead of running out of them now. We couldn't have arranged for a better scenario. Little did they know that their own eagle squadron which had been reporting in over the last few months had been planting plastic explosives in their underground city. Once the last of the hybrids were in the elevator shaft, the machimen had been instructed to drop more explosives down the shafts after them. It would be the elite hybrids last ride. The air supply vents would be stuffed with instant plastic sealant by the drones. Operation 3 Mile Down was in full swing. The eternals would end up minute men because that was how much time they had left.

We set down on the flattened top of the mountain near to the silos. We were part of wave two, and our mission was to dismantle the nuclear fireworks.

Lt. Robbins had decided to lead this assault himself, and I volunteered to go with him. "You must obey my orders, Travis. I don't want any lone renegades."

"Yes, lieutenant."

As we went through the gates of the compound, we met little opposition from anybody. It wasn't until we reached the elevator shafts that lead to the underground city that we first used our weapons. After an initial engagement with the enemy troops, Lt. Robbins had us pull back to some buildings, and called in the Machimen that were left to do combat with their own kind. "No need to give our lives needlessly," he told us. We stayed, using the buidlings for cover, and lobbed explosives at the enemy. Lt. Robbins sent a few of the eagles out to scan the tunnels above ground with their lydar and see what portion of the tunnels had yet to be destroyed.

It was at this point in the battle that I began to doubt the outcome of our success. Victory seemed out of the question. Wave after wave of the enemy came at our fighters. They seemed to have an endless supply of replicas from the factory. When we defeated one unit another would replace it. I looked around at our dwindling forces. It would soon come down to just us, the real men of the 110th Mountain Division.

I had felt much pride at that point in being a part of the men who belonged to the last human unit on earth. It was these humans who could not be put back together like humpty dumpty's that made my heart nearly burst, but I was also filled with an equal amount of fear. I had never even been in a street fight, and I was being pitted against what was said to be the best equipped and trained army in the world.

Then I remembered the story of David against Goliath that Good Neighbor Sam had read to us. None of King Saul's trained and battle hardened men had been willing to answer the taunts of the giant. It rested solely on a lone shepherd boy to quiet his jeering and insults. The question of defeat never entered the giant's mind. He was positive he would slay the young and small David, but something changed that fate, and it struck me in that moment that it was David's faith that had been the overriding factor. Could belief in this God of all alleviate my fear? I decided to give it a try, and asked for courage as we were moving out. I felt my legs move me forward. The hands that held my weapon were shaking and my stomach was full of nauseous fumes. I kept my eyes on Robbins who was out in front of me, and stayed just behind him and abreast of the line I was running in. Follow his lead, I said to myself, and kept moving forward with them and waiting for the fear to vanish, but it didn't. The panic sat in my stomach and waited for a way to come up. Just then the soldiers beside me opened fire. We were almost face to face with the enemy.

Instantly, I could smell sweat, blood, and iron mixed with dirt rising up through my nostrils. I heard the cries of the men lying on the ground. I looked behind me for an instant, seeking a way out, and I almost ran back behind the building where we had hidden just minutes before, but the darkness behind me was as daunting to me as the enemy in front of me. It was then I envied the eternals. They had no fear because they had stacked the deck and were assured of life. They were invincible.

Suddenly I was face to face with an armatron. I felt frozen, but suddenly his body just dropped belly down right at my feet. I had witnessed my first miracle. I had managed to shoot without realizing it. Smoke was pooling around him and rising up towards me from a hole in his back. I had not killed a real person yet, and I took a small comfort in that. I knew there were also humans and clones among the enemy because blood ran in rivulets from some of the bodies. Somehow seeing that tangible evidence of spilled blood gave me courage. The SG were down to the last resort as well. They were expending life. I kept firing until the noise from both sides ended. To my astonishment I was still standing. I felt a majesty I had never experienced enter my being. I was alive and all around me were the broken, dead, and dying bodies of all species. I didn't have a chance to reflect fully on my emotions just then because Lt. Robbins grabbed me and pointed after some enemy soldiers running in the distance. "They're headed for the silos."

"Instant melt down," I managed to say. "That's only good for one thing. Grilled cheese sandwiches."

"I don't have any bread," Robbins answered.

We were far behind them, but caught up with them when they stopped to open the silo doors. Luckily the power grid had been destroyed, and they couldn't lift the bomb bay doors by themselves. Without warning, Lt. Robbins jumped out from behind the debris we were hiding behind and let go his fire power. I followed his lead. In seconds the enemy was down and silent. He turned to look at me. "I feel faint," I said sliding down on my butt and letting out a sigh of relief.

"You did fine."

"My legs and arms felt like Jell-O. Still do."

"The important thing is you kept going. You didn't stop."

I looked at him then and he looked back. Did my face reflect the terror I felt on the inside? Is that why he was looking at me so closely? "You'll do better next time. It gets easier," he said patting my leg. According to his words I surmised that he had some questions about my performance because it sounded like a pep talk.

A few of the men in his unit came up to us. "Targets one, two, and three have been destroyed, sir."

"How much opposition is left?"

"About four regiments, sir."

"Where are they positioned?"

"By the perimeter of the shafts leading to the underground city."

"I need four men to help run the lydar across the top of the compound where we believe the tunnels to be. Shaw, you head north with your man and scope out the tunnels, and Bristle, you go south. Bomb all the remaining targets. I want no structure left underground."

"Sir!" the young men saluted and hastened to their job.

We were alone again. "We need to protect these silos and dismantle their triggers," he was saying to me as he was smashing in the door to the nuclear silos which was known in the military, he said, as the hot box. From there they could send laser and microwave missiles and nukes to anywhere in the world, but we had rendered them useless by EMP, I said to Robbins.

"We don't want them to be used in the future, either," he answered.

When we had the doors open, he threw a carton of sizzle and search bombs into the room ahead of us. The sizzlers moved like little black snakes writhing on the ground as they sent their white spray ahead of them and then they lay still and waited to strike a second time. When a species coughed, moved, or talked the sizzle and seek munitions zeroed in on them. They were black flying eel like weapons that flew at speeds you could hardly see while they emitted a high-pitched whistle that was terrifying. Next you saw smoke rising from where they had hit and then the hole where they had bored into the enemy target. It was instantaneous. "They're so small. How do they leave such a big hole?" I asked Robbins.

"They have gyrating spinners that come out on contact and expand to more than five times their size. Imagine your little finger suddenly swelling to the size and width of a fist."

We waited for the white fog to drift away. When we were sure there was no species left to defend the room, Robbins said, "You cover the door. I'll detach the detonator wires."

I was shocked he trusted me to protect him, and scared out of my wits. "I'm going to shoot anything that comes down that hallway," I warned him.

He laughed. "Just make sure it isn't one of ours."

There were glass windows in each of the rooms and I could see panel boards with all kinds of computers and high tech equipment set up in long rows that covered the entirety of the room. Bodies were slumped forward in their chairs with their heads fallen over the command key boards. I could sort out the human or hybrid ones because of the blood. The other species just left debris scattered all over. They were now what Robbins considered a 'leave on site' cadre of dead. The hybrids would bloat and rot and explode in time like regular human corpses.

I was jittery and kept looking at the hallway to make sure no enemy was moving in on us. My hands were sweaty, and I could feel them sliding down the iron portion of my weapon. My fingers were so tight on the trigger I could feel them spasm, so I began moving them one at a time to relax the muscles. It seemed like Robbins was taking an eternity to complete his mission. "Hurry up," I shouted.

"Want me to melt us down and about five hundred square miles along with us?"

Suddenly I saw bodies coming around the corner and I almost dropped my weapon. My heart pounded so that it actually hurt. The beats were slow and protracted, and just when I thought my chest would explode, I realized it was one of our own men.

"One hundred ten mountain division here, sir," I heard him yell the warning we had agreed on. There were ten or more soldiers behind him. In seconds I heard Robbins running up to the front. "Good, it's you, Masters. I want you to start dismantling the detonators in the other room. Post a look out. Travis, you can start helping me now."

"I don't know anything about what you're doing."

"It's a simple pop and snip job."

Before I knew it, he was making his way back to the row of panels and boxes where he had been previously. As I followed him, I took note of the triggers he had already dismantled. I noticed that the green buttons were hanging out of the metal plates that had been covering them, and their inside wires were strung out and cut. "See this set of wires?" he said showing me the green ones. "Cut them. Then use your screw driver to pry off the metal covers on top," he continued, "like you're opening a bottle of beer. They just flip right off."

I laid my weapon down and popped the first plate off. I flinched when I cut my first set of wires and held my breath. I had to tell myself to start breathing again. Just then a round of laser fire sounded from the hallway and I felt my stomach lurch. The sweat pooled under my arm pits. I had left my gun down the row. I made a lunge to retrieve it, but kept myself low to the floor and then continued to crawl behind one of the desks that was towards the front of the room and looked over the top of it. I could see the others shooting at the forces coming up the hall. Glass began shattering all around us and men were falling over dead. I saw the enemy retreat behind the corner of the wall and they were throwing little bb sized chemical beads all over the floor. In seconds the floor was on fire. "Your candle wax now," I heard one of them yell.

I just stood there and watched it happen. With them covering the hallway, there was no way to put out the fire without being shot. I was about to be crisped like a slab of bacon. That was when I heard a familiar voice speak loudly. "Alpha commander one zero niner in pursuit of hu-manimal forces. Don't use your weapons on us. We are targeting the control rooms. Repeat we are from Alpha squadron. We are in pursuit of the hu-manimals."

I wanted to jump up for joy. Niner's warning was working. He and his squadron were not being shot down. Instead the enemy was holding their fire as the drone squad approached and flew by them. When the drone squad was directly parallel to the entire enemy force, they opened fire on them and blew them across the corridors into what Niner called fractions. By the time the SG forces figured out the drones had opened fire on them, it was over. There were only cheers for the eagles from our side of the army.

The battle for the entire compound went on until late the next day though it had seemed to me to go by much more quickly when I looked back on it. Skirmishes broke out less and less, and we basically stayed behind for one reason: to make sure all the tunnels were caved in and no life forces were detected on the scoping devices. We felt the explosions beneath our feet off and on all day. They were like tiny earthquakes that rolled the earth beneath us. A few times the blast sent pieces of debris into the air above ground. The explosions had been so powerful as to blast through three miles of solid rock and reach the surface. By the time those eruptions had detonated we had already moved outside the perimeters of the city.

We had a routing victory, but Captain Reynolds' forces had not been as successful in their fight at the Utah base. They were being assaulted by returning forces that had not been present when they had first attacked, so we were on our way to help them. We took the latest jet fighters and tanks that were in workable condition and headed West.

From the air, the destruction was formidable to look on. The buildings and homes of the compound were scattered and splayed over the landscape as if some giant megaton dinosaur had sat its butt down on it, and then trounced over the rest of the city on his way out. It was amazing to me the amount of devastation a few hundred men armed with sizzle and seek pellets and plastic explosives had inflicted in a couple of days. It was also sobering to realize that almost half of the humans in our force had been lost. We had paid a high cost. Niner had about one hundred and fifty of his squadron left. Both Wudgey and Axle had survived and came along with me in the sky jet.

Niner informed us that his unit was in need of recharging and would need to stop before we reached Utah. While the drone force recharged, Niner gathered information from the enemy by using his Alpha identification and call numbers. He was posing as a survivor of the attack on the base in Denver. Needless to say, the Utah base was very suspicious of Niner's questions and gave only limited information to him.

We did learn that the base had called in reinforcements from a third base in Arizona. This base was on the map that Niner had shown to us and it was to be our next target after Utah. It was not a primary base and had no Life Centers or nuclear capabilities. However, we set up a defensive position to combat their arrival from the south and sent forces on ahead to stop their advance.

A day or so later we landed in a wooded area with a clearing and parked our sky vehicles as close to the trees as possible. We had barely gotten out of the doors to our vehicles when we were opened fire on from the trees across the valley. I reached for the weapon that I had left on the seat of my sky car, and just as I did, a hail of laser dots broke the windows above my head out. I jumped back in the car and lay down across the front seat. It was then that I heard Niner come in on my computer monitor. "Cease fire. Those are humans firing at us."

"Humans?"

"You are killing your own kind."

"Who are they?" I screamed at the monitor.

"That is not known."

"I thought you were supposed to know everything. Now is not the time to tell me you don't."

"I am sorry about your memory, Travis, but you have been told many times. I am only as good as my creator."

"We'll have to do something about that," I said mostly to myself as I rolled up my jacket and put it on the end of my weapon and stuck it out the broken window and waved it to the enemy. "Hold your fire. Hold your fire," I was yelling.

When the firing stopped, I got out of the jet slowly still holding my weapon in the air and waving it back and forth for the forces to readily see.

"Do you wish to surrender?" a voice called from across the clearing.

"We are humans. We do not wish to fight against you if you are humans."

"There is a new law against humans. They are wiping us all out."

"We have just blown up the Denver base and are on our way to help other human forces trying to fight in Utah."

There was no answer, but I could see that two men had run out to help a wounded man who was laying in the snow. I could see the blood clearly against the whiteness.

The man I was communicating with stepped out alone. "You are the ones who attacked the base?"

"We are part of the same force, and are on our way to help others who are mounting a similar attack."

"You have enemy SG jets and equipment and some of your soldiers are dressed like SG troops."

"Spoils of war. We needed clothes, weapons."

"Do you have food?"

"Tons of it," I yelled back as I got ration meals out of the back of the trunk. My throw didn't send the light weighted meals very far towards the other side. "Special delivery," Niner said swooping by and picking up a carton of food in his talons.

I watched as the delivery was made by the man's feet. Soon men ran out to get it and cheered after revealing its contents.

"Where you from?" the man yelled.

"Manhattan."

"Texas," he answered back.

It wasn't long before our two sides were intermingling with one another and talking. I was truly happy. Things were looking up. Men and women from all over the southern parts of America had joined forces. There was over five thousand in the new group. The man from Texas was Cooper Smith. The others had joined up with them along the way when the SG's had begun rounding humans up. They had been over ten thousand strong a year ago, but the battles they had fought had reduced their force to half its original strength. I showed them pictures of the way we had left Denver and they let out such a roar that I thought an avalanche would start in the mountains around the valley. Cooper was eyeing Niner and said, "I was going to ask you about those SG drones."

"We've been reborn," Niner broke in. "Reprogrammed by the wizard here," he said flapping his wing against me.

Cooper looked at me and laughed. "Wizard, huh?"

"I only call him that," Niner told him. "We were headed to see the true wizard when this all began."

"He read the Wizard of Oz," I told the group.

"I have never read a book, so I have never heard of this wizard," Cooper said.

"I will tell you," Niner said. "I read the Instruction Manual and found out there was a being who formed all of this out of the darkness. He breathed into the first man he had formed out of the dust of the earth."

"A remarkable tale. I have heard of a similar one that was true."

"There was a man among us for a while that gave off higher readings than I had ever seen from a man," Niner said very intent and seriously. "I think he was a messenger from the north, from beyond the brightest star where the third heaven is, and where this wizard resides."

"Where is this man you met now?" Everyone started asking.

"Vanished," Niner said spreading his wings out as far as he could stretch them, and the crowd was immediately silenced.

I wanted to shut the bird up so I said, "I'm afraid I gave him too much imagination."

"Oh, so it is you who are responsible for his programming."

"He may have started up my thinking, but I have the ability to learn as all humans do now," Niner said. "I will one day be real. The wizard will breathe into me."

"If this heaven is above to the north of the brightest star then you must believe in aliens like over half of the population," one little boy said. "My father says not to believe in them."

"I am speaking about the Great I Am," the bird came back quite loudly. "He is no space man or alien. He is the sole creator of life."

"We will never get to other planets. Everyone knows that by now," the child said.

"We do not have to get to him. He is coming back for us. He is coming to earth to get us."

"Your drone speaks of the banished book?" Cooper asked.

"Yes," I said producing a copy.

Cooper sat holding the book in his hands and read the title. "Basic Instructions Before Life Ends," he said softly. "No, this is not the book that was destroyed. This is not the Bible."

"Yes, it is. Look at the first letter in each word," Niner said. "Joseph told me they had put a new cover and name on it to hide the original title." Cooper tore at the binding and ripped it off from the book revealing the original binding. It was black and there were gold letters on it that spelled the word Bible.

"It is the Holy Book," Cooper said. "Cora, your prayers have been answered. We have found a Holy Book."

"I have a copy of it in my memory banks," Niner told them. "Anyone who wishes for a copy may ask me to ezip one to their Compaq," the eagle offered.

"No," the woman said taking the book, "I, for one, would like to hold it in my hands and touch the pages." Suddenly the woman looked up at me. "May we borrow it?"

"Keep it. Share it with the others."

"You are filled with the truth," Cora said.

"Niner is more of a believer than me," I said.

"Show me where it says he is coming back," the woman asked Niner, guiding him away from us.

"And the part about the third heaven beyond the stars," a girl said, sticking her tongue out at the boy as the group moved away to a separate area.

Cooper and some of the others kept looking skyward from time to time. "We have seen jet cars flying to the mountains over there. They have been coming back and forth over the last few days."

"Do you know where they have been going?" Lt. Robbins asked him.

"Yes, to what looks like a big rock, but it is not. There are two sets of rail like tracks in the snow where it glided to its resting place."

THE WIZARD OF All

"Yes, it is a disguised ship of some sort."

"Oumaumua," I said looking at Robbins for a second. "Can you take us there?" I said turning back towards Cooper.

"Put on your skis. It is down in the valley."

"We'll fly. It's faster."

Plans were discussed briefly, and we were on our way. The older women were left behind to safeguard the children, and a smaller cadre of men were also left to defend them if need be. Most of the young women joined us. This group of men and women were not married and there were not many children among them. They were more from my class of people: the ones who couldn't afford all the extras in society like marriage certificates or children.

Lt. Robbins tried to explain to the women that they should stay behind but they were of the mind that they should pay their way. The unisex mentality was prevalent among this new group of over throwers. They had lost the distinction between the sexes many d's ago. From a distance it was hard to tell the men and women apart.

We fit as many men as we could in our jets and sky cars and I was glad to have John Robbins with me again. I liked him. He was young and sure of himself though somewhat aloof, but I attributed that later quality as stemming from his military background and his physical training. I had seen him with his wife and children. He was warm and caring. He touched his children often and played with them. All children should have such parents. If I could say I had formulated any ideal of what a man should be, it would be the lieutenant. I suddenly became more curious about the man and I looked over at him. His hair was short like mine. "Why did you decide to choose a career in the military?" I asked him.

"I didn't." He turned to look at me looking at him. "My father did."

"You knew your father? But how? You're so young," I said rather confused.

625

"He was a military man. He convinced me that was the only way to be allowed a wife without going into debt and to be allowed to raise your children as your own.

"That's an old and obsolete way of thinking, isn't it?"

"I suppose it is, but that's a rather unfair assessment because now you know the end of us. You've seen the future. Granted, we humans have our shortcomings. We change our minds and can't be trusted. We are limited in intelligence and short lived."

"A better than average answer," I said and let the idea drop. I was focused on steering the jet car because I wanted to be at the controls if we were attacked, so I wasn't looking at him anymore, but I felt him staring at me.

"How did you ever arrive at reprograming the government drones and robos?" he asked me.

"By accident. I only meant to reprogram Niner to have a companion to chat with. They had a syntactic program laying around in a sporting goods store somewhere in the east and there you have it."

"Remarkable that you were able to remember the steps to the surgery without remembering, if you know what I mean."

"It was weird how that worked. You've helped destroy my delusion that I was a rather fast learner," I said laughing.

I was looking at John, so didn't see Niner fly up beside the jet car until I heard him flapping against my side of window. I pushed the button to release the back window and he flew in. "Turn your screen on," he ordered. "There's something you should see."

I pushed the button immediately and was stunned by what I saw. Niner was live streaming a picture of thousands upon thousands of marching soldiers."

"How far ahead?" the lieutenant questioned.

The eagle lifted his wing and pointed down out the window just in front of us.

"There."

"We can't fight against this," I said. "I'm turning around."

"Never show your tail feathers," Niner said.

"To go on is suicide."

"I'm not sure they are real," the bird continued.

"What are you squawking about?"

"Just keep flying straight ahead."

"Are you crazy? We'll crash right into them."

"They maybe just a hologram."

"Maybe? Why don't you know for certain?"

"New technology. Now turn this iron bird around and act like a hero." Since Niner was pointing a taser at my head, I obeyed his directive.

"Sorry, Trave, but there is only one way to tell and that is to fly directly into them."

"Then I'm closing my eyes," I said.

I heard the sound of two distinct but simultaneous "No's" reach my ears. I did have my eyes closed, but opened them out of curiosity and terror. I didn't want to crash without knowing what I was crashing into, and as luck would have it, just as I opened my eyes for a peek, we were about to run head long into the marching column of soldiers. They looked solid and real enough to me. Their weapons were drawn and I braced myself for the end. In the next second, we flew directly into the oncoming soldiers, and to my relief passed through them. I felt Niner patting the back of my neck and head with his wings. "I was right," he said in a bragging sort of way. "What about that, huh?"

"You, you weren't sure," I stuttered at him.

"Almost," he said smiling. "I can make the adjustments to my radar now."

I pulled the nose of the jet car upward again and we left the shadow world of the fake holograms behind. I was not yet fully recovered from the scare we had just flown through when I spotted the enemy who had been left behind to guard the rock on the ground.

"I think things will get exceptionally real from here on out," I said sarcastically.

Just then lasers flashed past us. One hit the wing on the left side and it shook the vehicle sideways with a jolt.

"Let me out," Niner declared.

"I have half a mind to make you ride this thing out," I said.

"I have explosives," was all he needed to say to make me roll down the window to accommodate him. In seconds I heard his flapping and felt a breeze from the open rear window caress the back of my neck. It felt good and I decided to leave the window part way open while I maneuvered to a lower altitude so Cooper and his men in the rear seats could jet pack into the battle. I could see all the other jet cars making the same adjustment as I turned my head around to see Cooper and his buddies checking their gear. "Okay, brace yourselves. Back door opening," he said giving me the thumbs up sign. They climbed onto the wings and I heard jet packs burst on with a roar. In seconds I could see them drop below us; their weapons drawn and ready.

Soon we saw a giant erose shaped rock jutting up from the snow more clearly. It was long and tubular in length, and much larger than I had expected.

"Fly over it. Let's see if we can spot anything," said Robbins.

When we were directly over the object we could see that there were buildings and what looked like a city built into the side of the giant structure and on top of it.

"It cant's be a ship. I don't know how it could possibly get off the ground," Robbins said in between whistles. "It's the size of a small planet."

Just then a squadron of jets rose straight up from behind the far side of the rock. "Enemy at three o'clock," he yelled at me. "I'll load our ammo."

Originally we sky jetters were to fly in behind Niner's crew and spearhead the second wave of our attack at Utah, but we could not load the bombs until the moment right before the attack. John Robbins was switching the bombs from the holding lodge into the firing chambers. I could hear the whirr of the machine engage as the weapons were transferred from the loading hold into the firing jets. They were taser level eight rounds and could do maximum damage. Level eight's also had an advantage in that they created a blinding light show before they exploded.

Robbins turned to me. "Ready?" he asked handing me the goggles to save my eyesight from the flashes we were about to set off. I didn't say anything as my throat was dry and I felt a sudden sensation to cough. "Tell me when the fighters are below us," he added as we continued to climb higher into the clouds. I was watching the scope on the dashboard in front of me. When the target finder blinked red on the scope, I yelled, "Now." Robbins let them drop. The bomb release was designed to be handled by the pilot, but the button on my side had malfunctioned during our practice attack and Lt. Robbins had to create a new release system, so he had installed the new button on his side of the car. We had a few rounds of the tasers, the old smart bombs, and a few of the new sizzle and seek bombs that were designed to lock on 8 targets and take them all out at once. We had arranged to drop them in that exact order so the sizzlers could mop things up.

I couldn't see the jets gauges over the blinding flashes of light the explosions created. I didn't like flying in the first place, but being forced to fly blind as a bat with only navigation really made me nervous. Just as I was fighting my panic attack, I felt a hit come on my side of the jet car. I looked and saw smoke coming from the left retractable wing. Just then the engine sputtered and choked. Suddenly it was very quiet in the front seat, and I felt us dropping quickly. We were in a downward nose dive. I had seen the world go around like this once before as a child on the tilt-a-whirl ride at the fairgrounds. I saw Robbins pushing on the buttons madly on his side of the sky car. "I need to discharge the bombs that are loaded so we don't explode on impact," he was saying. It was more information than I needed at the moment, but before I could become more frightened, I felt the weight of the craft tip as the bombs were released and I heard them hit the ground. I could feel the blast as it shook us from underneath, but the craft had managed to right itself. We hit the ground hard some thousand yards ahead, and I felt one of the tires blow out on impact, but we were plowing forward. I couldn't keep the car from veering to the right after the tire popped, nor could I slow it down. I struggled with the steering until we were headed in a straight line again, but there were tanks and jet cars and various pieces of military equipment in my path. I felt my teeth snap together as we side swiped the first vehicle and kept going. We hit a few more tanks and armored cars before finally bouncing into some trees, which proved to be immovable.

Before we could get out of the car, I heard firing in back of us. I took another look into the rear view finder and saw an army running towards us and firing an arsenal of weapons. "Help me tip this thing over and get it pointed in their direction," Robbins was saying. "That way we can shoot back. We still have some sizzle and seek bombs."

By this time he had run around to my side of the car. "Wedge this rock under the side. It will help us get the car bouncing so we can flip it over," he said grunting to roll the boulder under the belly of the tipped sky car. We managed to maneuver the rock underneath the portion of the sky car that was up in the air, and then we began pushing down on the car until we got it rocking back and forth faster. Finally the jet car finally fell over like a giant whale breathing its last. It landed with a thundering noise, but it was on its side. We had done it. Now the firing tubes were pointing straight at the rushing onslaught. Since the guns were mounted on the wings, one firing tube was up in the air and the other ran parallel to it along the ground. Robbins jumped into the sideways car and fumbled for the launch button. I could hear him pounding on the dash board as I fired my laser weapon into the crowd. Just when I thought the firing tubes were jammed for good, I heard the swish that rockets make coming out of a bottle on the fourth of July. Stream after stream of sizzle and seeks came out of both launch tubes now and they were hitting their marks. I was watching the flying snakes bore into the approaching bots inner machinery and explode. "Let's get out of here," John was yelling at me while heading in the opposite direction.

When we were beyond the road and into the trees, we stopped to catch our breath and survey the damage. The jet was beyond fixing. The rock like ship or asteroid lay a few meters away in an open patch of snow on the valley floor. "That thing is bigger than Manhattan," I said.

"Do you think it's an alien probe?" the Lt. asked me.

"I'd be guessing, but I know someone," I smiled and put in a call to Niner on my computer phone.

Some minutes later Robbins pointed skyward. "I think I see him. What's he doing flying back and forth?"

"Gathering intelligence."

We both watched as Niner and his squad battled the enemy drone jets until they had wiped them out of the sky. "Niner can be my wing man anytime," the Lt. said, trying to get his communicator cell to work. "I think I landed on it when I hit the ground, and damaged my tail bone to boot," he said rubbing his butt.

"I'll ask him what data he has the object," I said typing into my k com.

Niner was answering my question as he made his descent and set down in front of us. "Of course I know what this ship is," he said. "It's one of those ark things, like in the manual."

"It looks like an asteroid, not a boat," I said.

"There is an astral city, a beautiful, magical place aboard. See?" he said streaming live pixels to us on his screen. In between the rocky crags on the south side of the rock, I could make out glistening spires and towers of skyscrapers rising up and set in a planed off section of the asteroid. It was larger than Manhattan and had as many buildings, but they were shining like unmined diamonds. "Have you run an analysis on it?"

"Of course, Trav."

"Do we have the technology to destroy it?" Lt. Robbins asked.

"Oh, no we do not want to destroy it. It contains every seed and plant and human form of life in it's pure genetic DNA state."

"It is not a ship of war?"

"It has the capabilities to destroy life, but it was sent that it might preserve it."

"Who sent it?"

"I will tell you after I show you the stores inside its warehouses."

"These buildings are made of ground crystals, honed until they glisten and they are indestructible. It is the hardest substance I have come across in this universe," Niner continued.

The next scene he showed us contained the inside of the store house units which consisted of rows and rows of shelving of a sort with a myriad of small rectangle storage drawers less than an inch thick. There were thousands and thousands of these tiny bins. Each was labeled with the names of trees, plants, and animals. "Inside each drawer is the seeds and DNA for the planned generations to come that are to be planted after the fire and the ashes have prepared the soil for the new earth. A new shining city on a hill is going to be built which shall stand for a thousand years. Then the last battle will be fought and the dragon will be vanquished."

"Another war after this?" I said feeling defeated.

"The greatest armadas ever seen shall arise to fight the battle, but there will be only one lone fighter that fights for mankind in that day and that is the son of the wizard. He will be mounted on a white horse and thousands of his army shall be poised behind him. He will speak a word and the dragon and his minions shall be banished."

I sat down on my butt. "A good story, but did Asphorsh merge with this intelligence on board? Is there any way to tell what he downloaded into himself?'

"I was told by the guide that showed me these rooms what they guided him to," Niner told me, trying to chuckle, which came out like drunken hiccups.

"Well, what did they give him?" I asked to stop his raucous noise. "Sorry," Niner said, and changed the scene on his monitor to reveal a large safe like object marked with two letters. It was guarded by rings of glowing pulsars. It was clear that it had been opened and its contents withdrawn for the doors stood open. As Niner zoomed in on its doors, I could read the initials E.T.

"Extra Terrestrial DNA," I said out loud at the same time Robbins did.

"Guard one thing above the others and it will be thought to be more precious," Niner said looking at us and still cackling, "and that is exactly what Asphorsh thought, too. Human minds think alike," he said trumpeting his awful drunken laugh again.

"Well? Tell us what it really stands for you plastic coated pterodactyl," I said plucking a feather out of his tail region.

"Ouch," he said pivoting around towards me. "End times. ET stands for end times."

"What was in there? Some sort of virus?"

"The DNA of the original serpent dragon. The one that was born of the light of the stars, the one that shone like the morning sun."

"Asphorsh is becoming a dragon? How much power will he possess?"

"All power accorded to a being of his magnitude, which is universal power, but it lasts a short time and then he is reduced to crawling on his belly."

"I want to see that," I said. "I want to see Madison choke on the crumbs of earthworms."

"No. It is too dangerous to do, Trave. Let it go. Watch over the treasures that are left on board the starship and keep them safe. In the spring you are to send forth planters and sowers into all the earth," Niner said in a serious manner.

"John?" I said turning to the lieutenant. "Can you protect the vessel without my help?"

"Of course, but I wish you would do as Niner suggests."

"I didn't think you were superstitious."

"I prefer to call it cautious," he said. "Besides you don't know how long it will take for Asphorsh to transform."

"Damn, I wish he hadn't gotten away," I said. "Niner, find Asphorsh. Send me his coordinates. I'm not going to wait for him to gain more power. He needs to be stopped before he can destroy anything else."

"That is not for you to do," Niner said to me. "I told you the wizard destroys him when the time has become full."

Niner took flight from a rock next to my shoulder. He was high in the sky when I called out to him. "Forget all this wizard stuff. There is no wizard."

I still had him in my line of sight. His feathers seemed to have a sheen and a life of their own under the light of the sun. "Joseph knew," he called back. "Believe."

What I did believe was that Good Neighbor Sam was mixed up in this somehow though not the way that Niner would have me believe. We were closer to the structure now and stopped to look at it. "Asphorsh left guards behind," Niner reported to me by text.

"How many?" the lieutenant asked.

"A small force of only eight remain to cover the doorways to the chambers inside. He wasn't expecting to have to fight an army, you know," Niner answered via John's k com.

I was staring at the vessel as Niner talked. From a distance the object looked simply like a boulder shaped outcropping of the mountains themselves. "If we didn't have its coordinates, I would never have given it a second glance," the lieutenant said to me. "It looks like part of the landscape."

After John spoke, I looked again at the mysterious asteroid like ship resting across from us in the woods. He was right. I marveled at how brilliantly the camouflage had been adapted to fit into this specific terrain. John called for a backup unit and we waited until they arrived to take out the SG guards who had been posted outside. I left the fighting to the trained men and went in with them only after the outside was secure.

To our surprise, steps automatically descended to the ground when we were positioned directly below the entrance, and we climbed up to the shining city. The outside door opened and we went inside when the sergeant signaled the all clear. The lieutenant left two men to guard the door and sent the rest in to secure the entire city, but before they able to begin their mission a voice greeted us. "Welcome, travelers. Dr. Newman and John Robbins."

"Who gave you our names?" I asked.

"It has been known since the beginning who was to come," the voice answered.

"Right. Tell me who you are."

"If you do not believe what I first told you, why would you believe the second?"

John laughed beside me. "He's got you there, Trave."

The voice reminded me of Joseph because whoever it was had that annoying characteristic of answering a question with a question.

"Is Joseph here? Do you know him?"

"There are many here that go by that name."

"Where do you come from?"

"Beyond the third heaven."

"Where's that?"

"It is the genesis of all."

"And, of course, the wizard lives there?" I shouted, pointing my weapon upward as if I was going to use it.

"You cannot use your weaponry in here."

"We'll see," I continued in an even more sarcastic voice as I tried to fire my laser at the walls. The gun's trigger would not move. John, seeing the problems I was having tried to fire his. He looked at me and shook his head. "No firearms can work in here," he said reading off his cell. "The report of my finding says there is a shield consisting of waves which render them useless. Even if they could work, the walls and structures are made of Trinchon crystalline quartz which is indestructible."

"I've never heard of it."

"It doesn't exist on earth," the faceless voice spoke up again. "Please, travelers, step over to the large monitor at the center of the room. It is time you received your instructions."

Before we could walk to the center of the circular room, the monitor came on and began a virtual tour of the city which the voice told us was not a city, but a repository for all the DNA of every living thing. Then the voice told us exactly what Niner had already revealed to us. After the ashes had settled over the winter and the soil had been prepared, reseeding was to begin. "Each seed silo will open only when it is time to plant that specimen," the voice informed us. "There is no chance for error." Then the voice gave us the rest of the instructions. Only man would repopulate the earth. All humans and animals were to report to the ship when the fires began and stay until spring. It was the only safe place while the fires cleansed the earth. The ship would orbit the heavens until it brought us back to earth again in the spring. Then the ancients would descend to earth with us to rule over all men and every living thing. However, after a millennium, this wise and goodly ruler would loose the dragon again bringing about the final war on the planet. The King would subdue the dragon with the sword of his tongue. Then would come a lasting peace. War and strife and hatred would vanish from the stars and be brought to remembrance no more. Even their words and their concepts would be lost and forgotten forever. Men would not kill one another again. Tiny kittens would sleep in viper's nests and be unharmed. Children would walk among lions." Then the monitor went suddenly silent. We were stunned. It was a lot to take in.

In a moment, John was on his computer and notifying those at the fort in Banff. He gave them the ships' coordinates. "You're not buying all this garbage he tried to sell us?" I asked.

"What harm is there in keeping our people protected just in case?" he said. "I love my wife and children. I don't want them caught in the fires he warned were coming," I kept staring at him and he continued. "What if what we were told is true?"

"What if it's a trap and they are just trying to get all of us together in a nice little package so they can kill us with a single blast?"

"I don't feel threatened," he said in a low voice and looking me in the eyes.

My computer buzzed and I looked at it. "Niner's sent me the location of Ashforsh," I said.

"Do not go to the stronghold of the enemy," the voice said without warning. "Revenge belongs to the wizard."

"Yeah, you sound like Joseph, now. He was always a little late."

"You have been warned, traveler."

"You didn't warn me, you just said don't go."

"I do not tell the future of men's destiny."

"You just did that for over an hour," I said.

"That was of mankind. You are an individual. You have been warned whether you choose to acknowledge that or not."

The voice was silent, and I headed for the door. "I'm not going to be able to change your mind am I?" John said.

"I have to see justice carried out."

"You don't trust the wizard."

"There is no wizard, John. I helped Asphorsh and the others dream all these terrors up, remember?"

"Can I ask something of you first?"

I gave him a brief nod. "You can try."

"Wait until the others arrive and are safe inside the city here."

"I'll do better than that, John. I'll help you set the satellite coordinates to wipe out the subterrean cities and the Life Engineering labs for Utah."

"That has already been calculated," the voice said. "An interstellar satellite will trigger the hit with plasma ionized gas like that contained in the stars and the sun. That power is unlike any source that has touched the planet since its creation. Its wall of energy will disintegrate the city to atomization particles in seconds when it destroys the earth to make way for the new world which will come."

"What's atomization particles?"

"Dust that is as fine and as invisible as you see floating in the sunlight."

Hours later the doors to the silo opened up and those that we had left behind at the Canadian fort came inside. Once they saw the two of us standing inside, they quickened their pace and John's wife came and hugged him. Upon seeing me she said, "Nice to see you again, Travis." John took one of the babies in his arms and kissed his wife. Others pushed their way around us. "What is this place?" someone one asked.

"It is our refuge for now. There is a video stream that will explain it on that monitor over there. Gather around and you will be told all that we know," John said guiding them towards it.

"Walk me to the door," I said to John as the ring played again from the beginning and the voice repeated its message to the newcomers.

Suddenly the video message that was being played stopped, and the voice spoke directly to me. "There is no changing once the path has been chosen, Travis. Joseph told you that."

"Okay, where are you, Joseph? You can come out now," I said turning in circles and looking for a secret door to open. It was then I saw Zel pushing her way through the circle of people towards me. "I'm going with you," she called out.

"You don't even know where I'm going."

"Yes, I do. Your mission has been the same since we started. I know you. You wouldn't just give up."

"Wait until I get my men organized and I will be the third charm in your locket," Robbins said. A sharp whistle brought his men to us and we started towards the exit. "Let's go slay a dragon," he said as the door to the rock like structure opened.

Within an hour we were back in Denver. Robbins had his men assemble around the perimeter of the ruined fortress while me, Zel, and John continued flying over the area and awaited coordinates from Niner. The destruction we had left was visible, but it was also probable that some of the underground city was still intact. A second attack would instill a greater victory. "The fortress of the gods is in ruins," the lieutenant said looking down into the holes that we had blasted into the earth. "Sure you don't want to save anything down there?" he said turning to me.

"I'm for burying it all." I turned to Zel. "Are you sure about destroying the clones?"

"I have never been surer," she said smiling.

"You won't live forever anymore."

"Let tomorrow come," she yelled jumping into the air and waving her arms.

Suddenly a beep came on my computer. Niner was sending us Asphorsh's coordinates complete with skype pics. He had returned to his mountain eerie retreat. "One on one, Madison," I muttered mostly to myself. "Keep him on the ground, Niner."

"Something's going on here, Trave," Niner replied. "There's rumbling and thunders underground. I can't get an accurate reading on what's happening."

"Get out of there, Niner. Clear the whole squad out."

We were just flying over the spot that Niner had given us when I thought I saw the mountain heaving and sighing like a runner who is out of breath. Smoke and flashes billowed out from seams all around the mountain. I could smell the toxic fumes and the steam rising up blinded us as we flew into it. "Eruption," I said as I veered into a tight circle and did a one eighty back the other way.

Just as we flew out of the mist, I witnessed Madison's jet car exploding. Instantaneous evaporation. "Something must have sparked his liquid quartz tank," Robbins said.

"That was easy," Zel said. "The war is over."

"Too bad it took more than fifty years and over 200 billion lives," I said just as the warning light blinked a recharge/refuel signal at us. "I'll have to set her down."

"Bad news, Trave, Zel," Niner's voice came over the K-phone. "He wasn't in it."

"That means he's on the ground like us. We'll find him."

Once we had landed, I saw a line of soldiers coming across the seam in between the mountains. They were on foot and had no vehicles. There were a few skirmishes going on in the distance, but otherwise it looked quiet. We set off in the snow and waited at the bottom of the hill until it was night and then made our way up and over the rocky outcropping back the way we had come. We still hadn't found even one of our men, or a single drone. "I'd have thought Niner would have found us by now," Robbins said looking at me.

"I lost my computer phone back there somewhere. It must have fallen out of my pocket," I said as I sat down on a rock. "I have no way to contact him." I took off my boots and was rubbing my feet in my hands. "My toes are frozen," I said pressing them harder into my palms.

"Let's hole up here, and wait to be found," Robbins said. "I think you have the right idea about how to warm your feet," he said taking off his boots.

It was not until a day and a half later that Niner found us. In the distance we could still hear the explosions of the battle. The Eagle Commander had told us that most of the battle was won and that they were exploding the underground facilities now and fighting the human hybrids. "Getting messy," he had told us. "There's blood everywhere. It shows on the snow quite clearly."

Within the hour a jet car arrived. We were given food and a slug of whiskey laced coffee to warm us. "You need to get back to the ship. It is scheduled to leave. Do not miss its launch, Trave," Niner warned. "It is the greatest rescue of mankind ever to take place."

I got up and started loading our gear into the jet car and yelled at Niner to give me a hand. Wudgey had joined us from somewhere and stood beside us. The robotoid had lost Axle in the battle and had his parts in a box beside him. I didn't say anything to him. I just rested my arm across his back and left it there. I was busy watching the others get things packed up for the trip back and I was thinking about all the others that had been lost that day. Captain Reynolds was dead and so were more than half the men.

"Will you help make Axle into a functioning robo again?" Wudgey finally said without looking at me.

"All the king's horses and all the king's men couldn't put him back together again," I said to him. It was a stupid thing to say, but I couldn't think of anything else. I needed to convey the new world that was coming into being. Life was a onetime happening again. You had one chance to get it right. It was vital that you made the most of the time you were given.

Just then I heard a whistle and then a big explosion. Suddenly I felt a hot blast of air carry me backwards. I was at least forty feet from the jet car when I hit the ground. I could see the vehicle was in flames from where I lay. Somehow Wudgey and Niner were beside me.

"Why? You put Niner together again. You reanimated him," Wudgey said striking his fist angrily at the box the pieces were in so that it rattled and clanked. I thought we all must have been alright because he was continuing with the conversation he had started with me before the missile had struck the jet car. The only difference was that we were all lying on the ground.

"I won't do it again," I answered quietly while I focused on Niner who was spread out face down in the snow. I couldn't speak very loudly and I felt my strength was gone. It was then I realized I had been hit.

"Is that because you're dying?" Wudgey said and turned to look at me with the most amazing look on his face.

"This world wasn't made for immortality. Even the rocks finally break apart and fall to the ground. Rivers dry up. Plants and trees die."

"Humans die."

"Yes, all of us," I said.

"I thought you were afraid of death. You tried to keep the end from coming."

"I still fear death."

"Then why?"

"It's the only road there is."

"Then you have chosen to believe in the Wizard of all?" the robo said getting up.

I was trying to smile as I was patting Wudgey on the back. I didn't want to get into the reasons behind any of my thoughts.

Not too far in front of us they were burying the dead, and I watched Wudgey limp slowly over to where the soldiers were assembled. They had dug a single pit and bodies were being lowered into it together. After the last man had been taken care of, Wudgey handed Lt. Robbins the box with Axle's remains in it. John took the box and had it lowered into the grave. "Would you add his name to the list, lieutenant?"

Robbins nodded.

"Write, Axle, friend to Wudgey."

"Sergeant, did you hear that?" the lieutenant asked the man next to him.

"Yes, sir."

A twenty one gun salute sounded in the distance, and the flag was raised to half-mast as the trumpet sounded over the valley in the early dusk. Day is done, gone the sun. It was all too real. In moments the sun would fall beyond the mountains.It was Niner who drew my attention away from this scene when he gave me a nudge with his wing and spoke. "I'm scared, Trave. I don't want to die."

"Take hold of my hand."

"I need to tell you something," Niner said. "It is the reason I am afraid of death now."

"I'm listening, Niner."

"I've been afraid since the last time I died. I waited for the wizard, but he didn't come. When I died it was just blackness, Trave. It was like I had never been."

My heart stop beating in that moment. Niner had found the end of hope. He knew that the unreal could not be made real. Damn the cruelty of it all.

"Take hold of my hand, Niner. I will see you over."

"Is that possible?"

"I have never heard that it's not," I told him.

His voice lost its clearness and it sounded raspy. "Then you will have to go first, Trave. You'll have to find the way."

I couldn't find the words to answer him or the strength.

Not much time had passed when I heard him speak again. "Crazy isn't it? You wanted above all else in the world to have life and I wished to find death and the wizard at the end of it to be made real."

The eagle turned and touched my arm with his wings and found it was already cold.

"Trave, I'm still here," the eagle whispered and began to sob in half hiccup like sounding snorts.

In the last moments I saw movement in the hazy outline the world now resembled. I thought it was Zel, and when I heard her speak, I knew it to be her.

"Why are you crying?" she said touching the eagle.

"The wizard didn't come for me. Trave was supposed to take me with him, but he didn't.

"It could be a while, " Zel said trying to soothe him as Wudgey sat down beside them. "I've got time," Niner said to Zel before he turned his attention to the robo. "See that bright star to the north, the one that twinkles and outshines the rest, Wudgey?" the drone said pointing his wing towards the sky.

The robotoid looked upward. There was only a tinge of blue left in the sky where Niner pointed. The rest of the sky had turned purple and darkish like the mountains it mirrored to the west. "That's where the wizard resides."

"He has a different name," Wudgey said. "Why do you call him the wizard?"

"Look around at this world he created. It is magic, wouldn't you say? He made it all out of the great void. He spoke it all into being."

"That is why you believe he will come back?"

"I believed that once."

"The wizard will come," I heard Wudgey say.

"No, he has already come for Trave and the others, and I am still here."

"You are still alive."

"Trave did not take Niner with him as he promised, Miss Zel" Wudgey said turning to her. Then quickly turning back to his friend he said, "He lied to you in his last moments, Niner. Do you understand? He lied."

"Only to make things bearable," I heard the eagle say.

"Why aren't you angry?"

"I have seen truth. Truth is truth whether I am real or not."

The tears streamed down my face. I was a man who had played God and now the cruelty and reality of it was too much to bear. I needed forgiveness.

My eye sight was growing dimmer, but I could see Zel backing away from us. I saw her as only an outline, a shadow as she unslung the weapon from off of her back and took aim. I feared that one or the other of my friends would turn around to look at her, but they didn't. Both stayed facing the other way and Niner had his wing around Wudgey.

Zel shot Niner first, and then Wudgey turned slightly to look back at her to see what the noise was, and that's when the next laser shot struck him.

He made a much bigger fire and explosion than Niner. I could smell them burning next to me. I was fearful that Zel's shots had not been accurate and that one of them would cry out to me, but they didn't. At least I believed they didn't. Then a sensation came over me, a feeling so warm it could melt the moon and so strong it could pull down the sun.

Robbins and a few others ran up to Zel. "It was a merciful act," he said.

She said nothing as she picked up my last journal from out of my pocket. "This is all that's left," she said holding it out to the lieutenant. "Once there was a man, and a drone named Niner who dreamed of freedom and believed in the wizard of all."

"Do you think it wise to speak of the drone?"